A Silent Game of Spies

Book One of The War of the Royals

By Brittanny Davis

Copyright 2018 by Brittanny Davis

For my mother,

who first inspired me to write

This has been a Silver Lining Production

PROLOGUE

Sometime near the end of the Twenty Years' War

Luvian

Luvian dodged another arrow as he surveyed the rocky terrain. While it gave no soldier an advantage from twisting ankles in unseen holes in the dirt and tripping over rocks, it had chased the Eastern Alliance's Northern 20th Regiment into a trap that was closing rapidly. Ormon infantry climbing up to the right, while Ambsellon archers scrambled slowly upward to the left.

Luvian strained to hear a retreat signal, but none came. He shoved his sword into the neck of an Ambsellon archer. As he yanked it out, he saw another soldier of his regiment. "We need to retreat!" Luvian yelled to him.

"Aye, but who to draw us back?"

An arrow penetrated his comrade's shoulder. "Bloody hell!"

Luvian saw the man's Sergeant rank barely visible under blood. "Sergeant, I'll find a lieutenant. You draw the troops back. You be acting Lieutenant."

The sergeant nodded curtly and yelled, "Retreat! Retreat!"

With very little persuasion, the 20th immediately retreated toward the east. Luvian found the unattended horse of a dead soldier and swung himself into the saddle. He kicked the horse's sides, praying he wouldn't catch an arrow in the back as he rode off in the direction of Command.

What bloody fool had stationed them there, he'd like to know. Some arse whose only experience with war was in his father's courtyard, no doubt, he fumed.

Then he pulled his horse back. The Command camp was trampled and bloody, glowing embers in the dirt sending wisps of smoke into the air. Tents littered the campsite, ripped and burned, and dead soldiers of all rank scattered the ground with arrows and spears protruding from their armor and ringmail, their blood dripping into the mud with no prejudice.

Stunned, Luvian searched the ground for traces of the battle. Ambushed by a sizable mounted force, the battle had been over before half of them had swung a sword. Luvian's eyes narrowed with contempt. Just the sort of behavior they had come to expect from this enemy. But a Command camp. That truly was loathsome.

As he urged the horse forward, Luvian's horse whinnied nervously at the smell of fresh blood. The Command Tent itself was ruined, its burned shreds flapping in the regretful breeze. Luvian dismounted and ducked in the tent, not sure what he would find. He found no one, dead or alive; only ashes of the tent remained.

He certainly knew now why no retreat had been ordered. New ranks would be issued, of course. Luvian then set to looking among the dead for the Officer in Command. After stepping over all the bodies in the campsite, he found no Captain. Had the Captain escaped, or been taken prisoner?

Luvian set to looking for tracks outside the camp. Ah. In the bushes behind the Command Tent. Perhaps as many as ten men had trampled the bushes in a frantic escape, and two horses as well. At least someone had survived this massacre.

He led his horse through the bushes, following the trail of the survivors. He knelt and studied the ground. Blood. Luvian frowned. That did not bode well. At least one wounded. To have survived that ugly scene only to die on the trail would truly be a travesty. He kept his sword ready in case the survivors had been followed. He wanted no surprises.

More and more blood dotted the leaves of the ground. Finally, Luvian found a liveried soldier propped against a tree, his neck lolling to one side. Blood had drenched the man's blue livery, still seeping from a gut wound. Luvian sighed. Gut wounds were a terrible way to die. A dagger lay in the man's lap, left for him by his comrades, possibly for protection, but most likely to take his own life. The blade was clean, however. Death had claimed the soldier before the blade had been necessary. A blessing, Luvian thought.

He dismounted and knelt beside the soldier, reaching out for a memento to give to a loved one who would miss him. Command soldiers always had such trinkets.

Just as his hands neared the man's uniform, the man drew in an enormous, rattled breath and sat up straighter, his brown eyes round.

Luvian was thrown back in shock. *Luvian, you arse, why did you not check to see if he was alive!*

"Sir, I – you. You're alive! I thought you dead, sir."

The liveried man reached out his shaking hand to Luvian's, grasping him. "I fear I am not much longer for this life." His widened eyes read Luvian's uniform. "You. You are of the Northern Regiment."

"I – yes sir, I am. I can get you there, just – just hold on a little longer sir. Let me patch you up –"

The soldier's breath wheezed out in a weak attempt of a laugh. Even that winded him. "No, son. But you have a good heart." He took another breath. "In my –" He paused, as a wave of pain overtook him. "In my inside breast pocket. Are the maps of all the Northern Regiments and –"

The soldier was fading fast. Maps? "Sir?" Luvian prompted him.

"Ah, the maps. Of all the Northern Regiments. Our Command was – ambushed. We were – betrayed. A spy." With a sudden burst of strength, the soldier grabbed Luvian. "Soldier, it is now your mission. To get these documents to the Captain. You have no other mission. Do you – understand?" the man panted.

"Yes, sir," Luvian replied solemnly.

"Good. You're a corporal? I've just promoted you to a – a Sergeant. Sergeant –?"

"Luvian, sir."

"Sergeant Luvian, get these maps to the Captain of this Command. Give them to no one else, do you understand? That is imperative," the man insisted weakly.

Luvian nodded.

"No one else. My name is Corlander. Just tell him my name and he will know – I am in charge of all such – documents. See that he is safe." Corlander sat back against the tree, exhausted.

"But, sir. How will I know who the Command Captain is? What is his name?"

Corlander smiled weakly. Blood dribbled from his lips. "Sergeant, in this time of war, I – I dare not tell you. But you will know. You will know. Give my love – to my...."

His eyes stared off suddenly, seeing nothing. Luvian sighed and closed their glassy gaze. He had seen more men die than he cared to think of during this damnable war. This man – Corlander – was a true hero, to the drawing of his last breath. And now Luvian was saddled with a new mission. Find the Command Captain.

He disliked rummaging through Corlander's uniform with him still warm. But he found the maps and what looked like other documents as well. A brave man's blood stained their parchment but they were still legible. Corlander had saved them from the attack and payed for his bravery with his life. Luvian found no trinket nor memento to return to a family but would do his best after the war to find the man's family.

Standing, he saluted Corlander. His horse whickered behind him. "What? He was a good man. He deserves it," Luvian told his horse. Patting the horse on the neck, he swung up and urged him forward. His horse flicked an ear at him as if amused and plodded forward.

The attackers seemed quite arrogant in their assumption that they had left no survivors. Had Luvian's own regiment attacked a camp, they would have dispatched scouts to ensure no one escaped. Just simple battle sense.

But now... the tracks in the dirt were spreading out. Which to follow? He had been sworn to give documents to the Command Captain. Luvian knelt and studied the ground thoughtfully. Why had the small company spread out?

They had divided to get the most important asset – the Captain – through enemy lines. By creating distractions to either side, and surrounding the Captain with the most men possible, the small company had snuck the Command Captain through.

Which meant, Luvian thought, that he was now behind enemy lines himself. He had only been approximately two hours behind his quarry. So where was the enemy now?

In silence, he followed the tracks the Captain's team had left. Why had they turned back toward the north at all? The fighting was thickest in the north. But Corlander had insisted that they had been betrayed, so they had set out on a fool's errand unknowingly. Luvian fervently hoped that the company was still alive – to have survived that massacre at the Command Tent, sneak through the woods all this way, only to step straight into a trap…. If he ever found the bastard who had betrayed them, he would crush his neck in his bare hands.

Finally, a familiar sound reached his ears. The sound of metal on metal confirmed what the Command Tent survivors had found – fighting had indeed been awaiting them.

Luvian patted Corlander's documents safely against his breast and urged his horse forward, though he watched all about him for enemy scouts.

As he rounded the next hill, a spear landed in front of his horse, embedding itself in the dirt. Luvian swung out of the saddle as his horse reared. His heart pounding, he searched all around him.

"You!" a voice hissed. A red-headed man covered in leaves stepped onto the path before Luvian.

Luvian swung his sword around defensively.

"Put that thing away. What regiment are you with?" hissed the man, obviously a scout.

"Northern 20th."

"Ha. All but demolished, I hear."

Luvian's eyes narrowed and his jaw clenched. "Oy! They were mates of mine. You'll keep your mouth off them, may they rest with the gods."

"Fair enough. A test. But partly true, I fear," returned the scout.

"If decent leadership had placed us where we wouldn't have been cornered, we wouldn't be in such standing," Luvian grated.

The red-headed scout held his hands up in surrender. "I quite agree, as it happens. A number of regiments were given false information, placed where they thought no enemy would attack. And then were ascended upon from all sides."

Luvian thought of the last stand his comrades made before retreating. "Then who is to blame? We can't fight this way."

"Not my place to speculate, mate."

Luvian thought of the maps he had been dispatched to deliver. "I've been tasked to deliver something to the – Command Tent. Know where it is?"

The scout rose an eyebrow. "The Command Tent? Well, that's bloody well specific now, isn't it?"

"Corlander sent me."

The scout's face changed. "Who did you say?"

"Corlander. Corlander sent me before he died."

For a moment, the scout stared at him, then he seemed to make his mind up about something. "Come on." When Luvian paused, the scout snapped, "Well, do you want to get to Command or no? I said, come on."

Luvian reached out for his horse.

"Leave the horse. He'll find his way to camp. Now keep it quiet."

Luvian tried to emulate the scout's silent footsteps with painstaking effort. After a while, the scout signaled for a stop. "Rushby. My name, that is," he whispered. "Yours?"

"Luvian. Well met."

"Aye. There's fighting around that ridge, but it gets worse the farther we go. Command is set up in the thick of it. No sense." Rushby knocked his curly red head with his knuckles. "Makes no sense to me, but maybe that's why I'm a scout and they're in golden helmets, aye?" He snorted quietly.

"Aye," Luvian nodded agreement.

"We'll be heading north, which is mainly Ormish soldiers. Infantry, a few archers, longbows and crossbows." Rushby cocked his head as he sized up Luvian's armor. "I can see you're no stranger to the battlefield, so you're aware of their tactics."

"Aye," Luvian growled as he glanced down at his armor. Muddy, splashed with dried blood, dented to one side where a heavy shot from a mace had bruised his ribs. The blue of his Eastern Shield tunic was scarcely recognizable now.

"Sergeant? Lieutenant...?" Rushby trailed off in query.

"Sergeant." That would take some getting used to, mused Luvian.

"Ah. Well, Sergeant, we will be making our way there," Rushby pointed. "Just follow me and whatever you do, don't start playing the hero. Corlander sent you to Command and that's your only mission." Rushby stared at Luvian frankly. "Are you ready?"

They ran. Luvian marveled for a moment at Rushby's speed and then concentrated only on matching it, and then simply keeping the red-headed scout in sight. Ignoring the clashing of sword-to-sword combat and battle cries of enraged men all about him, Luvian jumped over downed men and twisted to avoid rivals as he sprinted after Rushby.

Suddenly Rushby came to stop. "Do you see Command? Up there?" he yelled over the din of the battle, pointing toward a striped gold and blue tent in the distance. "That's where we're headed, in case you're out here on your own," he panted.

Luvian heard the unspoken words of every soldier underlying Rushby's directions: *In case I don't make it.... In case I die....* He nodded shortly. With an intent look, Rushby saw that Luvian had divulged his true meaning and slapped him on the back.

"Right then!" Rushby dashed off, darting in between combatant soldiers. Luvian ran behind him, straining to keep sight of the scout around the men fighting all around him. He felt an arrow zip past his neck and thanked the gods he had not been one second slower.

Finally, Rushby led him into a heavily guarded Command Camp. He was right; it was in the thick of the fighting. What a ridiculous place to set Command, especially after the massacre of the last location.

"Stop! State your name and business!" Two guards with swords blocked Rushby and Luvian's progress into the tent. They stopped, panting from their run.

Rushby stood tall. "Lieutenant Rushby, Scout First Grade, with Sergeant Luvian."

The guards immediately snapped to stiff attention. "Lieutenant, sir!"

Luvian marveled, for he had not known he had been in the company of a Lieutenant, but said nothing.

"I've escorted Sergeant Luvian here on a private mission to Command personally from Major Corlander."

The guards eyed each other nervously. "Sir, yes, sir!" They escorted Rushby – *Lieutenant Rushby* – and Luvian inside the Command Tent.

So Corlander was no liveried servant but a Major. If he'd known, he would have paid the man more respect....

Inside the blue silk Command Tent stood two Lieutenants in decorated uniforms leaning with frustration over a map of the region. Luvian glanced about the tent but found no Captain.

Luvian thought of Corlander's words. *"Get these maps to the Captain of this Command. Give them to no one else, do you understand? That is imperative. No one else. My name is Corlander. Just tell him my name and he will know."* He thought of all the man had sacrificed for the blood-stained parchments hidden behind his armor, and wondered just how deep the betrayal lay, if Corlander would not even tell Luvian the Captain's name.

"And who are our guests, Corporal?" asked one of the Lieutenants.

The Corporal who had escorted Luvian and Rushby inside the Command Tent saluted and responded stiffly, "Sir, Lieutenant Rushby and Sergeant Luvian here to see you, Sir." He turned to Rushby and Luvian. "This is Lieutenant Hawthorne and Lieutenant Fannion."

Rushby nodded at him.

"Very well," commented Lieutenant Hawthorne. "And why are you here?"

The Corporal drew in breath, but Rushby stepped forward and said, "Corporal, I'll take it from here. Dismissed."

The Corporal knew a dismissal when he heard it, and though he saluted and spun on his boot heel, Luvian caught a nervous glance at Lieutenant Hawthorne and Lieutenant Fannion.

Rushby told the two Command Lieutenants then that he had escorted Sergeant Luvian from his position on the trail with important news only to be delivered to Command.

"Well, then, man, here you are. Out with it." Irritation colored Lieutenant Fannion's voice and his face showed plainly that things of far more importance than Luvian's message required his attention. Luvian instantly disliked the man but refrained from retorting in any disrespectful fashion.

Luvian took a deep breath and stood to his full height. "Sir, I need an audience with the Command Captain."

Both Lieutenants stared at him and he felt Rushby's amazement next to him.

"Sergeant... Luvian? Whatever message you have you may convey to us."

"With due respect, Lieutenant, sir, I was told to give my – message – only to the Command Captain." Let there be ambiguity in his errand so that none could report details to a spy, Luvian thought. Such was the nature of his mission, after all.

Under his breath, Rushby said, "You've got brass ones, I give you that."

The Lieutenant frowned and huffed, unaccustomed to disrespect. "And just who gave you such a – *message*?" He repeated Luvian's choice of word but let it drip with acidity.

With no choice but to both ignore the bastard's condescension as well as his prodding for information, Luvian replied, "Major Corlander, sir."

The Lieutenants exchanged a glance and then the bastard strode around the table and leaned against it, tapping a quill to his mouth.

"Interesting, you see," Lieutenant Fannion told Luvian as he cocked his head, "because we had heard the Major was dead."

"Sir, he is now, sir. Attacked in an ambush at his last Command post and left for dead on his way here. Sir." Luvian allowed his tone to remain even as he reported the facts.

The two Lieutenants shot a glance at each other. "Guards. Out. You, Rushby, you stay."

The guards exited quickly.

Lieutenant Hawthorne, a dark-haired, rigid man, approached Luvian. "The Northern 20th? You're a long way from home, Sergeant." A steely blue gaze prompted Luvian for more details.

"Aye, I am. Not a soul with a sense of leadership in that regiment left. We decided to retreat and I made for the Command Tent for a Lieutenant to lead us. What I found was the whole site, bloody and burned to the ground. Ambushed. Not a survivor left, sir."

The Lieutenants glanced at each other.

"Behind the camp, I found a trail of men who had escaped and followed it through the woods. It was there I found Major Corlander, with a gut wound, nearly dead. He told me what happened and tasked me with this mission. So, I've made it to your camp to find his Command Captain. His message is for him alone, by order of Major Corlander."

Lieutenant Hawthorne and Lieutenant Fannion weighed his words. "Certainly you may give us the Major's message," Lieutenant Fannion finally responded. "After all, the import of a dying man's mission – how sane was he, after all? He couldn't have been in his right mind."

Lieutenant Hawthorne considered. "Still."

"Sir, I swore to give this message only to the Command Captain," Luvian, now irritated, let go of conventional military terms of respect.

"I'm afraid that's just not possible," Lieutenant Hawthorne told him, his face stoic.

Luvian stared. "And why is that? Where is he? Is he in the mess tent, then? I'll see him there." He started to turn around.

Rushby laid a hand on Luvian's arm. "Sergeant –"

"Sergeant, the Command Captain is not in the mess tent, more's the pity."

"Oy – are you two are running things? This is just as bad as back home. How are we supposed to win a war when the Captain is missing, the Lieutenants are idiots, and the Command is camped in the center of the fighting?"

"What did you say?" Lieutenant Fannion was furious.

Rushby tried to hold Luvian back, but Luvian himself was enraged. He strode to the center of the tent, brushing past Lieutenant Hawthorne and Lieutenant Fannion as if they were fleas. Pointing to the maps pinned to the table, Luvian demanded, "Oy – what's this? Is this your local Regiment?" He did not wait for an answer but walked around the table, studying the war plans and shaking his head with disgust. He saw strategies for a forward movement to the east, which would leave the men bare to the west and the north. Luvian snorted.

"Who designed these? Some fool fresh from his daddy's courtyard. And right there, in the middle of it all, Command. After the last massacre. And you wonder why we're fresh out of men. We're too busy defending your silken tents and your cheese and your grapes!" Luvian pointed at the corner where a table of refreshments stood.

"How dare you, sir!" Lieutenant Fannion stepped forward, his fair face reddened with rage.

"Oh, I dare, I dare. How dare you! Ask yourselves that, setting up in the middle of the worst fighting! We lose half our troops to circling around your silken arses, when instead, you should set up your camp up here, or here, or here! And let the real soldiers do the fighting!"

Luvian knuckled the map in safe, easily defendable positions. "We'll send riders to and from with reports but you, you silken types, you're next to worthless."

"Luvian!" Rushby warned him loudly.

"No, sir, I'll be heard! The whole of my regiment is gone now due to some fool placing us in a near indefensible post. Real leadership, and real soldiers, not just pampered jackarses wanting to impress their daddies back home."

He stared at the map. "Move this tent here," he pointed to a remote location on the map. "By end of day, and let the soldiers start doing what they trained to do. That's this tent, your mess tent, all of it. Here. Get out of the line of fire, by end of day.

"Now. Where is the damned Command Captain?" Luvian growled.

Lieutenant Hawthorne and Lieutenant Fannion exchanged glances.

"Well, he's not dead, is he?"

"Oh, no, not dead. At least, not that we know," Lieutenant Hawthorne rolled a hopeful eye skyward. But then he glanced at the map.

"Bloody hell. You've got him out there? Fighting? While you're in here?"

"He's rather hard to control – stubborn actually. Once he gets it into his head to do something, there's nothing to be done for it," Lieutenant Hawthorne explained.

"He's got a point," Rushby confirmed.

"Not you, too."

Rushby held his hands out to his sides. "Sorry, Sergeant. It's true."

"And where is the Captain, then? If he's not dead yet?" Luvian grated. All of them, idiots, especially the Captain.

Lieutenant Fannion glared at him and Lieutenant Hawthorne squinted at the map. "Here, I believe, last we had word. He left two days past."

Rushby let out a long breath. That did not bode well.

Luvian turned his attention to Rushby. "And what's there?"

"Well…." Rushby glanced at Lieutenant Hawthorne and Lieutenant Fannion and then abandoned all formality. "Only about the craziest area of the battle."

Lieutenant Hawthorne's eyes rounded and Lieutenant Fannion's mouth dropped open.

"He told us there was barely any action there!"

"And that's why you need more scouts. That area's seen heavy fighting for days now. Either he knew that and duped you, or he had no idea and ran off straight into a maelstrom."

Both Lieutenant Hawthorne and Lieutenant Fannion had the grace to look guilty.

"What was his last communication?"

"*All was well, no problems to report*, received this morning," Lieutenant Fannion's voice was unsteady. Luvian did not like the man a bit, but his shaken demeanor went a long way toward redemption.

"Well, let us hope all is still well with him, aye?" Luvian raised an eyebrow with disgust.

"You, Sergeant, are out of order!" roared Lieutenant Fannion.

"Please, Lieutenant, you are too kind. Now. Where can I get a fresh horse and some rations? It seems I have a Captain to find deep in the middle of enemy territory. With luck, I will not have to deliver my message to a corpse."

"OUT! OUT!" screamed Lieutenant Fannion, pointing at the tent flap, his face incensed.

Rushby stirred Luvian around before he could say anything else. "Come along, come along, Sergeant, let's not say anything else you'll be sorry for."

"Sorry? I'm not sorry! REMEMBER! BY END OF DAY!" Luvian bellowed to the Command Tent behind him.

"Brass ones, my friend, did I say? Big ones. You'll be lucky not to court martialed for that scene in there," Rushby steered him toward the mess tent.

"At least someone spoke sense to them, sir. May be the one time during this whole bloody war someone does," Luvian ducked under the mess tent flap and picked up a bag of rations.

"Well, mate, it made for sheer entertainment, I'll tell you that much." Rushby picked up a bag of rations as well.

Luvian looked at him in puzzlement. "Sir, what's that you're doing? Stealing me an extra bag? That's trouble, speaking of court martial."

"Ah, well, just say you inspired me back there, Corporal. Doesn't happen often, so bask in the compliment while you can. I'm taking you to the Captain."

Rushby read the disbelief on Luvian's face. "Well, move along, then, move along. We've an idiot out there to save, haven't we? And if you tell anyone I called him that, I'll disavow all knowledge of it. Besides, scouts know all the best trails, aye?"

Luvian accepted the scout's help gladly. He stuffed the rations in his rucksack and turned to Rushby. "Where are the stables?"

Rushby shook his head. "No, mate, no horses. Cavalry makes for easy targets. The Ormish out there are mainly archers. Might well as paint your back red. We'll run."

Luvian's mouth dropped open. "Run."

Rushby smiled. "Ah, and the giant is suddenly speechless. Don't worry, mate, you'll make it. Just swing your sword if you have to and keep up."

That worried Luvian. He was known for strength, not speed. "And if I lose sight of you?"

"Well. Kill the arseholes. And look for the Captain. He's the idiot wearing the stupid gold and blue helmet. You'll know it when you see it. Only –"

"I know, I know, sir, you never called him an idiot." Luvian nodded and Rushby grinned.

"Now you have it. Ready, then, Sergeant?" They stood posed on the edge of the combat zone.

Luvian hoisted his rucksack and pulled his sword loose. "Aye. I am now."

Rushby gave him a quick nod in return and sprinted off. Luvian followed him.

Several times, thick fighting forced them to stop. Luvian was almost glad, for at least fighting in one-man combat, he could regain his breath. Rushby whistled at him twice to break him out of the fighting. If the Captain was as thick as those other two mush-headed, mealy-mouthed morons, then Luvian feared for the regiment, and, indeed, the fate of the message Major Corlander had charged him to impart. What Captain would place himself in harm's way and leave his subordinates behind to puzzle out the outcome of the war? Fool. Luvian sucked in air as he ran past Eastern Alliance and Ormish soldiers alike.

Finally, Rushby stopped ahead of him, panting. They knelt below the line of sight and gulped in water. Luvian swept his brow of dripping perspiration. "How much further?"

Rushby took in a few deep breaths, and then jabbed a thumb eastward. "Still some fighting up there, mind."

"No different than what we're in the midst of, I expect."

"Aye. Just keep up your stamina and, of course, stay alive." A tired smile lit Rushby's features.

"Aye. I want to tell this Captain that you called him an idiot while you're still alive."

"Ah. I'd like to see his face on that. Right then, on we go, our Captain needs us," and Rushby was off.

Just as they topped another ridge, the battle strengthened in intensity. Ormish infantrymen attacked Luvian and Rushby from all sides. Luvian worried – after all this way, it would be awful for Major Corlander's message to get lost when he was so close to delivering it. He also worried – if the battle was this intense, had the Captain survived? What would he do with the Major's message if the Captain was dead?

Rushby grabbed him. "Pay attention!" He yanked him forward. "He should be about this area, somewhere. Keep your head down!"

The two of them surveilled the area, dodging Ormish soldiers as they searched for the Command Captain. Luvian had no idea who he was looking for, other than a gold helmet. He was relying on Rushby.

Suddenly he saw a flash of gold. Craning his neck, he grabbed Rushby's arm. "Is that him?" he yelled over the din of the battle.

Rushby strained his neck and pointed in the Captain's direction in confirmation. Together, they ran up the ridge to the inner circle of guards surrounding the Captain.

"Captain! I've a message for you!" yelled Luvian.

The Captain was just a young man, his own age, Luvian would warrant, and hardly old enough to have achieved the rank of Captain. Nevertheless, he had no business being in the thick of this fighting, and he suddenly vowed to personally escort him back to the Command Tent.

A cross look manifested upon the Captain's face. "I'm a bit busy, you may have noticed! Give it to someone else!" he yelled back.

"Captain, sir, I cannot. Major Corlander bade me tell you his name and that you would understand."

An odd look crossed the Captain's face then. "Fall back!" he called to his circle of men.

After the men had fallen back to a site where they were not being attacked, Luvian stepped forward.

"Sir, this is Lieutenant Rushby, Scout First Grade. He saw me safely here. My name is Sergeant Luvian."

"Well met, soldiers. Lieutenant? Did you speak with Major Corlander?"

"No, sir, I've only accompanied Sergeant Luvian. I'll be returning to my camp now, if it please you, sir."

"As you will, then, Lieutenant. Take rest as you can and good will follow you."

Rushby saluted the Captain smartly, who returned a salute and a nod of dismissal.

"Returning?" Luvian grabbed Rushby's arm.

"I said I'd get you here. I said nothing about staying." Rushby smiled toothily. "I have a regiment to get back to. Which you would do well to stay away from, given how you left it."

Luvian snorted and grimaced a bit.

"But I'm going back to see that they move that tent. By end of day, aye? I'll keep them in line for you."

Luvian smiled. "Good man."

They grasped forearms. "See you on the other side, then," said Rushby.

"See you on the other side," returned Luvian.

Meanwhile, the Captain had downed a fair bit of his waterskin. "Well then, Sergeant, let's have it, what's this message you were sent to give me? You have my full attention if Major Corlander sent you."

Luvian glanced about them. Soldiers stood all about them and at any moment, those papers could be lost should he take them out. This was hardly the place or time.

"With all due respect, Captain, a quieter time and place would be best –" he trailed off.

The Captain snorted and gave a wide gesture about them with his arm. "Sergeant, if you hadn't noticed, we're on a battlefield. Where had you supposed we might find a quiet time and place?"

He had a point. Perhaps by night, when the fighting came to a rest for the evening.

"If you please, Captain, Major Corlander insisted. I meant no disrespect."

"You keep mentioning Major Corlander. When did you last see him?"

"Not four hours ago, nearly dead from a gut wound in the woods. His Command Tent had been ambushed and he had escaped. He died, sir, in front of me."

A look of regret passed over the Captain's face. "I was in that Command Tent. Several of my men, the Major included, helped me to escape. It seems you were fated to meet each other if he has given you a message for me. He was a good man."

"Some of his last words to me were to keep you safe. I –"

"Captain! Incoming!" yelled several soldiers all at once.

"Shit!" swore the Captain.

"Captain, with all due respect, you need to head north, out of the line of fire, and back to the Command Tent. They need you there!" Luvian insisted.

"I left Lieutenant Hawthorne and Lieutenant Fannion there. Perfectly capable!" called the Captain.

"Again, sir, with all due respect, Lieutenant Hawthorne and Lieutenant Fannion couldn't find their thumbs if they shoved them up their arses!"

The Captain threw an outraged look at Luvian. "Sergeant, you have overstepped your bounds!"

Luvian swept the scene around him with an arm in imitation of the Captain's earlier condescension. "Captain, where are the bounds on a battlefield?"

The Captain's eyes narrowed and then an Ormish swordsman made it through. The Captain slashed downward with his sword, killing the man.

Luvian reconsidered the Captain. He had skills and was unafraid to use them, and he had experience on the battlefield, for crusted blood smeared his face and his armor. Albeit not a respectful swing in the eyes of an ArmsMaster, the Captain had buried his sword in the neck of their opponent with might and main, killing the soldier swiftly if terribly. Luvian decided he approved, even if the man was in harm's way.

Their eyes met over two more unlucky opponents whom they dispatched. The Captain placed a bloody boot on another Ormish soldier so that he could yank his sword free while Luvian kicked an Ormish soldier's beheaded skull out of his way.

"Very well. You've earned my respect, Sergeant. And, it seems, the Major's, or you would not be here."

"Sir, if you've any battle sense at all, and I think you have, you must return to the Command Tent."

Pure disdain at the thought made the Captain roll his eyes.

"You have to lead the troops. We sent Command to the North so they'd be out of the way of the fighting...."

"We?" asked the Captain. "Who is this 'we'?"

Suddenly nervous, Luvian answered, "Well, me. Just me, I did. Captain, sir, they were located in the center of the fighting and the men had to protect them instead of fight the enemy. What's the sense of that?" He realized then that he was treading on dangerous ground. It may well have been the Captain who set that plan up. He might find himself swinging from a rope.

The Captain stared at him and then nodded. "And how did you accomplish this?"

"Well. I went in and – I yelled at them, sir."

The Captain chortled. "Now that's something I'd actually like to have been in the Command Tent for, just to see their faces. And how did they respond?"

"Lieutenant Fannion yelled at me to get out. But I think they'll have moved camp. Lieutenant Rushby is assisting them," Luvian told the Captain. "With all due respect, Captain, sir, you should be there. You've been out here, you know where the fighting is, you know where to place the men."

The Captain studied him for a moment before saying, "Very well. You give a convincing argument. And you're right. I know where to place the men best now."

Luvian breathed an inward sigh of relief and a cheer.

The Captain pulled the nearest soldier aside – "Corporal, a word –" Luvian listened to him outline brief plans for his return to the Command Tent as soon as possible. The Corporal immediately saluted and turned to the rest of the Captain's unit to inform them.

Just then, a group of Ormish infantrymen rounded the hill, roaring a battle cry.

"Captain! With me!" yelled Luvian, beckoning the Captain to the top of the hill so they could escape to the north. It would not be honorable, but nor would the Captain's head on a spike serve any purpose.

The Captain struggled visibly with his decision: stay and fight, or run to the Command Tent. Luvian saw it on his face. He was going to stay and fight. Luvian knew he would do the same. Damn the man.

But more and more Ormons were pouring onto the battlefield. Luvian saw with horror the Ormons overtaking the small camp they had just been conversing in.

"Captain!"

The Captain immediately made his way up the hill to Luvian, his eyes wide with the need to flee.

Luvian stretched an arm down and pulled him up. As they gazed down, the Captain murmured, "There's no one left to call a retreat for...."

The entire site was swamped with Ormish soldiers. Almost as if they had been told the Captain had been there. Odd, Luvian thought....

And then an arrow struck the Captain. "Captain!"

"My shoulder – I'm fine. Damn it!"

Luvian turned to look at the Captain's wound but an odd gleam caught his eye, a reflection in the Captain's plated armor....

"Captain, get down!" Luvian hollered. He shoved the Captain down and threw himself into the air in front of him.

And then pain lanced through his entire left leg. A crossbolt – lodged in his thigh.

"Sergeant! Sergeant! Are you –" the Captain's worried face appeared above Luvian.

"Crossbolt – sonofabitch! We have to go *now!* Keep low!" grated Luvian, the pain in his leg growing worse with each step. "Get behind that wagon!"

"They'll be on us in no time." The Captain's face looked worried as he looked down at the arrow protruding from his shoulder.

The two of them dashed for the broken-down wagon and slid down behind it.

"You're going to have to pull it out," panted Luvian.

"Pull it out?"

"Don't be such a baby. I can do it if you like. But I warn you, I'm not at my best at the moment, as you might have noticed."

Luvian watched as the Captain winced. "Whatever you do, do it quick. We've got to get on the move. They'll be looking for survivors."

That made sense to the Captain and was all the impetus that was needed. The Captain sucked in a deep breath, gritted his teeth, grasped the arrow, and worked it out slowly. Blood flowed freely from the wound around it. Luvian gave the Captain credit for not crying out.

"We've got to get you to Command. But first you've got to get rid of that helmet. Anyone will recognize you in it." Luvian reached over, grabbed it, and tossed it aside.

That was it, of course. The Ormish recognized the golden helmet. That was how they knew to attack the site they had just occupied. Damn.

The Captain suppressed his outrage as the logic of the idea slowly washed over him. Luvian craned his neck around the wagon and saw no one. Good. He stood up and limped painfully over to some of the dead soldiers.

"Well, come here then," Luvian gestured at the Captain. If he disliked losing that precious, gold-plated helmet of his, he was going to like this even less.

"Your armor. Take it off."

"What?"

"Shush – you want to wake the dead, do you?" Luvian waved at him to squat down.

"Take the armor off – I'm sure you've got more of your fancy gold suits wherever it is you come from. The Ormish will be looking for a bastard in gold plated armor with a stupid gold helmet. So let this dead bloke wear it and they'll stop looking for you."

Luvian tossed the Captain the dead man's helmet.

The Captain glared for a moment at Luvian and then began a painstaking process of jingling and stripping off the armor. Luvian belted it onto the dead man, though his leg was shooting jabs of pain up his side.

"Now then." He walked a bit around the dead soldiers, looking for a man of the Captain's height. "Here." He nudged the man. "Trade clothes with him."

The Captain's eyes bulged out. "You're joking."

"No, no I'm not."

"Do you have any idea who I am, Sergeant?"

"Right now, you're a wounded Captain that I've got to get back to Command. Other than that, I really don't care who you are," Luvian stared at him. His patience was wearing thin.

"You really don't know, do you. No idea." The Captain seemed amused.

"Can we do this later, maybe, under cover, maybe when you're wearing armor again? I'd really like to get back to a regiment, sir, if it's all the same to you, no disrespect intended."

"Where are you from? You and I have the same accent, I think."

"Romeny."

"As am I. I've pledged to serve my life to Romeny. As this ring indicates." The Captain held up his hand, where a gold signet ring gleamed.

Slow comprehension washed over Luvian. He suddenly thought of all the things he'd said....

"You are...."

"Rhutgard Firthing of Romeny."

"Crown Prince."

"Yes, Sergeant. And I believe that you saved my life back there –" he gestured at Luvian's leg, "for which I, and our country, will be forever grateful." His penetrating blue eyes stared at Luvian. *Romeny blue*, he thought.... For once, Luvian found words deserting him.

"I – Your Highness. I – Forgive me, please." He fell to his knees. There goes any thought of court-martial... he'd be lucky to see the inside of the Palace dungeon for the rest of his life. Did they still draw and quarter folks or just lynch them....

A bit amused, the Captain – His Royal Highness – held up a hand. "Still Captain, please. And did you really not know? Refreshing. I thought Major Corlander told you."

Unsure what question to answer first, Luvian blinked, at a loss. "Captain, sir, Major Corlander told me only to get these documents to the Command Captain. I asked for a name, but he told me I would know once I arrived, and that telling me would endanger the mission." He paused and then dared to add, "Captain, sir, Major Corlander believed that there was a serious betrayal. He knew not where or whom, but he believed it ran deep."

The Captain nodded and kept his thoughts to himself. He then asked, "What documents are these? Major Corlander was my –"

Luvian stopped him with a hand. "No, sir! If we are being watched – we may yet be in enemy territory."

Frowning, the Captain glanced around. "True. We should find cover. And have a look at that wound."

Luvian stared at the Captain and swallowed with difficulty. How to tell the Crown Prince of Romeny that his clothing was unacceptable for this mission? He cringed. Well, there was nothing for it but plod on in his usual fashion.

"Ah. Captain, sir. You've yet to change your clothes out." Luvian gestured to the dead soldier.

The Captain stared down at the soldier for a moment, his mouth falling open. Then, in a hushed voice, he pointed at the corpse. "I will not change my clothing with that man!"

Luvian sighed then, pain from the crossbolt stabbing up his leg. "With all due respect, Captain, what offends you more? The fact that the man's clothes are a commoner's, or that he's dead?"

A glare and a frown met him, though the Captain remained silent.

"Truly?" Luvian's temper blew. He wrestled the corpse's trousers off and held them up to the Captain. "Here! Put them on!" A slight curl of distaste of the Captain's lip as he accepted the trousers disgusted Luvian even more.

"I'm trying to get you back to Command and if you look like an expensively dressed fop, you're going to stand out immediately. If you're dressed like a regular man, at least you'll stand a chance."

The Captain slipped on the trousers gingerly and brushed them off. "They're – itchy."

"Itchy? You mean to say they're not velvet? They're homespun by a woman who made wool clothing for her husband to keep him warm. Begging your pardon, Your Highness," Luvian bowed with exaggerated sarcasm, "but this is what your subjects wear every day."

The Prince cleared his throat and looked down at the trousers he now wore. He brushed them again with his hands and responded with dignity, "They will be quite satisfactory."

Luvian blinked. He had expected more of fight. Inwardly, he credited the Prince yet again.

"And with these? Do we dress him with these, then?" The Prince gestured with his velvet trousers.

"No! Burn them. We don't want the enemy thinking you were anywhere near here or they'll be on our trail," Luvian told him.

"Burn them? But we can't leave him – you know –" And the Prince gestured to the dead soldier.

"Uncovered?" Luvian supplied a more palatable word than *naked*. He chuckled to himself. The Prince was, after all, wearing a dead bloke's clothes. He was quite sure that this was a war story that would never be hailed in the gilded halls of Fairview Palace.

"Still –" the Prince insisted.

"All due respect, Captain," Luvian rolled his eyes behind the Captain's back. He had a feeling he was going to be using that phrase quite a lot in the next few hours.

But the Captain was stepping over the few corpses that littered the area. "We can't leave him – uncovered – like that."

"Sir. I really don't think he minds, wherever he is. He was a soldier. In fact, if he knew his trousers were going to be worn by a Prince, he'd be quite happy to have donated them and told all his friends about it over his cups in the pub later. We really must be leaving."

But the Prince had found a cloak and had yanked it from beneath another corpse. Spreading it over the soldier from whose clothes he had taken, he said, "Now. He won't be – uncovered."

"He truly did give his services to the Crown, didn't he?" Luvian observed solemnly.

"Yes, he did. Although I'm sure that's not what he thought would be expected of him when he signed up to 'donate his services'...." The Prince gazed down at his new clothes.

For some reason, Luvian found that funny, but folded his lips back to hide a grin. Of all times to laugh. His mother had raised a better man.

The Prince cleared his throat and coughed. Then he glanced at Luvian. Luvian saw that the Prince, too was holding back laughter, and they both burst out laughing. Soon, they could not stop, and they were bent over in hilarity. Luvian felt like a naughty child.

Finally, they stood straight. Both of them wiped tears from their faces.

"We must be going," the Prince said.

"Aye, we must. But Captain – one last thing."

"What's that?"

Luvian pointed down at the Captain's boots. Expensive, oiled black leather, probably water resistant....

The Captain grimaced. "No."

Luvian raised an eyebrow at him.

"Very well – but I'll not burn them. After I'm back at Command, I'll have need of these, and certainly no need of someone else's – boots. These were tailor-made," the Prince insisted.

Luvian sighed but relented. Royalty.

They found a soldier whose feet were the same size as the Prince's so he could wear a different pair of boots. Luvian threw the Prince's boots into his rucksack, along with a combined collection of rations, flint, and water. Dislike was evident on the Prince's face. "This is robbing the dead."

"Captain, they don't care a bit. If they were about to set out on a journey with them wounded, they'd do the same."

This argument convinced the Prince and he nodded. "But first –" and he held up his velvet trousers. "Let's have a look at your wound."

"It's fine, Captain. We have to get along. Time to burn those trousers and move on."

"Not until we tie that leg off. You'll be bleeding the whole way and you'll be a hazard to us both, between leaving a trail of blood for anyone to follow, and blood loss. You'll pass out half way there. So go on. Drop your trousers." The Captain snorted. "I had to. What's wrong, Sergeant? Too scared to show your arse in front of your Prince? You've been doing it ever since I met you."

Luvian glared at him. "Bloody hell." He reached under his armor and unlaced his trousers.

Pulling the strings loose was the easy part. Pulling his trousers down – hurt far worse. Luvian inched them down little by little. The cold ground underneath his bare arse was the least of his worries – his thigh was on fire from the sudden movement.

"Go on, Sergeant. Stop whining about it, don't be a baby, we're going to have to pull that bolt out soon enough."

Luvian glared at the Prince. "You're enjoying this, aren't you?"

"Oh, you've no idea. But that – that is shitty, and it's not going to be easy coming out." The Captain pulled out some of the waterskins from the rucksack, and then started ripping his velvet trousers into strips.

"Wait." Luvian grabbed his hand. "Do you have any idea what you're doing?"

"Yes. Field first aid. I'm going to tie this off. Now bite down on this. It's going to hurt." The Prince shoved a thick chunk of wood in Luvian's mouth. He would probably be glad not to hear Luvian yelling at –

And then his leg burst into pain. He screamed around the wood and bit down as hard as he could.

He looked down and the Prince was tying the strip of velvet into a tight knot. The Prince glanced up at Luvian and handed him a waterskin. "Drink. This is going to hurt."

Luvian refrained from being a smartarse. His leg hurt too much and nothing sprang to mind other than wanting the pain to stop. He gulped at the waterskin and handed it back, panting.

The Prince drank from the skin himself, his eyes never leaving Luvian's. Then he held up the wood. "You might want this back again."

Luvian said nothing but inserted the wood back into his mouth. Then the Prince dumped water all over the wound. It felt like fire. He elected to close his eyes. He didn't want to know when the worst happened.

He felt the bolt pull out of his thigh – he had no idea how deep it had been lodged. A muffled scream went on and on around the wood in his mouth.

And then he felt water flood his open leg. "Sergeant! Sergeant? The bolt is gone now."

Luvian opened his eyes. Panting, he saw the Prince busily wrapping blue velvet strips about his leg to bind the wound shut. *Oy!* What he wouldn't give for a bottle of whiskey! A string of expletives escaped him.

"I quite agree," murmured the Prince.

After several more bindings, the Prince sat back, satisfied. He held up, with a bloody hand, a broken silver crossbolt. "Want it?" His voice was tired but mildly amused.

"Fuck, no!" Luvian, still panting, sat up and laced his trousers up. He noted how shaky his fingers were, as did the Captain.

Wordlessly, the Captain handed Luvian a full waterskin. "Take a few minutes, and then we'll be off."

Luvian nodded shortly. He gulped at the waterskin. This wound would take time healing. With luck, a Healer was stationed at Command. For now, he would have to ignore the pain and move as fast as possible. The import of his mission was now doubled. He no longer had just a Captain to see to safety, but the next King of Romeny. Bloody hell.

⁕

"Stop, stop. You're pushing too hard. We aren't going to get there tonight. We'll need to make camp," the Prince told him.

Privately, Luvian was happy to hear him say that. He knew his bandage needed changing; blood had been trailing down his leg for the last mile. How had he and Rushby run the entire distance?

The Prince glanced around a small, covered copse. "This will do for tonight. It's nearly twilight. We'll get there tomorrow. You set up camp and I'll get some firewood."

"No," Luvian objected as he set basic necessities around their small camp. "No fire. It will alert enemies."

The Prince thought for a moment. "You're right. But we need to light a small one to boil some water." When Luvian objected again, the Prince told him, "To sanitize your wound. And mine. I insist."

Luvian sat down gratefully, the pressure off of his leg at last.

The Prince eyed him as he said, "Besides. If anyone is tracking us, fire and smoke will certainly be the least of our worries. That trail of blood will lead them straight here. We'll have a look at that wound and change out the bandage."

Luvian realized then that he was being directed by a Prince accustomed to having his orders carried out at all times, rather than a field Captain with soldiers who might have more experience and knowledge of the world than he. Luvian kept his mouth shut.

The Prince lit a small fire and boiled a bit of water. "Go on. Let's see, then."

Luvian grit his teeth and inched his trousers down to expose his wound. The blood had seeped through the velvet bindings some time ago, but there was nothing for it.

The Prince pulled out several more strips of velvet. "Sergeant, this is going to hurt."

"That's what you said the last time," Luvian grumbled. He eyed the steaming water with concern.

"I did. But you might want to bite down on something just the same."

"On what? A pine cone?" snapped Luvian as he glanced about the wooded ground.

"Anything but a finger."

Again, Luvian recognized the Prince's authoritative tone. He found nothing to bite down, however, and gestured as much.

"Then don't scream," the Prince returned in a quiet tone. He glanced around behind him, indicating the need to keep their presence quiet.

Huh. Don't scream. Cheeky bastard. All the same, Luvian covered his mouth with his hand.

And in the next second was immediately glad he had. The water was not boiling, but hot enough to hurt nearly as bad as the removal of the bolt itself. He did not scream, but he did drive a groove in the ground with the boot of his other leg.

"There." The Prince glanced up at him. "The worst is over." As he tied tight velvet strips about Luvian's wound, he murmured, "Who would have guessed, that imported velvet from Hardewold would have such excellent use in battlefield medical care?"

Luvian snorted. Certainly not he. Although they did make an excellent whiskey.

"Well, that's it then. Do us a favor and cover up your arse?" The Prince's mild jest brought a glare from Luvian, but he pulled his trousers up all the same. His wound was on fire, but he appreciated how much worse it would be had the Prince not dressed it. Mopping his head of perspiration, Luvian knew he'd need to thank him properly.

At the moment, the Prince was tending to his own wound. He was fortunate the arrow hadn't lodged in his sword shoulder.

Finally, as they chewed on rations in the last remaining light of the day, the Captain suddenly sat forward. "Let's have a look at these documents, shall we?"

Luvian slipped a hand under his armor and pulled the documents from beneath his tunic. Major Corlander's blood had dried to brown stains on the parchment, Luvian saw as he handed the documents to the Prince.

The Prince met his eyes as he accepted them. "You took these from Corlander?"

"Major Corlander told me he had them and to take them to you, but died before he could tell me more." Luvian repeated the entire conversation.

"A shame." The Prince's face took on a faraway look. "He was a good man, and a good friend. He was a faithful servant to my family, and I knew him my entire life." He looked suddenly at Luvian. "A true and loyal servant to his last breath. I was told only that he had fallen behind, not that he had taken a wound." He looked at Luvian then. "It would seem, then, that there is a threat in my own Command. A betrayal. A spy." His eyes narrowed. "And I wondered why at each station we were attacked by such a rigorous enemy."

"Sir, if you please, back at your Command, I was told that the last communication they had received from you was just this morning: *'All was well, no problems to report,'* after two days of being gone."

The Prince sat up, startled. "I sent no such message."

Luvian stared at the Prince. "None, sir? Would it not have born your Royal Seal?"

"I sent no message at all. You noticed that we were far too busy to sit down and write messages. No birds about."

"If I may ask, Sir, why did you choose that region to fight in?"

The Prince sighed. "Too many of my men died, and for no reason, back at Command. Right before my eyes. We were ambushed, no other word for it. And now I know why. I was given to believe that this region had only a little action. I needed to get out of that damnable tent. I wanted, I suppose, in some small way, to avenge the lives of my men by fighting out here."

Luvian blinked. His respect for the man rose, royal or not. "Well, it's probably that which saved your life. You might have gotten a gut wound to the stomach yourself, as did Major Corlander."

"Ha. Whoever is behind this probably assumed I'd die out there on the battlefield instead. If my father found out I'd been fighting in the heaviest of battlegrounds, he would disown me." A tired smile tried and failed to pass over the Prince's face.

"Well, Sir, you did your men and your family, and your country proud out there. That I can tell you."

The Prince's blue eyes met Luvian's. "Thank you, Sergeant." He cleared his throat. "Let's have a look at what Corlander died to protect, shall we?"

He unfolded the maps and tilted them in the dying sunlight. "I'm not sure this makes any sense. Why did he want me to see these?"

Luvian pointed with a stick to different regions. "My regiment died there. Mostly cornered by the Ormish and Ambsells, of which we had no prior intelligence. The 21st was supposed to meet us here. The 19th was supposed to be stationed there." He continued to point at the few Northern regiments that he was aware of.

The Prince shook his head. "No. No, Sergeant, that's not right. These two regiments were stationed here and sent to back up the 10th and the 14th until the Southern detachments arrived with supplies."

Luvian stared at him. "Well, Captain, the dog's wagging its nose instead of its tail because that sure as shit isn't right. "I never heard no such thing. If anything, the North needed supplies."

The Prince overlooked Luvian's rebuke and shuffled to the next parchment. "This – this is all troop action. I don't understand what he's trying to tell me." He shuffled through the next several parchments. "All maps!" he swore.

"With all due respect, Captain, was that not what his function was?"

The Prince sighed and rubbed his eyes. "It was."

"Sir, it's too late, we can't see anything anyway. Put them up, Captain."

"You're right." The Prince folded the documents up but then said, "Here. You keep them. You be my new mapper." The Prince handed him the documents.

Luvian blinked. "Sorry, what?"

"Keep them. You're the only one who knows the story of what took place between you and Corlander and saw for your own eyes the burned down Command Camp. You keep the documents. There's obviously something that Corlander wants me to figure out that I'm just not getting. Besides, my face is far more recognizable than yours. If they take me alive, you can take those on to – to…."

"Sir?"

The Prince was quiet for a moment.

"Sir, I think you need to consider that… your Command station is no longer safe."

"Sergeant, I think I agree with you. But who to trust? Those two Lieutenants?"

Luvian pffed. "Hawthorne? Fannion? They may be idiots, but I'm not sure they're traitors."

"And that, Sergeant, is where I may be more experienced than you. Politicians and spies are not so very different – I've been surrounded by the former my entire life, and hopefully not the latter very often. Most notably, however, they both lie and put on excellent performances, an occupational requirement. So how would we know if anyone in my Command was a spy? Surely if he has sent me and my soldiers into ambushes without being detected, his competency as a spy is most renowned, wouldn't you agree?"

"You will need a guard back at Command, then, Sir," Luvian remarked as he tucked the parchments back under his tunic.

"Perhaps. For now, let us rest. I'll take first watch. Get some sleep, Sergeant."

Suddenly, Luvian awoke. It was daylight, morning, judging by the sunlight streaming through the trees. The Prince was dozing against a tree.

Keenly aware of both his sore leg and the need to piss, Luvian scrambled up. The Prince opened his eyes.

"What happened to second watch?" called Luvian as he relieved himself against a tree.

"Never came," replied the Prince.

Luvian limped back and stared down at the Prince. "You should have woken me."

"You needed the rest."

Luvian did not argue the point and began clearing the camp. He drank several swallows of water from a waterskin and handed it to the Prince.

He accepted it and told Luvian, "Sergeant, I require your services for a few days longer." Water dribbled down the Prince's chin as he took several gulps.

"Of course, Captain."

"I thought about a number of things over the course of the evening, and I've decided upon my best course of action." The Prince let out a deep breath. "I will not be returning to Command. I've no idea what Corlander was trying to impart to me with those maps, but there is something of dear value in them, he made that clear. Keener minds than mine need to make sense of them. In short, my father needs to see them."

Luvian blinked. "Your... your father? As in, the King? Of Romeny?" *Bloody hell.*

"Yes. For many years to come yet, I hope," answered the Prince.

"Right. And, if I may ask, Sir, just where is your father located? Please don't tell me he's stationed out on the battlefield as well."

"Well, no, of course not!"

"I thought I would ask, as you were out on the battlefield yourself, in the thick of it. Last place you ought to have been, by the way."

"Yes, we have established that. And why," snapped the Prince. "My father is at home in the capital, at Fairview Palace. Had your fun now?"

Luvian permitted himself a small smile. "Thought I would ask, at least." Then he sobered. "Fairview is a few more days from here than your Command. I make it...."

"Two days with two wounded men, allowing for good weather. I know this land, if not its people," the Prince informed him quietly.

Luvian wondered how much it cost the Prince to admit that.

"Right then."

"Here," the Prince tossed him a thick branch, stripped of limbs and about as high as Luvian's head.

"What's this?"

"Use it to put your weight on." When he caught Luvian's surprised expression, he intoned dryly, "You'll find I can be extraordinarily resourceful, you know, when I'm not fighting for my life in the wrong battlefield or stripping dead men of their clothing."

Luvian chuckled and gave an awkward bow. "Your Highness."

The Prince accepted the perceived gratitude but then warned Luvian, "And whatever you do, do not call me *Your Highness*. Even commoners not in the Army will turn in a Prince on the run for gold."

Luvian knew the sad truth of that. With his good leg, he kicked leaves over the small campfire the Prince had made to heat water for their wounds.

"You know we're going to look like deserters," he observed. He tested out the walking stick the Prince had made. Sturdy. And if he was going to walk a good pace clear east to Fairview, he was going to need it.

"Yes. We'll need to come up with a story."

"Discharge."

"For us both? I'm still able to fight."

"Well, so am I," Luvian returned.

"Our commissions are expired?"

"In the middle of a war? No. If we keep losing soldiers the way we have been, we'll need farmboys out of the fields." Luvian did not explain that only a quarter of the Army was comprised of commissioned soldiers; the rest were enlisted men who were fighting for their country.

He started chewing on his dried rations as they moved onward. Army rations were better than nothing at all, but Luvian would be glad to get some real food in his belly. The thought of the Prince not having a buffet of cheese and grapes and fresh meat, however, made his ration taste much better. But as he limped on his leg, Luvian was reminded that it was the Prince who had bound his wound and gone without a full night's sleep so that Luvian could rest. He sighed inwardly.

The day turned into an eternal hell of limping and leaning on the walking stick that the Prince had given him. When they stopped to rest, he refused to admit just how grateful he was to sit down and take the pressure off his leg, though on occasion, he caught the Prince eyeing him with something like concern.

During the afternoon, the Prince asked suddenly, "Sergeant, I never asked. Where are you from?"

"Fairview, sir. Same as you. Though, my people are a bit less refined than your own, I expect."

The Prince nodded and conceded to that observation with a rueful expression.

That gave Luvian a sudden idea. "You know, Captain...."

The Prince glanced over his shoulder.

"We may have the same story, being discharged for medical reasons, but no one will believe you're just an ordinary man. All due respect," he added.

"What's that supposed to mean? Aren't I wearing homespun clothing...?" The Prince stopped and looked down at himself. "What's wrong with me?"

"Sir, it's – well." Luvian trailed off. They had agreed to pretend they were brothers, and that the Captain was escorting him home to their kin in Romeny. As they both were injured, they planned to exaggerate their injuries should they meet anyone on their way to the Palace. "No one will believe we're brothers because you talk and act the way you do."

The Prince frowned at him. "Like...."

"Sir, I'm a commoner. And I talk and act like one. You're a royal, sir. You talk and act like one, with all your manners and your words."

"Then what do you propose? How am I to act if we meet someone?"

"There. You see. I would never say that. *How am I to act. What do you propose.* Captain, if you please, Sir, just let me do the talking."

"You! But –"

"Aye, sir. Not to take it personal, but I blend in. Would you say I'd blend in among your people, even if you dressed me up in silks and satins?" Luvian prompted.

The Prince's blue eyes narrowed. "I see your point." He cleared his throat. "Very well. But let us then make every attempt to avoid speaking to people," the Prince eyed him sternly.

Luvian snickered. "What, you don't trust me?"

"Careful, Sergeant." With a heavy sigh, the Prince admitted, "You're quite right, however."

They resumed their trek, dry leaves crunching beneath their boots. "You shall have to teach me, then."

Luvian started. "Sorry, what?"

"Teach me. To talk like – like you."

"You mean a *commoner*. You were going to say *a commoner*." At this, the Prince threw a baleful glare over his shoulder at Luvian. "And the answer is no. No. Huh-uh. No way. Not possible. I mean – all due respect, but – Your Highness – you just can't."

"I can, and I will. And you will teach me. And I told you not to use that honorific."

Luvian snorted. What of any of that made a lick of sense? "Honorific? Sir, not a commoner anywhere has ever heard of that term, and if they have, they probably think it's a disease they can catch. You see?"

The Prince grabbed at Luvian's tunic sleeve. "And that's why I need you to teach me! I insist!"

Bosh. This was ridiculous. Easier to stuff an egg back into its shell without a crack.

The Prince must have read his face, for he intoned in a deeper voice, "I insist." And there it was. A royal decree.

And if he failed, what then? He'd lose his head? At the least, the Prince would sound ridiculous. Either way, Luvian would still need to do the talking should they meet anyone during the rest of the journey.

So they passed the rest of the afternoon with Luvian coaching the Prince on how to speak as a commoner. In awe at that sheer lack of understanding the royals had of their own subjects, Luvian restrained himself a number of times from simply staring at the Prince in disgust. For the Prince truly was attempting to learn, as an eager puppy might, but phrases such as *why, of all things!* and *upon my word!* were just not in the normal commoner's day-to-day language.

His vocabulary was appallingly obnoxious. Luvian tried a number of times to explain that no commoner would use such words, nor even have heard of them. But the Prince was stubborn – by dark, as they sat against trees in their camp, he was trying to instruct Luvian on the benefits of his royal education.

Finally, Luvian's patience snapped. "Oy! I don't care about your bloody *ed-u-ca-tion*. With all due respect. Sir, half your subjects can't hardly do their numbers and less than that can't read. Do you think your precious vocabulary is going to impress them, should we come across one or two of them between here and Fairview? Sir?"

"Let me tell you something. My mother learned her letters and her numbers because she and my father run a business, and they have paying customers. I learned from them. But most of my friends only make their marks and they can do their numbers enough to get their wages. Do you think, Sir, that they care about your Treasury up in the Palace, or these maps we're carryin'? They just want to keep living their lives without anyone raisin' their taxes so they can put food on the table for their little ones. If they know the names of all your siblings, that's an impressive thing, Sir. Mostly, they just know you and your parents. They'll never leave the couple blocks they live on. They count themselves educated if they know the names of kings in Delsynth and Hardewold, but they truly impress each other if they know all the names of the people in the Market Square. Readin' and writin' counts nothin' to them."

Luvian heard his street accent creeping in, but it was best that the Prince truly understand who his people truly were. He had some romantic idea of them, born and passed down to him, no doubt, by some tutor and his royal family. Luvian couldn't fault him for his upbringing, but if he wanted to understand his people better, he needed to lose the veil that blinded his eyes.

The Prince had remained impassive during this outburst. Now, however, he said, "Are you done?"

Luvian snorted. "Not nearly." But he said nothing else.

The Prince rearranged himself against his tree. Finally, he said, "I think it best that we pick this up tomorrow morning."

Again, use of vocabulary. *I think it best?* This was going to be harder than he thought. Luvian shrugged. "I'll take first watch."

The Prince started to protest, but Luvian stopped him. "You hardly slept last night. I'll wake you for second watch."

Satisfied, the Prince nodded and laid down on his cloak. "Be sure to," he murmured around a yawn as he rolled over and closed his eyes.

"Sergeant." The Prince nudged him with a boot. "Time to be going."

Luvian sat up. The crisp air of early morning assaulted his senses. Yawning, he stood and stretched. The damp fog that lingered in the trees would serve to mask their progress. So far, fortune had accompanied them on this journey. He prayed they wouldn't lose it.

Luvian swigged some water from his waterskin. If they didn't find some water – a stream, a brook, anything – soon, their water would fall below a critical level neither of them cared to confront each other over.

The Prince ran his hands through his golden locks and neatened his appearance as he waited for Luvian. Oy. Royals. Luvian brushed himself free of dirt and debris and stood, leaning heavily on the crutch Rhutgard had fashioned for him.

Glad of the extra rations he'd procured, he chewed on his breakfast as they set out. His leg was sore – the cool air had set into it and he continued his limp and lean routine. He mulled over whether they would reach Fairview by tonight or if they'd have to make camp again. This close to the city, Luvian knew how important it was that the Prince not be recognized.

They tramped along in silence until the sun finally peaked over the horizon, breaking through the mist.

Finally, Luvian asked, "Sir, what will you tell your father when we arrive?"

The Prince tramped a few more paces through the leaves and then said tiredly, "The truth. That there is betrayal in the ranks. And that we know not where."

Or who, thought Luvian, thinking of Major Corlander's eyes as he died. He would need to send word to the man's family – but no. He would inform them himself. If not for Corlander, the whole of this war might have gone in a different direction altogether. In fact, the Prince might even be dead by now….

That! A noise – up ahead in the distance. Someone trying to be stealthy and not succeeding. "Captain!" he whispered, clutching at the Prince's sleeve. The Prince had heard it as well. They immediately dropped to the hillside and froze.

Every nerve in Luvian's body jangled. Laying in the leaves, Luvian stared at the Prince's widened eyes and saw the Prince was just as alarmed.

He took in half breaths, smelling the earth and the dead leaves. "Soldiers?" whispered the Prince. Luvian shrugged. If soldiers were up ahead, then the two of them were just fucked, plain and simple. Obviously, enemy soldiers would execute them, or worse, keep them for questioning, which meant ultimately a very painful existence and then a grisly death. The Prince would be ransomed, of course, but his own fate in enemy hands would not be as secure, Luvian was sure. And Corlander's documents would be lost.

And if Eastern Alliance soldiers awaited them, then at best, they would be court-martialed for deserting, but at worst, hung from the nearest tree. Deserters in time of war were severely frowned upon. No questions were asked until after the rope was cut from the tree. They certainly would never believe that the man in homespun clothing claiming to be His Royal Highness of Romeny was sane… they would hang him first, and then make apologies to the King later.

Again – there it was! Someone was stepping quietly through the leaves up ahead. Clearly, they knew Luvian and the Prince were there. The Prince loosened his sword in its scabbard.

"Who are ya? Show yerselves, I know yer out there!" came a woman's voice. "I've got a knife!"

The Prince collapsed with relief upon the leaves. Luvian buried his head under his arms, letting out a long breath. Then they looked at each other and shook their heads with a shared release of anxiety.

Luvian stepped forward first. He held up a finger to remind the Prince. "Remember who we are!"

The Prince nodded and shooed him forward.

"Oy! Here! No harm intended," Luvian called, waving his arms.

A woman in a gray homespun dress stepped out from a tree. And she did, indeed, have a knife, though it was her vegetable knife. She had a woven basket of vegetables on her arm and they had clearly disrupted her harvest.

Luvian immediately adopted a far more pronounced limp and then glanced at the Prince. The Prince then recalled that he, too, was to act much more injured than he was, so that a medical discharge would be more believable. He immediately bent over and assumed a sickly stance.

Luvian leaned on his walking stick and groaned as they approached. "Sorry for the fright, we mean no harm. Just on our way home from the battlefield. Discharged."

Her face, creased and windworn, and shrewd gray eyes took in their bloody uniforms, though she kept her knife out. "I can certainly see why. Was it medical, then?"

"Aye. Bloody bastards. Everywhere we turned, they were on us. And more coming."

"Well, boys, I'm sorry for that. They're everywhere now. Never knew it so bad. Where ya headed?"

"Me 'n' my brother, we're headed back home. Had enough of the wide world."

The woman chortled. "Don't they all want to leave and see the world and once they're out there, they can't figure out what to do with themselves. Well, you soldier boys, ya've sure earned a place at our table. I've got some stew ready. Come on in and rest yer bones a bit before ya move on."

The Prince was silent throughout this exchange, thankfully, but Luvian saw an avid curiosity alight on his face.

"My name's Ernestine," called their host, "but I'm mostly called Ernie. My own boys run off and gave me grandchildren years ago. Don't see them hardly enough at all," she mused. Ernie led them to a worn log cabin sheltered under several fir trees.

As she led them to the door, she warned them, "Mind ya wipe yer feet. The husband don't do it near enough. If he did the sweepin' and changin' out of the rushes, I'll tell you what, he'd wipe his feet every ten seconds, he would," Ernie clucked.

Luvian and the Prince both made a point of wiping their boots. Ah. Inside was a warm, cozy home such as he hadn't been in for months, and with food ready over the fire…. Luvian wanted to collapse with exhaustion, feeling safe for the first time in months.

"Sit yerselves down, I'll be about with some stew. It's only rabbit, my husband hasn't shot a deer in a month a more. It's the war, ya know. Soldier men have found all the deer. Not," Ernie turned and looked at them with an apologetic smile, "that I'm blamin' you. Just they marched through and now deer is scarce."

The Prince sat forward then. "What was that? Who? Who marched through?"

"Why, the soldier men. Ambsellon, I think it was. Right through the city, if you can believe it. I never knew that had happened before. But they wiped the deer fresh out of the forest, not a buck to be found for miles, says my husband."

Luvian found himself staring and swallowed. A lump had formed in his stomach and he suddenly had no interest in food. Troops – marching through Fairview. That hadn't happened for – well, at least a hundred years. He knew the Prince would know.

Luvian cleared his throat and dared a look at the Prince. His face had turned to stone and his mouth had dropped open. He couldn't imagine what he was thinking, but right now, they still had to be medically discharged soldiers on their way home.

As soon as Ernie turned her back, Luvian delivered a sharp kick to the Prince's ankle. The Prince turned his attention to Luvian with a thunderous expression, but Luvian stared him down. It would not do to lose their cover now when they needed information so desperately.

Ernie was scooping stew into bowls for them. As she set bowls down in front of Luvian and the Prince, the Prince said, "Ah, Madam –"

Luvian kicked him again in the ankle. Ernie laughed merrily. "*Madam*. Such pretty manners he has, your brother. Where'd he pick those up, aye?"

"Ah, well. He was always trying to impress the ladies back home. 'Course, Dad thinks he's a pansy, but, me, I don't think so. He's just a show-off is all," Luvian nodded at the Prince across the table as he shoved hot stew into his mouth. Knowing him as well as he had come to, Luvian could see that he was smoldering, but was also taking the reminder of his environment seriously. Later, however, Luvian feared for his life.

The door behind them opened and closed. Luvian and the Prince both froze and waited, every nerve on alarm to find out who had just entered the cabin.

"What's this? A show-off? Surely not referring to me?" boomed a deep voice under a shadow that fell over the table.

"You wiped yer boots, did ya?" Ernie stood with a hand on one hip and an accusatory wooden spoon pointing at the door.

"Yes, Ernie, if I wiped 'em once, I wiped 'em a thousand times, I keep tellin' ya, woman. I'm gonna start wipin' 'em on your arse if ya don't stop hecklin' me. Now."

The Prince and Luvian both relaxed in minute increments as they recognized that Ernie's husband had joined them. Luvian hoped fervently that one day he would stop startling at the slightest noise and go back to living his life the way he used to.

A man of enormous stature approached the table and, as he shed his cloak, he stared down at them, demanding answers. Idly, Luvian was amazed that such a tiny woman as Ernie and such a huge man as her husband were a pair.

"Who's this at my table? Soldiers, by the look of ya."

"I was just tellin' them, Petyr, about the soldier men who marched on the city."

"Oh. Aye. Hasn't happened in a hundred years, the way I heard it," he frowned.

Luvian stared at the Prince, whose jaw had clenched, and said, "Bastards."

"Aye. Took all the game outta the wood on the way through. But what's this? Who are you two?" Petyr sat down at the table and Ernie served him a bowl of rabbit stew.

"Brothers, both medically discharged," she told him.

Petyr's skeptical brown eyes looked from Luvian to the Prince. "Both brothers, medically discharged at the same time?"

"Aye," started Ernie, but Petyr interrupted her.

"Let them tell it, woman." He looked at them and crossed his arms on his chest as he sat back in his chair. "Well?"

Luvian had felt less nervous his first day on the battlefield, and if truth be told, he'd damn near pissed his pants after he saw the bloody corpses out there.

"We was stationed in the same regiment, so we got moved about quite a bit."

Petyr held up his hand and stopped Luvian. "What regiment was that?"

Luvian was beginning to get angry. He had not served and killed more men on the field than he could count in the name of his country and the Eastern Alliance just to get interrogated by a woodsman.

Evenly, he returned, "The Northern 20th. It don't exist no more. It's gone. Ormish wiped it out."

Petyr's brow furrowed and he looked down at the table. "I apologize, soldier. Our table is yours. We can't be too careful these days. Deserters sneakin' round in the woods. We have to protect our own."

The Prince spoke up then. "That we do. That we do."

"So yer brothers, then. If ya don't mind my sayin', you don't look it much." Petyr rolled an eye back and forth between the Prince and Luvian.

"Petyr, let them be. They're guests, and medical discharges from our Army," Ernie protested.

"That's all right. Happens all the time. I takes after Mum. He takes after Dad, clear as day and no mistakin' it." The Prince met his eye over the table and shook his head ever so slightly at the personal jest. Then he filled his mouth with stew and nodded to confirm Luvian's story.

"What about him? He's a quiet one," Petyr observed as he nodded at the Prince.

Luvian thought fast. "Ah, well. He took a hard knock to the head. There's times he's not quite right now. Home's the best place for him, I think. I just leave him to his thoughts, ya know?"

"Right. Might be yer dad'll have to support him the rest of his life. He looks like a strong enough fellow. He could get a job out in the fields," supposed Petyr.

"Aye, that he could," Luvian returned politely. Now that he'd like to see!

They needed to leave as soon as they could. Ambsellon soldiers in Fairview – and here they sat talking of the Prince of Romeny working as a farmhand. It was time to leave. If their mission wasn't important previously, it was dire now.

"Well," Luvian pushed his empty bowl forward, "we really must push on. We've got to get home to our folks in Fairview, especially if there's still soldiers about, as you say. Don't want to get caught out in the dark with any lurking deserters." Luvian stood up.

The Prince followed his lead.

Petyr stood as well. "Son, if yer headed to Fairview, ya might want to consider that –

could be maybe yer folks met with, well...." And he looked at Ernie.

Ernie stepped forward and put her arm around Petyr, where he sheltered her. She reached out her other arm gently. "An untimely end..." she supplied kindly, concern on her face.

Luvian looked at the Prince and then back to Petyr and Ernie. "Yes, well. I – we – got us some cousins down in Ivy Town. We could always head there if we need to."

Petyr raised an eyebrow. "Ivy Town. The village?"

Luvian recognized yet another test. "No, just a spit of folk livin' on the water outside Ivy Gate. Right there on the Rosh. If we have to, we'll just take the ferry on down and hope for the best."

Satisfied, Petyr said, "Right then. Well, fill yer waterskins before ya leave, we've plenty in the water barrel to spare for our Army boys."

Luvian and the Prince filled their waterskins gratefully and set out to leave.

As they were headed down the path, Ernie came running down. "Here's a bit of bread for ya both," and she handed them each a small chunk of bread. "I know it's not much, but maybe it'll help in the times ahead. Good will follow ya both."

They thanked Ernie and slid the homemade bread into their rucksacks. And as she passed Luvian, she whispered loudly, "And I don't believe for a second yer brother's a pansy. Find 'im a good wife an' he'll find his wits again." She winked and turned back down the path.

As Luvian limped forward, he knew he was going to pay dearly for his remarks.

They kept up their exaggerated pain until they were sure that they had not been followed by Petyr. As they rounded a hill, Luvian glanced at the Prince. His face was a mixture of stone, fury, and concern, his jaw clenched. If soldiers had marched through the city, what of the Palace? The King?

Luvian drew in a breath, but the Prince stopped him with a raised hand. "Don't. Say a word. I need to think."

And so Luvian left the Prince to his thoughts, which surely were of more import than his ever would be.

An hour passed while he limped through the leaves. How had Ambsellons ever made it past our guard, he fumed. Fairview had been indelible through the years – all knew that invading the city was a fruitless endeavor. This sounded more like – a planned attack that insiders had planned... and planned well. Luvian dreaded actually seeing the city. If they had been attacked with little warning, and by Ambsellons, no less.

"Do you... smell that?" The Prince stopped and sniffed the air.

"Aye. Smoke. I've smelled it for at least a mile, Sir," Luvian replied grimly. "Could be someone's burning a camp fire," he said hopefully.

"Perhaps," the Prince replied shortly, unconvinced.

As they continued on, the smell of smoke permeated the air and what could be seen of the sky through the tree cover had turned grey. Finally, a flake of ash drifted past them.

"Sergeant, they have burnt my city."

Chills tingled down Luvian's spine. He would never forget the Prince saying that.

"Perhaps – perhaps not – Sir...." Luvian trailed off. He had never felt so useless.

The Prince turned to him, not having heard Luvian's remark. "I must get into the city immediately. Do you understand?" His voice a dangerous, low tone, the Prince's face was set in an expression Luvian had never witnessed before.

"Yes, Sir."

"Now, we must pick up our pace, as fast as your leg will allow."

"Of course, Sir. But, if I may, Sir, will it not be dangerous for you to appear in the City? Will you not be recognized, Sir?"

"I must get into the Palace. I must see if my father is alive! Do you understand, Sergeant?"

"Aye, Sir, I do. And it with the utmost respect for your life that I ask again, will you not be recognized in the City? The Ambsellons will surely recognize you, Sir. How do you plan to get into the City, and into the Palace itself, if it is overrun with soldiers?"

"There is a back way into the Palace, tunnels, that we as children often snuck in and out of. I know not if it has been found, but I must try, do you understand? And as for appearing as a Prince." He gestured down at himself. "Do I look a Prince to you? You've seen to that. I'm not wearing silks and satins, as you say, nor gold plated armor, am I? Perhaps they will look past the Prince and see the commoner, if fortune is with me."

"Now that's the first time I've ever heard that expression used that way," replied Luvian dryly, as normally commoners wished to be seen as Princes. "Very well, then, Sir, after you. Let's take back your City."

Luvian was pushed past his endurance limping on his walking stick, for they ran as best Luvian was able. He knew the Prince was keeping him as protection, else he would have snuck into the Palace by now. Luvian didn't mind. He had sworn to Major Corlander to keep this bloke safe, and so he would, at least until he was in his velvets and satins again with his maps in hand. Then he would consider his oath fulfilled.

More and more ash filled the air and finally they stood from the hillside looking down at the city of Fairview.

A burned and blackened shell met their view. Smoke still drifted up lazily from building still smoldering. Luvian felt all the air whoosh out of him. This was the capital city of Romeny, and it had been sacked. He realized his mouth was hanging open and he shut it.

Taking a deep breath, he looked up at the Prince. He stood, immutable, except for his eyes, which took in every sight he could see from their vantage point.

"Captain?" Luvian prompted.

The Prince remained silent. Of course he's got nothing to say, Luvian thought. Just look at that. Bloody hell.

"Captain? We need to go, Sir. Now."

"Sergeant. I ask of you one more thing."

"Aye, Sir."

"Kill any Ambsell bastard you see."

"With pleasure, Sir!" Luvian set foot after the Prince's sudden stride forward. Rarely did the Prince swear, but this occasion warranted it if any.

Their footing down the hill was unsure. The Prince took up a thick branch much like Luvian's to steady himself until they arrived in the City proper. Luvian wondered where the Guard was. Normally, no one would be able to enter the City from any angle, not even from the woods. But as he strode further into the city, he thought he knew.

People stood staring wide-eyed at nothing in the street, wandering nowhere in particular, their clothes covered in soot. Children cried for their parents, tears trailing tracks through the dirt on their faces. One small child looked at Luvian with her thumb in her mouth, her other hand out, demanding food. Their eyes all looked soulless.

Most of the buildings had burned to the ground. Blackened shards of lumber shot upward as ghostly reminders of the buildings that had once stood. And everywhere, ashes swirled in the air.

Luvian bent to give the small girl one of his rations, but the Prince grabbed his arm and pulled him close immediately. "Don't!" the Prince whispered fiercely.

"What? What the bloody hell is wrong with you? She's hungry, can't you see that?"

"Aye. They're all hungry, Sergeant. They're starving. But if you give one of them food, you'll need to give all of them food!" the Prince whispered again.

Luvian struggled to loose his arm from the Prince's tight hold. "Why, you bloody bastard –"

"Shut up and do as I tell you. Look straight forward. Don't look at them. Hear me now? Don't look at them. Do as they do. Act as if you've been through a battle. Act as if soldiers have run through your city and burnt it to the ground while you slept. Stare down at the ground, like they are. They're in shock, soldier. Here," the Prince pulled him down and glanced around quickly to see that no one had observed them. "Rub some of this soot on your face. Go on." The Prince ran soot through his own hair and over his face.

Taken aback, Luvian rubbed dust and soot about his clothes and skin.

"I want to help them too, Sergeant, but if we do, then we'll cause a scene, and if we cause a scene, then soldiers will notice and that *cannot happen*. Do you understand me?" The Prince demanded affirmation.

"Aye, Capt –"

"And no more rank. We are not Captain and Sergeant now." The Prince glanced around for anyone who might be observing them, then whispered, "Take off your armor and your swordbelt and stuff it in your rucksack. Hurry up." He was doing the same as he glanced around nervously.

"With all due respect –"

"Stop saying that. If someone overhears us, they'll turn us in for money. Or food. We need to pass as commoners. Which means that you need to do the talking again. Understand me?" whispered the Prince fiercely.

Luvian nodded. "It's just… well, what do I call you if I don't use… rank?"

"…Mate will do," the Prince shrugged with impatience. He pulled Luvian along again, staring at the ground. "Remember, don't look at them."

"Aye… mate."

Some women crying in what had been a marketplace rankled Luvian, for he feared the Ambsell soldiers had claimed them as war trophies, but the Prince clutched at his elbow tightly. "Fuckin' bastards," muttered Luvian.

Soon, two Ambsell soldiers passed them, dressed in full regalia, laughing with each other. He felt the Prince draw in breath as if to confront them and saw his fist clench.

"No, no, onward we go, mate," Luvian nearly hauled the Prince forward. The Prince threw a furious glare at Luvian but consented.

Finally, the packed mud and dirt street became cobblestone, though even the stone buildings in this well-to-do district showed damage from the fire, with scorch marks and soot traversing their structures.

A carter drove his wagon past them, dead bodies weighing it down. Luvian glanced at the Prince. His eyes were round at the sight, but the smell of the decay was even worse. Luvian himself nearly gagged. He wondered where in Fairview was there to bury such a mass amount of bodies. He knew of nowhere and hoped that they weren't being dumped in the Rosh, their only source of clean drinking water….

"This way," the Prince suddenly pushed Luvian to the left.

A look up at the Palace told him that it was well-guarded by Ambsell soldiers. He hoped this was not a fool's errand. He knew the Prince had to get into the Palace, but Luvian did not want either of them to lose their lives trying. Morosely, he wondered if there was any point… that Palace looked well-fortified on the outside.

Looking about for anyone who might see them, the Prince yanked Luvian aside. "Right then. We'll head to the back of the Palace and hope we don't get shot down by archers on the towers."

"Sorry?" Luvian stared at him.

"Did you think the Palace wouldn't be armed? Just stay low and follow me," whispered the Prince.

He'd said nothing of archers. Bloody hell. He was going to sneak along and not even know if a crossbolt was coming his way. At least on the battlefield, he knew it was coming, he could see them. All this bloody sneaking around had him on edge. If he was manning a tower, he'd shoot first and ask questions later, men sneaking around by the castle like they were.

Finally, the Prince waved him over to a clump of weeds. "This is it. I think, anyway."

"You think?" Luvian rolled his eyes and shook his head.

"It's been over ten years since I've last been here, so you just settle it down, *mate*," snapped the Prince.

Luvian shrugged in response.

The Prince looked up at him. "Well, don't just stand there, dig!"

"What?"

Together, they dug through the clump of weeds until they reached a stone door. In relief, the Prince sat back on the grass in the dirt and weeds they'd just dug up. "Thank the gods, it's still there."

"Mate, we're only half there. We've still got to get in," Luvian told him frankly.

The Prince's blue eyes narrowed. "You're a real pessimist, aren't you? You couldn't just be happy about it, could you? Has anyone ever told you that? That you're a complete pessimist?"

Luvian glared at the Prince. Before he could check his tongue, he retorted, "And you're a real pain in the arse, has anyone ever told you that? I'll bet not."

"Not nearly as much as you are," crabbed the Prince as he brushed the stone door free of dirt and grass. "Don't say this, act more like that...."

"Yes, but only one of us will live to regret it, and I won't say who," returned Luvian as he stood up to pull the door open.

"That –" the Prince stood up himself and they both took hold of the rusty door handle. At the same time, they both heaved.

"...Sounded suspiciously like treason to me," finished the Prince, panting. He brushed his hands clean of rust and dirt.

Luvian scoffed. "Depends on who lives to regret it." He brushed his own hands free of dirt, then handed the Prince flint for the tunnel.

The Prince struck a spark on a lantern hanging within the tunnel, then lit another lantern for Luvian. They closed the door behind them, and Luvian hoped fervently that no one would pass by on the outside and make note of the freshly unearthed grass and weeds, much less the tunnel door.

"Well, mate, you're inside the Palace," Luvian said. "What now?"

The Prince turned to him with a rueful expression. "I've got to get into the Throne Room. And I need to find my father." He took a long breath and stared at Luvian. "Or," he said quietly, "I may be the King of Romeny myself."

Luvian started. The King of Romeny, standing here next to him, in an underground tunnel. Bloody hell. Gods be good, he hoped not.

"Well, then, mate," he returned evenly, "we need to get you into the Throne Room."

The Prince turned around and, his lantern held high, headed down the tunnel with a brisk pace. Luvian himself was still recovering from the idea that this – this – spoiled bloke that he'd been chiding, in all good fun… might right now be his King.

Finally, they reached the end of the tunnel, and a rusty ladder reached down to grant users access to the Palace above. Luvian couldn't help but wonder if all of this would be for naught if they couldn't get through up above.

The Prince set his lantern down on the stone floor. "Shh," he told Luvian. Ha. As if Luvian needed to told to be quiet in a palace overrun by Ambsells. Nevertheless, he held up his own lantern so that the Prince could see his way up the ladder.

At the top of the ladder, the Prince stopped and listened. Heartbeats went by, and the suspense of not knowing what was happening gripped Luvian.

Finally, the Prince stepped down a rung and signaled for Luvian to follow him. Luvian wondered briefly if he was climbing up to his death.

The Prince placed his hand on the trap door above him and shoved it open just a bit, so he could stare out into the room around him. Luvian's breath was sucked in – he found it impossible to breathe.

Then the Prince shoved the trap door open all the way and pulled himself up. He beckoned at Luvian to hurry and pulled him up out of the tunnel. Together, they closed the trap door so that it made no noise as it fell shut.

The Prince grabbed Luvian and pointed toward the wall. They stood with their backs flat against the wall, waiting to see how active the Palace was with Ambsell soldiers. Silently, Luvian pulled spiderwebs from the tunnel out of his hair and beard.

After a few minutes passed, the Prince seemed satisfied. He jerked his thumb in the direction of the next hallway over. With painstaking effort, they tiptoed to the next room over.

Luvian, for his part, was in awe of the palace. Never had he expected to be in the presence of the Prince, and certainly never in the palace. But it was just stone. He was quite disappointed. Though the floor was polished, all his childhood beliefs of palaces and knights were now dashed. The Prince, of course, was a knight, and he was a glorified arsehole, and the palace was supposed to be golden and beautiful and here it was just a hunk of stone.

They snuck carefully into an enormous hall. Luvian then revised what he'd thought of the palace not being golden and beautiful. This room was gilded and bright, and painted art and tapestries of amazing feats of courage hung from the walls, while the floor itself was shining marble. Crystal chandeliers sparkled in the sun that streamed in from windows and balconies where fragrant flowers hung in decorative containers. It was more than Luvian could take in.

The Prince tugged on his sleeve and nodded toward the front of the hall.

This was the Throne Room, or else another enormous golden chair sat in some other hall on another dais, thought Luvian. All seemed well....

The Prince seemed satisfied and pulled him toward the back of the room. "So this is your home," he whispered.

The Prince looked at Luvian for a moment and then shrugged. "Maybe. Maybe not." He pressed himself against the wall outside a door at the back of the Hall, listening.

"Ambsells?"

The Prince let out a long, pent up breath. "No." He opened the door and beckoned Luvian to follow.

"Father!"

A richly dressed man with chestnut hair and a crown encircling his head stood leaning over a mahogany desk. Three men attended him, who all looked up in amazement.

This – this was the King of Romeny, thought Luvian faintly.

The King stood straight and stared at this person who had addressed him uninvited in his study. His eyes took in the sight of the Prince for several seconds.

Well, and why not, dressed in filthy commoner's clothes as he was, smelling of smoke, unshaven.... He certainly looked nothing like a Prince. And, Luvian thought at that moment, he took pride in that.

"Rhutgard? Rhutgard, is that you?"

"Father, I'm home! I had to sneak into the City."

"My son! Thank the gods! I had heard the worst!" King Galvin came forward and hugged his son. Then he stepped back, holding the Prince by the shoulders to inspect him. "But what is this you're wearing?" He wrinkled his nose.

Luvian wanted to laugh but didn't dare change his expression in the front of the King of Romeny. So like a royal.

"I – it's a long story, Father, but I'm here now." Prince Rhutgard accompanied King Galvin briskly to his desk.

"Yes, yes, and I need you at my side –"

"Your Majesty, if I may interrupt, who are these people? I do not know them." Prince Rhutgard gestured around the room at the three people in front of King Galvin's desk.

King Galvin's face registered surprise at the interruption but complied with his son's request. "That is my steward –"

"Your – steward?" Prince Rhutgard turned and waved a condescending hand to the steward. "Dismissed."

"Rhutgard!"

Ignoring his father, the Prince walked over to the other two counselors. "I don't know them either."

"He is Angoth and he is Brestle. They have been my war advisors throughout these last months of war. As you can see, I've many documents we've been making more sense of. We have a number of supplies that need to be redirected –"

"Redirected? And where would they need to be sent?"

Immediately, Brestle answered, "To the Southern Regiments, Your Highness. They are in need of it most."

Luvian looked down at his boots to conceal his disgust. Here was the betrayal. All the way at the top. Major Corlander was right. And they had the ear of the King.

But the Prince was not so easily deterred. "And what of our cavalry?"

Angoth and Brestle shared a look and then Angoth answered, "I think it best for them to continue in the Riverlands. It would take too much time to send them elsewhere at this point." The older man was patronizing Prince Rhutgard, looking down his nose at him as one did a child whose knowledge of such information was helplessly miniscule.

Luvian stared at his boots, trying not to clench his fists. He glanced up to see the Prince's face for just a fleeting moment. The Prince stood in front of both Brestle and Angoth.

"Wrong and wrong. Both wrong. Guard! Take these men to the dungeon and throw them in the traitor cells! See that they're kept far away from each other and keep a watch on them. I'll speak with them before end of day."

Two guards stepped forward and immediately grabbed both Angoth and Brestle.

As if realizing how far he had overstepped his bounds, Prince Rhutgard then knelt in front of the desk and knelt. "Your Majesty, I most humbly beg your pardon. Those men I know to have committed treason."

A stern look on King Galvin's face, he stepped forward and placed a hand on his son's shoulder. "Rise, Rhutgard. You are forgiven."

"Thank you, Your Majesty."

"Well, and how do you know them to be false, may I ask?"

Prince Rhutgard looked at Luvian and then told King Galvin, "The biggest city in all of Romeny is starving, Father. My advice is to redirect half of our supplies here. And the rest of them to the Northeast, where the fighting is heaviest. As to cavalry. Your Majesty, we've had no cavalry for months. They were sent North from the Riverlands and then ambushed by the Ormish. They killed the men and took the horses. It was a complete loss to the man. Hardewold is sending in cavalry and men and possibly supplies to the Riverlands, but that will take two weeks yet in good weather. Shaw has its own fight and can't help us. I've no idea what Delsynth is doing but if they've men to spare, we could certainly use their Spears."

King Galvin was silent as he digested this news. He took a deep breath. "The Northeast, you say? The heaviest? And you know this how?"

Prince Rhutgard looked at Luvian and then at King Galvin. "Because I barely escaped with my life. I was fighting in the middle of it."

"What!" King Galvin's mouth dropped open in shock and anger, but Prince Rhutgard stepped forward and continued.

"Your Majesty, may I introduce to you –" Prince Rhutgard glanced quickly at Luvian and then back at King Galvin – "Lieutenant Luvian. Because of him, I am here today. He nearly lost his own life in order to save mine."

Somewhere inside, Luvian marveled at the promotion. He had gone from Corporal to Sergeant to Lieutenant in less than a week, and now he'd been promoted by the Prince before the King of Romeny himself.

He stepped before the King and knelt awkwardly, for his injury would not allow him to kneel.

"My son, do not kneel before me, it is I who should kneel before you. You have saved my son's life, and for that, I and my son will forever be in your debt. As a father, I shall always be grateful to you. As a King, your country will always be grateful to you, for you have secured its royal bloodline." King Galvin walked up to Luvian and extended his arm. "Please," and pulled Luvian up.

"Thank you, Your Majesty," replied Luvian in a hoarse voice.

"Captain, have you any other news I should be aware of?"

"As a matter of fact – if you recall Major Corlander, Your Majesty?"

"I do, of course."

"First, you should be made aware of his passing. He was murdered by attackers who hoped to kill me, except I escaped. Major Corlander managed to steal several important documents for me but because he died before he reached me, he entrusted them to Lieutenant Luvian. Lieutenant?"

Luvian had almost forgotten about them, so accustomed to them being next to his skin was he now. He pulled them from beneath his tunic and handed them to the Prince, who handed them to King Galvin.

King Galvin accepted them, looking sadly at the dried blood that stained them.

"Be sure to send his family notice of his passing and, and –"

Before he could hold himself back, Luvian spoke up. "Your Majesty, Sir, permission to speak, Captain?"

"Of course, Lieutenant."

"Sir, I was hoping to notify his family personally, if I might. Since I was there in his last few minutes, and – during his passing. His last thoughts were of them."

The Prince and the King looked at each other and both nodded. "Of course, Lieutenant, that would be fine."

The King set the maps down upon his desk. "And now, let me see what he had that was of such great import."

"I was not able to determine the best plan of action based on these. I needed to see your information, Your Majesty."

"Well, Captain, I can see why. I hold here entirely different maps. We will need to renegotiate areas of the most need and find where our men have resurfaced. But we can draw lines and boundaries later. Right now, I can see that the Lieutenant is badly in need of a Healer and the both of you need food and rest. I will send for you later this afternoon."

"Thank you, Your Majesty."

Luvian recognized a dismissal when he heard it, even when it was delivered by a King to his own son. He turned to leave, leaning heavily on his walking stick.

"Rhutgard –"

The Prince looked over his shoulder. "Father?"

"It's bloody good to have you back."

———

Luvian was losing patience. The Healer was clucking over his leg and her complaints were neverending. She mostly spoke to herself aloud but occasionally she addressed him outright. She had to cut the stitches open again and sew his wound back together, which alone put him in a sour mood, but she had given him woundwort, which helped numb the pain.

"I just can't imagine why anyone would ever stitch that way. And velvet no less. Mm-mm-mm, what were they thinking. Bits and pieces of thread stuck in there now, lucky to be alive you are...."

"Oy, it was battlefield surgery. If it wasn't for that stitching, I'd be dead. Better alive with shitty stitching than dead, aye?" he finally snapped.

The Healer huffed at him with a disapproving stare. The nerve of him, using profanity and speaking to a Healer thus, said her expression.

"You can go now," she brushed him away with her hands.

That was fine with Luvian. He was tired of sitting with half his arse out in front of a woman he didn't know. Women always had something to complain about, but he didn't need one stitching his leg up while he was bare-arsed in front of her.

He limped back to his room in time to see the Prince leaving. "We've been summoned."

"Right then, I'll be out in a minute." The Prince had probably burned his commoner's uniform, Luvian mused. Whatever else he had done, a new Lieutenant uniform had been supplied for him. He did not feel like a real man in it at all, he felt like a dress-up doll, pampered and laced and shiny. Just like a noble, gods help him.

The Prince noted the new uniform. "If it doesn't fit, just ask for the tailor, he can adjust it for you."

"It's fine, Sir, thank you."

"What's wrong, Lieutenant? Was the Healer not careful enough with your leg?"

The Prince snickered.

"Careful? Is that what you'd call it?" grumped Luvian.

"That's just how she is."
"Well, let me tell you, Sir, she was no fan of your stitches."

"Well, nor was I. Do you think I've sat around embroidering my whole life? You were lucky I even had a needle."

Luvian snorted. "You wouldn't have needed a needle if you had been in the damn Command Tent, Captain."

The Captain chuckled. "Fair enough. To be fair, would you have wanted to stay in that tent with those two?"

"Not an extra minute more than I had to be," Luvian smiled as he limped. The woundwort was starting to wear off, but the Healer, damn her twittering, had given him quite a supply of it.

They entered King Galvin's study together. "Ah. Back again. Very good." King Galvin had a goblet of wine in his hand. "Red? It's Ghivernish."

Luvian shook his head. He'd grown up in a brewery. Wine was just not part of his palette. More importantly, he was on duty.

But the Prince signaled for a goblet. Luvian struggled from rolling his eyes. He would be so glad to get out of this palace and out of these pretentious clothes. He needed to get home and see that his family was well, since the Ambsells had marched through.

"Come, Luvian, have a drink. We've several hours before us. What will it be? Brandy?" asked King Galvin.

Luvian stared at the King. *Brandy*? Whoever drinks *brandy*? Where would you even procure it?

The Prince, however, read his face plainly and stepped in to save Luvian. "I think the Lieutenant drinks something a bit stronger, Father. You're a whiskey man, aren't you, Lieutenant?"

Luvian blinked. Well, then. If they were going to drink, then whiskey it would be. On the King's gold, no less.

They spent the next two hours trying to make sense between the documents Major Corlander had sent and the misinformation the King had been operating with.

Frustrated, the Prince slammed his golden goblet down and ran his hand through his hair. "I need more. Guard! Bring us those two miscreants from the traitor cells." He looked at the King and Luvian and said, "I need to know exactly where they have stationed their spies. We can't rearrange our troops if we're going to have them ambushed all over again. We're stuck here in our own palace."

"Only until the Ghivernish get here," King Galvin held up a finger.

"Yes, I know, Father, but we are still stuck here. And we don't know which of your people is loyal. You need to get rid of them all."

The King's blue eyes bugged out as he sat back in his chair. "All! Have you lost your mind?"

"Father, we trusted someone and they let people into Fairview. First, we will have to take back our city. Then, we not only have to cover the cost of rebuilding our city, but we have to feed and station troops here, and we have to feed our starving and soon, our sick. And we've likely run out of places to bury our dead, so the Rosh River will be polluted. We'll need fresh water sent in. And we have no one to rebuild. We've lost our journeymen, our apprentices – our commoners are half gone. We'll have no food ourselves. We'll need those supplies redirected here."

"Your Majesty! Your Highness!" A guard slid into the room, out of breath.

King Galvin said tiredly, "Yes, what it is it?"

"The two men in the traitor cells, Your Majesty. They're dead. Hung. The guard who was watchin' them, gone. No trace of him anywhere. Can't tell if he done it hisself and run, or if he was paid off to look the other way and then run, but them two, they won't be talkin', Your Majesty."

"Shit!" yelled Prince Rhutgard, swiping several of the maps across the desk and onto the floor.

Appalled at Prince Rhutgard's reaction, King Galvin nodded to the guard and told him, "Very well, thank you," dismissing him with his hand.

As soon as the guard had closed the study door, King Galvin stood up and roared, "Just what is the matter with you!"

"Don't you see, Father? They were your link, they were connected to whoever is betraying us. They were killed to keep them from telling us anything!"

King Galvin stared at him for a moment and then walked over to the window. He stroked his beard, looking out at nothing. Luvian wondered what he was thinking.

Finally, the King turned around. "I want letters sent out to Hardewold, Shaw, Delsynth, and Ghiverny. I want the Eastern Shield Alliance to meet. Here, in Romeny. This guessing game can go on no longer. And make it clear to Hardewold that he needs to attend no matter what his hounds are hunting at the moment. This is imperative and if they do not attend, I will consider their lack of attendance a personal offense against our Alliance.

"I have no idea from where this betrayal has sprung, nor how deep it runs. It may have roots in each country, and we cannot afford to ignore it. We must stand together against this threat to the Eastern Shield. Someone is systematically dismantling our alliance from the inside. If Romeny has taken such a strong hit, imagine what Ghiverny, Delsynth, Shaw, and Hardewold have suffered. Our Alliance must plan together, not flop about like a dying fish on the shore. We will not let this common enemy take us down.

"Write that out, yourselves, in the best language you can. Send it with my personal seal. Two birds to each country. You send the birds yourselves. Rhutgard, you are right. I can no longer trust a single man in this Palace. You will be in charge of planning and I want you to start by finding me new men for my household. And fire that steward. I can lay out my own bloody clothes for a few damn days."

For the next two days, the Palace was a flurry of activity. Prince Rhutgard and Luvian sent birds that very afternoon and were anxiously awaiting replies, but in wartime, did not expect any for at least a week.

The Prince had sifted through his father's immediate staff. He admitted personally to Luvian that a number of them were utterly lousy at their jobs, but he would only dismiss them if he believed them to be falsely aligned – disloyal to the Crown. Employment would be scarce enough. Others the Prince sent out of the Palace without even allowing them to pack.

Luvian said nothing but raised an eyebrow at the third dismissal.

"Lieutenant? You have something to say?" the Prince demanded, reading the Luvian's skeptical expression.

"Nothing, Captain."

"They're traitors. I've sent them to be with their own kind! They needn't pack!" huffed the Prince with contempt.

"No, Sir."

The Prince stared at Luvian for a moment, realizing that Luvian was merely agreeing with him rather than voicing his opinion. "Well, then, out with it, man. What would you do with them?"

"I'd throw all their treacherous arses in the dungeon, all together. Along with two of my best spies, and a couple of guards I trusted. I'd have my guards leak that the torture was just unbearable and the prisoners weren't surviving long enough to tell the royals anything of use. Then I'd let those bloody traitors start snitching each other out, one by one, like the rats they are.

"But that's just me, Captain."

The Prince listened to this suggestion with a mixture of shock and curiosity, as if seeing Luvian for the first time. He nodded slowly. "But Lieutenant, Romeny does not torture prisoners."

"Maybe we should start. Captain." Luvian returned his gaze evenly.

The Captain blinked at the rawness of the suggestion, horrified. "My father would never approve such a measure! Nor would I! Lieutenant Luvian, we are talking about the torture of human beings, of deliberately causing terrible, unimaginable, unthinkable pain to our fellow men. And women. Torturing – is strictly forbidden for a reason!" the Prince's blue eyes were enormous with disgust and loathing at the thought while he berated Luvian.

Luvian waited until the Prince finished his tirade. "I'm sure the women, children, and men of Fairview who were raped, lynched, stabbed repeatedly, beheaded, and burned to death by the Ambsells would agree with you, Sir."

As this sunk in, the Prince's narrowed blue eyes fixed upon Luvian with resentment. Luvian decided that very few people spoke to him with such frankness.

Finally, the Prince ask through a clenched jaw, "And what would you have me do, Lieutenant?"

"Open the torture room. You do still have one down there, don't you?" As the Prince's eyes grew wide, Luvian held up a placating hand. "I didn't say *use* it, I only said *open* it. That alone will make news. Rats will desert before you can throw them out. Once you start throwing them in cells, either they'll hang themselves, or give our men information we can use.

"And keep a close watch on your new staff. See if any you entrusted with their positions suddenly sneak out. Have them followed – see where they lead and find out what information they harbor."

The Prince looked thoughtful. "It will be hard to sneak any of our men past the gates, but it can be done."

Then he focused on Luvian directly. "I make no promises with the torture room."

Luvian shrugged. "Just an idea, Sir."

At the noon day meal, the King asked for a report on his new household staff. The Prince and Luvian glanced at each other. Luvian looked down at his plate.

"I've got a plan that will... test the loyalty of all of your staff, Your Majesty. I think it a very good plan. I expect to start tomorrow." The Prince did not miss a beat as he explained this aloud, though Luvian knew if King Galvin knew what the Prince was really planning, the Prince might find himself locked in the dungeon.

"Excellent," replied the King around his goblet.

Seconds dribbled by like minutes, and Luvian held his breath. He knew the Prince was holding his own breath, scared that the King would ask for details.

Instead, King Galvin said, "I need a new report from the Treasurer. I have no idea what's left to spend for Infrastructure, but whatever is left needs to be doubled, tripled. As soon as we get these damned Ambsellon bastards off of our doorstep, we will need to rebuild, and that will cost money. Lumber, steel, iron...."

Both Luvian and the Prince melted with relief.

That afternoon, the Prince found Luvian standing on the balcony of the Throne Room.

"Lieutenant? Are you well?"

"Yes, Sir."

"Come back in, we've use of you in Father's study."

Luvian took a deep breath and turned to the Prince. "Your Highness, if I may...."

The Prince discerned Luvian's use of the honorific *Your Highness* and immediately remarked upon it.

"Lieutenant?"

"I've – I've…." Luvian stopped. He had been wrestling with himself all afternoon on how to approach the Prince. He had fulfilled his oath to Major Corlander, seen that the Prince had received the documents, seen that Prince was safe, and aye, even seen that the King had received his documents. He'd helped the Prince as much as he could. But he felt that now his oath had been fulfilled, and he was anxious to see his family. How to express this to a Prince in his Palace while he and his father the King were bombarded inside by soldiers from Ambsellon, with unknown traitors walking their very halls? Thus, he wrestled with himself over whether to even ask for the time to leave at all. Luvian would never forgive himself if either of them were assassinated with him not in the Palace.

"Come on, man, out with it."

"I wondered, if – if I might check on my family. Just check on them, and return." Luvian scraped a hand across his chin nervously.

"Luvian. Have you family here in Fairview?" asked the Prince suddenly.

The Prince's use of his first name shocked him. But he sucked in a breath and nodded. "Yes. Yes, Sir, I have. In South Fairview," Luvian replied quietly.

"But, but Luvian…." The Prince held him by the shoulders. "Why did you not ask to see them before now?"

Luvian looked the Prince in the eye. "I was fulfilling my mission, Sir. I'm a soldier."

The Prince said nothing but stared at him for a moment. Then he nodded. "Good man. Of course, of course you can take leave to see your family. Take all the time you need, Lieutenant. We'll sneak you out the way you came in, and if the stable on 8th Street is still standing, take any horse you please."

Luvian took care to look as inconspicuous as possible among the city dwellers. He could not stand to see them drifting lifelessly in the streets, but knew that the Prince was right, however a vile truth it was. If he stopped to feed or help one lost soul, he would create a scene, and he could not attract Ambsellon soldiers, especially since he was headed home.

All that remained of the burned homes he passed were their packed dirt floors and their scorched brick hearths, perhaps some iron pots. Still, families crutched in them, having nowhere else to go.

Other people wandered the street, their hands outstretched, hoping for money or bread. He shook his head to discourage them – he couldn't bear to look them in the eye. He became a soldier to protect people from this. He never thought to see it happen in his own city, aye, in his own neighborhood.

Children ran in rags, some even naked, their parents dead or missing, unable to care for their young. Luvian knew that Romeny's poverty level would spring through the Palace roof now. Three dogs fought over a dead horse haunch as if it were just a turkey bone. Luvian closed his eyes to the grisly sight.

The farther he rode, the worse the damage to the homes, to the people. Flies buzzed in black swarms over the dead bodies upon the streets, for carters had not yet wheeled this far. The stench was such that Luvian covered his hand over his nose and breathed through his mouth. People had vomited near the bodies.

Here, not a dog nor a cat was to be seen, for they were like to be tonight's supper, and a lucky catch at that. Overturned Market wagons lay unattended, and Luvian saw a little boy and girl huddled under one of them for shelter. Businesses he remembered seeing his entire life were blackened or gone altogether. He dreaded rounding the next corner.

His heart in his stomach, Luvian stared at the brewery he'd grown up in.

Blackened poles shot up toward the sky, for the roof was gone. The window frames were there still but no glass remained in them. No door stood to greet customers. The stable was gone entirely.

Luvian blinked, for his eyes had been staring too long at the sight. Finally, he dismounted. He tied his horse to a stump outside the remainder of the brewery. He saw that no counter stood anymore, no shelves behind it. Just a shell of a building, like the others. No tables. The pine planks were gone – only packed earth remained for the floor.

He took a breath and stepped in.

A breeze drifted across his face. Odd, that, in a brewery. Suddenly, he heard a scurrying. Luvian drew his blade. Rats? He stepped forward.

Then he looked down at the ground.

A scorched body of a woman, encircling another dead body. Where the woman's body hadn't burned was a dress, covered by an apron....

Luvian felt his stomach loosen. But just then he heard a noise.

An old man sat in the far corner of the bar against the wall, rocking back and forth, covered in soot and dirt. His white hair stood out in all ends, his grey shirt had dried blood on it. His hands shook and he had soiled himself.

The old man squinted up at Luvian. "Is that you, Matty?"

Luvian dropped his sword. *"Pappy?"*

He sat down next to his father. "Pappy. Pappy. What happened? Where is Mum? Where are the others?"

"Matty?"

Luvian sucked in his breath as he stared at his father.

"No, Pappy, no. I'm Luvi. Luvi. Pappy, where is Mum?"

"Oh, Luvi. Good, Luvi. Your mum is wearing that brand-new frock I got her. Isn't she pretty in it, isn't she?" His father, a ghost of a smile slipping across his face, pointed a shaking hand toward the other end of the brewery.

Luvian blinked. "Yes. Yes, Pappy, she looks, looks wonderful." Tears ran down his face. "Come on, Pap, let's get you up. Let's get you up and washed off."

A kindly smile crossed his father's face as Luvian lifted him up gently. "Matty? Is that you? Back so soon? We have to get another pot of stew started."

"Aye, aye, Pappy, it's me, Matty." Luvian choked on his tears as he replied.

He smoothed his father's hair back. Pappy had always dressed so sharply, even with his apron on. Luvian found a stool in the kitchen, still sturdy enough for his father to sit on. "Here, Pappy, here, sit down. I'm going to clean up a bit."

"Oh, that's good, that's good." A happy smile spread across his father's face.

Luvian stepped out of what was left of the kitchen in shock.

"Luvi, is that you?" asked a cautious voice. An older woman stepped in, shading her eyes against the sun. "Well, I'll be if it ain't Luvi, back from soldierin' off in the war."

She walked up to him and looked him up and down. "Look at you, all fancy, how about that soldier uniform, my, my." She brushed the shoulder of his uniform. Luvian cursed the Prince inwardly for his choice of formal military attire.

"Mags?"

"Aye. Glad you're back, little Luvi. Glad you've come back to us."

"Cassie? Is that you, my love?" called Luvian's father.

"Yes, dear, it's me, back from Market, love," called Mags around her hand toward the kitchen. She gave Luvian a sad look and patted him on the shoulder. "I'm so sorry. He's lost his mind, you know. They're all gone. Luvi, I'm so sorry. So sorry."

He screwed his eyes tight. There would be time for mourning later. His Pappy needed him right now. "… How?"

Mags smiled kindly. "It was just the fire, dear. It weren't no soldiers."

"Just? Just the fire?" Luvian growled.

Taken aback, Mags took on a mother's frown and said, "Well, now, it coulda' been like lots of folks, where the soldiers had their fun and sport first before they burnt down the place. You hear me now, Luvi?

He swallowed and took a deep breath. "Aye. I'm sorry, Mags."

"'S'all right, little Luvi. Ya've had a nasty shock."

"Is that you, Cassie?" called his father again.

"Yes, love, it's me, I've come back from the Market. Wait 'til you see what I've brought," called Mags. She pulled out a small loaf of bread out of her basket.

"You've been caring for him," he said.

She shrugged. "We all do what we can. He and I, we came up together. We knows everyone in the neighborhood." Then Mags sighed. "Knew."

"I'm sorry, Mags, I haven't asked. How has your family fared?" asked Luvian politely.

"Same as yours. I'm the only one left. 'Cept some would argue as I lost my mind years ago." She smiled a small smile and patted him on the shoulder. "I'm glad you're back, Luvi."

"So am I. But can I ask a favor of you?"

"Of course, child."

Luvian found the idea of being called *child* refreshing, given the sights he had seen and the actions he had committed. "I need to run an errand, and then I should be back for good. Can you watch out for him?"

<hr>

All the different ways that Luvian had practiced speaking to the Prince were forgotten now that he stood before him.

"How is your family, Luvian?"

They stood out on the balcony before dinner, where Luvian could see the start of the sunset. Wind ruffled his hair.

"I...." Luvian stared at a fixed place before him to keep from showing any emotion, and then, once he had himself under control, he said, "Captain, Sir, I must ask a boon of you."

The Prince's eyebrows shot up. "A boon? Well. By all means, Lieutenant, ask." Curiosity and concern colored his face.

"Sir, if I may...." Ah. Bloody hell. "Sir, my family is dead. All but one. My brothers, my sister, my mum, all dead. My father survived, but 'is mind is gone completely. Our brewery burned to the ground and he's exposed every night, starving to death." Even as he explained this, he saw the Prince's face change to sympathy. "Sir, the boon I ask of you is this: may I resign my commission that I might take care of my father and rebuild our home?"

The request took the Prince by surprise. He immediately recovered, reading the pain registered on Luvian's face. He knew that nothing would cause Luvian to leave his life as a soldier unless it was dire. He also knew that nothing he did would keep Luvian at his side, whether his commission resignation was granted or not.

"Lieutenant Luvian. Your request to resign your commission is granted."

The Prince stood stiffly to attention as a Captain then, saluting Luvian. "Lieutenant Luvian, your watch has ended. May you go with good will."

Luvian, barely hearing the words, for he had never expected to hear them in reference to him, saluted the Prince. "Captain, Sir. May you go with good will."

The ceremony was necessary for all soldiers retiring from duty, or those who had passed on.

"Luvian. I am so sorry for the loss of your family." The Prince reached out a hand to Luvian's shoulder.

"Thank you, Sir, that's kind of you." Luvian still felt numb by the entire ordeal.

"I will have builders and funds sent –"

"No, Sir, if you please, just my soldier's wages," Luvian told the Prince.

"But –"

"Truly, Sir. My soldier's wages. Besides, Sir, if you don't mind my saying, you'll need all the coin you can get to rebuild elsewhere." Luvian gestured out at the rest of Fairview City.

The Prince sighed. "That's the sad truth. But some can be spared for a war hero who saved my life, at least...."

"Hah. War hero. What's that? There are no war heroes. Just soldiers doing their duties, Sir."

"Ah," the Prince nodded, a small smile playing on his face. "Luvian, I shall miss you around here. Who's going to be an arsehole to me? Everyone here will just bow and say, *Yes* or *No, Your Highness.*"

Luvian scoffed. "Well, Sir, if it's an arsehole you want, just turn and look in the looking glass." He grinned and clapped the Prince on the back, something he never thought he'd do.

The Prince's eyebrows shot up. "Are you trying to say I'm an arsehole? Certainly you would know what one of those was. I'll tell you what, if I need any advice from an arsehole, I'll yell down to South Fairview and have them search about for a big, hairy lout named Luvian."

Luvian chuckled. "They know me well down there, I'm afraid."

The Prince's mirth faded and he said, "Best of luck, mate. Let me know if I can be of any assistance. Ever."

Luvian woke to a noise outside the brewery. He scoffed, for at the moment, outside was also inside, until he could put up a roof.

The clop-clop of horses stopped outside on the street and the sound of boots hitting the pavement reverberated through the brewery. Perhaps he would put up a door first. The echoes were almost too much to bare....

Knowing that only soldiers were likely to be riding horses, Luvian refrained from drawing a blade.

Two soldiers ducked into the brewery. Luvian released his pent-up breath, for they weren't Ambsells but soldiers of Romeny.

"Lieutenant Luvian, Sir!"

Both soldiers stood to attention, staring at him.

Mags stepped out of the kitchen behind him. "Lieutenant, huh? Lieutenant Luvi, well, I'll be."

Luvian sighed and stepped forward. If he didn't acknowledge their formality, they would continue to stand there.

"Sir, we come from the Palace."

So this is what it feels like to be retired, Luvian mused. He nodded. "And?"

"First order: ...." and he glanced at Luvian nervously.

Luvian glanced at his uniform and then snapped, "Get on with it, Corporal."

"Yes, Sir! First order: The Prince has decided that instead of your resigning your commission, you shall instead be listed as a Retired Lieutenant."

Luvian raised an eyebrow at this. He sniffed something odd about that but was unable to determine just what.

He gestured for the list to continue.

"Second order: The matter of your soldier's wages, Sir." The Corporal gestured, and the Private brought out a small wooden box containing his wages. Luvian thought immediately that he would need to bury that somewhere, for people in the streets had turned to looting and theft. If anyone tried to rob Luvian, they would lose limbs, and in a very unpleasant fashion.

"Third order: A gift, from His Highness, the Prince."

The Private brought in a wooden crate and together, the Corporal opened it.

Inside the crate was a set of fine glassware. Here, both Corporals glanced at each other.

Luvian backed away from the crate. "No. No. Tell His Highness that I appreciated the gesture, but that I couldn't accept his generosity."

The two soldiers swallowed and then held up a glass. The Corporal then informed him, "Sir, His Highness told us that you would say that, and that we should do this –"

Here, he dropped the glass on the ground, where it shattered into fine shards everywhere. "He told us to then say that he knew you would not accept it, but since the crate was now an incomplete order, the Crown could not accept it in return, so you must now keep it."

Luvian shook his head. Sneaky bastard.

"And finally, Sir, Fourth Order:…." The Corporal paused.

"Well, what is it, Corporal, get along. And don't smash anything else on my floor."

The Private brought out another crate.

"His Highness has sent you a crate of the finest whiskey kept in Fairview Castle, to bless your brewery, and hopes that you might, upon occasion, send up a toast."

Luvian stepped forward and stared downward into the crate, full of bottles of whiskey that probably cost more than an entire year's wages each. He nodded.

Then he looked at the two soldiers awaiting his direction. Bloody hell.

"Corporal, tell His Highness that his gifts are most appreciated. And that I might even try a red one day."

"Yes, Sir!" The soldiers stood to attention. It was not for them to ascertain the meaning of his message, only to bear it to its intended recipient.

Luvian realized that they were continuing to stand there for him to dismiss them. He shook his head. He wouldn't miss the Army at all, he decided.

"Dismissed!"

APPROXIMATELY TWO YEARS LATER

"Luvi!"

Luvian heard his name called but he was too busy. He couldn't hope to keep up with the demands of the customers if he was running his mouth. "Mags? The stew?"

"Already started," she called back.

"Luvi!

It was Tank. Surely Tank could deal with unruly customers himself, that why he worked there. Army man with no family left, big as an ox, tougher than –

"Luvian."

"Take care of it yourself, Tank, I'm too busy."

"I think you need to see him." Tank was serious.

Luvian sighed and crisped his hands free of flour. "Donvan, keep kneading the bread."

"What? Me?"

"Yes, you! You've seen me do it a hundred times. There's nothing to it. It's just for a few minutes. I'll be right back!" Some days, Luvian missed the Army.

He stepped out of the kitchen and the customers of the brewery, talking, laughing, filling the air, was a welcome sound to his ears. He'd grown up with it.

"Well? Tank?"

Tank was suddenly very covert, taking steps toward the door. "He asked for you, Luvian."

"Did he, now. Maybe he's got a tab to pay."

A hooded stranger stood by the door. As Luvian approached him, he turned.

Luvian glanced upward into the cowl of the man's cloak.

The blue eyes of the Crown Prince of Romeny stared back at him, along with a mild smile.

"Don't say anything. Just step outside with me."

Bloody hell, thought Luvian. "Tank…?" Surprise had rendered Luvian speechless and so he gestured about the brewery in a show to indicate that Tank was now in charge.

Out in the stable, Luvian finally was able to collect his senses. "What the bloody hell –"

The Prince held up a hand. "Hush. Keep it quiet." Then he smiled. "How are you, Luvian?"

"I'm well enough. But I think you've clear lost your mind. This is not the area you should be in. If someone knew you were here…. I mean this is South Fairview. Bad folks on the street after dark, depending on the side of the street."

"Well, a friend once told me I need to keep abreast of all of my subjects, not just those in my social circle," the Prince said dryly.

Luvian scoffed. "A friend like that must have known South Fairview back in the day." Luvian craned his neck around the Prince and sized up his bodyguard. "I hope he's as good with a blade as you need him to be."

"As do I. Although I'm not half-bad myself, rumor has it," he chided.

Luvian conceded to that.

"I merely asked where the best brewery in the area was, and without fail, I was directed to The Brew House. Be proud, my friend, be proud. You have a wonderful establishment here," said the Prince.

"Aye, thank you," Luvian answered. He sensed something more.

"You should build up."

"No, I've got too many customers as it is, and not enough employees –"

"No, Luvian. Not *out*. *Up*. An upstairs." The Prince pointed upward with a finger.

Luvian stopped and stared at the Prince in his cowl. An upstairs? But then that would make The Brew House....

"Make it a tavern," said the Prince. "Just a suggestion. It would bring you more business."

Bloody hell. He hated when the Prince was right. It made a lot of sense. But he certainly didn't have the time, much less the man-power or the wages to build anything beyond what he already had, so it was just a pipe-dream.

"And your own business? How goes that?" Luvian inquired.

"As well as can be expected," the Prince replied, shrugging.

"Congratulations on your new bride," Luvian said, offering his hand.

"Ah, thank you. Marriage of state, but all the same, she's lovely."

Luvian was glad then that he was free of the bonds of such societal impositions. He was free to marry who he pleased, have children when he wanted, live where he wanted....

"I've been looking for names, actually," mused the Prince.

"Names?"

"Yes, for horses."

"Horses. What makes you think I know anything about horses, other than riding one?"

"Well, I always thought I might name a son after a friend of mine who saved my life once, but that wouldn't be appropriate, I'm told, so I'm looking for the names of horse's arses. Know any?"

Luvian took this in and then realized what the Prince was actually conveying. "No!" he whispered. "She's with child!"

The Prince's blue eyes sparkled with joy and he nodded. "Yes. No one knows yet, just her, and me. And now you, of course. So don't tell anyone!"

Luvian dropped all pretense and hugged the Prince. "Congratulations! That's wonderful!"

Then he laughed and held up a finger. "Just don't name him after me. I think you'll agree, one horse's arse in your life is more than enough."

They laughed quietly together.

"Now, let me tell you a better way out of here –" and he whispered more covert instructions back to the Palace for the Prince.

He brushed flour onto his hands from his apron as he entered his Brewery. Build up. Luvian glanced up thoughtfully at the ceiling. The Brew House and Tavern… it had a nice ring to it….

APPROXIMATELY 6 YEARS LATER

Tank leaned over the bar. "Luvian!"

"Not now!" Luvian was shoving another loaf of bread into a hot oven. Fortunately, it was quiet and he would be able to take a break in a bit, but he'd see that loaf rise first. That baker. What did he know. Luvian's bread was better and everyone knew it.

"Luvian!" Tank leaned over the bar again, this time with more insistence.

Luvian brushed his hands free of flour on his apron. "What! What's wrong?" He checked the level in the stew pot as he passed by. "Mags!" he called. He looked at Tank. "We need more stew."

"Mags went to the Market for vegetables. She'll make another kettle when she gets back. Luvian!" Tank insisted on Luvian's attention by standing in his way.

"Oy! What, man?"

Tank glanced around surreptitiously and whispered behind his hand, "Do you recall that bloke who came to visit back before we built up?"

Luvian's eyes snapped to Tank's. "What of him?"

Tank pointed with a barely discernable finger in the direction of the stable. "He's here. In the stable, askin' for you."

Bloody hell. This couldn't be good. Luvian stripped off his apron and slipped out the back of the kitchen, calling, "Donvan, watch the bread in the oven!"

Luvian stepped into the stable, where the smell of hay, horse manure, and horses assailed him. He heard a fly buzz past as he looked about.

In the corner, a shrouded figure stood, cloaked and unremarkable.

Luvian shook his head and passed by the horse stalls. He glanced around for anyone else, but the two of them were alone. He cleared his throat.

Rhutgard Firthing, King of Romeny, threw back his cowl and smiled at him.

"Your Majesty," Luvian knelt before him.

"Luvian." The King offered his hand and Luvian kissed his ring to swear his allegiance.

"Rise, Luvian. Of all people, I can't stand to see you kneeling before me."

"Of course, Your Maj –"

"And do not *Majesty* me."

Luvian nodded and swallowed. "Well, then, ah. Sire?" He felt the need to lighten the mood. "Welcome to my stable. Again. May I ask what brings you to South Fairview? Surely not the scenery."

The King smiled at Luvian's jest, though something about his demeanor was serious. Perhaps it was the weight of the Crown, mused Luvian.

King Rhutgard changed the subject. "You built up, I see. The Brew House and Tavern. Entrepreneurship suits you," he smiled.

"Well, owing to your idea, of course."

"It looks good. You've done very well for yourself, Luvian."

"Thank you – er –" Luvian was at a loss as to how to address the King. The King of Romeny, standing here, in his stable, with muck and hay and flies….

The King held up his hand. "Just a thank you."

Then he drew in a breath and let it out. "My old friend, I hate to come here today. You have done so well for yourself, you are so content in your life, in your world, and as it should be." The King stared off suddenly.

Luvian's eyes narrowed with concern. "What's wrong? Is there trouble?" He crossed his arms on his chest and waited.

King Rhutgard frowned. "You are one of the few who would ask that and truly mean it with concern, rather than social platitude."

Luvian read the King's face and saw how he was struggling with what he needed to say. "Out with it, man."

"Luvian, I need to call in that boon you asked of me those years ago."

Luvian let those words wash over him. Somehow, they didn't sink in. He thought his mouth was open.

Finally, he said, "I – I don't understand."

The pain on King Rhutgard's face was evident as he looked at Luvian. "My friend, all those years ago, you came to me, asking a boon of me, because your family needed you.

"And now, Luvian, I am coming to you, because these many years later, my family needs me, more than I can ever say. Because of that..." and Rhutgard's face drew up in pain here, for the pride of a man, a husband, a father, and a King warred across his face, "I have come to you. In possibly my most desperate circumstance to date."

Luvian heard these words, but still could not yet bring himself to comprehend them. Finally, he said, "Maj –"

Immediately, Rhutgard covered his mouth with a hand. "Shh! Not here. Nor at all! And do not use my name. As you say, this is South Fairview."

Taken aback, Luvian held up his hands, and Rhutgard released him slowly.

"Mate! You want to tell me what this –" and Luvian swooped about the stable with his arm, "craziness is about? Are you well? Because you seem quite mad to me."

"I'm not, though it feels it. I assure you, I would not bring this to you unless I had no choice. You are the only person I can trust."

Luvian looked into the King's eyes and saw sanity there, but he knew that whatever the King had to say, he did not want to hear.

"Go on, then."

King Rhutgard drew in a deep breath, shaking his head. Luvian decided the King looked like many soldiers just home from battle: wide-eyed, nervous, staring about him, and startling at every noise. It had taken Luvian himself at least two years to get past that feeling of always being watched by the enemy, and still he woke from nightmares.

"Do you remember when last I came to visit you?"

"Aye, I do. You stood not far from this spot, as I recall," said Luvian.

The King nodded wryly. "Hennolynn had just conceived." He drew in a great breath and let it out slowly, staring down at the hay, though Luvian knew it was not hay that his mate was envisioning.

"I was so sorry to hear, my friend." He laid a hand on Rhutgard's shoulder in sympathy.

"Yes, well." Rhutgard recovered and put on what Luvian had deemed years ago as the "royal" face. "She took a fever while she was with child and died. As did my unborn son."

Luvian was at a loss for what to say. Surely Rhutgard had been given so many condolences since then, he was tired of them. Luvian didn't want to add to a bad memory by stumbling his way through another apology.

Then Rhutgard cocked his head a bit. "At the time, I thought nothing of it. For of course, it seemed a plausible explanation. She had taken fever over the last two days. But now, I wonder. For she was nearly to term...."

Luvian raised an eyebrow. That was quite a suspicion to entertain. But he held his tongue. Women took fever all the time.

"Then there was my father, not a year later," Rhutgard continued. He sighed and glanced upward. "How I do miss him."

"I am sorry for your loss, mate. I liked him." Luvian was surprised to hear of King Galvin's death, for he seemed a robust and hearty man.

"Thank you, my friend. He like you as well." Rhutgard's face took on a thoughtful look. "They, the Royal Healers, I mean, claimed he died of choking on a fishbone. Imagine that. A fishbone." His blue eyes refocused and he stared sternly at Luvian. "If I am said to have died in some trivial, inconsequential manner, Luvian, I want you to circulate rumors all throughout Romeny that I died in a swordfight, or spearing a bull, or even fucking my wife if you must, but nothing like choking on a fishbone." He rolled his eyes. Then he sighed. "The thing, Luvian, that I found odd at the time, was that my father never ate fish. Didn't care for it. He was found of ocean fish, but not river water fish, and so he generally only ate it if compelled to, such as at feasts with guests." He shook he head. "And we were not feasting."

Luvian raised his eyebrows. That was odd indeed, given the state of affairs he'd left the Palace in. He wished he'd known of that; he would have insisted that Rhutgard launch an investigation – fire all the cooks, sniff out any possible traitors, as before. A woman dying of fever while with child, that might be overlooked. But a healthy king not a year later, in such a sloppy manner? Obviously, whoever committed the regicide did not take the time to find out what the king's eating habits were.

"You see why I was quick to take a wife. I was chastised by many, but I had no immediate offspring, with only my brother as my successor, and he is but eight."

Luvian nodded. He had thought Rhutgard had married rather quickly after assuming the Throne, but he was too busy here at the time, for the tavern was being built and he was still running the brewery as well. He'd had no time for speculating upon the doings of the Royals.

"My next wife, I hardly knew. Aolynn, out of Ghiverny. She was with child within just six months, for my advisors are relentless when it comes to rulers with no children. Once she conceived, all seemed well." Here, Rhutgard's eyes narrowed.

Luvian shook his head and frowned. He did not want to hear the rest. "All seemed well... until...?"

"Obviously, I had no evidence that my father had died of anything but... well, choking on a fishbone. Nor did a woman dying of fever while with child seem out of the ordinary." Rhutgard's brow was furrowed and his blue eyes were glittering.

Luvian crossed his arms. "Mate. What happened!"

"Aolynn was sick for her first two months. Aren't they all, though, aye?" Rhutgard shrugged. "She wanted such things – odd fruits and, and – turnips, of all things. I hate turnips." He shook his head.

Luvian glared at him. "Is there an end to this commentary soon?"

Rhutgard sighed and looked back at Luvian. "All seemed well, a normal – well, pregnancy. Then she suddenly took ill. Her Healer couldn't explain it, the midwives couldn't explain it. She remained bedridden for all the rest of the pregnancy. Aolynn died in childbirth. The oldest of my sons has always been sickly due to her pregnancy – I, in fact, do not expect him to live long enough to assume a Kingship, though it pains me greatly to admit this. He is well in all ways, just a very sickly boy, pale and frightens easily. He stays locked up in his library with his tutors and his books." The King drew in a long breath, his face gloomy.

Luvian knew how much it pained Rhutgard to admit this. Rhutgard had been a father's ideal son – Rhutgard had been a strong child who had excelled at statescraft, horsemanship, swordplay, and no doubt attained the rank of Captain as much through his own military ability as through his father's influence.

Prince Merridon, however, Rhutgard's son, was nothing like his father, if what Rhutgard had just disclosed was true.

Luvian was unsure of what to say, for nothing he could say would change the sad course of Rhutgard's story.

King Rhutgard looked down and kicked at some of the hay with his boot. "Do you believe in coincidence, Luvian?"

"'Course I don't. You know that. And nor do you."

"I don't. But I'm not the only Royal whose country this is happening in." King Rhutgard fixed Luvian with an even blue stare. "I thought that might help convince you, before I go on. Shaw's wife, the Queen, that is, died in a hunting accident. She was an excellent horsewoman, but the leather on her stirrup to one side was sawed through partially, as by a knife. One of my men told me that. Shaw didn't believe it until he had a look himself.

"Ghiverny's brother, second in the ascension, to whom he is closest, died by drowning, out ice-fishing. Fell under the ice and couldn't get back up in time before the ice closed over him. No one could reach him in time to save him.

"Ghiverny is heart-stricken, and it turns out that he did not need much convincing by me, for a few of his immediate advisors have recently *retired* or found their deaths."

Luvian stared, spellbound by this tale.

"Now what, you may ask, do any of these other – *unfortunate* – incidents have to do with me?

"Simple. I was present at each of them."

Luvian started.

"Still coincidence?"

"I stopped believing in coincidence the day I stepped on the battlefield."

"As did I. Perhaps sooner."

"So what are you suggesting? That someone, or a group of someones, are targeting you? Or Royals? Or is the Eastern Shield being threatened again?" asked Luvian.

"Luvian, I've no way of knowing. But I am the Eastern Shield, the leader of the Eastern Alliance. Romeny is the Shield itself, and I am its King. I have played every scenario through in my mind. Perhaps they think me young and so easily overthrown. The Twenty Years War may be over, but Ambsellon and Ormon to the North can strike again through the Mantle Mountains. Romeny has not yet recovered to her full fighting strength yet, and Fairview still remembers the soldiers who marched through. I know I will never forget them.

"Shaw is young and small yet. Ghiverny is such a part of Romeny's bloodline, we are near to one country – they are our oldest ally. But they are far enough to the North that a sudden direct hit on Fairview, as before, or even Romeny itself, will still require them at least two weeks to regroup and arrive with troops and aid. Ormon and Ambsellon each have twice Romeny's numbers.

"Something is not sitting well with me. I know not what, but I trust my gut, as a soldier. I know something is afoot."

Luvian knew Rhutgard was right. But the King was not done.

"Which brings me to this: I'm sure you know of my latest marriage." Rhutgard shook his head. "It was near everything I could do to secure her hand, for, say my advisors, I am considered by some to be *'haunted'* now – girls beg their fathers, *'no, Father, please,'* for apparently, should they wed me, they are like to die here." Rhutgard snorted. "Would you believe? There was a time when betrothal proposals and ladies-in-waiting poured into the Palace."

Luvian scoffed. "Tripe. What tripe – don't believe such shit."

"Ah, but such is the world of politics, my friend," smiled the King sadly. "But nevertheless, I married a wonderful woman –"

"So I heard. Congratulations… I hope…?" Luvian trailed off, unsettled.

Rhutgard nodded, a smile on his face finally as he pictured his wife. "Principea, out of Ghiverny. And I have kept her by my side, watched her every bite, and overseen her every move since the moment she arrived. Truly, she thinks me mad, I'm sure."

"Well, then, she's got good instinct. I like her already," Luvian quipped.

The King snorted, but the smile did not leave his face. Luvian decided Rhutgard truly loved this Queen of his. And that was just as well.

"But this brings me to the issue that brought me here. Finally," Rhutgard conceded.

"Forgive me, mate," Luvian held up a placating hand to interrupt him, "but you said something a bit ago that I have a question about."

The King gestured. "Go ahead."

"Perhaps I heard wrong, but did you not say, *the oldest of my sons*? I admit I am a busy man in my small world," and he gestured toward the brewery, "but I'm sure I would have heard if more Royals had been added to the King's family."

A slow smile spread across the King's face. "You never miss anything, do you? And what a fool was I, to have missed that. I'll need to be more careful," he thought aloud.

"Sorry? Mate? The issue of children?" Luvian prompted the King. Royals. Always drifting off in daydreams this way and that. Though, to be fair, Luvian conceded, Rhutgard certainly had more that most to think about. Nightmares more than daydreams....

The King shook himself. Taking in a deep breath, he was finally silent.

Luvian felt like shaking him. What the bloody hell. To come all this way and tell him this whole gallish story and then just dry up like an old prune. He felt like kicking him in his royal arse.

Rhutgard turned about and stared at one of the beams. "Do you remember our trip, Luvian? When we were practically strangers still, and couldn't think of anything to talk about?"

Luvian's mouth fell open. Bloody fucking royal. Standing here talking about shit and not getting to the point. Oy.

"I remember," he said.

"We talked mostly of Army things, military, because we really had no common ground. But you did tell me about that month you'd spent stationed in Dinsmore. Do you recall that?"

Luvian did not recall any such thing but had no chance to respond, for the King then said, "You told me about the woman you fell in love with there. Remember her? Ruth?"

Luvian's eyes rounded and for once he was taken entirely by surprise.

"I? Told you that?"

King Rhutgard turned and regarded him with something like amusement.

"Aye, my friend. Don't worry, I shan't repeat it to anyone," he said with a tired smile.

"Huh." Luvian, still amazed, said, "Well, to be honest, I was in quite a bit of pain."

"True, that you were. I never heard a man curse so much."

Luvian started to get annoyed and then realized the King was only teasing him.

He hadn't thought of Ruth in years. They had spent one entire month together, while he had been stationed in the Dinsmore Valley, and he still a Private. He had snuck out every night past curfew and stayed with her, sleeping under the stars beneath an Army-issue blanket in the patch of wildflowers outside of camp. He had risked everything for her green, green eyes.... Being AWOL as a soldier during wartime was severely frowned upon, even if it was just for a woman....

The King cleared his throat, bringing Luvian out of his reverie.

"If I may?"

"Aye, uhm – right, then." Luvian found himself stumbling over what to say. He hadn't thought of Ruth in years, but now all he could see was her smile. Damn Rhutgard.

"This brings me to why I've come."

Luvian's eyes narrowed and he crossed his arms. "What has Ruth to do with any of this?"

"Ruth is widowed now, this last year."

Luvian smelled a plot and raised an eyebrow. He didn't like it, didn't like it at all.

"And what has that to do with me?"

"She has two little girls, ages one and two, by a soldier who just passed."

"Again, mate, what does this have to do with me? Obviously, I'm sorry for her loss, but as you can see, I've a business to run." He brightened. "If she needs a place for her family, she can stay here in one of the rooms," he suggested.

The King nodded, a small smile playing on his face. "That's good of you. But do you recall that I mentioned 'of all of my sons'?"

Luvian's mind jumped quickly. "Surely you don't want your sons and her daughters...."

"Oh no – no. But what you don't know yet is... that my wife just gave birth."

Luvian's eyebrows shot up. "That's fantastic, man!"

Rhutgard hissed at him, "Shush, shush, keep it down!"

Luvian glanced around. "Well, truly, that's wonderful! Now you've two sons, aye? Congratulations, mate!" he whispered, truly elated for his friend.

The King was grinning. He lifted his eyebrows conspiratorially. "Actually... I have three now."

Luvian looked at the happiness in the King's blue eyes. "Twins!"

Rhutgard nodded. "Twin boys. Just last week."

Luvian grinned. "Even better! How can I sneak some of that fine Palace whiskey out here for us to toast to?"

Rhutgard shook his head and his smile faded.

Luvian stared at him. "Bloody hell, man, what's happened? Is it the Queen, did she take ill?"

"No, no, nothing like that. She's fine, and so are the boys. I had them under my own guard every single day, I watched everything she ate and drank, and almost no one knew she was with child. We'll announce in a few days. She has just stayed sequestered, claiming to have felt ill all this time. Which," he rolled his eyes, "only served to feed the rumors swirling about my haunted wives," he chuckled.

"But all healthy. Thank the gods, mate, thank the gods," Luvian said.

"Yes, and they will stay so, by my every breath," Rhutgard's tone was serious. "For they are the line of succession to my Throne, and my blood. If some easily explained, plausible death or illness should befall them, may the gods forbid it, then I will have proof, undeniable proof, that my river has been poisoned. Do you believe me?"

"I understand, mate."

"But do you understand why I am taking all precautions? For just last spring, the King of Shaw's youngest sister recovered from an illness that only her childhood Healer was able to heal. He was called to her bedside as a last resort by the King, acting on a thought that he was considering since his wife died. Unbeknownst to her current healers, Shaw sent a private bird to his sister's old Healer and had the old man, half-blind now, brought to her bedside. Within two days, she was up and walking around again, whereas before, she had been coughing and near to death. Shaw's sister is twice down in his line of succession," said the King quietly.

"What do Shaw and Ghiverny have directly in common with me, besides my having been present at their loved ones' demises?"

Luvian knew at this point that it was better to say nothing and wait for the King to continue.

"They are smaller countries who both border Romeny. Everyone knows how much the Ormons have craved Ghiverny for their own – but no one has ever penetrated the Wolf Wall. Perhaps, if they cannot take the Wolves from the outside, whoever this unknown enemy is will take them from the inside.

"As with Shaw. Shaw is such a small kingdom, but it runs the lower River Lands. It is protected by all of the Eastern Shield on every front, and so might be more easily dismantled from the inside rather than invading.

"We've just seen how expensive wars are. The Twenty Years War – the only countries who weren't ultimately depleted were, of course, Ambsellon and Ormon. Delsynth has its Spears. The Coastal Alliance –" Rhutgard scoffed. "A few lousy ships and some regiments. They will need years yet to recover.

"Hardewold, I think he is glossing over his losses. That old Hound." Rhutgard snorted, then a thoughtful look crossed his face. "He needs to look to his own House. The changing of the guard isn't far along from now. I don't think anyone would dare to attack the Hound, but if they put some well-grounded people inside, come the changing of the guard over there, the new King could well be led astray...."

Luvian saw suddenly how fragile these rulers really were. If the commonfolk only knew.... "And Delsynth?"

"Psshhaw. There he sits in that iron castle of his. I think he sleeps in a cod piece. I can't imagine anyone dismantling that castle, or his bloodline. He's a crafty old bastard. You should have seen me arranging my marriage. I near had to kneel at his feet."

"Right then. So... mate. I think you and your peers are right to watch out for yourselves. No such thing as coincidence. You being the Eastern Shield, as you say, you need to step up and make sure each of those other Thrones aren't being watched by the wrong eyes. You're the Eastern Shield. It falls to you to take on that responsibility. If you know you're a target, then you should assume all your other soldiers, your Captains, are too, so see that they get their Houses in order. And sooner than later. And if they don't like it, or it puts them in an awkward situation with some advisor or that lordling, then they don't need that advisor or lordling. Clean out their Houses, from tower to scullery. What's more, call them in for a meeting, as your father did before you. Remember as he said, if they didn't like it, he would consider it an act against the Alliance. You may not be in the Twenty Years' War anymore, but mark my words, there is a war going on. It's a silent one, and you don't know where it's being fought, nor by who. Mate, you are right back where you started when I brought your arse back here to Fairview. Just now, your house is a whole lot bigger, spans a lot more land than it did. Find the traitors, mate. You know how I'd do it.

The King was nodding slowly. "You always know exactly what to do. I wish I could put you on my staff of advisors."

Luvian scoffed. "Even if that were a possibility, that would last a day or less. Picture it: me trying to listen to some spoiled lordling's idea of how to run a country. Nah. I'm exactly where I need to be, mate."

That's when the King nodded sadly.

"*Bloody hell.* Here it comes. I knew something was coming. Knew it."

The King looked away for a moment, as if debating how to start.

Luvian's temper snapped. "Well, shit – just get on with it, will ya – ya've told me this much! Or maybe ya could've led into it with whatever it is. *'Oy, Luvian, I have somethin' for ya –* instead of running me around – spit it out, aye?"

"You have kin. In the Dinsmore Valley."

"What?"

"Yes. You have kin up in Dinsmore."

"Oh, have I now. Funny how I don't recall them."

"They're near to death, and all of your family on that side will be attending her until she passes," the King told Luvian.

Luvian said nothing for a moment. But the King was serious.

He stuck a finger in the King's face. "You're mad. Mad."

Rhutgard waited.

Luvian continued. "In case ya haven't noticed, I'm not leavin' to go anywhere to see anyone's fake dyin' kin. I'm runnin' an establishment here and I'm workin' my arse off to do it! What the hell. What do they feed you fools up there?"

"Are you done?"

"Not nearly. What the fuck would I go to Dinsmore for?"

"So you could marry your wife," the King said.

"My wife. Did you not hear me say, that I'm too busy to do such a thing, I'm runnin' an establishment here. An' if it's Ruth you're talkin' about, she's welcome to stay here with her family. I don't need no wife and certainly don't need no family. Bloody hell. You really are an idiot. Mad. Absolutely fucking mad."

"Luvian, keep your voice down." The voice of the King of Romeny suddenly issued a royal command proper.

So Luvian stood there instead, glaring with fury at Rhutgard.

"A wife, Luvian. Besides, when do you ever find time to get laid?" said the King of Romeny.

Luvian punched him square in the jaw, utterly infuriated. Panting, Luvian suddenly realized that he had struck, aye, punched, Rhutgard Firthing, First of His Name, King of Romeny and Holder of the Eastern Shield. Men had been hung just for running in a king's path before.

Rhutgard, his blue eyes wide, stood up, holding his jaw. He spat blood out in his mouth. He stared at Luvian with all the authority of a king and Luvian realized that it was only their friendship that kept him from being arrested.

Rhutgard rubbed his jaw. "Perhaps I deserved that. I apologize, my friend."

Luvian massaged his fist. "Bet that's never happened before."

"What? Getting struck?"

"And apologizing," Luvian shook his head and then smiled a bit. He was still disgusted, but Rhutgard had apologized.

"Now explain why it is you're wantin' to marry me off and make me a father near overnight. Am I cut out of husband, father cloth to you, mate, do you think? Am I? I run a brewery." He gestured in the direction of the kitchen and bar.

Still rubbing his jaw, the King replied, "Just the fact that you've questioned it tells me that you are. Damn. I think you loosened a tooth."

"Did I? You know there's a perfect cure for it. Works every time," commented Luvian.

The King, sensing his friend's sarcasm, narrowed his eyes. "What's that?

"Pulling the fucker out."

Rhutgard glared at Luvian.

"Right then. Get on with this bloody fuckery you'd have me doing. Marryin'." Luvian scoffed.

"It's Ruth, Luvian, and she has two small girls."

Luvian remained unconvinced. "Funny, I got that part already. What aren't you tellin' me? Why would you," and he pressed on Rhutgard's chest," give a shit about a common woman in Dinsmore that I told you about near ten years ago? And not because I loved her back in the day, and I know you're no match-maker. You need something."

"Luvian, you are the one person I trust in this world, other than my wife. You have saved my life on more than one occasion, and I will never be able to repay that debt. Nor will the Crown. Nor... will my children."

Luvian's face changed. "Sorry? Your boys –"

Rhutgard nodded and said, "Will be, gods be good, happy and healthy, at the Palace, with my wife and I."

Luvian relaxed but was still confused.

"But my daughter...." Rhutgard trailed off and stared at Luvian directly.

What? "Daughter? When did you have a daughter, mate?"

"My wife... she had two boys... and a girl."

A number of thoughts clashed in Luvian's mind at that moment, for the end of the plot he'd sensed suddenly started pulling together around him, and he felt prisoner, for he now knew he had been deftly pursued and trapped. He also realized that Rhutgard was shrewder than Luvian gave him credit for... a well-executed maneuver. Damn the man.

"Your daughter." Luvian swallowed quietly.

"Yes." Rhutgard watched him warily.

"Just born?"

"Yes, with her brothers, last week. In the best of health."

"And why am I going to Dinsmore?"

"Luvian," Rhutgard sighed. "I have three sons, one not like to live past twenty. Two are hail and hearty for all their six days of life in this world. But my brother died last spring, leaving just two cousins closest in the line of succession.

"Someone has their thumb in the pot, as you said, and I cannot help but wonder if they may well be trying to dismantle my country. I have to protect my children, and my bloodline. Daughters carry on the bloodline more so than sons, as all know. It's been decades since people have had to do such a thing, but I – we – the Queen and I – have decided to hide her away until she comes of age, so that no harm comes to her." Here he paused.

Luvian knew this happened all the time. Daughters carried the bloodline truer. He wondered what cousin, what duke, duchess, earl, whatever royal would be raising the little girl. Perhaps that was to be his errand. Deliver the babe to whoever she was to stay with. Again, he sighed. Could the King not have led with that, and maybe have saved Luvian a sore fist?

"Her identity is never to be known, until she comes of age."

"I understand, mate. But, I have to tell you – I'm no good with babes. Where is the girl now? That's what you want me to do, isn't it? Take her to – wherever she'll stay?"

The King looked at him with a mixture of expressions. "You could say that, yes."

"Then – where is she?"

"She's with Ruth. And no one knows who she is, except Ruth."

Luvian's eyes suddenly narrowed. "You told me I was to marry Ruth. Was that a joke, then? Why has she got your baby daughter?"

"She is well protected, I assure you. You will attend the bedside of a dying family member for near a month there in Dinsmore. While there, you will rekindle your affection for Ruth and – marry. She will immediately take with child – my daughter, though no one will know that. By the time your kinswoman "passes," you will return here. Take your time returning, so that Ruth will have time to grow with child. When you return here, she will remain sequestered until such a time as she will have delivered. And so my daughter will be here, where I would trust her nowhere more."

Luvian listened to this, unsure of what most was objectionable. He stood in shock.

"Luvian?"

"Aside from the fact that – that – you've given me a kinswoman who doesn't exist –"

"Who will pretend to be ill and who we will sneak out of the village shortly before you leave – Happens all the time."

Luvian was still spluttering. "Aside from that, then, *mate*, you're marrying me off to a woman who already has your daughter, but is going to pretend that she is ours when we get married –"

"That's a rather simplified way of describing it –"

"Is it? Which is the most simple part of it? I'd say none of it if you were to have asked me, but you didn't ask me, at all, for none of it. And while I'm most happy to have Ruth, her children, your child – I don't think you thought this through completely. Does your wife know who I am?"

"Yes," Rhutgard replied with dignity.

"You're insane. You're mad! Both of ya, then, fuckin' mad." He managed to lower his voice at the very last moment and hissed. "Are you tryin' to tell me you want me, to raise your daughter, here? Do you see where you're standin'? Mate, this is a bloody brewery. A tavern! Your daughter is a princess! What were you thinking when you thought of lettin' your only daughter grow up –"

"With the biggest arsehole I know, in a brewery, a tavern, the best in all of South Fairview? With a war hero, a strong military man, a fighter who's loyal first to his family and second to me, the Crown, whose arse he has saved at least twice? Yes, it took quite a lot of thought to convince my Queen to allow my daughter to grow up amongst not just ordinary folk but pickpockets, thieves, and criminals. Exactly... where no one... would ever think to look for her...."

Luvian was speechless. He could only shake his head at the notion of a royal child in his home. His home, his brewery – loud, bawdy, fights, beer, clanging, laughing, music late into the night.... A royal child in the midst of all that....

"You. You're just flat out."

"Excuse me?" asked Rhutgard.

Luvian sighed and shook his head. "It's a South Fairview term. When there's no other word for it, that's what we say. It's just *flat out.*"

"Well, then." Rhutgard gestured uselessly.

"She'll not be getting that fancy royal education here, mate. Are you so sure now?"

"We know that. Just as long as she can read and write and – her numbers," Rhutgard stumbled over the unfamiliar common term for arithmetic. "She can be tutored once she comes of age."

"Rhutgard. Please. Man. Think this through. She's going to grow up in a brew house, a tavern. The people will not look kindly on that when she comes of age – you know best how society and perception work. Trust me. You don't want her to grow up here," Luvian pleaded.

"Yes, Luvian, I do. Or she may not grow up at all." Rhutgard said frankly.

Luvian finally sighed. He saw that the King was immutable. "I see I can't change your mind then."

The King shook his head some. "No." Then he said, "Luvian, I am trusting you with my family, my child, my only daughter. Do you understand what I'm doing? I am trusting you with not just my life but hers as well." The King's face was serious.

"I do. But – mate."

"Luvian?"

"You can't come back here again. Ever. Her life is in your hands as well."

The King's jaw was clenched. "I know that. I do." He reached in his mouth and felt about. Then, with a sudden cringe, he yanked out his tooth. "But a part of me will always be here with her." He gave it to Luvian. Luvian clutched the bloody tooth in his hand and nodded.

"I'll see that your business is taken care of by the very best while you're gone. After all, my daughter will be living here," the King managed to smile just a bit as he rubbed his jaw.

"Might want to get this replaced, mate," Luvian said as he held up the King's tooth.

"No, I don't think so. Every time I feel that empty spot in my mouth, I want to think of her and why she's not with me. And every time, it will renew my incentive to root out these bastards who are behind this treason."

"As you will, then, mate."

"See that you leave immediately, please," the King told Luvian.

"I will, at top moon."

"Bring her back safely, Luvian, please." The King was trying to keep up a show of bravado.

"Mate, relax. Congratulations are in order. We're both fathers now. Of course, I think my youngest takes after me, but what can I tell you. I'm usually right about these things."

The King swallowed and smiled at Luvian's jest, appreciating the levity.

As he turned to leave the stable, Luvian called quietly, "Good will follow you, mate. I'll take the best care of her."

———

PRESENT DAY

What a grace she had. Some days, Luvian swore he saw her father staring out at him from between those golden ringlets. And where, folks always asked did she get those eyes? Romeny blue, he wanted to say, from her father, of course. Sometimes she even laughed like him.

He shook his head as he watched her clear the tables clean of tankards. Luvian never let her out on the floor when customers were out and about. She objected to this, and his older girls teased him for favoring her. Ah, what children didn't know about the world. Or at least his.

On her tenth birthday, a parade was thrown uptown in the Palace District, for the War Heroes of the Twenty Years War. A Corporal from the Palace visited The Brew House with a special medal for a war hero of the highest degree. The girls hadn't known he'd been a distinguished soldier until then, but Ruthie stared at it and glanced at him. Tank's eyes grew round at the distinguishment. As a veteran from the war, Tank recognized what the medal stood for.

Idiot, thought Luvian, what was that crowned idiot thinking....

Luvian had thrown the medal in the wooden box that Rhutgard had sent him when he'd resigned his commission. Inside the box held one other item – a tooth.

Right now, Luvian knew as he watched his youngest daughter, that when they finally came for her, he was going to get some of that specially fine Palace whiskey that he kept hidden away down in the cellar, and he was going to go out in the stable, and get good and drunk.

But for now, Luvian looked down and swiped a damp rag across the counter top of his bar.

⁓

End of Prologue

Theldry

On and on he droned. Crimson bougainvillea vines blew in the breeze and she stilled her fingers to keep them from drumming the table with impatience. She stared at her china plate, with no appetite for the pastries and fruit that lay arranged on it for her.

Minutes stretched on while Theldry waited for an opportune moment to interject but the subject of Naval holdings in Banker's Bay was just not affording it. Finally, she sat forward.

"Father –"

"Don't interrupt your father, Theldry," her mother chided mildly.

Her brother snickered and threw a grape from his morning breakfast bowl at her.

She threw it back with force so that it hit him between the eyes.

Immediately, Bronn pointed, and, regardless that his mouth was full, complained, "Mother! Did you see that?" Theldry rolled her eyes at him. His excelled at that victim act – she could think of no one who annoyed her more!

"Theldry!"

Ugh. Her mother was so – so perfect! "Mother – he started it! How can you not see that!"

Since neither parent was looking at him, Bronn smiled wickedly at Theldry, with grapes in front of each tooth and his eyes rolled up into his head.

"Theldry, you must act more like a princess." The Queen of Tortoreen looked at Theldry with a quiet grace and told her, "Now. Sit up, and –"

"Oh, and that was him acting like a Prince!" Theldry protested. She slammed herself back into her cushioned chair.

"Theldry, Bronn is nine. You are fifteen."

"Exactly! Why can I not leave yet! Father! *Please!*"

"Theldry, I have had this discussion with you. Twice now. I'll not have it again."

She stared miserably out across Kelving Bay. "All of my friends are –"

"Yes, my child. All of your friends are married or betrothed. I am aware. But they are not you, and you are a princess. When I find you the right match, then off you shall go." Her father brushed his fingers out across the breakfast table to animate the idea of sending her away.

"But. Can I not at least – visit at court? Some of my friends, perhaps?" Theldry wheedled, hoping to win him over. The breeze blew the veiled curtains behind them gently.

He turned a stern glance down his nose. "What, so some baseborn squire can get you with child in a back hallway somewhere? I think not. You'll not be some lady-in-waiting to a misplaced duchess simply because you tarnished your reputation. You will be a duchess, or perhaps even a princess in your own right – if we find you the right match. But you must be patient. And of that trait, I know you have precious little."

Theldry did not say more, for she did not want to anger her father. She glanced away sullenly.

Her father turned in his seat and looked at her square on. "Theldry, you may yet come to understand this some day. Your friends are of noble blood, yes, and they have found good matches, I am sure, the best their families can make. You, however, are different. You are a princess. I have alliances to uphold, contracts to support, and a country to protect. Royalty does not have the option of marrying for love, nor for pleasure. We must abide by our duty at all times. Royalty is a duty. Duty before love, always, Theldry. Duty before love."

"And that's all I am then, a bargaining chip, a tool, a – a stamp on a contract to you, Father?" Theldry inquired of her father.

He looked down at her. "If it must be so, then yes."

Topher

He stared around the bare walls of his cell. He missed his own cell, where he had lived for nearly six years now. But since he was to take the Final Oath, he had one last week in seclusion to pray. In this ugly, barren, enclosed little space.

All of his possessions would be disposed of or distributed to other members of the Order, should they prove useful. Topher didn't believe such would be the case, save perhaps his blanket. They did not keep possessions.

He was supposed to be in deep, fervent prayer with The One God, casting off the unholiness of his soul in here. Topher sighed. Four bare walls did not induce any sort of commune with The One God now any more than they had before. He expected his flippancy over the last six years toward this religious aspect was now catching up to him. When he took the Final Oath in two days, The One God was surely going to exact his penance. *Topher, you fool....*

Being locked in this cell for the last four days hadn't shed any more illumination into his soul than he'd seen when he'd first arrived here.

Topher remembered sitting alone at his parents' table when he had heard a deep voice outside bellow, "Callon, son of Storran!"

Topher had been ten. He'd immediately frozen and looked around for his parents.

The deep voice bellowed again, "Callon, son of Storran!"

Topher stepped outside timidly. He glanced all around, but neither his parents nor his siblings were to be seen.

A wooden wagon stood ominously in the dusty road. Topher recognized the man calling his name as one of the men from the County, who dispensed Healing, business services, and educational needs to the people, but Topher did not know his name.

"Callon, son of Storran, approach!"

Topher was suddenly very nervous and wanted to run away. In the back of the wagon, he saw three lads of his own age. Had he done something wrong? Where were his parents?

A man suddenly appeared from behind the wagon, dressed in black robes.

Topher's parents appeared behind him. His father patted Topher's head. "You be a good boy, son."

"What? Da?"

His mother bent over him and enveloped him in a hug, crying. "Always remember, Callon, that we love you," she whispered.

Now he was truly afraid. *"Mum?"*

The robed man stepped forward, a stern expression on his face. He raised his eyebrows expectantly.

Callon's mum pushed him forward. His little sister appeared at his Mum's side, her thumb in her mouth. She started to trot after him. "Callon?"

"No, baby girl, you stay," Callon's mum grabbed her hand.

"Where's Callon going, Mummy?"

Callon was forced to look forward as the County Elder took his hand. "Callon, son of Storran." He then handed him to the stern man in robes, who nodded. He gestured for Callon to step up into the back of the wagon with the other lads.

What had he done? Where was he being taken?
"Mum! Da!"

His parents watched as the wagon suddenly hitched forward with a rickety jolt.

"Callon!" His baby sister was crying. They turned around and walked into the house without a word.

He pressed himself against the wooden slats, trying to see his house and the cornfields as the wagon rolled away.

"No use, Callon," said one boy.

"Yeah, better say your good-byes while ye still can, Cally boy," said another. He snickered. "Get it," he winked at the other boys.

"Lay off him, you were a bloody mess when they collected you, weren't you, then," said the third.

Callon stared at each of them. "I – I don't understand."

"What's to understand? You've been collected."

Callon shook his head. "What's *collected?*"

The three lads looked at him with pitying expressions.

"Wow. You really are rural, aren't ya?
"Lay off the lad." The largest boy seemed to be in charge.

"No. I want to know, what is *collected* mean?" Callon insisted. He had never heard of it.

"Well, outside of the cornfields, in the big, wide world –"

"Don't be a wad!" the largest boy kicked him.

"Fine, you tell it, then!"

A cough from the robed man driving the horses suddenly got their attention. They looked up to see the man staring at them with a baleful glare. Chastened, they quieted down and the robed figure turned around again.

"Look, Cally boy, you know as you're ten, you mostly apprentice out."

"Not me. I'm working my da's fields."

The largest boy snorted.

"And ye told me not to be a wad."

"Who are all of you?" Callon demanded.

"I'm Sechaill, from Roarden North. That's a city, in case ye don't know what one is, country boy," laughed the obnoxious lad.

"Just shut it." The second boy, who had said very little until now, introduced himself as Gilroy, and told them he'd been living in an orphanage in West Mabon. He said, "Lots of orphanages give collections to the Order. Some of them need to clear out the space, and some of them just need the money. Some of them might just want to get rid of a boy or two." Gilroy shrugged. "I don't care one ways or another. As long as it gives me three squares and roof."

Callon stared. What did that mean for him? What was *The Order?*

The largest boy spoke up then. "I'm Alden. From ArkenHeights –"

"That's also a city, in case ye didn't know, country boy," Sechaill couldn't resist interjecting with a laugh.

"Wad," and "Prig," came Alden and Gilroy's unison reprimand.

"Aye, well, and why not? I might as well get it in now while I still can, shouldn't I?"

"I still don't understand. I'm supposed to work my da's fields –"

"Callon. Got any siblings? Lot of mouths for your mum and da to feed?" asked Gilroy.

"Any crops go bad lately? Need help in the fields?" asked Alden.

Callon stared between the two. "I'm the oldest, I have two more brothers an' a sister. And we lost our crop last year, but my da says it'll come in just fine this year."

Alden looked disgusted and stared out the slats of the wagon. Gilroy said nothing, just looked away.

Sechaill, however, jumped in. "Cally, boy, ye been bought and paid for. Ye see that now, don't ya'. Your da put up a notice in your village, or whatever that was that we just left, for The Silent Order to come and collect you. The Village sends notice to nearest Order and they come and collect you. After they buy you, that is. Wonder what we cost in today's world, do ya think? How do ya word a message to get rid a' kids, aye? *"Ten-year-old selfish prig, runs like a loon through the streets, come and collect 'im before I hang him from the rooftop?"*

Alden and Gilroy snickered in spite of themselves.

"Really, Cally, boy. Ye' never heard of the Collection?" asked Sechaill, as serious as he could be. He leaned forward with interest as he saw that Callon was did not comprehend.

"They're the Silent Order. Everyone knows them. For being, well, obvious." Gilroy nodded his head up toward the driver. "They're monks. It's a religious order."

"They're not all bad," said Alden. "They rescue slaves, and they work with the Royals. Healing. Stuff like that."

"Maybe I'll get to work with a Royal. Ye think?" Sechaill's face turned merry.

Gilroy and Alden boy snorted. "Fat chance of that."

"Why, what's wrong with me?" he demanded.

Alden said, "Well, for one, the Royals, they don't want arseholes."

Gilroy snickered.

"Pfff. The Royals are arseholes. I'll fit right in," quipped Sechaill.

Even Callon smiled weakly at this.

The robed monk turned around and glared at each of them. The three of them assumed properly respectful demeanors until he turned around again.

As soon as the wagon moved forward, Sechaill sent a profane gesture forward in the direction of the monk. All three boys snorted laughter, covering their mouths to keep from being overheard.

"Seriously, I head they whip ya if ya don't behave there," whispered Sechaill behind a hand.

"They whip anyone if they don't conform," said Alden. "I knew a friend who had both brothers collected. He came home twice and they were gone. He's still there," Alden mused.

"We must be worth a good copper, maybe two then, ya think? They always scare us as kids, *If ya don't behave, I'll have the Silent Order come and collect ya. If ya don't shut that mouth, I'll have the Silent Ones shut it for ya!*" Sechaill said.

Alden and Gilroy both nodded, remembering the same warnings.

"Silent?" asked Callon. He swallowed. He really was a country boy. He could count the amount of times he'd been to the County Market on two hands, for otherwise, he'd always stayed at home, helping his da in the fields or else his mum with the chickens and the other chores.

His three new companions stared at him.

"Cally, boy, let's just say, today is the last day anyone will ever *hear* from us again." Sechaill winked.

"No one will ever need to tell *him* to shut up again," said Gilroy, nodding at Sechaill

"Aye, so sad. The world will have lost such a great –"

"Shut up!" Gilroy and Alden both laughed at him.

"Why?"

"Callon! You're so thick, boy. You're joining the *Silent Order*. As in, *Silent*. You're never going to speak again, not after today. Got it now?" Gilroy told him, exasperated.

Callon stared at him in shock.

"Did ya *hear* him, Cally boy, because it's the last ya'll hear of again, I guarantee ya." Sechaill was for the first time, entirely serious.

"But, but why?"

"Because. You swear your vows, you're trained up, and finally, after you're trained up, they take your tongue out. Silent forever," Alden explained.

Callon shrank back against the wooden slats of the wagon. "No!" How could he get out of the wagon? "No! I need to get out!"

Gilroy leaned over and shushed him immediately, while Alden pushed him away from the back of the wagon. "Stop. You don't get to leave now. You're the property of the Silent Order!"

"Leaving the Silent Order is punishable by death. If you run away, and they find you, they will execute you. Anyone will. If anyone recognizes a member of the Silent Order who deserted, they execute the member, then keep him 'til a monk comes to get him. Then they'll be paid by the Order."

Callon was horrified. How had this happened to him?

—⟨⁕⟩—

Topher had read that everyone remembered their Collection vividly. He certainly did. They were rounded up no differently than cattle, their heads shorn, and then the induction began. They lost everything from their prior lives, including their names. *Callon* seemed such a strange name to him now. Sechaill, Alden, and Gilroy were now Brothers Ewan, Kegan, and Levvan, though, Topher thought darkly, and each of them had taken the Final Oath already.

Inductees received a very rigorous education, far more so than most Royals, Topher knew. Scribery, arithmetic, Healing, history for hundreds of years of all the land, heraldry, agriculture, animal husbandry.... Some who were better with their arithmetic focused on accounts, while those who worked best with writing worked in scribery and history. Some orders produced soaps and waxes, honeys, and other such items that they occasionally sold to the Markets. Many of them, after they were trained, were sent to a village, county, city, or Royal, who had need of The One God's services.

Inductees took their Initiate Vow after their first week was completed. After five years, they took their Second Vow, during which they were assigned a group of Brothers to focus more directly their abilities for the next year.

And then, like Topher, they were assigned a small cell for one week, to cast away the last six years, and before that, all of his entire life, to become as one with The One God before offering his soul to him forever.

Topher was no closer to communing with The One God now as he had been four days ago, nor a year ago, nor six years ago. He truly believed in The One God, and Topher believed that The One God believed in him... but he just was not ready for his tongue to be burned out of his head. Perhaps he liked the taste of food too much, or just the idea of speaking. Becoming a verbal eunuch scared him more than anything else.

For the final week, they wore navy colored robes. They were only allowed to leave the cell for prayers, at sunrise, noon, and sunset, as all the Brothers did. He, however, had to return to his cell. His food was brought in to him.

He occupied his time with exercise. Meditation was impossible, for he was unable to concentrate at all. He barely slept. Topher saved two of his pears and taught himself to juggle, but after two days, even that held no attraction, and, of course, the fruit was so bruised from their several falls upon the stone floor, that he'd needed to eat them.

All he could do to pass the time was recite dates of important events in history, but this morning, Topher finally snapped. The cells, of course, were not guarded. But he had to get out. He opened his door quietly, so that it would not creak.

Glancing around, Topher waited for one Brother to pass by upon the green before he swung his door open.

He snuck around to the back of his building and cowered in the bushes, breathing in the fresh air as if each were his last.

When finally Topher had enjoyed enough of the sunlight and the breeze, he stood and stepped cautiously toward the corner of the building to peer around.

A wizened Brother stepped in his path suddenly. Topher almost dropped to the ground with shock, his heart in his throat.

The old Brother observed Topher's navy robes and then looked at Topher's face. He traced what Topher knew were dark circles beneath his eyes with a finger, and then, with a kindly smile, patted him on the shoulder gently, almost as if he recognized Topher's struggle. And then he continued on his way. Topher knew many other Brothers would not have been so accommodating.

Topher could still hear his heart pounding. He immediately slipped around the building and back into his cell, before any other Brother could catch him.

Perhaps the Brother recognized that he looked like all members of the Order did before they took their Final Oath. Miserable and scared and half mad....

Topher knew from reading that he would only become a Brother if he took the Final Oath. But how he would miss the taste of raspberries, and cherries....

He'd also read that quite a few Brothers died while taking the Oath or immediately after. The Healers were always present for the Oath, and Topher and the others knew that during the Oath, many broke their Vow of Silence by screaming. Not a good way to start off your service to The One God, Topher mused. He wondered if he would scream. He kept biting his tongue, probably because he wouldn't be able to in a few days.

Those who screamed during their Oath were heard across half the facility, both due to the sound of the voice, and because there were so few voices heard at all. But heads everywhere looked up, listened for a moment, nodded with realization, some with sympathy, and then all the Brothers returned to their task at hand.

Some Brothers did not survive after taking the Oath, for it took at least two weeks to fully heal, if not more, during which the new Brother was sequestered. If a member did not survive the Oath, or a Brother took an infection or fever and passed on immediately following, then they were considered by the Brothers as unworthy to serve in The One God's view.

Members could refuse to take the Final Oath, Topher knew. But they were seen as unfit to serve, and made to carry out the worst of jobs, live in the worst of living conditions, shunned on the grounds. Most of them eventually gave in and took the Oath.

Topher sat there on the floor. He'd seen Brothers yawn before, seen them with their mouths open, and just seen a scarred stump for a tongue. He was just not able to envision himself tied down with a pair of red-hot tongs inside his mouth....

He drew his knees up to his chin and took a deep breath.

That was it, then. He would run.

Rhutgard

"And?"

His advisor stared at him with a chilling gaze. "They have proved no more productive than...when they were recently questioned."

Rhutgard sighed and looked away from the man for a moment. Finally, he looked directly into the man's empty gray eyes. "You're torturing them, aren't you." It was not a question.

The man's gray pallor registered no emotion, but he acted as if he were taken aback. Rhutgard frowned. Such were the men whom he employed to force information from his enemies. He could delude himself no further.

"Your Majesty," the man feigned shock with ease.

"Enough with that. How long have we had them?"

"They were captured three days ago, Your Majesty."

"And how long have they been in the dungeons?"

"Two, Sire."

Rhutgard frowned. Found scouting into Romeny territory, the Ormon soldiers were captured and sent immediately to Fairview for questioning. After two days, very little information had been gleaned.

"Shall we continue, Sire?" His crooked palms curled together almost eagerly.

"No. What has your man done, rack them? Pulling their bodies apart further will accomplish nothing if they have given us nothing by now. Throw them in a cell."

"But, Sire..."

The barely disguised disappointment on the man's countenance nauseated Rhutgard. Men like this sadly had their place in the land but he could bear to look upon this man no more. "Cells. Now. Go." Rhutgard waved a curt dismissal.

He turned and strode down the deserted corridor, feeling filthy. He stopped in front of a glass window and gazed out. His father and even his grandfather had prepared him for being a king. He had always known as Crown Prince that he would have to make difficult choices. But he had always believed those choices to be such as choosing between this tariff and that, settling Council disputes, finding ways to fill the royal coffers.

He gazed at the hazy reflection of himself in the glass window. He did not like who he was becoming. His father, King Galvin, had been a hero to him, had trained him in diplomacy, the art of war, heraldry, history, and strategy. He had seen that his education as a Prince was tailored specifically with an eye to ruling one day.

Now, as Rhutgard gazed at his reflection, he wondered if his father, and indeed, his grandfather, were faced with the choices he had carried out. If they had tortured men. Those men were mere scouts, young men, not even officers. Brothers, sons, husbands, fathers even, perhaps. And now they sat in Rhutgard's dungeon, broken men, merely for fighting for what they believed in, as every soldier fights for what they believe in. Rhutgard stared into his own eyes, searching for answers.

He wondered if his own sons would ever have to face such choices as he had. He hoped not. Rhutgard would not leave his sons wondering if he had committed such atrocities. He would teach them the truth about such things, so that they were truly prepared for their futures. For he had wished numerous times to talk to his father more about being King, for he had become King himself younger than he would have wished.

For now, he would teach his sons to be righteous, especially in times of war. The people must be ruled by honor, above all. He stared out over the courtyard.

Ellia

Ellia swiped a damp rag across the drying pint rings on the bar and eyed the South Fairview workmen seated about the corner table as another burst of raucous laughter erupted from them. They accepted new pitchers from Ellia's sister Hasley readily, not noticing as the ale slopped over their empty pint glasses. Today marked the end of the workweek for many of the tradesmen and workers, but the workweek at The Brew House was just beginning.

Torchlight flickered throughout the common room as the heavy oaken front door swung open to allow Metz and Ron through. They waved to their fellow friends and apprentices and were beckoned over to join them.

"More pitchers for that crew," Hasley rolled her green eyes with a half-smile as she tossed her head in the direction of the rowdy corner. She circled behind the bar and set down empty pitchers.

Rowdy hoots of laughter went up from the corner, and one of the men clambered up on the table, tipping dangerously as he did, his balance skewed by ale. Mags poked her head out just then and noted the table. "Time to send Tank over?"

Hasley considered for a moment, but Ellia said, "No, he's a regular. His wife just had a baby last week. Let him drink while he's still allowed out of his house." She smirked as the corner started singing, "Hang from the Rafters and Shout!"

"Ha!" Mags sniffed. "As long as he goes home to his own rafters tonight, we'll be fine. We only got one room left," Mags warned them before disappearing behind the waving kitchen doors.

Already? The tavern rooms were usually not full until Sixthday. Hasley threw Ellia a worried glance. When all of the tavern rooms were rented, travelers and customers who wanted to stay the night could sleep on the common room floor, or even in the stable. On the occasion that a drunken customer took offense to the idea of taking his repose on the floor or became belligerent, Tank either discouraged him or threw him out. Tank's looming stature alone usually dissuaded unruly behavior in The Brew House and Tavern, but he also ended the brawls that broke out now and again with a few well-placed clouts, then threw the stunned and dazed recipients into the street by their collars.

"Mollie!" Mum called, craning her neck behind the bar. "Where is that girl! I need her upstairs!"

"She went to the down to the cellar to fill the pitchers," Hasley supplied with an apologetic face.

"Ah, sure she did. She knows she's supposed to be working the chambers," Mum whirled with frustration and narrowed green eyes. "When she comes upstairs, you send her up to me."

"But Mum, I'll work upstairs, I'm old enough now!" called Hasley.

"No, you're not, girl, you stay down here. You and Ellia stay down here with tables where Tank can keep his eye on you."

Hasley drew in breath to protest but Mum cut her off with a stern look down her nose and a finger in the air. "I told ya, now, no. And send your sister up to me soon as she comes up."

Hasley heaved a great sigh of indignation and glared out over the rowdy bar.

"I don't know why you keep asking," Ellia shook her head at her sister.

"Shut up, you. You're not allowed on the floor. You don't get grabbed and slopped on with ale by the drunks," snapped Hasley. "I want to go upstairs and work where it's quiet."

"Mollie would trade with you, you know that. Besides, she has to clean out the rooms. Chambers, linens." Ellia wrinkled her nose at the idea of soiled linens and chamber pots. "You can have it. I'd rather work down here."

"All you have to do is fill up pitchers and tankards and bowls. You just have to stay behind the bar. Just wait 'til Pappy sends you out on the floor. You'll see," Hasley's green eyes sparked with disgust.

Ellia wasn't allowed out from behind the bar. Pappy always said it was due to her age. She was sixteen, though, and Hasley was out on the floor when she was sixteen, Ellia had often protested. But Pappy had insisted, and once he made his mind up, he stared you down with that stare, and there was no changing his mind. So only when the bar was empty did Ellia come out from behind the bar, to sweep and clean the tables.

And Mags sent her to the Market more often now, though she always sent Ellia out on errands when Pappy wasn't around to hear. Ellia had the sneaking suspicion that these errands were more designed to get Ellia out of The Brew House and into the neighborhood. Twice she had been sent to the Market Place to pick up vegetables for the stew that she knew Mags had enough of, but she said nothing. Sometimes Mags gave her a little extra coin and told her to get herself a bit of a treat, so Ellia bought some candied orange slices or sugared cherries.

Mum often saw Ellia return but said nothing. She would lean against the frame of the swinging kitchen doors and give Mags one of those indiscernible looks that Ellia knew meant more that she was saying. "What?" Mags would say innocently. Mum would shake her head and smile a bit before disappearing upstairs. Mags would wink at her and tell her, "Ya got to get out there once in a while, haven't ya, girl?

But for now, Ellia wasn't going anywhere. Neither the pitchers nor the tankards would fill themselves, and she would keep them full for the sake of the customers, for Hasley's wrath was not to be taken lightly. Hasley frowned and grabbed two more pitchers for the men singing "Hang from the Rafters and Shout!"

A Silent Game of Spies

"Hang from the Rafters and Shout"

We can all dance the jig
If they serve pints that are big

We can all send up laughter
Straight to the attic rafter

Oh, hang from the rafters and shout! (Shout!)
Hang from the rafters and shout! (Shout!)

We can all run and dance
If there's a hint of romance

So string up a fair tune
That we all might prance like loons

Oh, hang from the rafters and shout! (Shout!)
Hang from the rafters and shout! (Shout!)

Let us toast then and sing
Be us stable hand or king

Let us take pints and drink
Tankards and pitchers can't think

Oh, hang from the rafters and shout! (Shout!)
Oh, hang from the rafters! Hang from the rafters! (Shout!)

Hang from the rafters and shout! Shout! (Shout!)
Oh, hang from the rafters and shout! Shout! (Shout!)

"Hmm!" she sniffed. "I'll give them something to shout about, just see if I don't." And she marched off in their direction, ale sloshing over the sides of the pitchers she carried.

Ron

Cradwick was asleep. Asleep was a nice term for it, as the master blacksmith was most often passed out from drink during the days. Ron himself now provided most of Cradwick's smithy services and interestingly, no change in skill had been noted or accorded by their customers. A truly gifted smith, Cradwick had long been a member of the Romeny Blacksmith Guild and a respected member of the community. Ron fought to keep the old man's reputation stainless.

He left a full jug of wine where the old man's hand would grasp it and slipped out the back. The cool air of the small alley blew across his face, always a welcome respite after the heated confines of the forge. Ron tugged at the strings of his tunic and turned onto Wagon Way.

He nodded at customers and acquaintances upon occasion as he made his way toward Market Square. Ron was impatient as a blacksmith's apprentice. Almost two years had passed already. He tried not to let his frustration overcome his features.

Ron fingered over cloth he knew was poor quality silk and expressed polite interest along with other customers in a spice merchant's embellished story of new merchandise. He paid the baker's apprentice for fresh loaves of bread, bought vegetables, and smiled at the shy girl at the fruit stand while her mother wasn't looking. She smiled shyly back and took his copper for the pear.

Every four days was a market day, by Cradwick's rule, and today was no different. Ron turned and glanced nonchalantly about the square. After a wagon passed, Ron's eyes met those of a dingily dressed man across the square, who bit into the round of a pear.

Ron sighed inwardly and looked away. His assignment would continue.

Tyndie

Lynza hurried Tyndie along. "So, you're Tynda. You'll have to hurry a bit more if you want to do this job. Your Auntie says you're a hard worker down there in the kitchens, and I never known her to be wrong."

Tyndie could hardly believe her luck. No one ever made it out of the kitchens, they just worked their way up. She was just a kitchen girl, and a lucky one, at that, for after her mum passed, they'd kept her on out of sympathy.

Lynza grabbed her hand and forced Tyndie into a quicker pace. "Come on, come on, hurry it. You'll be a runner, bringing cups and the like from the kitchen to us, the servers. But you can't be late, understand?"

Tyndie nodded, breathless. "Good. Now I know you don't know the layout of the castle yet, so you'll be runnin' about with me for a few days," Lynza explained as they rounded a stone corner, "but only for a few days. You got to learn quick. We're short-handed. That's why your Auntie said we should take you on. She's a good soul, she is."

They arrived at a dusty set of stone steps that Lynza skipped half of. Tynda nearly lost her footing twice.

"Come along, you'll learn to run these steps soon enough. Now, in you go," and she pushed Tyndie into a small room where three other women sat, polishing silver and cleaning cupware.

"When we're not serving, we keep extras on hand here, and we polish the silver," Lynza explained. "Now here," and she held out a maid's dress and apron. "Change out of that ugly rag and put this on. Keep it perfect, for you'll only have one other, for when it gets cold. If you spill on it, you'll best switch it out with the laundress quick as you can. The Royals will be seein' you, and if you look anything but starched and perfect, you'll be sent right back to the kitchens again. If you're lucky," Lynza added.

Tyndie looked down at her old kitchen dress. It had been washed so many times, it was grey now, and thin in several places, even though she'd always worn an apron. She was almost reluctant to change out of it, as if it were a vestige of her past. She felt all the women's eyes staring at her. Self-consciously, she accepted the new dress and turned around, letting her old dress fall to the floor.

She fingered the starched cloth of her new dress – it was stiff and rustled as she picked it up. She slipped it over her head. "Oh, and find some time to bathe when you can." Lynza sniffed with condescension from somewhere behind her.

"Lynza, stop ridin' the girl. It's her first day," clucked one of the other ladies.

Tyndie held her peace and slipped her new apron over her head. It smelled of fine soap, the same soap as came from the laundress. Not a single wrinkle at all. She took a moment to marvel privately at her luck. With the exception of having to run everywhere... this was a wonderful turn of events for her.

"I'm not ridin' her. She needs to bathe, is all. How often do kitchen girls bathe, is all I'm saying," protested Lynza.

"Lynza. You're lettin' your bitch show again," said one of the other ladies, and then they tittered.

Tyndie turned around to see Lynza roll her brown eyes. "Fine, have it your way."

Just then, an older, burly serving woman bustled in with a silver platter of empty dishes. As she relinquished them into a barrel of clean water, she complained, "That damnable little pup!

Someone should throw his skinny arse into a kennel and let him howl for his slops for a week or two and then let him see just how lucky he is. Better still, send him back home to his –"

Then she stopped, standing up straight. "Why, Tyndie, girl, is that you? Come here, love!"

Tyndie, happy to see someone who cared for her existence, approached her Aunt Renne, and was immediately enveloped in an enormous hug. Aunt Renne pulled Tynda back by the shoulders and held her chin up, studying her face. "Child, if you don't look more and more like your mum every time I see you, may she rest with the gods."

Then she stood up. "Now then. You'll be following Lynzie about for a few days, get the lay of the castle. We're short of staff and we've been working double shifts. But you've got your mum in you, you're smart and you learn quick. Do as Lynzie here says and you'll be on your own in no time."

Aunt Renne smiled and patted Tyndie's shoulder fondly. Then she gave her a quick hug, but whispered in her ear, "And don't let her be too much of a bitch to ya, Tyndie girl, aye," she chuckled.

<hr />

Tyndie sighed. She was only carrying a jug of water, just to start off slow, but she couldn't remember whether she turned right or left here. HarCourt Castle was immense, far more so than she had imagined previously.

Lynza remained unconvinced that Tyndie was at all able to carry her weight, but the other women recalled to Lynza her first few days. She sniffed and said she supposed everyone had to learn at their own pace.

Yesterday, Lynza leaned against a stone wall during one of their few breaks. As she bit into an apple, she looked Tyndie up and down.

"I suppose you think I'm being hard on you. Might be." She bit into her apple again, glancing down at it. "But how else you gonna learn, Tyndie? A girl who's bad at her job has no job. And your Auntie can't watch out for ya forever, can she now?

"Now mind what I told you. Never look a Royal in the eye, not ever. You just be invisible. All you do is pour the liquid and maybe someday, you might serve some food. Right now, you're just bringing us water and soon enough, maybe, cider and wine.

"Curtsy like I taught ya. Say whatever they want you to say, whatever they want to hear. And that's no matter where ya are, serving or not. Just be like you're not there. The less anyone sees you, the better. Especially as, you're cute enough to look at, you don't want the wrong eyes seein' ya, and ya know what I mean." Lynza chucked her under the chin. "Speak right, too, don't be usin' slang. Save that for our off time." Lynza took a final bit of her apple and wiped the juice from her chin. "You got all that?"

Tyndie had nodded. She had learned it best to say nothing at all to Lynza, for like as not, she would find fault with whatever she ventured forth with. Tyndie doubted that Lynza would even take kindly to a compliment. She wondered off-handedly whether Lynza had always been such a bleak personality, or if someone or something had caused her to act like this. Perhaps it was just the job. Lynza wasn't but maybe a few years older than Tyndie.

And now, she arrived later than she was expected with her water, for in trying to find her way through the back passages, she had taken two wrong turns and had had to double back. Lynza glared at her as she snatched the jug and swept out of the room.

Tyndie had started using all her time memorizing the castle corridors and the back passages. But still, she was not quick enough, even though she ran. She had most of them memorized now, yet still she arrived later than Lynza preferred.

The first time she arrived punctually, Tyndie relished Lynza's surprised look before it faded.

Still, she was only punctual half the time. Her goal was to be early all the time.

Tyndie walked the dimly lit North East Corridor. She had found how valuable discretion truly was. Two days ago, just as she neared the end of the third-floor corridor overlooking the gardens, she heard muffled voices. Not wishing to be observed, Tyndie glanced around. If she ran back down the corridor, she ran the risk of being heard. She looked up at the wall, where a dusty, wall-length tapestry hung. She gulped and slipped behind it.

Then she recognized the voices – a squire was fucking a maid against the wall just around the corner. Tyndie stood there, barely breathing, her eyes rolled upward in disgust, captive to the entire event. Tyndie peeked out once and saw the young maid, a pretty blond girl, with her skirts up about her waist while a squire rammed into her continually, proud of each thrust. Though the maid cried out with pleasure during the entire affair, Tyndie caught just one eyeroll and wondered how the squire couldn't see that she was feigning her every moan and wail.

Just as Tyndie was beginning to get truly impatient, the squire finished, panting and attempting to articulate meaningful expressions. Finally, Tyndie heard him brushing off and straightening his clothing.

"All right, there, love?" Tyndie heard him pat the maid's cheek before he turned around. The sound of boots on stone cobbles faded as he disappeared down the hall.

Tyndie peeped out at the maid. She was smoothing her hair. As she hiked up her bodice and rustled her skirts straight, the maid muttered, *"All right there, love?"* in imitation of the Squire. Then she said, "Fuck you, ya bastard," and turned down the opposite hallway.

Tyndie was just truly grateful than neither of them had turned down her passageway, for they may have seen the tips of her shoes protruding from beneath the tapestry.

And yesterday – she had nearly been caught. While it had been far more interesting than a Squire poking a maid in a back corridor, it had also been ridiculously more dangerous. Not only had no tapestry been available to shelter her, but the lords in the corridor were speaking – aye, yelling, in fact. A clandestine meeting that had gotten out of hand. One lord had paid in advance for a service that had yet to be delivered by the second lord.

"Will you lower your voice!"

"I will not lower my voice –"

A menacing voice replied, "Get a hold of yourself, fool. We are in this together. I have not yet had the opportunity to fulfill our arrangement. Such things require time! Time and planning. And patience, of which you have little. This is why I excel at my job. Do you see, then?

"Drury, if anyone should find out of our connection –"

"And how should that happen? We know each other as passing acquaintances here only. I might add, Stanson, you sought my services of your own accord, not the other way around," hissed Drury in foreboding tones.

"Is that meant to be a threat?" Stanson's enraged voice rose again.

Drury's voice replied lowly with an intensity that frightened Tyndie, "I make no threats. I merely act on need."

It was clear from Stanson's silence that he was cowed by such intimidation. Tyndie wondered what service Drury had sought Stanson's assistance for.

After Stanson remained silent for a few heartbeats, Drury said, "Very good. We understand each other now, do we not?" When silence met his inquiry, he continued. "We are not to be seen with each other, nor speaking to each other. At all. Go back to your apartment, fuck your mistress, do - whatever it is that you do. But we do not know each other. Now go." And Tyndie heard whom she presumed was Stanson leave down the stone corridor, all too quickly.

She did not dare to look out from where she cowered in the dusty, unused foyer around the corner, glad of the darkness that hid her. Tyndie knew that Drury still stood there, on the cobbled stone of the main passage. Her heart was in her throat, for she was sure he could sense her somehow.

After a moment, he seemed to shake himself and turned on his boot heel. Not until she was sure she was alone did she step out of the dark foyer.

The next day, the entire castle was buzzing with news of a young lord who had fallen into the moat the night before, drunken, and drowned. Tyndie's thoughts immediately turned to the hushed conversation she'd witnessed between Drury and Stanson, but she shook it off. Lords took to doing ridiculous things all the time when they were drunk.

But two days later, Lord Stanson was killed in a hunting accident – trying to spear the boar himself.

Tyndie heard the lords snickering about it, for they were amazed a horse had even been able to carry his fat arse into the forest. And why had his Squire allowed him to spear the boar? It'd been far too long since Lord Stanson had even been hunting, did he even know how to use his sword anymore? They laughed about the sexual connotation of the remarks. "Found dead trying to stab a piggie," and they all laughed.

Tyndie was the only one who was horrified at what she truly knew had happened now. She wasn't sure whether to feel bad for the Lord Stanson or not, for now she knew he had hired Lord Drury to assassinate the young man who had drowned in the moat.

But what she did know for certain – that Lord Drury was an assassin, and that she had witnessed his plans.

Ron

He ducked beneath the protruding iron Brew House sign, its hinges creaking slightly in the afternoon breeze, his eyes adjusting from the brightness of the sunlit street to the torchlit tavern. Ron had grown fond of the knotty wooden planks of the tavern, fragrant with stew and bread, its tables ringed with ale from the pints and tankards of many an uproarious eve.

This afternoon he had to himself. Almost all customer orders were complete. Only a set of doorlatches for an artisan expanding his shop remained. Ron had planned to work them himself this afternoon instead of seeking a mead at The Brew House, but Cradwick had roused himself from his bed to take up the hammer and tongs. In a blustery haze, Cradwick had stumbled about the forge, then sent Ron to the woodmonger. Though a plentiful stack of lumber rested behind the shop awaiting use, Ron knew Cradwick was grasping at the fringes of an old routine and so hastily bowed with obeisance to his master before setting out upon the needless errand. Cradwick would, if custom served, soon sit down for a rest and a sip of wine, and be snoring by the time Ron returned.

Ron glanced at the table he usually preferred to take a meal at, but found it occupied. With nonchalance, he slid onto a stool at the far side of the bar and loosened the strings of his tunic.

"Why, Ronnie," came the warm voice of the innkeeper's wife from behind the counter.

"Miss Ruth," he dipped his head respectfully to the green-eyed, smiling matronly woman as she smoothed her dishtowel across the bar surface.

"Pshaw, those manners. Someone raised you right," she chuckled. "How is it you're here this time of day?" she asked as she set down a full pint of mead and a plate of fresh brown bread before him. Inwardly, Ron smiled. Had he been frequenting The Brew House so often that they knew his preference without his ordering it?

"Master Cradwick had a special project he wanted to work on." Ron's lie came with a practiced ease.

"He's a gifted talent, he is. When he takes to a project, you know it'll be done just right." She pointed up at the oil lamps. "He did those for us years ago. Imported the iron and all."

Ron noted the deft craftsmanship and agreed with her.

She patted his hand and disappeared behind the swinging kitchen doors.

He was just spreading butter on his bread when Ellia pushed airily through the swinging doors. "Oh!" Her blue eyes rounded with sudden surprise. "I didn't expect to see you there, Ronnie. Have you got the afternoon off, then?"

"Some of it," Ron admitted. "Have some bread with me?" He held up a slice of bread.

Ellia smiled. "Oh, no. The help doesn't eat with the customers," she replied with a hint of mischief.

Ron held the bread toward her insistently. "What if the customers insist?" He smiled and held it out.

Ellia shook her head and accepted the buttered bread. "What my father would say if he saw me right now...."

"I won't tell him if you don't."

"Fair enough, Ronnie." Ellia bit into her crusty slice of bread as he buttered another slice. He hated to admit, while Cradwick was loyal to the baker, Ron really did prefer Luvian's bread. He bit into his own slice and washed it down with mead.

Just then, the hinges of The Brew House door creaked open. Ellia looked with curiosity over his shoulder. He watched her expression become guarded and she immediately stood up and brushed the bread crumbs from the bar.

Ron turned on his wooden stool to behold Denward walking up to the bar. He was a regular, but an odd one. He rode in every three or four weeks, sat on the same bar stool, and usually even asked the same questions, if phrased differently. He sensed Ellia's growing discomfort, and in a raised voice, called, "Ah! Denward! Good to see you again, friend! How is the world outside of South Fairview?"

In all actuality, Ron would as soon spit on a viper than call Denward a friend, but Ron's raised voice brought Luvian sauntering through the kitchen doors.

Luvian was an immense man, tall and compact, with shrewd dark eyes that knew when you were lying and also, Ron was sure, how to lie. Ron had decided many months ago that Luvian was one of the few people he totally respected, and possibly feared.

"Ellie, see to the stew, please."

Luvian's low voice immediately sent Ellia scurrying back into the kitchen, though Ron knew she was glad of the excuse. Nor was Luvian ever angry with his daughters – they climbed all over him like kittens.

Right now, Ron enjoyed watching Luvian fix Denward with those shrewd eyes. Luvian tossed a damp rag over his shoulder before he leaned his meaty arms on the bar. "Denward. Welcome back. What'll you have today?"

Denward frowned. His lined face framed brown eyes and an upturned lip that always seemed scornful. His condescension had bought him no friends in The Brew House. As he was about to draw breath in to place his order, Ruth appeared from behind the swinging doors. Ron was sure Ellia had run upstairs to get her.

"Master Denward. We love having you back, you know that. What'll it be? Your usual, then?"

Luvian's eyes never left Denward's, though he addressed his wife. "Ruthie, run down to the cellar and bring up a pint of that special stout we keep on hand for Master Denward here."

"Of course." Ruth smiled warmly and slipped behind the kitchen doors.

"How about some of that stew I saw your youngest girl go back for? You know I like that. Stew, things all mixed together, you never know what's in it."

"Aye, that's why we keep our special recipe close and personal, Master Denward. Family recipe, I'm afraid. We don't give it out. But I've got a pot back there almost ready. About to boil." Luvian's tone was respectful, but a steely evenness underlied it.

Denward nodded slowly. Ruth swung through from the kitchen then, with a tall pint of ale. She set it down with a smile. "Only our very best for you, Master Denward."

He sipped it and set it down. "Luvian, I don't see how she stays with you."

Wow, thought Ron – the balls on this bastard. Every time he came, he needled and poked like this.

Luvian smiled a rare smile. "Well, that's easy. She's blind to all my flaws."

Ruth smiled up at him. She hugged him and he encircled her with an arm. Ron smiled inwardly. He rarely saw them together, but when they were, Luvian and Miss Ruth had eyes only for each other. He could only hope for that one day.

But Denward, of course, had to sour the moment by saying. "No, I don't think she's blind at all. I think she's just a very tolerant woman." He took another swig of ale from his pewter pint. "Speaking of eyes, where did your youngest daughter ever get those blue eyes? I'd have thought she'd get her mother's eyes. Or yours, Luvian…." Denward trailed off.

Mags walked out with a bowl of stew, hot from the pot. She set it before Denward stiffly, saying not a word, and turned her back around.

"Gets it all from her mum – beauty, luck, grace, charm – I'm a lucky man, Denward. You should find yourself a wife and settle down. You wander too much. Find a woman who'll give you children, keep you busy," Luvian said calmly.

Ron was trying to decide whether there was an underlying message behind Luvian's words or not, but Luvian's face was unreadable, as Ron often found.

Denward scoffed and answered, "Children and a wife. I think not." He swallowed all of his pint down and set it down on the bar with a clank. "That'll be all." He flipped his coppers for the pint on the bar and left, though the stew had gone untouched.

Ruth stared after him. "That was a short visit."

"Not short enough," Luvian rumbled, crossing his arms against his chest with a frown.

"Special stout?" asked Ron. "I didn't know you had any new ales in stock."

Luvian snorted and couldn't resist a half smile as he looked down at Ron. "Believe me, lad, you don't want any of this stuff."

"Why is that?"

Ruth grinned. "Because we have Tank spit a luger in it before we serve it."

Topher

Last night, Topher had snuck into the Food Hall and stolen several fruits and vegetables for his journey. He knew they would not look for him until tomorrow, unless fortune was with Topher and the Brother who delivered his meal in the morning did not notice he was missing when he slid his tray in onto the floor. If Topher's absence went undetected at first, then Topher would have a few more hours before they started looking for him.

Topher crouched in the bushes behind the outer Order building, a solid, stone representation of Topher's chance to turn back.

Topher looked up at the stars and breathed in the cool, clean air. Sitting in the darkness alone, staring up at the starry sky, he realized he had never in his life been unaccompanied by a Brother, or even his parents before that. He was sixteen years old, and alone in his life for the first time. A smile of pure joy spread across his face and he dashed forward.

Heedless of any Brother who might witness his escape, Topher ran and ran, exhilaration speeding his sudden journey into the night. The moon lit his flight, and Topher ran for what he knew were miles, breathing in the cool night air, the wisps of the green meadow grasses brushing the tips of his fingers.

Finally, exhilaration turned to a heated, slowed jog, and soon, Topher stopped altogether. Though the evening was a chilled one, sweat dripped down his temple. He bent over, breathless.

Still, however, he was amazed at the pure elation his new-found freedom brought him. His heart pounded in his chest.

Topher knew it was time to direct his path. He believed the Brothers would watch for him in the direction of Harper Hill, for while it was a day or so farther away, it was more populated and would offer more advantages for a runaway Brother as well as shelter and food.

That was why Topher was running west, toward the smaller villages and eventually north toward Roarden North. A city of that size could hide any Brother and offered nearly any employment opportunity, and surely by then, his hair would have grown out. He had decided to stay in Corstarorden, for he knew little of S'hendalow, and the Free Lands offered nothing. Tortoreen was treacherous for someone of little experience with dealings in the outside Land, Topher knew, so he decided to stay where he was.

He wondered if the Brothers would look for him back at his family's farm. Topher had read that runaways occasionally returned to their families. But Topher wanted nothing to do with his family. A family who took their chances with a few coins for seed to sow in the earth over a son to love held no loyalty for Topher. And any Brothers who returned to the family who sold them as such were foolish. For if that family had sold them once to the Silent Order, then they would sell them again. All for coin.

No, Topher had planned the details of his escape very thoroughly. He knew how to live off the land, though he hated to attribute those skills to both his family and the Brothers. It was his cropped hair that marked him most as a runaway from the Order, so until it grew out, Topher would hide himself away, sleeping by day and running by night.

Near the end of the evening, Topher wandered into a small village. Barely a village at that, just a spit of a few huts and homes, with a well in the center, and a brick oven.

Once Topher was sure no one was about to observe him, he stole silently through the mud into the center of the village. He gulped thirstily at the well, then took stock of the small village. One home had a lantern burning in the window, which helped him step closer. He saw laundry hanging on a line and immediately slid a man's roughspun woolen shirt off. He helped himself to a set of trousers at another home, though they would be enormous on him.

Topher glanced up at the moonlit sky, sending a prayer to The One God for forgiveness. Theft was an unholy act, of course, but he had to wonder if burning a man's tongue from his mouth was not also an unholy act?

Topher took great pains to sneak about the village without noise. Just as he was lifting two eggs from beneath a sitting hen, however, two hound dogs started barking, baying at his presence.

His heart in his mouth, Topher immediately ran with his ill-gotten booty, across the village toward the woods as fast as he could.

Behind him, he heard a man holler, "Shut up, ya fuckin' dogs!"

"You shut up, Bertrand, they're just dogs, now go back to sleep!" came a woman's irritated voice.

Once Topher was out of the village and back behind the forest line, he collapsed against a tree. That was just pure luck. If those dogs had been loose, had run after him....

As soon as he recovered from his fright, Topher stripped out of his navy Final Oath robe and stepped into the roughspun trousers. Fortunately, there was a drawstring in them, which he pulled as tight as he could about his waist, but anyone who saw him would wonder at the sight of them. Next, he slipped the tunic over his head.

Topher hadn't felt the feel of such roughspun clothing since he was a child. Though he felt the cold though them, that was unfortunate. He debated what do with his robe. At least it was warm. He couldn't leave it behind for someone to find, nor could he burn it, for someone might find the ashes. He decided to keep it hidden in his rucksack and would use it to lay on, or if he had to, a cloak of sorts if the weather turned too cold.

Topher stared down at himself. The feeling of trousers rather than robes was odd after all these years. Then he scoffed and stuffed the robe in his rucksack with disgust. Topher headed deeper into the woods, planning to walk all day and all of the next night as well. Finally. He was free.

Kendrick

He held the thong of the long bow until he was absolutely certain... and released.

"Perfect!"

"No, not perfect. The outer rim."

"Well, close enough –"

"Kendrick! What are you doing out here?"

Kendrick closed his eyes for a moment, fighting for patience. "Melleck, please, take these, I've a feeling I'll not be needing them now."

Melleck accepted Kendrick's longbow and quiver, saying nothing.

"Father! Out for a bit of work on archery," Kendrick called. His saw his father striding rapidly down the green, his cloak flapping in the wind behind him, suggesting his father's displeasure. Kendrick turned around and took in a breath for what he was sure was going to be an unpleasant exchange.

"Where is your brother?"

"I've – no idea. Out picnicking perhaps, to entertain our new visitors?" Kendrick raised a hopeful eyebrow with his innocent tone.

"The two of you were scheduled to be hunting today. Imagine my surprise to find out none of the horses in the stable were out," commented his father, his eyes glaring at Kendrick. He gestured for Kendrick to walk with him into the Palace.

"Father, I –"

"Kendrick, you must understand the importance of keeping to your schedule. If I need to call upon you, I must know where you are at all times," his father's blue eyes snapped at him.

"But –"

"Keeping to your schedule is part of being a Prince. You and Keldrick must learn this. It is your duty. When you see your brother, send him to me!" His father stared at him emphatically, and then turned on his boot and left.

Kendrick unclutched his fist. He would not swear where others could see him, after all, that was his duty as a Prince, he thought sarcastically.

He smelled his mother's perfume and turned around. She laid a sympathetic hand on his shoulder. "Mother, I swear, he is still fighting the War. The War has been over for years now, does he realize that!" Kendrick spat in a whisper.

His mother patted his cheek but said, "Darling, you have no idea what he is going through. None at all. If only you knew what he has done for you...." And she looked at him directly, her azure eyes refusing to surrender.

Finally, Kendrick tore his gaze from his mother's. He trusted her, but he believed her to be naïve to Father's faults. Sullenly, he muttered, "Yes, Mother." He sighed. "But if only he would –"

"Kendrick," the Queen, not his mother, was talking then; her voice warned her son only slightly that he was to say no more on the subject.

He thought for a moment, then decided to push his luck. He was nothing if not his father's son. "I'm sixteen and a man grown. When is he going to realize that?"

The Queen delivered a cool stare to her son. "Your father knows far more than you will ever know, both about you and your brother, about this country, and about how to run it, and that, at the moment, is more than I can say for you. Be glad I have told you that, and not your father, for he would not be so kind. When you are truly a man grown, you will respect your father's authority and not second-guess him, and only then, my son, will he consider you equal to the task of sharing rule." The Queen observed her son a moment longer, and Kendrick, reeling from his mother's sudden attack, watched her swivel about gracefully and leave him with his mouth open in shock.

Rhutgard

He sat down on his mahogany desk, his eyes faraway. Principea came to his side and looked at him with that half smile that he loved so well. She laid her hand on his shoulder.

"You think I am too hard on them."

She shrugged slightly. "Perhaps a bit."

Rhutgard covered her tiny hand with his own and drew her in front of him. Sighing deeply, he shook his head. "They have no idea what is happening around them. None at all. I don't know if that is best for them, or if I am failing them as a father."

Principea brushed her lips across his forehead with a small kiss. "Rhutgard, these are terrible times. They have yet to know what is happening. But – he is right, dear. They are sixteen. Men grown now." She looked at him with sympathy on her face.

Rhutgard stood up and walked about the study, his blue eyes clouded. He rubbed at the stubble on his chin as he stared out the window for a moment, then turned around.

"Sixteen. At sixteen, I was –" And he trailed off. Sixteen for him had been vastly different than for his sons, who rode about on – on picnics, and hunting expeditions, and archery practice.

"At sixteen, you had command in an army. But there was a war going on at the time, Rhutgard," Principea reminded him. "There is no war right now."

Rhutgard snorted. "There is, Sweet Pea, just not one being fought on a battlefield." He strode to the portrait of his father and gazed up at it, as he had so many times before, eyeing each of its minute, painted details. He sighed. "I miss him so much. He would be able to help me so much right now...."

"I know how you miss him. I wish I had met him," commented Principea. Then she said, "I think it's time that we had a new portrait of you done. I'll have one commissioned."

Rhutgard scoffed and waved his hand in dismissal of the idea. "No. I could hardly sit still for the last two." He continued to gaze up at his father. Putting his hands on his hips, he read the title entered below on the gilded frame. *"'King Galvin Firthing, the Victor of the Twenty Years War'"*. Rhutgard sighed. "What would the portrait of me be named, *'King Rhutgard Firthing, the Unaccomplished?'"*

In disgust, he shook his head and stalked across the room.

"My love, your accomplishments are so many. But few know of them...."

"Yes, and that's the truth of it." Rhutgard studied his wife. He rubbed his jaw, an old habit that he barely recognized. Suddenly he said, "What if something were to happen to me? No one would know she was out there. No one would believe she was truly mine, ours, if I were to die...."

He worried about this more and more as the years passed. Only Principea knew his pain. She said, "They are sixteen. Is it time, then?" He detected a hopeful tone in her voice.

Rhutgard thought of the serious turn of events that had taken place over just the last year alone. "Not yet. Soon, but not yet...."

Luvian

Luvian was not so busy between baking and the brewery itself that he did not know who his customers were. He was well aware of who his regulars were, and who came into his brewery without invitation. Specifically, soldiers.

Rarely did Crown soldiers make their way into The Brew House and Tavern, for South Fairview was generally mistrustful of soldiers, even Crown soldiers. Crown soldiers usually meant that taxes were being collected or that someone was being hunted for a crime, and, of course, South Fairview was a breeding ground for criminals, especially since the War. Poverty had risen and criminals took to theft and even good folks made unwise decisions upon occasion just to survive. Such was South Fairview. But in The Brew House and Tavern, Crown soldiers drank their first pint free, and Luvian made a point to set an example to his patrons that Crown soldiers were protectors, not bullies.

Of late, however, more and more soldiers were stepping foot in his brewery, and not Crown soldiers, and nor were they in uniform. Luvian could always recognize a currently enlisted soldier, as could Tank, having fought in the Army themselves. Straight backed, chin up, hair cropped, clean shaven, eyes watching about him for the enemy....

The last year alone had seen a rise in soldiers passing through. They were taking the Silver River up and getting off at the docks, said the fishmongers in town, those who knew how to listen and watch. Others said they came in on horse outside the Brace Fort, then sold their horses for wagons and come up into Fairview direct that way. Either way, they were coming into Fairview from the south, and that meant they were stopping at The Brew House and Tavern.

Depending on the length of their trip, they might ask for a room. Ruthie wanted to refuse them rooms, lie to them about having availability, but Luvian said no. He wanted to know what their business was. And as a rule, he rarely turned paying customers away, even when he didn't like them. Just good business sense. King or beggar, the coin still spent the same, his Pappy used to say.

All Luvian had learned was that wherever these soldiers were headed, they were moving through South Fairview as a waypoint. And he still was not sure where they were coming from, for their coin was Rommish.

When soldiers did stay overnight, Ruthie rummaged through their belongings while the soldiers drank downstairs. She occasionally found something of importance, maps and coins of other countries, but otherwise just nonsense as travelers would carry. These men were paid to keep themselves hidden in plain sight. Luvian was tired of watching them pour through Fairview, and more and more of them as time passed. Something was wrong, he knew it and he didn't like it.

Today, a group of soldiers in common clothing strode in and sat down in the corner. It was just early afternoon and Luvian would bet they only wanted to pass through. Usually, when soldiers came in, he was inside the kitchen, and Tank would sneeze twice to let him know that he needed to step out to the bar. Today, however, he happened to be stocking the shelves beneath the bar with freshly cleaned tankards when the four soldiers walked into his brewery.

They inspected the bar as they sat down, nodding and shrugging with an arrogance that immediately pissed Luvian off. Hasley stepped out of the kitchen, for she'd heard the creak of the door open and knew to check for new customers to welcome. But Luvian told her in a low voice, "Get back in the kitchen, girl."

"O-okay, Pappy," Hasley stuttered, shrugging as she turned on her heel and returned to the kitchen.

Luvian tossed his dishrag over his shoulder and strode over to the corner. He nodded to the table of frequent customers behind the soldiers, who held up their tankards to him in good will.

"I always like to see new customers here. What'll you be drinking today?" he said as he studied each of their faces. Fair hair and complexions.... A bit sunburned, or, perhaps their sunburns had faded. Luvian guessed they'd gone up the Silver River – no woods to shelter them from the sun.

"Ale all around – you do have ale here, do you not?" asked the nearest of the four in a patronizing tone.

Luvian held to a respectful demeanor and smiled, trying not to clench his teeth. "Oh, yes, we do, being a brewery, man. We have the very best of stout in the area, I'll have four brought right up. And send over some bread to break your fast, shall I?" He smiled a gritty smile and turned about.

"Tank, our very best for these men!"

Tank nodded and disappeared in the direction of the cellar.

Luvian met him downstairs. His eyes took a moment to adjust to the darkness of the cellar while he leaned against one of the barrels.

"You want to do the honors or shall I, boss?" asked Tank, holding out four tankards.

"Split the difference," Luvian said, and they both hawked up their best globs of spit they could and dropped them into the tankards before filling them with ale. It had become a challenge between him and Tank, whose glob was the biggest. They decided it depended on who had eaten recently, so it wasn't really a fair fight, but they competed nevertheless.

"That one. That one goes to the arsehole who ordered," Tank held up a tankard.

"You think so? I like this one, actually." Luvian held another one up.

Tank shrugged. "If you say so, bossman."

Luvian shrugged. He gathered the other two tankards, filled them with ale, swirled the ale about, and then stepped upstairs. Such were the finer points of his life, the smaller things that entertained him nowadays....

The light of the afternoon streaming into the bar met his eyes and he stepped over toward the table. He decided on Tank's choice as he set the tankards before the soldiers and took a private moment to enjoy his spite as he watched each of them drink thirstily.

He brought over two large baskets of bread and a slab of butter. Unfortunately, he was too far away to hear what they were talking about, and their mouths were mostly full as they ate bread anyway.

Luvian leaned on his bar and pretended to be interested in the people passing by on the street.

But just then, Ron and Metz walked in. Good kids, apprentices nearby, mused Luvian. What an age to grow up in. At their age, he'd been serving in the Army two years already....

"Ronnie, Metz." Luvian smiled a genuine smile as they sat down at the bar before him. "Your usual, then?"

"Always," Metz, with a smile, slapped the polished bar twice with emphasis. Ronnie held his finger up for one pint of ale.

Luvian eyed the corner again before he disappeared behind the kitchen doors. Wordlessly, Halsey supplied him with a fresh basket of bread and a small slab of butter. Even from behind the kitchen doors, she knew to serve the customers, and what they wanted. Such a good girl – they'd run this place long after he was gone, Luvian knew.

Quietly, Luvian set the basket and their two pints down. He kept a surreptitious eye on the corner of soldiers as he made idle conversation with his young customers.

Finally, they stood up. Luvian met Tank's eyes across the room. He knew this was about to end badly.

Tank wandered casually over to collect payment. Suddenly, what happened next was a blur. Luvian heard who he recognized as the team's commander in charge tell Tank to "Put it on our tab."

Tank was a large man, even more so than Luvian, stronger, taller, and without doubt, a man to be reckoned with in a fight. Which is why Luvian took him on when he rebuilt The Brew House. Luvian was sure that Tank tried to convince the soldier to pay up his tab, but in watching the soldiers' expressions, that did not meet with an arrangement to transfer funds as requested.

Within seconds, the commanding soldier's face was laying against a nearby table, with Tank holding his arm behind his back. The rest of the soldiers stood up, jarring their tankards upon their table as they did so. Tank gave them a single look that dissuaded them.

The table of men behind them had stopped talking to witness this spectacle, craning their necks around to watch. Ronnie and Metz twisted around on their bar stools to observe. What was it about violence that everyone loved to see, Luvian wondered idly.

"Let me up!" spluttered the soldier. "Let me up," he demanded again, his other arm flailing around uselessly, looking for something to grab on the table. Tank looked bored and began to lean on him, ever so slowly.

Luvian couldn't help but enjoy this. But, business was business. Still, he took his time approaching the table.

Tank leaned on the soldier just a bit more, his arm looking unnatural in that pose. "Ow, ow, ouch, son of a bitch, you bastard, let me up! Let me up!"

Luvian finally stood in front of the soldier and leaned down to stare him in the face. "Do we have a problem here?"

"Tell your man to let me up!"

"Well, my friend, he gets his wages from me. He only does that if someone hasn't behaved himself in a fashion as is expected from our patrons here at The Brew House and Tavern. Maybe lots of other ale houses let their customers act in ways such as we might consider dishonorable, but here at The Brew House and Tavern, my patrons have come to expect a certain quality of behavior from the customers who pass through. So Tank here is just giving you what we call a *friendly reminder* to watch your manners, mate. You watch yours, and we'll watch ours. Understand, then?"

The soldier glared at Luvian with fury but was silent.

Luvian slapped Tank on the shoulder. "Tank, let the good man up. I'm sure he and his friends would like to pay their tab now."

Tank let the soldier up slowly and Luvian stepped back behind the bar.

The man's face was red with rage. His compatriots pretended that they had not noticed anything from the ordinary had happened, not wishing to risk their commanding officer's wrath.

The man rotated his forearm back and forth. He spat something lowly to his nearest officer, who then handed him some money. Glaring at Luvian across the room, the commanding officer tossed a silver at Luvian for payment.

Luvian caught it with ease but then threw it back at the soldier who had supplied it to his commanding officer. "We always like making new friends here at The Brew House and Tavern. First one's free of charge." It flashed in the sunlight as it flew through the air. The soldier caught it nervously and stuffed it into a pocket.

The commanding soldier's eyes glittered with fury and the four of them stepped out into the street.

"I'll get the slops bucket, shall I," called Tank, as in the fray, the tankards on the table had spilled over onto the wooden floor.

Luvian turned around to see the heads of Hasley and Ellia peeping through the kitchen doors. Had they stood and watched the whole thing? Girls and their silliness!

He waved his hands at them. "Get back in there! Go on – shoo!" He heard them giggling as they turned and ran into the kitchen.

Luvian turned and looked at Ronnie and Metz, seated at the bar in front of him. Metz held up his tankard. "To Tank, the man of the hour!"

Ronnie smiled and held his own tankard up. "Aye, to Tank!"

Luvian nodded. "Aye, to Tank."

Tank moved back behind the bar as soon as he finished cleaning up the slops. "Arseholes, aye?"

Luvian agreed. "Aye." He shook his head, puzzled as he leaned on the bar. "What I can't figure is their accents. They're not Northern. And not Rommish."

Tank thought for a moment and shook his head. "Couldn't place it, either."

"Some sort of Coastal, maybe," Luvian mused.

Ronnie cleared his throat then. "Sounded Western, I think. I mean, it could be…." He trailed off.

Luvian looked down at Ronnie. "Western? Why do you say Western? Have you ever heard a Western accent before?"

Ronnie's face turned innocent as he shrugged. "I – no, just knew someone from there once, I think." He shook his head and took a swig of ale. "I'm probably wrong, it's been a while." He smiled disarmingly.

Luvian frowned. Then, over his shoulder, he called, "Nick! I've got a job for you!"

Ronnie washed down the last of his ale. "Want me to follow them for you?"

Luvian looked at Ronnie and shook his head. Nice kid, this blacksmith's boy, but he knew nothing about the street. He smiled down at him.

"Nah. That won't be necessary. Besides, I don't think they'll be back."

———

Luvian was never wrong. He hated to be wrong, he was hardly ever wrong, but today, tonight, he was wrong. *Bloody hell.*

"About a full house tonight, Luvi," Mags called.

"Excellent," Luvian nodded.

Nick waved at him over the top of everyone in the kitchen but Luvian shook his head, signaling *not now*. Nick jumped in the air and waved both hands over his head urgently, insistent on Luvian's attention. What news could he possibly have of such import that he must speak with me now, Luvian grumped. A full house bloody well trumped information any day of the week.

Donvan removed the warm, crusty loaves of bread, holding the oven ajar for Luvian to slip in the dough. One day, Donvan would be able to run this kitchen... almost as well as he could. Luvian had this kitchen working like the cogs in a wheel. He liked to think his Pappy would be proud. He eyed the kettles – one full and the other half full. Tonight was going to be a good night, even if the day had started out rough.

And then he heard Tank sneeze. Twice. And then a third time, which meant the rough equivalent of, *get yer arse out here now*. And then he heard a whistle, which was Tank's way of making sure he heard him over the noise and bustle of a full house. Times when people were singing and dancing, uproarious laughter, jokes, times it was hard to hear back in the kitchen.

Luvian immediately dusted his hands free of flour and pulled his apron over his head, tossing it aside on the counter.

"Luvi?" Mags had heard Tank's signal and Hasley and Mollie had come bustling into the kitchen.

"Keep the girls in the kitchen, Mags."

He stepped out behind the bar to see what Tank's concern was, not sure what to expect.

And there, standing under the torchlight of the street outside The Brew House and Tavern, were the same four common-dressed soldiers he and Tank had dismissed earlier that day.

Which was, he suddenly realized, what Nick was attempting to tell him.

Luvian quickly assessed the situation as best he could from inside. At least they had no torches, that was good. But they were, however, barely able to stand they were so drunk. And their commanding officer – a sergeant, Luvian judged – was out in the street laughing maniacally. His obnoxious personality had been magnified by an afternoon spent drinking, and now he was here to avenge the wrong done to his honor earlier today. *Bloody hell.*

Tank caught his eye across the room.

Ruthie appeared out of the kitchen doors, glancing about nervously. "Luvi?" Her tone was worried.

"Ruthie, get four of our very best stouts for the gentlemen about to come in the door," he commanded quietly, his eyes never leaving the front door.

He heard the kitchen doors swing closed behind her.

Ronnie and Metz were seated back at their stools. Ronnie cleared his throat and sat up. "The very best?"

Luvian looked down at him. "Aye – we always save the best –"

"Special stout for your special customers. I recall your telling me once what that meant."

Luvian raised an eyebrow. "Did I now," he returned quietly, but he watched the door. He nodded in the direction of the door. "You see who's back?"

Ronnie was already twisted around in his seat, watching the door. Metz was slurping at his stew, oblivious to their exchange. Luvian wasn't surprised, the place was packed.

"Don't stare," warned Luvian, directing Ronnie to turn around. He wasn't going to encourage those bastards if he could help it.

Tank moved in closer, slowly, 'til he leaned against the bar. Ruthie reappeared with four full tankards of ale. She set them just below the bar.

She stared up at him and glanced at the men outside the door. "Who are they?"

"Just a bunch of drunks, no one special. Go back inside, Ruthie. We have this handled."

She looked worried but retreated all the same.

Finally, the four commonly-dressed soldiers entered The Brew House.

Luvian stood up straight and walked to the center of the bar. "Back so soon?" He didn't frown, but nor did he smile. Tank walked forward to stand in front of the bar.

The soldier Luvian deemed a sergeant cackled and pointed at Luvian. "The barkeep. Do we drink for free again now, too," he hooted.

Tank stepped forward, but Luvian, stepping from around the bar, held him back with an arm. "No, my friend, allow me."

As he advanced toward the sergeant, he addressed him in a loud voice, "I think you need to find another place to drink." Luvian crossed his arms and stared at the sergeant, blocking further entrance into the brewery.

The grin faded quickly from the sergeant's flushed face. He swayed slightly on his feet, though he still stood his ground. "Are you – denying us service?" The idea seemed fascinating to him, and Luvian decided he was as much an arsehole at home as he was standing in his bar here tonight, for apparently, no one had ever denied him anything he'd ever wanted.

"Denying you service?" Luvian pretended to think for a moment, throwing sarcasm at the sergeant. "No. I am not refusing to 'serve' you. I, as the owner of this establishment, am refusing you entry into it. They're something slightly different, although," and he made a great show of leaning forward and sniffing, "in your current condition, I doubt you'd be able to distinguish between the two." He coughed pointedly and waved in front of his face. The combined odor of ale and spirits surrounding the sergeant was enough to make a horse gag. He was surprised the man was able to stand, much less function.

"You lowlife, uneducated son-of-a-bitch! Back away this instant and let us pass!"

Luvian's eyes narrowed. "Back. Away. And leave."

The sergeant snorted over his shoulder and laughed. "Do you see this?" His compatriots snickered.

And then the sergeant reached out and tried to shove Luvian. The action served only to knock his balance off, for the sergeant was not only drunk, but a man of a far smaller stature than Luvian.

"That – was a very bad decision," Luvian told him. The sergeant reached up his fist to throw around a punch, but Luvian caught it in his own fist. He dragged the drunken sergeant over to the bar and slammed his face into the bar between two patrons.

Behind him, the other three soldiers had run in to support their sergeant. Luvian saw Tank grab two of them by the necks and slam their heads together. They slid down into an unconscious puddle of drunken haze on the wooden floor. The remaining soldier stood staring up at Tank, as if weighing his options. He threw his fist back to swing at Tank, but Tank caught it and suddenly the soldier started howling in pain.

More and more of the customers at the tables became aware of the fight and the atmosphere hushed as they stared.

"You bloody bastard!" yelled the soldier. "You've broken my bloody hand!" He clutched at his hand and held it against his chest.

Then Luvian felt the sergeant beneath him move slightly, and saw the soldier with the broken hand suddenly slip his good hand inside his pocket.

"Don't do it!" Luvian yelled. "Don't you do it! Don't you draw!"

At the same time, he heard Ronnie yell, "Luvian! Knife!"

Tank pulled the knife from the soldier's pocket and dropped it on the floor, where he stood on it with his boot. But Luvian twisted awkwardly to pull the knife that the sergeant had reached for out of his pocket.

"Guests in my establishment do not draw weapons! Especially not upon me!" Luvian growled. He whirled the sergeant around as he spoke and slammed him down on a table where two regulars were sitting.

Luvian forced the sergeant's hand upon the table with one hand, and with the other, drove the knife into it, straight through into the table below.

The sergeant screamed. In incredible pain, he was unable to move, for whichever direction he moved caused the blade inside his hand to cut into even more flesh. He was left to stand bowed forward in a very awkward position.

The patrons at the table wore a mixture of lurid fascination at the hand pinned to their table by a knife, and the horrible drunken breath forced upon them by the sergeant's stance.

Luvian cast an eye at the two soldiers on the floor but they were still unconscious, fallen upon each other in a heap.

Tank had picked up the other soldier's knife. Holding it to the soldier's throat, he waited for Luvian's direction.

"Now. Hear me. This is my establishment and I am the proprietor. I may refuse anyone I please, but I always refuse those who have given me no reason to trust them once already, and that would be you. South Fairview does not look kindly on strangers, and South Fairview looks out for its own. Every man in here has seen your face, all four of you, and they will remember you tonight, and they will tell everyone else in South Fairview about you. We here remember the War all too well, and we have come back proud and strong. So you take yourselves out of South Fairview, and do not come back. And then you leave Fairview, and then you leave Romeny. And stay gone.

"Tank?" Luvian pointed at the door.

Tank pushed his captive soldier toward the door, trickles of blood streaming into the soldier's collar where Tank held him by his own knife point. As soon as the soldier was outside, Tank heaved up the two unconscious soldiers and shoved them out the door into the night.

Luvian grasped the sergeant by the back of the neck and squeezed. Then he yanked the knife up out of his hand. The sergeant screeched with pain.

Luvian dragged him to the door by the neck and before he threw him into the street, he grated menacingly, "Now stay the fuck out of my bar!" Then he shoved him out and turned around.

"I'll get the slops bucket, then, shall I?" called Tank.

"Aye, Tank."

He looked down at the knife in his hand, the blade bloodied. He'd never seen a hilt like this before. Enraged suddenly with the invasion of the outside world into the safe, ordinary, quiet and content life that he had constructed here, Luvian turned and tossed the blade across the brewery, where it sank forcefully into the wooden wall and quivered.

Luvian was suddenly aware that the room was hushed. He turned about and stared around him. His patrons were staring at him like lost children.

"Well, what are all you lookin' at? Drinks on the house! To South Fairview!" The sound of tankards clanking in widespread agreement and cheers all over filled The Brew House and Tavern.

Ron

Even aside from the true purpose behind Ron's visits to the Market Place every four days – both Cradwick's and those his employers requested – Ron just enjoyed getting out of the forge and wandering aimlessly with no actual purpose. Even a small Market Place such as South Fairview provided was better than nothing at all, and sweating in that steaming, sooty forge.... He'd learned fast enough, but he would be grateful to move on to another assignment. Ron had had all he could take of the continual ringing of the hammer on steel, and the heat of the fire, the coals, the ashes....

So Market Place days every fourth day were near holidays for him. He scoffed at himself – how far he had fallen. The South Fairview Market Place, a holiday.

Nevertheless, he had taken to the people here. They were wary of strangers, but Ron had come with references that had impressed them. Falsified, of course, but these people didn't know that. They were good people, and he felt bad deceiving them –

And then he narrowed his eyes. The second he grew a conscience, he would lose track of his real assignment.

Ron had been posted here almost two years now. He would be, in all actuality, eighteen in just a few months, though the workmen here believed him to be sixteen. Ron pretended to be a likable, all-around, friendly apprentice, the South Fairview sort of street boy these people all recognized. It was this ability that had gotten him placed here, his employers told him. His conscience did rise up to nag him on some nights, but he had learned to squash it.

He really didn't know what he was doing here – stay, observe, report. Spy. Very well and good. Such assignments only lasted about three months, perhaps four. But near two years? He was reporting the same thing over and over. Ron had begun to wonder if his employers had forgotten him – or if they simply wanted him out of the way. After all, a placement in South Fairview? The shittiest part of the entire capital of Romeny? At least station him in Fairview Proper, or even in another Rommish city... Bridge Port, or Sunderham, he'd even take Ashtonport.

At the same time, on nights when he lay awake, pondering the meaning of life and of his ever-ongoing post here, Ron considered that perhaps South Fairview was an excellent station, especially for someone like him, just coming up in the ranks. Overflowing with all the scum and criminals a city could offer, South Fairview hid away every villain in its alleys and back corners. They all smiled and nodded at you in the street, and many of them looked entirely respectable, all while they picked your pocket in passing, or sneaked into your home in the night to lift your valuables.

Perhaps Ron had been sent here to study them all. For he'd seen them all as he walked past them in the street and learned their tricks himself before he had even arrived.

He knew which of the street gangs were responsible for what type of crimes. The Castle Grates, for example – they were the largest street gang in most of Romeny and spread from just south of Fairview Proper to South Fairview. While they spent most of their time thieving and stealing incoming river imports up and down the Rosh River, they were otherwise harmless. They retreated to the tunnels beneath the streets through the grates in the streets and were near impossible for the Crown Guards to catch, and so they named themselves the Castle Grates, but more usually the Castle Greats, as they were mostly successful at lifting their targets. They rarely resorted to killing, though.

Smaller gangs were just petty competitive block and street gangs, struggling for dominance over their own several blocks, occasionally resorting to beatings or even killings. The Crown Guard would step in on a tip and clean out the streets from time to time, but they never quite quashed them. Every city had its villainy, and South Fairview was the humming life of Fairview's.

Ron breathed in the clean, crisp air. Observation of petty street crews and thieves were a complete waste of his talent. Unless, of course, his employer wanted a spy with extraordinary blacksmithy capabilities, for those he was certainly developing.

The smell of sandalwood and cedar blew along in the breeze. He took his time, glancing over the intricate carvings etched in wood at one wagon, nodding with polite interest to another vendor who attempted to sell him jams and jellies. Ron was not fond of figs and he knew this vendor filled most of jams and jellies with fig and very little of them with berries, as he liked to coax passersby with.

The delicate tinkling of bells sounded at another wagon, where the matron sold intricately embroidered cloth and occasionally, lace. Her fingers were rough and calloused, and Ron knew that she did all of her own clothwork herself. Ron also noticed that her hands were slightly shaky, and, upon occasions when neither she nor anyone else was observing him, he left a few silvers for her. She was growing older and would need to put money away and hire an apprentice. He liked helping the people who deserved help.

On rare occasions, a spice merchant made his way through South Fairview, having traveled successfully through the RiverLands. Though he usually only bore mustard seed, cinnamon, pepper, curry on occasion, and a few others, the folks of South Fairview used their few coppers to buy his wares immediately out. Ron wasn't sure he trusted the man, but he pleased the residents, and his merchant papers were up to date, or he wouldn't be selling here in the Square.

Finally, he bought a plum today instead of a pear. The shy daughter of the fruit vendor hid behind her mother. Ron pretended not to notice her, but he had the feeling that the fruit vendor knew he was feigning. He paid for his fruit, nodding respectfully to her, but she glowered at him until he passed on. Ron didn't blame her. He was, after all, for what she could tell, sixteen, while her daughter was probably fourteen.

After he passed, he snuck a glance over his shoulder. The girl was looking downcast after him. Ron smiled and rolled his eyes. She brightened. He winked and continued down the cobblestone street. Ah. If his mother could see him now…. He could just hear the scolding. He looked down at his leather boots for a few steps with a small smile playing on his face. *Too much of a flirt*, she'd say, *be a gentleman*….

Yes, mother… he thought fondly.

Ron let his smile fade. He looked up after he double-checked to see that his tunic laces were still loosened and tucked backward.

He stood on his side of the cobbles, as always, and glanced with nonchalance across the street, waiting for his employer's representative to show himself.

It was a simple code to follow, really. Ron polished his plum with his sleeve and shaded his eyes with his hand. He was running out of simplicities – he couldn't appear impassive much longer. On a whim, he bent down and brushed dirt from his boots.

While Ron was bent over, he saw his employer's representative amble into view across the street.

Ron stood up and yawned, though he watched the man. Usually, it was the same person, but occasionally not. Sometimes, he dressed in impressive noble attire; others, he looked to be falling down drunk with half his tunic untucked and a suspender half down his shoulder, his hair sloppy and unkempt. Today, he looked as most other South Fairview men, a simple tunic and woolen breeches, leather boots. But at all times, his face was guarded and his eyes were sharp, just as today.

Today, he tossed the apple in his hand a few times before he took a bite of it, though he did not look in Ron's direction. Once he turned in Ron's direction, Ron bit into his plum and turned back in the direction of the Market Place.

In a few seconds, he glanced in the reflection of a vendor selling glassware, but saw no sign of his representative. How, Ron marveled, did he *do* that? He had tried to follow him upon occasion at first, but then received a blank slip of parchment at the forge with an apple peeling nailed to it by a knife. Ron didn't need assistance to figure out that he was not to follow his representative again. Though that merely served to raise the level of Ron's idolatry for the man's sheer ability. He had spent the next year working on his vanishment techniques – his goal was to melt away unseen, to disappear as softly as smoke. A year and a half later, Ron was certain he'd made it half-way to his goal. He was quite light on his feet – but as for melting away…. He had yet to melt away unseen.

Ron grew impatient. He wondered just what was being delivered. Ron never knew ahead of time what was being delivered, but often it was a piece of work already completed by a master craftsman, ready for a mysterious customer to pick up, and thus the secret to Ron's success as Master Cradwick lay in his drunken haze nearly every day. Most South Fairview customers only wanted nails, handles, horseshoes, and items of other similar simple nature.

Ron knew he was only to give his absence an extra twenty minutes, but he always threw in ten more in the event of unforeseeable circumstances, such as Cradwick rousing himself during a delivery.

Ron still took great personal amusement the day they delivered an iron trunk, trimmed with intricately carved bronze bracings and adornments. Being made of iron, the trunk was quite heavy. Ron had turned back onto Wagon Way that day to see his two representatives, glaring at him from down the dusty path, where they leaned against the neighboring business.

Just as they were about to drop off their heavy delivery, Master Cradwick had roused himself from his drunken haze and stumbled out to the outhouse, where he was taking a very loud, and it seemed, a very long shit. Ron's representatives had been forced to wait until Master Cradwick had cleared the contents of his bowels before delivering the trunk. Ron had waited until they had left before he stepped outside for a good belly laugh, imagining their repulsed faces, over and over.

It was a simple code, though he got it wrong the first time. Every time he went to the Market Place, he was to unlace his tunic laces and fold them inside. He would also buy a piece of fruit. Then he would wait at the start of the Market Place wagons until his employer's representative met him across the street. Ron would wait and watch for direction, and then take a single bite of his fruit, which indicated understanding and acknowledgement.

His representative always had a piece of fruit as well. If he juggled it, as he had today, then at least one delivery would be dropped off at the forge, usually in the back. Most often, jugs of wine mixed with sleeping potion were delivered for Cradwick and left regularly in the back; these were never made note of in the Market Place.

Deliveries of craftsmanship or sometimes supplies for the forge that were not found or imported to South Fairview were left at the forge. Ron wondered what he would find today when he returned. He had found all sorts of things, breastplates, kettles, lanterns, even a sword once.

If two men stood in the Square talking to each other face to face, then when Ron returned to the forge, someone would speak to him with information. If two men stood in the Square side by side, then information would be left for Ron at the forge. If the two men stood side by side talking, then he was to go to The Brew House and wait to be approached for further instruction.

If Ron needed to give his representative information that was important but not an emergency, he was to write it down on pigeon parchment and leave it under the back rafters of the forge before he left for the Market Place, then buy two pieces of fruit.

If Ron needed supplies unavailable to him, he should write the list down on pigeon parchment and leave the list under the back rafters before he left for the Market Place, then kick his boot twice on the cobble.

If there was some sort of trouble, Ron was to leave both his tunic laces open on the outside instead of tucked inside.

Once he observed his representative's instruction, Ron was to tug his laces farther open and take a bite of fruit to indicate that he understood, and then leave. They were never to actually meet each other's eyes, nor acknowledge that they saw each other, nor that knew each other in any way whatever.

Every two weeks, Ron was to write on pigeon parchment all that he had observed and leave it under the rafters. He never knew who collected it or of what importance it served, or even who it ultimately was read by in the end, but he continued to perform this duty. Much of the time, what he wrote in such tiny letters was almost word for word the same as previous weeks. So little changed in South Fairview. Ron really strained to watch and listen for more of note and interest, but truly, nothing else beyond the usual South Fairview villainy, nighttime goings-on, criminal disturbances, and plots occurred.

Although, of late, he had been recording the rising number of incoming soldiers. Soldiers dressed as commoners, who, to a practiced eye, stood out more than they would as if uniformed. He recorded their incoming, their actions, and what they did while they were in South Fairview. Ron had to admit to puzzlement as to the reason they were passing through more and more, and certainly as to why they posed as commoners. He wondered also where they were going. But that was ultimately for his employer to pass judgment on.

And Ron had heard nothing thus far from his employer. He only knew that he going to continue at this post. The only other way he might leave it was if his representative did not show. If his representative did not show on a meeting day, then Ron was to do absolutely nothing. He was to continue his routine as normal, go to the Market Place every four days as Master Cradwick bade him, buy a piece of fruit, but not look for a representative. He was just to continue his work as an apprentice, continue watching and listening, as usual, for one full month. If a representative showed in the Market Place who used the protocols, Ron was to disappear that night – get out of Romeny altogether and stay low for at least three months, until he deemed it safe to find out what was happening. Otherwise, after one full month, he was to disappear with no word to anyone, and return home. In either event, though the former more so than the latter, he could assume the mission was either over or compromised.

Rarely, however, was he taken by surprise. He had been recording the movements of these soldiers, whether they came in by river or by Southern Romeny, and how they left. He had built up a small – effective, but small – network of informants who were happy to throw in a few whispers of input for a few coppers or, depending on the information, perhaps, a bronze.

No one expected the lad with the blacksmith apprentice sigil on his tunic to be keeping abreast of such shady events. He even had the sister of a Castle Grate who sometimes gave him the times of the next ferry takeover if, she insisted, he bought one of the soaps from her wagon. Usually, Ron paid her extra for the soap and dropped it into a shopper's basket on his way home. What was he to do with lavender petal soap?

But yesterday, he had been surprised, and little surprised Ron. Actually, his mind was still reeling. Luvian – Ron had not given the innkeeper the credit he was actually due. Ron knew that Tank was a veteran of the Twenty Years War. Everyone could see that on his face – the big man was quiet, still kept himself in what Ron would consider nearly prime fighting condition if not entirely. Somewhere behind that silent face that rarely smiled, Ron believed there to be a tortured soul, appalled somehow at what he had done in the War, forcing himself to relive it every day in penance.

But Luvian. Luvian was almost as big a man as Tank. Dark eyed and swarthy, his arms were thick and it was clear he was quite strong, even covered with the flour of the bread he took such pleasure in baking.

Until last night, Ron believed Luvian had always worked with his family here at The Brew House, and so most of South Fairview said. His father before him had built the brewery, and Luvian and his family lived and worked here. Ron knew that during the Twenty Years War, soldiers came through and burned the brewery to the ground and that Luvian, his father, Mags, and Tank rebuilt it.

The skill Luvian showed last night against those soldiers proved that he was more than a simple innkeeper, however. While Tank was just an Army soldier, Luvian had some serious combat training.

Ron recalled needing to close his mouth twice. Once when he watched Luvian slam that soldier onto the table and pierce his hand with a knife – neatly between the tendons, Ron recalled noticing, very neatly done…. And twice when Luvian tossed that same knife with enormous force clear across the bar, where it sank to the hilt into the wood. Not just once, but twice last night, Ron had reassessed his opinion of the burly innkeeper.

He knew he had called out to warn Luvian about the soldiers drawing their knives, but his warning had gone as unheeded as a small boy tugging at his mother's skirts, for both Tank and Luvian were well aware of their captives' actions. *Soldiers never forget*, the saying went. And now Ron knew one more new thing about South Fairview – that Luvian had fought on the battlefield during the Twenty Years War, well enough to have accrued deadly tactics such as what he still practiced perfectly last night.

Ron considered. The man was just an innkeeper. A veteran. Was it even worth reporting?

Tyndie

Tyndie called her The Shrew now.

Lynza crossed the room in three quick strides and grabbed her arm. "Where have you been? We needed ya two hours ago!" she hissed.

Tyndie was taken aback, having just entered the room for her shift.

"I – I just came from the bath," she stammered, surprised at the sudden attack.

Lynza squeezed her arm. "Well, where've you been of late? Can't find ya when you're needed, what use are ya?"

Tyndie managed to hold her tongue, for she was practicing her speed. As The Shrew had told her when she'd started, a girl who wasn't good at her job didn't have a job. And Tyndie was working to see that she was at least good, if not better. And she had gotten fast, too, she was racing through the corridors and flew up and down the stone steps now. She'd also dropped weight, for she had to tie her dress and apron tighter.

But how was she to know when she was needed? Tyndie worked later and arrived earlier for all of her shifts, and never complained about working double shifts. In fact, she hardly spoke a word, particularly when The Shrew was around.

She was punctual and occasionally even early all the time now, curtsied perfectly, and had yet to drop a thing, which The Shrew had warned her dozens of times not to.

Tyndie looked down at her arm where Lynza was squeezing it. She was trying to hold back her indignation, but her eyes had already flashed at Lynza and worse, the other women had seen it.

Stupid bitch, she sniffed as she stared into Lynza's brown eyes. Then she wrested her arm free from Lynza's grasp, rested her glare on Lynza for one final second, then marched into the room.

Waiting for reprisal, Tyndie started counting. But nothing came of it, and she even saw Hermia look down at the silver cup she was polishing with a smirk. Tyndie guessed that The Shrew had halted in shock behind her, for Manda said in a warning tone, "Lynza, leave her be. She's not yer little pin cushion." Manda, next to Tyndie's Auntie, had worked there the longest, so Manda's directives were to be minded as Auntie's were.

Tyndie got to work polishing and saw that she sat on the other side of the room from The Shrew. Today, they would be serving near all afternoon, for there was a small feast in the Great Hall. It was only for King Reaghann's immediate cabinet and visiting diplomats and emissaries, Auntie said. But it would be a long afternoon anyway.

It was also Tyndie's first feast. Auntie told her if she'd ever been tired, then take how she felt then and expect to feel exhausted. "And do keep that cute little face out of the way – the gods know you don't want one o' them bastards to decide he's got an eye for ya. Know what I mean, girl?" She chucked Tyndie under the chin with affection.

Tyndie did, thinking of the maid and the Squire she'd happened upon when she'd first started. She also knew what happened to maids who came with child. Of those times when a lord decided he wanted to lay with a maid long enough to get her with child – he'd never acknowledge a child from between the sheets. Maids had but a few options. They could leave the castle if they had the means and bear the child as a bastard. Lots of girls with the last names of seasons to indicate that they were bastard children, and boys with the directions on the map were born, all over the city, and in all the orphanages.

Some maids were just plain foolish and begged the lord to acknowledge the child. Such silliness, Tyndie reflected. Lords refused to stain their reputations, nor that of their wives, if they were wed. They pretended not to know the maid. Tyndie knew coins were exchanged in secret for "problems" to disappear, whether the maid just left the castle, or she suddenly was just ill of food poisoning and not with child at all. More like as not, Tyndie knew, maids just took wormwort and miscarried the babe without telling anyone. Or they met certain midwives outside of HarCourt Castle for a procedure to rid of the babe. But Tyndie knew most women were careful enough. They didn't want to risk such procedures, for they hoped to one day have babes of their own.

Her stomach growled as she stood against the wall. She hadn't had time to eat, and it would be a long afternoon. Fortunately, with the minstrel music and the chatter throughout the room, it was loud enough that none of the lords heard her stomach's protest, though Hermia, next to her, glanced at her underneath her lashes and risked the tiniest of smiles. Trying not to smile when you really wanted to laugh was so hard.

The feast itself did not help. They were only half-way through the stuffed pheasant and candied yams. Baked parsnips dressed with berry relish lay steaming in covered platters waiting to be served with roasted chickens in orange sauce, chilled mint strawberry soup, cheese, and, of course, more honey butter for the oncoming crusty loaves of bread on the table. Her Auntie was right, she was already tired.

Then Tyndie saw one of the men seated at the table. Any humor she might have found in the evening immediately died. Lord Drury! He was seated close to King Reaghann, which meant that he had the ear of the King more often than these other dignitaries. *Sittin' with the salt*, her Auntie said.

This was the first time she'd seen Lord Drury since his menacing conversation with Lord Stanson. Tyndie drew in a deep breath, smoothing her facial expression. *Stay invisible. Ya don't want the wrong eyes seein' ya....* This instruction had now taken on a whole new meaning for Tyndie – words to live by, truly live by.

Somehow, Lord Drury knew she was thinking about him, for he turned slightly. He glanced at the man seated next to him but decided that he was not what had caught his attention. Though his sudden curiosity had not abated, Lord Drury directed his gaze toward King Reaghann again, his face inscrutable.

Tyndie let out breath she didn't realize she'd been holding.

Ellia

"But Pappy –"

"Everyone's talking of it –"

"You hear people whispering about it –"

Ellia's sisters were speaking in unison, excited. They had been needling Pappy for the past five minutes, wondering, trying to discern any truth to the rumors they had kept hearing.

Ellia had heard talk of war occasionally as well, as customers spoke about it at the bar in worried tones, hushed and glancing about as if by speaking quickly would keep trouble away. Most of South Fairview remembered the Twenty Years War, for the soldiers had marched through and put the torch to all the city. Pappy had left the Army to help GrandPap rebuild the brewery, he told them when they were young, for the soldiers had burned it right to the ground, but he built on the tavern as well.

"Enough!" Pappy finally roared. "There is no war!" He shoved the dough into the oven with force and then clisp-clasped his hands free of flour so fast that flour dusted his grizzled beard.

"But Pappy, I even heard the fishmongers tell of it down at the docks," Mollie continued, just as if Pappy had not lost his temper.

"I don't care what they were saying down at the docks. And just what were you doin' down at the docks? You shouldn't have been all the way down there. I keep tellin' you that!" Pappy raised a finger at Mollie. Ellia heard his street accent creep in to his speech. That only happened when he got emotional about something.

Mollie's green eyes focused on his finger as she stammered, "Mags sent me, she told me to go...."

"Well, you just never go down there again without a chaperone. You take Nick. If you ever go again, which you better not," he warned her.

Privately, Ellia wondered what use Nick would be as a chaperone. Tall and skinny, she doubted Nick weighed more than a hundred pounds, much less that he could throw a punch.

"Yes, Pappy," Mollie breathed out a long, exaggerated sigh.

Pappy turned and eyed her. "Mollie girl, you don't want to go there with me." Pappy's quiet tone was stern and even.

Ellia could not see his face, but she had occasionally been the recipient of that tone, and knew those dark eyes were drilling into Mollie with the intensity of a red-hot poker.

She wondered if the war had made Pappy that way, if he had been a carefree, smiling, laughing boy before the Twenty Years War, or if he had always had that deep, brooding intensity.

"Yes, Pappy," Mollie, finally cowed, replied sullenly.

"Pappy, haven't you heard the talk, yourself, though?" Halsey threw all caution to the wind.

The last thing Ellia saw was Mags roll her eyes.

"*ENOUGH*! There will be – NO MORE TALK – OF WAR – IN MY KITCHEN! Now everybody out! That's all of ya! Out! Now!" Pappy bellowed, his muscled arms waving them all toward the doors.

Ellia and her sisters nearly stumbled over each other in their hasty exit through the kitchen doors.

Mags wandered through with her head held high, stately and proud. She looked down her nose at Mollie and Hasley. "Ya had to push him, didn't ya." She shook her head with something like disgust as she walked past the bar.

"Ya have to know he hears the rumors," pouted Mollie.

The three of them leaned their elbows on the glossy bar.

"Yes, but you didn't need to keep pushin' 'im," Hasley scolded.

"Me! I stopped, you're the one who kept it goin'!"

"Me? You're the one who started it!"

Mollie bapped Hasley behind the head. "Brat!

Hasley's mouth dropped open, then she bapped her sister back. "Brat yourself."

"Both of you, stop!" Ellia laughed. "You're both brats!"

Her sisters turned to look at her. Hasley sniffed and Mollie leaned around and bapped Ellia on the back of the head.

"Pap's little Golden Girl. *'Yes, Pappy', 'No Pappy'.*" Mollie simpered.

"With them pretty blue eyes," Hasley smiled adoringly as if she were staring up at Pappy.

Ellia bapped them both. They all giggled, but a group of patrons came in then and they all called, "Welcome to The Brew House and Tavern!"

Ellia, troubled, scraped her broom across the floor. It was still quiet enough that she was allowed out from behind the bar, for the work day was not yet over.

Ellia wished they wouldn't talk of war to Pappy. Something had happened in the war that had changed him. He rarely spoke of it, and when he did, he got a faraway look in his eyes, and when Mum was present, she would lay a hand on his shoulder and pat him just so. She'd say, "Come, love," and he'd draw in a great breath.

Pappy never talked about his wound. When the weather turned especially cold, he limped, and sometimes he would limp before bad weather came. He claimed it told him that trouble was coming to town. Pappy strove to an enormous degree to hide his limp but now and again, a customer would ask how he received it.

Ellia had seen him answer that question at least a dozen times now, and he always answered it the same way. The smallest of smiles would slide over his face and he would gaze out the window, though she could always tell that it wasn't the street Pappy was seeing. "Just in the right place at the right time," he always said. And then the customer's next drink was always free.

Of late, Ellia noticed Pappy had become more affectionate. She didn't know how to respond to that, so she just took it in turn. Sometimes, she would find him watching her. Pappy would be leaning against a door jamb, or over the bar, just gazing at her.

Today, she had looked up to see him watching her with the faintest of smiles as she swept. Ellia said nothing and pretended not to notice, though not before she saw his forehead crease. He looked sad, almost wistful, as he turned and stared out the window, far ahead down the street.

She didn't know what it was Pappy saw far ahead down the way, but Ellia wished it would stop making him so sad....

Ishbel

Ishbel watched as he adjusted himself, tucking himself comfortably into his trousers. As he pulled the laces of his trousers tight, he slipped between her curtains without a look back at her. She waited for a count of ten heartbeats, for some men returned – they left articles of clothing behind, or begged her not to tell their wives, their mistresses, or, even worse, Ishbel sniffed idly, had the stamina to start again, which was became more and more rare the older they were.

But he did not return. Ishbel rolled across her mattress and stood up. His man juice streamed down her leg, but she wiped it away with a linen cloth, then cleansed herself. She wiped the rest of her body clean with rose water, and then dusted herself lightly with petal powder.

With contempt for her last customer, she rubbed almond oil into her nipples. Just because they protruded did not mean they could be twisted, pulled, bitten, or sucked off, though men, and even women occasionally, persisted in trying.

She rearranged the veils over her body and had barely begun to smooth her hair when Gobin entered. Always on time. His eyes traveled up and down her body, inspecting his merchandise. He nodded, satisfied, and picked up her soiled linens. At least he provided well for his whores. Ishbel knew of numbers of slave owners who beat their whores, starved them, fucked them, and even damaged their bodies.

Ishbel had been with Gobin for what she thought was five years now. In Pavilion City, one lost track of the seasons, for the temperature remained almost always the same, temperate and nearly tropical. He was her third owner, and, she hoped, her last. Gobin was very pleased with her, for she had island blood in her. Her tan skin and green eyes was a special attraction for men, as most whores looked as most other women, fair complected with brown, red, and blonde hair, and green, blue, or brown eyes.

Special attraction or no, Gobin still charged two silvers for her as he did all his whores. And they had to be silvers, not coppers equal to the same amount, for he wanted no whores stealing from him. Better a whore than a thief, he said, though there were times when Ishbel couldn't tell the difference.

She had not always been a whore. She and her family had lived on the outer coast of S'hendalow, and so she herself was not an islander, though her mother was. Ishbel had not known her mother long enough to learn from where she had actually hailed. But pirate ships had come through after the Twenty Years War, enjoying the lack of naval patrol now that many of the naval vessels had been destroyed. A pirate ship had captured Ishbel and her family and sold them to slavers. She had been perhaps five at the time, but she'd never seen her family again.

Ishbel's first owner branded her shoulder, which now was only a smaller scar, though a scar nonetheless. She had lived in a cage with other slaves, shackled and chained when she wasn't working in the kitchen. The callous around her ankle took years to finally disappear, long after she'd been bought by her next owner.

Her next owner bought her and branded her shoulder on top of the old brand, and Ishbel was set to working in the kitchens, usually chopping vegetables and fruits, stewing pottages, and such light work as a ten-year-old was able to do.

Then her master lost a portion of his wealth, and she was placed on auction at the age of thirteen in Pavilion City, along with his other slaves. Gobin happened to see her and immediately bought her for her exotic appeal. She had not yet dropped her skirts.

But Gobin's tattoo was on her shoulder now, and Ishbel admitted that, of all her owners, he had treated her the most gently. Of course, for he did not want to mar his merchandise. Men wanted beautiful women, not bruised fruit.

Gobin set down another basket of fresh linen cloth for her. He screened the men whom he allowed into his pavilions. Any men he suspected might bruise his fruit he did not allow back. Occasionally, he judged a man wrong, but generally, Gobin read men's characters well enough. He nodded shortly at Ishbel and scooped up the two silvers on her bureau before he ducked out.

Ishbel was not alone for long before a new customer slipped between her curtains.

She let her eyes travel up and down him with a desultory gaze. She smiled slowly and patted the mattress next to her.

Usually, Ishbel could read a man just by taking in his face, but this one was a bit of a puzzle. Hmmm. She liked puzzles. His clothing – dusty, gritty. He had traveled recently, a lengthy distance and probably from the west. The color of his clothing – nondescript, neutral colors. Odd. Most men preferred at least one color, usually a tunic, of dyed blue or russet. A dark vest over his tunic, and a cloak of another neutral color.

His gray eyes studied her in return, his dark hair had very little gray in it, but his stubbled chin revealed his age with gray shot through it. His boots were leather....

All of his clothing was of good quality. He set down a heavy rucksack and threw his cloak to one side. He set down two silvers on her bureau, which glinted in the sunbeam streaming in over the top of her outer curtains.

Ishbel had still not formed an opinion of him, other than that he was the most mysterious man she had ever seen.

His gray eyes ran all over her, taking in her entire body. In a gravely tone, he asked, "What's your name, girl?"

Ishbel considered. She flipped through her mental inventory of facades that she used with men, based on her first impression of them. Unable to draw upon one she thought would suit this man best, she chose the basic paradigm.

"What would you like it to be?" She pursed her lips suggestively. She always made it a game, figuring out a customer. Usually she had him figured out as soon as he walked in the door, so she only needed to confirm her opinion. This, however, was going to be a treat.

He frowned. "That wasn't the question. I asked what your name was. What was the name you were born with?"

Ishbel blinked and then raised an eyebrow. Occasionally men styled themselves intellectuals who wanted conversation first, and it was these men who asked the names you were born with. Whores always, as a rule, chose a name not their own. You didn't give that away, that was personal. You chose a name that was believable, even something that, based on your impression of the customer, you thought they'd appreciate. *If you want a good actor, hire a whore or a politician*, ran the saying.

But something about this man made Ishbel decide upon the truth. She studied him for a second and decided he could tell if a person was lying. "Ishbel," she told him, dropping all pretense.

He nodded then. "Very good then, Ishbel." He sat down in front of her on the mattress and started pulling off his boots.

Unsure for once of how to proceed, Ishbel raised up on her knees behind him and placed her hands upon his shoulders.

He stopped. "There will be no need for that." He turned and looked at her from face to navel. "You are a very beautiful woman, Ishbel, and on another occasion, perhaps I would take pleasure – great pleasure – in your abilities. But I am here merely because I want to quietly go through some paperwork, sit comfortably here with no interruption, and possibly even lie on a mattress… without fear of a knife being stuck in my back."

Ishbel stared at him. Never had a man said such a thing – not, at least, about being murdered. Plenty of men had come just to lay with a woman and do nothing at all, but not just to escape the outside world and possibly hide away from an assassin.

He raised his eyebrows at her, demanding acknowledgement. "Do you understand?" he asked quietly.

Without a word, Ishbel nodded, and then the man said, "Good." He dug in his vest, and pulled out another silver. He held it up before her.

"For your service today, and your silence."

Ishbel's eyes grew wide as she stared at the silver. She had never had money before, not even a copper chip. A silver – that was more money than – she could even fathom ever owning. Gobin did not allow his whores to accept money. Even if they were paid money, he took it from them. If he were to find out that Ishbel had money....

Ishbel met the man's grey eyes over the coin. Then she took the coin.

Rhody

The King's Royal Torturer – if King Rhutgard actually called him such – was placed in possibly the best position they could have arranged. A spy as the Torturer – Rhody wondered who had placed him. For clerics, diplomats, cabinet members, Healers and other household staff not only ran the risk of being discovered but were often unable to turn conversations to such that they might glean information worth sending home. Nor, Rhody, pondered as the pain sent shivering up his body, were they even able to get close to individuals who had information of the sort King Hewart found of interest.

Rhody had known that he would be tortured, for that was the mission. He and Wyngroth both had trained for this. But Wyngroth, twat that he was, had gotten wounded enough during capture that he had died during torture, and now the entire mission rested upon Rhody's shoulders.

They had trained for much worse, of course. Over the years, Ambsellon had heard a mixture of rumors float north from Romeny. That they never tortured anyone at all, of course, was predominant. But also, that, since the changing of the guard, with the new pup Rhutgard on the throne, the torture was so bad men died within hours, barely able to speak of the crime they'd committed, be it treason or even simpler crimes. Occasionally, spies reported that it was merely a hoax, a ruse, to frighten and discourage such espionage in Fairview, even Romeny itself. No one believed that, though. They believed the new pup had the set of balls his sire and aye, even his grandsire before him never had. Others said it was merely just the rack he used.

And so, Rhody and Wyngroth both had prepared for the worst of torture devices before they left Ambsellon, in the event that their man here was not in place as expected. But Rhody was relieved to see only the rack. Other torture devices of a horrendous nature did sit in the room, he'd seen when he was dragged in, but they did not look used of late, at least not in the fashion Ambsellon used their own.

The Torturer and Rhody had exchanged a great deal of coded information. However, Rhody was concerned that the Torturer had taken a bit too much pleasure in the physical job. Rhody, once he had felt that *pop!* in his lower back, decided to end the charade. Lack of control had never been a strong point of his.

The Torturer had, of course, tied his rope bonds loosely, but nevertheless, he should have stopped the rack by now. Rhody had been prepared for just such a situation and had worked his wrists and ankles nearly free, though the rough hemp of the rope had scraped skin away until blood ran freely. Rhody wasn't sure which was worse, the tickle of the blood trickling down his skin, or the pain of the rack, both of which he was powerless over.

He eyed the Torturer's set of knives, set out upon a set of brown linen, undeniably old bloodstains. Any of those knives would serve once he broke free.

Finally, Rhody pulled his wrists free, then yanked his ankles out of their rope bindings and jumped away from the rack. He knew the Torturer had already reported all the Ambsellon information to – whomever his contact was, or so he'd indicated as he rolled the rack this morning.

Pain lanced through his body as his bones slipped back into their rightful places, and he panted. The Torturer, surprised, stared at him. Undoubtedly, a prisoner had never escaped him before. Clearly, the Torturer had been down here too long.

Rhody sprang forward and grabbed one of the knives from the table, ignoring the pain his movements took. Before the Torturer could move, Rhody had plunged the knife into his gut and then across the man's neck. Arterial blood sprayed forward, and Rhody took great pleasure in watching the man who had planned to pull his body apart clutch at his neck and slide to the stained stone floor. His eyes bulged, his head lulled to the side then in death. *Arsehole.* Rhody shoved the man with his bloody foot away from where he'd fallen again against his legs.

Then Rhody took in several deep breaths. His time from here was extremely limited. He glanced about. Ah. The Ambsellon uniform he'd arrived in. And Wyngroth's. Pain medication had been sewed inside the upper hems. He bent and slipped the knife the knife between the thread, then immediately chewed on some of it.

Though Rhody nearly gagged at its awful taste, he knew he would savor it in just a few minutes. Something had *popped* in his lower back and that would make his trip over the Mantle Mountains a rougher one than he could have hoped for. He found Wyngroth's medicine as well, vowing to ration it after today.

Rhody slurped thirstily from the water bucket, for it had been probably two days since he'd had liquid to drink. Once he stood again, he immediately had to bend back over, for he was lightheaded. *Twat*, he thought. He'd received training on just this. How was he going to get of this fucking dungeon, this castle, much less back home? Lightheaded! *You fucking pussy, stand up and get your fucking arse out of here!*

Rhody splashed water across himself to wash the dirt and blood from his hair and body, for he knew he stank of two days' worth of torture. Naturally, there was no soap here. But to pass muster upstairs, he needed to look – and smell – decent. Hopefully, the bruises on his face had not yet blackened. He believed the Torturer had left his face alone now that he thought of it, though his body was another story. Broken ribs, something in his spine broken, black and purple bruises all about his body....

After the fastest bath he had ever taken in his life, Rhody finally smelled free – or so he hoped – of dirt and blood and urine. He could not, of course, don his Ambsellon uniform, though he looked fondly at it.

Rhody took a deep breath to hold in the pain, and then bent to pick up the Torturer's arms. He grit his teeth and started pulling the man toward the farthest torture machine in the back of the room. There, against the wall in the dark with the cobwebs, he dumped the bastard. It wouldn't do for them to find the arsehole immediately. If Rhody hadn't been wounded, he'd have strapped the Torturer up on the damn rack himself and then tortured him.

Panting, Rhody studied the device the Torturer lay against for a moment. Even he did not recognize it. Well, give some credit to Romeny, then. And a good resting place for this arsehole.

Rhody knew there was a guard stationed outside the Torture Room. What a shitty post, he mused. But were there ever two, he wondered? He doubted so, unless any prisoners were dropped off or transported. Wearing the Torturer's uniform to escape in was a last resort only, for the man had stood a foot taller and had sported several more inches about the waist. Aside from which, Rhody thought with disgust, the pervading stench of perspiration and unwashed body odor would definitely raise eyebrows, even if the ill-fitting uniform did not.

He'd take his chances with the guard outside. Rhody snatched the keys from the dead Torturer's belt and then stole forward with the knife toward the door. He searched through the keys for what he hoped was would fit in the dungeon door and held his knife ready, for as soon as the guard saw him, Rhody would need to spring into action. This would be either a very quick encounter, or a painful and bloody one. In his weakened condition, he hoped for the former.

The metallic *chink* of the key in the lock of the dungeon doorway alerted the guard, though he only turned his head slightly in Rhody's direction, a passive expression on his face. Of course, thought an idle part of Rhody's mind as he reached out toward the dungeon guard, who else would be coming and going but the Torturer?

Rhody placed a firm hand over the guard's mouth to silence him and squeezed his neck in the crook of his elbow so tightly that the guard lost his breath. He sagged, unconscious, though he would wake with quite a headache. Best of all, he had not seen his attacker, thought Rhody with pride. He dragged the guard back inside and pulled the man's uniform off. It was a bit tight across the chest, but otherwise fit well enough. He leaned the man against the Torturer and chained his arms and legs to the torture device. If he was loud enough, someone would check on him.

Rhody glanced down with distaste at his Rommish guard uniform. Red, blue, and gold. Soon enough, it would be red, gold, and silver. Any country who had chosen a rose, even if fit was wound round a sword, deserved to be conquered. Rhody scoffed. Pussies. Fucking Romeny.

He could not wait until they finally owned this stupid country. He belted his uniform and attached the keys properly.

He walked carefully up the stone corridor. Rhody hoped against hope that no one would recognize him for the prisoner he was. Finally, he ran into a young guard at the opening to the dungeon level, but Rhody merely looked down and coughed when the young guard saluted.

Rhody wanted nothing more than to be on his way out of this stinking castle before his imprisonment was discovered, but he had one last errand to complete. Based on the coded directions that bloody Torturer had given him, he knew how to get to the pigeon loft.

Twice, two younger soldiers snapped to and saluted him with a stiff hand, which he dismissed. He wondered what his predecessor had done to get stationed down in the dungeon, for clearly, he was of rank enough to be saluted as uniform denoted when seen.

Finally, he stepped out into the green and found the pigeon loft. He crossed the grass as quickly as possible without calling attention to himself. Once he ducked inside, Rhody glanced about. Ah. Both Ambsellon birds, right as the Torturer described. Up on the second level, set apart from the rest.

He glanced about for parchment, then set to writing his messages to King Hewart. Coded, of course. When Rommish birds flew in, their communications were immediately brought to the King, never read by anyone first.

A trickle of sweat ran down Rhody's neck, and not due to nerves. This miserable country's heat was intolerable. When they did take it over, he would stay behind. Bears did not belong so far south. Rhody loved the cold and the snow and even the ice, he supposed as he dipped his quill into the ink.

"Bared the bear. Look for the cub in the cave beside the spring."

He wrote both parchments with the same message and stamped them with the Castle Seal of Romeny. Rhody affixed the messages to the pigeons' legs, then tossed them both into the air. If one didn't make it to King Hewart, the other would, or so he hoped.

It was not his place to speculate how King Hewart planned to explain this move toward Romeny without informing Ormon. As such long-time allies, they rarely made any militaristic moves without informing the other, and certainly not one to such a measure as King Hewart was planning.

But Rhody himself heard the King say that "While Munsolrysche has had his arsecheeks frozen to that ice chamber pot of his, we have waited these many years for him to ready a plan with us to move against the Eastern Shield. No more! Let us ahead! We have the troops, we have the Navy, and we need no Ormons! We are the *BEAR!*"

And now, now Rhody could leave. He found his way to the stables. Rhody patted down a fine-looking stallion. It would be a shame to sell him later on the journey, as he'd probably have to, but at least the beast would fetch a good price.

The stable hand stood staring at him, his mouth open.

"Well, what are you looking at?" The castle idiot, probably. Well, he seemed to keep the horses in good order. He tossed the boy a copper from his predecessor's pouch. Surprised, the moron caught it. Huh. His reflexes weren't bad for a moron.

Rhody turned and led the stallion out of the stable. He kept his head down, hoping none of the guards would stop him on his way out.

Luck was with him as he walked toward the gatehouse. He swung up on top of the stallion and urged him through. The clop-clops of the hooves on the cobbles was the sweetest sound Rhody had heard in days. Sweet escape. *"Yah!"* He urged the stallion into a gallop down the cobbled street.

Kendrick

Kendrick had just completed currying Rosie down when he'd heard boots enter the stable. Kendrick was really not in the mood for company, nor for exchanging platitudes with some courtier looking to improve his station for the week. Riding for him was serious, and he'd been out all day. He believed he might even be slightly sunburn across his face.

And soon enough, he'd be taken to task for it, by nearly every adult of authority in his life. That's why he loved riding so much. He could leave his life behind, no diplomacy, no politics, no tutelage in anything, no bowing and kissing of hands, no *Highnesses*.... His father wasn't about to stare at him with that... that *look* that without a word, implied how much more he expected of his son.

Well, sighed Kendrick, Keldrick got that *look* too, but not near as much as Kendrick, for Kendrick was second in succession to the throne, where less was expected from Keldrick. Kendrick could only wonder what his older brother Merridon went through... no wonder he hid himself away all the time. Maybe it was to hide himself from Father....

Rosie whinnied gently and flicked an ear. She turned her graceful head around to observe him. She always knew when he was in a rotten mood. But this time, he was just pushing too hard with the brush. "Sorry, girl," he murmured, and patted her neck. She flicked her ear again.

That was when the soldier walked into the stable. Rarely did soldiers ever sign out horses from the stable. And certainly not prison sergeants, if Kendrick had read his uniform correctly. Even more so, he had chosen one of his father's favorite horses, Windy. But the oddest thing of all, was that he had glanced at Kendrick for a moment and then said nothing at all. Not a *Your Highness*, not a bow, not a salute, not even a *sir*. Instead, he'd treated Kendrick as – now that he thought about it – a common stable hand. And then actually tossed him a coin. Whatever would Kendrick do with a coin? Everyone knew who he was, and what he looked like, even if his tunic was stained and untucked from riding. Particularly each and every guard in the Palace. So just what had happened?

Rhutgard

Rhutgard rolled his eyes toward the ceiling and let out a long breath. "Do we know where he was heading?"

"We think so, Sire. He won't return to that same village we found them in –"

"Kantletown."

"Uh, yes, Your Majesty." The lead scout seemed surprised.

"This is my country, after all," Rhutgard tried not to sound sardonic but the attempt, he was afraid, turned out more patronizing then anything. "I fought near there when your parents were your age." Then he closed his eyes. Not only did he sound old, but he was being an arsehole. This boy was a scout, and good at his job, or he wouldn't be standing here. Rhutgard could just hear how Principea would scold him....

He turned around and faced his advisors. Staring at the lead scout, Rhutgard looked him in the eye. "Your name is Canton. Canton, I owe you an apology. You didn't deserve that. I was being an arsehole."

The boy – possibly nineteen at most – blinked at him, speechless.

Now Rhutgard really was annoyed. He kept a very close guard on his tongue and then between gritted teeth, said, "Bask in the moment, son, for I rarely apologize to anyone." Then he smoothed his expression to a show a calm demeanor. "Carry on," he gestured.

As Canton was still speechless, the second lead scout quickly spoke up and told Rhutgard, "We feel certain that he will instead run to Wintonville. He's injured, and he will need to rest. He will also need to trade that horse for money so he can make it through the mountains." The second lead scout coughed. "Or so he thinks."

"I will miss that horse," Rhutgard mused.

"How long would you like us to follow him?"

"Only to Wintonville. Recapture him there. I've other plans for him, plans that do not involve torture," he added.

"The messages, Sire?"

"I've plans for those as well," Rhutgard said, smiling faintly as he looked down at the unrolled messages on his desk. He was not entirely sure what,

"Bared the bear. Look for the cub in the cave beside the spring."

meant, but they all felt certain that King Hewart in Ambsellon knew to look for his lost spy in the immediate future at a before-planned destination. The bear was, after all, the emblem of Ambsellon.

Rhutgard was not going to reveal all of his network to this group standing in his study. Over the years, he had built up an inner network of informants, something he knew many kings did. He wondered what his father's had been like. He knew Father must have had one – it was a war, after all, and twenty years long. Maybe he had inherited it from Grandfather. But what had it been like.... Father had been canny, sly....

Rhutgard changed his network regularly – reassigning men suddenly for no reason, sending them to the other ends of the country or even other countries, to different cities, towns. And quite often he sent them places from where he needed no information at all, just to keep his informants guessing.

But oh, how it wore on him. He would rather be fighting a war on the battlefield than this silent war of spies. It was much like a game of Ice – the ultimate game of strategy, but he was tired of moving his living pieces about his live board, and occasionally, lords, noblemen, even royals died. As long, Rhutgard sighed, as none of the royals were any of his own, he thought as he rubbed his jaw absently.

He dismissed all of them, except for Stanyard. Stanyard he had recruited himself, his very first. Stanyard he had found during his first visit to the prison cells, nearly dead of neglect and starvation. Stanyard's hair had hung in greasy long wisps over his sunken face, which had been little more than skin stretched tautly over a skull. And yet – and yet – Rhutgard still remembered those gray eyes followed his every move. Stanyard had pretended to be barely conscious but a sharp intelligence stared out of those sunken gray eyes.

Stanyard had been a spy from Ormon, a rare find. His mother was Ormon, his father Ambsellon. Apparently, the men who hired him disavowed all knowledge of him once he was caught, though Stanyard explained to Rhutgard that once he was in Rommish borders and half the contacts he was supposed to have met never showed, he believed that he was supposed to have been caught. Poor planning was not an Ormon trait. But he had spent three years down in the cells, with no more enlightenment on his mission than he did today.

Stanyard's allegiance was wholeheartedly Rhutgard's now, though. Rhutgard rescued him from the cells; such an action was unheard of in Ormon and Ambsellon, particularly for spies. Rhutgard had visited him regularly and learned as much as he could about both countries, for book learning and the battlefield were nothing compared to an actual native and son of both cultures. Eventually Stanyard began to trust Rhutgard, once he decided that Rhutgard wanted nothing from him other than the understanding of the worlds he had grown up in.

Soon, Rhutgard started asking Stanyard's opinion on state matters involving Ambsellon and Ormon. After this proved fruitful, Rhutgard finally sat him in a Cabinet meeting. When the lords sitting at his table inquired of Rhutgard an introduction, he simply replied, "This is Lord Stanyard, one of my most trusted advisors." The Cabinet members glanced at each other, some with curiosity, others with misgiving, for none of them had heard of Lord Stanyard, nor even known that Rhutgard had been speaking with such a man.

Stanyard's abilities as a spy were an enormous advantage. Occasionally, when he knew what a man was saying was truth, he would cock his head to the right, as if interested. If Stanyard knew what the man was saying was deliberately an utter falsehood, he would cock his head to the left. Either way, Rhutgard knew to regard the individual's commentary carefully, and follow it up further as necessary.

When Rhutgard asked if he wanted to return home, Stanyard replied, "Return... home? I come from no home. I live here now." Rhutgard had nodded, pleased. But he made it very clear, that at any time, Stanyard was free to return to the Northern Countries.

Rhutgard also told Stanyard that he needn't work in service to him, that he was free to leave the Palace at any time, live as he liked. Stanyard implied that, though he had never been contacted in any way by his former countrymen, nor felt any allegiance toward them, his life was likely to be a short one should he leave the Palace.

Rhutgard also, however, made it even more clear, that, while Stanyard was free to leave at any time, he was not free to take up his former occupation working against the Crown. Stanyard did not need this ultimatum to be further detailed for him to understand what would happen if he were to violate Rhutgard's trust. But Rhutgard did not believe that would happen.

Now that the scouts had cleared the study, he looked at Lord Stanyard. Master of Spies, Lord of None. Stanyard had switched the Ambsellon birds out long ago, so that they would fly to Miller's Tower. The man who kept pigeons there was a retired Crown Lieutenant and loyal to his last drop of blood. He sent birds to and from the Palace regularly.

"And what will you do with the messages?" inquired Rhutgard's Master of Spies. "Or have you not decided?"

"I've decided," Rhutgard said. "I'm going to send the Bear Cub's message, just as it is, to Ormon, straight to the King. Let us see how Ormon appreciates being left out of Ambsellon's plans. And then let us sit back and see who starts fighting first."

Lord Stanyard smiled. "I, for one, will enjoy watching."

Keldrick

Keldrick joined his brother in the hallway. "Do you know what this is about?" he asked Kendrick.

"No, not an inkling."

A Royal Summons was more than a *visit me at your leisure* and *you are on my schedule, so attend me on time* and certainly more than a *drop by my study by day's end*. A Royal Summons was an executive order issued by King Rhutgard Firthing, whose word was law. One did not disobey the King of one's country... even if he was your father, mused Keldrick as he straightened his surcoat.

They arrived at the entrance to the Great Hall, barricaded shut and guarded by the King's Guards. They stepped aside to allow Keldrick and Kendrick inside. The Great Hall doors boomed shut behind them, and Keldrick expected to see an impressive array of diplomats, envoys, ambassadors, and the like in attendance.

What he saw nearly stopped him. No one sat in the Great Hall. Had the messenger given Keldrick the wrong time? But no, Kendrick had received the same time as well. Were they early? Or worse, late?

There on the dais sat his father on his throne, in all his kingly attire.

"Approach us." He beckoned them with a formal wave.

Ah, the formal Kingly "We." Keldrick recalled his first Royal Summons at the age of six. Keldrick had been told that Father would be sitting on the throne up on the dais. Keldrick would be not allowed to approach or speak to Father at all during the ceremony. Keldrick had understood that well enough, but what he had not understood was that Father used the royal "We" throughout the ceremony. As soon as he began to use the "We," Keldrick had immediately become confused. Of whom was he speaking? Who was "we"? Was Father speaking of himself and Mother and his brothers and Keldrick? Father kept saying "We have decided…" and "We have chosen to…" but Keldrick was terribly upset, for he was so confused.

His older brother Merridon had not helped matters by laughing at him. Several of Father's counselors, Keldrick's tutor, and other people he had not known had covered their mouths to hide amused smiles. Keldrick, flustered, kept asking the people around him, "Who is 'we?'" Finally, his tutor had escorted him from the Great Hall. It had been Keldrick's greatest embarrassment for some years to follow, though he finally found it humorous himself, as he did now. He wondered if every time he heard the Royal "We," he would recall that day….

He and Kendrick advanced toward King Rhutgard, their demeanor stiff and formal as required.

"Your Majesty," they both murmured.

"Follow Us." King Rhutgard rose from his purple cushioned throne and stepped down from the dais. They glanced at each other behind his back. Kendrick shrugged, and they followed Father into his study behind the Great Hall.

"Close the door."

Keldrick closed the door. They were now alone with their father. Not even Lord Stanyard was with him. That was odd, Lord Stanyard almost always attended Father at his side.

Father – King Rhutgard… Keldrick knew when he had to distinguish between the two… stood behind his great mahogany desk and gestured for Keldrick and Kendrick to sit down in the wooden chairs across from him. Keldrick circled behind his brother and seated himself. Keldrick tried not to frown with concern – but he felt as though his father the King was going to reveal something important.

Once he and his brother were both seated, King Rhutgard gazed down at them for a few seconds. Keldrick hated that look, that Romeny blue-eyed stare that measured and judged you of worthiness, and left you wondering if you had been found wanting.

Mother told them both upon occasion that they looked almost exactly like Father did at his age. Well, Keldrick thought to himself whenever Father delivered this same penetrating, intense stare as he was right now, he was never going to glare at his own children the same way....

"We have decided to allow you into more of our meetings. As you are of age now, We think it best to expose you to what is – and has been... occurring about the Kingdom of late. Other than, of course, social engagements."

The King kept his voice even and did not allow sarcasm to color his last comment, though Keldrick knew it was implied particularly toward Kendrick.

King Rhutgard observed their faces for a response to this news, but as Princes, they had been trained to remain impassive. The King nodded once. "You shall start off by merely listening and watching, not contributing. Any contribution you should have will either be shared with Us or Lord Stanyard privately.

"After you have learned which Cabinet member speaks for what interests, We will give you more responsibilities, allow you in different meetings, perhaps. For now, this is how you shall begin. Anything Lord Stanyard tells you, follow as if We have given you the order Ourself.

"How speak you?"

Keldrick and Kendrick both agreed in firm declarations, though Keldrick's mind was spinning.

"Very good, then. Dismissed."

Ron

Ron had wandered about South Fairview for half the afternoon, for Cradwick had roused himself suddenly. He had declared it to be a Market Day, though it actually was not. So in a half-drunken haze, Cradwick had sent Ron to the Market so that he might gather materials that, of course, they actually did not need. But on days when Cradwick took it upon himself to take up his trade, Ron stayed out of his way. Some days, he forgot he had an apprentice altogether. He wondered just how strong the sleeping potion they mixed in his wine truly was.

However, the afternoon off gave Ron a chance to wander into the neighborhoods he normally didn't get to see during the daytime, for he usually only snuck out at night. He trudged along through the mud of Miller Street, keeping a sharp eye out for some of his informants. Miller Street ran up into the north border of South Fairview, where sturdier homes stood and a more well-to-do sort of folk inhabited the area, or at least, well-to-do for the southern end of Fairview.

Miller Street became Chandler Blvd., and here Ron stood with the cowl of his grey cloak up around his face.

While Chandler Street boasted far fewer criminals in residency, it still attracted them, for pockets to pick had more coin and homes had a more lucrative treasure to be lifted. However, due to just such this criminal activity, Chandler Street and its local neighborhood had its own constabulary, however minor in number, and they also depended upon each other to watch out for suspicious occurrences.

Just as Ron was about to step off the corner of Chandler Street, he spied a familiar figure leaning on the house across the street. Was it… Nick? Nick, of The Brew House and Tavern, who worked for Luvian?

Ron immediately stepped backward again and quietly slipped unseen behind the greengrocer so as to observe Nick.

Nick was leaning against a stone home with a practiced nonchalance that Ron recognized as one of his own postures. What was Luvian's Nick doing so far north of South Fairview, and of The Brew House and Tavern? Was that what Luvian meant when he told Nick, *"I have a job for you?"* No. Luvian was too forthright to be involved in such dealings. And yet, there Nick stood. Perhaps Luvian was unaware. Ron considered and decided that Luvian was unaware of very little in his brewery.

Ron had respected Luvian previous to the night he'd nearly killed those soldiers, but now Ron's level of respect had grown far beyond his original assessment. A veteran of the Twenty Years War with highly specialized combat training, right under his nose, working as an innkeeper, and Ron had missed him completely. Ron still was unsure whether to include Luvian in a report or not.

Across the street, Nick stood up, casually, slowly, calling no attention to himself. Ron admitted to being impressed. Nick suddenly turned his head a little, as if he knew he was being observed. Ron shrank immediately behind the unsuspecting greengrocer, hoping the wagon would hide him. After a few moments, Ron chanced a glance around.

Nick had slid up the street-facing window of the residence and was just sliding in! Ron's mouth dropped open. Nick – a thief! His observation skills were no longer serving him, of that he was certain – he would need to sharpen them immediately. What else was The Brew House and Tavern hiding that Ron was unaware of?

Ron knocked a few pieces of fruit to the ground from his stance behind the greengrocer. As soon as the vendor bent over to pick them up, one by one, Ron stepped across the street with a casual pace. He glanced about, saw that the vendor was polishing his fallen wares with the sleeve of his tunic, muttering to himself.

No one else watching – excellent. Ron hopped up on the half-open window sill and slid in silently. He knew how to enter buildings unnoticed, of course, he just rarely used the ability.

Once inside, Ron immediately smelled the last bit of candle smoke, snuffed out, Ron presumed, by Nick. Ron let his eyes adjust to the darkness of the home and stepped quietly against the walls so as to avoid the creaks of wooden planks in high traffic areas that would give his presence away.

He didn't have far to go, for he found Nick in the next room. A small study of sorts, where shelves held a number of bound books and a desk that was covered with a shuffled mess of unrolled parchments. And Nick stood above them, holding a candle.

Ron cleared his throat.

"So it's you, is it. I knew someone had come in, but Ronnie boy, you continue to surprise me. Almost as bad as me, now," said Nick in an indifferent tone as he continued to scan the document he was reading.

"No, no I am not. I'm nothing like you," Ron whispered. "I'm not a thief."

"Ohh," Nick clucked. "Thief, that's such a strong word. I prefer to say that I *'acquire items by unconventional means.'"* He stood up straight. "And you needn't worry about whispering, there ain't no one here. Obvious. If there was, I wouldn't be here, now would I?" And he cocked his head to look at Ron as if he had shared something that was a common piece of knowledge amongst all people.

"I'm not letting you leave here with anything that wasn't already yours to start with." Ron crossed his arms firmly. Nick could be a smartarse if he chose, but that did not change the fact that he had broken into a family's home.

Nick scoffed. "Well, good, good, Ronnie boy, because I didn't come here to take anything. Honest, I wasn't here for thievin'. And a fair amount a' time, I'm not." Nick winked at Ronnie, taking pleasure in explaining his actions.

Ron's eyes narrowed. "Then... why?" He waved an arm around them.

Nick took in a deep sigh of something close to exasperation. "Information, Ronnie," and he tapped the side of his temple. "Information."

"Really."

"I think you'll find, Ronnie, although," and Nick's eyes narrowed here with speculation as he gazed at Ronnie, "I think you already know, that information is more valuable than any trinkets or baubles. Not to say I'd turn down a good deal of gold, but information sells for gold these days, if you get it from the right source. What do you think, Ronnie, Would you agree?"

A cocky half smile slid across Nick's face, with a knowing expression that told Ron that his actions in South Fairview had not gone unnoticed. Now Ron was truly concerned. Nick was usually a likable enough fellow, placid, occasionally a bit of a jokester. The girls and Mags at The Brew House and Tavern often called him PicNick, which Ron had always assumed was simply an affectionate food-related nickname, as Tank was short for Tankard, though no one knew Tank's real name, except perhaps Luvian.

This, this skinny street lad was threatening Ron with what sounded like extortion, and he didn't like it one bit.

"I'm sure I don't know what you mean," Ron replied evenly.

"Really? That's a right interesting sigil you got on your tunic, Ronnie, my friend. Bein' a blacksmith's apprentice as you are...."

But Nick never finished his sentence. Ron had grabbed Nick by the neck of his tunic and pulled him close until he was staring him the eyes. "Yes. Yes it is. I work for Master Cradwick. And you?"

"I – I work for Luvian. Of course."

"And the name *'PicNick?'*" Ron insisted. "Does Luvian know?"

"PicNick – was my street name for Picking Nicks, pickpocketing. And later, Picking Knicks, as in Picking Knick Knacks out of the Market Place. Then, I gots good enough to pick locks, so they called me NickPics, as in NickPicksLocks. And NickKnacks, though I didn't stay with that gang long – they was nearly all cleared out by the Guard.

So then I started workin' for meself and," Nick sighed, "not doin' so well at it, when Mister Luvian found me in the Market. He saw right through me.

"He said, *'You was about to pick that old woman's basket clean of bread she saved up a week to eat, boy, and she hasn't got any more coin and no family to help her. Do you and your kind ever think that maybe you hurt the people you steal from?'*

"And he had picked me clean up offa' me boots, and slammed me up against the bricks, and I was petrified, nearly pissed me trousers.

"I actually never knew a person who had thought about them folks we'd taken from. And Mister Luvian, he said, *'Where are your parents, boy?'*

"And I told him as how I'd never known them, I'd been in an orphanage 'til it burnt down in a fire when the soldiers came through. I told him I was just hungry and needed somethin' to eat was all.

"Mister Luvian says, *'What's your name?'* I told him the orphanage headmaster had called me Nick, for Nickolas. So Mister Luvian brought me back to the brewery and gives me some bread and some stew and says I can earn an honest wage working for him doing odd jobs about the place and that I can stays there. But that the instant as any single thing, a copper chip, a goblet, a fork, anything goes missing, or his patrons suddenly can't find something they walked in with, he will deliver me into the Guard's hands by the back of the neck personally.

"Me, I figure, I got me a warm place to sleep, three squares a day if I wants them, easy work, it don't get much better. And them girls is sweet lasses, I keeps an eye out for 'em when they leaves the brewery just to make sure they're safe. But I also have an arrangement with Mister Luvian too. He ain't stupid, he told me once. He says he knows I'm probably up to things he don't want to know anything about. But that that might work for him, because if I know the bad sort of folks in Fairview, and they comes into the brewery, I can just lets him know, and they'll be escorted out. That way, ain't no villains and scum in his place of business and the brewery would be known as a reputable and safe place to go.

"And that's what I do for Luvian. But you – I sees you about, Mister Ronnie. Not as innocent as I thought at first. Couldn't believe mine eyes, I thought when I saw ya down by the docks one night.

"And Mister Ronnie, I give you credit, you're good – but what I ain't never figured out, is what you're doin' hittin' that bloody anvil. I watched ya for a while, tryin' to figure ya out, an' you was all respectable, nice, all-around apprentice from down the block, but I never did get a take on ya. So, I gave up. Imagine my surprise to see you in here tonight. Thievin', Mister Ronnie? I wouldn't a' taken ya for a thief. Or was you just followin' me?"

Ron had listened with some interest to Nick's story, but kept in mind that the story was nevertheless a deflection from the original question. To keep from giving information away, you can do a number of things, he thought, anger, enamor, flatter, frighten, tell a story – as Nick had just done – deflect with another question, even change the subject if possible. Some people are even able to feign illness – coughing, sneezing, fainting, fits.

"Nickolas, I do believe you and I may be of use to each other. You know I am more than I seem. You've been quite straightforward about your many uses and talents. I suggest we trade information." Ron let his suggestion trail off to see Nick's reaction.

"Hmmm." Nick stroked his chin thoughtfully. "The idea has possibilities, it does. You tell me your contact."

Ron snorted. "After you."

"Hmmm. It seems, then, Mister Ronnie, that we are at an impasse. It was a good idea, though." Nick started walking toward the window they'd both entered in.

Not only could Ron not afford to let Nick tell his contacts about his identity, and even break his cover, but Ron could not risk his own identity being discovered.

"I suggest you reconsider." He stood in front of the window.

Nick stared at him. "And why is that, Mister Ronnie?"

"For starters, I can go through all of the entirety of South Fairview, up right into Chandler Street. Any lock I find that has been 'picked,' will be replaced by the very best locks for free by Master Cradwick himself. In the interest, of course, of neighborhood safety and community." He watched Nick's face change. "That's an awful lot of locks, Nick. What say you now?"

Nick's eyes narrowed. "Fine." He scowled.
Ron smiled. "To the future exchange of information."

Ellia

Mister Ulmerton stepped aside as he walked in the door to let in the Captain. The Captain strode in with a jaunty step, his tail raised high in the air behind him.

"Oy, the Captain's back!" called one customer. He raised his pint to the Captain.

"Everyone salute the Captain!" called another. Most of them yelled "Cheers!" and held up salutes to the grey striped tomcat.

Ellia loved watching The Brew House customers salute the grey striped tomcat whenever he walked about the floor. They dropped pieces of bread for him or gave him a bit of a pat, while the Captain rubbed up against some of them. The Captain was something of a mascot for The Brew House and Tavern.

Ellia remembered when she first found him sitting outside. As soon as she had lifted him up, he had begun purring. Ellia knew her father was not fond of the dogs his patrons often brought inside with them, for they often occasionally made messes inside, or worse, fought with each other. But this was a cat, and it was cold outside....

She had hugged the cat close and brought him inside. "Please, Pappy? It's cold outside." And both of her sisters had held their breath and pet the cat, looking up at Pappy as well.

Pappy's glare softened, as it always did when Ellia begged him. "Fine. But make sure he's fed. And keep him from messing in my brewery!"

Magpie had snorted as she always did when Pappy gave in to Ellia, and Mum just smiled and shook her head up at him. Mum recognized how powerless he truly was, for whenever Ellia put her mind to something, she usually got it. Although it usually came with a *"Ah, bloody hell! Fine, then! Now get out of here before I change my mind!"* And Ellia would laugh and hug him tight and tell him how much she loved him.

Ellia and her sisters had squealed with delight, which alarmed the cat. Ellia had held him closer and crooned to him to calm him.

"What are we going to name you, cat?" she had questioned him as she held up the cat before her and looked into his green eyes. He had stared back at her doubtfully.

Pappy had then spoken up. "I've got the perfect name for him. Call him *Captain*." He grinned just a bit as if a private joke had struck him. Mum smacked his arm. Pappy had looked down at her and spread his hands out in feigned innocence. "What? I think it's the perfect name. Why not?"

Mollie had objected and offered up Fluffy for an alternative, and Hasley had suggested Stripe.

"No," Pappy's tone had been firm. "He may be your cat, but it's my bar. Captain it is."

Magpie had leaned over and scratched the cat on the head. He had immediately started purring. "Well, and why not. He'll make the rounds, and he'll keep the rats away."

Pappy had snorted and glanced at Mum. "Ain't that the truth." Then he had waved Ellia and her sisters out. "Well, go on, go on, out of my kitchen! And take that bloody cat with ya!" But Ellia and seen a faint smile on his face as he turned back to kneading his bread.

⁓

Ellia didn't know his name, but whatever it was, he stumbled with his empty pint up to the bar. He was in no condition to order anything but water. And she had a headache – tonight just seemed louder than usual, though for a busy night, it was no different than any other.

He made it to the bar, glad to have arrived so that he could lean on it. Ellia watched the drunk open his eyes as wide as he could. Likely he was seeing two or three of her right now and was trying to focus on at least one of her so that he could order. Ellia sucked in a breath for patience and presented him with her usual how-nice-to-see-you smile.

"What'll it be?" When Ellia was at her worst, her conversational tone and smile was at its best.

The drunk slapped the bar with his hand, and a cloud of ale breath drifted toward her. She held her breath in as she had countless times before.

"I'll have another ale!" He slammed his pint down on the bar. As with so many customers when drunk, he did not realize that he was shouting rather than ordering in a normal voice.

Ellia nodded and took the pint from him. "Mister, I think some tea might be best for you. Maybe you'd like some cider." She gave him a winning smile.

He frowned with confusion as he tried to decipher her suggestion. Too ale-sodden to process her gentle recommendation that he had drunk enough for the evening, he felt about on the bar for the empty pint glass he'd brought her.

Ellia flicked a quick glance about but did not see Tank. She sighed. He must still be upstairs helping Mum get rid of a belligerent customer. And she didn't hear Pappy behind her in the kitchen, which meant he was down in the cellar to get more ale. Well, then. She'd take care of the drunk herself.

"I said… I wanted me some… more ale!" The man's insistent tone implied that the worst was yet to come.

Ellia leaned across the bar, mindful of his stinking breath. "Listen, my friend. It's tea, or water. Choose."

Outraged, the drunk slurred, "You… don't get to decide… decide… what I… get to drink! And I! Wants me some ale!"

Ellia glared at the man. She looked down at the pitchers full of ale waiting to be distributed by Mollie and Hasley.

Then she picked up a pitcher and threw its entire contents into the drunk's face. "Good! You got ya some! Now get out of our bar!" Ellia spat.

Ice cold ale cascaded down the drunk's face. He tried to keep his eyes open, while his mouth gaped like a fish. His wet hair hung in wet, dripping, streams. Ellia stood with her hands on her hips, incensed and waiting for him to leave.

Unfortunately, he took a step and then slipped and fell on the floor. When he didn't get up, Ellia knew he had either passed out or hit his head. Either was fine with her, she thought as she took a towel and sopped up the ale that had landed on the bar.

Just then, Pappy burst through the louvered kitchen doors. "What was that? I heard a splash!"

Ellia turned and smiled brightly at him with all the innocence she could muster. "Just some ale that spilled on the floor, Pappy." She hoped he wouldn't walk around the bar to investigate. And that the drunk wouldn't suddenly stand up….

Pappy's brow furrowed and his head bowed. Those dark eyes of his regarded her, fixed and unblinking as he looked down his nose at her. He always seemed to *know* when she was hiding something. Ugh! Ellia loved her Pappy dearly, but she hated that look so! It was if he was peeling her apart like the layers of an onion, looking for the actual truth.

Just as Ellia wondered if he was going to question her further, Pappy's eyes narrowed and he sighed. He nodded and backed his substantial frame through the kitchen doors. Just as he had so many times before, Pappy was capitulating, preferring oblivion and ignorance to the actual truth.

Ellia let out her breath and glanced around. Still no Tank. So she rolled the slops bucket over and nudged the drunk out of the way.

"What's this?" Mags asked. She had come from downstairs and seen the drunk lying on the floor. Then she watched Ellia's face as she attempted to formulate a plausible excuse. She put a finger to Ellia's lips. "Never mind, pet, I don't want to know. Let's just get him out o' here."

They each picked the unconscious drunk up from beneath a shoulder and tossed him into the muddy street.

Mags clisp-clasped her hands. "You can mop up after 'im though, I've another kettle of stew to start up." She winked at Ellia. "You be more careful, girl." And she disappeared behind the kitchen doors.

Later into the evening, the noise level had risen substantially. Pappy was, of course, quite pleased, for they even had two exhausted customers staying in the attic tonight after a five-day trip from Hardewold.

It was rowdier than usual, and even Mum was working the floor tonight. Usually, Pappy had stopped making bread by now, but he decided to make several more loaves to feed the extra tenants who were going to be sleeping on the floor passed out later.

Ellia was tired. The drunk they'd thrown out in the street earlier had only served to sour her mood, though of course she kept her expression and voice cheerful, as always. It seemed that half of South Fairview had visited tonight at some point....

And then another drunk stumbled up to the bar, right to the seat where the last customer, a long-time patron, had just vacated. Ellia watched him warily. She'd already dealt with one drunk tonight, she was in no mood to exchange pleasantries with another. She glanced around for Tank but did not see him.

"Ah. A little one, aren't ya. Even better," called the man in an accent she was not familiar with. Mostly, only South Fairview folk came to The Brew House and Tavern, and occasionally, travelers from Shaw, even as far away as Hardewold. Was he from the North, then?

He stumbled up to bar. "You go on and head up to my room, little girl."

Some of the customers at the bar glanced over at him, and then at Ellia. Not all of them were long-term customers, but most of them knew that she was the innkeeper's daughter. Which, she sniffed, made her off limits. All of them knew that, and if her Pappy, or Tank heard this... arsehole, now....

Ellia said evenly, "I'm the innkeeper's daughter, and this isn't a brothel."

Naturally, Ellia and her sisters were accosted in such a manner by men upon occasion, since it was, by definition, a pub where men drank large quantities of ale that caused them to act fearlessly. Men often believed that the barmaids of The Brew House and Tavern were available for sport and personal enjoyment, as in other pubs, winesinks, taverns, and brothels, though Pappy and Tank discouraged such behavior immediately. On such rare occasions as when Pappy and Tank were unavailable to protect them, however, there was little recourse but to fend for themselves.

"I don't care... who you are. I said, get up in my room, girl, and wait for me there." The man's brown eyes stared expectantly at her. He was a man who was accustomed to having his orders followed. Then he grasped her forearm, which lay on the bar.

Ellia's mouth fell open as she stared at his hand. She jerked her arm free as if a snake had crawled around it.

"And I don't care who you are!" A boiling bowl of stew that Mags had left on the lower counter to cool was sitting in front of her, and she picked it up and threw the stew in the man's face.

He screamed in pain, clawing at his face. The other men sitting at the bar said nothing, though all their eyes grew wide. They each picked up their tankards and took a drink, and a few of them nodded, though the customer sitting nearest Ellia brushed a piece of carrot and celery off of his shoulder before he took a drink. None of them said a word, and they all ignored the man shrieking in pain behind him.

Ellia still did not see Tank or her Pappy, and the men were singing on the other side of the bar, so the man's shrieks were drowned out by their raucous song.

So Ellia left the bar and placed her hands on the man, who was dripping with hot stew. She turned him around and marched him toward the door. "And don't come back!" Ellia called after him one she had shoved him outside.

Ugh. Now she had stew on her arms and there was a trail of stew leading from the bar. She sighed. The slops bucket, twice in one night.

She was nearly finished swiping the mop back and forth when Tank sidled up next to her. He frowned at the floor, then at Ellia. "That's my job." Tank took the mop from her. He said nothing, but his face demanded an explanation.

Ellia did not feel like explaining. "It's just – flat out."

Tank rose an eyebrow and turned to look at the man who sat out in the street, crying and picking at his burned face. "Anything to do with him?" He jerked his head in the direction of the front door.

Ellia smiled faintly. "Maybe...?" Tank was someone else who was impossible to lie to.

Tank eyed the burned man in the muddy street, then looked at Ellia. "That there is not a returning customer."

"He better not be!" she flared.

"Like that, was he?" Tank dipped the mop in the slops bucket to rinse it. "Ellia, what did I tell you about that?"

She stared at him for a moment, then gave up. "He started it. He did, I promise." Tank had a way of drawing the truth out of you, even when you didn't want to say a word.

"But I've told you. If you can't handle a customer, and your Pap or me ain't around, then you just go –"

"Inside the kitchen," Ellia and Tank said in unison. "But I handled him just fine, didn't I? And at least I didn't punch him." She smiled a little at him. Tank had showed her how to hit, just in case she was ever in the Market Place and she needed to fight back.

Tank shook his massive head at her. "You go inside the kitchen. I've known you girls since you were all babies and I'm not going to see something happen to you now. What would you do if your ran your mouth and a customer had a knife?"

Ellia stared up at him. "Yell for you?" She smiled a little, hoping to coax Tank into a less serious mood.

He glared a little at her, then looked down at the floor he'd just swabbed. Then he leaned on the top of the mop handle, gazing out at the man sitting in the street. "Boiling hot stew. Wow."

"Yeah," Ellia sniffed. "Waste of good stew."

Tank rolled an eye at her and shook his head. "Well," he took in a big breath, "at least it wasn't ice cold ale. Hate to waste ale."

Ellia remained mute to that remark.

As Tank rolled the slop bucket about, something on the floor caught his eye. His eyebrows raised up. "That's a lot of ale here, stuck to the bar here." He cocked his head.

Ellia smiled and said, "Hate to waste ice cold ale."

Tank rolled his eyes at that and mopped up whatever ale she had missed earlier, then disappeared with the slops bucket into the kitchen.

_____

Near the end of the evening, as the pub was emptying out, Ronnie sat down at the bar. Ellia genuinely liked Ronnie, for he was around her age.

"So," and he smiled. "What's with that gent?" He tossed his head over his shoulder in the direction of the street. Was that jerk still out there? Why wouldn't he just leave?

Ellia rolled her eyes.

"Heard he got burnt a bit." Ronnie snickered and shook his head.

"Yep, well that can sometimes happen when you piss off the barstaff," Ellia announced airily.

Ronnie's eyebrows shot up. "Is that right?" He stared over his shoulder for a bit, then looked back at Ellia. "He'll have some boils for a bit, but he'll get past it. His pride, though, can't speak to that."

Ellia sniffed. "I could have punched him."

Ronnie stared. "Punched him? You? A girl?"

"Tank's a veteran and he taught me how to punch if I ever get into trouble," Ellia confessed.

"Well, forgive me, but isn't that what Tank's for, to make sure you don't get into trouble?" asked Ronnie.

"Aye, he is, but he was upstairs and Pappy was downstairs, and him –" Ellia nodded in the direction of the jerk sitting in the road – "he was sitting right where you are now."

"So, this barstool is sort of consecrated, a holy barstool of sorts." Ronnie glanced down beneath the bar to study the stool, then his head popped back up above the bar. "No stew here."

Ellia laughed. Ronnie always made people smile. She needed the laugh.

"And remind me never to piss you off! Punching people and such," Ronnie whistled.

Somewhat embarrassed now, Ellia confessed, "It was only once. The Captain was sitting on the bar up here, and a man sitting next to him said he wanted to make the Captain part of his stew. He even put a knife out on the bar. So I punched him." Ronnie was laughing. "Pappy made me apologize. But he's not allowed back here, either." Then she held up her right hand and flexed it. "I had to ice my hand for a week!" They both laughed.

"Well, darlin', I'm glad to see you smiling. You know, *turn off the light with a light heart.*" He smiled. "But I'm actually here to pay up tonight's tab, so...." Ronnie laid out all of his coppers for the evening with a few clinks onto the bar. "I shall *depart* with a light heart."

On his way out the door, he winked and waved. Ellia felt much better now that she had talked to him.

Tyndie

She arrived just slightly out of breath. Only Manda was there. Good, no one to berate her.

Manda eyed her for a moment, then she set the silver tea cup she'd been polishing aside. Standing up, she said, "Tyndie, girl, I've made my mind up on you."

Tyndie immediately froze.

"No, no, relax. I've decided I'm going to help you out." Manda smiled and beckoned Tyndie closer. "Now come with me."

Intrigued, Tyndie followed Manda. No one had offered to help her since she had begun, unless she counted The Shrew, and that wasn't really help, she had been instructed to train Tyndie.

Manda looked back at Tyndie. "Well, come along. We don't have all afternoon, do we, girl?"

Tyndie quickened her pace to keep up with Manda.

"I have decided to teach you something that will help you far beyond your skipping up and down the stairs and dashin' around corners. And mind you," Manda's voice dropped as they entered a main corridor, "no one else knows about it. Not any of the other girls, and certainly not Lynza."

Manda stopped and glanced both ways at a major thruway. They she looked back at Tyndie. "Does it sound like somethin' you're interested in, Tyndie? Because if I teach it to you, you can't show it to anyone else."

Mutely, Tyndie nodded, though she suddenly had a thousand questions to ask.

"All right, then. Come along." Manda led Tyndie into a hallway that had no special rooms but a set of steps into a foyer.

Manda beckoned her down the steps, then stopped. "Mind you, I didn't teach this to Lynza or no one else, an' that was for a reason. Some people just aren't head smart," and Manda tapped her temple. "And others you just plain can't trust. Then there's some who are both," she mused, and Tyndie thought Manda had a few people spring to mind.

She reached into her apron pocket and pulled out a piece of chalk. With a small *snap*, Manda forced it in two and gave the other half to Tyndie. "You're gonna need this. And don't lose it. If you ever need more, let me know, quietlike, and I'll find you some. Now, keep it hidden in your pocket." Manda rolled the piece of chalk into Tyndie's hand and slipped her own into her apron pocket.

Tyndie tried not to let her bewilderment show, but she was completely baffled. What was Manda showing her? And the chalk? Manda continued on.

"You're not afraid of small spaces, are ya, girl? Hm, ya've probably never been in one small enough to say. Only one way to find out. And whatever happens next, you have to be silent. Understand me, Tyndie? Do you?"

Tyndie nodded.

Manda studied her for a moment. "Good. Understand now that you'll be the only other person who knows about this. Besides me and your Auntie Renne. Now –"

And she felt the mortar along the wall, pressing it. Suddenly, there was a minute *click*....

And the wall moved before Tyndie's eyes.

Tyndie's mouth fell open. The stone wall had turned outward, revealing a whole new hallway behind that which they were standing in.

Manda turned around to observe Tyndie's reaction. She laughed quietly behind her hand. Then she pulled Tyndie inside, and pushed the stone door back into place. As she was about to shut the door, she paused and glanced at Tyndie. "Unless you'd like to head back upstairs...?"

Tyndie shook her head vehemently. She was fascinated. There were even lanterns lit far down the dank hallway. She was speechless. Finally, she looked up at Manda.

"This, Tyndie, was the secret to your Auntie's and mine success. And mind you... no one ever taught it to us like I'm showing it to you now. We came across it by sheer chance, and nothing more. Of course, we were not much older than you are now, and ah, we were just wee slips of girls back then." Manda sighed and patted her belly. "Of course, we'd never have seen it if we hadn't noticed a manservant we had oh such a fondness for.... He had the nicest –"

Tyndie coughed. She in no way wanted to hear the reminiscences of her Auntie and Manda as girls when they were in love with some manservant! Ew! Especially when she was standing here in a – a secret passage of some sort? Certainly a secret passage took precedence over reminiscing on long ago heart throbs?

Manda looked down at Tyndie and chuckled. "Just you wait, Tyndie girl. One day, you'll be my age and you'll be thinking about that young Squire who made your heart go pitty-pat every time he passed ya." And she chuckled some more.

Tyndie nodded agreeably, but as soon as Manda turned her back, she thought, *Ha, not bloody likely!*

"Now here," and she handed Tyndie a tallow candle. "Always leave a candle in here somewhere. And always take one in with ya – can you imagine being all alone in the dark in these tunnels?" Manda shuddered at the thought.

"Someone's still using these old halls," Manda mused, or there the sconces wouldn't be lit." Manda pointed up ahead to the light down the hall.

Once they arrived at the wall sconce, Manda lit Tyndie's candle and her own.

She followed Manda through the corridor, taking in her surroundings with awe. Moisture from somewhere in the walls caused a dank smell to pervade the tunnel. The flickering of Tyndie's candle caused shadows to jump and dance as she crept after Manda. Tyndie let her hand trail along the rough, damp walls until a spider hopped onto her hand. Tyndie managed to keep from yelping with shock, but jumped back and shook it off her hand.

Her heart in her mouth, she hurried to catch up to Manda.

"Here we are, Tyndie girl." And they stopped, for there were four hallways to choose from. "Me and your Auntie, we called this the Hub, for it took us just about anywhere we need to go. That way," and Manda pointed, "will bring you out right near the kitchens, and I'll show you. That way there," Manda showed Tyndie one of the darkened staircases, "takes ya straight up to the Ladies Bowery, but you won't be servin' them, at least not yet, so you won't need to take that way.

"Now that stairway, you don't never want to go up. It goes into the Lord's Quarters, where all the courtiers are quartered. And you ain't got the first lick o' business being up there. Not now, and not ever." Manda turned a stern eye on Tyndie. She wouldn't look away until Tyndie nodded dutifully.

"Right, then. That corridor only takes you down to the middle of the second floor, not a room, but a well-placed passage, lots o' traffic, so mind your comin's and goin's if you go through there.

"And always use the chalk."

Tyndie pointed at an "x" marked by chalk against the Lords' Quarters stairwell. "Like that?"

Manda inspected it closer with the light of her candle. "That's an old mark," she mused.

Tyndie made as if to erase it with her hand.

"No, no, don't. Might be someone will look for it again. Leave it. We use the chalk on the outsides of the corridors. To show where the passage doors are, as they're invisible on the outside. You'll get to remember them, but usually there's a bitty piece of chalk on the floor in front of the door to mark where the door opens. Keep your eyes open the next time you explore the castle, and you'll see them. This Hub network isn't the only group of tunnels, Tyndie, there's lot of them. I still see chalk now and again, though I ain't lookin' for it, and in places I never figured it for. Me and your Auntie only used these few here."

"But Manda, who designed them all?"

"That I can't say. HarCourt Castle was built hundreds of years ago. I expect this one here was meant to help smuggle the lords and ladies out if the Castle came under attack. But there's lots of these here tunnels. Really, I think the few people who use them are just waitstaff, manservants and folks like me and you who have to serve their lords and ladies with speed. And I haven't seen no one around these entrances in years. But you just be careful in here. Always take chalk, in case you get lost, and to find the door on the outside."

"But what about finding the doors on the inside?"

"Simple enough. The wall sconce is lit on the opposite side of the wall. You'll see. Every time a wall sconce is lit on the opposite side, that's where there's a door. But, and hear me now, Tyndie, you listen and you watch to make sure no one is around before you go in and out of these tunnels. Make sure no one ever sees you."

"And here's what I'll tell ya last, and ya remember this if you remember nothin' else."

Manda took her by the shoulders and looked her in the eyes.

"We all know that sayin', *Watch the wall for its eyes and listen to the wall for its ears.* But maybe now that sayin' makes a little more sense, aye?"

Hosh

Hosh never minded the fog out west in the islands, for at least the winds pushed it inward toward land. But here in the Riverlands, the fog just settled over you like and hung there, trying to smother you like a wet wool blanket, he mused. Damn fog was wetter, somehow, too. That come with the climate. Muggy and muddy – made for a lousy combination.

Plenty of sailors said, "Hah! You think these Riverlands is bad, you should sail down to the Swamplands. Now thems is muggy." And they would detail all sorts of interesting stories about horrible smelling mud that sucked you down and wouldn't let you back up, long, ridge-backed land monsters with pointed teeth that swallow a man whole, snakes as long as a mast and thick as your waist, and not a breath of wind, not ever.

Hosh could always tell if a man was lying, and most of these men was just blowin' the same old wind at the same old sail. Men who had actually made the trip kept to themselves, didn't want no one to hear about it. Makin' that trip was near impossible, so tellin' folks about it would be next thing akin to askin' fleas to jump on rats. They didn't want word to reach the wrong ear.

But as long as there was water and a paddle, Hosh would be standing at the helm. He had a good nose for rotten fish, and Storden reeked of it, and growing worse. Hosh didn't know what it was, but he hadn't served the most of the Twenty Years War just to retire in a neutral country whose seas were starting to get rocky.

He wondered times when he steered this ferry up and down the Rosh about what he'd left behind. Not much. Couple of grave markers for his brothers and parents. Somewhere out there was that son, and now a grandson, maybe even more. But hell, Hosh had been stationed on an island that was little more than a fort – that was Anchor Island. Archer Island no different. No one lived there but navy men when they weren't at sea.

Just five years into the Navy, docked at Leedsport, Hosh had himself a night of fun at a local pub and a bit more than fun with a local girl. They docked again three months later. Her name had been Shellie. She goes by Shella now she's a grown woman now, Hosh mused.

The girl was frantic, found him at the docks and told his she was with his child. Beggin' for Hosh to marry her. Hosh was bewildered. Marry? A child? He couldn't think straight at the time. He believed the girl that it was his child, for he'd taken her first time easily enough and no doubtin'.

But Hosh hadn't no money for a hearth and a home, none even for himself, much less for a wife and a babe. He never was proud of himself for turnin' her down. Quite hated hisself for it, when he was past a few pints or three, in fact. But so it was. He wasn't so old hisself, hardly past twenty and no one to tell him, "Hosh, ya fucker, marry the girl," for his parents and brothers died at the start of the Twenty Years War when Ambsellon and Ormon soldiers marched through Storden.

Storden was neutral to all the countries, for hundreds of years now, and didn't contribute nor assist no country, just imported and exported a bit. In war times, no one was supposed to harm any Storden citizens, but that didn't stop the Ambsellon and Ormon troops from takin' what they pleased in his parish and then burnin' it.

His dad and brothers had fought back and they'd got killed for it. His mum sent him off toward the cliffs, tellin' him to *"Run, Jom, run!"* And then an arrow caught her straight in the back. Her eyes had just stopped seein' suddenly. Hosh sighed. He could barely remember what her eyes looked like anymore. Sad, that.

So Hosh had run, just as his mum told him to, for what was left to him in a burned down, empty parish with no family or villagers? The first building he saw in Haliport, the next port past Leevesport, to was a naval yard. Hosh had been fourteen, and full of guts and fire when he made his decision. Who could burn him down at sea on a neutral Stordish ship? Hosh entered boldly and claimed that he was sixteen, for to join the military, men had to be of age.

The recruiter eyed him and raised his eyebrows, clearly doubting that Hosh was of age. But he glanced at the soot and blood on Hosh's shirt and said, "All right, son, if you're sure. This ain't gonna be no apprenticeship, you know. Just so's you're sure." Hoss had written his name with clumsy letters on the parchment in reply.

He'd sent Shellie a good share of his wages whenever he came into port. When he next came into Leevesport, he found out that she'd married a man. Hosh wasn't proud of himself for sneaking up to their house in the dark and peeking in like some sort of thief, but Shellie's husband – well, he looked like a good enough bloke.

That rankled at Hosh for some reason. More so, for he'd been holding Hosh's son. Hosh's boy. There he was, his son, in another man's arms. And then Shellie walked past, and her pregnant. Hosh nearly ran from the house, where he damn near lost his belly against a tree across the dirt street. He'd made his choice. That was his fault, his choice. Best he steer away from it altogether.

Hosh never did stay away completely. Times were he'd sneak past on occasion. Hell if that boy of his didn't look just like his oldest brother Krighton. And now Hosh's son had a babe of his own, just a wee boy.

Hosh shook his head. Nothin' that way but sheer quicksand, sheer quicksand. Hosh had seen the babe just twice, enough to see his boy was goin' to be a good father.

And then he left for the East Riverlands. He had no ties to Storden, after all. Nor did he have ties here to the East. He'd just packed up what he'd felt like taking with him and set off, figuring on stopping when he felt like it was time to. And he took the ferry up the Silver River, straight up into the Rosh. A river wasn't an ocean, but it was still water, Hosh had thought at the time, and Romeny was a safe enough country, bordered by three other strong countries. And there he had hung up his boots.

Easy enough to get a job at the docks. Even easier piloting the ferry up and down the Rosh at night. They couldn't keep a captain on the night ferry for longer than a few weeks. Hosh took on the R.C.S. Night Crawler easy enough. He knew he was still a young enough man, by all standards, that he could take a younger wife, give her a babe or two. His wages were plentiful enough. But Hosh just didn't think that now, at his age, he could stand the squallin' of a babe and havin' to change it.... Hosh didn't know -

The Night Crawler hit something to port and she rolled over it. Hosh sighed. Another bloody barrel....

He stepped down, hearing the river waves make exception as the Night Crawler slipped over the barrel. Hosh leaned out on the starboard edge, net in hand, for the barrel to surface. Depending on what was in it, it was going to be wicked hard to pull up by himself....

Oh hell. Another one. Not a barrel. Did these bloody fucking idiots not know that wood fucking floats, he asked himself. And it had been such a quiet night.

Hosh tossed the anchor, glad no one was aboard but himself. Then he took the boat hook and pulled it in. Roped to the barrel was another dead body. Hosh was glad no one was on this stretch of the river or they'd certainly be in horror. He netted in the barrel and dragged the rest of the poor bastard aboard.

Hosh shook his head. Someone, or someones, had taken care to open the barrel and stuff some stone brick in it, for they certainly didn't want this one found. But the barrel top had eventually opened and moved about on the river bottom, best Hosh could tell from the condition of the bloke's face. His face was quite a bit nibbled off by fish, but all the same, the skin below his clothing was relatively intact yet. But bloody hell, the man stank – shit! River mud is river mud and it always stinks, no matter what it comes up with, he thought.

Hosh rubbed his face and grimaced. Riverweed attached to the man's boots trailed water down the planks of his ferry. Damn it, he'd have to spend extra time swabbing the deck now for mud. Hosh never expected when he retired from the Storden Royal Navy that he'd ever swab a deck again, and damn sure not for a fucking dead body, but here it was, another one.

Hosh poked at him with the end of the boat hook. Nah. At this point, he just didn't care no more. He remembered the first few floaters. The first guy, he thought, well, he was just one unlucky son-of-a-bitch. Not for just his death, but what happened after. For Hosh, after he'd made his run, he'd gotten off at North Rosh Port and hung about for the next day. The town was all abuzz about the floater. But it was what they all said that smelled the fishiest.

For the port's Medical Man, or whatever this country called them, had announced that he died of sheer drowning after being drunk. And Hosh knew damn better than that, for he'd pulled him out of the river. He'd seen enough floaters and dead bodies aboard ship with stab wounds to know just exactly how that man had died. And he'd died of a nasty gut wound. His clothing wasn't terribly bloodstained, either, and he hadn't been eaten up much, nor too stiff, so he hadn't been up the Rosh too far. Clothing was of decent quality, too. Somebody missed that man. But Hosh knew better than to say a word.

About a month later, another floater turned up. Bloke had been strangled, best Hosh could tell. He netted him aboard and into a burlap sack, and in front of the widened eyes of the passengers that night. He expected they went home with nightmares. But that bloody bloke, he'd been strangled, sure as shit. His eyes bulged out and his neck purpled all about in a ring, he hadn't been in the water long. Fish had nibbled at him a bit, his nose and part of his eyes gone, but he wasn't too stiff yet either.

At first, Hosh thought maybe it was the Castle Grates. But he eventually dismissed the idea, for really they only wanted what was in the barrels, and they stayed to the docks. He'd never known them to kill folks. Maybe once or twice had he heard of them threatening anyone, but that was the only violence he'd heard of. What's more, the Castle Grates, if they had beat anyone bloody, or even killed some unlucky bloke, they'd want the notoriety for it, they'd put the bloke out before the Castle with a note, for all to see, not dump him in the river in the dead of night.

So Hosh didn't know if these poor bastards were coming from the east or west side of the Rosh, but his gut told him it was the west side.

Of late, nearly every three weeks floaters turned up. Some of them were tied to barrels. Land folk didn't understand – you don't tie things you want to sink to things that float. Fucking rafts float, boats, ships all float. Why would you tie a dead body to something... that floats? Idiots. Tie them to stone.

Hosh dumped them on the east side of the river. He had no idea why people were getting killed and tossed in the river as they were, but it was happening more and more. If it got much worse, Hosh just might pack up, somewhere where it didn't smell so fishy....

Topher

Patience in all things, counseled The One God to his earthly children. Topher sighed and plucked a brown hair from his head. He studied all one inch of it. Still, after one month, his hair was the one thing holding him back. Topher glared at it and flicked it away.

He had been following a rivulet, a brook of some sort that he knew was not on any map, but it was headed northwest. As long as he camped next to water, Topher was able to provide for himself.

He used his old Order robe as a tent, draping it over sticks. While Topher wanted nothing to do with the Order whatever, and wanted to burn the robes, he grudgingly admitted the robes themselves were only cloth and served to shield him from the cold and the elements. Topher figured if anyone ever searched him and asked him about the robes, he would tell them that he found them back in Harper Hill in the woods.

Mostly, Topher traveled by night and slept by day, though upon occasion, if he was near a farm, he would steal out at twilight and pluck vegetables from the rows, usually carrots and cabbages. He found some beets once, but he had to push them back in the ground, for he had never been able to stomach beets, not boiled, raw, nor any other way. Topher was not hungry enough yet to force beets down.

Last week, he found some wild strawberries growing in the woods and, after sitting in the center of the entire patch, Topher gorged himself on them without an ounce of guilt. In fact, his chin and fingernails stained red with strawberry juice, he pulled all the rest he found and dropped them in his rucksack for later.

He had become quite a gifted thief, however, and quite ashamed of himself for this new art of his. Topher was even covering his tracks in the dirt behind him. For from village to village, he was sure people had to talk. He only stole two or three eggs from each village, some vegetables from the farm, and now and again, a shirt or two, so that just in case someone spied him leaving, he'd be able to change clothing quickly.

But Topher never forgot the day when he was walking alongside the woods line, with the sun at his back. Suddenly, he decided to whistle. He couldn't fold his lips the right way to whistle. He had forgotten how to whistle. Odd, that. Topher tried a few more times. Once he was sure his lips were set right, he started to force wind through his mouth and succeeded in spraying spittle all over his chin.

Topher looked to the sky. Was this The One God's amusement for Topher not taking his Final Oath? Showering himself with spit? He wiped his face with the back of his hand. He tried a few more times unsuccessfully. Topher felt the back of his neck heat with embarrassment.

Just as Topher was about to give up, a watery, single note sounded. Topher's eyes widened. He hadn't whistled since he was child. He whistled several times more, though it sounded pathetic. He'd whistled better as a child.

Then Topher suddenly realized something. He was no longer a child... but no longer was he a member of The Silent Order....

"My... name... is... *Topher.*"

It was the first time he'd used his voice in over six years.

Ishbel

Gobin stuck his fat head into her pavilion. Ishbel was just swiping a linen cloth across her stomach, exasperation fueling her movements.

"Got a complaint aboutcha'," Gobin commented. His face demanded an explanation.

Ishbel sniffed. "Didja' know. Was it the bloke who just did this?" And she turned around so that Gobin could observe the bite mark on the back of her right shoulder, where blood was still seeping. She shook her head with disgust. Would that the bastard had bit the other shoulder, and maybe he'd have bitten one of her scars off, or her tattoo.

"Bloody cannibal. Shoulda' let me know as he was leavin' and I'd've taken care of him." He picked up her soiled linens.

Ishbel held back her scorn, for short, plump Gobin was not a match for most customers. Thus, he kept a wooden club at his side, though Ishbel doubted even that was effective. But it lent Gobin a sense of dominance, and so she and her peers said nothing of it, or at least not to his face.

"Sop it up and then go to the baths." He turned and walked out.

The baths? Ishbel considered. They bathed each week, and she had just been two days ago. Gobin was in a generous mood today. Ishbel could not fault Gobin for seeing to their needs. Fresh linens for cleaning themselves from each customer, always water, and decent meals each day.

But of course, this was to line his pockets, and to do so, his merchandise must be in perfect working order, Ishbel frowned as she dabbed at the blood on her shoulder. She had heard horror tales of other whores…. They spent the time they were not with customers chained to each other, living in cages like animals, whipped, water from buckets thrown upon them to bathe, flea-ridden even.

Those were just horror stories, though, Ishbel mused as she sat inside the hot spring. Steam rose into the air from the water. Ishbel always found the idea of a natural bath amazing. Several other people sat inside the spring with various expressions of repose.

Ishbel rubbed the lavender petal oil that Gobin provided for them into her skin and then slipped slowly into the hot water. It always took her breath away at first, but as she emerged herself, she relaxed, relishing how the water calmed her taut muscles.

Until the water sank into her open wound, and she sat up immediately, her eyes widened from the sudden sting. Ishbel held her breath and sank beneath the water for a few moments, swishing her hair around. She could almost pretend that her whole life was different down here, where it was warm and safe, no pavilion, no bed, no Gobin, no people….

But her breath always ran out, as did her dream.

Ishbel returned to her pavilion and laid down on her mattress to nap. They always took rest as they could, and one of the first things a whore learned was to fall asleep quickly, for she never knew when her next customer would arrive, day or night.

— ⚬ —

The rustle of her pavilion curtain woke her. Either it had been a slow day, or Gobin had allowed her time to rest, for she'd been napping since late morning and the position of the sun in the sky told it was late afternoon.

Two silvers clinked upon her bureau. Ishbel rolled over on her mattress and hid her surprise, for the nameless man who had visited her a month ago stood before her now.

Ishbel immediately thought of the silver she had hidden as she raised up on one elbow.

He eclipsed the sunlight streaming in from the top of her. "Napping?"

"Resting," Ishbel said. It implied a less lazy disposition, for napping gave the idea that she was not skilled enough to have a steady stream of customers.

Mister Nameless nodded and allowed his rucksack to slide to the ground next to her bed. He was still wearing the same sort of clothes as before, Ishbel noted.

He studied her with a cocked head for a moment. Then he sat down next to her and began to pull off his boots. Ishbel returned his scrutiny surreptitiously, though she doubted he was completely unaware of her covert appraisal.

Mister Nameless – for what else was she to call him? – turned to look at her. His eyebrows furrowed with intelligent curiosity. "What do you see when you look at me?"

Ishbel smiled faintly. Many men asked that question, always the same, usually phrased in different words. She was wont to answer honestly, but if she knew the truth would upset them, she would lie and give them a wonderful impression of themselves. If they only wanted to hear a story they could leave with that helped them believe in themselves, that strengthened their confidence, then she gave them that. Ishbel long ago hated that question. She had a number of wonderful replies that she just changed slightly, depending upon the man. Such a useless question.

But this man wasn't looking for a confidence builder, nor someone to reflect back his strength to him. He was looking for a description. Mister Nameless never ceased to amaze her, she'd say that.

Ishbel crawled across the bed to sit in front of him. She took him gently by the shoulders. He held up a hand in warning.

"No, no, just –" And she waited while he finished removing his second boot. Then she turned him gently about on the bed so he was facing forward.

Ishbel held her hands up in front of Mister Nameless so that he could see her actions as innocent only. She then reached out a finger and traced his face.

"Your face – it is, tanned, windworn. Wrinkled," she told him, "but not from laughter. From squinting." She pushed back some blond, sun-streaked hair from his face and tucked it behind an ear. "Lightened from the sun. You are outdoors often, though your hair is usually darker."

Ishbel lined his mouth with two of her fingers. He tried to pull away. "Not enough laughter, no laugh lines here. A strong jaw." She ran the top of her hand under his chin. The bristle there had grown beyond stubble but not long enough for a beard. "You prefer to stay clean-shaven, but either you don't have the chance often enough to shave, or you think it best to appear scruffy as you do now."

Mister Nameless raised an eyebrow at this last assessment, but said nothing.

Ishbel pulled the neck of his tunic aside lightly with a finger. She thought he would jump but it appeared he was used to her touch now. "As often as you are out in the sun, you are not dressed in the clothing of the nobility, or at least not often enough, for your tan line –" and she traced her finger down his tan across his collarbone – "matches the tunic you're wearing now.

"Your clothing is of good quality, not of the nobility, but sturdy. Your boots, good quality, if sandy, a bit dusty." She raised a slight eyebrow at the sand on the floor. "All the same color clothing – neutral, made to fade in. Except, perhaps, this dark vest...? Which could hide you in the darkness...?"

Ishbel stopped and stared into Mister Nameless's light brown eyes.

He nodded slowly. "Extremely perceptive." He studied her face. "For how long will two silvers last me?" he asked, shading his eyes beneath an upraised palm.

"Two hours." Interesting. Ishbel was curious as to what sort of man Mister Nameless would be, and almost sad that she at last would find out, for she had enjoyed trying to figure him out.

"Is there a way to shade the sun?"

"Of course." Ishbel stood up and pulled the reed blinds down from across the bed. She didn't care for the afternoon sun herself, but it was always the customer's choice.

While her back was turned to Mister Nameless, he asked, "What's that? On your back?"

She had nearly forgotten, but turned with a desultory smile. "Just my marks of enslavement." Ishbel looked at him through lowered lashes, hoping to dissuade his attention.

He frowned and pointed. "Not those. The other shoulder. It wasn't there before."

Ishbel blinked. How had he known that?

He watched as she tried to formulate a plausible explanation. Then he shook his head. "I'm sure I don't want to know." Then he rummaged around in his rucksack. He came up with a small vial. "That will likely scar if you don't attend to it." He tossed the vial to her across the pavilion.

Ishbel surprised herself by catching it, unawares as he'd caught her.

"Keep it. I'll buy more. There's plenty of it out there –" and he swept a hand toward the rest of the Pavilion.

Ishbel nodded once in gratitude. Gobin did not allow them to accept gifts, but this one she thought she would keep, for, after all, it would keep her fruit from bruising....

Now that his boots were off, Mister Nameless swung his legs up onto her bed. Ishbel slid up next to him, assuming her best pretense.

Mister Nameless sighed as he looked at her. He took hold of her wrist with a gentle hand. "Under ideal circumstances, I would greatly enjoy," and he let his eyes run down her body, "availing myself of what I am sure are considerable talents. But.

"These are not ideal circumstances." Mister Nameless grimaced. "Do you know what I want when I come here?"

Ishbel felt the ruse was over and so she sat up and looked at him, waiting expectantly for him to continue.

"I want a place to be invisible, where no one will know me, where I can just – lay back for an hour or two and be – safe. Does that sound odd to you?"

Odd, of course it was odd, Ishbel had never heard of such a thing. Yet it was his earnestness that caught her, and she schooled her facial expression and demeanor into one that would not offend him.

"You say two hours?"

Ishbel nodded.

"Then… wake me half hour before I must leave, for I have paperwork to ready." Mister Nameless's eyes searched her face. "Do you agree?"

She nodded, at a loss for words.

"Good." And he laid down next to her. Within just minutes, Mister Nameless was deeply asleep.

Ishbel hated to wake him. She'd never seen someone fall so deeply asleep so quickly. She had so many questions, and she knew she'd never get a single answer for any of them. People were hunting this man, so much so that he found safety in her pavilion. And yet the worn pommel and swordbelt next to his rucksack told her that he had no trouble defending himself….

"You're watching me sleep."

Ishbel smiled a little. What a puzzle he was.

"Only debating how to wake you," she said quietly.

Mister Nameless opened his eyes. He looked at Ishbel, then all around her pavilion. "A half hour yet?"

She nodded.

"Very good then."

Ishbel watched as he straightened a number of parchments from his rucksack, then pulled his boots on.

As he stood up, he pulled a silver from inside his vest and handed it to Ishbel. It flashed in the sun.

She stood up beside him and looked up at him. Then she rolled her hand over the silver. "I did nothing. Keep it."

A slight smile lifted the side of Mister Nameless's mouth. "Exactly." He thought for a moment, then looked about her pavilion. "For your continued silence. And, if not for your 'service,' then for your… companionship." He stalked across her pavilion and, feeling about the top wooden beam, he found the other silver. He placed the second silver there.

"Good will go with you," she murmured.

Mister Nameless nodded shortly as he slipped between her pavilion curtains.

Suddenly, Ishbel was brought back to reality. Gobin would be appearing in seconds. She poured water on some linens and threw them into the collection basket. Next, Ishbel mussed her hair and her veils.

Out in the Pavilion, Ishbel heard the faint voice of Mister Nameless telling Gobin on his way past, "Best I've ever had! Best girl yet!"

Ishbel smiled a bit.

Gobin came in then. "Satisfied bloke, sang your praises." He picked up Ishbel's linen basket and watched as Ishbel straightened her hair. "What'd you do for him? Couldn't shut up about ya out there."

"Oh – well. He was easy enough. Let him do all the talking, he had most of the bed. He even passed out for a few there – exhausted."

Ishbel didn't look at Gobin as she told him this, she was rearranging her veils. But she knew it would never occur to him that a whore would ever lie to him.

"Well done, well done," applauded Gobin. "If he comes through again, I'll send him straight to ya."

Ishbel hoped so. For he would need a safe place to stay.

Munsolrysche

"Bring me *that* one!" He pointed toward the red head and pulled his fur farther up around his shoulders. Sometimes he cared if it hid his stomach, and other times he did not. It wasn't as if anyone was going to say the first word to him about it.

The servant looked at him with a mixture of fear and concern. "Which… which one would that be?" His circumspectness was disgusting.

Munsolrysche told him, "The *redhead*, you farking fool! Are you deaf?"

The servant looked out upon the floor of the Great Hall where numerous women covered the floor of the Great Hall, most of them wearing only fur coats, all dancing to minstrel music.

Plainly frightened, the servant left. Good, Munsolrysche rolled his eyes. Maybe he'd find a set of balls out there….

Just then, another servant showed at his shoulder. "If it please you, there are several redheads on the floor. Which one would you like, Your Majesty?"

Munsolrysche glared at this new interruption at first but then backed down. He did like redheads. The more of them, the better. But where was the one he'd had his eye on? He stood up and concentrated, searching the floor for the redhead he wanted. Be damned, he thought, there were at least four reddies out there. There!

Munsolrysche grabbed the servant's elbow and he pointed. "That one, there! With her titties hanging out! I fucked her once before," he announced as he sat back down on his throne. "She had a cunt like fire, ha ha!" he directed this last comment to the lord sitting nearest him.

Could be he was drunk but it didn't matter a fucking bit. He rose a toast to Lord WhatsHisName. "To Reddies!"

The lord returned his toast with a rousing tribute, and they both drank down the rest of their goblets.

"Ah. Much better." Munsolrysche signaled for more wine and saw his reddie being escorted up the hall to him. The night was about to get much, much better. "And there she is." He turned to Lord WhatsHisName in a fit of good will and asked, "You want one? There's two or three more out there, you can have one."

The lord leaned over and said loudly enough to be heard over the minstrel music, "I'm married!"

Munsolrysche stared at him for a moment. What had marriage to do with fucking? "I didn't ask if you were married, I asked if you wanted a reddie for the night. Oh, bloody hell, ya fuckin bastard, I'll keep them for myself!"

Just as his reddie was stepping foot toward the front of the Great Hall, Nabol appeared at his side. Nabol – that was never a good sign. Munsolrysche would dismiss him right away.

"Your Majesty," whispered Nabol in Munsolrysche's ear.

"Nabol?"

"Yes, Your Majesty?"

"Look around you, what do you see."

Nabol did not look around but responded, "Dancing, Sire."

"Aye, that's right. And Nabol, there's a reddie walking up right now as we speak who's going to –"

"Your Majesty, I apologize, but this is something I believed you should hear. Right away."

Munsolrysche's eyes narrowed. "Nabol –"

Nabol whispered in his ear. "Ambsellon has been moving against Romeny. We just got word from Romeny."

Munsolrysche's celebratory mood deflated immediately. He stared up at Nabol.

"Do you trust it? Who's the source?"

"It came direct from the Palace, with the Castle seal." Nabol stared at him, oblivious of the joyous atmosphere. "Come see the message for yourself, Your Majesty."

"Damn." Munsolrysche stood up from the table. At that very second, his reddie appeared before him. Ah, fuck. One half of him was ready to stay, of that there was no doubt. Of all the fucking times….

"You, stay and wait for me, I have a quick meeting and then I'll be back." He tore his eyes away from her. "Don't let her leave. If the meeting lasts longer than the dancing, send her to my rooms." His servants bowed and murmured various forms of acquiescence.

"All right," King Munsolrysche snarled when he entered his study. "Let's see what that bastard Hewart has been sneaking around doing! Fucking Ambsellon!"

And Nabol handed him the unrolled pigeon parchments.

"'Bared the bear, look for cub in the cave beside the spring?' What the fuck is that supposed to mean?"

"I would guess, Majesty, that it is encoded," offered Nabol.

"Of course it's fucking encoded, Nabol! People don't go around talking like that normally, do they! They don't say, *'dicked the dick'* or –"

King Munsolrysche slid into a chair and held his head in his hands. "Bloody hell," he mumbled as he screwed his eyes shut. Opening them, he said, "Never thought the day would come when our closest ally would stab us in the back."

"And it doesn't do that I'm drunk on top of it." He stood up on drunken, unsteady feet and stared at Nabol. "Who else knows of these?" King Munsolrysche held the pigeon parchments up.

Nabol stared at him directly. "No one but you and I, Your Majesty."

"Not my wife?"

Nabol kept the same implacable expression in place as he replied, "No, Your Majesty, Her Majesty the Queen knows nothings of these."

King Munsolrysche was drunk but he still heard an unspoken *"yet"* following Nabol's words.

He rubbed absently at his chin. "Keep it that way. I'll tell her myself." He blew out a breath of pure loathing. The woman was the worst bitch he'd ever known – the Ice Islands were warmer than her cunt.

King Munsolrysche had his own network of spies and informants, and she had hers, of that he had no doubt. What concerned him, drunk or sober, was not knowing, especially on nights such as this, which of those spies worked for both King and Queen.

"Send a servant in. I need refreshment."

Nabol bowed his head and approached the door.

A servant immediately scuttled in. "Your Majesty?"

"Get me...." What would help him think clearly? "Tea. Bring me tea. And honey it up well," Munsolrysche called as the servant turned to leave. Munsolrysche could never bear tea – tasteless crap with leaves left over at the bottom of a dainty china cup. Tea was a woman's drink, for women who sat up in boweries.

Ambassadors from his Coastal Alliance visited and they all drank tea – he never did understand it, but it was said to sober you, and to heal you, he mused, and so he could think of nothing better. For this, Munsolrysche could not be drunk. But he knew he would have one shitty headache come morning....

"This seal," and a loud belch interrupted him. Ah – that would be that stuffed goose coming up – or the stewed cabbage.... Well, coulda' been a fart. Munsolrysche smacked his chest with a clenched fist and then continued. "Are you sure of its authenticity?"

Nabol smiled slightly and returned, "I compared it to the other Royal seals we have received, Your Majesty. It is genuine."

A knock sounded upon the door of Munsolrysche's study then.

"That would likely be your tea, Your Majesty. I'll let him in, shall I?" suggested Nabol.

"Yes, yes," Munsolrysche waved his approval at Nabol and then stared down at the unrolled messages.

"Get me maps of Romeny and Ambsellon."

"Yes, Your Majesty," Nabol replied. First, he set out a cup of tea for Munsolrysche. Cheese, berries, grapes, and a slab of bread with a cup of honey butter had also accompanied the tea.

Ah, this fucking tea. What did they say in the kitchens when the found out their king was asking for tea, Munsolrysche wondered idly as Nabol unrolled the Ambsellon map before him. They were all pinned to the wall, but these maps offered more thorough details, featuring the smaller towns, villages, parishes, smaller rivers, and other designations of possible interest. And, yes, mused Munsolrysche, perhaps even *springs*.

He swallowed his tea as a child swallows his medicine. It was honeyed well enough, but still bitter to his palate. He threw the rest back and picked up a slice of bread. Munsolrysche was not hungry, but the bread would help sop up he didn't know how much red wine he'd consumed tonight, and this move of Ormon's would require his full attention. That bastard. He lathered honey butter over the bread and then wandered around to lean upon the map.

"So this – this cub. He's returning to a cave beside a spring. How fucking many springs can there be? And caves? Pisspoor message if you ask me. Hewart's people drink bearpiss for beer."

Munsolrysche stared all over the damned map.

"We're assuming that he's even going back to Hewart." He buttered another slice of bread. "He might be staying in Romeny. If he sent those with a Royal Seal, he was well-placed."

Damn Ambsellon. Munsolrysche had silently been redoubling its strength – and that was a juicy little tidbit he'd shared with no one, not even this – fop standing before him who only *Majestied* him as it suited him. Munsolrysche was certain Nabol bounced his ball on both sides of the court, which was why he kept back the choicest information. He harrumphed to himself and hoped that *she* knew Nabol bounced his ball on both sides of more than just one court, or probably only one. Munsolrysche snickered to himself. *Balls*, that was. He crammed his bread inside his mouth.

"Well, then. Let us send a message to Hewart, that fucking bear." Munsolrysche crammed the rest of his bread into his mouth.

Nabol's eyebrows shot up.

"A message?"

Fucking fop. If only the little shit didn't know so much, wasn't as smart as he was, Munsolrysche would replace him for an advisor with a real pair of balls, and a brain. Who was loyal only to him. "Yes, Nabol, that's what I said. I've warmongering to do." He kept the disgust he felt out of his voice.

"Now we're going to need some pigeon parchment, some ink –" and then the fart came. Loud one, too – about time, it'd been building up. Ah, definitely the stuffed cabbage.

Nabol coughed politely and cleared his throat.

"And then," Munsolrysche continued, "we'll send him a reply. You can duplicate the Romeny seal –"

Here, Nabol's eyes widened. "Duplicate it, Sire?"

Little fucker. He hated when people repeated everything he said. "Yes, Nabol," Munsolrysche sighed. "I know you can do it. You have all the tools you need, just make it as believable as possible." More was the pity, thought Munsolrysche. Someone with that particular skill set disturbed him, for who had or could he send birds to in Munsolrysche's own name? "I'll send two birds from here."

Nabol was careful not to register surprise. For if he had, Munsolrysche would have genuine confirmation of Nabol's double-siding it. Smart little shit.

"As you wish, Your Majesty." Nabol brought new pigeon parchment over to the desk. "What would you have the messages say?"

Munsolrysche rubbed at his chin for a minute. There was no decoding a message such as that. So he'd send an equally bizarre message back, and see what it brought in return.

He'd send two messages, of course, but he would select the birds himself. Long ago, Munsolrysche had bought the silence of his birdman, and as such, the birdman appeared to act on the behalf of any who stood before him. But the birdman had switched out two of the pigeon's cages. Two cages bound for Hewart himself had been redirected by his wife, may the gods torture her soul. The birdman purchased two new birds from the village and these two he would send to Hewart tonight.

"Your Majesty?" prompted Nabol.

"Write this: *'Borne cub awaiting near the spring.'"*

Except for the scribbling upon the desk by Nabol as he wrote the messages out, the study was silent. Munsolrysche could not help but wonder what Hewart would think when he read these messages. Munsolrysche wanted to be there himself, to watch the bastard's face.

He heard the quill fall upon the desk and Nabol blew upon the parchments.

"I've finished, Your Majesty."

"Good. Give them to me, get your sealing wax, and let's go."

Nabol looked surprised. "Go, Your Majesty?"

"Yes, I said, let's go. To the pigeon loft. After you, Nabol." And Munsolrysche pointed at the Study door. That way, he could keep an eye on the little fucker.

Finally, up in the Pigeon Loft, they threw up open the door. Cold air blasted in.

"Nabol, you get your sealing wax ready, now, and I'll get our Ambsellon birds out."

Munsolrysche had brief Squire duties – oh, so many years ago now – helping a birdman in Norgroth Castle, and while that position lasted little more than a month, he remembered enough to know how to pick up a bird.

Nabol had his back turned to him, warming up the wax. Munsolrysche smiled. Little shit.

Munsolrysche took out the pigeons who actually flew to Hewart at Wellacobre Castle, one by one. They were sleepy and pliable, and he held them gently.

"Now roll those messages up tightly, there's a lad, right – and stamp it quick." Munsolrysche waited while Nabol repeated the process again.

Munsolrysche checked both birds to see that the messages were tightly rolled and the seals affixed to them had dried.

"Now then. Nabol?"

"Your Majesty?"

"Open the window."

"Yes, Your Majesty."

Cold air blustered in, but it only invigorated Munsolrysche. For now, there was a plan afoot, and even better, his wife had been powerless to stop it.

He threw the pigeons into the air and watched them as fly into the darkness. He wanted to grin, but that would only alert the little spy. For a moment, he was tempted to toss him out the window as well. Damn this Kinging. One would think it gave you all the freedom in the land, yet times it backed you into a corner and scolded you like a drunken god.

Like as not, this little ball-bouncer would head straight to the Ice Cunt and tell her every word. Unfortunately, their brother ally was stabbing them in the back – that was a matter of state important enough for her to at least know about, though as previously agreed, the bitch need not show her face unless it was a ceremony or function of supreme importance.

"Very well. Ambsellon stabs us in the back? Let us see how he likes his knife."

Selby

Preoccupied, Selby's steps brought her to the end of the drab passage way, where the dazzling colors of a stained-glass window lit the stone cobbles in a brilliant display. At least some light shone into her day today, she thought as she heard her black skirts rustle about her to a stop.

Of late, everything preoccupied her. Selby despised this lack of focus. While she knew she was allowed this preoccupation, she could not afford it.

Just then, a manservant walked past her, struggling to balance the awkwardness of what she knew was a wall-length, rolled-up tapestry.

"Stop!" she commanded the servant.

Selby watched as the man recovered from his fright – she had startled him and now, though he was no longer frightened of her approach, he was still frightened of her. Quite, she thought as his eyes grew larger and larger.

 The manservant started to drop the ungainly tapestry so that he might honor her, but Selby shook her head and lifted a hand. "Don't. Your hands are quite full with this… tapestry."

The manservant was petrified, she saw. "What is your name?"

"Dannel, Your Majesty."

"Dannel. Dannel, do you know what this tapestry shows?" Tapestries most always showed great feats of courage or ceremonies. This one, Selby saw, was dusty, and yet it was being carried in the direction of her quarters….

Dannel shook his head, too afraid to speak.

"Very well. Dannel, do you read?"

"Y-yes, if it please you, Your Majesty."

"Good, then. At the very top of that tapestry, Dannel, nailed to the wood, is a gilded plate, which tells us the date and the title of this tapestry. Read for me the tapestry's title."

Dannel found the gilded plate and craned his neck about to read it upside down. He had to sound it out, but soon the entire title was *"King Gwalter Malstroud Torran Rournebourke, Spearing the Boar, RainsCourt Falcon Hunt"*. Selby arched an eyebrow. While history had been a favorite subject, she could not recall if King Gwalter had reigned two hundred or three hundred years ago... But she caught the undertones of this tapestry nonetheless, for where else could a servant possibly be taking such a tapestry?

"Thank you, Dannel. And where are you to deliver this tapestry?"

Dannel paled. "To the hallway outside your new quarters, if it please you, Your Majesty."

Selby nodded imperceptibly. "And who directed you to do so?"

"My – my master, Lord Graystone." Dannel swallowed.

Selby saw how scared the man was. "Relax, Dannel," she told him kindly. "From this day forth, you will work in my household. You will report downstairs to the Castellan.

"But first. Lay that –" Selby waved her hand with disgust at the tapestry – "ancient dust trap down and find Lord Graystone. Tell him to attend me. Here. And now," she added.

After she was alone in the passageway again, Selby stepped up to the rolled-up tapestry. Dust particles floated in the sunbeams that shone in on it. With a slippered foot, she rolled it open, taking care to keep dust from settling on her gown.

The more Selby saw of it, the more the rage in the pit of her stomach grew. Her eyes narrowed, she kicked it so that it rolled back up completely. A puff of dust floated into the air – disgusted, Selby sneezed twice. Another thing she hated – being locked indoors all the time.

Having viewed just half of the tapestry, Selby saw that it showed two things – mainly an enormous display of male hunting pride and, of course, chauvinism, she added sourly to herself. But in the arrangement of the figures and their weapons, there was also the underlying sexualism, as in so many works of art. And Lord Graystone would have that hang outside her quarters.

"Lord Graystone," Selby said evenly when the man arrived. Obviously, he had taken his time, for the man did not look concerned at all, nor out of breath.

"Your Highness, I beg your pardon, I did not know –"

"Not *'Your Highness,'* Lord Graystone. *Your Majesty*. And you would do well to remember that."

Selby could not help but enjoy the emotions at war upon Lord Graystone's face. She had enraged him, a respected Cabinet member, well-regarded by society, and a fierce political advocate, she knew. This last was unfortunate, but *he* was *her* pawn, not she his. And he would do well to remember that as well, she thought nastily, wishing she could tell him so.

Lord Graystone dropped all pretense then. In a stiff tone, he returned, "Not until your Coronation, *Your Highness*. There are cousins in the bloodline who also have a claim to the throne."

Selby heard his deliberate insult. And yet, this – man, this simple, ordinary man. Did he think he was going to harm her with his little words, and his little plots? She just had no emotions left. Save perhaps disgust. Selby dearly wished she could tell him what a ridiculous arse he was, but... that would serve such a small purpose ultimately, and if she didn't need him, she needed the good will of his peers.

"And yet I have sat the throne these six months, Lord Graystone. As a Cabinet member, I'm sure you are familiar with our Clemongardian law, which states that the next surviving child of a reigning monarch assumes the throne once that child becomes of age. It does not say *'son'* but *'child'*. As I am both the next surviving child and certainly of age, I therefore, have the first claim to the throne of Clemongard. However, should that law not be one that you comprehend, Lord Graystone, perhaps my father's will, which was signed by him and stamped with his own seal, will instead persuade you. For it states the line of succession as being the royal Stevanrhut children of my family – all of whom now are dead... but me."

Selby let her last few lines linger before him, knowing that they echoed in the hallway.

Lord Graystone remained silent, though his eyes glittered. Selby would need to bring this bastard to heal, and quickly. Should he get too out of hand, her battle amongst her squabbling little Cabinet members and so-called advisors would become a war.

She decided to throw the bastard a bone, though for her, it had been one of contention among herself and her personal advisors.

"Now, Lord Graystone. You mentioned a good point." Selby paused for drama's sake, just so she watch his curiosity pique, even if it was with reluctance. Then she decided it was more just to piss him off. She let the pause lengthen and knew Lord Graystone was seething inwardly.

"My Coronation. I will set a date, and soon. As you can imagine, other things of far more importance have been taking up my time other than the planning of a Coronation.

"And this." She toed the tapestry, then arched an eyebrow at Lord Graystone.

"Your Highness –"

Selby immediately held up a hand to stop him. She would bring this bastard to heal, for her father's sake, if no one else's.

Lord Graystone's nostrils flared and his eyes turned cold. His lips curled with distaste as he said, "Your... Majesty."

He didn't say a word, but his cold, brown eyes conveyed every bit of hatred he felt for Selby at that moment. She smiled at him as if she were pleased with a subject who had just knelt to kiss her ring. *I hate you too, Lord Graystone.*

"Carry on," Selby waved him with her hand.

Glaring at her, Lord Graystone said, "With all due respect, *Your Majesty* – you are moving to the Lords' Quarters."

Selby had announced this move, and instead all of the Lords' Quarters, and more specifically, the King's Quarters, be switched to the other side of the Palace, and the Ladies' Quarters to be switched to the Lords'.   What an uprising that had stirred, like horses running from a stable on fire. They thought it was just the silliness of a young girl at first.

First, she found them moving her own bed from her room toward her new wing. "What is that?" she had demanded.

"Your – your bed, Your Majesty," the menservants had said.

"I can see as much. *That* – is the bed I slept in for all the years I was a princess. Did you not just call me *'Your Majesty'*?"

They looked at each other guiltily and immediately returned in the direction of her old room to reassemble her bed.

Selby couldn't bear to sleep in her father's bed, and her mother's quarters were not suitable for a reigning monarch.

Finally, she had taken up quarters in the guest wing. She could not believe that she was sleeping in the guest wing of her own Palace. That was when she got the idea to switch the quarters around.

Her advisors were, not surprisingly, horrified at the idea, and full of opposition. Selby told the servants that the King's Quarters were now the Queen's Quarters, and there hadn't been a reigning Queen in nearly three hundred years, and so any recent guidelines for reigning Queens in their own Palaces were far out-of-date. Selby then gave all of them her most baleful stare, which she'd seen both her mother and her father give, and suddenly servants immediately began moving furniture.

But tapestries....

"Not at all, Lord Graystone. The Lords' Quarters have become my quarters, the previous King's old chambers will now be the current Queen's chambers. And, therefore, all of the women will be joining me.   The Lords will just sleep on the other side of the castle. It's just a room to sleep in, after all, Lord Graystone. If you find your new quarters not to your liking, then I will, of course, allow you to retire your post and return to your estate."

If Selby had been a man, she was sure Lord Graystone would have exploded. However, there he stood before her, his eyes not moving from hers. Finally, he said, "I'm sure that my new – room will be quite satisfactory, Your – Majesty."

Selby relished in just how difficult it was for the man to spit that out. Aloud she returned graciously, "Of course. The Palace is taking every measure to ensure that all of its residents are comfortable.

"But –" and she let her eyes boar into his. "The matter of this tapestry."

The slightest of smiles slipped across his face, visible only fleetingly.

"It's an excellent choice, Your Majesty –"

Selby held her hand up to cut him off. "I'm aware of your choice, as well as its detail. Do be sure, however, not to send any more of your choices to my wing. I will choose my own art. Also – so you are aware. Menservants will be in low demand in that section of the Palace for, well, rather obvious reasons. My own staff will be in place.

"This –" and she toed the dusty tapestry on the stone cobbles, "you may return from where you took it. And that will be all for today."

If he could have bared his teeth and growled, Lord Graystone would certainly have done so. Instead he said, "Easily done, just let me have my man come to pick it up."

Queen Selby looked down at Lord Graystone. "If you're referring to Dannel, he's been reassigned. He now works for me, here in the Palace. Since this tapestry was your idea… *you* pick it up, and you return it yourself."

Her father would be furious at this move of hers, but, Selby thought as she watched Lord Graystone purple with rage, she was not her father….

Myrischka

Myrischka clenched her fists and let her eyes roll back for a few moments. But only a few. Showing emotion was a weakness. She hated women who tittered with excitement and dramatized each second with outbursts of meaningless tripe. Rather than ladies-in-waiting boring her in a bowery, Myrischka preferred to surround herself in the social company of men in the library or a downstairs study, perhaps. However, participating in this activity too regularly was unsuitable for a woman of any station. So, Myrischka engaged herself in sporting events that men pursued – ice fishing, hunting – when weather permitted, of course.

On the rare days her husband stirred himself to join them, Myrischka feigned an abrupt excuse not to attend. She found the snow, the crisp air, the frozen icicles hanging from the trees, and just being outdoors, liberating, invigorating. But to see her husband waddling around, his boots punching squeaky prints in the snow, waving his arms about as if he were some formidable force to behold, nauseated her.

Now, Myrischka was just annoyed. She opened her eyes and gestured with her hands impatiently. "Up."

He stopped.

She rolled her eyes. "Up, up! That's enough!"

Nabol's head emerged from beneath her white, fur-trimmed silk gown, his face glazed. He looked up at her from the floor where he knelt, as a puppy looks eagerly at its master for praise. She wanted to kick him aside as she would a puppy, but Nabol had proven far too useful to toss aside just yet.

Myrischka waved him with exasperation in the direction of the water basin. "Go on." That been fair at best. She stalked toward her table and donned her white fur mantle. She heard Nabol splashing water across his face from the bowl across her chamber. Myrischka could not help but take immense pleasure in knowing that the tongue that spoke to Munsolrysche by day was the same tongue that licked her whenever she pleased. And that fat bastard didn't even suspect. She permitted herself the faintest of smiles, one of deep satisfaction.

Although it had taken Nabol at least four months to get it right. But, Myrischka

conceded, it wasn't as if she had the equipment he really preferred to wrap his tongue around. And if she had, then she would be King, not that stupid bastard who sat on the Gold Throne now. She sniffed with disgust.

Nabol appeared at her table before her, his hair wet from where he'd slicked it back with water. He truly was an idiot, she thought.

"Now tell me again, did he actually use the word *'warmongering'*?"

Nabol nodded. "Yes, Your Majesty." His innocent child's expression was more than she could bear now. She had to plan the next move.

Myrischka's idiot spouse had never been accounted for as a consideration. That he had discovered this at all was the worst luck, to an absurd degree.

"Go. You may go." She dismissed Nabol with a curt wave in the direction of the door to her quarters. "And Nabol –" Myrischka added. "As always, you will tell no one."

Nabol nodded solemnly as he closed her door without a sound.

Myrischka flipped her mantle up as she sat into a cushioned chair before the crackling fire. She stared into the dancing flames. That fat fool had no idea those birds he sent would fly directly back to her. At least there was that small boon. But he knew of the whole plot now, or some of it, and was planning a war of all things. What an arse. When it had taken her so long to finally get King Hewart to get off his pacifist, cushioned throne to move against Romeny on his own, now? *Now?* Now Munsolrysche wants to declare war on Ambsellon? Fucking idiot!

Myrischka's spies riddled Ambsellon, and she had finally placed them as high up as to whisper into King Hewart's ear the benefits of moving on his own into Romeny. It had taken her nearly two years, but finally her fruits were ripening.

How that damnable message got sent to Munsolrysche, Myrischka could not imagine. That was what came of trusting Ambsellon men, she supposed.

But the Romeny man they planned for this mission was so well-placed, a torturer, what could possibly have gone awry, Myrischka fumed as she glared at the fire, where the remnants of the message lay in ash. She had a network of men in Romeny as well as Ambsellon, though Ghiverny was harder to penetrate.

And finally, just as Romeny would have been taken unawares, with a lack of men, no troops from its Shield, Ambsellon would have sacked Fairview. Taken the Palace, killed the King, and even with luck, his pups.

But her fat fuck of a husband had to find out. How, how, how.... Myrischka racked her brain. Or who? Ambsellon, perhaps? Betrayal? She arched an eyebrow, leaning her chin on her fist, her lips pursed as she considered numerous alternatives. And none seemed plausible.

To have read the original message wrong, backward, in fact. Myrischka sniffed with disgust. That, too, was a small boon.

Wherever, whoever had survived, if either or both of them had, they were waiting here in Ormon, waiting to spring on anyone but the aforementioned designee, the cub. And soon enough, the information they had learned in Romeny would be in her hands, via the cub....

Ron

Nick was signaling him from the stairwell. And not very secretively, either, for an individual who spent a significant amount of time on the street. Ron ran a hand through his hair, allowing him to shake his head ever so slightly. If nothing else, he wanted to finish his noon-day meal.

Luvian stepped out from the kitchen then, his forearms lightly dusted with flour. He leaned both hands on the bar.

"So. Ron."

Luvian's use of only *Ron* rather than *Ronnie* caused a pit of apprehension to settle in his stomach. Ron hadn't fought on a battlefield, but he knew how to employ the use of such verbal tactics. They played with your mind and distracted you. Ron strengthened his resolve.

"Did you get enough stew?" asked Luvian.

Odd question, that, thought Ron, but he'd play along. "Of course, always. And always excellent."

Luvian's dark eyes were studying him, not blinking. Aloud, he said casually enough, "That's because we always put just enough vegetables in it, we never add too many. And we simmer it, we never let the pot overflow. Family recipe here."

Luvian's eyes continued to penetrate Ron. From nowhere, he placed a basket of fresh bread in front of Ron. And then he glanced quickly down the bar where Nick had been standing, but had disappeared. Then he looked into Ron's eyes again.

"Be sure to give our regards to Master Cradwick."

Ron knew that Luvian's underlying message was *if you don't keep your private affairs out of my bar, you won't be welcomed back*. He wondered how Luvian had found out, and then, considering Nick's lack of subtlety, decided it couldn't have been hard to notice.

"I absolutely will," Ron replied quietly, in the same tone that Luvian was using.

Ellia, who had been clearing the other end of the bar top, stepped up. "Pappy," she scolded as she slid her arms around Luvian's arm. "Don't look at Ronnie like that. He's one of our favorite customers, isn't he?" Ellia smiled at Ron.

Then she looked up into Luvian's serious face. "Are you getting enough sleep, Pappy?" Worried, she raised a slender finger up in his face in imitation of Luvian scolding the girls. *"Now you see here, and listen good. If you don't get enough sleep, you won't be worth spit out there on the floor."*

Ron couldn't resist a smile. Luvian's serious demeanor melted, though with reluctance, as he turned and gazed down at his youngest daughter. Finally, a smile tugged at the corners of his mouth.

"Yes, daughter," he sighed as he capitulated with a shake of his head.

"Now, that's better. Go on, go, back in the kitchen, take care o' that bread. And be sure to get more sleep!" Ellia called after him, still in her Ellia-as-Pappy imitation.

Luvian's smile was for Ellia's benefit as he turned about, but he still affixed a quick stare in parting at Ron. Ron lifted his eyebrows briefly in understanding.

After Luvian's considerable frame was no longer staring him down, Ellia turned around. She stared down at the basket of bread. "Hungry?" she inquired with a disarming smile, for Ron had already eaten a basket.

"Ah, no," Ron shook his head. "Your Pap brought it out for Master Cradwick."

"Oh, I see." Her blue eyes gazed off over Ron's shoulder. "I worry about Pappy sometimes. You know? Maybe you could talk to him."

Ron choked down his swallow of ale. *Thanks*, he thought, *but no*. Luvian was the last person he wanted to talk to just now. Ron suspected Luvian could pick apart even the most accomplished of liars. He kept coughing – damn if hadn't swallowed that ale wrong!

Ellia slipped around from behind the bar and patted him on the back. "Are you okay? Ronnie?"

In a watery voice, Ron held up his hand, clearing his throat. "I'm fine. Fine." He coughed a few more times.

After Ron could look at Ellia without spluttering, he suggested, "Ellia, I'm surely not the one to talk to your Pap. Maybe Tank? They were in the Army together?"

She placed a hand on his from across the bar. "But Ronnie, that's why you're a better choice. You aren't in the Army. You didn't serve, you don't remind him of the War, and you're a local boy. He likes you," Ellia insisted.

Ron sucked in a deep breath. How to say that he was likely her father's least favorite person just now...? No, he hadn't served in the War, but....

Ellia's big, blue eyes stared at Ron, beseeching him.... Ugh. She got that trick from her father, no doubt. He felt himself relenting. Now he knew what it must feel like to be Luvian....

"I... I can try," Ron mumbled. And there it went, zip, all his training, right out the window.

"Thank you, thank you, Ronnie!" Ellia grabbed his hand with both of hers. Her smile lit up her whole face.

Ellia ran around the bar and squeezed his shoulder in thanks. "Lunch is on the house!" she whispered with enthusiasm. And with that, Ellia danced off to other side of the bar to sweep.

Ron gestured uselessly in reply. How – how had she done that? He was glad his employer hadn't seen that. Ron leaned his head on his hand and stared up at ceiling.

"Fell for 'em, didntcha'? Ha ha." Nick chortled some more.

"What? What are you talking about?" Ron did not like to be seen out in the open with Nick, even if they were standing in a shadowed alley. Especially after Luvian's pointed hint. Ron pulled his cowl up a bit further.

"The blue eyes. The blue-eyed ploy. Works every time, I tell ya. You're not alone. Except on her mum. You'll hear Miss Ruthie tell her, *'You can look at me all you want, Ellie girl, but until those chores get done, you're not goin' anywhere, much less the Market Place.'* She even gets Tank.*"* Nick chortled again.

Somehow, Ron did not feel relieved.

"By-the-by, and today, I do mean buy...." Nick always loved to start off his tales of information with clichés. He rubbed his fingers together to emphasize "buy."

"Get on with it," Ron hissed. He planned to cut back on their arrangement. Nick had given him very little of worth, but Ron liked to have enough people on the streets that he could talk to at a moment's notice. He knew that Nick would enjoy not having to report to him as well.

"Well, now, South Fair is South Fair, isn't it, same comin's and goin's," commented Nick. Lately, the street people had abbreviated South Fairview to South Fair, and the regular residents had begun taking up the term as well. But Nick was prolonging this discussion deliberately, enjoying Ron's building exasperation.

Ron narrowed his eyes.

"All right, all right, if you're gonna be like that...." Nick shook his head. Then he leaned closer to Ron and, behind a hand, whispered, "There's some rich folks in town."

"That's it? Your big secret? Rich folks in town? Honestly, I –"

Ron was turning to leave, but Nick grabbed his arm. "No. You think that's nothin', right? Think about it. This is South Fair, mate. Rich folk, in South Fair."

Ron pulled his arm back and rolled his eyes. "So they're passing through, maybe they came from the west, or maybe they got off on the ferry." Ridiculous.

"In their nice iron carriage, drawn by pretty horses? Best of clothing, expensive luggages...." Nick ticked off on his fingers and trailed off pointedly.

Ron admitted to a small bit of curiosity now, but nevertheless, most reasons for wealthy travelers passing through South Fairview were easily justified.

"And... did they have a destination apparent?" Ron prompted, rounding his hand about with impatience.

"Nope, that's the odd thing. My folk all say they just rode through and round about. I mean to say, we South Fairs, we do like our town, such as it is, but it ain't no Fairview Proper. Ain't a one out of a hundred of us'll ever see a goldy. But them rich folks, you know they got goldies sittin' about in their shithouses to wipe their arses with." Nick snorted. "Ronnie, mate, them folks probably got shithouses made of gold, that's truth there," and Nick nodded his head with a jab in Ron's ribs.

Ron sighed at this exaggeration, but Nick was right. None of these people here had ever seen gold pieces, and many not even silver. So for what reason were these wealthy people in South Fairview truly here?

Ron mulled over this new development as he readied himself for his trip to the Market Place, for it was, after all, a fourth day. He found himself wondering how to report this to his employer.

Ron turned into the Market Place, lost in thought, considering how he would approach his employer soon. Then the whinny of horses broke into his reverie. He glanced up with surprise. It wasn't that he hadn't heard horses recently, but these horses were all a-jingle, with the trappings of the buckles and bits that attached them to an impressive iron carriage.

Nick was right, Ron admitted with reluctance. Lined with gold trimming, decorated with gold crests and accoutrements, the carriage was, without doubt, out of place in South Fairview.

Dressed in striped black trousers and a stiff black velvet greatcoat, the coachman directed the horses with a look of pure disdain for their surroundings. A whistle sounded from inside the carriage, and the coachman drew up on the horses. The carriage wheeled to a stop. Ron had never seen something so out of place before.

A woman with pale, golden hair piled elegantly upon her head leaned out of the window of the carriage. She outstretched her arm at the folk in the Market Place, her fingers stiff with contempt.

"Do any of you know where Master Chadlick can be found?" Her voice was bored and patronizing as she gazed out upon the shoppers on the street of the Market Place.

People glanced at each other. Ron knew two things at once – one was that poor people who were treated like scum by rich people were never going to help them of their own accord – and two, that Master Chadlick sounded a great deal like Master Cradwick. Even if any of the South Fairview people recognized this mistake, none of them were about to assist her. They paid enough in taxes. Why give the rich any more than they deserved, and for free? Ron saw that plain on their faces, even if this woman did not.

But the mystery was, what did they want with Master Cradwick? Certainly people of their means had access to a blacksmith in Fairview Proper, or wherever their destination was. There was certainly no need to go galivanting about South Fairview riling up the residents.

A man on the other side of the iron carriage leaned out. He caught sight of Ron. Unfortunately, Ron's blacksmith apprentice sigil, two crossed hammers over an anvil, was visible on his tunic.

"You! You! Come here!"

Shit. Ron glanced about him. So much for remaining hidden and observing.

He took a step back and glanced about him, wondering just how successful his chances of running for it were. Ron took another step back, his eyes darting about. He could run behind the vendors, fewer witnesses….

"You, boy, you!"

And then a man grabbed Ron and forced him forward.

Immediately, Ron began fighting, but his unseen aggressor pinned Ron's arms behind him with brute force. Then Ron was shoved into the carriage.

"Go! Go!" called one of the men, slapping the outer side of the carriage.

Ron saw nothing, for a burlap hood had been forced over his face. Still, he lashed out all about him for the door so that he could jump out, the window even.

And then a stunning pain to his head, and darkness….

Blurry.

"You're a bloody fool, you know that, don't you?" snapped a woman's voice.

Ron could not see. About his eyes a dark rag was bound. He struggled then, the details suddenly rushing back to him. But rope fastened his arms together behind him.

"When I get free of this, you are all going to die." Ron started pulling at his ropes.

Both the man and the woman chuckled. "Well, he's definitely awake now," she laughed.

"Oh, don't worry, you'll be free enough, boy. We're here for Master Cladwich. It is Cladwich, isn't it?" said the man to the woman.

"It's *Master Cradwick*," growled Ron.

His blindfold was untied. His nose had told him he was still in the wagon, but the curtains were drawn.

The woman stared up at the top of the wagon, bored. "Cradwich, Cladwich, whatever," she waved her hand about.

"It's *Cradwick!*" snarled Ron. "And what do you want with him?"

With even more affectation in her voice than before, she leaned over to address her male companion. "I personally can't believe they even have a blacksmith in South Fairview. Such a – a mudhole."

"They even have a Market Place. Who would have guessed?" laughed the man.

She sniffed. "If you could call that a Market Place. Really, it was just a, a Muddy Place," and she brushed at her skirts.

"Am I here," droned Ron, "for some significant worth or consequence? Because if you don't need anything blacksmith-related, then please, by all means, knock me out again. I can't listen to this tripe."

The two of them were silent for a moment. Probably at having been spoken to so rudely, Ron mused. He half expected to be hit again. Ron couldn't fathom why he was a part of this small company, but he hoped they would enlighten him soon....

She frowned with disdain, displeased at being addressed so.

He told Ron, "As it happens, we need the services of a blacksmith."

"We have been told that this... this Master Cladlick is the best in this mudhole."

The male gentleman continued. "And we are unable to leave until we get our horse looked at. She requires a new shoe." He held up a horseshoe that was slightly cracked.

Ron wanted to laugh. A horse could take them on for miles with a shoe such as that. And why did they not travel with an extra? What utter arses.

"That won't take but two hours at most," Ron told them. Assuming his arms were untied and he didn't kill them first.

The woman looked horrified. "Two hours!"

The man also looked stunned. "Why, we can make it to Fairview Proper by then!"

Ron shrugged. "Aye. Take it or leave it."

"Well, then. I think we'll just make it on our own," huffed the man.

Please do, thought Ron. There was no way he could possibly stand their company any longer than necessary.

She sniffed, her nostrils flaring. "Very well, then. Cut him loose." Then she thought of something.

"I've barely eaten today. Has this mudhole anywhere people can eat, save their own kitchens?"

She couldn't be more insulting. Then an idea brightened his throbbing head. "The Brew House and Tavern is a place people go a lot."

"Very good, tell us where it is."

"I – I –" Ron hadn't expected she would actually go for the idea. He'd been attempting to insult her.

"*I – I...?* Are you more of a moron that we originally thought? Or do you not even know where it is?" she snapped.

"Well, milady, it's not that I don't know where it is, it's just that.... Well. A lady such as yourself, of *quality* –" here, Ron had to choke the word out, for he would have preferred to call her a *bitch* instead – "well, milady, it's a tavern, after all." Ron raised his eyebrows, assuming she would pick up on his reference. Woman of quality never set foot in taverns and pubs.

"I understand what you're trying to tell me, boy. But does this place have food?"

"The very best. Ask them for their *very best stew* and their *very best stout*, and they'll take great pains to make sure you get it. They only do that for quality folk. Ask them for their family recipe."

Her eyes narrowed, trying to discern if he was telling the truth. "Very well."

And he was cut free and shoved out of the wagon.

Ron's only consolation as he rubbed the rope burn on his arms, was that Luvian and Miss Ruthie were going to enjoy taking extra special care of those two....

Ron walked home in the twilight of the evening. They didn't need to club him on the back of the neck like that, he grimaced. That was going to be bloody sore tomorrow. Ron decided that tonight, just for one night, he was going to take in a serious quantity of red wine, and not Cradwick's, either. But his own, stashed in a corner behind his small chest of belongings. And he would have one fuck of a hang-over tomorrow morning. And to be quite, *quite* honest, Ron did not give the first fuck about that. In fact, he mused, he would sleep long past the bloody roosters and the distant bell-tower. *Bloody club me on the back of the neck,* he sulked, *bastards —*

Ron's grumpy mental commentary was interrupted by the noise of a number of children yelling. Typical of South Fairview, he thought. No one minds their children…. Somewhere inside of him instantly berated him for that miserly and undeserved thought, but his pride was too wounded just now to care.

On the other side of the next street corner, a number of boys of varying ages, probably no older than fourteen, Ron observed, were laughing and ganged up in one pile. Ron crossed the street to get a better view.

Street boys, gang boys. Piled on top of some unfortunate little fellow. Ron thought idly that he wasn't the only one who would be sore in the morning, but whoever that poor git was, he was going to be in bad shape tomorrow.

"OY! All of you! Go on! Get out of here! You heard me!" Ron yelled.

The boys looked up then. Several of the younger ones ran off. Three of the older ones stood up and considered him. Was Ron seeing right? A twelve-year-old and two fourteen-year-old boys, thinking to take him on?

He scoffed and put his basket down. Ron opened his arms to invite any of them to try him. But first he said, "Let me tell you something. This is not something you want to do."

The three boys glanced uneasily at each other but stood their ground.

"Well then, come on. The ground over here could use a little more blood."

Ron's small, would-be assailants measured him a little longer, and then turned their backs on him, strolling down the street as if Ron was simply not worth their time. But he'd seen the whites of their eyes. Ron snorted at himself. Good. Something else he could get drunk over tonight. Scaring small children. *Cheers to you, mate, now you're really an arsehole.*

Then he heard a whimper. What the hell –

Down there on road, half-hidden against the building, was a tiny ball of a child. As Ron stepped closer, he found that the boy had hidden himself half inside the concave of the building, where the bricks had fallen away. The child's arms were covered all about his head and shoulders to protect himself.

All of Ron's disgust and anger dissipated. Those bullies.

Quietly, Ron stepped up. "How badly are you hurt, lad?"

The boy flinched and retreated even further into the brick of the building. Odd, that, though Ron. Damn it all, now his interest was piqued. Shit. He picked his basket up and squatted slowly next to the child.

"I'm not here to hurt you. Will you let me see if you're okay?"

The child did not respond. His tunic was filthy, old dirt stains ground into it, gray from age, and far too large for the boy. A street child.

Ron reached out an arm. "Can I see?" He placed a hand on the child's shoulder.

The boy jumped but after a moment, relaxed slightly. He peeked out from beneath his elbow.

Slowly, Ron was able to unwind the child from his tightly wound arms. Old scars on the boy's face told Ron that this was not the first time the boy had seen the harsher side of the fist. Right now, however, there was grime and dirt on his face. His lip was split, and blood ran freely from his nose. Ron didn't know what he hated more right now, the condition this child was in, or the bullies who had done this to him.

"Lad, what's your name?"

The little boy looked up at him with small green eyes. They considered Ron for a moment, as if, Ron realized, wondering whether Ron was even worth interacting with.

Then the boy shrugged. "Kylon. But they call me 'Pylon,' because they all "pile on" top of me." The lad tried to sound brave as he informed Ron of this last, but his eyes fell to the ground at the last moment.

Ron wanted to throttle every street boy he ever saw from that point on. But he schooled his expression to a kindly one, so that he wouldn't frighten Kylon.

"Kylon, how old are you?"

"Ten," said Kylon with another brave face, his green eyes wide in an attempt to convince Ron.

Ron looked down his nose gently, staring at Kylon until the boy finally admitted in a stubborn tone, "Eight."

Eight. He would have guessed seven, but street boys didn't have the proper food and nourishment that other children did. Then an idea sprang to mind.

"Kylon, when did you last eat?"

Again, Kylon had a ready lie for him, but Ron put a finger upon the lad's lips to shush him. Kylon looked at Ron's finger, cross-eyed for a moment, until he decided upon the truth.

He looked up at Ron. "Three days ago. It were burnt bread from behind the baker's."

Ron was suddenly glad of the bread he had taken home from The Brew House and Tavern. That unspoken conversation between him and Luvian early this afternoon seemed so far away now.

"Well, Kylon, I'm going to take you somewhere where you can have a good meal."

Immediately, Kylon started shaking his head in fear.

"Why not?"

"If they see where you take me, they'll just beat me again when I leave."

"Kylon, I insist. I have friends on the street who will watch out for you and make sure you are safe. I really do," Ron insisted, when Kylon looked skeptical. "Now, stand up. It's just a warm meal, and a safe place to sleep for tonight. No one will hurt you.

"And we can clean up that face of yours."

Reluctance warred in the boy's face and his eyes darted all about the street for the boys of the street gang, but the promise of a warm meal and a safe place to sleep won out.

Inside the forge, Ron set down his basket and gestured to Kylon to have a seat.

He dipped a cloth in the water barrel and sat down before Kylon. As Ron dabbed at the blood on Kylon's face, he couldn't help but feel badly for the lad.

"Kylon, where are your folks?"

Kylon winced as Ron held the cloth to another wound. "My parents died of fever when I was little." Amused at an eight-year-old's idea of *little*, Ron encouraged Kylon to continue. "My mum, before she died, she signed me over to the orphanage." Kylon sighed. "Then she died. And then I lived at the orphanage for a while. But they're not nice people there. They don't always feed you. And – well...."

Kylon looked off to the side, thinking of some nightmarish action. "So I ran away." He paused, and then said, "The boys on the street, they wanted me to join them, but I didn't want to. 'Cause I watched them, and they're mean to folks. So when they wanted me to join them, I said no. I keep saying no, and I can run faster than them, and hide, too." Kylon drew in a deep breath. "But sometimes they catch me anyway."

Ron finished cleaning the blood from Kylon's face. Underneath all that dirt was a clean face again. There were even a few freckles....

"Well, Kylon. Or do you want me to call you Pylon?"

Kylon's face was solemn. "I haven't gone by Kylon for a long time now."

Ron didn't think he could bring himself to call the boy Pylon. "Right then, lad. Let's see about getting you some dinner."

Ron put together a fast pottage and fed the boy some boiled vegetables and a bit of Luvian's thick bread as well. Kylon watched Ron's every move with large eyes.

"You know, Kylon," Ron said as they ate together. "They may call you Pylon, like *Pile On*. But there's a real such thing as a *Pylon*. You hear how different I say it, *PY-lon*, instead of *PILE-on?*"

Kylon yawned and nodded around his mouthful of bread.

Ron looked at Kylon thoughtfully and then said, "Lad, a PY-lon is actually something that's very, very strong. It holds other things up, like great big enormous towers and gates. PY-lons are huge, and very strong. Blacksmiths like me, and him back there, Master Cradwick, we use that term.

"*Kylon* may be the name your parents gave you, but you can go by PY-lon if you want to. If you want, you can stay here and help out here. You need a safe place to be."

Kylon's eyes grew round. "Like an apprentice?"

"A bit, yes. I'm the apprentice here, for now, but one day, I'll have my own forge, and Master Cradwick will need a new apprentice. And that could be you. If you want. Just now, you just sweep and do a few little things about and I'll see you get a wage."

Kylon was still staring at him.

"Now, Kylon, if this sounds good, then you go on and stay. But you cannot leave the forge here, because if those street boys find you, they'll beat you again."

Ron thought for a moment. "You don't have to stay either, Kylon," he said. Street kids were street kids, you couldn't rescue them unless they wanted to be rescued. "If you want to leave, I want you to take this with you." And Ron turned around and found the smallest hammer Master Cradwick had. He handed it to Kylon.

"Here. You take this with you if you decide to leave. Just use it for defending yourself and then run away, don't use it to beat anyone up with, you hear me? If I hear you're out there beating boys up with my hammer, I'll come find you and I'll beat you silly. And then I'll take my hammer back." Ron had kept his voice benign throughout all of this.

Ron stood up and dumped their dishes into the water barrel. When he came back in, he said, "Lad, you're fallin' asleep and so am I. Now, you sleep there –" and Ron pointed to the pile of hay on the floor, "and I'll be sleeping here." Ron walked toward his own bed and started pulling his boots off. Ah, that felt good.

He looked over his shoulder at Kylon. The boy was already stretched out on the hay. Ron picked up one of the extra blankets they had in the forge – hardly needed with the coals still burning all night – and spread it over the boy.

In nearly no time, the boy's breathing was even. Ron slid out a bottle of wine, crappy wine, but wine nonetheless. He drank so rarely, but what a day. He stared at this little boy. Someday,

Ron thought as he gulped a mouthful of wine down, this little lad might be Cradwick's new apprentice. Ron swallowed several more gulps of wine before he corked the bottle tight. He bloody well hoped so. He was tired of this assignment.

Tyndie

Royals. Tyndie sniffed. They found every reason imaginable to feast and throw banquets. Servants often got the left-overs, if they happened to be in the right place at the right time, but Tyndie was rarely so fortunate, in her current position or as a kitchen maid.

Today, for example. She leaned out a window. The set-up taking place down in the gardens for the banquet later today was immense. The mimes and the jugglers were practicing off to the side.

The King was constantly entertaining. Some frowned upon it, for it wasn't so long after his father King Cahall's death. But Tyndie heard others insist that King Reaghann was doing exactly what the people needed to see – reminding them that Hardewold was a country of means and might, and of great fortune.

King Reaghann had assumed the Crown earlier than expected, and King Cahall in such good health, they all said. Even Tyndie remembered when he passed, for all the bells in the entire city tolled at once for an hour. For a man of middling age, people sighed, they thought it just damnable luck. A man in such good health, a Twenty Years War veteran and hero, an excellent huntsman, a fine father, to die of food poisoning....

Tyndie thought she'd been nine at the time, and the kitchen staff had to scramble to find her a black smock. All of the city, even the castle staff, attended the procession of the King's funeral, all to pay their final respects to the King they had loved.

For an entire city present upon one street, most all of them were silent. Tyndie recalled being amazed at that. Only some sobbing, a bit of coughing and hushing was all the sound heard throughout the assembled masses that lined the street for miles.

King Reaghann, then still Prince Reaghann, headed the wagon that bore his father's casket. The wagon was the only noise that filled the air, only the clop-clops of the horses, whose saddles were trimmed in black and gold, and a bit of squeak from the wagon wheels as it tumbled over the cobblestones.

Entirely garbed in black, the Prince was pale against the startling black of his mourning attire, and his velvet cloak flapped slightly behind him as he passed. Tyndie stared up at him, for this was the first time she had ever seen a Royal, and not only did he look just like a normal person might, but he was sad just like she had been when her mum had passed.

And then, Tyndie would never forget, that, though the Prince continued to stare forward at the sea of thousands of people, he looked down upon her and met her eyes with his own green ones, just for a few seconds. Those green eyes had been the only mark of color in all his whole face. It had taken her breath away.

Now, years later, Tyndie really didn't care about that so much as she did some time off of her feet. She'd already worn through one pair of shoes, and Auntie had replaced them with some better-quality shoes that the cobbler had made special.

—⁕—

A stray strand of hair kept teasing Tyndie's nose, and she was not allowed to tuck it behind her ear, for that would call attention to herself, and both her hands were full. She blew up at it as she could, but the breeze simply blew it back again.

At least this banquet was outdoors. She loved being outdoors, and maids had so few occasions to get out of the castle. Their only job was to hold the refreshment water bowls today, as extra menservants were working the tables.

Honeyed apples and spiced plums had already been served, along with the bread, while the ham and leek pottage was still on the table with the chilled pear soup. They were slicing into their garlic roast and seasoned asparagus. Tyndie thought it might be sage and rosemary – she had worked in the kitchens long enough to tell her spices. Menservants also lingered serving gingered carrots. She knew pork potpies stuffed with bacon and berries would be the next dish, along with a side of cheese and grapes. Mulled wine would be served then, and Tyndie wasn't sure of the dessert, but cherry tarts and cinnamon pastries were often favorites at the Hardewold table. And her toes would be aching long before that.

Though she would not be dismissed for hours yet, Tyndie preferred being on her feet outdoors rather than inside the castle's dank stone walls. Outside, at least, there was a breeze, and sunlight, and grass.

Tyndie also passed her time listening in to the conversations of the dignitaries whom she stood behind. Most of the time, the talk was nothing but laughter and expressions of enjoyment of their meal, of friends and shared experiences. Tyndie had taught herself how not to yawn, in fact, so bored did she find most of the lords' banter.

Ladies' discussions were far worse. Tyndie was still working to keep a steady, calm expression, for a maid who rolled her eyes at what ladies before her said would surely be dismissed.

But the giggling and the dissembling, such obvious feigned and practiced behaviors disgusted Tyndie. All she heard from them was whose gowns were replicas of other ladies' gowns, who would never get betrothed at their age, who they wanted to invite to parties, and what men were supposedly not adhering to the strictest of social principles.

Finally, the guests stood up from the linen-covered tables. In small clusters of two's and three's, they seated themselves before the entertainment. Tyndie heard Manda heave a great sigh. This meant the afternoon was almost over. And Tyndie was so glad – her arms were aching from holding those stupid silver platters of refreshment water all throughout the meal.

She couldn't help but smile a tiny bit at the mockery on the stage. Tyndie always enjoyed the mimes and the jugglers. They helped to take her mind off her work.

Then the minstrels played, and the lords and ladies stepped onto the dais and started dancing. Tyndie hated to admit that she enjoyed watching the dances. They were all so graceful, them with their colored silks and jewels, their gowns aswish as they spun about....

Then Tyndie stared. Lord Drury! Lord Drury was out there! Her heart quickened. Well, of course he was, she scolded herself. Usually, she did not serve the lords placed closest to the King, which, of course, was where Lord Drury sat. Between her being so busy, and not having to see him, it had been easy for Tyndie to forget about him... almost. Though there were times at night when she couldn't sleep that she wondered... just how had Lord Drury pulled it off. How had he actually killed them both....

But now. Right there, dancing, up on the flower-covered dais. Tyndie kept her eyes lowered, but still watched him through her lashes. Most women would have considered him handsome. And he glided about with a grace on the dance floor from partner to partner with a charm on his face that hinted to each woman who stepped in his arms that she alone had captured his fancy. Lord Drury was exquisitely attired in light green and gold embroidered silks which perfectly complimented his deep emerald trousers, none of which made of him look overly dressed or foppish.

Tyndie watched him as he moved about with his peers. He laughed and smiled just enough, exactly as needed and when required, and the lords and ladies about him admired him. He blended in easily with his peers, and no one actually saw, really looked at his true face, thought Tyndie. Lord Drury's outer face was just a mask. His eyes were cold, and dead. When he smiled at people, he didn't care about them, it was just an act he performed. To Tyndie, Lord Drury wasn't handsome so much as striking. *Dangerous*.

⸻

Ah. Finally. Tyndie stretched. She had worked four twelve-hour days straight, which probably had something to do with The Shrew. At the end of Tyndie's shift last night, Auntie Renne told her that today, she had the whole day off.

So Tyndie when to her tiny room, only really large enough for a small bed and a place to put clothes in. She'd gone to sleep last night and hadn't woken until today around noon.

Tyndie took a quick bath and then planned to make herself very scarce, for she just knew that The Shrew would find a way to make Tyndie cover her shift tonight. But if Tyndie couldn't be found, then... too bad for The Shrew. She sniffed.

Besides, Tyndie had seen numerous places all about the castle where bits of chalk lay on the floor. Which was frustrating, for she had been running about on her feet for most of the last week with all these feasts. Today, though. She thought most of the guests King Reaghann was entertaining had left, and only the most important of them had stayed for the rest of the week.

Before she left her small room, Tyndie pocketed two tallow candles and a bit of flint. And the chalk Manda had given her had never left her pocket, of course, for she used the Hub regularly now on her rounds.

She wondered which passage to choose and decided on one that no maids or manservants – or The Shrew – would be like to discover her. And she had also seen something as she'd run about the castle that she'd been interested in exploring further… in front of the entrance ways of some passages were two pieces of chalk, side by side. Tyndie wondered what that meant. Manda had told her nothing about that.

And there was one right before her. With two pieces of chalk, side by side, as if to make a longer piece. Tyndie glanced about cautiously, then stepped back to check the stone castle corridors.

No one. Excellent. Tyndie smoothed her fingers across the mortar of the brick before her, pushing until finally the thick stone door swung open toward her.

She slipped in and pushed it shut. As soon as Tyndie's eyes adjusted to the darkness, she realized immediately that this tunnel was nothing like any of the others. Not only did a number of chalk marks stand out upon the dark rock of the wall, but up ahead, the rough wooden stone that usually lined the indoor of the other tunnels became smooth and polished.

Tyndie frowned and lit one of her candles from the flame burning in the wall sconce. Misgivings immediately arose about this adventure, but she stepped forward anyway.

Finally, up ahead, she found another imitation of the Hub, but she had no idea where any of the tunnels led. She continued further but then, after several paces, froze.

Voices!

Tyndie sucked her breath in – she immediately blew her candle out and flattened herself against the wall.

At first, she congratulated herself on her luck. The voices were stationary. Two men, their voices raised a bit, and in a confrontation of some sort. If fortune was with her, they would turn around and leave – go back the other way, wherever that led….

And then, they started making their way toward her, each with lanterns in their hands.

Tyndie knew she had no time to run back to the door of the corridor, and the smoke of the tallow candle she'd just blown out was still pungent in the air yet. She could only run.

Which tunnel to choose?

Tyndie heard the metal creaking of the lantern handles behind her, knowing the men were getting closer. Perhaps they would leave the way they came.

Any way she chose, Tyndie ran the risk of being caught. She remembered Manda's words: *"Just don't get caught, hear me, Tyndie girl?"*

Finally, Tyndie just turned the corner around the left tunnel of the Hub and crouched in the darkness, hoping to hear a clue as to where the men were headed, so that she might run the other way. Perhaps, if they did start down her tunnel, she could throw her apron up over her face and run in the opposite direction....

"You just make sure you vote how I've told you. I'm not going to tell you again, you hear me."

"I do, I do – but Canton, it's just –"

"Look. You do what you want. Vote right, nothing happens, you get a little windfall down the road, that can't be bad...."

And then Tyndie, crouched in the darkness, heard Canton continue, "But if you don't, my fine friend," and she heard Canton pat the other lord down on the shoulder, "those two boys of yours that you've been paying for, with that nice lump sum over to that little village in Tenpoole.... Your wife wouldn't like finding out about them, now would she?"

"Canton, I – It were just that one time. And they're good boys. My family couldn't take that."

Tyndie heard the other man sigh deeply with regret.

Canton laughed. "It's not just one time, the way I hear it, Canton, my man. 8th Street, the Boulevard Bank and Inn, the Red Rug...."

"All right, all right, all right," hissed the other lord. "So I enjoy a little extra recreation. That doesn't mean that you should extort me for to your own benefit! If my wife were to find out...."

"Ah, Lord Camby... don't you mean 'if your wife's *family* were to find out'? For they're truly the source of your wealth anymore. They're who lend you this reputation of yours. As to extorting you... Camby, that's such a harsh term. Let us think of this as a long-term arrangement, shall we? I need your vote on the Council two days' hence. And just consider, that alone will add to your social image and continue to bolster your reputation. You really can't lose. Now, let us go, and you shall draw up the paperwork. See that I get it tomorrow morning so that if I need to make changes...."

And they passed Tyndie back down to the entry of the tunnel. She nearly collapsed with relief. And she was disgusted – did all the strong pray upon the weak? Look at The Shrew, she mused. The Shrew would have continued to bully Tyndie if she hadn't stood up to her. But these lords – Tyndie had expected better of such folk, and yet they were no better than cup bearers themselves.

After Tyndie had gotten her breath back, she decided to follow the tunnel she was in. Soon, her curiosity was piqued, for the tunnel dipped sharply downward, and then, Tyndie was surprised to find, wooden paneling lined the walls. Where was she?

And then she heard voices – again… but they were outside the tunnel.

And one single light shone in around the bend. A hole in the wall!

Tyndie tiptoed to the hole in the wall and had to stand up on the top of her toes to look out.

The first thing she saw was the elegant art hanging far across the room upon warm, wooden paneling. And she saw bookcases built into the wall, full of leather-bound books. Tyndie knew how to read, but she couldn't possibly imagine reading books such as those. Then she saw ornately threaded rugs that stretched the length of the entire wooden floor….

Tyndie's eyes widened in shock. She had been in that room, just once, to serve a very small group of dignitaries. This was King Reaghann's personal study! Why was there a spy hole to look into it?

And then she heard one of the voices….

Lord Drury.

Tyndie moved over slightly so that she could view the entire room. It was only the slightest of holes, built into the wooden frames and she suspected that a tapestry was hanging next to the spy hole on the opposite side.

But Lord Drury and one other lord were sitting in the King's study – without the King.

Lord Drury sat behind King Reaghann's desk in a cavalier manner, his hands laced together on the desk. Tyndie could not see his face, but she guessed he must look inordinately proud of himself.

The other man sat across from him, a white-haired, distinguished older lord, well-dressed with a grave expression.

"And Shaw?" inquired the other lord.

Lord Drury shrugged. "What of him? He probably thinks his brother is dead by now." He waved a precursory gesture to the ceiling as if shooing a fly away. "Is he?" he drawled.

The other man returned, "No, not yet. Not that I have been informed, anyway. Would you like him to be?"

Lord Drury thought for a moment. "It's really of no consequence. No one knows he's here. His brother thinks he died on the way to visit us with his wife, bandits. But – why not. Keep him alive. He may yet serve a purpose." Lord Drury paused. "Or is he not worth saving at this point? How long has it been now?"

"Six months, I think. He's in a traitor cell – they're not fed so well down there. But I could have the turnkey feed him more often if you like," suggested the other lord, sounding bored.

"Do as you will, Hampsherd."

Tyndie was round-eyed. She had placed her hand over her mouth so that her breathing could not be heard – she wanted to run, and cry, and tell her Auntie, and hide beneath her pillow, all at once. But she was transfixed – she had to hear more.

Lord Drury stiffened suddenly and held his hand up to stop the conversation. He cocked his head, as if trying to hear something far away.

Lord Hampsherd didn't dare say anything, though he arched an eyebrow.

Lord Drury then shook his head. "Do you – do you – *smell* that?" He took in a deep breath of the air above him.

Lord Hampsherd studied Lord Drury for a moment, raised both his white eyebrows and then sniffed the air.

He shook his head and, with a penetrating look, told Lord Drury that he smelled nothing, but Lord Drury did not appear to hear him. He was concentrating. "I've smelled it before. Jasmine. With lavender, perhaps." He shook his head.

Lord Hampsherd came near to scoffing.

"Gardens? Perhaps a lady keeps jasmine and lavender in her window? Or perfume? Such a common perfume."

Lord Drury recognized the presence of his companion with a chilled roll of his scornful brown eyes and a single arched eyebrow.

But Tyndie could not breath. Her soap! The soap she bathed with was made of jasmine and lavender oils.... Her Auntie had given it to her as a gift last year – "so you don't have to smell like all that kitchen grease...."

That anyone could identify it from several paces away was amazing – but now she knew why Lord Drury always knew when she was close by. She would get rid of that soap immediately. He chilled her to the bone. What sort of monster was that man?

In silence, Tyndie slipped away from the spy hole and then scampered as fast as she could back to her room, petrified.

———

Tyndie was having trouble grasping the entirety of what she'd overheard. She knew already that he was guilty of assassination. But her mind was spinning... the brother of the King of Shaw? Imprisoned in one of the traitor cells of the dungeon?

As soon as she'd emerged from the tunnel, Tyndie had run to the laundress and swiped a bar of soap. She hated to throw away Auntie's gift, but if she smelled anything like it at all again, Lord Drury would know. Then she'd steamed herself in a bath, near scratching the skin off herself and lathering her hair to her toes with her new soap.

Tyndie was taking no chances with the jasmine soap. She wouldn't have it anywhere in HarCourt Castle. Tyndie snuck out onto one of the lower baileys, waited until no guards were passing by, and then tossed the jasmine soap into the moat. Its *ploop!* into the dark moat water immediately relieved her and she drew in a huge breath of relief.

⸻

The next day, Tyndie went to her shift as always, though her skin felt a bit raw. In hindsight, she mused, scrubbing her skin off with laundress soap probably had not been necessary, but at the time, she had felt filthy from what she'd observed, and the entire encounter had left her skin crawling. Bumps still raised when she thought of Lord Drury's cavalier dismissal of the life of the King of Shaw's brother.

This was one of the times when Tyndie actually wanted to be busy – she was still overwhelmed and needed busywork to calm her nerves.

And with King Reaghann's guests still in attendance, there was still plenty of work to be had. Right now, they were polishing the silver for the King's personal dinner that evening. All Tyndie was doing was concentrating on her work, which soothed her.

"Tyndie, girl, run bring us some water, love," called Auntie Renne. Even she sounded tired, and she had been working this job the longest. And Tyndie recognized that running to get water was a break of sorts. Tyndie was thankful, for constantly rubbing at silver for hours made her hands sore.

After she had fetched the water, she took her time wandering back. She was going to need a little off-time, considering the serving time they'd be doing later –

"You!"

Tyndie looked up.

She nearly dropped her pottery jug of water on the stone floor.

Lord Drury stood in her path, staring at her.

All she heard was blood rushing in her ears. Something in her recovered her training.

She dropped a perfect curtsy, staring at her shoes. At the last moment, she adopted Lynza's North Hardewold accent. "Milord."

She hoped he couldn't see that she was trembling.

"Haven't I… seen you before?" asked Lord Drury, trying to place her.

"As it please you, milord, I'm just a kitchen maid."

Tyndie dared to steal a glance at him through her lashes. He was studying her shrewdly.

"And where are you taking that?" Drury gestured to the jug.

"If it please you, milord," and Tyndie curtsied again, "I just started working upstairs polishing silver. They asked me to fetch them some water." She curtsied again.

Tyndie kept her chin glued to her chest and continued to stare at her feet. All she could hear was the pumping of her heart in her ears....

She didn't dare to look up, but he had paused long enough for her to know that he was considering her story, or her, or both, perhaps.

Finally, Lord Drury shook his head. "Yes, you and your – jug of water – go." He waved his hand at her in condescension as he passed.

Tyndie nearly melted with relief but remembered to curtsy. "As it please you, milord," she murmured, though Lord Drury had stalked past her already.

After he had passed around the corner, Tyndie flattened herself against the cold stone wall, allowing her head to fall back against it. If only she wasn't in a public corridor, she would have slid down in a puddle on the floor and cried. So that was what it was like to talk to an assassin....

And then her crockery water jug fell to the floor and broke, letting water spill everywhere. "Crap!" Tyndie whispered to herself. Tyndie toed all the pieces of the jug back against the wall and watched as the water seeped into the stone cobbles.

By the time Tyndie had filled another jug with water from the well, she was tired of climbing stairs and wanted to hide where she wouldn't be found in the open again by Lord Drury.

But when she finally arrived, every single woman was sitting still, their knees together, a stack of silver in their laps. Tyndie stepped into the small room and saw no one else but them, so she set the jug down. Instantly, her heart began to pound again. She looked at each woman's face – Herma, Manda, Lynza, Farina, Auntie....

Their faces each were still as stone, their eyes round as they sat in their chairs, burnishing the silver. They were petrified, Tyndie saw.

He'd been there! Him! Why?

The look on each woman's face said plainly that there was a line drawn between her and them, and she had crossed it. They were frightened into silence, Tyndie saw. He must have told them, *"If you see her, do not tell her that I was here...."*

Well, that was it, then. Lord Drury did not believe in coincidences. If just the slightest thing concerned him, then he eliminated it, like Lord Stanson. And now, Tyndie thought, she was the new Lord Stanson.

Manda lifted her chin almost imperceptibly. Slowly, so that none of the other women noticed, Manda tilted the platter she was burnishing in her lap up so that Tyndie could see the bottom side of it.

Manda had chalked an arrow on it. Once Tyndie saw it, she wiped it off. She nodded just a tiny bit in direction of the door.

Run, Tyndie, run!

———

Tyndie sat on the cold stone floor, scrunched up between the walls of the tunnel, staring at the flame of her tallow candle as it flickered. It was a tunnel that she knew went nowhere, so she should be safe here. For she, too, was going nowhere, at least for now.

That bastard. That bloody bastard, she thought suddenly. Now she was sitting in here, in the shadows, jumping at every noise, at every drop of water that fell on the stone.

This was Drury's fault. Not hers.

He was an assassin. And known for it in certain circles, too, she fumed. Hired to kill men. And he took pride in it. She shook her head with disgust.

And then, there was this matter of the King of Shaw's brother. If she knew correctly, the King and his brother were twins. Tyndie knew very little of the world outside of HarCourt Castle, and even less outside of Hardewold, but Kings in the Eastern Alliance who had twin brothers, that was something people knew about, and something the lords and ladies spoke of at feasts and banquets.

Not only was King Rickstan's brother here, secretly imprisoned by Lord Drury in a traitor cell, but Lord Drury had killed the man's wife as well. While they were on their way to Hardewold on a state visit. And under King Reaghann's very nose. What a monster Drury was!

A small spider dropped silently, silently, silently down on a single thread and stopped, hanging before her. Perhaps it was observing her as she was observing it, thought Tyndie. She held the spider up on an index finger and it sat there looking at her.

Then Tyndie smiled. She thought of the man down in the prison.

Lord Drury had fucked up her life. Now Tyndie was going to fuck up his.

Hewart

"If it please you, Your Majesty –"

King Hewart ignored the servant. He always enjoyed Mulford's comedy, *"The Invasion of the Armies: A Very Long Tail."*

Hewart had sat in this same Great Halls for half his life watching tragedies and long, drawn-out dramas for theatre, for his lord father, may he rest in peace, had always preferred them. Comedies made light of that which they held most dear, of the wars and battles that men had died to win.

Hewart appreciated that. King Starthann had known nothing but war – against Clemongard, mainly, but he had planned the larger part of the Twenty Years War, years ahead of its formal commencement. King Starthann had sat at Grandfather's side, listening to tales of war, learning war strategy – Hewart wondered times if *war* had not been the first word off his father's tongue in the cradle. King Starthann had been a very serious, stern man, and stalwart to the last, but there had been no laughter in the man, and he had rarely smiled.

But Hewart as King was made of different stuff. He honored the dead, the sacrifice of the soldiers who had died in the service of Ambsellon, the wars, the battles. He had nominated three more days throughout the calendar year as honorary veteran and military holidays.

So if he wanted to enjoy comic theatre, no complaints should be made. And really, *"The Invasion of the Armies: A Very Long Tail?"* The 100 Legions War had been five hundred years ago, or so he thought… his memory for history was not at its best anymore, it might be seven hundred years ago. The point of the damned thing was that it was all of the countries fighting until they ran out of men and gave up – as the dog chased its tail throughout the whole play.

"Begging your pardon, Your Majesty, it is of some import…"

Hewart cracked his neck to both sides and then looked up at the servant. "Boy. You do see that we've got theatre here?"

The servant looked as if he might piss himself as he nodded. Little runt. Hewart sighed. "Well, go on then, what is it?"

The audience laughed. Damn. That had been his favorite part. The runt lowered an ornate silver platter. Upon it rested a sealed note.

Hewart glared at the servant and snatched the note. He pulled the seal apart and read three neatly inked words: *"News from Romeny."*

From Romeny? Hewart sat up straight in his throne. That was of note. Had it been from Ormon, he would have brushed it aside – Ormon could wait. But Romeny – he rarely received news, and certainly not correspondence from Romeny.

Hewart leaned forward and jabbed Sturgund in the shoulder. Annoyed, Sturgund turned to berated whoever had jarred his attention away from the play. Then he saw his father beckoning him with a finger and immediately leaned forward.

 Hewart stood up and, with regret, left the Great Hall. His Kings Guard started to follow him, but he shook his head. "I'll be back soon enough." They nodded with unease, for their one calling in life was to ensure Hewart's safety. Hewart had found the idea of a Kings Guard unnecessary at best – he was perfectly able to swing a sword.

Furthermore, a patrol of guards trailing along after him like puppies made him look weak. He could hardly tolerate it, but after the end of the Twenty Years War, death threats had been made, aye, and nearly carried out, he mused as he considered the scar on his back. And thus – he walked about with this pathetic retinue of liveried sword swingers.

As soon as Hewart closed the door to his study, his son stared at him.

"What the bloody hell –"

Just then, Hewart's chief advisor, Levonroth, entered from the back of the study.

"Perfect timing, as always," grumbled Hewart. How Levonroth knew when Hewart to attend him, he would never know. Hewart knew there was an answer, and whatever it was, he didn't want to hear it.

"Always, Your Majesty." Lord Levonroth bowed.

Lord Levonroth had served Hewart's father before him, and therefore came with only the highest of references. Hewart had been changing his father's household staff out for his own after his father's passing, from Cabinet members to Gate Guards.

"And why should I keep you on?" Hewart asked.

"You shouldn't," replied Levonroth.

Intrigued, Hewart had asked, "Why is that?"

"Because I know far too much."

"About...?"

"Your father. This kingdom."

Hewart had frowned at him, unsettled. "Would you hire you, if you were me in this conversation?"

Levonroth, who had known Hewart for the better part of his life, raised an eyebrow and stared at Hewart. Then he had said, "If I were you, I wouldn't be having a conversation with a servant. I'd have the balls to hire him or throw him out the gate."

Hewart had never forgotten that conversation. Needless to say, he had hired Levonroth, but also punched him for speaking to him in such a manner. No other man had spoken to Hewart in such a manner prior to that, nor had any man henceforth.

Levonroth continued. "We have received word from Romeny."

"And?" Hewart asked. He leaned forward upon his desk. Something about Levonroth he'd grown to hate – he really drew things out. He could just lead with the information. Times he just wanted to throttle the man. Just give him the fucking basics, man!

"It's odd, actually." Even Levonroth seemed puzzled, which was a rare thing. He presented two pigeon parchments and placed them, with unbroken seals, upon Hewart's desk. Sturgund leaned forward from his leather seat in front of Hewart's desk.

"Have we not been waiting for word from Ambsellon, rather than Romeny? Both of those are Fairview seals, Sire."

Hewart picked up one of the rolled-up pigeon parchments and examined the seal. He looked up at Levonroth. "Have you seen this seal? It's a Royal Seal of Romeny. From the Palace itself."

Sturgund asked, "Is it authentic?"

Hewart had included his oldest son in much of his business over the last three years, be it simple commerce, trade, royal necessities and ceremonial events... and strategies unknown to all the rest of the land but himself. And, of course, Hewart sighed, Levonroth.

After studying the seal briefly, Hewart nodded. "Authentic. I rarely receive written communication from Fairview, but I recognize it well enough."

Hewart glanced up at Levonroth. "What the bloody hell are they doing still in Fairview?"

Levonroth gestured with doubt.

Hewart sat down in his chair behind his desk, then popped the seal off the pigeon paper and unrolled it.

"*'Borne cub awaiting near the spring.'*"

Hewart looked up at Levonroth and Sturgund. "What the bloody fuck is that supposed to mean?"

They, too, bore expressions of confusion.

"Father, read the other."

Hewart twisted the seal off of the other pigeon parchment. This one had best make sense....

"*'Borne cub awaiting near the spring,'*" he read. "Bloody hell!" Hewart tossed the parchment off his desk.

Levonroth hurried to pick it up. He examined it and then the first. Then he stared with reluctance at Hewart and shook his head slowly. "I've no idea."

"What does *'near'* the spring mean? What happened to Ambsdale? I was supposed to collect the information at Ambsdale from the two of them once they made it back over the border," insisted Sturgund. "That doesn't say anything about a cave at all."

Hewart stroked his beard thoughtfully. Finally, he said, "I don't like it. I don't like it at all. It stinks. Something about it stinks."

Levonroth suggested, "Perhaps the initial reports of torture were worse than we heard. Whoever sent that may have had his brains too – scrambled, perhaps, to send something sensible to us."

Hewart rose from his chair and paced around his study. No. Something was wrong.

"That Ormon bitch...." He turned around and glanced at them. "Would she have sent this?"

Both of them looked surprised.

"From Fairview Palace?" asked his son.

Slowly, Hewart nodded. "Somehow, though, somehow... she has a hand in this shit. She's not innocent. Any bitch who plans to force her husband's hand... that's no one I trust, even if it benefits us in the long run...."

Hewart remembered feeling a bit of respect for the Ormon Queen – albeit reluctantly, for she was just a woman – when she had outlined her plan for Hewart to move on Fairview, on Romeny while they lay hibernating, as she called it, which had pleased Hewart, since he was the King Bear.... And then she could sweeten her husband into joining Hewart against Romeny, and then the Eastern Shield, for much of the Shield had not yet recovered from the Twenty Years War....

For all the bitch's whisperings, Hewart did not trust her farther than he could spit.

And this... this bloody note. The men they sent off were supposed to meet in Southern Ambsellon and wait for Sturgund to meet them and report home to him with their information. Their return trip home was plotted out ahead of time, their note to be sent home pre-arranged.... What the bloody hell was this?

"Father –" Sturgund's voice was impatient. "I know the note is not written as we arranged. But let me ride out to Ambsdale and see if either of the men are there."

"No." Hewart placed his hands on his hips. "We do not need this information. We have fought countless wars without information from inside spies. And won, I might add. Something about these messages stink. I trust my gut. As will you one day, for sometimes, it will be the only source of information you'll have. No offense intended, Lord Levonroth," Hewart nodded to his chief advisor.

Levonroth shrugged. "None taken. Sound advice, I might add. Though, I do hope, young Sturgund, that I will not need to advise you in the same capacity as I have your father and grandfather. May that day never come." Here, he nodded in deference to both Hewart and Sturgund.

Hewart smiled tiredly, but Sturgund rolled his eyes. "Yes, yes, yes, Father, may you live forever, but –"

Sturgund, who had also begun to pace with impatience about the study stopped, for Levonroth had coughed politely and Hewart had produced a loud and lengthy clearing of his throat.

This is my son, who will one day sit my throne, Hewart mused. May he mature substantially before then and now....

Sturgund suddenly looked up, at both Levonroth and Hewart, aware that what he'd said had been offensive. A round "o" suddenly overtook his features and he gaped like a fish.

"Sturgund, if you act like this in public, then I despair of you," Hewart sighed as he looked down the bridge of his nose at his eldest son. "At least finish what you were saying."

So chastened, Sturgund continued in a more respectful tone. "I only hoped to say, Father, that, perhaps what was expressed in those parchments was a coded clue, something the sender attempted to let us know. If we decode the message, we might know where to find our men, for obviously what the arrangements we agreed upon with them before they left for Romeny have changed.

"The word *spring* is still mentioned, and *cub,* and those both mean Ambsdale and me. Therefore, do you not think it then prudent for me to at least scout out Ambsdale? Our men may be awaiting me. Forgive me, Father, but I do not think after their sacrifice for the Crown, that it is just of us to leave them without the support we promised them."

Hewart and Levonroth flicked a glance at each other at the close of this speech.

Ah, his son. If he could just keep his dick in his pants and those fine ideals in his head, he would make a fine king one day, a fine king....

Sturgund, swing a sword, shoot crossbolts? Oh, yes, with the best of them. Had he a brain for business, for accounting, numbers? That he did, and better than most, even if Hewart were to admit, himself. The boy's memory, it soaked things in like sand, and it never forgot a thing. He was better at strategy than battle, but he'd not fought on a battlefield before, either, mused Hewart. Not yet. But the boy – he had too much passion – passion for women, passion for ideals, passion for justice.... And those latter two, if not all three, would get him killed.

"My son – did you not hear me when I said that something about this stinks? I trust my gut, and my gut says that something is wrong," Hewart insisted.

"I, too, believe things are not as they seem," protested Sturgund. "But how will we find out for sure if we sit about this desk, wandering about hemming and hawing? Are we not bears, are we not creatures of action?" demanded Sturgund.

Damn that boy of his. Damn him. Right in the balls. Too much of himself in him, grouched Hewart. He glared at Sturgund.

"Very well –"

"Excellent –"

"*But* – a detachment of men shall accompany you," finished Hewart.

"*What?"* The despair on Sturgund's face was tangible. "A detachment? Whatever for? I can take care of myself!"

"That I don't doubt," returned Hewart. He readied himself for what was going to be a number of protestations. This was woman's work. His wife was cold and dead in the ground these five years past, bless the woman. Hewart didn't fault the woman for taking a fever, but she would have handled this stubborn child far easily than he. Women take care of unruly children, not men. Hewart was a king, not a bitch full of milk for pups to nip at.

"A detachment will only call attention to me. Aside from making me look weak," Sturgund glared.

Levonroth cleared his throat. Hewart and Sturgund switched their attention to the chief advisor. He was tapping his chin thoughtfully.

"Might I suggest a compromise…?" Before either Hewart or his son could reply, Levonroth continued. "Send a small detachment… but have it follow at a discreet distance behind you, a few hours, let us say.

"We, of course," Levonroth gestured at Hewart and himself, "will choose the men ourselves." Though this was intended as compromise, Levonroth's sturdy delivery of the idea made it clear that that the plan was now complete and would be set in motion.

Neither Hewart nor Sturgund cared for the plan entirely but it was better than any other.

"Ride out at first light, then. And by the gods, boy, don't take any foolish risks. There is nothing right about this." *Not a damn thing*, Hewart added silently.

Ron

He woke slowly, basking in the glow of the sun on his face.

As he opened his eyes and sat up, two things instantly jarred Ron out of his half-asleep state. One, that the red wine from last night had indeed, resulted in a hangover, for he'd drunk the better part of the bottle. And two – a very sore lump had risen over night on the back of his neck. Between the two, Ron's head was pounding.

"Ow," he muttered as he prodded the welt were those arseholes had clouted him yesterday.

Ron yawned and slid out of bed.

The clump of hay where Kylon had fallen asleep last night was empty and no blanket either. Ron sighed and shrugged. Street kids. The hammer was left behind in the center of the anvil, however. Odd, that, Ron mused, but right now he didn't pause to consider its ramifications as his head was pounding.

He stepped outside for some water and heard a rustle. Customers?

Instead, Ron found Kylon sweeping the stables clean. The boy looked up. He pointed to his neatly folded blanket which hung over a stall and then admitted with a guilty expression, "He – the master – he started…" and then Kylon's voice dropped to a whisper. Behind his hand, Kylon whispered, "He started *snoring* – and I couldn't sleep – so I came out here and slept." He shrugged up at Ron in apology.

Ron looked down at the ground in amusement. Aloud to Kylon, he smiled. "He's been known to do that, I'm afraid. I've learned to sleep through it. You'll get used to it soon enough."

Ron chugged several gulps of clean water from the water barrel down and then told Kylon, "Now, let's put some breakfast together."

Ron normally did not eat breakfast, but growing children needed to, especially growing, undernourished, soon-to-be blacksmith apprentices. Well, if the boy stayed, that was.

He watched how quickly Kylon – or perhaps Pylon – consumed his breakfast, and knew he'd have to take a trip to the Market or the boy would be eating hay for lunch.

Most of the morning was spent explaining to Kylon what the tools of the forge were, how they operated, and what blacksmiths did. He even pulled the tongs out of the forge and molded a bit of steel on the anvil for the boy.

Twice, he gave the boy a bit of a break. And why not, for an eight-year-old's attention wandered and waned after just a few hours. Ron, too, needed the break, so he could splash some water on the pulsing lump on the back of his head.

The second time he stepped outside for a drink at the water barrel, Ron saw something rustling in the breeze against the forge.

Nailed to one of the wooden beams were two cored apple skins over the top of a blank piece of pigeon parchment.

Shit. Ron was to go to The Brew House and Tavern and wait to be approached with information.

And he was convinced that this visit would be concerning the people in the carriage yesterday. How was Ron supposed to work that into a covert conversation, when what he really wanted to say was, *"Two bloody knockers kidnapped me and threw me into their carriage!"* That should make for some interesting conversation. Or maybe he'd just show them the lump on the back of his head.

It was only snoon but if Ron picked up groceries from the Market Place and placed an order at the tailor for a tunic and breeches for Kylon's size, it'd be after noon and Ron could stop at The Brew House.

Ron cleaned himself up and told Kylon to watch the forge until he returned. Once he told Kylon that he wouldn't be gone long and that he'd be returning with groceries for lunch, Kylon brightened. Amused, Ron recalled vaguely eating everything he could stuff in his mouth while he was growing up.

Ron browsed about the Market Place for the extra amounts of eggs, vegetables and fruits he'd need to feed his own small apprentice, and bought two loaves of bread from the baker as well.

The tailor eyed him with curiosity when Ron described the measurements for Kylon's tunic and breeches but asked no questions. If the boy stayed on for two weeks, then Ron would have a small sigil stitched onto Kylon's tunic, just a small one, without his name, but the same crossed hammers and anvil as Ron's.

—⟨⟩—

Finally, Ron stepped into The Brew House and Tavern. What Ron wanted was a good pint, for whatever it was that his employers had to impart, it was serious enough that it couldn't wait until the next Market Day, and so a good ale would help Ron wash it down. And possibly even numb that bump on his neck.

The Captain crossed his path as he stepped toward the bar. "Captain," Ron gave the tomcat a precursory salute and then slumped into his bar stool.

Hasley set his usual basket of bread and bowl of hot stew before him, though her smile was an absent one, for she immediately moved on to new customers who sat down at a table across the bar.

Ron stretched his visit out by dipping a slice of buttered bread into his stew, waiting for someone to arrive.

Ellia brought him a pint of ale, for which Ron was grateful. Not often was The Brew House and Tavern busy at noon, but it had its days. Usually, only a few customers strayed through.

A man seated himself one barstool over from Ron. Ah. Finally. He placed a pear on the bar. He ordered a full loaf of bread from Ellia to take with him. Ellia smiled and disappeared behind the swinging kitchen doors.

After she was gone, the man commented, "I see you took the boy in."

Ron, confused, thought, *that's what they're here to talk to me about?*

Ron continued to stare at the wall before him, but returned lowly, "He'll be of no trouble."

The other man responded just as covertly, "See that he's not."

Then Ellia returned from the kitchen with a warm loaf of crusty bread. She smiled while the man paid her and wished her a good afternoon.

As Ron's Market Place representative turned away, his elbow knocked the pear to the floor, though he appeared to take no notice. Ron recognized that this stunt was for his benefit alone.

Once Ron heard The Brew House door creak to a close, he casually reached down and added the pear to his basket. But there was a piece of pigeon parchment, folded into such a tiny wad that it was almost invisible upon the wooden planks. Ron swiped it up and slipped it into his boot.

It was everything he could do not to hurry through the rest of his meal, for this had never happened. Even meeting like this in The Brew House was highly irregular. But, as he pushed his empty pint and stew bowl toward Hasley, he decided on a whim to order a full loaf of Luvian's bread to take with him. After all, Kylon was like to eat him and Master Cradwick out of the forge, so why not have a loaf of Luvian's bread to himself? And he could also follow the representative's example....

Ron was sure the pear was for him to follow the code, per usual, indicate his understanding once he received his information. He'd let it sit out in front of the street for one of them to see after he'd bitten into it.

Once he arrived back at Cradwick's forge, Ron stepped with silence behind the stable, so that Kylon would not know he'd returned. He drew in a deep breath and pulled the pigeon parchment from his boot. Amazed at the care taken to wad it into such a tiny square, Ron finally unfolded it and tilted it toward the sunlight to read it....

By the time Ron finished reading the parchment in full, he found his mouth had dropped open.

He read it a second time.

And then a third....

Myrischka

Reclining with her feet before the fire, Myrischka was entirely relaxed.

"Is it done, then?" she asked the Guard. A mercenary, he had been a part of her network for years now. She would ensure that he was richly rewarded.

"Yes, Your Majesty."

"Hmmm." Myrischka considered. "How?"

He glanced down at her for a second. "You've never wanted to know before."

She stared back at him, waiting. After all, none of the others had been a child of hers.

"Under the ice." He cleared his throat briefly. "He was – unconscious. Didn't know it was happening."

Fortunately, the man stared straight ahead while saying this. His hands always behind his back at second attention, but Myrischka liked that he never patronized her, as one in his profession might.

Myrischka felt a distant touch of disquiet; she recognized it as such and shrugged it away. She had only borne children to remain Queen. She allowed herself a personal fondness for them while they were very small, but beyond that, they had been of no use to her.

Myrischka folded one of her legs across the other. "And the other?"

"Our men are waiting for Hewart's cub." Her mercenary shrugged. "Whether he's unaccompanied or escorted, enough men are waiting to fulfill the task."

Myrischka smiled slowly. "Good," she purred. "Bring me his head if you can." She breathed in a deep, satisfied breath, imagining the look on Hewart's face when he received his son's body, bereft of its head.

"As you like." The mercenary nodded his head. Another thing she liked about him. He didn't Majesty her repeatedly. He understood his purpose and rarely overstepped his bounds. In fact, Myrischka did not even know his name, and she appreciated that in a mercenary.

She held up her hand. "I still have not received those pigeons. That troubles me."

The merc glanced at her, as if expecting a question soon.

Myrischka brushed her hands in the air. "Pay it no heed now. Two days of information gleaned through torture cannot be of consequence. Do you have a man in place waiting for them, should they arrive?"

He inhaled and replied, "I do. As soon as they cross the Green Gates, we will accompany them, then – relieve them of their burdens. So to speak. As pre-arranged."

She nodded slowly. Excellent. She despised loose ends.

Myrischka looked back up at her mercenary, disguised as a Palace Guard. He stood still as ice, staring across the room as he waited to be addressed, as if she did not exist.

"Very well, then. I've had a long day, and I barely slept last night, so I shall be retiring to my chambers." Only part of that was true. Nabol had been preoccupied with something last night, for he had simply not gotten it right. His report from Munsolrysche had been more entertaining. She had finally just thrown him out.

Myrischka stood up and rose a hand to cover a yawn.

Her pet mercenary nodded and, turning sharply on his boot heel, exited her rooms.

— ⟨⟩ —

He had closed the solar door. Good. Once inside her bed chamber, Myrischka nudged her slippers off. Then she stalked over to the corner of the room. Bare and devoid of art, she stared at it. She'd never thought to use it again. But now she smiled....

Myrischka shoved at the unseen door with her shoulder. Part of her was impressed that it actually opened still.

She slipped inside the hidden chamber, lit the wall sconce from the candle in her lantern, and continued down the marble hallway.

After she'd given Munsolrysche his children, Myrischka had her entire chambers rebuilt, the entire wing completely redesigned. Now she had an entire wing to herself and only entertained as necessary. But – she had kept this private marble hallway. Munsolrysche probably forgot its existence long ago. Well, she thought, as she slipped down the marble floor in her bare feet, that would be a risk she would have to take.

Finally, she arrived at the other end of the hallway.

She shoved the door open, peeping into her husband's bed chamber. Myrischka held her breath, listening, her back against the wall. But no – the only noise was the crackling fire and the snores of her husband in that enormous bed.

She padded into his room on her toes. The thick carpet felt much warmer than the ice of that marble hallway.

With contempt, Myrischka stared down at this man who ruled Ambsellon, who snored before her, unaware of her presence.

Myrischka slid silently into his bed, slowly as ice dripping from an icicle. Munsolrysche stopped snoring for a moment, as she lay there, staring at him, but then immediately began snoring even louder.

Myrischka climbed atop her husband then. Gods, he had grown even fatter then she recalled. She took the fattest pillow on the bed and forced it over his face. He saw her just long enough for his eyes to widen with hatred. She smirked at him and covered his eyes as well. He could make no noise whatever.

She had to straddle the bastard – he kicked and flopped like a mating walrus. Just as he slowed, Myrischka took out the knife. She plunged it into him – into his fat belly, his neck, his shoulders –

The blood sprayed all over her, of course, and dripped from her chin. She sank her knife into him once for every single year of marriage, and for each child she'd had to bear him, remembering how he'd ridden her like a drunken pig fucking a sow.

And then, at the last, she took both hands and sank the knife into his heart. She left the knife there. Poor Nabol, she snickered. It was his bootknife, after all. A gift for a child from a soft king, engraved. She had snuck it from his boot last night. He had probably noticed it was missing, but how to ask her if he had left it in her rooms?

Finally, she crawled off the fat fuck. The pillow had fallen off and his eyes bulged in death.

Ugh, the blood was getting sticky on her hands. Just as much a pain to clean up after in death as he had been in life. She shook her head with disgust.

Myrischka slipped back into the marble chamber, extinguishing flames as she went.

The knock sounded upon Myrischka's oaken door some time past early morning. She slid out of bed and tied her mantle tightly about her as she padded to her door.

A number of Palace Guards – Kings Guards, of course – stood in her hallway. They all bowed with the sharpness that their stations demanded.

"Your Royal Majesty," the first guard proclaimed.

Myrischka sighed with impatience. Burning her clothing last night had taken longer than she'd anticipated. She'd prodded it with a red-hot poker in the fire to be sure absolutely no trace remained, and then inked a number of numbers down on parchment. She'd thrown that in and half burned it, so that it appeared as if that had been what the she'd burned of late. Myrischka in no way believed her rooms would be searched, but she was merely safeguarding herself in all ways.

Dryly, Myrischka answered, "I presume there is a reason you and your men have awoken me?"

The Kings Guard bowed again. "With greatest apologies, Your Majesty, but there is."

Myrischka waited and then, with a roll of her eyes, spun her hand around. "And…?"

"It's His Royal Majesty, the King…." The guard trailed off, unsure how to proceed.

Myrischka sniffed. "What, then? Has he gotten his dick frozen to another ice statue again? I've told you then and I'll tell you now, I won't take care of that again. Hot water will take care of that, and frankly, in my opinion, the hotter, the better." Myrischka pretended extreme annoyance – actually, recollecting the first scene, the annoyance was no act – and started to close her door.

The Kings Guard coughed - he was too young to have heard that story – and immediately said, "No, Your Majesty, if you please – the King is –" And he leaned closer. "He's dead."

Finally, she thought. She schooled her expression. All knew there was no love lost between them, therefore, a show of sadness and tears would be unrealistic. She took a deep sigh and leaned against her door jamb, crossing her arms. After a few seconds, Myrischka shrugged. "Well, then. Let us change the guard. Send for a bird for Bryranth at – wherever he is now, and have him return at once."

The Kings Guards exchanged worried glances and shuffled their feet.

Myrischka arched an eyebrow. "Do you not know where Bryranth is? Riversberg? Wessex? We must change the guard at once."

The Kings Guard who had been addressing her told her, "Prince Bryranth returned home not three days ago. He was seen dining in the Great Hall just two nights past."

Myrischka frowned. "Well, then! Why are speaking to me? Speak to the Crown Prince – he is now the King. Long live King Bryranth!" She gestured, annoyed, to send them on their way. She wanted to smile, for they were quite flustered.

"If you please, Your Majesty. Prince Bryranth is not to be found."

"And have you looked in all the ladies' quarters? He is his father's son, after all. I'd try even the maids'. Toll the bells, if you must, that might get his attention."

"If it please you, Your Majesty, we have looked throughout the Palace, and throughout the city. Prince Bryranth is not to be found. Thus, we have come to you."

Myrischka stood straight. "Not to be found? Did he leave again? Hunting? Ice fishing? Come now, he is our new King!" She allowed irritation to creep into her voice.

"No horses were checked out, and no tracks in the snow around the Palace, Your Majesty."

She sighed and shook her head with an air of disgust. "Very well. How did the man die?" Myrischka backed away suddenly and covered her face. "Not fever? Not plague?"

The Kings Guards shook their heads. The leader immediately negated her inquiry. "No, no Your Majesty, the King was not ill." He dared to step forward. "If I may...?"

Myrischka pulled her mantle about her.

He leaned down to her. "The King was *murdered*!" he whispered. He looked horrified.

Myrischka had wondered what this moment would sound like, and now she knew. How delicious, how satisfying....

She wanted to grin, laugh.... But, of course, that was impossible. Myrischka pretended shock. "Murder? What brings you to such a conclusion?" she questioned aloud, feigning disbelief. She acted as though they were simply being dramatic. Mainly because she wanted to see what they knew....

The Guards' eyes grew round and though they maintained their forward stance, their eyes looked all about, probably from shock as well as the absolute knowledge that the King had, indeed, been murdered. Myrischka wondered how many people knew now – the bells hadn't tolled yet.

The main Guard leaned forward and told her, "He were strangled, Your Majesty, and... stabbed as well. While he slept."

"Your Majesty, with the deepest of pardons," asked the Kings Guard behind him, "but, do you own a knife?

"How dare you! This is Her Majesty, The Queen of Ormon!" hissed the Main Kings Guard.

The second Guard lifted his eyebrows and held his ground.

"Your Majesty, please forgive him," uttered the Main Kings Guard.

Myrischka yawned and smiled. "Not at all. He's the sort of man we need in our ranks. Do – please." She allowed the twelve Guards in.

"I own two knives." Myrischka padded across her fur rug to her desk, her mantle rippling behind her as she strode. She tied it tighter once she stood behind her desk.

Opening the first drawer released a woodsy smell that she'd always enjoyed. Myrischka picked up her hunting knife, a gut hook at the end and partially serrated, one that she'd carried on countless hunts. She laid it before them on her desk. "My hunting knife, as most of the men I hunt with will confirm. A truly excellent tool. Unfortunately," and Myrischka sighed, "the weather has not been accommodating of late for hunting." Her disappointment on that fact was real.

She enjoyed how some of the Guards eyed it with hesitation.

Then Myrischka slipped her hand along the mantel of her fireplace. She held up her other knife and laid it before the Guard as well. "A betrothal gift from my uncle. The hilt is ivory, my initials inlaid with silver."

"That will be quite enough, Your Majesty," the Main Kings Guard said as he turned a glare over his shoulder at his compatriot. Though she did admit, they looked at the knives with some curiosity. Myrischka never once considered using a weapon of her own for just such a reason.

"If you'd like to examine them...?" she gestured smoothly.

"No – no. As it happens, we already have the –" and the Main Kings Guard took a deep breath. "The murder weapon. That is to say, the knife that killed him."

Myrischka turned a look of purest contempt upon them. "And yet you stand here in my chambers? Having awakened me? When you cannot find the King-to-be and you have the weapon who killed the King-who-was? What nonsense are you about?"

The guards had the sense to look guilty. "You're here, telling me someone has slaughtered the King of Ormon. You have the murder weapon. Are you not wasting precious time standing in my chambers instead of looking for the person who committed this heinous crime?" She waved her hand emphatically. She had to convince them, after all.

But soon enough, the bells would need to be tolled. Before he started to stink. More so than he normally did, she smirked to herself.

"We ordered the gates closed as soon as we discovered the – his body," the Main Kings Guard informed her.

"Well, there's a start," she commented dryly. "Have you any idea who would do such a thing? Other than, of course, all of the Eastern Shield? Who had access to him day-to-day? What would have caused someone in his social circle to commit such an act of violence?"

Ugh. Did she have to handhold them through the entire process? The knife had Nabol's initials inlaid upon it, after all.

The main Kings Guard bowed and gestured for his men to leave. "Yes, Your Majesty."

"And do find Prince Bryranth. We need to change the guard, after all. And I want the bells rung at noon. Have his body wrapped and –" Myrischka brushed her hand in the air, for she had no idea how kings were laid to rest once dead... particularly one in her husband's condition – "seen to as tradition accords."

The main Kings Guard bowed.

"I expect a report at mid-afternoon on your progress," Myrischka called as he closed her door.

Then she smiled.

Sturgund

He pulled up on his horse, his breath fogging before him. Very few people were out. And a clear blue sky, no snow – no reason to be indoors. Not even children playing. In truth, Sturgund was only on the outskirts of Ambsdale, yet he expected to see more folk out, more of the streets shoveled. Instead, his horse was squeaking through the fallen snow as she stepped ahead.

Sturgund knew his father had sent a small detachment far ahead of him as well as one to trail him. It was just his way. And possibly why the people here were hiding indoors. Or so he'd prefer to think.

Sturgund really hated when his father was right. For his father was not one to just move forward with a new set of circumstances, no. Father wanted you first to acknowledge that he was right, at least twice, and then he would refer to the incident or dialogue for two, perhaps three days following. And then he would bring it up among company simply to embarrass you and gratify his ego, Sturgund brooded.

But this time – Father was right.

Not to say that Sturgund did not believe that something about this mission was off – for he had. But his entire life, Sturgund had plagued himself with *"what if's…?"* As King himself someday… *may that be a long, long time from now*, he added, as he always did whenever that thought crossed his mind… Sturgund's rule would introduce more opportunities… more possibilities for the people, new and better ideas, he would break them out of the same old rut they had been slipping and sliding about in. In short, he would rule with more optimism.

And perhaps, Sturgund would finally be the king who broke into Clemongard, for he and his countrymen were tired of stagnating next to Ormon, staring at Romeny…. Clemongard was the real jewel.

But right now – the gut Father didn't believe he had was nagging him.

It was the Ormon Queen who had contacted them first, via her contacts with Father and Levonroth. She set this entire miserable adventure in folly up. And behind her husband's back.

Was it so hard to believe, perhaps, then, that he would be stepping into a trap…? Hmm. Sturgund pondered how else her note might be considered as he prodded his horse forward.

"'Bared the bear, look for cub in the cave beside the spring…."'

Sturgund guessed the cave still meant Ambsdale, given the caves behind its waterfalls. But… what if it was read backward….

Spring upon the bared bear cub when he arrives in Ambsdale?

What if those men were never to arrive in Ambsdale at all? What if this were a trap to lure him to a location where men would kill him? And all a plan of the Ormon bitch....

Sturgund knew then that he was right. He wheeled his horse about in the snow and backtracked her at a sudden gallop.

Immediately, an arrow struck his horse. She screamed and crumpled into the snow. Sturgund had enough time to leap from the saddle.

Where was his attacker? He drew his sword and turned all about him, wide-eyed with shock.

Suddenly a number of men crept out from their positions behind homes and bushes, their gaze all fixed upon him. He counted one, two, three crossbows, a longbow, three swords....

Sturgund couldn't hope to fight them, and likely he couldn't out run them. His heart was pounding in his ears.

He would not have it said that a Prince of Ambsellon went down without fighting to his last drop of blood.

"Well, then, have at it! You hid yourselves long enough! Come out and get a bite of me!" Sturgund yelled.

And then they did. They ran straight at him. Sturgund swung as he could. The first man, scruffy and dirty, Sturgund speared in the neck, for he would bleed out quickly and he could pull his sword out with ease. Dark blood gurgled out of the sword wound left behind and the scruffy man fell into the snow, clutching at his neck.

The second man, a mercenary, wore leather armor. Sturgund buried his sword into the merc's sword arm and watched as the man screamed. The sword flashed in the sunlight as it fell in the snow. Sturgund heard the *whoosh!* of a nearby arrow just released and immediately hid behind the merc. In a second, Sturgund was glad he had, for the merc was thrust forward upon him. The point of an arrow protruded through the man's neck. Blood sprayed all over Sturgund – just an idle though passed through his mind that he was glad his mouth was closed. The man continued to spurt blood, but he would serve as shield until he could perhaps find a horse – though Sturgund had a sinking feeling he wouldn't make it that far. Crossbolts and arrows... against him on foot... the odds were not good....

And then men screamed a battle cry. *"For Ambsellon!"*

Several men ran forth and stood around Sturgund, fully armored, others running forth to confront his attackers.

Sturgund wiped the blood from his face, then yelled, *"For Ambsellon!"* and threw the mercenary's body to the ground. He remembered little beyond that, merely swinging his sword and reveling in the blood that burst forth.

He did recall a glinting axe from far above him, falling, falling... and that he hit the ground, hard....

Tyndie

Tyndie was so bored. Not that she would prefer running about on her feet, but she at least would like to be out in the open rather than passing time in these dank tunnels.

First, she caught up on her sleep. Laying her face on the bare, dank rock of these passages disturbed her – she couldn't bring herself to do it. Besides – there were rats! So Tyndie slept propped up against the walls.

Tyndie was fairly certain two days had passed, if her stomach was to be trusted.

She had begun negotiations with her stomach. At first, she was not going to slip out and steal food out from the bowls outside the tunnels in the middle of the night. For she surely did not want to get caught. If she was caught, she would lose a hand, sure and simple, and would likely be thrown in the dungeon cells.

Then her stomach protested so much that she could not ignore it. So Tyndie decided instead to sneak into the kitchens at night. She could pass as a kitchen maid still, and there was so little activity there after dark.

Tyndie waited until she knew the moon had risen before she stepped out of the tunnel near the kitchen. Silently, she stole down the kitchen steps....

"Tyndie?"

Tyndie almost jumped out of her skin.

But it was only Eliza, a kitchen maid near Tyndie's age that she'd worked closely with.

Eliza glanced over her shoulder and then whispered, "Tyndie, girl, what you doin' here!" Her eyes were round and her face worried.

Tyndie tried to play nonchalant. "Why do you ask?"

Eliza grabbed her arm. "Don't you play silly with me. A man, a *lord –*" and her voice dropped even lower – "a scary one – he come by but two days past, lookin' for ya." Eliza looked Tyndie up and down in the firelight of the wall sconce. "You ain't with his child, are ya?"

Horrified, Tyndie whispered, *"No!"*

Eliza shrugged. "Well, then...Tyndie, I don't know what ya did, but ya can't stay here no ways. He weren't no nice person. You need to leave this place." She paused. Her brown eyes lit up over her freckled nose then. "Tyndie, I got cousins in Presfield – they'd take ya in –"

Tyndie nodded. "What did he say when he came?"

"Well, ya know, I'm the first one by the door, so he asked me." Eliza gulped. "He asked if a kitchen maid who looked like you had stopped workin' with us and gone upstairs to work recently.

"I could see he weren't no nice person – and I knew he was talkin' about you. So's I told him we had a kitchen girl long time ago who transferred out but I never known where she went, and that it mighta' been you, but it weren't my place to know such things."

Then she took a good look at Tyndie's face. "What you got on your face? Your face is dirty," and she reached out toward Tyndie.

Tyndie pulled back out of the way. "You can't tell anyone I was here. I was –"

And there it went – she swallowed down the last remnants of her pride. "…Looking for some bread…." Gods, she felt pathetic.

Eliza stared at her with an open mouth for half a second. Then she grabbed some baguettes from the corner workshelf. "They're a bit burnt, and I ain't had a chance to throw them out yet. But if that's what ya want…."

A troubled look on her face, Eliza threw another look over her shoulder. "Ya know ya should leave. You best be hiding yourself somewhere good," she scolded Tyndie. "But I'll keep puttin' the burnt ones over here, in the corner for ya. An' when I see they don't get picked up no more, then I'll whisper a prayer to the gods and hope ya made it outta' here well and good.

"Here, these are startin' to bruise, too." Eliza threw Tyndie a clump of green grapes.

"Thank you," Tyndie whispered. Eliza hugged her suddenly. "You be careful, Tyndie girl!"

So Tyndie now had burnt bread to crunch through, enough to fill her belly.

After a day of sulking and seething, Tyndie had calmed down. She finally decided to spend her time following all the hidden tunnels. She was surprised at where they led her – many of them led only to bed chambers, while some led to solars. Others led to corridors that weren't in use.

But Tyndie found two hidden tunnels that disgusted her – one led to a room which had another spy hole in place. The King's bed chamber, if she was to judge by the richness of the décor, the size of bed itself, the art upon the wall…. Why would anyone want to spy upon the King while he was in his bed chamber, she mused.

Well, of course, she could imagine all sorts of unsavory reasons, but she was nevertheless disgusted at the idea. She wondered if the King knew of this tunnel and toyed with the idea of leaving a bit of chalk outside the door. A King should know if he is being watched.

The other room tunnel was similar, for it led to what Tyndie presumed was the Queen's bed chamber, though its furniture was shrouded in dust sheets, for King Reaghann had not yet married. This belonged to the previous Queen. Tyndie wondered what sort of people spied on Kings and Queens while they were in their bedchambers….

And then the tunnel led her back to King Reaghann's study. No one was in it this morning, nor did she expect there to be, for the royals were yet in the Great Hall, breaking their fast.

But last night, Tyndie had snuck down here to peep through the spy hole of the study – and been enthralled. For King Reaghann himself had walked in just then, alone and unattended.

Part of Tyndie felt quite guilty for watching what he believed to be private moments. But another part of Tyndie felt as if she were now his invisible guard, somehow. And so she watched him.

Tyndie watched as the King unfastened his deep green surcoat and tossed it carelessly upon a chaise lounge. He pulled his black leather boots off with a barely audible "Ahh," and sat them neatly next to each other on the side of his desk.

As King Reaghann seated himself down in his chair, he loosed the laces and the tunic beneath his chin. Then he reclined back comfortably in his desk chair, crossing his stockinged feet upon his desk.

Tyndie smiled as she watched this. The King of Hardewold seemed so… normal now.

From his desk, he pulled open the first drawer and removed a stack of parchments. He gazed at the top of the first parchment, then balled it up and tossed it across the room. "Arsehole."

He gazed at the top of the second and third parchments as well.

"Arsehole, arsehole," and tossed each parchment across the room after he balled them up.

Tyndie, hidden in the shadows behind the spy hole, was beginning to thoroughly enjoy herself.

King Reaghann took an interest in the next parchment and scanned through the first half. Then he balled it up abruptly, scaring Tyndie in her position behind the wall. "Not bloody likely!" That parchment got tossed across the room as well.

King Reaghann read the next two parchments through. He appeared to consider them worthy, for he set them off to the side.

His next parchment made him scoff. "Bloody hell. What a fucking idiot." He tore the entire parchment up. "There you are, Lord Canton. That's what I think of your proposal."

The king stretched and yawned in his chair. Alarmed suddenly, Tyndie covered her mouth with both hands, for now she had to yawn, and she couldn't be heard in the shadows. The King would surely think he was going mad if heard a yawn suddenly – he'd think the wall was yawning.

King Reaghann picked up the rest of his parchments – obviously proposals for bills and tariffs from his Council members, thought Tyndie. He shuffled through them quickly, just glancing at their titles and authors.

"No, no, definitely not, maybe, maybe, yes, possibilities, joking, arsehole, no, arsehole, definitely not, definitely yes, maybe, yes, arsehole, yes."

At her spy hole, Tyndie was grinning as she watched the King separate all the different proposals based on his knowledge of the Council member, rather than what the proposal might state. She recognized that he knew what the proposal read anyway, but she had enjoyed watching King Reaghann cut his pile of two dozen down to possible six in less than fifteen minutes.

The King got up from his desk then and threw all the proposals he'd designated as "arseholes, no's" and other negative titles into the fire. Then he walked around the study and picked up the few crumpled up balls of parchment. One by one, he tossed them forcefully across the room into the fire, with great enjoyment on his face.

"Best part of my night," he muttered.

Then the King walked over and picked up his green surcoat, slung it over his shoulder, and strode out of the study.

Tyndie wanted to laugh. He had left his boots behind.

──────

Eliza was good as her word – she left burned baguettes off to the side each night for Tyndie, last night with an apple that wasn't bruised at all, and the night before, two plums that looked more as if they'd simply fallen rather than bruised.

Tyndie was ready to sneak out of the castle, but the question was when? Part of her told her just to run – she had her destination after all. But Tyndie was quite sure that a man as dangerous as *Lord Drury* – how she hated him now! – had the castle gates watched for a maid of her description. Despicable… he was just that precise, thorough, for how else had he become so good at this other… pursuit of his? And a simple maid leaving the castle in broad daylight would be remembered, for maids rarely left the castle – or at least not dressed as such. Tyndie would have to steal a common dress from the launderer's at night before she left.

All this, just so she could sneak out of HarCourt Castle undetected – and hope to find work who knew where? All she bloody knew was this castle. She'd grown up here. All Tyndie knew of the wide world beyond these castle gates and the city outside it were the tales she overheard others speak of. HarCourt Castle was the only world she knew. And now – Lord Drury was ousting her from it.

It was him that kept Tyndie from having left days ago. It always kept coming back to *Drury*. That smug countenance, those cold eyes.

She wanted to strike back, right as hard as he had. She wanted to see his reputation trampled, wanted to see fear replace that smug expression, and a stricken demeanor take over his condescension. Tyndie had lost everything, and was forced to live in the shadows. She would see Drury – she would never call him *Lord* again, for the word *Lord* suggested a person of honor – lose all he held dear as well… his reputation, his standing with the King, perhaps even his title….

And so, Tyndie yawned, she passed her time in the tunnels, the unknown bowels of HarCourt Castle, crunching on bread, watching over King Reaghann, and searching for unknown passageways to prowl.

⸙

Spy holes were her favorite. Tyndie was astonished at first at the idea that people would really listen to others from inside these tunnels. Many of these spy holes looked into unused rooms and chambers now, but once she knew where on the walls to look for them, Tyndie was both disgusted and amused that people were so curious, or perhaps deceitful as they were. She imagined men like Drury made use of such spy holes quite often. Drury himself... Tyndie decided he paid others to do such work. She could not imagine him tiptoeing about in her tunnels – she had started to think of them as hers – ducking beneath the spiderwebs and stepping around the puddles of dripping water, even stepping quickly to the side as a rat ran past....

She followed one hidden tunnel for some time, and she nearly stopped, but found finally that it opened up above her. Tyndie climbed an old, rickety ladder and pushed a trap door above her, hoping that its hinges wouldn't creak and alert anyone up above.

Tyndie pushed it up only enough to peep out around her. Hay fell all about Tyndie, and she realized that she had opened a trap door near the stable. The smell of livestock and manure confirmed her theory. The stable could be of use in the near future, Tyndie mused, though she had never even been near a horse. She took great care to let the trap door back fall down in silence.

Two more hidden tunnels ran near to the guards' barracks, and while Tyndie wasn't sure if they were aware of its existence, she certainly was not going sneak in and find out. She could hear men to either side of the walls, laughing and yelling at each other. Tyndie retreated from both tunnels as quickly as she could.

The next tunnel Tyndie came upon took her farther and farther below the castle, and she shivered, for she knew she below the castle now. The walls were no longer smooth castle brick was simple subterranean black rock. Upon occasion, a wall sconce was wedged into the tunnel wall, and Tyndie lit it, for she'd stolen candles three times now from the chandler and she needed to conserve her tallow as best she could.

Finally, she arrived at the end of the tunnel. With reluctance, she pressed her face against the end of the tunnel, hoping to hear voices that would indicate what sort of room this tunnel had led to, whether she would be safe here or not.

Tyndie decided this was no safe place, however, and yet that it was still exactly the place she'd been searching for all along. The dungeon.

But were there guards outside the door? Would they see her open the door? And worse, what if the door didn't open from the outside? Tyndie's own foolish curiosity might lock her down in the prison.

How ironic, and what a stroke of luck for Drury would that be. She would be trying to break someone out and instead, she would lock herself in.

Tyndie lit the wall sconce before the door. Chalk marks scratched the rock there, but she saw how old they were. In fact, there was no chalk at the bottom of the floor by the door. Yes, Tyndie thought, staring at the rough wall, there might be a way of getting into this dungeon on the other side of the door... but like all dungeons, there was no way of getting back out.

With a sigh, Tyndie slid down the wall with discouragement. She hadn't come all this way not to be able to get out again.

The wall sconce flickered then, casting shadows on her legs. Tyndie arched an eyebrow. Of course!

She knew she couldn't block tunnel doors open with a piece of wood – she had discovered this the hard way early on, for the stone wall had crunched a piece of wood in half and Tyndie had had to skulk her way through the castle back to another tunnel door.

And often, rock was not a viable door stop either, for it was unreliable and might pop out at any time, or it might also be crushed. Both wood and rock made noise that would call attention to the tunnel door's existence as well, and down in the dungeon... Tyndie could not afford to be seen or heard

But her shoes.... They were made of leather with wooden heels. The door couldn't break those. A sly smile crept across Tyndie's face as she unlaced her shoes.

She didn't much like the idea of mucking up her stockings, so she took those off as well, feeling rather disgusted at her sudden vanity. Still, the less she had to sneak out at night and wash, the better.

Ugh – the floor was cold, and wet, and... muddy, disgusting. This shoe thing had better work, or she would find herself locked in a bloody prison with no bloody shoes, she mused with worry.

Then Tyndie pictured Drury's face and chinned up, taking in a deep breath.

She shoved the door open. Her bare feet held no traction, slipping and sliding in the mud, but after a few seconds, the door budged open.

Tyndie made a face – a dank, stale smell floated into the tunnel, enough to gag a horse. Tyndie listened at the crack of the open rock door, breathing through her nose. Just as she was beginning to wonder if maybe she had opened the door into the sewer after all, she heard a distant voice, a moan.

And then a clanking. Like a tankard upon bars, and then several tankards, as if they were being dragged across prison bars, to and from. She had reached the dungeon after all.

Tyndie sucked in a breath and stuck her head inside the dungeon.

Nothing. No one. Darkness and the stench of human decay. Tyndie yanked her head back in, panting. She gagged a bit, for it was the most unpleasant place she'd ever been in.

Tyndie, what the bloody hell are you doing?

She could be well on her way to the ocean by now, instead of standing here, in the dark, with her bare feet freezing and mud between her toes…. She didn't owe these people anything. If she was smart, she'd pull her stockings back up, get her shoes back on, and get out of this bloody castle tonight.

And Tyndie truly, seriously considered it. But then her eyes fell on the old, scratched chalk marks on the wall, and she thought of Drury's smug face, and King Reaghann in his study, being played for a fool like ticks upon a dog….

Damnit. She rolled her eyes and picked up her shoes.

Tyndie bent down at the corner of the open door and after a few seconds, had placed them where the door would fall against them. She studied them. She hoped she'd see them again soon….

Then she stepped into the filthy, underground cave that was the HarCourt Dungeon.

Tyndie took several steps, her back against the rock wall. Her eyes finally adjusted to the darkness, but no one was in the cells before her. A stroke of luck or not, Tyndie wasn't sure.

She reached the end of her corridor and finally heard a conversation far down the next corridor. Guards!

Tyndie peeped around the dungeon wall.

Four guards in HarCourt uniforms were squatted on the floor, playing at dice and laughing. Tyndie pulled her head back in and nearly scoffed. And she was worried about being frightened. But how to find the traitor cells?

The block ahead of her was black and empty and the block she had just snuck up had but one torch burning. What if Tyndie had to slip past the guards somehow? How awful to have made it this far, only to not find the prisoner, or worse, she worried, get lost. Tyndie immediately chalked a mark on the bottom of both walls.

"Sounds like it's time to feed the folks, they's gettin' restless," yawned one guard.

"Damn – that's twice now," complained another.

"They do that when they get bored. Fuck 'em. I'll feed 'em when I get good and ready. Three threes," replied a third guard.

"Really, why don't you go feed you whole one prisoner, Joshik? We could give ya a hand, don't want ya to overwork yaself."

The other guards laughed.

Tyndie listed to the dice hit the stone of the dungeon floor before whom she presumed was Joshik say, "Oh, my traitor boy? I fed him yesterday. He don't need to be fed. Maybe tomorrow. If I feel like it."

And they laughed.

Tyndie's eyes grew round. She threw a look back down the corridor she'd just crept up. She had been in the traitor wing all along!

Tyndie silently snuck down the wing, finding no one in any of the cells. She was nearly in despair when she reached the end.

In the very last cell, crouched in the far back corner, was a body.

Tyndie wasn't sure what to do – what if the dungeon guard decided to come back down the wing? She decided that unlikely. None of them were going to interrupt their game for prisoners any time soon. If she had to, Tyndie could make a run for it and disappear into the tunnel, and then out of HarCourt Castle, no one the wiser, and these dungeon guards would just think she'd disappeared in the dungeon.

So she took a chance and lit a candle, but covered the top of it close with her hand.

The man in the cell held his arm up against the light. He'd not seen light in a very long time, Tyndie saw with despair. How sad!

Tyndie lowered her candle and, with a glance up the corridor first, she snuck up to the cell door. She could see the man's face now.

His beard covered much of his face, though it was mostly brown. Dirty and stringy hair hung down his face in tangles. But behind his hair, Tyndie saw green eyes. Sad green eyes, hiding from the candle glow under a scratched arm. His face looked smudged, but something about the way he sat, and the shape of his face... it reminded her of King Reaghann....

"A kitchen maid? Are they charging for a look now or do they even know you're down here...." The man's voice was hoarse, gravely, and full of dejection.

"It's you, isn't it? You're him," Tyndie whispered. It was. It was him! The Duke of Shaw, King Rickstan's brother. She had found him....

He regarded her and said nothing for a moment.

"What do you want with me, girl? Don't you know, I'm a traitor? Hence," and he waved up at the top of the cell, "the traitor cell?"

"No, no you're not. You and your wife were attacked on your way here. I know who was behind it, I heard him talking about it. He's killed two other people, too. And he wants to kill me," Tyndie blurted out in a quick whisper.

King Rickstan of Shaw's twin brother sat forward. "How do you know all this?"

Tyndie glanced down the corridor. "I'll be back. You can't say anything about me being here, anything at all, do you understand? Now here," and she tossed him a baguette of bread. "Keep it hidden."

She took a deep breath and whispered, "I'll be back as soon as I can. Remember, not a word. I'm going to rescue you, my lord!"

Ron

"So's why ya want t' talk t' me, Ronnie? I thought we agreed to, you know," and Nick pulled at his collar.

They were leaning in the twilight against the side warehouse by the South Fair docks, and this was tonight's last shipment. Fishmongers and shipmen called to each other from ship to docks.

They weren't likely to be noticed since the men were scrambling to finish before the last of the sun sank.

Ron sighed. This wasn't easy, asking for help – especially from Nick, of all people.

"The street boy I took in?"

Nick nodded. "Told ya he'd run away. It's just what they do, mate. Sorry t' say."

Ron shook his head. "No, no, nothing like that. He's still with me." *That's actually a bit of the problem,* worried Ron.

"No shit? That's a surpriser. Well, Ronnie, give it a bit of time...."

"Nick, quit the shit for a moment and listen. I need you to...." And Ron trailed off. Wow. This was harder than he thought it would be.

"To...?" Nick rolled his hands around to prompt him.

"Look out for the kid on the street."

Suspicion made Nick lean on the building and cross his arms. "I thought that's what you was for, Ronnie boy."

"Well, in case I'm – not around."

"Not the hell around? Where do you plan on bein'?"

"Look, Nick. All I'm asking is, will you have your people keep a look out for the boy, even if he's not working for me? As you say, street kids...."

Nick's face demanded further explanation.

"You know I have my people, but they're not like yours – mostly not street folks. This kid, he's a good one. He was in an orphanage before but ran away –"

"Which orphanage?"

"28th Street, I think he told me once."

Nick nodded. "That ain't no nice place. Walkin' nightmares in there. Good for him, runnin' off."

"So the street gangs keep beating him up –"

"Ronnie, that's a street boy's life, it is, I swear to you –"

"Nick, just listen for once? He refused to join them because he said they were mean to people, and every time they catch him, if he doesn't join, they beat him up."

Nick studied him for a moment. Then he looked out toward the sunset and the docksmen. "Ronnie. You can't rescue every bleedin' pup –"

"He's eight, Nick. He pretends he's ten."

Nick was quiet.

"Scars on his face…."

"Damn you to every hell, Ronnie!"

"I've already bought him a new tunic and breeches, new shoes. He's a good kid, respectful. Learned his letters and numbers at the orphanage…."

"If he's so bloody fuckin' wondaful, why wouldn't he be stayin' with you? All I mean to say, Ronnie, for all you run your mouth, you ain't that bad of a git. Warm place to stay, three squares and a roof. I can't says for the Master – frankly don't see him so much about no more but –"

"Just – Nick! Promise me – South Fair honor – you'll look after the kid on the street when you see him – and by that, I mean you and your people." Ron had Nick by the balls now – between South Fair, honor, and all of his people, there was no way that Kylon wouldn't be taken care of somehow, if he didn't stay with Cradwick.

Nick glared at Ron. "Yeah, all right, promise – I gotta friend the lad could shoulder under if he needed to. And yes, no little street shits will be jumpin' his skinny arse.

"But you – there's somethin' stinks. And I don't mean smithy soot, neither. Ronnie, you got somethin' cookin' an' right now, I'm thinkin' it stinks…."

———

Ron worked more with Kylon. Cradwick was already drinking wine with less sleeping potion in it. By the time he was drinking regular wine, hopefully he would recognize Kylon formally as his new apprentice.

Kylon had a lot to learn, and in so little time….

Hewart

This was his stern face. Probably he wore it quite often, but today it was sterner than usual, for it masked the enormity of his emotions – they were just a… a conglomerate, and all of them useless.

Hewart was accustomed to conspiracy. Conspiracy was part of what colored the Royal Bears' bloodline, for hundreds of years. Networks of spies and infiltrators from generic informants to scouts to deep cover agents and even, he mused testily, double agents, had spun the wheels of war for Ambsellon for countless generations.

He'd had a whiff of this conspiracy, but only a whiff. All of it was an oddity, every single sliver of it, and so he had, against his better judgment, dismissed what his gut was insisting, demanding of him at the time.

Never, Hewart thought, never should he have let Sturgund leave.

All but three of the soldiers he had sent with Sturgund had survived, and one of them would no longer be serving, for his leg was broken and like as not, he'd walk with a limp for the rest of his years.

A knock sounded upon the door of his study. Hewart shook his head but Levonroth opened the door to admit the servant.

Hewart stared at the servant, who held up a trembling tray before him.

"Somebody had best be dead – else take that rot away!" growled Hewart.

The servant paled but continued to stand before him.

Levonroth advanced quickly to the servant and smoothly removed the parchment from the silver tray before Hewart upended it in the servant's face.

He strode to the velvet curtained window and stared out at the gray day. Snowing.

Behind him, he heard Levonroth pop a seal open.

"Your Majesty –"

Levonroth rarely was speechless, so this must be worth listening to. Hewart unclenched his teeth and wandered to his desk. He leaned on his desk chair.

"Well, are you going to tell me or do I have to guess?" Hewart snapped.

Surprise was replaced by amusement as Levonroth looked up from the parchment. Hewart suddenly realized how rarely he had seen Levonroth smile, but right now, as he gazed at Hewart, a smile crossed over his face.

"Sire, news from Ormon. His Majesty, King Munsolrysche of Ormon, is dead. Murdered, in fact."

Levonroth than folded his lips in to hold back a laugh.

Hewart's eyes grew round. "Well, I'll be. Son-of-a-bitch. I'll be."

He sat down in his desk chair and realized his mouth was open with astonishment. "Son-of-a-bitch." Hewart thought of all the meetings, battles, wars, the feasts and ceremonies.... "I knew the man – what, forty years or more. And murdered?"

Levonroth nodded.

"Does it say how?"

"No, Sire."

"Harrumph." Hewart crossed his hands over his chest and rocked back in his chair a few times. "Be damned," he finally said. Then he realized something. "Shit. That means funeral services. And the swearing in of the new king – and – and – all that bloody mess."

Ambsellon and Ormon had been allies for so long no one even counted the years anymore, except historians. Brother countries nearly, though not literally.

But, just as any other ally, as soon as the changing of the guard of a new ally took place, they immediately were at the side of the new king, to swear allegiance. More so with Ormon and Ambsellon – their Ambassadors immediately stepped up to the task of aid and support. Hewart remembered distantly the prior Ormon Ambassador, explaining much of Ormish customs, politics, and formal requirements back when he had taken the throne.

And all that bloody paperwork they'd need to sign - fortunately, his Ambassador was a canny one. Hewart forgot the Ambassador's name most times, but Levonroth oversaw the better part of the communications from him.

The main part of this Hewart was hating more and more that he thought about it was the bloody trip to Ormon. Across the mountains, and in this weather. To that miserable ice mountain they considered a home. Ambsellon lived most months of the year in cold weather, and rarely saw grass, to be sure – but the temperature in Ormon dropped far below what Ambsellon lived in year around.

Between the trip over the mountains, and staying for who knew how long, Hewart hated the idea. And... part of it was this gout in his leg. It wasn't gout as far as anyone else knew. He told the Healers that it wasn't gout, so they said it wasn't gout... but privately, Hewart knew it was the onset of gout. A lengthy trip over the mountains with a long retinue of followers would take forever, and then a prolonged stay in a miserably freezing cold country.... Such was the reason why Hewart always invited the Ormish to Ambsellon.

Not attending an Ormon Royal funeral, and an Ormon Royal changing of the guard, was out of the question. Unthinkable. Bloody hell. The next few months were going to be miserable.

Levonroth popped open the seal of the second message.

"Funeral private – please do not attend. Will send details for Changing of the Guard ceremony. All prior messages to be disregarded." Levonroth stopped reading and then commented, "It has the Queen of Ormon's seal."

Hewart relaxed in his chair. "Well, some luck to come out of that. No one wants to traipse across those bloody mountains at this time of year. Or ever, frankly. Who's the new king going to be? Can't ever remember the boy's name… begins with a 'b'." He knocked his knuckles on his desk.

"Bryranth," Levonroth supplied.

"Ah. Well, then, long live King Bryranth. Odd sort of name, isn't it. Wonder how the old man was murdered…."

Levonroth shrugged. "I can't imagine, but I do have a few men in the Palace over there. One has managed to station himself fairly high up. He sends a bird each week to one of my men. Mibol, Mabol, I don't recall his name, but I'm sure we'll find out what happened soon enough."

"Ah. Excellent," replied Hewart. Levonroth had a plum in every pie. It wasn't that Munsolrysche was a friend, per se, but as long-time allies, they had planned numerous battle skirmishes, fought the Twenty Years War through, sat side by side in feasts and ceremonies, occasions of all sorts…. Yes, Hewart decided, he would raise a toast to both the man and the King tonight, and likely drink himself completely drunk.

A thought crossed his mind then. "The seal is authentic, I suppose?"

A snort of disgust came from across him. "How might we know at this point?"

Hewart's stern face replaced his curious expression.

Never had he ever been so proud of any of his children then he had when he found out about how the bastards had ambushed Sturgund, alone in the snow, hardly anyone to assist him, yelling for the enemy attackers to charge him….

The three survivors had been too far away at the time to assist him just then, but had seen and heard everything, and reported the entire scene, word for word, blood for blood, to Hewart.

As a father, Hewart looked at his son's body and died over and over again inside. He could remember upon an occasion or two chastising Sturgund to be more careful in his swordplay and his riding lessons, and the boy replied with that happy-go-lucky charm, "Don't worry, Father, you still have two more sons!" Hewart had told Sturgund that he was never, *ever* to joke about such a thing, not *ever*.

As a King, Hewart had wear a brave face and allow no one, not even Levonroth, to know the kaleidoscopic emotions he felt, for he had a number of actions, ideas, he wanted to follow through on.

Sturgund, however, sitting before him, was of a single mind. Someone had been ordered to kill him. His blood had been spilt and he would not rest until he found out who.

The boy – Hewart could no longer call him a boy, not now especially – sat there, bandaged, when he should be abed. He was furious, and he wanted to find out who had tangled this mess, who had ordered his death.

Sturgund's arm had nearly been hacked off with an axe, and the back of his head had struck a rock as he'd fallen into the snow, or such was Hewart's report. Whatever had happened, he'd been unconscious when they'd arrived back at the castle, two of the soldiers taking turns carrying him.

Hewart had hovered about in the Healer's wing, and they had tried to shoo him from the curtained bed but he'd refused.

So many Healers surrounded Sturgund, Hewart could hardly see his son, and Levonroth pulled outside. "Give them space to work," he'd commanded in a whisper.

So the two of them stood just outside the curtains waiting anxiously.

At one point, Sturgund regained consciousness and started thrashing about on the bed. "What the fuck! Get off me, you bloody wench!" he'd shouted.

Hewart and Levonroth had stared in surprise at each other, for Sturgund was always so courteous and well-mannered.

"Drink it!" came the hiss of one Healer.

"Fuck that! I'm not drinking some bloody potion – let me up – get off, me, woman!" All Hewart and Levonroth had heard was the twittering of Healers about Sturgund and his thrashing about in the bed. Hewart had hated to find humor in the situation, but to hear his son screaming so had brought the smallest of smiles to his face.

Then Sturgund's thrashing had stopped for just a few seconds. "Did you just – slap me! Do you know who I am?"

The Healer had snapped, "I don't bloody care if you're a Prince or the Bone Man. Now drink it down or it's the Bone Man will be comin' for you!"

"Here. Tastes wretched," Sturgund had said after a few seconds.

"So sorry, Your Highness, we don't age our life-saving potions to perfection," the Healer had retorted with sarcasm.

Levonroth had covered a smile with a hand. Hewart had then glared at him and immediately Levonroth's smile had disappeared.

"I – I –" and Sturgund yawned. Then a *ploof!* sounded against the pillows.

"Is he out?" one Healer had asked.

"Finally, thank the gods! What a mess he's in –"

Once Hewart had been assured from the Healers that Sturgund was not going to die, he had taken the reports from the soldiers who had waited for him.

So proud Hewart was – Sturgund yelling a battle cry, expecting to die but going down fighting. He'd killed four men on his own before Hewart's men had arrived to assist.

But men were waiting all about to ambush him, mercenaries with crossbolts and arrows… men Sturgund couldn't have hoped to fight off. They had known he'd be there, they had bloody well known…. And according to that report, if Sturgund hadn't rolled out of the way at the last moment, he'd have lost his head to that axe.

Between the actions of that heroic soldier pulling him out of the way in the snow, and Sturgund holding his arm up to protect his head – well, Hewart hated to think what might have happened. Someone wanted his son's head…. And with the Ormon king's murder….

Perhaps Hewart should look to himself now, he thought suddenly, for an attempt upon the son to rise to his throne, and possibly him next? Hewart was now very sick as he stared at his bandaged son across the desk.

Sturgund's arm was bandaged very tightly, and he had to keep it elevated. The back of his head was also bandaged, and Hewart knew his son had taken a very hard hit on the back of a rock that might well have killed him itself. But when Sturgund showed up at Hewart's study this morning shortly after Levonroth, Hewart considered for just one moment telling the boy to go back to his rooms to rest. Then he saw the flash of his son's eyes and silently opened the door.

Levonroth had hinted a bit about Sturgund perhaps needing a bit more rest, but Hewart had smiled, for Sturgund had grown up overnight.

"I'll rest after I kill those bastards."

Nabol

At first didn't think his balls could shrink any higher up than they already were. Now he couldn't even feel them anymore, or anything else, for that matter.

Nabol had been asleep when they'd pounded at his door. All he'd had time to do was sit up before the castle guards had rammed down his door.

"Are you Nabol, servant to His Royal Majesty, King Munsolrysche?" asked the foremost guard.

Nabol had nodded.

"We find you guilty of the regicide of His Royal Majesty, by means of your knife!"

He had blinked. Shock had washed over him. Had he wanted to kill the bastard? Of course, he was such a pompous, disgusting arse. Would he have done so? And by his own knife? Nabol was smarter than that. Poison, perhaps, had he ever decided to kill Munsolrysche, but....

It mattered not. They had stuffed him in one of the old crow's cages, high above the Palace. It was a means of torture, for it had spikes inside and was too small for a man to sit comfortably in any position. But in this weather – freezing cold weather....

The spikes had drawn blood, but the blood froze nearly immediately after they'd hoisted the chain. Finally, the guards set him on the crow hook. They threw ice and snow at him from down below on the tower top, though most of it didn't reach Nabol – the cage was too high.

It must have been that bitch who had stolen his knife, for he'd missed it two days ago. Gods, what a bitch. And she knew that he could hardly ask either of the Royals if he'd left it in their suites. Conniving slut.

Nabol had known nothing good would have come of that bitch having his knife. But framing him for the King's murder? That was beyond his expectations.

Nabol had been out here nearly half an hour now, and he knew, naked as he was, that his entire body was frostbitten. He wasn't shivering anymore, and he knew his body was shutting down.

At least now he could act like himself – up here, in the swirling gray wind and ice, where no one would see. Instead of the silly, petrified runt they believed him to be. He thought of his family, his parents and siblings, the house he'd grown up in... just one last time....

Nabol opened his eyes for a second. "To Ambsellon!" he croaked, then closed his eyes and fell asleep.

Myrischka

The hour-long castle and city ringing of the bells had been the longest hour of her life. Actually, perhaps not, once she thought of it. The first time he'd fucked her had taken about the same amount of time, and it had been no different than a drunk pig fucking a sow. Wedding nights were to impress guests, not the bride and groom, she mused. Had it been her choice, she would have just taken his cloak, his monstrous ring, repeated the words, and such have been done with it.

But simpering had been required, and an enormous cloth-of-gold gown, jewels woven into her hair and wound around her neck, a tiara.... All of it for the guests to ogle.

Myrischka nearly cut the bell-ringing short so addled had her mind become by the tolling. The people had never even seen him or been spoken to by him, and he didn't give two shits about anything but that enormous gold throne.

She had ordered Nabol placed into a crow's cage. The Guards wanted to flay him alive and let him die in a traitor's cell, which actually she had liked the idea of, but Myrischka wanted to appear both gracious and vengeful, so she ordered them not to flay him, but place him into an old crow's cage. Not only would he bleed up there, but he would freeze in under an hour.

So in Myrischka's first act as Queen, she met both the needs for vengeance against a man who had committed regicide, as well as the Guards' need for blood.

Nabol actually had intrigued her of late. When she allowed him to sleep in her chamber – a rarity – he spoke in his sleep upon occasion – and some very interesting things came forth. Nabol was either a very good liar – or his parentage was partly Ambsell. Or possibly both. But when he was asleep, he suddenly was not the Nabol Myrischka knew, but a man with heavily accented Ambsell speech, who spoke not a child's "if you please" servant's demeanor, but instead with a sort of militaristic bluntness.

Bryranth was still not to be found, she was told. Some hazarded that perhaps he had met with a similar end as his father, and all in listening vicinity frowned. Others worried that Bryranth may have left the castle and did not even know of his father's death, even though numerous birds were sent.

Myrischka listened to all their fears with a patient demeanor, for this time period was crucial. Transitioning from King to Queen would be difficult on this masculine-focused society. And once it was clear that Bryranth was not to be found, they would reach for the remaining bloodline, though she and her pet mercenary had disposed of those individuals months ago, and quietly. Fever, hunting accidents, slips on the ice…. Not one of the original bloodline remained, not even a babe.

Her own bloodline was a match, but many cousins ago. Though that mattered not, for she was Her Royal Majesty, and had been for almost twenty years now. Myrischka liked her chances.

She encouraged the Council members to send more birds, to send men by horse. Eventually, Myrischka knew, they would tire of trying empty options and turn to her to run this castle.

But first, she thought as her black mourning mantle rippled beyond her, they needed to think she cared.

Tyndie

Tyndie was still recovering from her encounter with King Rickstan's brother. She sat on the tunnel floor, gnawing on some bread, with her feet propped up against the other wall. Tyndie realized she didn't actually know the prince's name.

But she hadn't much of a plan to break the man out of his cell. She would need the key, obviously, but what if the dungeon guard didn't have a key? Wouldn't it be just like Drury to have the key himself?

The more and more Tyndie considered the idea, the more she realized she was right. Drury would never leave such a thing to chance. The brother of the King of Shaw, escape HarCourt Castle to tell his story? No. Drury had that key.

Not that Tyndie knew how to escape HarCourt at all, much less the castle, with a Prince of Shaw. If Tyndie could sneak out unseen in plain clothes from the castle, she could easily get out of the city. But not with him. She needed to plan an escape.

She sighed with irritation and crossed one leg over the other. This was far more complicated than she had anticipated. What if someone recognized the Prince, even if he did look like a sewer rat now? And smell like one, she mused, wrinkling her nose as she thought of the dungeon.

Steal a horse? Tyndie knew Princes could ride horses, and in his weakened state, he wasn't likely to walk or run far. But the Castle gates went down at night, and they couldn't steal horses by day, for they'd be seen.

She'd sneak men's clothing for him from – somewhere – so he could change out of his prison dregs.

But before all else, Tyndie would have to break the prince free of his cell. And that meant.... A key.

From Drury.

She hugged her knees to herself.

Finally, Tyndie took in a deep breath. She didn't know where his office was. And she would have to watch him to find out. But first – she would have to change clothes, and bathe… for his sense of smell was unnerving. He would know if she was near.

Why was she doing this again, she asked herself? She looked at the tunnel walls.

Because you're living in a tunnel and Drury's not. Because that prince is living in a cell and Drury's not, whispered Tyndie's conscience.

Yes, but rather a tunnel with a way out than a cell without one, Tyndie told herself. If she got caught.... And if Drury caught her – then he'd just kill her.

After a week of living in the darkness, seeing only by torchlight, eating burnt bread and bruised fruit, the idea of death actually wasn't as disturbing as it once had been.

Living in a cell, however, without her freedom, after running about the way she had, wherever and however, all over the castle, that was a different story. Tyndie sniffed. She knew every inch of this castle now, and knew where to look for what, and for whom. This castle was almost as much hers than it was the King's, except that she was on the inside of the walls, and King Reaghann was on the outside of the walls.

If only the King knew what she knew, and where.... Tyndie almost hated to leave him behind. For with Drury here, she knew the King was in danger – if not physically, then by other means.

She thought of all the parchments he'd tossed about. Surely, his Council members were under Drury's thumb, just as Tyndie had heard Lord Canton extorting Lord Calbry.

Tyndie toyed with the idea of leaving a note for King Reaghann before she left, but what King would believe the word of a kitchen girl over a well-respected lord?

Tyndie had discovered a spy hole into what she believed was the Council chamber, but if her memory served her, they would not meet for another week. Tyndie hoped to be gone by then. She often wondered if all castles were as riddled with secrets and deceit as hers was, or if it was just HarCourt.

—⟨⟩—

The bath had been luscious. Steaming hot, to be sure, and Tyndie was sure half her skin had peeled away, but at least the dirt of the tunnels had bubbled free from her skin and her hair. This time, Tyndie did not scrub herself raw with launderer's soap, as someone might notice the scent through the walls if she passed by a spy hole. But she did grab two bars of soap, for she had an idea.

Tyndie was dismayed at the amount of dirt floating in the bath when she stepped out of the water. Had she really gotten that dirty? No wonder Eliza had stared at her so.

She stepped into a new maid's dress and apron that she'd also filched from the launderer's. Now, at least, she wouldn't smell – or look – like a sewer rat herself when she went prowling about the castle, searching for Drury's office.

If the worst happened and Drury did see her, Tyndie knew that she could step into any of her tunnels and disappear behind the walls. He would never know what happened to her or where she'd gone, but Tyndie did know that he would double his search efforts. Right now, Tyndie mused, Drury probably thought that she had left the city and so had dismissed her from his mind.

But what she had to do was find him first.

Tyndie decided just to position herself outside the King's study. Where else would Drury be most likely to go? For if she found him, Tyndie could follow him at a steady but discreet pace behind him.

Hours stretched on like days as she sat before the King's study. Finally, Tyndie heard the laughter and talking of men passing by in the corridor outside the study doors.

She stood up on her tiptoes, but no one entered the room. Then Tyndie had an idea – she ran to the Council Chamber.

Lords were filing in! Seating themselves about, voicing platitudes to each other.

And then Drury….

Tyndie's eyes narrowed and her lips curled with aversion. A convivial smile in place, Drury patted the shoulders of friends he passed, while others called his name in greeting. That…

man… who glided so easily amongst the King's Council members… *he wants to kill me….* Tyndie's nostrils flared with hatred.

And, of course, he was seated just a few seats from the King. *Sittin' with the salt*, thought Tyndie.

Every Council Member rose as one entity when King Reaghann entered, and they all bowed and uttered, "Your Majesty," in unison as well. But as the King stepped toward his seat, he faced Tyndie for just one moment, and his eyes looked at the ceiling, his face indifferent. Then he turned and motioned the Council to sit down, and called them into session.

She watched with interest for a while, and wondered which of the Councilors the King thought were arseholes, based on his disgust of their proposals. But his speech was courteous and well-delivered, even when he disagreed.

Tyndie, finally bored, slid down the wall the paneled side of the inner wall to listen. After a while, she heard some of the Councilors repeat the same proposals, only reworded. Did they think the King an idiot? She wished she'd brought a plum but then immediately squashed the idea for of course, for *Drury* would *smell* it. Tyndie wished then that she could fart so he could smell *that* – a perfectly chosen expression of her true feelings for the man. Arsehole.

Just as Tyndie's head was falling on her chest, she heard King Reaghann's polished golden chair scrape back on the polished marble floor of the Council Chamber.

"You have all submitted your proposals," and there was a loud stacking of parchment upon the table before him, "so I will make every effort to consider them. My lords, until our next meeting, we are adjourned."

Tyndie jumped to her feet. Many of the Councilors looked surprised, so Tyndie decided that King Reaghann had ended the meeting abruptly. Good, she thought. All they had been doing was blowing up their egos over and over amongst each other and even arguing a bit. Infrastructure and tariffs on new exports, and tariffs on market goods, and taxing incoming ships from the Coastal Countries…. Tyndie didn't know what most of that meant but apparently King Reaghann did.

As Tyndie watched the King leave his chair, Drury stood out in his path. Drury hadn't spoken a word throughout the entire meeting, but whatever he spoke to the King about now, was in hushed tones too low for Tyndie to hear. The King nodded and gestured with an arm to follow him. Tyndie rolled her eyes.

Then she raced through the tunnels to the King's study, hoping that the King was on his way to his study.

Tyndie arrived ahead of them, for she heard their voices outside in the corridor. But she had to sit and cover her mouth, for she was out of breath and she couldn't afford to be heard behind the wall.

"– you see why I thought I should bring this to your attention personally," Drury was saying as he and King Reaghann walked into the King's study together.

"Yes, I can see your thinking behind this – it sounds like a possibility worth exploring," commented the King neutrally as he sat down in his study chair.

Drury, not to be dissuaded, also sat down, for Tyndie heard the leather cushion of the chair across from the King's desk *swoosh* with Drury's weight.

Tyndie dared to peep through. Drury had crossed his legs comfortably and laced his hands, as if this study was his and he was entertaining the King, not the other way around. Tyndie fumed.

Not to be intimidated, the King asked, "And the river project? What is your view on the river project? Do you have papers drawn up on that yet? I recall you mentioned once that you were looking into that with an …interested partner…?" King Reaghann sounded innocent but Tyndie suddenly recognized it as a version of Drury. A political strategy, delivered flawlessly. She smiled behind her hand.

But Drury suddenly sat forward. "Forgive me, Your Majesty –" and he sniffed the air.

Tyndie's eyes widened in the dark and she immediately moved from the spy hole and slid down on the ground.

She heard the King's chair squeak – he must have sat forward a bit, she thought. "Lord Drury…? Are you well?"

"Do you smell… that… in the air? Soap, perhaps, of some sort?"

The King cleared his throat and told him, "I believe the rugs were laundered just last week. Otherwise, I smell nothing."

The King's words were civil but Tyndie detected a slight note that said he thought Drury a bit mad.

"No, no. It's gone. You're right, of course. The rugs. And I do have paperwork on the river. I'll have it brought to you. Tomorrow, perhaps?"

"That would be fine, Lord Drury," King Reaghann returned smoothly.

"Right then, a good afternoon to you," Drury told the King.

Tyndie heard the doors to the King's study shut. She did not dare to stand up.

She heard the King shove a number of parchments into his desk drawer and stand up. As he was walking away, Tyndie heard him the King mutter, "Pompous bastard."

In the shadows, Tyndie snickered silently.

— ⁗ —

An enormous risk, these balconies, thought Tyndie, though they had proven a successful gamble in the end. And what a new idea – she had been lurking through the tunnels... perhaps now she could follow the balconies about....

She immediately dismissed the idea, for in the tunnels no one, or probably no one, would ever see her. On a balcony, she could be seen at any time, and get locked out, worse.

Which gave her the idea to unlock all the balcony locks, even if they stayed closed. That way, she could push them open and hop in if need be. But as to being seen by someone, that was the main risk, especially if they stepped out onto the balcony themselves.

All the same, today had been a success, Tyndie mused. After Drury had left King Reaghann's, Tyndie had scrambled to step out to the upper level corridor where the Lords' and Ladies' Quarters were. She wasn't sure if he had passed yet or not, but all there were outside the corridor were stained glass windows and curtained balconies. And then she had gotten her idea.

Tyndie had glanced both ways down the stone corridor and then stepped outside on the iron balcony. The fresh breeze would cover the scent of her bloody soap. How was she supposed to bathe that the man would not smell her, what was he, an animal that he could distinguish people's scents? Did he know all people's scents, or was it just hers, she wondered with disgust.

For a while, Tyndie grasped the wrought iron railing and stared out. She had never been this high up, not outside at least. She wondered how many lovers had stood out here, grasped in passionate embraces, hidden from view. An ivy vine caressed her cheek in the breeze. From here, Tyndie could see all of the east side of HarCourt Castle, its moat, the forest and hunting grounds beyond it.

Just as Tyndie was hiding between the walls of the balconies, reveling in the sunlight and fresh air, wondering how long it had been since she had seen sunlight, Tyndie heard boot heels sound inside on the stone corridor.

She dared not move, for it could be anyone. And if Drury stopped and smelled the bloody air just one more time, Tyndie wasn't sure what she would do. She could not abide the man.

But she was in luck, for the wind rustled the curtains next to her ever so slightly, and the boot heels continued at a normal pace.

Just before they disappeared altogether, Tyndie peered around the curtains.

Excellent. It was Drury. She dared to step out into the corridor, where she tiptoed after him, hugging the wall.

At this point, Tyndie knew she given all caution up, for if Drury turned suddenly and saw her, it would be a run for the next tunnel, and he might easily catch her before then.

A pair of lords passed just then, laughing, and Tyndie stepped away from the wall. She curtsied, but said nothing. They never saw her, and she gulped.

She thought Drury had slowed down up ahead, where the end of the corridor ended, so she immediately stepped behind the curtains of another balcony, though it was closed. Praying that he would not see the tips of her shoes poking out from beneath the embroidered curtain, Tyndie heard the hinges of the door open, then shut.

Tyndie smiled with satisfaction behind the dusty curtains. She knew now where Drury's quarters were.

Drury had taken all afternoon to leave, and Tyndie's legs were exhausted from standing still. Just as she worried that he wouldn't leave at all, possibly barricaded himself in for the evening, the man stepped out.

Tyndie took care to hold her breath as he passed. She watched after him as he passed. He had bathed and donned new clothes for the evening. Perhaps he would guest with another lord for dinner, she hoped.

And now was her chance....

Tyndie, her heart in her throat, stepped out of the curtains and up to Drury's door. Well, she thought, as her hand touched his brass doorknob, there was no turning back now....

She pushed the door open and closed it quietly, barely breathing.

Drury's chambers were just like him – richly adorned, carpeted.... Gilded artwork hung from the stone walls, and embroidered curtains framed his windows. A low fire popped occasionally.

Wouldn't it be nice to throw fresh manure all over the entire room – so he could hold his snobby hand up and sniff the air.... *Is that... shit... I smell?* Tyndie reveled in her personal daydream with a nasty smile.

She sighed and walked about the chambers until she found Drury's desk. Good. She sat down in his chair, feeling a bit like Drury must have when he'd sat in King Reaghann's chair. Tyndie felt dwarfed in it.

Then she sat back in it and crossed her legs up on his desk, enjoying the naughtiness she felt. Tyndie hadn't grinned this way for months.

Tyndie stuck her chin up in the air and waved her arm condescendingly around the way Drury did while he had sat at King Reaghann's desk. *"Everyone is a lower life form... than me,"* Tyndie declared aloud in imitation of Drury.

Then the chair fell over, spilling Tyndie onto the carpeted floor.

Blinking in embarrassment, Tyndie stood up and righted the chair. *Tyndie girl, what are ya doin'?* She could just hear her Auntie scolding her. *Well, Auntie, it's a long, long story....*

Tyndie brushed her dress clean and faced Drury's desk. Her eyes narrowed. The holder of secrets. She'd best get to work soon, or the arsehole would return....

In the bottom drawer on the left, she found love letters. Love letters! Psssh. Who could love this bastard? And one of them from a lord! Tyndie wondered nastily if Drury had killed them too, or if he just read them sometimes when he needed a good laugh.

In another drawer was a number of parchments from other lords outlining policy concepts, nothing of interest. She slammed it shut.

The top left drawer held tariffs and taxes, accounting and such. Tyndie rarely did her numbers and didn't see that they looked useful, so she rolled that drawer closed as well. She found nothing of special interest in the bottom right had drawers, either. The right top drawer, however, Tyndie found a number of parchments, all from lords, and not all of them Councilors. On the top lay an old parchment titled at the top, "RiverWorks".

Tyndie gave serious thought to stealing it, but then not only would some innocent manservant come to a terrible end, but anything she might be able to use of Drury's would suddenly be locked up tight... elsewhere.

And she needed a key.

Tyndie glared at the top drawer. It had better hold the key to the Prince's dungeon cell, or....

She tugged and found it difficult to open. Edging it from side to side revealed only that inside lay only pigeon parchment, extra quills, and ink. Damn!

Tyndie tried to push the drawer closed, but it was stubborn. She reached under the desk to pull the drawer closed from below, but...

Her fingers found a sliding door. In the drawer!

Immediately, Tyndie fell to her knees and twisted around for a look. Carefully, she pushed the compartment aside. And was rewarded with not just one, but two keys.

She grinned. Tyndie held them up, staring at each of them. Enormous, of sturdy iron, Tyndie guessed this key unlocked the Prince of Shaw's cell.

But what of this key? Smaller, brass, yet still sturdy.... This desk did not lock. Tyndie considered. Perhaps the King's desk in his Study locked? But no, if it did, the King left it unlocked.

Perhaps the King had something in his chambers that he locked.... Tyndie frowned at the key. To take it or no? Finally, she decided she wouldn't have another chance to sneak into Drury's chambers – in fact, she never wanted to be in here again, much less chance the risk... so she pocketed them both, one in each apron pocket, so they wouldn't clink against each other as she walked.

She slid the compartment door shut and then pushed Drury's stubborn desk drawer shut. Ha. Now, she held a little power over him, her and her soapy scent.

But what of all those lords.... He wasn't back yet. And she could write, if not in calligraphy.

Tyndie now knew the names of all the Council Members… but here, in front of her, she had access to all the lords who Drury associated with…. Was that not a key in itself?

Her eyes narrowed again as she smiled. She pulled out a piece of parchment and then, flipping through each lord in Drury's top drawer, jotted down every name. Tyndie blew on the parchment, especially where she'd blotted it with ink – it wasn't as if she'd practiced her calligraphy with the ladies in the boweries – and then she rolled it up.

Tyndie brushed the desk clean. If she knew how to do anything, it was how to clean up, so she cleaned up all traces of her sitting at his pretentious desk. Much as she wanted to leave a piece of launderer's soap in each drawer, especially his little hideaway drawer, it couldn't appear that she had been present in any way.

Bloody hell! Boot heels! Down the bloody corridor! How was she supposed to get out?

Tyndie for sure did not want to spend all night under the bastard's bed! And he for sure would smell her long before the night was over….

The balcony! He had a balcony! Thank all the gods before, now, and to be, her mum used to say….

Tyndie stirred the fire, so it would smell more of wood and fire than soap, smoothed her footprints from carpet with her shoes, and slipped out onto his balcony just as Drury opened his door.

Tyndie scampered down the balconies and jumped out before her hidden tunnel door.

Once in the darkness again, she fell to the floor with an enormous sigh of relief.

After Tyndie's heart started beating again, she slipped out both keys from her apron, and held them up before her. Then she pulled out the parchment of lords' names that she'd scribbled. Staring from hand to hand, a sly smiled passed over Tyndie's face.

She was going to bring him down….

Ron

Ron guzzled at his second pint. He was going to need the fortification for this. Luckily, neither Mollie nor Hasley knew it was his second pint, for a number of workmen were celebrating at the tables of The Brew House and Tavern.

He thumped down a belch and saluted the Captain as he strolled out of the kitchen, his tail high with indifference.

Ron had grown to love this pub, with its warm pine floors, its polished bar, the many iron torches and candelabras all about lighting the floor.

Ron sat on this one barstool, for it faced the only part of the bar that had not burned down during the Twenty Years War, when the Northern soldiers marched through and put the torch to the bar. It stood as a vestige of the past, stands for today, and will be the future, Luvian liked to say when people asked about the different color of the wood.

Ron glanced around at all the men sitting at the tables. For half past noon, the pub was oddly full. Ron threw back all the rest of his pint and wiped his face with his sleeve.

Tank and Luvian escorted another common-dressed soldier out of the bar, though he offered no complaint. As Luvian was striding toward the bar with Tank, Ron laid two silvers on the glossy oaken bar and stepped through the door onto the street.

Ron rolled up his tunic sleeves as he walked along the dusty street. With a precursory glance at the first few vendors' wares, Ron half-smiled to the people behind the wagons.

He stuffed his hands in his pockets and stepped out of the way as a dog ran past. Up ahead, Ron saw a wooden wagon, near the end of the Market. His eyes widened and he thought of the rich folks who had thrown him into the wagon. And, Ron thought with irritation, clobbered him on the back of the head. He still had a bruise there.

Ron studied the wagon. Red curtains were drawn and four sturdy coach horses stood before it. The wagon looked fairly sturdy, though its luggage rack was near empty. Two men leaned against the back of it casually.

The door opened just then, though it obstructed his view of the person. Whoever it was climbed up into the coach seat.

Ron sighed. He glanced down at the clothier's cart next to him. A white length of silk hung haphazardly at the end of it.

Coughing, Ron skimmed it off the cart as he passed and slipped it up into the inside of his sleeve.

South Fair Market Place. Small children ran freely, screaming and unattended. The body odor of unwashed workmen in old, patched, roughspun clothing. Ramshackle buildings that bore the scorch marks of the Twenty Years War. Old men with tanned and wizened faces tossed dice with each other, laughing and pointing back and forth at each other's luck. Young women holding babes in their arms as they filled their baskets. A Healer's tent, with pungent odors drifting out. The hopeful expressions on the vendors' faces, a fishmonger, a chandler, a glazier....

Finally, Ron had reached the fruits and vegetables. Several customers stood about the carts. And there... there was a familiar face, just near the wagon. Perfect timing, he thought, though this was going to be the only good thing that came of this....

Ron snuck the silken hood down his arm. The second he was behind her, Ron threw the hood over Ellia's head, picked her up, and pushed her into the open wagon.

Who knew she could scream so loudly? Thank the gods the driver had a way out of South Fairview. Definitely not Ron's favorite assignment.

While she was screaming, shrieking, and kicking, the coachmen were gesturing to people outside in such a manner as to indicate that actions of a very – intimate – nature were occurring inside. So Ron heard laughter and chuckles as they creaked past. Ron grimaced at the very idea.

Ellia got one solid kick on his shin. That one would leave a mark, he knew. Ron swung himself up sideways on the cushions and propped himself up against the side of the wagon.

One of the coachmen had gagged and bound Ellia before they'd left the Market Place, and she had fought like a spitting wildcat. Ron sat there against the wall of the wagon, miserable with guilt. He hated looking at her like that.

For several miles, she had thrown every ounce of energy against the bonds, doing all she could to break free of them. Ron expected nothing less – he would have done the same. The bonds, however, were anchor knots and tightened the more one pulled on them.

Finally, two bangs came upon the ceiling from the coachman. They were outside of Fairview. Ron took in a deep breath of relief and let it out slowly, letting his head fall back against the side wall.

The ride became bumpier as the wagon was no longer upon a road but following a dirt track.

"All right, Ellia, we're not in the city anymore, so if you scream, no one can hear you but us... so –" Ron reached inside Ellia's hood and pulled the silken tie down that held her gag in place. "I'm getting rid of your gag."

Ellia was silent for a few moments. Finally, she said in a deadly low voice, "Wait until my pappy hears what you've done. He owns a brewery. When he finds you, he will crush your skull in his bare hands."

Ron looked up at the ceiling of the wagon when he heard that and nodded uncomfortably. He did not doubt that Luvian was capable of just that. Ron rubbed his hand across the stubble on his chin and cleared his throat. He had a job to do, all the same.

"Ellia, there's something that you need to know. And it's not –"

"Stop. I know your voice. Do I know you?"

"It doesn't matter. Now this isn't –"

"No, it does. Have you been in my pappy's brewery? I recognize your voice."

"Ah, girl, stop interruptin,' will you!" Ron insisted.

Ellia was silent.

Bloody hell. Why him. Now he really felt like an arsehole. Yelling at girl who was bound, hooded, kidnapped.... Quite the gentleman, Ron, he thought.

"All right, then." And he pulled off Ellia's hood.

Her blue eyes grew round when she saw him.

"Ronnie! Ronnie, you *arsehole!*" She immediately started kicking out at him.

Well, there it was and no denying it. He'd never heard her use such a word before, though.

"Ronnie! Why would you do such a thing! You pig – you, you –"

"Enough! Now let me explain like I was trying to do to start with!"

Her blue eyes shot sparks at him but she quieted enough to listen.

"Let me just... try to explain..." and he trailed off. He still had no idea how to explain this. How, he thought, are you supposed to explain this? Of all the most important things in the instructions, Ron fumed, they left *this* out.

Those blue eyes kept staring at him and whatever he was planning to say just disappeared. Ron hoped it hadn't been especially worthy....

"Well?" she snapped.

Ron had practiced all sorts of approaches and some of them had seemed worth trying, yet in the end, he knew it would be whatever came barreling out of his mouth.

"Right. Ahh. Once, long time ago, these two mates were real close friends, back in the Twenty Years War –"

"Honestly? You're going to sit there after you've bound and kidnapped me and then tell me a war story? Do you really know how many war stories I've listened to? Only most every man who ever walks into that brewery talks something of it." Ellia's lips were a thin, red line and her blue eyes were dangerous.

Ron blinked. Not only had she just insulted veterans of the Twenty Years War, but she was seriously getting on his nerves. "Honestly? You're going to sit there and be a spoiled little Pappy's girl, who won't sit still and listen while someone's trying to explain why you've actually been put in the position you're in? I mean, really, you just sit there and sulk and I'll keep it to myself." Ron swung his legs back up on the cushions and then studied his fingernails, pretending to ignore Ellia.

"All right. Tell me." Ellia's concession was a forced one, a sullen expression on her face.

"Okay then. Long time ago, these two veterans, they were real close mates of each other, they saved each other's lives back in the Twenty Years War. They stayed in touch, like mates do."

Ellia said nothing, but her eyes said everything. Those blue eyes were furious. So Ron attempted to draw the story out as long as he could, just to piss her off. The had a long enough trip ahead of them, after all.

"… and one day, one mate comes to the other. They trusted no one else in all the world but each other, you see. And that mate, he visits his friend and tells him that he's hidden a child away. He told his friend that he wants no one else in all the land but his friend to raise his child. He'd been getting death threats, you see, other children had died, wives had died, neighbors had died…. And it was the best thing he thought, for this new babe if he hid it away and had his best mate in all the world raise it, cause that man, he was a strong, cautious type and he'd never tell anyone, not ever. And he'd raise the babe right. Until it was time for his friend to take the child back."

Ron knew he was making a complete disaster of the story, but he had at least piqued her interest. She had not drawn any conclusions yet, however….

He paused.

Ellia shrugged at him. "And…."

Ron shook his head. Well, shit. There was no going back now.

"That babe – is you, Ellia. He hid you away because daughters carry the bloodline truest. And he asked his best mate, your Pappy, to raise and protect you. Until you came of age…."

Ellia stared at Ron for a few seconds. Then he watched a genuine smile tug at her lips. It turned into a laugh. She laughed and laughed, leaning forward as she chortled.

"I have to hand it to you, Ronnie. You are a gifted storyteller. You even pulled me in with the two veteran mates…. A sweet story."

Annoyed, Ron glared at her. He'd just spent the last ten minutes telling the girl about her life and she sat there laughing. She really was annoying. He would be so glad to be rid of her. Her and her Romeny blue eyes….

Finally, Ellia stopped laughing. She watched him.

Then she said, "I have two sisters, and my mum and my pappy are Ruthie and Luvian and we have a brewery."

Ron still said nothing. What was there to say? He'd told her everything there was to know. Almost.

Finally, he cleared his throat. Quietly, he asked, "Anyone ever ask you about your eyes?"

Ellia's eyes grew round as she recalled dozens of remarks about how she looked nothing like her sisters or her parents…. She shrank back against the wagon cushion.

Suddenly she looked to the side, out the window. Tears streamed down her face.

"Did – did they ever – love me?" Ellia choked on the words.

Defeated, Ron leaned forward on his knees. "More than you will ever know."

A long silence went by. Ron had no idea what to say. Nothing he could say would make it better, and he couldn't fathom the pain the girl was feeling. Tears rolled down her face silently. He had never felt so useless.

Ellia sniffed and turned toward Ron. She rubbed her face on her shoulder, for she was still bound. "So...." She trailed off and looked down at the wagon floor. Then she took in a long, shaky breath and tried again. "So, so who are my actual parents, then?"

Ron stared at her for a moment. Well, this was going to be a moment she'd remember for the rest of her life. Make it good, he thought.

"You, Ellia, are actually the last child and only daughter of Rhutgard Firthing, the First of His Name. You are, therefore, Her Royal Highness, Mirelle Ginnessa Rochilda Firthing of Romeny.

"And I," Ron sat back against the cushions, "am Prince Ronan Martel of Ghiverny."

———

He sat back against the wagon cushions. "Now, remember what I told you, right?"

Ellia – *Mirelle* – nodded a few times, the anxiety in her eyes clear. She looked like a frightened child.

Ronan had finally cut the tight rope surrounding her. The girl rubbed her arms and hugged herself. The first thing she did then was look out the window. Unfortunately, thought Ronan, there was very little worth looking at, just wide-open meadowland.

Mirelle hadn't said a thing since he'd told her who she was.

Tears had rolled down her face now and again, but other than that, there was no other expression. She was in shock, of course, and who wouldn't be? A person just finding out the parents they knew and loved all their lives weren't really your parents? That your siblings weren't really your siblings? That your actual parents had sent you to live with someone else until... well, until it was convenient?

Ronan couldn't imagine what the girl must feel like just on those ideas alone, but she had also found out she was the daughter of the King of Romeny. A girl who, all her life had grown up in a brew house, working behind a bar, serving pints, just finds out that she's a princess.... Ronan could not imagine what the King had been thinking, other than that Luvian would be her fiercest protector.... And in these recent times, when nobles and royals were finding mysterious ends... perhaps King Rhutgard hadn't been

too far off the mark. But a brew house? The people would never believe she was his daughter, even if she did look like her brothers.

Which made, Ronan realized suddenly, Mirelle a cousin… twice removed, now that he puzzled it through. Ghiverny and Romeny blood was so intermixed it was impossible to separate.

"All right. Just allow me to talk with them, and we'll be brought up to rooms right away. You were horrified from the attack, and need to rest and regain your strength."

Mirelle nodded again.

Outside, on the back of the carriage, Ronan hastily changed into a suit of lavender and plum in the luggage case. Rather rumpled, he thought, but finally, no more roughspun trousers, no more smelly soot…. Ahh. With a knife and a razor, Ronan shed the long, commoner, workman hair he'd been sporting for nearly two years and designed the best he could a nobleman's style. Then he slicked it back with water. He was starting to feel like himself again.

Ronan swung around the wagon and up front to sit with the coachman. The coachman looked at him, eyed his change in appearance without a word, and told him squarely, "Your Highness, we'll be arriving in just a few minutes." He nodded at the estate gatehouse looming in the distance.

Finally, the horses hit the bricks of the avenue leading up to the gateway. The coachman slowed the horses and several men from the estate ran up to the wagon.

"My – my lord?" asked one, unsure of their guest's identity.

The coachman called, "You have the pleasure of guesting His Royal Highness, Prince Ronan of Ghiverny and his lady from Fairview. Please note that we were set upon by bandits while on the road. All things of value were taken, as you can see, even our wagon. The lady must be treated gently, as she has suffered a terrible fright."

As the men of the estate listened to the coachman, their faces grew more and more alarmed. Ronan was mildly amused – however, the ruse was necessary, after all.

The gate swung closed behind them and the guardsmen ran to inform different household staff of their new guests and new requirements.

Ronan jumped down onto the brick. He found Ellia – Mirelle, he corrected himself, knowing immediately that it would take a long time to get used to – peeping out at the estate from behind the curtains.

He opened the door and, with an extended hand, helped Mirelle step down from the wagon. She was all a-gawk at the estate, her blue eyes wide.

"Ronnie – is this a castle?" she breathed.

The poor girl. If growing used to her new name would be hard for him, growing hard to her new identity would far harder for her. He tried to squash some of the amusement, for this was merely an old estate – an excellent estate, and its family highly esteemed by all, to be sure – but still, just an estate.

"No, Mirelle," Ronan told her kindly, "this is an estate that we'll be visiting."

Color stained her cheeks. "Oh...."

The coachman drove the wagon and horses toward the stable. Ronan offered Mirelle his arm and she accepted it, but as she stared about her, she squeezed his arm inside her own.

As they walked into the courtyard, the Seneschal hurried out.

"Your Royal Highness, we at House Emberly welcome you graciously. I was just alerted to your travel troubles. Please be sure we will take every measure to see that you and your lady....?" Here the Seneschal trailed off, waiting for an introduction.

"Lady Ellia, of Fairview," Ronan told him.

"Ah, yes. We will take every measure to ensure that you will be comfortable and made to feel safe –" here, he looked at Mirelle and bowed very low.

"Thank you," Ronan told him in a rolling tone. "Those bandits took everything from us, our wagon, our luggage, even – as you can see –" And Ronan gestured up and down at Mirelle's cotton dress. "She's extremely traumatized, as you can imagine. She's hardly said a word for miles."

Guilt struck at Ronan for this last, though it was true. He hated to use Mirelle's misery as part of their ruse, but it added to their overall credibility.

"Of course, of course, we're having rooms prepared for each of you as we speak," the Seneschal hastened to reassure them as they walked toward the main hall entrance.

Inside the receiving hall, Mirelle stared all about her. Even Ronan was impressed. The Emberly family kept a middling estate, but their reputation was stainless, and their rumored affluence was considered remarkable in the social circles who still spoke of them. The Emberly family had withdrawn from court life long ago, though they remained prominent in some political realms.

The creamy marble floor was polished to a high gloss, and a crystal candelabra hung overhead.

Two maids curtsied before them and held out their hands toward Mirelle.

She immediately looked up at him, her blue eyes scared, her faced troubled. "Ronnie?" she whispered.

"Lady Ellia, they'll take you to your chamber. You'll be able to rest there, like we spoke about just a little while ago. And then I'll see you this evening at dinner." Ronan hated to let her go – she looked as terrified as a cornered rabbit.

—⟨⟩—

Ronan felt like a new man. A real bath, new clothing, his beard shaved off, sleep in a real bed....

The staff had offered immense apologies for the small chamber, that it was only a guest room, but that the state chamber would be ready for his repose by the evening. Ronan didn't mind at all, for they had been given no notice that they would be guesting a prince and a lady until they had actually stridden into the receiving hall.

And Ronan's chamber was twice as large as the entire forge he'd been living in for the last two years. Ronan was not at all troubled, nor would he mind if he stayed in this chamber for all the rest of his visit, which shouldn't be but a few days at most.

Cheese, pastries, and an assortment of fruit sat on his sideboard, all of which he'd been nibbling at, along with some bread and a rich red wine. Ah, he had missed wine as well, thought Ronan as he took another swallow. But it would not do for him to appear drunk the night he met his host.

Ronan had held up a slice of thick, white bread, pre-sliced and begun to butter it, but with a pang, he suddenly longed for Luvian's instead. Ronan stared at the slice in his hand for a moment and then laid it down, both with guilt and the knowledge that it would never quite measure up to Luvian's recipe.

A knock sounded upon his door.

"If you please, Your Highness, Lord Emberly's dinner is about to be served, should you like to attend." The steward bowed low.

Ronan smiled. "I should, thank you."

The steward led him around the corridor and down an elaborate marble stairway. Not many private estates boasted this sort of wealth, he mused as they stepped downward, or at least they did not spend it upon the inner décor. But he knew the Emberly family had been of extraordinary means.... He glanced up, his thoughts jarred.

A maid was walking with someone down the steps just behind them.

Was that – *Ellia?*

Ronan held a hand up to pause the steward. He knew his mouth was open, but the change in her was striking. From brewhouse girl to...

Her golden hair had been brushed until its waves gleamed, kept from falling into her eyes by a small royal blue circlet that matched her eyes.

She wore a simple royal blue velvet gown, trimmed in gold and cream embroidery. It trailed slightly behind her as she stepped down the stairway.

Ronan recognized then that Ellia's *"listening to customers' boring stories"* look was frozen upon her face, which had always helped her appear interested even when she was thinking about other things. Ronan reminded himself then that she was playacting as Lady Ellia when in fact, she had been a brewery girl her entire life.

He extended his arm then, and she accepted it calmly. He had never seen her outside of her ordinary barmaid dress and apron – it was if that Ellia and this girl here before him were two different people.

"If you will, Your Highness," and the steward gestured forward.

"Of course," Ronan said, blinking.

Ellia – *Mirelle*, he corrected himself – was stiff and silent as they appeared in the dining hall.

Lord and Lady Emberly stood before them at the far end of a linen-covered mahogany table. For all that Ronan and Ellia had arrived with no warning, they had still prepared quite a feast. A beautifully decorated mallard duck was the centerpiece of the table, with an orange in its mouth and small pastries arranged along its back in such a way as to indicate feathers.

White and orange cheese wheels stood in the center of bunches of grapes. Soup bowls stood awaiting use, and several steaming platters of silver hid their servings. Servants stood with bowls of water and goblets of wine, ready to wait upon them.

"Your Royal Highness, it is our great honor to welcome you to Emberly. I do wish we could have provided better fare, I'm afraid this is all we have for you tonight. More is on its way as we speak.

"This is my lady wife, Polenna."

As Lord Chazland of Emberly, the third of his name, hastened to make apologies for the fare of their food, he bowed low to Ronan.

"Well met, Lord Chazland. I appreciate your hosting us at such short notice. Please let me introduce Lady Ellia of Fairview."

Lady Polenna said, "Fairview? I thought I knew all the Fairview girls…."

Ronan heard Ellia at his side take a deep breath. He realized that between table etiquette and a social vixen such as Lady Polenna, Ellia was going to be far out her depth, and he would not be able to answer for her, nor explain everything all evening.

"Lady Ellia is still feeling poorly from our encounter, but she did want to make an appearance, for of course, she wanted to make your acquaintance, Lady Polenna, and yours, Lord Chazland, naturally," Ronan immediately improvised.

"Oh! You poor dear," Lady Polenna immediately responded. To a nearby servant, she said, "See that Lady Ellia is served in her chambers, please –"

A sudden commanding voice interrupted them.

"That will not be necessary."

An older woman, a grandmother at least, thought Ronan, but still handsome, had stridden into the room. Her proud carriage dwarfed everyone in the room and her sharp, blue eyes took in the entire scene in a matter of seconds.

"I am surprised, Grandson, that I was not made aware that a Prince of Ghiverny was attending us."

Ronan saw power radiating off of this woman as she stared across the table at Lord Emberly.

Lord Emberly cleared his throat to save face and then responded, "Grandmother, I was not aware —"

"Yes, Chaz, I know, you were not aware." The Duchess of Emberly herself looked rather nauseated and then told the servants that Lady Polenna had just directed to serve Ellia, "You needn't serve her in her chambers. I actually was made aware of their presence myself shortly after their arrival, you see, and their difficulties upon the road. Lady Ellia has had chambers made up for her at my estate, where she may be sequestered as long as she needs to be. After all, what she's just gone through is a singularly terrible event. I shall see to her needs at my estate personally.

"Come, Lady Ellia. It is a pleasure to see you here safe at last. Why, I knew your mother and father, and my — I knew their parents when they were just children. You will have a chance to tell me everything, child, but first, you need rest."

Ellia had gratefully ducked beneath the Duchess of Emberly's outstretched arm like a baby bird.

"Lady Emberly..." Ronan called out with some alarm. Obviously, she knew of Ellia's true identity, for she had just provided the highest pedigree to satisfy Lady Polenna's inquisitive and gossiping nature. The Duchess of Emberly knew everything about everyone in most of the land, and if you were in her good graces, then you were truly a gem to behold in all social circles.

But why had Ronan not been told of the Duchess's involvement? It was Ronan's understanding that Ellia — *Mirelle* — was his charge....

Just as she and Ellia were leaving, he called out, "Lady Emberly —"

She stopped and tuned half way around. After looking him up and down from head to toe, the Duchess told him, "Ronan, is it? Well, young man, you seem to have done well for yourself. I knew your father when he was a prince half your age. You look like him, you know. The Martel men always do. And what a fireball your father was. Hm. Well, you've a good meal here, don't let us keep you waiting." And she smiled slyly.

And then she walked away with Mirelle.

Luvian

Luvian sighed and turned around. That was most odd. That was a bit of a Week End night, an evening, and a busy noon day all at once.

Fortunately, he'd baked more bread yesterday, more from sheer boredom than anything. At least he had a few more loaves left for tonight, but he'd be busy kneading for the rest of the evening, that was sure. And, now he thought, Donvan would be too.

He replayed the afternoon in his mind. All three tables in the corner were lively and hungry, burning through bread and stew, drinking down pitchers faster than Hasley could serve them.

The back two tables had been quiet but still hungry. Mags had switched to the next kettle of stew and started readying ingredients for a third. Hasley was up and down from the cellar with new pitchers.

Ruthie had called Mollie down to assist finally.

A juggler and his two mime friends were passing through on their way to their next event and so entertained the crowd. Entertainers ate and drank for half price, so long as they were worth their salt and the crowd was pleased.

Tank called him out of the kitchen to remove a common collared soldier, but the man left without argument. Which was also unusual – they never came alone and were always arrogant morons.

Suddenly, Luvian realized there was hardly anyone left at all in the brewery. Just two regulars in the corner and two more who sat in the table in the sun up front. No one at the bar.

That was it. No one at the bar. Near everyone had emptied out, almost at once.

And he'd found two silvers sitting on the old bar. No matter if you bought everything on the menu and stayed a night, would you pay two silvers, Luvian thought, his eyes narrowed into slits, an eyebrow arched.

Something. Something. He knew it, but he didn't know what.

"Ruthie! Get down here! An' bring Mollie with you!" Luvian called loudly. He ducked his head into the kitchen. "Where's Hasley? And Ellie? Hasley, girl, get up here now!" Luvian knew she was likely down in the cellar filling pitchers. That girl would be an excellent brew keeper one day, she knew exactly what to do and when....

Hasley immediately jumped into the kitchen with two pitchers, just as Luvian knew she would.

"Ellie! In here, now!" Luvian bellowed. Something was off. Mollie and Ruthie stepped behind the bar, breathless.

"Luvi, what –"

"Pappy?" asked Mollie.

Mags and Hasley stood to the other side of Luvian.

"Hey, Pappy?" Hasley set the pitchers down and Mags leaned sideways on the bar.

"Family meetin', then, Luvi?"

Luvian clenched his jaw and breathed in and out slowly.

"I. Am. Missing. A daughter."

"Oh, no, Luvi, I sent Ellie to the Market Place to get me some vegetables for the stew. She went to the Market Place is all," Mags reached out a hand and patted his upper arm twice.

Luvian maintained his breathing at a slow and even pace, and then turned to look at Mags over Hasley's head.

"Why. Would you do that? You went yesterday and bought vegetables at the Market yesterday."

Mags suddenly paled. Her mouth dropped open as she tried to think through the last few hours' events. "I – but – there aren't any left. You can see for yourself, there are none left. None," she said in a trembling voice.

"Pappy?" Mollie asked slowly.

Just then, two Crown soldiers in blue and red uniforms walked in with a parcel.

Luvian felt his strength draining.

The first asked him if he were Luvian, the proprietor of The Brew House and Tavern.

"I am," he answered quietly.

"We have two things for you." The speaker continued, after judging Luvian's response. "A message." The soldier removed a scroll, slid a blue satin ribbon from it, and unrolled it. Luvian saw painfully neat calligraphy written upon it through the parchment.

The soldier informed him, "We were told to read it *exactly*, in the *exact manner*, as follows:

This message is from a grateful man

Who has been at the…

ROOT

Of all of your troubles

Since the start;

A grateful man

> *who can never hope to repay his debt*
>
> *but will always look at the flower*
>
> *sprouted from the*
>
> ### ROOT...
>
> *and know he made the right decision*

The soldier said no more but rolled the script up in silence and placed it on the bar for Luvian.

The second soldier opened a finely grained wooden box. He pulled out an enormous bottle of Romeny Palace whiskey and laid it quietly on the bar.

Then the two soldiers stepped backward silently, bowed deeply, and left The Brew House and Tavern.

Luvian stared at the bottle. It was all surreal, somehow. It wanted to wash over him, but stopped, just short, a moment frozen in time before him.

He swallowed.

"I. Have lost. A Daughter."

Luvian turned around and pushed the kitchen doors open blindly, headed toward the stable. "Pappy?" called the girls.

"Luvi?" asked Donvan.

"Leave me."

Mags pulled at his arm from behind. "Luvi –"

"Leave me."

A tear had already spilled from each eye.

Suddenly Luvian turned around. Back at his bar, he swiped the whiskey, then headed out to the stable.

Selby

Her fingers thrummed the gilded carvings of her chair.

At her request, the old chair had been removed and this one created. Enough jokes were made about a woman sitting in a man's seat – she did not need to be approving policy while sitting in a man's seat in her own Council Chamber.

Selby did like it, she admitted. It sat up higher that she might look, if not down upon her Councilors, than at least at eye level. And, of course, it was of a woman's dimensions, rather than a man's. And by the gods, more comfortable! More cushioned – for some of these sessions went on for ridiculously long periods, and, to be frank, that old chair left her arse sore.

Perhaps this new chair had a few too many adornments, but Selby wasn't picky. And it had to look the part, after all.

This Council Meeting was going to be a memorable one, she knew. Perhaps even historical. She would love to listen to what the walls heard when some of these Councilors left today....

And here they all came, filing in, half of them fat old men, growing fatter off the Clemongardian coin they turned to mint in this room. The other half were cunning and danced around diplomacy like maidens around maypoles. At least half of them had served twenty years at this same table.

Selby nodded to the scores of "Your Majesty's" as they walked in, but, as a woman, none of them would seat themselves until she permitted them or sat herself.

And so they stood, expectantly at the back of their Council seats. Soon, a silence developed, during which she looked each Council Member in the eye. Drawing out a lengthy silence was a power tactic, one she enjoyed employing. She used a number of them, for a queen not yet eighteen had to appear serene and impartial at all times. Such as today.

After both a quiet cough and a nervous clearing of the throat sounded within the room, Selby said, "Good morning, Councilors.

"Before you seat yourselves, please note that there are two parchments placed before your chairs. Pick up the first parchment, on top, and read it."

It had taken Selby half of the evening last evening to pen out all these parchments, but when she thought of all their political springs and traps that she had either had to deftly avoid at the last moment or had even fallen into upon occasion, this, this day, would be such a rich reward. And this morning, Selby arrived early and placed each parchment carefully, perfectly atop the other. Just for today.

Each Councilor was reading through the details of her Coronation, none of which she had included them on.

"As you can see, I have chosen a date for my Royal Coronation. I have, after all, sat the Throne now for over six months, and it is time for my Coronation. I expect all of you to attend."

Some of them drew in breath to comment, but Selby shook her finger at them just once, for not only was her Coronation anything that would be up for discussion, but they had another far more pressing matter to discuss.

"Now," she continued. "The second parchment. Many of you have served loyally and contributed to Clemongard's finest ideals.

"Because of your remarkable service to the Crown, your retirement is a rich one, well-rewarded, and know that the Crown is appreciative of your service. You are, of course, welcome to stay on within the Court, or retire to your personal residences, as you please, effective immediately.

"Those of you still have a seat at this Council, please be seated while your responsibilities and obligations from this day hence are explained to you –"

"Why you, you –"

"You can't do this –"

"You can't –"

"This is unlawful!"

… and several other similar protestations arose around the room from Council Members whom Selby had permanently retired. These men had served her father, not her. So, actually, had the men remaining, but she valued their input, their abilities, or their connections enough to keep them close.

Ah, again, to listen to what the walls heard, she thought as they filed out, arguing like wet hens. Selby wanted to smirk, however ungracious it was of her. She was never raised to be a ruler, so she was not accustomed to licking the wounds of old mens' pathetic egos every time they got a sliver under a fingernail. People were trained in such arts, but Selby had not been, so she wondered often just how much her reign would stand out from other rulers.

Left sitting at her Council table was less than half of her Councilors, many of them alarmed and wide-eyed.

One Councilor still seated, Lord Lemrond, sniffed and laid his parchment on the Council table.

"No. I was given this seat by King Garmond of Clemongard. I will not be *allowed* to keep it by a girl who sits his throne, daughter or not." He shook his head and stood up.

"Then," Selby returned smoothly, for his words to her sounded dangerously close to treason. In fact, she was right, for her guards behind her immediately slammed their spears to the floor. "… if you do not leave, you will be removed from this Council Chamber. Lord Lemrond, your Council retirement privileges are hereby revoked. You will leave Court at once, permanently, to return to your personal estate. Or, perhaps, you should leave Clemongard altogether…." Selby suggested dangerously.

Lord Lemrond's eyes widened with outrage. "This is outrageous. It's unlawful."

Selby beckoned one Ericorian guard to follow her to her Council Chamber door while the other Ericorian guard forcefully removed Lord Lemrond by his collar to the door.

He hung there before the door from the Ericorian's hand when she signaled the guard with an upraised palm to stop.

"It is lawful. I am the Queen of Clemongard. I am the law."

She gestured then at the Ericorian guard. He threw Lord Lemrond out of the Council Chamber, where he landed on his arse on the marble and skidded into the wall.

Queen Selby smiled and closed the door to her Council Chamber.

Now that Selby had called her own Council to order, she gazed around at all the empty seats. Though she had been quietly researching new replacements, she first had to see how her current Councilors upheld their new positions. Once she had established their abilities to work as a new conglomerate, she would choose new Council Members that would fulfill the gaps left.

Feeling pleased with herself, Selby asked, "Any questions?"

Lord Dansherd, an older gentleman with white sideburns and a compact frame, leaned back in his seat. He laced his hands over his stomach. "I have."

Selby nodded for him to continue.

"Are these… men, your guards, necessary, here in the Council Chamber?"

"You mean the Ericorian?"

"Well, of course. Over our Crown Guard, that is," replied Lord Dansherd.

The Ericorian were Clemongard's finest warriors, trained in all manners of weaponry and war, and only those of the highest honor, the best fit, and the utmost able became Ericorian after the most rigorous of training. Selby saw no reason why Ericorian should not have them as her personal guards.

"I, of course, have the highest respect for our Crown Guard," Selby returned with a practiced grace. "They are our Royal Guard, and Clemongard's defense from start to finish, and the finest of men.

"We have thousands and thousands of fine Crown Guard. There may be perhaps two or three fine men… who make a poor choice… upon occasion." Selby allowed her last words to linger for just a few seconds, for she truly did appreciate the daily sacrifice of her Crown Guardsmen. "And also," she continued, "there is the matter of uniforms. Any non-soldier with… unsavory intentions… might possibly purloin a uniform."

Selby saw the various expressions upon her remaining Councilors' faces – curiosity, interest, shock, astonishment, complacency….

She continued. "You recall that not yet seven months ago, King Garmond and all three of my brothers were… lost… at RainsCourt, a castle our family has known our entire lives, and for generations, of course."

All eyes were on Selby.

Selby had very personal beliefs as to whether the reports sent back from RainsCourt were true – slipped on the icy stairwells, fever.... When her brothers and father had all been in the best of health before departure and all of them, including herself, knew those steps inherently... and never had ice formed on them at any time of the year.

Selby herself had remained here at FalconRise at the time and felt sure that if she had accompanied her family to RainsCourt then, she too, would be dead as well.

"Since I am the last remaining of the immediate Stevanrhut Royal bloodline, I think it only wise to protect my promise to the people of Clemongard in the best way possible, and that starts with securing my life.

"Sadly, anyone can masquerade as one of our beloved Crown Guards, though we hope that is never the case. But, as you can see," and Selby gestured to the nearest Ericorian behind her, "it would very difficult to infiltrate the Ericorian ranks. Sheer height requirements alone would impede most attempts, though our Ericorian men are also tattooed and their uniform requirements are of a different nature." Selby waved at the Ericorian's hair, for their hair was shorn very specifically.

She bestowed a smile upon Lord Dansherd. "You'll grow accustomed to their presence."

Lord Dansherd nodded slowly, though he studied the Ericorian at her side from head to toe.

"Which now brings me to the subject of my Coronation. All preparations are being made, so you need only see that those within your villages, townships, parishes, and cities are alerted. This will be a small affair, and only the most prominent of Lords and Ladies may attend, as well as those whom I have already invited. That list will be provided for you before our next meeting, but before you send word to anyone, I will approve the list of those whom you propose to invite. Be sure to have that list ready by our next meeting as well."

Selby believed her Councilors to still be in shock from the dismissal of their compatriots and so they remained silent as they nodded in assent. Hm – a first. She held her amusement back.

Ah – so close. "Your Majesty, I do have a concern that is somewhat related...."

"Lord Fraynard. If your concern is noteworthy then by all means, please share it."

"You are, as yet, unmarried." Lord Fraynard had brown eyes set close together and a habit of rapidly blinking twice, which he did now. He also had frizzy brown hair that hung just over his eyebrows, shot through with grey. She did not know which irritated more, the frizzy hair, or the rapid blinking. As he continued to double-blink at her, Selby imagined small pins propping his eyelids up and decided the blinking, yes, definitely the blinking.

Selby cradled her hands over her elbows and replied, "I am actually aware of that fact." She braced herself for another argument on this very subject.

"You're one to speak of protecting the bloodline, Your Majesty, with all due respect, but you must provide a line of succession for it. You must marry and provide an heir," Lord Bralwin commented. And not for the first time, Selby thought tiredly.

"Let us take one event at a time. First, my Coronation, in six weeks."

She paused. Two years ago, one year ago even, she would never have thought herself needing to fend this very moment off. Now.... She sighed.

"You do all realize, that I am wearing black, don't you? From head to toe?"

Her Councilors glanced nervously at each other, realization dawning upon them.

"Yes, that's right. I am in mourning, my lords. I lost a father and three brothers just six months ago. Four dear family members at once."

Though she would have loved to asked them what in the names of all the gods were they thinking, Selby elected instead to say quietly, "While they meant little to you, and their loss has made little or no difference in your lives, they meant a great deal to me and their loss has echoed tremendously through my life.

"I fully expect to wear mourning for a period of one year, as is expected of women, Queens or otherwise. And I expect each of you to respect the thought that entertaining thoughts of courtship and betrothal prospects are highly inappropriate. There will still be men with marriageable designs six months from today."

Again, Selby's Council Chamber was silent. However, each Councilor was nodding with respect. She knew she would not need to address this subject further.

"Now. We have another agenda to pursue." Upon her own papers, she had a copy of the day's agenda, which she slid down the marble Council table.

And now the silence would come to an end, Selby thought smugly.

Near the close of the meeting, Selby leaned her head in her hand. "All right. One last thing. Lord Branshaw," and she swung her attention to the Council whose pewter hair always seemed fly-away.

He raised his eyebrows. "Your Majesty?"

"You are my RiverWorks Councilor. I need bridges. The Rournebourke, particularly, for the distance between BrevisPort and the Mickel Bridge is just too far. The Trellis as well. People are traveling far and away from their destination just to get to a bridge.

"Lord Branshaw. This should not be nearly a frightening a prospect as you've suddenly become." The man had suddenly taken in a deep breath and become very apprehensive.

"Oh. Frightening, no, Your Majesty, not at all. It's just – it could be – costly."

Selby frowned. "The Crown is giving you the coin for this project. These bridges will be sturdy, brick, and designed by a Crown architect. You need only provide the best locations."

"Right. Right then," replied Lord Branshaw, though he did not sound convinced at all. One Councilor coughed and another pulled at his collar.

Selby turned to the side in her seat and cocked her head.

"If I didn't know better, Councilor, I would think that you're concerned about this prospect."

Lord Branshaw saw that she was studying him and realized that he would not be able to hold back his objections.

"Well, Your Majesty, it's simply that – rivers do overflow their banks, in flood season," he offered weakly.

Selby raised her eyebrows. "Interestingly, I was aware of that fact."

"And they do sink below their banks in drought periods...."

Did he think her an idiot or was he one?

"Keeping those important facts in mind, Councilor, the necessity of bridges, water beneath them or no, is to allow and even encourage our citizens to travel. This means that trade will increase. What that means, is that coin will, if you will, *flow* into our Treasury.

"Also – travelers from other countries, Storden, even the East, will be more likely to visit once they see how many Clemongardian destinations are accessible.

"More bridges means more travel, and more travel means more access. I expect your ideas by our next meeting, Lord Branshaw. Beyond that, I expect to see your research – proposals on bridge placements based on yearly weather issues, citizen demographics, land, etc.. The start date for this project will be no later than four months from today, Lord Branshaw."

Lord Dansherd cleared his throat, recognizing that the meeting was ending.

"Yes, Lord Dansherd?" Selby was not overly fond of the man, but she was fond of his connections, and so humoring him was requisite.

"Just one question, Your Majesty. What do you think your father would feel of your sitting on his throne?"

"I'm not sitting on my father's throne, Lord Dansherd. I'm sitting on my own.

"Today's meeting is adjourned."

Selby stood up from her chair and watched her Councilors bow before her as they left. Lord Dansherd seemed pleased with her answer, for he gave her a respectful nod before he left. That battle had been won, she thought, though Lord Branshaw looked increasingly nervous as he left the room. Her eyes narrowed.

Selby didn't wonder what her father would do. She was too busy doing it herself.

The Council Chamber doors closed and the room was silent. Ah. Finally. Alone.

Well, nearly alone. She had her two Ericorian with her.

Selby turned around and stared at them, tapping a finger on her mouth.

"You. Your name?"

"Durain, Your Majesty."

"Durain, please approach."

Durain immediately stepped forward.

"Walk with me." Selby walked half the length of her Council Chamber, then crossed her arms.

"I know that you two heard all. What did you think of that man, Lord Branshaw?"

Durain immediately replied in one tone, "Ericorian have no opinion, Your Majesty."

Selby frowned and shouldered her hair behind her. "Durain, right now, I need you to have an opinion. I don't trust anyone else. My father and my brothers were murdered six months ago, and people believe that they just *fell on the steps*." She sniffed.

"Durain. I am not asking you to become a Council Member. But that squirrely little man that just left. There is something about him that I don't trust, and I need to know what it is." She peered up at the man. Those height requirements were impressive, but at the moment, it was making her neck hurt.

Durain suddenly glanced down at her. Ah! A spark of singularity, an individual behind those blue eyes. She knew it.

"Durain," and Selby leaned forward, "do you... know of anyone who could find out information for me? Whom you personally, *you*, trust? Someone who could, maybe... watch Lord Branshaw... someone of the utmost discretion?"

Durain swallowed calmly. His face was like stone, Selby thought.

Quietly, he told her, "I do."

Her heart skipped a beat and her mouth dropped open.

"Would you like an introduction?"

"No!" Selby whispered. "No! It would be best for ... that person, and for me, for us, that we never meet. And perhaps, that person might find other... people of similar natures who could provide services of the same manner. If so, they would be greatly rewarded." Selby stared up at Durain with all seriousness.

He nodded just slightly. "Understood, Your Majesty. It will be seen to."

Selby's breath whooshed out of her. "Thank you, Durain."

She was a new Queen – and the first lesson she was learning was that she could not do everything by herself.

Varley

The detestable squalling of those babes. Could no one shut them up? It seemed wherever he went, he heard them. He threw a glance over his shoulder. Two wet nurses were marching by with each brat at the tit. He sucked in his breath with disgust and turned around again.

Varley remembered right after they were born. Once family members were allowed to view them, he had finally stepped in, performing his duty as the supposed loving elder brother ought. The first thought that passed through his mind as he looked down at the two of them, twin boys, was that their faces looked like rumpled little tomatoes with small, screaming mouths.

And they hadn't stopped screaming since, the wretched creatures. Colic, some whispered in corners. No, Varley rolled his eyes, just poor breeding, what else did they expect from a lowlife Wescarl twat from Kipper Cove?

They should have removed her by now, to another residence, that was just tradition, but for everyone's sake – and sanity – Varley might just insist upon it. Father was so enamored of them. Quite possibly impressed that he could produce children still, though Varley wondered if the babes were his. Time would tell. Though… terrible things were known to happen to small babes in their cradles. So tragic. Truly a loss it would be, Varley thought with a mixture of amusement and loathing. He suddenly understood why so many babes died so young… parents just couldn't take their bloody fucking squalling and squashed them with pillows. Or something.

Whatever occurred, Varley now had company in the succession arena. Though he himself would be upon Father's throne long before such a consideration would ever be necessary. And a wife of excellent breeding would provide sons that wouldn't spit up on his imported velvet surcoat the first time he picked one of them up.

Finally, Varley could hear himself think again… they were gone. He continued to eat his breakfast.

One of his servants stepped to his side and bowed. "Your Highness." He held a silver tray before Varley with a pigeon parchment atop it. Varley accepted the parchment and dismissed the servant.

Curious, Varley snapped the seal and sat back in his seat.

Ah. The Ormon Queen. She never sent him correspondence with her own seal, nor signed her name, but Varley knew her personal handwriting by now.

"King Munsolrysche dead. Unexpected involvement by ES. Do nothing at this time. Wait for further communication."

Irritated, Varley wondered what had happened. The changing of the guard would certainly slow her plans down, though that would be a bit difficult with no son to pass the crown to.

He hoped the plans had not changed entirely. ES. He did not like the idea of the Eastern Shield involvement. Was Myrischka losing grip on all her ice up there? Varley did not like that idea. She was supposed to take Ambsellon for herself, and leave him to take over Clemongard, the first Storden King with a set of balls in hundreds of years. And after that....

She could have her Eastern Shield. He wanted the West.

Tyndie

Ugh. The mud down here. Tyndie smirked... to lock Drury down here.... He'd go apoplectic in ten seconds. But the idea of forcing him into a cell? That certainly had its charm... hmmm.

Finally. She held up her tallow candle and peered into the Prince's cell.

He held up an arm and blinked beneath it. Of course – the candlelight was too bright. Tyndie lowered her candle right away. She took a deep breath. Well, at least he was still alive.

"I was starting to think you a daydream."

Tyndie scoffed and then immediately regretted it. For look at this man's miserable life – forlorn and desolate, never seeing the light, near starved....

"No, my lord, not a daydream." Tyndie glanced down the corridor. Had she heard something? "He's not coming, is he?" she whispered.

The Prince lifted his eyebrows. "No. I know the sound of his boots. I know the sound of everything in here, actually, now," he mused aloud. "But no, he's not coming. Still, keep your voice down," he told her in a low voice.

Tyndie stared at him. He'd not even come to the front of the cell, he'd continued to sit against the dark, rocky corner, utterly hopeless.

She lay her tallow candle upon the black rock ground. Tyndie removed two baguettes of bread that she'd stuffed in her apron pockets.

As she was doing so, the Prince commented dryly, "Are they sending kitchen maids to feed the down and out now, are they?"

Tyndie glared at him. Still a stuck-up royal underneath all that dirt and dinge, she saw. "No, just the animals in the cages," she snapped, and threw both of them at his head.

He dodged them both with his arms and then picked them up from his lap.

Clearing his throat, he said quietly, "I apologize. That was unseemly of me. Thank you."

Unseemly. Silly word, only royals used such words, royals and nobles. Why don't they just say *stupid* and have done with it, Tyndie wondered. People would get along much better if they all used the same language.

Tyndie saw he was breathing in the smell of the bread appreciatively. He said suddenly, "I don't mean to sound ungrateful, but these are hard to hide in here...."

"Well, give them back and I'll be off with them." Tyndie outstretched her hand. Would you believe that!

"No – no, not at all," he said defensively, cradling the bread to his chest. "It's just – they're hard to hide is all."

Suddenly, the Prince raised a palm at her, listening. "He's coming. *Go! Go!* He'll be gone in a bit, but leave now, before he knows you've been here!"

Tyndie needed no further persuasion. She grabbed her candle and ran down the corridor and slipped into her tunnel. But she kept the door open just a tiny bit and blew her candle out.

Joshik soon tramped down the muddy passage, his considerable weight causing him to wheeze. Tyndie heard the prison keys clinking against each other on his key ring as he made his way toward the Prince's cell.

"Hungry yet?" Joshik snorted as the sound of an aluminum pan land upon the rocky floor. "Yeah? Well, 'ere ya go. Maybe ya'll be able to reach it if you lean out far enough. Or maybe ya won't." Joshik sniggered.

Then he raised his lantern. "Ay. Wot's that in there? Behind ya?"

Tyndie froze. Oh no – what had she done!

She could just barely hear the Prince. "This? It's a dead rat." Tyndie knew he was hiding the bread, for it was the same size and shape as a rat.

Joshik chortled, then laughed. "Well, then. Seein' as how you got yaself a right good feast in there, ya'll not be needin' this anytime soon, will ya?" He laughed some more and Tyndie heard the aluminum pan scraping across the stone floor.

Then Tyndie heard the sound of water running against the wall. But she nearly gagged after that, for Joshik was relieving himself against the wall.

"Can I have some water, please?" called the Prince.

Joshik snorted. "The only water you's gonna get is suckin' off my cock," Joshik called back as he clambered back down the hallway.

Tyndie sat there in the darkness, her stomach turned. Easily the most disgusting person she'd ever witnessed. And the Prince had lived down here every day with that man for months....

Finally convinced that there was no one else in the dungeon corridor again, Tyndie lit her candle.

Careful to avoid Joshik's addition to the mud upon the dungeon floor, she tiptoed back to the Prince's cell.

"Charming man," she commented.

The Prince scoffed and returned dryly, "You've no idea."

Tyndie held her candle over the pan Joshik had left behind. "What is this supposed to be?" She knew it was supposed to be food, but whatever it was, she didn't recognize it.

Inside his cell, the Prince held out his hands. "I don't know, and I don't ask."

She started to toe it over.

"No," he whispered, "I've got the bread. I'll be fine."

"Right then." Then Tyndie smiled. "I've got something for you. And us." She pulled the key out of her pocket, and with the candle, held it up so that the Prince could see it.

In the candlelight, the Prince's eyes fixed upon the key. He still did not move, but Tyndie thought that perhaps a gleam of hope sparked in him for just a moment.

Then he looked up at her. "And where did you get that?"

Tyndie glanced back down the corridor, worried.

"Don't worry, he's fed me, he won't be back for another two days," said the Prince.

Tyndie's eyes widened. In shock, she started to comment in anger, but the Prince cut her off. He split the air with a hand and shook his head.

Still horrified, Tyndie closed her mouth and stared at the man who was born a Prince for a moment. There he sat, cowering in filth and mud in the back of a dungeon cell reserved only for traitors, starved and beyond despondent....

Tyndie took a deep breath, resolving to rescue the man just for humanity's sake if not to piss off Drury, for he was entirely innocent.

"In the desk drawer of the man who is responsible for putting you here. And putting me, of course, in these tunnels...."

The Prince's eyebrows rose. "And how did you manage that?"

Tyndie couldn't resist a small smile. "Snuck in. But we don't have time to discuss it, for he might notice that it's gone, and if he notices it's gone, he'll come down here and check on you. Either way, he'll get a new key made and I might not find that one. He'll know there's a thief about.

"So we're leaving tomorrow morning, first light," Tyndie finished, breathless.

The Prince stared at her. He scratched at his beard then, and an odd look came over his face.

"And you have a plan for this?"

"Well, there's the moat..." Tyndie trailed off. "But I'm not a good swimmer."

For the first time, a glimmer of interest shone upon the Prince's face. "The moat is not a good idea. HarCourt Castle hasn't been invaded for hundreds of years for a number of reasons, but one of them is that it's heavily fortified, as I recall my history."

"What's *'fortified?'"* Tyndie asked.

"Without going into unnecessary detail, the moat specifically is designed to deter invasion. Beneath the water are sharpened spikes, both upward and on both banks. I'd really hate to escape the dungeon merely to impale myself on a spike in the moat. Or, I might add, be shot by an arrow from a soldier atop the baileys." The Prince bestowed upon Tyndie a kindly expression.

"It wasn't my first choice anyway. Too many eyes."

"Take horses from the stables?" suggested the Prince hopefully.

"And we both be caught as horse thieves? That will land you right back here, and me in here with you. I think not."

The Prince conceded to this and sighed.

"I actually do have a plan, but.... You will need to wash up, and...." Tyndie wasn't sure how to suggest to a Prince that he needed to shave and change from his rags.... She would not be surprised if he had lice....

He stared at her. "Wash up? Down here, in the dungeon baths, you mean?"

"No, I know of a place for you to bathe. Though of course it will be risky...."

The Prince continued to stare at her in disbelief. "Riskier than escaping, that is?

Tyndie held up the key with narrowed eyes. "You realize I could have left weeks ago."

He stared at the key again and held up his hands in compliance.

"You, he only wants to keep as his little dungeon pet. Me, he means to kill. So stuff the bow-to-Your-Highness routine because it's a cup girl that's gettin' you out of here. *Your Highness."*

The Prince cleared his throat and said nothing, the haughty expression gone now.

Tyndie continued outlining her plan then. "Now, the only reason we're not leaving tonight is – well, I've got some last-minute things I've got to finish. And the gate's always put down at night, so we can't leave at night anyway."

In a respectful tone, the Prince said, "That sounds right; most castles lower their gates as soon as it's dark and pull them up again at first light.

"But first…." And the Prince trailed off and looked up to the key, not wanting to say more.

"I was coming to that. We have to make sure this actually fits."

Tyndie took a deep breath and held the key before the cell's keyhole. Then she looked cautiously at the Prince. "You know you can't get out right now, don't you. I mean, we have to do this in steps."

"I do. You're the one who knows where I'll be going, remember. Without you, I'm still stuck down here, in or out of a cell," he responded quietly.

"Right." Tyndie took in a deep breath. *Please be the right key, please be the right key….* She inserted the iron key into the keyhole. It fit, but would it turn….

And with a clank, the key unlocked the door….

Tyndie's heart soared. Her mouth dropped open and she looked in at the Prince. He was sitting up straight, his eyes wide. He finally believed this might happen, Tyndie thought.

But she knew she had to lock the door again, and so she twisted the key back.

She was smiling, she couldn't help it. *Take that, Drury!* She hoped desperately that he hadn't yet discovered that the key was missing.

But then she heard boots on pavement again.

"Go! Go!" the Prince waved her away desperately.

Tyndie grabbed her tallow candle and ran down the corridor again.

"Thought I heard somethin' in here," announced Joshik once he stood before the Prince's cell.

"Just trying to get the food." The Prince threw what sounded like a rock against the wall, which landed in the pan of food.

Joshik gave a suspicious grunt, then snorted. He wandered back down the hall, muttering, "Lost 'is wits, he 'as."

Tyndie waited for a few minutes before she returned.

"I thought you might not return."

"He may be a problem," Tyndie mused.

"Joshik – his brain may only be a toadstool, but it does work upon occasion," said the Prince. Then he said, "He probably won't be back at all tomorrow, that's his routine."

"What a foul man," Tyndie whispered, wrinkling her nose.

"Ha," the Prince returned in something close to amusement. "You don't know the half of it. He's been known to nap down here. And he snores abominably." He looked up at the ceiling, shaking his head. "When first I was imprisoned, I went a bit mad. I did anything at all to occupy myself. One of the things I did, I counted things. Drops of water, bits of food, cracks in the walls. Well, the first nap Joshik took down here, I counted how many snores he made. When he woke, I told him that he'd snored 193 times.

"And then he lashed me, 193 times."

Tyndie's mouth dropped open in horror.

The Prince shrugged. "Now, when he naps down here, I count, but I never tell him. Usually, it's between 230-250 times. Unless he's been drinking, then it's closer to 500."

Tyndie stared at the man. She would never have survived down here. Bugs, and mud, and rats, and... and....

She shook herself. "I have this mostly worked out. Before I return, I'll have it completely sorted. I know everything about where we're going, and who will be where, and when. I'm the one who's getting you out of here. You're going to have to trust me, and do what I tell you to do, as I tell you. That means doing what the cup girl tells you. Can you do that?"

He nodded solemnly.

"Good. Then I'll be back for you tomorrow morning."

Reaghann

He rolled his neck around and sighed. When he opened his eyes, he stared up at the paneled sealing. The agriculture report he'd asked from Lord Wardston was not going to read itself, and yet here it was, full of fluff, so that it – and Lord Wardston – would appear full of information.

He let it flutter through his hands from front to back. Worse, whoever scribed it wrote in small, fine print. Reaghann slapped the report on his desk. His father would never have read this tripe – he delegated all this fine work to his Inner Secretaries.

But Reaghann was not his father, nor did he trust such information to Inner Secretaries. He did not want men he did not know running his kingdom, especially in such... uncertain times.

There, he'd admitted it. Reaghann propped his legs up on his desk and swallowed some wine from his goblet. For these were uncertain times. He could not explain why, or how, but he just felt it in his gut.

He had received reports of increased ship sightings in the Treasure Sea, from sailors who docked at the Singing River to as far north as Swindle Bay. Most of the sailors called them pirates, but too many pirates in one sea... equaled a coincidence, and Reaghann did not believe in coincidence. He had only been a child during the Twenty Years' War, but he'd listened to men who planned it, and if he'd learned anything, it was that there was no such thing as coincidence.

Increased activity also up the Rosh River into Shaw. And by no one special, no people of a specific quality or attribute that had been determined. Scouts found more travelers headed East in general, through the Free Lands, though all had plausible excuses.

More people – whether by land or by sea – were the result of three things: plague, money…

Or war.

And Reaghann would have heard of the first two long before now. In fact, the first two were the direct results of the third. *War always caused disease and financial opportunity, and usually the two were intertwined*, he remembered an advisor of his father saying during the Twenty Years War. So greed was a disease, mused Reaghann. Many of his Councilors would argue that concept, while others would applaud it. And still others would never recognize it within themselves.…

To hell with this bloody report. It would still be ready to bore him in the morning. Reaghann opened his drawer, ready to toss the report on top of his other papers.

And then saw those papers, neatly arranged. Again. This was the third time now.

Who was arranging his parchments for him?

To be sure, he actually found it interesting, the order in which they were arranged, from worth his time to utter tripe. But it only meant that someone – Reaghann could not imagine who – was going into his desk drawer and sorting his paperwork.

Reaghann considered each of his Inner Secretaries but again dismissed them, as he had the first two times he'd discovered this. Only Katham remained as a possible suspect, given his knowledge of Reaghann's interest on certain subjects, and Reaghann did not consider Katham likely, for he was a servant, a steward of sorts.

And then the back of his neck prickled.

He had missed it the first time, when Lord Drury had sat across from him, though he had smelled the slightest of soap scents. He'd dismissed it as launderers soap lingering in the air, perhaps after the dusting of his curtains or some such thing as servants did.

Oddly, he did not consider himself to be in danger. He took a sip of wine.

"I could use the company – come out and have a goblet of wine."

Reaghann thought he heard an intake of breath. Pleased with himself, he held up his goblet in an invitation.

"No? Very well, then." He picked up the report and then looked at his open drawer. On a whim, Reaghann said, "I assume it's you who has been rearranging my proposals for me."

There was a nervous clearing of a throat behind the wall, and then a quiet, distinctly female voice said, "Yes, my lord."

Surprised, he realized two things. One, that the speaker was young, and two, that the speaker was a servant.

"Well, then." Reaghann didn't want to frighten her off, for this was the most intrigued he'd been in months. "You got it mostly right, though there were two near the bottom I was interested in."

"If you please, my lord, I put any you considered arseholes on the bottom. Or those whose statements just repeated themselves."

Reaghann smiled a bit. "And how would you know who I consider arseholes?"

The girl took in a deep breath behind him. "The walls hear all, my lord. So it's said."

He raised an eyebrow. "If I thought anyone would believe me, I could call you in on treason charges."

She coughed and sounded suspiciously smug as she replied through the wall, "You'd have to find me first, my lord."

"Well, no one would believe I was conversing with someone behind the wall, anyway. And yet..." and Reaghann turned in his chair, "there you are, aren't you."

A bright green eye widened and then fell back from the spy hole he'd long ago forgotten about.

"Well, don't run off now, it was just getting interesting," Reaghann called lowly.

After a few seconds, the girl appeared at the spyhole again.

"I'm here – for a reason."

"One would presume so," he replied dryly.

The girl said nothing for a moment, but Reaghann believed her green eye narrowed a bit. He was only trying to coax her out, he wasn't trying to harangue her – surely whomever she was, she knew that.

Then the girl said, "I won't be back after tonight. I have – information for you that you have to believe. Just... tell me you'll trust me when you see it."

Reaghann's demeanor immediately changed. This he did not like the sound of. "What exactly does that mean?"

"My lord – I mean, Your Majesty –" the girl stumbled, "you're not...." She looked from side to side in an attempt to find the best way to phrase her next statement.

"Well, out with it, girl." Reaghann was suddenly impatient and he did not like the turn this conversation was taking.

"You're not exactly safe here."

Well, there it was, outed and matter-of-fact. As direct as one could hope for, Reaghann thought.

"Who are you?"

The girl was shaking her head. "I can't say."

"What's your name?"

"I can't tell you that, either. I'm going to be gone and you won't find me anyway, so don't search for me. I only wanted to tell you that… and to give you… some information that you – *you must know*, Your Majesty."

The girl was nothing if not earnest. And direct. Still, the whole idea sounded ludicrous….

"Do you at least promise to consider what I've come to tell you, and to… give you?"

"Give me?" repeated Reaghann. He thought for a moment. "First answer this. How often have you been in my desk to rearrange my papers?"

The girl cast her eye downward. "Three times now, my lord – Your Majesty."

"And how do you know how to arrange them?"

The green eye glanced up at him briefly, looked down, then stared at him straight on. "I watched you once when you were throwing your proposals about, lords you liked and didn't. And then… I watched a Council Meeting."

Reaghann's mouth fell. "A *Council Meeting*? How – is there really a – behind the…?"

The girl nodded.

Well. That was not good news at all. In fact, that frightened him a good bit. "And?"

She didn't reply.

"Do you have a name that I can call you, or will I just be speaking to you through the wall?" Reaghann asked, slightly irritated.

"I can't tell you my name."

Utterly perturbed, Reaghann said then, "Well, then Lady Green Eyes, what did you think of your Council Meeting?"

He watched her blink, then roll her eye.

"That interesting, was it?"

"I actually was almost asleep when you finally adjourned it."

"Well, we have that in common. I feel quite the same most meetings," Reaghann returned.

He thought she was smiling.

Then she grew serious and told him, "I have information for you. You need to believe me when I tell you that... that there are... certain people... who do not wish you well."

Part of Reaghann would like to have laughed. He'd known that his entire life, there were people who had not wished generations of his family well, and he was no exception. But Lady Green Eyes behind the wall was quite earnest.

"And how do you come to know this, exactly? Other than common knowledge....?"

He detected a sniff behind the wall. "That is... a long, long story. But – here."

And before Reaghann's eyes, a rolled-up parchment pushed itself through the spyhole toward him.

Well, he now had proof that he wasn't imagining the entire event. He stood up and pulled the rest of the parchment through the wall.

"What is this, exactly?" Reaghann asked slowly as he unrolled it. Names were hastily scribbled upon the parchment, names of lords he knew, some he worked closely with, even....

"People who do not wish you well," said his green-eyed friend behind the spyhole.

"Where did you get this?" Reaghann asked sharply.

Taken aback, Lady Green Eyes replied, "I wrote it, wrote the list down, myself."

"Well, that much I can see –"

"I'm sorry I didn't spend more time on my calligraphy up in the bowery, Your Majesty...."

"Am I right, to presume that you are chastising me?"

The green eye in the spyhole narrowed into a green slit.

"Very well, very well," Reaghann placated the girl with upheld palms. "But answer my question – where did you get this information?"

Lady Green Eyes behind the wall considered Reaghann for a moment. Finally, she answered, "From the desk of a... very bad man."

Just as he was about to express his irritation with that answer, Reaghann heard another paper being pushed through the spyhole. He pulled it through.

Names written upon it were divided into three sections.

He glanced up at her. "All right. I'm waiting."

"At the top, those men?" she said.

"Yes?"

"Those people are dead by his hand, personally."

"What?" Reaghann was shocked. Surely she was mistaken.

"That's actually why I'm leaving, or my name will soon be added to that list." She paused, then continued. "The second section, with all the names. They are people he consorts with in some way, some of them may be responsible for – other deaths. Or other… bad things."

"Other bad things? Do you even know how mad you sound?" Reaghann leaned backward and took a swallow from his goblet.

He could see her nodding. "Yes." She took a breath. "You needn't believe me. But I hope you do. Just hear me through and then decide. After all, I could have left days ago."

Reaghann glanced down at this second list, and then up at Lady Green Eyes. Then he leaned back against his desk. "Carry on, then."

She stared at him. She really did have striking eyes, Reaghann thought idly as he waited for her to continue. "Do you know the King of Shaw?"

Whatever did that have to do with anything? What an odd divergence. "Of course I do. King Rickstan. What of him? What has he to do with your story?"

She cleared her throat and looked down. "You know, then, of his brother. His twin."

"Yes. Prince Rilstrom. His wife is pregnant, or was. He should be a proud father by now. Again, your point?"

Her green eye had widened and then looked down.

"Come, Lady Green Eyes, I am losing patience. I enjoy a good intrigue as well as any man, but you need to hurry this along…."

"Your Majesty, did you know of a state visit from Prince Rilstrom and his wife several months ago, to visit you here?"

A state visit from Shaw? Of course not. He'd have known. In fact, he'd have been pleased to host one. Months ago, in fact, she said? No. He hadn't seen anyone from Shaw but the Ambassador.

"There was no visit. No visit planned. Of all people, My Lady of the Green Eyes, I think I would be the first to know. Neither the Prince nor his brother visited, nor was any visit planned."

"That's because you were never to find out of it. They were set upon by bandits while traveling here. She died, all the men traveling with them died, and the Prince himself was captured. He's been down in your dungeon, in a traitor cell all these months."

Reaghann reacted to this with a mixture of disbelief, shock, and anger. That was absolutely untrue! Unfounded. And he told the girl so immediately.

The girl pushed an iron key through the spyhole. "I found this in his desk as well. I overheard him talking about it all. That's how I know. He told the other man that he *'didn't care if the Prince lived or died at this point, although he may yet serve a use, maybe it would be best to keep him alive still.'"*

Sickened, Reaghann reached for the key.

"No. He's not there anymore. I've taken care of him. That man was telling Lord Hampsherd this – Lord Hampsherd knew all of it and is a part of the entire plan. You were never to know. The brother is escaped now and on his way safely home to Shaw, Your Majesty.

"I've sent birds – the real birds, not the fake birds - to the King of Shaw to watch for him and help him home, which explained to him the truth of what really happened. Because Your Majesty, all these months, he's been mourning the death of his brother and sister-in-law, and your people here let you think they were alive and well, don't you see?

"If your ally King Rickstan were to find out that you had his twin brother all these months that he's been locked up down in your traitor cell, you'd lose an ally, or worse, he'd cry war on you. Do you know who would set you up like this?"

Reaghann had sat through this entire story, frozen. Could it be, that the girl was completely mad? She seemed so serious, so intense.... He just could not believe it – Prince Rilstrom, locked in his dungeon and he hadn't even known.... Who would do such a thing?

"How... how..." He was at a loss for words.

"Not how, Your Majesty. Who." Lady Green Eyes stared at him.

"All right then. Who?"

"You have to promise to at least consider who I'm about to tell you."

"I've just found out I've harbored a man in my dungeon that the rest of the land thought dead. I think I can take a name," Reaghann snapped.

He watched her green eye narrow but didn't care. He decided she was being more speculative than irritated, anyway.

"This man, he is an – assassin. A very good one, that no one knows about. And he's very good at being among people – everyone thinks he's clever and witty – no one would see him as an assassin, unless you saw him in his private time, like I have. So when I give you his name, you have to trust me. I'll be gone in a few hours, from HarCourt altogether, before he finds me, too. I just wanted to let you know all this before I leave."

Reaghann nodded. He wasn't sure he wanted to know, but he waited just the same.

She pushed a scrap of parchment out.

"Lord Drury" it read. His head jerked up.

"I told you, you have to believe me. He is a very, very bad man. Here –"

And a silver flash was pushed out of the spyhole. It fell onto his carpet. Reaghann picked it up. A key. Immediately he recognized it.

"Where did you find this…" he breathed.

"In a hidden compartment of Lord Drury's desk, along with the key to Prince Rilstrom's cell." Lady Green Eye's voice was quite somber.

"This is a key to – something – of my father's. Something I haven't seen for years, not since he passed away…." Reaghann thought it was lost when they'd packed his father's belongings so that he himself could move into the chamber as King. But no, here it was. The key to the hidden chamber in his father's bed chamber…. And in Lord Drury's desk all this time.

Lady Green Eyes had his full attention now.

"Your Majesty, I don't know what you'll do with this information, but I only hope you'll put it to good use, and – be careful of yourself. Take caution. He is very dangerous, more than you can possibly imagine." Lady Green Eyes sounded terrified and that green-eyed gaze was intense.

"I'd like that dungeon key as well, if you please," Reaghann told her.

She paused and glanced away. "If you go down tomorrow and look in the very last traitor cell, you'll see where he's been held. Just wait until – just after noon tomorrow."

Reaghann shook his head at her. "You know, I could just open the wall and take the key from you, Lady of the Green Eyes."

She stepped away from the spyhole. "You know where the door is?" she whispered.

Reaghann smiled. "I like to think I know my castle a bit better than others who run about. Though obviously you know it at least as well. I saw my father use that door when I was a child. He used it fairly often. To be honest, I'd forgotten about it until the other day when Lord Drury sat here.

"It would appear that you know the tunnels far better than I do," he commented.

"They're everywhere," she whispered. "Look on the floor – wherever you see chalk, there's a tunnel – just be careful, and bring a candle to light the way."

"Chalk?

"On the floor. Outside, lying on the floor, you'll see chalk wherever there's a tunnel. Always bring a candle, Your Majesty, to light the way…."

Reaghann thought her voice was receding as she said that last.

On a whim, he bent forward and peered into the spyhole.

"Lady Green Eyes?"

But no one answered.

Theldry

She was still angry. Angry with her father, angry with how the land ran in general. All Theldry amounted to in this land was a cog in a wheel, one which made her father's land spin around.

Theldry's mother recognized after a week or two the change in Theldry's behavior. She visited Theldry and explained to her that this was just the sacrifice women were made to bear. And women had the privilege of bearing the bloodline truest, so to whomever Theldry was married, her children would be the sons and daughters of Tortoreen.

It had taken all of Theldry's patience to smile at her mother and nod rather than shake her and tell her how ridiculous that sounded. Pleased that she had imparted to Theldry the true role of a woman's life in the world, Theldry's mother patted her hand, believing that Theldry now understood what her responsibility was. Theldry waited until her mother left to shake her head with amazement at the idea, the utter absurdity of it.

That had been weeks ago. While men of her station themselves were often confined to arranged marriages that brought advantage and benefit rather than personal preference, they were consulted, given a choice – this woman or that, this woman beastly to look at, that one too fat or too skinny…. Theldry would never be paid such a courtesy, and nor had any of her friends.

She was a living, breathing person, not a good at auction to be sold to the highest bidder. Not to be traded for gains and profits. And yet, her father was only waiting until the best man paid the highest bride price, gave him the best advantage over all the others.

And so Theldry seethed in silence.

Of course, the buyer would be a man in the Coastal Countries, for the North had nothing to offer that Tortoreen wanted, other than a partnership during wartime. Neither did they know of any marriageable men in the North, and the one courtesy they at least were offering her was that she would freeze in such a cold climate.

Wrinkling her brow, Theldry couldn't understand her father's logic there. Partnership in wartime… surely having a daughter up in the Northern Countries would only serve to cement an alliance there, rather than just join up again. If Theldry were her father – she'd pack his daughter straight off to some freezing cold lord in the North and to the hells with if his daughter froze or not. That's what furs and fires were for.

Or perhaps Theldry's mother had intervened. Possibly, even, Theldry thought, a proposal had been sent and they had brushed it off. She considered that from a Northern Country King's point of view. If her father was a Northern Country King, what would he want with a Coastal daughter….

Hmmm. Not much. Theldry knew very little of the Northern Countries, other than that they only invaded Romeny and Clemongard regularly throughout history. Her tutors rarely expounded on history beyond the basics, from the Battle of the Banners forward. And there was no war now. The Twenty Years War was over before she was born.

Thinking as her father might, what could the North possibly offer other than a secure alliance during war? Not much. Ice? Rolling over on her bed, Theldry propped her feet upon her pillows, which caused her gown to slip down to her knees. *Yes, Mother, sooo unladylike…* Better be unladylike now before she was sold off to a husband somewhere, where propping her feet up would be sooo unwifelike….

At all times with her parents, mealtimes and otherwise, Theldry now was quiet and rarely spoke. She knew Father had seen this change, but he had not commented on it. Theldry endured meals in silence in the hopes that her father would choose a man based on her behavior more than her bride price, though she believed that prospects on bride price would ultimately rule over the new ladylike, Princess behavior she had recently adopted.

Ignoring her stupid brother at mealtimes had been a true test - for he really knew how to irritate her. Seated across from her, His Royal Bratliness was still able to catch her attention, even when Theldry turned a blind eye.

She finally considered him practice. If she could ignore Bronn the Brat, then she could ignore anyone. So she stared through his little freckled face with no expression whatever.

Upon employing this tactic, Theldry immediately discovered that this served only to incite further shitty behavior from Brat. He truly was a little shit. She could not imagine him upon the throne. King Bronn. King Brat, His Royal Shittiness.

Theldry hoped earnestly that when it came time to kiss her brother's royal ring someday and commit to him her loyalty and fidelity, that she could kiss his stupid ring, pledge her allegiance, and then, where no one could witness, make a face and stick her tongue out at him, so she could watch his face before all those people.

Theldry did exact her revenge upon him, for she passed him in the corridors most days when he strode off to his horsemanship lessons. She smacked him in the back of the head as he passed if he was alone. Who was he to tell? And why? His big sister, picking on him? No one would believe him, and if they did, they'd say he was sugar. A sigh passed from her lips. *Yes, more unladylike behavior, Mother*, but Theldry could not resist a snicker.

Now, Theldry wanted to know she was most likely to be traded for. What would benefit her father the most worth trading a Princess for.

Just around the corner from her where her tutor would be most likely to find her, Theldry heard a number of men laughing and conversing.

She dared to sneak past the corridor, hoping her tutor wouldn't catch sight of her. Perfect – she'd lost him again. Theldry knew that skipping her lessons was wrong and soon earn a scolding from her mother, but surely Extended Arithmetic was not going to be needed for a woman in her position in life… or anyone's. Simple accounting ought to be all anyone should know, shouldn't it, Theldry wondered?

What Theldry was more interested in… was these men…. They're all Council Members, she thought as she peered about the stone corner. Undoubtedly, they knew more of any interest to Theldry than Extended Arithmetic would ever afford her.

Theldry ran forward on an impulse and slipped in to the Council Chamber just as the door was closing.

Many faces of the Lords she recognized, though some were unfamiliar. Theldry stood behind her father, who sat at the head of the sturdy oak table.

Choruses of "Your Majesties" sounded from all about the table as the Council Members bowed. Theldry's father waved them down so that they might seat themselves.

Most of them remained standing, however, many of them amused or smiling, mainly due to respecting her.

"Your Highness," several said.

Father immediately threw a look over his shoulder. He did not want to yell at Theldry before his Councilors, but his eyes narrowed and she heard a dangerous intake of breath that communicated a serious displeasure with her.

"How good to see you, Your Highness. Are you joining us today?" asked one.

"What a delight to have you join us. A fresh face, if just for a day," said another.

With every ounce of grace, Theldry curtsied for the entire Council. She bestowed upon them the kindly and delicate smile she had seen her mother use before crowds and hoped it turned out the same on her own face.

"Splendid, splendid!" called the first. "Please, find Her Highness a chair."

One of the Royal Guards immediately brought a chair from the side wall, placed it next to Father, bowed deeply, and retreated.

Theldry snuck a glance at Father. His jaw was clenched but he suddenly forced a smile upon his face and a cheerful voice roared out across the Chamber, "Daughter, welcome to our Council. Do, have a seat." And he gestured at Theldry's seat as lords always did, though his brown eyes met Theldry's personally so that none could witness them. Hard and glittering, she knew even the sweetest of honey and sugar wouldn't soften the blow that she could see was coming later.

At first, Theldry was fascinated by the diplomacy the Council Members employed as they promoted their causes. Everything they spoke of seemed to Theldry rehearsed speeches, for occasionally they paused, then started again.

Father contributed little to the meeting – in fact, Theldry mused, he seemed little more than a gargoyle watching over a garden on a tournament day. Had he no opinion at all, or was he just there to mind them in case they lost control of themselves and jumped across the table at each other?

At first, the Lords were quite polite, tactful even. After an hour or so, Theldry suppressed a yawn and she saw one aged Councilor near the end of the table twiddling his thumbs.

And why not, for the subjects they tossed back and forth – were these what Theldry was really up for on the bargaining block? Mutton tariffs? Equality of sale between lake fish over river fish? Wool? Cattle straying into local parishes? At least lumber imports had some value, but then three of them fought over whether lumber imported by sea should be charged the same as lumber imported by land.

After the second hour, Theldry found Councilor Twiddling Thumbs down the table with his head nodding, attempting to stay awake.

Into the third hour, Theldry found that tact the Councilors had dealt earlier so freely had now given way to subtly disguised barbs. But she also realized something else – most everything they discussed was a reworded proposal of an earlier proposition, and often by another Councilor. She found that interesting, for then this could only mean that certain Councilors supported others in their efforts to convince their fellow Councilors to vote in agreement for their proposals. As an onlooker with fresh eyes, Theldry was amazed at what she saw unfolding before her. Perhaps Father had the right idea after all....

Down at the end of the table, one Councilor proposed a tariff on all incoming vegetables from Corstarorden, given the blight they had recently suffered.

Theldry's brow furrowed. That just made no sense at all to her. She'd seen the lessened amount of vegetables upon her plates of late. Why would they tax people who need the help with harvests, rather than assist them? Tortoreen certainly was able to extend the aid.

To speak up or no?

"Pardons, my lords," Theldry called, realizing that her voice had hardly been loud enough to be heard. She would have to speak up.

The entire room stopped speaking and Theldry saw every face turn toward her, including Father's. Well, she would take that beating when the time came for it.

Theldry cleared her throat and then, in a raised voice this time, called out, "Am I right to assume that you are asking to tax the import of a country who is selling us what is left of their crops after a blight killed off most of what they grew?

"Forgive me, if you please, but I don't see the sense behind that. If anything, we should lower the import tax on Corstarorden vegetables and raise the price for them in our local Markets, as they will be scarce.

"In fact, due to their scarcity, and because Corstarorden is and has always been a Coastal Ally of Tortoreen, we ought to send them aid to replant, for we certainly have the coin to do so. And so, in another year's growth season, we and they would have the regrown crops, and if necessary, we might even require them to pay us back by sending us a larger share of vegetables. That would, in fact, strengthen our ties to Corstarorden, would it not?

"And perhaps, in the future, should Tortoreen suffer similarly, one of its Allies might rise to its assistance."

The Council Chamber was silent. Theldry could feel her father's eyes upon her.

And that's when she saw the Councilor who proposed the Corstarorden Vegetable Tax glance nervously at the Lord sitting before him across the Council Table.

He then drew in breath and responded, "That is, Your Highness, a, a, wonderful thought. We should definitely give it some... consideration." The Councilor swallowed and, when he sat down again, he glanced across the table. The other Lord was resting his jaw in his palm, as if curious to see what happened next.

It occurred to Theldry just then that the Corstarorden Vegetable Tax was proposed merely as a money-making scam, not as a political device at all.

Several Councilors looked down at the table and others would not meet her eye.

Before her jaw fell open with disgust, Theldry immediately clenched her jaw shut.

All a scam. Look at them all. Dishonest. Corrupt. How many of them were liars? And her father? Theldry's breath was gone and she was speechless. How much of Tortoreen was run this way, of government, of any country?

A blight. Those poor farmers, struggling to make a living, and these – immoral Councilman, not worth the dirt those farmers planted their crops with, wanted to charge them taxes just to sell what was left of their harvest.

Then Theldry had a terrible idea... what if....

What if....

If there had been no blight at all? If there was just some sort of... brief sickness, like a fever instead of a plague in people... just so that the Councilmen could tax the farmers in order to put gold in their pockets?

Theldry stared at them and knew it to be true....

Topher

It was time. It was. It was time.

If he camped under another tree tonight, he'd scream.

Topher's hair wasn't long, as in apprentice long. Nor was it runaway-Silent-Order short, either. It was mid-ear and he had bangs in his eyes now. He thought that was worth taking a risk on.

He'd spent three and a half months sleeping outdoors, though two or three times, he'd found a deserted, rundown barn here and there, and slept like a king. Best nights of his life of late.

And what a bold thief Topher had become. Far more so than his first few weeks. His boots were a perfect fit, thanks to the cobbler's store with a weak lock in the back. A fresh loaf of bread cooling on a window sill, a berry tart once in a small village, half a jug of milk…. Not an accomplished thief, nor a gifted thief, but bold, aye.

Dogs had chased him twice, and once bitten him as he'd scrambled his way up a tree. In the dark, no one expected to look for a thief, they thought their dogs were running after animals.

And his clothes fit now, closest as could be expected. Topher had a cloak now as well, which helped keep the cold out the farther north he traveled. Sleeping on the ground had lost its appeal, however thankful for his freedom he was.

He'd also acquired a few coppers, though on each occasion, those were by mistake. Topher had a strict rule for not stealing money. People needed coin – whether it be to pay taxes, put food on the table for their little ones, buy seed for their fields or supplies for their trade…. Topher would not deprive them of that which they worked hard to earn. But in some of the pants he'd stolen, he'd found a few copper chips, so Topher had a small bit of coin.

Tonight, now, Topher was done hiding. He strode down the main boulevard of Landy Hollow, a town of middling size. While Topher was still southeast of Rorden North, he was only a week's walk, perhaps two at most. And tonight, walking into town among other people, would be a good judge of how other people accepted him.

He'd planned a getaway route, if he needed it, but Topher was certain he wouldn't require it.

No one thought any different of him. In fact, few people noticed him at all. Topher's heart soared. Though that was not a final conclusion, he knew. He still had to interact in a social setting with other people, and just the thought frightened him.

For what would he talk about? His past six years as a silent person in a religious order that wanted to cut his tongue out before he escaped? His parents who sold him for cornseed?

Topher had made up dozens and dozens of stories over the last three months of solitude, for though he was free, no longer a member of the Silent Order, and still had his tongue, he ironically had had no one to speak to and was still alone. But he had stories to rely upon for when he did finally rejoin society.

Like tonight.

And there was a small tavern near the end of the boulevard, for Topher had stolen about the town last night by moonlight and discovered the tavern. He had marked an escape route and a hideaway route, in the event that either proved necessary. But by The One God, Topher hoped to sleep in a real bed, under a real blanket, a hot meal in his belly tonight.

First, however, he'd be Arithist, from ArkenHeights. And there was Lancy's Finest, Best Tavern in Town, though Topher noticed the play on this was that it was the only tavern in town, and he didn't think there was another pub, either, though he hadn't checked the town so thoroughly as to be sure of that.

He nodded to a few people as he walked past them and ducked through the door of Lancy's Finest.

Immediately, the smell of sour ale, body odor, pine, bacon, and some sort of stew assailed Toper. Laughter burst out from table to table from coarse looking men. Some diced at their tables, others ate from pewter bowls of stew and shared conversation with their mates.

Topher stepped up to the bar and sunk onto a wooden stool. *Remember, you're Arithist from ArkenHeights, Arithist from ArkenHeights....*

Finally, the barkeeper with gray fringed hair running about the sides of his scalp tossed a towel over his shoulder and stood in front of Topher.

Topher stared at him. He wasn't sure what to say. Should he order his room first, or his meal... an ale, or maybe mead....

"Listen, what'll it be, huh? Bit busy to stare at ya all night, eh?"

"Right. I'll have – a room, please." Oops, he'd meant to say an ale. "And, an ale. And a, a bowl of stew."

The barkeep blew out a bored sigh. "Ya pay before ya stay. Two coppers, one more for the meal." He had obviously repeated that speech hundreds of times, mused Topher.

As he dug in his pocket for his copper chips, he caught the eyes of a man seated across the pub, at a table alone. The candles in the candelabra above him were blown out, so Topher could not see his face, only that he was dark-haired and bearded, propped up against the wall with his legs resting on the other chair. His black eyes met Topher's.

Just then, Topher's fingers found his copper chips. He laid them on the bar.

The barkeep bit each one. Topher pulled back a bit, trying to hide his disgust.

The barkeep caught Topher's expression and told him, "Got to be sure they're real."

"Real?"

The barkeep scoffed and pushed the towel around on the bar before Topher. "Ya never know nowadays, the things comin' through here. Got to check." He moved down the bar but returned with a pint that sloshed ale onto the bar. "Ya got Room 4, a winda' room. Bath water is first light, first come as first serve."

Then the barkeep moved on down the bar again. Topher swallowed several gulps of ale. His first ale, ever, and it tasted fine, very, very fine. A loud belch forced itself out, and Topher glanced guiltily around. Then he grinned. He could be as impolite as he liked from now on. But he expected to get that stew, and soon.

He looked around for a barmaid to inquire of, and instead found himself staring back at the mysterious man across the pub. Still seated with his boots propped up, the man had not moved.

Just then, a scratched-up pewter bowl of steaming stew with a wooden spoon sticking out of it was shoved at Topher across the bar. "Bread?" Topher called after the receding back of the barkeep.

"Bread's extra," called the barkeep, rubbing his fingers in the air for coins as he walked away.

Somehow, Topher doubted that, but this would be his first meal in months, and he really didn't care if bread was served with it or not. Just being inside among people was a wonderful feeling.

He pulled up a spoonful of stew, wondering what it was. Just some vegetables, but too hot to eat yet. Well, there was a cure for that, thought Topher as he swallowed down several more gulps of ale.

No belch. Ah, well, he thought as he glanced about the bar.

All these people and no one looked at him askance at all. What a wonderful feeling....

Then he met the eyes of the mysterious man across the bar, the man in the shadows. He held Topher's glance for no more than a second, but Topher saw him distinctly shake his head. Minutely, barely noticeable, and with something like scorn, and then his gaze flicked away.

And just like that, it was over.

And just like that, Topher's feeling of warm independence and oneness within the Land vanished.

Was the man a bounty hunter? Did he recognize Topher? Was he going to execute him, or capture him and deliver him back to the Order?

Topher barely tasted his stew, noting only that it was far too salty, which he recognized would make people thirsty and want to buy ale. If he drank much more of his ale, he would be completely drunk, and right now, he needed to be clear headed now more than ever.

Without finishing the rest of his stew, or his ale, Topher stole quietly around the bar and headed down his side of the bar toward the staircase. He'd sneak out tonight, out the window, since they'd given him a window room, according to the barkeep. Now that Topher thought of it, he wouldn't be staying the night, so he wanted his coppers back.

He bent to brush his boots free of dust, saw no one watching and that the barkeep was on the other side of the bar. Two copper chips were left on the bar next to two different empty bowls, and the barkeep had not collected yet.

Faster than lightning, Topher swept them off the bar and then slipped up the staircase silently. He wouldn't be staying but a few more hours if that long, and...

Was that bread?

Topher smelled bread.

He leaned around the corner. A customer had left an untouched half a loaf of bread on his dishes outside his door.

Topher swiped the bread smugly and opened the door to his room.

It wasn't much of a room, but it was a mattress underneath a roof, with four wooden walls, and a window. And it would have been nice to stay and have a bath in the morning as well, mused Topher.

But the longer he stayed, cramming bits of bread into his mouth, the longer he decided it was better just to leave before anyone might think to look for him.

Damn.

He forced the window open, climbed out onto its sill until he hung from his fingers....

Then he let go and fell to the ground.

It took a while before he was able to stand. Topher just sat down against the inn and panted for a while. A three-story jump. What had he been thinking! Bloody ale.

Thanks to The One God nothing was broken or sprained.

Finally, Topher set off down the boulevard out of Lancy's Hollow, heading northwest. He had to get out of there before someone found him.

He kept to the shadows and kept a brusque pace, albeit a gingerly one. *Three-story jump – Topher, you're an idiot –*

Just as he was scolding himself yet again, he saw a figure up ahead. Staying to the shadows as was he.

The figure up ahead halted and Topher immediately fell up against a building.

Then the figure began walking again. Topher had to leave – this was his getaway route, and with that mysterious man behind him, he couldn't risk slowing down. The end of the boulevard and Lancy's Hollow was so close.

Topher scaled the walls silently, hoping that whoever that man ahead of him was, he would hurry up and turn off a side street to his home.

Then the man ahead stopped yet again. Topher sighed with frustration.

The man ahead of him stepped into the torch light of the street, then put his hands on his hips.

Topher's jaw dropped.

"You!"

The mysterious man from the bar turned slightly and gave an annoyed glare behind him. "Do us both a favor. Stop following me."

Topher skipped up to him. "Me! Following you! I thought you were following me!"

"Lad, I don't know what instinct told you to get out of that bar when you did, but be glad of it. Why do you think I'm out here? I expect there's a thorough amount of blood being mopped up just now."

Topher's jaw fell open. "W-what? Blood?"

The man scoffed and rolled his eyes. He fell back into the shadows again and started walking forward.

Topher followed him.

"Stop following me," came the man's irritated whisper.

"I'm not. You're going in my direction. I'm – headed in the same direction."

"Listen, lad. I don't know where you're headed, and I don't know why or how. But you're not going with me." He paused but Topher could see the man's eyes as he glanced up and down at Topher's face.

"You may fool everyone else, but you think I can't tell a runaway Silent Brother when I see one?"

Topher's eyes grew wide but he replied, "I have no idea what you're talking about."

"No? That haircut hasn't grown out long, has it? Still got the same cut around the neck. They wanted to burn your tongue and you ran, was that it? Can't say I wouldn't do the same. But you're wanted now. You better learn how to hide real well. And I don't need anyone slowing me down. Understand me? You stay away from me, lad."

The man in black turned and continued further in the shadows.

"Who are you?" called Topher.

Elenorina

She always took her morning meals, and often her afternoon meals, outside. She believed one could never get enough fresh air. The sun had the converse effect, and she had taken great care to always wear a hat and sit beneath a tented gazebo or in the shade. So many ladies of her age hadn't cared for their skin over the years and now had wrinkles and age spots they might have prevented.

Elenorina sipped at her fruit juice. She did not care for tea so much as fruit juice, for tea stained one's teeth. So many of the older generation had stained teeth, and her own mother and aunts confided that they believed it had to do with daily tea consumption, so they advised that Elenorina drink it only amongst company.

Her long-dead husband thought such an idea bosh but she hadn't need to listen to all the things he thought bosh for too long, for he'd finally died at fifty-one of consumption in Fairview. Elenorina suspected Chaz had contracted it from some whore or other in Fairview, for he died in a hospice near a brothel. She had him recovered and buried here with his ancestors, though she'd first removed herself and Chaz II to her mother's home in Ivy Gate. One could never be too careful, and consumption had not reached that far south.

The thin curtains drifted lazily in the light breeze and she spooned more milk onto her berries. When she glanced up, Elenorina's new guest was striding down the green to her, accompanied by a house maid.

Hmm. That gait. She shook her head slightly. Too bold – she plodded forward as a horse trotted down the boulevard. That would need amending. Elenorina winced as she saw the girl struggle a bit with the gown that trailed slightly past her. Oh, my, she sighed. This would be quite the undertaking. *Rhutgard, Rhutgard, what were you thinking, child….*

Now that the girl stood before Elenorina, she took a final sip of chilled fruit juice and then rose.

"My lady," the house maid curtsied and then left.

"Ah. Lady Ellia. I trust you slept well?"

"Lady" Ellia struggled to appear calm, though her nod was a nervous one to Elenorina's practiced eye.

Elenorina stepped around her breakfast table and stood before the girl. "Ellia, I want you to know that I know your actual identity, for your father – that is to say, your other father, your Royal father – sent me a notice explaining all. You will be staying with me for a time, and so you can be sure that you are safe here.

"Now, Ellia, my name is Duchess Elenorina Chambourny of Emberly. But you may call me *Nona*."

She watched as this washed over the frightened girl.

"Ellia, my dear, I recognize this had been a terrible turn of events. Do understand something, child," and Elenorina place a few fingers beneath the girl's chin. She had always wanted a daughter. Granddaughters, and daughters-in-law, especially the grand-daughter-in-law she had now, were just not quite the same. She continued with kindness, "You grew up with parents who loved you, and who always will love you, dearly…." And Ellia's blue eyes glistened as they filled with tears.

"But you have a new family, a father and a mother, who have always loved you as well, who cannot wait to meet you."

Tears spilled down the girl's face.

"Ah, my child." Elenorina sighed. She had known this would happen. And why not? Anyone dearly cherished by their parents, then snatched up and removed forever and given a new identity – naturally would be heartbroken.

She pulled out her handkerchief and dabbed gently at Ellia's face. "Here is your first lesson, my child. Ladies, particularly Princesses, must never cry in public, nor never before other people."

Elenorina pressed her handkerchief into Ellia's hand and rolled the girl's fingers over it so that she might keep it.

"Of course, we ladies are not infallible, are we? So, how do we avoid looking as if we are crying?" Elenorina patted Ellia's hand and let a small smile play across her face. "You sneeze. Pretend to sneeze into your handkerchief. Twice if must be, but dab at your face and all will believe your tears are a result of your sneeze. Unless you are at table. Never sneeze at table. Cough at table, for other diners will believe you swallowed a bit of food or drink wrong. Then you can dab at your eyes."

Amazement and a bit of amusement illustrated Ellia's expression. Then the girl yawned. She covered her mouth with the handkerchief right away, and her expression changed to a guilty one.

Elenorina reached out and told her, "Don't ever yawn. It's considered terribly rude, the height of rudeness. The best way to keep from yawning is to take in a deep breath through your mouth, the second you feel a yawn starting. Of course, you may yawn in your bed chamber, but never among people, ever."

"I'm so sorry," Ellia said, her blue eyes wide.

"Oh, darling, you needn't be. You don't know any of these things yet. That, of course, is why you're here," Elenorina told her.

"When will I meet them – my other parents, I mean?" she asked.

Elenorina took in a long breath. "Well. You won't be going there yet. You see, dear, all the people will suddenly discover that they have a new Royal Princess that's been hidden away. And you must pass muster, as they say, at Court. But they will discover where you grew up, and so... not only must you convince the Court, but also the Romeny people, that you are truly a Romeny Princess. And so you must be perfect, in every way.

"Which, means, my dear, in all kindness, you must first learn to be a Princess."

Elenorina waited for Ellia to object, but the girl said nothing. "Therefore, while you are here, you will be my charge. I will be instructing you in all things such as History, many of the Arts, your social graces, of course, that will go without saying. Do you ride?"

Ellia blinked at her. "You mean a horse?"

"I'll take that as a no. We'll remedy that and start you on some horsemanship lessons."

She stood back and assessed Ellia. "My, but you do have your mother all about you. And I dare say, some of her mother as I recall. Her slight frame, which is a good thing, though for childbearing…. Well, let that be as will be, you're young yet. All you really have of your father is – of course, those ruddy eyes. *Romeny blue always breeds true*, they say. Of course, you do look exactly like your brothers, just a feminine version, so no one will ever question your identity once they see the resemblance. They, of course, have his jaw…."

"Milady Nona…" started Ellia.

"Just Nona please, and you need say "My Lady' to no one. Though in fact, do be sure to say it as *'My Lady'*, rather than *'Milady'*…"

Ellia flushed. She had beautiful white skin, Nona mused as she waited for Ellia to continue. "Nona, will they… my brothers, I mean, will I, like them? Will they – like me?"

The poor child. She pictured the twin boys. They were rather like Golden Retrievers – happy all the time, easy going, never serious. If anything, Elenorina thought they would adore her, the thought of having a new sister. But she did not want to get the girl's hopes up. History had shown throughout the generations that sibling turned against sibling when least expected…. Though she did not expect any such thing here.

"Child, I think they will love you."

Ellia visibly relaxed.

"Now, I've arranged for the seamstress and the tailor to attend us, for you must have dresses for all Court occasions ready. You'll not be wearing them here, understand, but it takes time for them to be designed and crafted. You'll of course need simple gowns for daily wear about here as well. Such a lovely complexion – light green might suit you, and rose, for blues will just make you fade away beneath those eyes of yours. We'll let the tailor decide, shall we?"

Just then, Prince Ronan strode into view.

"Well, young Ronan," Elenorina announced as he approached them.

"My lady, Your Highness." Ronan bowed.

"Ronan, we agreed that we will not be using that honorific while Lady Ellia visits us, unless we are told otherwise."

Ronan bowed. "As it please you, my lady. I just received a bird."

Elenorina did not like being interrupted, and her morning so far with Ellia had just been interrupted. Crossly, she replied, "Did you."

"I received orders that I was to remain here and – as – Lady Ellia's personal guard." Ronan tried to conceal a grimace. Elenorina knew he had worked for some time in a commoner position watching over Ellia, and no doubt was ready for a hiatus. Whether it was a return to Martmain Palace in Ghiverny or some more exciting station within the Army, she did not know, but she hoped he could at least not be an arse while he remained at Emberly.

"Well, you will need to have your belongings transferred from Chaz's estate to my personal estate so that you might carry out your orders, for Lady Ellia will be staying here with me."

"Yes, my lady. What will you be teaching her? She already reads and writes, she knows her basic arithmetic –"

"Are you having a Ronnie moment? Did you forget that I am standing right here? You needn't speak over me as if I'm some sort of child," Ellia cut in.

At the same time, both Elenorina and Ronan told her, "It's rude to interrupt." And then Elenorina continued to Ronan, "Why, History, of course, of all the Countries. Geography, certainly. A bit of the arts. Those subjects in which Princesses are instructed, young Ronan." Elenorina did not like being questioned – she was accustomed to giving orders, not having her orders questioned.

"Perhaps you might teach her Heraldry, for then she will recognize those in Court to whom she is speaking, for they will test her, just to be merciless."

"And I shall be instructing her in social graces as well, which you appear to have lost over time. As well as Horsemanship, though perhaps you may do that, as you are acting like a horse's arse at the moment," Elenorina snapped.

"Social graces and horse's arses. You both may not believe this, but I am right here – and you propose to teach me of rudeness while you speak over my head as if I'm not in front of you at all. One subject you needn't instruct me in is listening – for that I can do just fine!"

Ellia swept her gown around, the golden waves of her hair flying in the air as she strode away.

She had her father's temper, mused Elenorina, that was clear.

Selby

Selby gripped the balcony rail and leaned out, enjoying the fresh air. And the privacy. Stars were nagging at the twilight to disappear. Soon, she could retire to her chambers for the evening, slip out of this wretched, itchy black gown and into a silky robe, then enjoy some cider before her fire. And if she dozed off, then all the better....

A male throat cleared behind her. Selby ignored it and sighed. How long until she could retire for the night... perhaps she would have some cheese and bread sent to her rooms before she arrived....

Again, the same throat cleared itself. Her brow furrowed. This had best be good – it was far too late in the day for any sort of conversation, frivolous or otherwise.

Durain stood a few paces behind her. A respectful distance, of course, Ericorian would never broach her personal space unless necessary.

He glanced once at her and then coughed. A fake cough. Ah. The information she had asked for. She beckoned him closer. "Approach."

"Your Majesty."

Selby nodded to acknowledge him.

He advanced again but stayed away from her on the balcony. "About what you asked." Durain stood straight and did not look at her, as was required of his station.

Selby nodded and leaned on the guardrail.

"Go ahead."

"My – source. Followed the man you asked about. That man spoke to another person, who paid him several silvers. The conversation was similar to –

"'Bridges? That cannot be done. Our people can't get through if there are bridges along the rivers.'"

"'I realize that. But she is insisting. What would you have me do?'"

"'Put her off, of course.'"

"'I cannot, she wants an in-depth report, the land, the people, the locations, by next week's meeting. She wants it to start no later than three months from today, she said.

"'Shit. That's a queen for you. How long does it take to build a bridge?'"

"'Three months at most.'"

"'Then misinform her – tell her the project has begun, but delay it. Do what you must. She cannot know. Our men have to get through.'"

"'I am aware.'"

"'I want regular updates. If you must, build bridges that fall apart in places that can't hold them. If enough goes wrong, perhaps she'll give up. Women are flighty like that, they never stick to an idea long enough to finish it through.'"

"'If this falls through, it'll be your arse.'"

Durain paused. "The source was unable to determine the other man's identity, but is sure that he is Ormish."

Selby was staring into the night. Her mouth was open, she realized, but she didn't care. Was this happening? Ormish? The Ormons? She couldn't breathe.

That little bloody bastard, sitting at her Council Table. A traitor.

No. No. No. There was some other explanation. Yes. This was just being interpreted as –

Durain cleared his throat again. "Your Majesty."

No. No.

But she found herself saying, "Go on." Her voice sounded so distant.

"My source knows an architect – a loyal man, loyal to the Crown, who will build your bridges easily, while these men misle you. He only needs your –" Durain coughed. "He requires the finances and protection, since these men may assail him or harass his efforts."

Selby blinked. "Is this man trustworthy?"

"To the utmost. He is from a long generation of Crown Guards, and he fought ten years in the Twenty Years War, constructing siege weapons. He has been an architect ever since."

"Hire him immediately," she told Durain. "Have a list made of materials required and I will send coin that it may be purchased. As well as Ericorian so that he may have protection from any who might harass him as he builds. Is he familiar with bridges? Rivers?"

"He has lived his entire life on the Rournebourke, Your Majesty."

Selby sighed. "Excellent."

"There is more."

Selby nearly laughed. More? Surely there couldn't be more. How might there be any more horrendous news than that which she had just been informed of? Ormons – or someone at least – wanting access up her rivers?

She closed her eyes and waved her hand about for Durain to continue. Selby took in a deep breath.

"As you asked, Your Majesty, my source – reached out to more people that he trusts. He found out that Storden has built a number of new ships, Your Majesty. Galleons. They are building them in a number of shipyards, at least two he knows of and one other he suspects."

Storden? Building galleons? Whatever for? Storden kept its own Navy, to be sure, and in so doing, protected itself during wartime as necessary, but Storden had for hundreds of years been neutral. It neither assisted nor protected others in wartime. Building *galleons?* The idea shocked her, almost as much as the news just prior.

Storden aiding a country by building galleons…. The idea was preposterous. As much disband the Eastern Shield. The one country Clemongard had never had to worry about was its neutral neighbor to its south, Storden. The country supplied nearly all its own needs, traded little. They were Clemongard's immediate ally, of sorts, though the King never signed treaties with anyone.

And now, galleons….

Why, her Navy couldn't handle a war – not with numerous galleons….

Durain cleared his throat.

"Please – tell me more, by all means…." Selby stared up at the night sky above her. A nightmare? Yes?

"My source suggests you rebuild your Navy, quietly."

Selby glanced to the side, up at Durain. "Quietly? How might I do that? Every shipyard I own is in a quite populated town."

Durain nodded. "He thought that your Royal shipwrights had not been building ships for some time…."
Selby's head snapped around at this. "And yet I have been paying them?"

Durain stared straight into the night, silent.

Furious, she fumed. Drumming her fingers on the guard rail of the balcony, Selby waited until she could speak calmly again. Thin-lipped, she asked, "Perchance, has your source an idea that I might build my ships – galleons, in fact, *quietly*?"

"He has."

Selby's eyes suddenly narrowed. "Durain, I must ask. You trust these sources?"

"I do, Your Majesty."

"Very well, then. I'll hear this idea. For I must admit, I am curious to know where I can build ships quietly, for it seems my shipyards are no longer my own, my shipwrights are no longer my own, for all they take my bloody coin…."

And then Selby stopped abruptly.

She could suddenly hear her father…. *"Selby, Selby, stop, wait, take a breath. Now, calm down and stop over-reacting. You're being dramatic."*

And her mother…. *"Selby, darling, relax. A Princess must be collected and composed at all times, my love."*

Selby drew in a deep breath, held it, and let it out slowly. Both so true. And yet neither of them were ruling a country at the age of sixteen.

That, of course, was why this was happening. Why the North would be attacking her. Even Storden awaking from it sleepy, neutral slumber. Because she was such a very young Queen. And these people – these vile, insufferable, beastly people who were contaminating her life and trying to obstruct her reign.... They didn't know her very well. What they deserved would come to them in the end.

She cleared her throat and brushed her dress.

"Durain, what was this idea?"

"His idea was to send lumber along the Storden-Clemongard border to Ainsley-by-the-Sea and build a shipyard there, hire a number of trustworthy shipwrights, and keep the ships you build on the North side of the channel, where the Storden patrols won't see them. And since Ainsley-by-the-Sea has been deserted for so long, no one would look there anyway, for ships or a shipyard...."

Selby's eyebrows rose. The more she thought of it, the more she liked it. Ainsley-by-the-Sea was an old family estate that hadn't been used since probably her great-great grandmother's day. No staff had been kept there to run it in at least twenty or thirty years.

"He thought to turn the estate into a shipyard then? Both sides of the estate?"

"Yes, Your Majesty."

Selby liked the idea more and more. "Tell them to use the entire island. Turn the entire estate into whatever they need, barracks, anything at all. They have my full support." She paused. "To be clear, Durain, these new ships – they will be – galleons? For I'll not pay for anything less."

"Yes, Your Majesty." Durain's voice was quiet.

"That will require an awful lot of lumber, which will need to be transported across country...."

"He wondered if you might not let the idea slip that you were thinking of rebuilding the estate for a summer home, so that if anyone saw the movement of lumber, wagon drivers might simply describe it for the rebuilding of the Queen's old estate."

Selby nodded. "They think me just a flighty young girl, why would they investigate further. Excellent.

"However." And she rolled her eyes up to Durain. "This will not be cheap. Wars are cheap. Simply running Clemongard itself is not cheap. I will need to divert coin – a great deal of coin – into a fund for this – new summer home of mine. And my Council will not approve, I can guarantee you that."

Selby wondered from where the coin for this new Navy of hers – her Galleons would possibly come. Her Councilors were cunning and just now, before her Coronation, anything could happen.... She tapped thoughtfully at her lips.

Durain cleared his throat.

No, please, no, not more. Selby couldn't take anything more.

"Go ahead. Your source...."

He paused, then shook his head and glance at her quickly.

"You?"

"I – have a possible idea. It's not my place, Your Majesty, I know."

"Durain. I need your ideas, and it is now, without doubt, your place to disclose them to me," Selby told him calmly.

Durain nodded slowly. "As with your shipwrights, it may be that your treasury may not be – all it seems. Your Majesty."

Selby's eyes widened at the thought. Well, that would mean –

"Your Majesty, I know of a man whose brilliance with accounting skills are unsurpassed. Ericorian, you might say, but with arithmetic. I trust him completely. If you like, I could ask him to look at the Royal Treasury, the books, and see if all is correctly reported. If not, I – I am only Ericorian, Your Majesty, but I would divert what you have that is not reported to you to another fund as soon as possible, one which only you can access." Here, Durain looked at her steadily for a moment, then looked away.

Selby was open-mouthed. Would this list of horrors never end? Silently, she nodded her assent. Then, she told Durain, "I don't seem to be able to trust anyone right now. Except you, Durain."

She let out a deep breath, then said, "Tell this arithmetic-minded gentleman of yours that when he approaches me, so that I will know it is him, he must use the word "march" in just one sentence, but also "soldier" before the Treasury Door, to prevent a coincidence from occurring.

"If he does not use that code, strictly, he shall be executed."

Selby watched Durain for a sign of emotion, but none showed. Ericorian had always impressed her, just as Durain did now.

"I cannot thank you enough Durain, for this invaluable assistance, for your involvement. Without this information – Clemongard would be blind to what might well be an attack from her enemies, completely unprepared."

Durain said only, "It is a part of the oath we take as Ericorian, Your Majesty."

"Then, Durain, I am so fortunate that it is your dedication and allegiance serving me and not another Ericorian's. Most fortunate. Clemongard's thanks will never be enough."

"Yes, Your Majesty."

Ah. He was back to being an Ericorian again. One man a part of many, dedicated to a single purpose, to a single country. But Selby, now standing in the darkness, thought she had seen his chin raise slightly with pride.

Tyndie

She'd barely slept. How was she supposed to sleep anyway? Every single noise startled her from her skin. Now, not just the possibility of just anyone coming down these tunnels was conceivable, but Drury, and even King Reaghann, though she'd far and away it be King Reaghann she stumbled into down here than anyone else.

And how, exactly, would that conversation go? Ha. *"Are you Lady Green Eyes?"* He would only have to hold up a lantern to decide that.

She'd thought it cute, actually, for no one had ever remarked upon her appearance, except to make sure *the wrong eyes* didn't see her. Was King Reaghann the wrong eyes or the right eyes?

Tyndie had deliberated over whether to leave written instructions in his desk about what she knew, but had decided it was too much of a risk, for anyone might sit at his desk, Drury, for example, and rifle through his paperwork. So she had decided to speak to him directly and had been relieved to find him in his study.

Tyndie wondered if Drury had missed his two keys yet. With luck, he wouldn't miss them until she and the Prince – Rilstrom, now that she knew his name – were gone. What a terrible shame, his wife with child, he'd lost not just his wife but a child as well. Tyndie just hoped he could follow her directions and not decide he knew better than she did when it came time to leave.

She had snuck up to the pigeon loft as soon as twilight had fallen. She'd never written so small before and had to burn two pages of pigeon parchment before she finally got it right –

"His Highness, Prince Rilstrom of Shaw, thought dead, has, unknown to all, been kept in a dungeon traitor cell. On a state visit, Lord Drury had him kidnapped, and has kept him imprisoned unknown to King Reaghann. I have set him free but you must find him before Lord Drury does. King Reaghann never knew of the visit. He will be told after this is sent. – Anonymous"

— ⟨≈⟩ —

Tyndie wrote it out twice, to be sure it would arrive. She looked for the Shaw birds, but when she found the Shaw cages, both labels read, "Shaw." – with a small dot after them. She stood there, wondering what that meant, and then looked behind the cages at the birds. Their labels read, "SHAW" and there was no dot after them. Tyndie glanced at all the other cages and saw that most of them looked the same, with labels written in capital letters.

Tyndie decided then that, given what she knew about Drury, those birds in front never went to Shaw at all, but flew to someone Drury knew, so that he was aware of all correspondence between Hardewold and Shaw. How obvious. Maybe it took a servant with an eye for detail who was used to cleaning to pick up on that. Tyndie scoffed.

She pulled the birds in the back cages out one by one and wrapped her parchments about their legs, though while she sealed the second with the general Hardewold seal, the pigeon pecked her and now she had a scab on the back of her hand. Miserable bird. But they flew off nonetheless.

So she had sent birds to Shaw, ousting Drury and telling them that the Prince lived. She'd told King Reaghann about Drury and all he'd done.

Now all that remained was to rescue the Prince.

Tyndie heaved a great sigh and banged the back of her head against the tunnel wall. She stared up into the darkness, where somewhere, the tunnel ceiling loomed.

If all went well, in a few hours, she'd never see these tunnels again….

The fourth bell tolled distantly. Well. This was it, then. Tyndie sucked in a deep breath. She slung the bundle that she'd been staring at for the last three hours over her shoulder and followed the flickering of her tallow candle into the dungeon tunnel.

If a year ago, back when she was chopping and peeling vegetables, scrubbing them clean, a year ago over in the kitchens, with Eliza and Killey and Rosie… if someone had told her that she'd be living in the dirt down in some hidden tunnels below the castles that no one knew about, that an assassin wanted to kill her, that she'd be sneaking into the King's desk and talking to the King through the wall, watching Council Meetings, and helping a Prince from another country sneak out of the dungeon – Tyndie would have laughed herself silly, 'til she cried, in fact.

Yet here she was. She'd lived almost a month in the darkness now, at least as best she'd figured. Not the same as the Prince, for she'd had her candles, the wall sconces, torch lights, bathwater, food from the kitchens…. And freedom, most of all. Tyndie could have left at any time.

She hopped over a puddle and stood to the other side of the tunnel as a rat scurried past. Rats no longer bothered her. Tyndie wanted nothing to do with them, to be sure, but she didn't yelp if one passed by, as she did during her first week. And she knew where spiderwebs were likely to be now. These were her tunnels, after all.

Tyndie wondered what King Reaghann was going to do with the information she had given him last night. Or King Rickstan. She hoped at least one of them believed her, for someone had to stop Drury before he killed anyone else. When the Prince arrived home, that should in itself be proof enough of Drury's crime, but it would be a long trip.

She pushed the tunnel door of the dungeon open and peered about for Joshik. Good. No guards. Tyndie crept toward the Prince's cell and held her candle up high.

"So soon? It's not first light," he questioned her as he scrambled to stand up while he shielded his eyes from the candle glow.

"What did I tell you about following my directions?" she whispered as she held the iron key up with emphasis.

Prince Rilstrom held his palms up and shook his head from side to side, making a clear show of silence.

"Good," and Tyndie took an enormous breath. If all the acts she'd been committing up until now weren't treasonous, this certainly was, and she would hang for it, if she was lucky. That is, if she was caught. She could live in her tunnels for another month and never be found.

Tyndie inserted the key, let it clank open....

And tugged the grimy cell door open.

Its rusty hinges creaked abominably and echoed down the passage as it swung open, prickling every hair on Tyndie's scalp. But she looked up at the Prince.

His eyes were wide and his mouth had dropped open, but he looked scared.

"Your Highness," and Tyndie curtsied. She outstretched an arm toward the corridor.

Prince Rilstrom then stepped out of the cell. He turned to look back at it.

"Oh, bloody hell, we haven't got all day," said Tyndie and she took hold of the cell door and swung it shut. "Let Joshik explain that. Now let's go, hurry up," and she spun around and stole down the passage again.

She glanced over her shoulder. "Or you can stay if you like...."

The Prince shook himself then and rushed up to join her.

Tyndie held her tunnel door open for him long enough to step in, then stepped in herself. On a whim, Tyndie slipped a piece of chalk from her apron pocket and, up near the top, close to the door, she drew two "x"'s. Then she slashed them both out and smiled with satisfaction.

Prince Rilstrom had watched this with curiosity. "What was that for?"

Tyndie turned her gaze to him, still smiling. "Well... it's a long, long story. Now," and she held her candle up. "Let's go."

—⁓—

"Where are we, exactly?" asked the Prince.

Tyndie knew he was frightened, for he was exposed and could be caught at any moment. He hadn't been nervous in her tunnels, even once they'd run down a few castle corridors and into another tunnel.

But now Tyndie was pointing at a tub of water in the launderer's room. She wanted to tell him to relax, for if he had to run, she could get him to one her nearest tunnels, and they could disappear before anyone knew where they went. Six months of living in the dungeon in a tiny cell had twisted his mind, as it would anyone, though, so Tyndie was patient.

"It doesn't matter where we are. This is where you're going. And hurry up about it. Go on, get in. And wash your hair first, that's what people will see when they look at you."

He looked down at his rag then and up at her.

"Oh, of course –" and Tyndie turned about. She hadn't actually thought of him as a person until now, she realized, how sad. Of course they were to still observe manners, humility. *Tyndie girl, were ya gonna stare at a Prince in his privates?* came Auntie's voice in her head.

"Oh hells, it's cold!" breathed the Prince behind her. Bath water sloshed over the sides of the tub.

Tyndie couldn't suppress a small smile.

"Ahem," and she stepped backward, holding a bar of launderer's soap out. "Remember, your hair...."

"Right, right then...." And more water sloshed over the side of the tub. Tyndie hopped forward to miss being splashed.

"Gods –" and the Prince's teeth were chattering. But she smelled soap in the air suddenly, so she knew he was scrubbing.

Just as Tyndie was about to tell him to step out of the bath, she heard the Prince stand up and water run down into the tub.

He cleared his throat quietly. "Have – have you a towel?"

Tyndie's eyes grew wide. She turned her head a little over her shoulder. "I'm so sorry, Your Highness, but we're not in the castle baths, we're in the launderer's." Oh. She hadn't meant for that to come out as sharply as it had.

She was going to have to keep a tight lock on her tongue from now on – she was going to be traveling with a Royal.

Tyndie hastened toward some of the white linen sheets hanging up to dry overnight. "Sheet?" she offered in an obliging tone.

The water was still running off of the Prince into the tub. "Ah. No. If it's found missing, or – worse, it will set off an alarm."

Well, that was true, thought Tyndie. She covered her eyes with her hand and made her way back toward the tub.

Two dripping wet feet hit the stone and then the Prince asked, "What, then, will I be wearing, if I may ask?"

Well, she couldn't make it over to her bundle blinded as she was, could she?

How could this get anymore awkward? "Could you... please?" And Tyndie twirled her finger about in the air for the Prince so he would turn himself about.

"Oh, yes, right. Of course." She heard wet feet slapping about on the stone. Good. She should be safe then. Tyndie slid across the floor with her hand held up against the side of her face to shield her.

Oh, gods. She'd seen a Prince's arse. Of all the things in the Land. Tyndie rolled her eyes. She would be *so* glad when they finally got out of here. With her eyes screwed tightly shut, Tyndie fumbled about in her bundle and pulled out the neatly folded uniform she'd snagged from the barracks. Some poor soldier woke up yesterday morning without a stitch to wear, but compared to a Prince who needed to escape from a dungeon, Tyndie rather felt one need outweighed the other.

"Here. Do – do please – hurry." Blindly, she held out the uniform to the Prince behind her.

She heard him pull the wool uniform on and placed the boots in back of her as well.

"Is it safe to turn about yet?" Tyndie inquired. "We really must go, the fifth bell will toll any second."

As she spoke, the fifth bell tolled.

"Yes, I am fully dressed. The boots –"

"I hope they're the right size, I wasn't sure," Tyndie said as she turned around.

"They are close enough. Tight, but I can slit them open on the insides."

The first thing Tyndie saw was the water. It was black. Entirely black. There was no seeing through to the bottom of the tub.

Then she looked up at the Prince. A soldier stood before her. With flesh, not mud, for a face and hands. And his hair, it was actually lighter than her own. Tyndie blinked.

The last toll of the bell stopped, jarring Tyndie.

"What of this?" Prince Rilstrom gestured self-consciously at the tub of filthy water. He held up his prison rag as well.

Tyndie shook her head. "Just leave it behind. And throw the rag into the water. Let them make of it what they will. The last thing they'll think of is an escaped prisoner. Now let's go."

Once they were back in her tunnels, she led the Prince to where she spent most of her time camping out.

"You've been living here." The Prince stared about, noting her lanterns, candles, the blanket and pillow she'd filched. Tyndie had learned the best times and places to thieve what she needed. And while she knew that thieving was wrong, and that if caught, she could be jailed at best, lose a hand or even executed at worst, Tyndie felt that her tunnel life had been imposed upon her by no choice of her own, and so if she stole a little to survive, then so be it.

Tyndie did not reply but instead held up a pair of shears. "For your hair. And that beard."

"You don't happen to have a – looking glass, have you?" asked the Prince.

Tyndie closed her eyes. Patience, she thought, he is a Royal. "Do you see one down here?"

Humbled, the Prince replied, "Right, of course." And he held up the shears to his beard.

Then she produced the dress from her bundle. "Turn about while you're doing that."

"Whatever for?"

"If you please, Your Royal Highness, it's my turn to change clothing." There went her sharp tongue again.

Without a word, he turned around. Tyndie heard the snip-snips of his beard and hair falling from the shears.

It was strange, having another person here in her shelter. She felt extremely self-conscious as she dropped her maid dress to the floor. Tyndie couldn't remember wearing anything other than a castle dress, even as a child at her mum's side. Her mum had spun a tiny version of a castle maid dress for Tyndie.

And this felt so – strange. The gown slid all the way down to Tyndie's ankles. She was sure it was satin, for it glistened in the torchlight. There was nothing for her shoes but hope no one noticed them, for shoes were just not sitting about for thieving as often as dresses were. Those she had seen hadn't been in her size.

Tyndie let her hair down from its servant bun. Odd, her hair about her shoulders like this. She brushed it and twisted some of it into a small braid, as was a common hairstyle for ladies of nobility. Tyndie was glad there was no looking glass down here, for she would never recognize her reflection.

Tyndie turned about to check on the Prince's progress. Whole tufts of long hair lay about on her tunnel floor and on his uniformed back. Her first impulse was to reach out and brush his back clean, but she halted at the last second. The man hadn't been around other people for six months, and he had shears in his hand… who knew what his reaction might be…. Slowly, Tyndie withdrew her hand and made a note to herself that she would have to be very careful with him in the future.

"If you please, Your Highness?" Tyndie asked quietly. He was taking far too long, and they needed to slip out unseen, before too many people saw them.

He turned about on the stone floor with raised eyebrows. Just as she thought, he was making a mess of it. Tyndie sighed with impatience.

"Allow me?"

The Prince licked his lips and then handed the shears to Tyndie. "All due respect, sir, you have to look as a soldier would."

She chopped the other side of his hair and cropped it around his ears, hoping it was about the same height on both sides. She kept it even across the back of his neck and thinned his hair the best she could. Who would have thought peeling and chopping vegetables would come in such handy, she mused, enough to help her trim a prince's hair. She kept her humor to herself. What a long, long story would this be... she wondered if she'd ever get to tell it someone someday... ha, her, cutting a Prince's hair down in a secret tunnel of a castle....

"All right, your – your... beard." Tyndie stumbled over this, for this was the closest she had ever been to a man before. Color stained her cheeks.

He had trimmed nearly all of it, anyway, but some of it was left. And they had to move on, already.

"I think I can take care of that," the Prince said quietly and held out his hand for the shears.

Gratefully, Tyndie swallowed and handed him the shears.

"We do have to hurry on, though. If it please you, Your Highness."

"Understood."

Tyndie rolled her maid's dress into her bundle and stuffed the blanket in as well – she was sure she'd need it, wherever she went.

The Prince held the shears to her and turned about.

Wow. He looked – normal now. Though quite thin, his cheeks were clearly sunken. She hoped no one would consider that too out of the ordinary.

Tyndie had stolen several regular loaves of bread from the kitchen the other night as well as last night, and had given it a fond, last look around. The Prince would need to eat – a lot – before he passed muster by passing folk.

He studied her. "You look – quite different," he remarked. "No longer a maid?"

"Maids rarely ever leave the castle. People would notice if they saw me leaving in a maid's dress. You – you'll be escorting me from the castle."

The Prince looked down at his uniform. "Wherever did you get this?"

"I stole it, from the barracks," Tyndie returned, masking her impatience. She wanted to get out of this castle before anyone noticed that anything was amiss. And if they were lucky, out of the city. And then she would be able to breathe....

"The barracks! You, in the barracks?"

"Well, there's a tunnel there. And it was at night, and they were asleep. It was lying over the edge of his bed. I don't know what rank it is...."

The Prince glanced at his arm and then nodded appreciatively. "Sergeant."

"Well, Sergeant Rilstrom, you're escorting me from the castle. I'm a lady-in-waiting who's been dismissed but won't leave and is causing trouble. You're taking me to my family in the city."

The Prince nodded as he thought this through. "You've got it all figured out, haven't you?"

"Have to. Now keep your head down and don't meet anyone's eyes. If soldiers pass by, turn to me and act like you're yelling at me, so we don't run the risk of you being recognized as a Prince. Or worse, not being recognized as a Sergeant." Tyndie held up a hand before him. "May I?"

The Prince had shrunken from it but steadied himself. "Yes, yes, of course."

Tyndie brushed his uniform free of clipped hair. "There. Now." She picked up her bundle. "Shall we?"

The Crown Prince of Shaw looked at Tyndie for a moment, took in a deep breath, then tugged his uniform down. "Lead the way."

⸻

"Let up," said Tyndie from between clenched teeth. "You're bruising my arm."

The Prince was squeezing her arm as if it were a raft and he couldn't swim. "Sorry," he muttered.

Walking straight and stiff, the Prince advanced proudly, but Tyndie knew he was at least as petrified as she was. He wore his headdress down lower so that the sun shaded his face more.

The Prince's eyes had watered the second they'd stepped outside, and he'd stopped. She had hissed at him, *"Let's go!"* but he'd refused to move, for he was breathing in the fresh air. Tyndie watched him inhale several breaths as a thirsty man might water and decided they could spare a minute or two. He hadn't smelled fresh air for months, after all, nor felt the sun on his face.

Then he moved forward toward the Castle Gate with her. No one looked at them askance at all, for, Tyndie thought, just like a servant, no one looked twice at soldiers.

Just as they were almost at the end of the drawbridge, another Sergeant stopped in their way. "Stop!"

Tyndie's insides froze.

"Sir!" The Prince stood rigidly to attention.

The Crown Guard before them asked nothing of Tyndie whom the Prince had by the arm. Instead, he reached out and pointedly brushed dirt off of the Prince's shoulder.

"Watch you take better care of your uniform, Sergeant."

"Yes, sir!"

"On your way," and the Crown Guard strode past them toward the Castle.

The Prince said nothing but continued to haul Tyndie forward until they stepped off of the HarCourt drawbridge. From clenched teeth, he said, "I damn near pissed myself back there."

"Me too!" she whispered.

———

"I don't feel right, you know, having stolen all this," the Prince told Tyndie as he leaned against a tree, staring into the fire. They were both spread out, waiting to fall asleep in the chill of the night air.

"Well, Your Highness, don't think of it as stealing. Think of it more as... *privately commissioned.*"

The Prince snorted. "That isn't much better."

They'd stolen a horse, another change of clothing for the Prince, a commoner's dress for Tyndie, two more loaves of bread, some coppers from a cheese vendor who was far and away over pricing his wares, several bunches of grapes, and two cloaks. Tyndie had also stolen a boot knife from a pair of boots sitting next to the side door of someone's home, but she hadn't told the Prince that. She was going to need protection, after all.

Once they'd broken free of the city, they had both relaxed enormously. For the chances of being found once outside the city decreased dramatically – after all, no one would have recognized them, nor knew when they left, nor in which direction. And as for Tyndie, well, she would see to it that Drury never found her again.

The horse – a fair enough little mare, though an old one, the Prince had said - had borne them several miles west of HarCourt, though Tyndie knew it would take many, many more miles, possibly a week, before the mare arrived at Roadstone, the Capital Palace of Shaw, from where the Prince had left to start with.

As for Tyndie herself, she'd changed into her commoner's calico dress, seeing as how no noblewoman would ever be seen unaccompanied by any Lords with only a Guard, and walking the countryside at that.

Tyndie still felt odd in any dress other than her maid's dress, but now that she was free, she knew it wouldn't matter anymore what she wore.

Tyndie sighed and started dividing up the bread. He would need far more than she would, for he needed to put weight on, so she gave him a larger portion.

He sat up from his tree in the dark. "What are you doing?"

"Dividing up our portions," she answered calmly. She suspected this he was not going to accept this well.

"Whatever for?"

"Because you're going home to Shaw. And I'm not going to Shaw."

"What?" Prince Rilstrom leaned forward in the darkness. "What do you mean, you're not coming with me?"

"Your Highness, if I've learned anything, it's that people you trust may be the people you have to watch out for. I sent those birds to Shaw last night, so I don't know when they'll have arrived...."

"By this afternoon."

"Good then," Tyndie responded. "With luck, they will be watching for your arrival." She paused in her packing. "Or... they may be watching for your arrival... if you follow my meaning, Your Highness.

"We never really did know who Drury was working with. So, if I were you, I wouldn't trust anyone, anyone at all, unless you trust them absolutely. Don't follow the roads, stick to the forest. For once they realize you're missing, and they will, they will be looking for you, from both Shaw and HarCourt.

"In fact, if it were me, I would walk in to Shaw dressed just as you are, right into your Palace, in that Hardewold uniform, and then go to see your brother the King, so no one will recognize you between here and there."

Prince Rilstrom stared at Tyndie, digesting this. She saw after a few minutes that he realized it was the better idea, rather than waiting to rescued along the way home.

"And where will you go?"

Tyndie stared at the Prince directly in the eyes and lied. "North of here, to Delsynth. I've kin there, cousins. They'll take me in." It was almost word for word what Eliza had said. Just not anywhere near Tyndie's destination.

The Prince studied her for a moment, unsure whether she was being truthful. He finally nodded, as he knew he would never find out anything else. "Very well, then." He sighed and told her, "I wish you'd reconsider. I – and my country – owe you a debt that will never, ever be repaid."

Tyndie almost smiled. What would she do at Shaw, at Roardstone Palace? Go back to serving obnoxious Lords and Ladies again? She thought not. But she knew the Prince meant well.

"As it please you, Your Highness." She held up his bundle. "Ration all this. I know you'll want to eat good food again, but don't gobble it all right away. You'll need to ration it until you get home safe, understand me, then?"

Tyndie felt the need to explain all this to him, for she'd be gone just as soon as the Prince fell asleep, and he was just a mere babe in the forest – Royals, alone, in the forest? Hunting was one thing, but survival another. She felt a pang of guilt – but she couldn't take the risk of being found in his company by anyone who might be working with Drury, or even Drury himself.

He gave her a serious nod, the reflection of the fire dancing in his eyes.

"And remember – they'll all of them, east to west, be looking for you on the roads. So stay off the roads and stay back in the trees. Understand me?"

Prince Rilstrom smiled gently and replied, "As it please you…" then he paused. "…I don't even know your name."

Tyndie thought for a moment, then she met the Prince's eyes.

"Shadow. My name is Shadow."

Volnyxx

Life was peace. Peace was life. Unless there was war. If there was war, then war was life and life was war. This was what he was trained to do. Delsynth Stafford Spears knew nothing else.

And right now, life was peace. Volnyxx was part of a small Spears unit bought to serve Lord Tranick. It wasn't Volnyxx's place to offer opinions, and thus he was silent each day. Spears never offered their opinions on anything; their sole purpose was to fight.

But, though his tongue was silent around his employer, and he offered no opinion aloud, Volnyxx's mind was alive with convictions. Just because he stared straight ahead and acted as though he were brainless did not mean he heard or knew nothing. All of his Spear comrades saw and heard all, but acted entirely deaf and, to an extent, blind. They only stared straight ahead and heard nothing, saw nothing. Though it was the greatest kept secret among themselves, the best joke. The things they saw and heard….

Volnyxx's current employer disgusted him. An ugly, pudgy man who, when alone, farted and would wave his hand behind his arse to dispel the odor. This job often tested the limits of Volnyxx's abilities to keep his face emotionless.

The worst had been several months ago, soon after Volnyxx and his unit had been hired. Lord Tranick hosted a masquerade, which had started out normally. But soon after the minstrels began to play, the guests began dancing and removing their clothing. Soon, every guest in the room was dancing without a stitch on their bodies, neither Lord nor Lady. And many of them needed to be covered up, so as not to offend the gods if for no other reasons. He remembered a few of the other Spears catching his eye – remaining expressionless, of course – but catching each other's eyes, as if to say *"Bloody hell!"*

But right now, Volnyxx and Capperton were watching over Lord Tranick and his guest, Lord Pralter. Capperton was on the far side of the study, so was unable to hear what Volnyxx was listening to.

And Volnyxx was not pleased.

"… I brought this first to you, Pralter. I actually am considering it," Tranick said as he leaned against a small table. "I mean to say – think of it. All she wants is the key to Ghiverny. They've never gotten through by means of invasion and if we give them all the supply routes, the times, the roads, the troops…. She'll take over Ghiverny and then get rid of the whole lot of the Delsynth bloodline for me, which puts me on the Delsynth throne. And Delsynth and Ormon – will be allies," explained Lord Tranick.

"Hmmm. Hmmm. I think… that it just might work. I like it, Tranick. You do hear, what they're saying about her up there, don't you?" Pralter said to Tranick.

"Which rumor is that?"

"The main one, really, that she killed her husband as he lay in bed. That she was the one who killed him, slashed him up and gutted him like a holiday pig, I've heard. But they don't say a thing before her, she's taken the whole country under her thumb now."

Lord Tranick chuckled. "Well, I don't care. I'm not married to the bitch."

Pralter chuckled as well. "And what do you propose to do with this, then?"

"Well, Ambsellon will take over Ghiverny, and I'll have a throne. There will be a lot of time to decide who's on what side of the tourney when it comes. I wanted to give you the chance though, to jump in first. It is only a proposal, she just sent it a few days ago, but…."

Suddenly, Lord Tranick turned and looked at Volnyxx. He marched up to him.

Volnyxx appeared surprised. "My lord? Are you well? Is anything wrong?" He moved his spear frontmost and center.

"How much of what we were talking about just now did you hear?" asked Lord Tranick suspiciously.

Volnyxx shook his head and stared at him. "I'm sorry, my lord? Did you – do you need assistance?"

Tranick looked up at Volnyxx with narrowed eyes for a moment. Then he just shook his head and walked away.

"They really are brutes. Big, dumb brutes. That's what my coin bought." He snorted.

Pralter reminded him, "Ah, perhaps, but come a battle, you'll be happy for them. Now, where were we?"

Treason. They were speaking of treason, that's where they were. Against the Eastern Alliance and Delsynth.

Volnyxx stepped quietly next to Capperton. Once at his side, he jerked his neck in the direction of the study door.

Capperton frowned. "Sir?" he whispered.

"Take a break."

Capperton arched an eyebrow but said nothing as he left.

Volnyxx moved against the wall silently, until he was standing behind the two bastards.

Within seconds, he'd stabbed their guts, twisted their necks, and stabbed downward into their lungs.

Before they made too much of a mess, he flung both of them from the balcony.

"Not in my country, you won't."

Ishbel

Ishbel stood in the entrance to her pavilion, watching as Gobin left with his two silvers and the soiled linens from her last customer.

A curious noise caught her attention just then and she glanced over her shoulder. Just then, a figure was slipping in between the outside curtains of her pavilion.

Having a pavilion that faced the open edge of Pavilion City onto the grasses had its advantages. Ishbel had been with Gobin the longest, and so, once this set of pavilions opened up, he'd snatched them, even though he admitted he overpaid at the time. But the fresh air drifted through and Ishbel could see the sun, there was less noise....

Gobin had trusted her with the open pavilion, and most of his whores, in fact, as he said, "Where are they going to go, dressed like they are?" And he was right, covered in transparent cloth only, many of them were barely literate at all and considered this the best job they could ever hope to get.

Ishbel was barely literate herself, but that didn't stop her from wondering what happened to Gobin's whores once they became too old to be of interest to customers. No one wanted old, rotten fruit, as he would put it....

And how would any of them attempt escape? With what money? They would need new clothes, for a start, and where would they go? Food? Pavilion City was set a fair distance away from most towns or villages.

Not that Ishbel had ever entertained the thought of escape seriously, only played it out in her mind idly. The idea really was just fanciful at best.

The downside to having a pavilion opening up to the open air was the weather. Sometimes the sunsets were unbearably brilliant, and she needed to pull down a reed blind to block the light streaming in. And naturally, inclement weather. Gobin had her pavilion reinforced with sliding wooden doors off to the side, to protect from storms and cool temperatures. Though it was so warm year around here that cool temperatures were rarely a concern.

Ishbel's pavilion did not, however, protect against the odd individual slipping in from the outside without paying....

Eyes wide, Ishbel immediately charged around her bed to confront the individual.

But her words died on her tongue. For it was Mister Nameless. It had been nearly six weeks. Ishbel didn't really know whether to assign him a time table or not, but six weeks appeared to be his theme.

Nameless held on to the far side pole that supported her outer pavilion, and swung about it.

Ishbel caught him and propped him up on her shoulders. At first, she thought him drunk, but the only smell about him was not of drink, but thick and coppery....

She didn't need a Healer to tell her that was blood.

"Oh, hells below, what have you gone and done to yourself...." Ishbel dragged him over to the side of her bed and laid him down face first on the grass mat next to it.

Mister Nameless was only slightly conscious – he patted his pocket inside his vest. "Silvers. Just – in case."

Did Ishbel really want to take money from a man who seemed to be dying on her rug? Well... Gobin might inquire. Upon occasion, men did stumble in without checking with Gobin first, but the girls always treated them the same, silvers first.

So Ishbel delicately felt about in Nameless's vest pocket until she found the shape of two silvers. She thumped them both onto her bed and then stared down at Nameless.

"If you get me into trouble, I'm blaming it all on you. You hear me?" she told him lowly, but Ishbel doubted he heard anything.

Ishbel squatted down on the grass mat next to him and inched his black leather vest off. Sticky blood had soaked into the back of it. Ishbel shook her head but then her jaw dropped with shock when she saw the man's back.

What had once been a non-descript colored tunic was now drenched in blood. Not much ever took Ishbel's breath away, but she had never seen blood like this before.

With a cautious glance at her entry, she sat down onto her knees and snagged the bootknife from Nameless's dusty boot.

Just as she peeled the shirt up from his skin to cut it in two, he whispered, "No – I need the shirt –"

"No, love, trust me, you don't. All it is now is a bandage, if that."

And she sliced the shirt up from its hem to its waist, where it began dripping with blood as she held it up. The shirt separated in two with a damp rip and a small spray of blood onto her thumbs. Ishbel peeled it off the man's back, thinking at that point that it was entirely possible he might die there on her floor.

Open and gaping like fish gills, three stab wounds oozed blood slowly. Each time Nameless breathed in, they opened, exposing raw flesh, and as soon as he breathed out again, they closed, spurting forth a small trickle of blood.

"Gods, gods, gods. Who did this to you…" she whispered, more to herself that to him.

Well. What more was there than to patch him up? He'd paid her for her silence, so she couldn't take him to a Healer.

Ishbel rumbled around in her small nightside drawer. She had a small variety of medicines, only such for what small cuts and scratches the girls might incur during the course of a customer's visit… but nothing quite for a wound such as this. She did have some numbing ointment, however, some sweetspice…. Ah. And the needle and thread she was looking for.

Ishbel's stitches were lousy, but stitching was the last of her interests – in her time off, she preferred just to sleep. They slept whenever they could. She forced the thread through the eye of the needle. This was going to take a lot of thread….

"My friend – I'm not going to lie to you. This is going to hurt… so you just take a bit of a nap, all right, then?" Ishbel waved some sweetspice under Nameless's nose and he fell asleep. He was too weakened from blood loss to fight her.

Ishbel saw him pass out, then dabbed the openings of all three wounds with the numbing ointment. The Healers swore it had healing properties as well, so Ishbel would use anything she had.

She poured water in each wound as well so they wouldn't infect, and then got to work stitching.

When finally Ishbel knotted the last wound shut and sliced the thread with the knife, she sat back on her legs, exhausted. She felt the stress drain from her body. Only luck had kept Gobin from sending in a customer, and it was still early afternoon yet. She smeared the closed wounds with more numbing ointment and then let him breathe in some more sweetspice. She couldn't have him waking up if she had a customer.

Ishbel scrubbed the inside of Nameless's vest of blood and dressed him in that, while she stashed his bloody shirt beneath her nighttime stand. She would dispose of that the next time Gobin sent her to run an errand.

Then she collapsed upon her bed, exhausted from stress.

About a half hour later, Gobin sent in a customer. Ten minutes into rolling about on Ishbel's bed, he stopped.

"Ay. Who's that?"

Damn. "Who's who?"

"'Im. Down there. On the floor."

"Oh. Him. Don't need to worry about him. Here, look at me, love," and Ishbel forced his face to look at her face. She ran her hands through his greasy hair and smiled, ignoring the drop of perspiration that dropped down on her face from his forehead above her.

"Right, right." He calmed down and started chugging along for a minute but then stopped again. "But what's he doin' in here? Sleepin'? Don't want no bloke wakin' up when I'm in here. Paid good money to be in here."

He sat up on his knees.

Bother. "Him? He passed out. He won't wake. But you, dear, you're wide awake, aren't you...?" and Ishbel ran some sweetspice under his nose.

He blinked in sudden confusion. "I – I...."

"Yes, love, I know. It's been two hours already. You have been amazing, really," Ishbel stood him up and dressed him quickly before he fell over.

She walked him out of her pavilion entry. "Do come back now, we'll give it another go!" she called after him. He was stumbling down the Pavilion pavement. He waved at Gobin as he passed.

Gobin saw Ishbel standing in her entryway. "That was... quick...?" he commented.

"He's only got half a nut-sack. He keeps trying, he says, just in case." Ishbel smirked at Gobin. "I gave him my best, poor man, but he wanted to leave. He was too embarrassed to stay."

"Ah – right then."

"Here's my linens for you. And these." Ishbel scooped up the man's silvers and her linen, which she'd only had to wipe her face with.

After Gobin left, Ishbel realized belatedly that, according to some of the other whores, Gobin was a eunuch – he only bathed on days that none of his own whores would ever be present. That explained why he never fucked any of them. Perhaps, Ishbel thought, she should have chosen a different excuse....

Now that was alone again, Ishbel checked on Nameless. His wounds had seeped a bit through her stitching, so she dabbed at them with one of her linens.

Soon, Gobin brought in a new customer, and Ishbel gave him the same treatment with the sweetspice that she had the prior customer.

As soon as the second man was on his way down the Pavilion, Gobin walked up and asked, "What was wrong with that one?"

Ishbel swiped her arm across her temple as if she was exhausted. "Gobin. I'm thinking he really likes the men. You know? I even acted like a man for him? Pretended to be one for him, talked like one... but he just couldn't, wouldn't. And he left." Ishbel shrugged and shook her head.

"That would make explain a lot...." Gobin stroked his chin thoughtfully.

"What's that?"

"He said he saw a man in there."

Ishbel stared at Gobin and threw together her best act. "Really. In here. Not yet today, there hasn't been. Gobin, do send me a real man next time, please."

He chortled as he strode away with his silvers and her linens.

Once she was back inside, she squatted down next to Nameless. "You've got to wake up, come along."

He opened one eye. "Gobin?"

Surprised, she shook her head. "No."

Dryly, Nameless asked, "Do you treat all your customers like that?"

"Like how?"

"Sweetspice?"

"You knew it?"

"Recognized it right off. As for me, I probably needed it. As for them.... Drugging your customers... what would Gobin say," and he clucked his tongue.

"I only do that when I have men passed out from blood loss on my floor, so you're quite welcome," Ishbel admonished. "What we need to do is get you to the baths."

"The what?" He raised himself up on his elbows and stared at her.

"Baths. Pavilion City has two natural baths here, springs. They're supposed to be healing, but either way, you need to get those washed out, to keep infection out. And yourself washed as well, I might add."

"And you also need a new tunic. The other is ruined, of course. I know where to get you a new one of those."

He nodded then and told her, "Use the copper chips in my vest. Ten should be enough for a decent one.

"But these baths...."

Ishbel glanced either way outside her pavilion. No Gobin, no curious eyes....

She took Nameless's hand and yanked him out of Gobin's territory.

"All right. Now you can act normal. Which I don't know yet what is normal for you, but perhaps act like these other folk..." Ishbel suggested and smiled.

Nameless snorted but grimaced at her in a ghost of a smile. She could see that he was still in an enormous amount of pain.

"Well, then, here we are —" Ishbel held open the door to her favorite place — the baths. Steam drifted toward them from inside.

"A public bathhouse. Wonderful," muttered Nameless.

"Natural hot springs open to all bathers," Ishbel admonished and gestured for Nameless to continue through.

 Standing at the steps in the corner of the hot springs, Ishbel unfolded one of her towels and held it up between them.

His brow furrowed.

Ishbel smiled with amusement. "Well. Go on. Take it off. You don't bathe with your clothes on, now, do you?"

Nameless glared at her over the towel barricade, then slid his boots off one by one.

She rolled her eyes upward to give the man privacy as she heard him unlacing his trousers and held the towel up a bit higher.

"You're worried about humility? I'm impressed," said Nameless in a wry tone. "I have a full nutsack, if you were curious, and the whole thing works just fine."

Ishbel handed him the towel and nodded at his gest. "I might already have known that." She smiled slyly. "How do you know I didn't molest you while you were passed out?"

"Well, if you did, and I rose to the occasion, then I need some of that sweetspice for myself. Just a shame I don't recall a second of it." Nameless wrapped the towel about himself and stepped into the hot springs.

He winced once the water seeped into his wounds but immediately clenched his jaw.

"Don't fall asleep in there," Ishbel warned. "Can't have you drowning. I'll be back with your new shirt in just a bit and then we'll dry you off."

She chuckled a bit – for all of his objections, Nameless was sliding further down into the water, inhaling the steam, relaxing.

———

The clothier had raised an eyebrow at Ishbel's purchase, given that whores rarely bought clothing, far and away men's clothing. Ishbel told her it was a replacement for a customer for one of the other girls, and the woman's eyes widened and she said no more.

When Ishbel returned to the baths, Nameless's head had lolled back along the cement. She knew the feeling. If it weren't that Gobin would come searching for her, she'd spend all day there.

But Ishbel had been gone too long already. She slipped out of her outer wrap, out of her pavilion veils, and slid into the water. Soon she had brushed her skin free of dust and swished her hair about in the water. Then Ishbel climbed out and drip-dried as quickly as she could before she donned her clothing.

She twisted excess water from her hair as she padded over to where Nameless was half-asleep and nudged him with her toe. "Time to go." Ishbel placed his new tunic on top of his trousers and held up the towel for him again.

Nameless opened his eyes and stood up slowly. "I think my entire body is wrinkled."

She smiled and he accepted the towel. As he wrapped himself in it, he remarked, "I see you've availed yourself of the water as well."

"I have to look like I've been here, haven't I?"

Nameless nodded to this. He handed her the towel, for he'd already pulled his trousers up and his boots on. As he let the tunic fall over his shoulders, he noted, "Perfect size." He looked up at her. "Thank you."

"You're welcome. I always know the sizes of my men. Occupational requirement."

Nameless nodded a bit and then stumbled. He glanced quickly around to see if anyone had seen him.

"You, on the other hand, have an altogether different occupation, and you need an awful lot more water. And food. And rest."

He glared at her.

"Glare at me all you like, Mister Nameless, but you should know something, I never take no for an answer. And I always get my way." Ishbel glared at him right back until he gave up and acquiesced. "Now come along."

⁓

Once Ishbel had fed Mister Nameless, and made him drink an enormous quantity of water, a bit of color seeped back into his face.

At this time of day, early evening, to be precise, whores in Pavilion City rarely had company. Whores in brothels were just starting their evenings, but whores in Pavilion City were winding their business day down, for merchants had left. Pavilion City did not rent rooms – there were no taverns. Merchants sold, bought, met with other merchants, whatever they came to do in Pavilion City, but by late afternoon, they were all deserting Pavilion City in droves. Many of them slept in their wagons, and many others left earlier in the day in hopes to make it the next parish, village, or town on their way.

Most Pavilion merchants closed up their wares and retired to their own pavilions after nightfall, just as any other market.

So Ishbel felt a little safer with Nameless in her pavilion now that it was early evenfall. With luck, no one else would enter.

Ishbel had lit a few lanterns and a candle or two, but otherwise, let the twilight settle her pavilion for the night. Nameless lay on the grass mat next to her bed, with a blanket and a pillow.

Propping her head up on her elbows, she looked down at him from her bed. "So… are you going to tell me how you got those knife wounds?"

"No."

Ishbel hated curiosity. "Are you going to tell me why you got them?"

She thought she heard him smile down there on the grass mat.

"No."

Ishbel frowned. "What about your name, *Mister Nameless*. Are you ever going to tell me your *real* name?"

"No."

She dropped her head into her pillows. What an irritating man! She rose her legs up at the knees and dangled them around with boredom. Then she asked, "Are you ever going to tell me anything at all?"

"How about, you ask an awful lot of questions for pillow talk."

Ishbel's mouth fell open. "You. You. You are really a – a rogue."

She heard him chuckle.

He raised an upright palm in the lantern light. "I try…."

"That's it. That's what I'm going to call you. *Rogue*. That's your name from now on. *Rogue*."

"*Rogue*? Not something better, like *Champion*, or *Conqueror*?"

Ishbel's eyes narrowed. "You should be lucky I'm not calling you dead."

He ignored that and was silent for a moment. Then he swiveled his head around to face her.

"What have you heard here? Since I was here last?"

Ishbel recalled their original agreement and looked thoughtfully down at him as flipped through the last several weeks since she'd seen him.

"Ah," she held up a finger. "Soldiers."

His brow furrowed over his gray eyes. "Soldiers. How do you mean. What kind, who?"

"Not for certain, that's the odd thing. I know soldiers, they've all got their hair cropped and such. These soldiers, as who've been passing through, they're not in uniform. None of them, at all. Oddest thing. My guess is, Stordish."

That got his attention. "Stordish. Why would you say that?" He propped up on his elbows.

Ishbel shrugged. "I know my complexions by now. Fucked a few by now –"

"Don't say that."

Ishbel smiled faintly. "All right, as you say. But I know the Stordish boys, and some of these soldiers were Stordish."

"Why, were they wearing the same colors as Storden, or…?"

"No, but…" and Ishbel trailed. She cast her eyes to the side. Finally, she said, "I recognize a Stordish tattoo when I see it. There is only one country in the Land as tattoos the head of a bloody pig on themselves…."

"It's a boar's head, Ishbel."

"A boar is still a pig, Rogue. If it squeals like a pig and fucks like a pig, it's a pig."

He looked very much as if wanted to say something to that, but thought better of it. Then he said, "All right, so just Stordish soldiers, possibly?"

"Others, but I can't tell. They're soldiers, in small groups, threes and fours, sometimes larger, but never in uniform. I don't where they're headed or which way they're leaving for. And I don't know what country they're from, which usually I'm pretty good about. They don't look Eastern, not really, I will say that much," Ishbel mused.

"And also, a lot of lumber."

His grey eyes studied her. "Lumber. What do you mean, lumber?"

"I mean, Rogue, lumber. Trees. Lumber."

He rolled his eyes. "I know where lumber comes from. Are you sure it's lumber and not – sandalwood, or – cedar perhaps?"

Ishbel narrowed her eyes. "Do you think I'm new to this place? Look where I live. Look where I've been living for the last several years. I know sandalwood, I know my cedar. And I know the smell of fresh cut lumber straight from trees. I've no idea why it's here, don't know who's selling or buying, or where it came from. But there's been lumber passing through."

"Also," Ishbel suddenly remembered. "Horses. A lot of them, too. They had to build on extra stalls. No idea why, or what types of horses. Maybe for Royals, breeding or such. But there's been a lot more horseflesh in the City of late. Can't tell you any more than that."

She looked down at him. His eyes were closed. Ishbel listened – and she knew a man well enough to know when he was asleep for his breathing was soft and even.

Good. The gods knew he needed the rest. And she certainly did – that bloody man had turned her day upside down.

Ishbel took in a deep sigh and closed her eyes. In just instants, she was asleep.

But when she woke in the morning, all traces of him were gone... even the shirt she'd stashed beneath her nighttime table... and two silvers lay curled in her hand.

"Damn Rogue...." she murmured.

A'dair

He leaned on his fists over the desk. Another day of repetitive nonsense. He shuffled it all and pulled out what was more worth his attention – the people. Diseased fish in Arzua. Request for assistance after fires swept through the fields in Melm. Bandits ravishing the roads along the northern border to Pavilion City....

Now, most of governing fell to him, though few but the immediate household staff and some of Father's most senior Cabinet members knew that.

That did not mean A'dair knew what he was doing half the time. Father had not trained him for this.

To take over the Throne, yes. To take over the Throne at perhaps... forty-five, fifty years old, or even older, yes. To take the Throne at twenty-one – no. To watch his father wracked with pain, dying daily before A'dair's eyes of the wasting disease – never.

His younger siblings did not understand why their father was closeted in his bed chamber, taking no visitors, so it fell upon A'dair's shoulders to explain that Father was ill with fever and they would likely become ill as well were they to see him.

A'dair had been lying to so many people now for so long that he had lost count – from family to Cabinet members to the Court and even the people, when chance afforded him time away from the Palace, he grabbed at it with both hands.... Was this what is was like to rule? Assuming the throne was merely assuming a mantle of finely woven dishonesty?

If it was, mused A'dair, then either his reign would be a short one, or he would make monumental changes around here, in mass proportions.

"Your Highness." A liveried servant of his father's stepped into the study.

A'dair nodded at the man, awaiting the worst. At his point, he always awaited the worst. Or, perhaps it was more waiting for the best....

But no.

"Your Royal Father asks to see you."

"Thank you."

A'dair slid all the papers into one neat pile and stacked them atop the desk before he placed them in the second drawer. He had chosen the second drawer for himself, as Prince. It didn't feel right, putting paperwork into his father's desk drawer, but since he was governing in place of his father, he, as Prince, took over the second drawer instead. He rolled the drawer shut and left his father's study.

A'dair hated walking into this room every time now. And he hated himself for that, how uncharitable it was to think so. Women – Healers, of course, brought in fresh flowers each day that his father might smell and see them. Personally, A'dair wondered how well his father could smell or see anything now.

Once a tanned and robust man, muscled and active, a man who laughed, danced, joked, a man with rich auburn hair and brown eyes, but now... now the feeble figure was nearly lost in the feather pillows he lay propped up against.

What was left of his hair was just a gray tuft atop his temple. The lines across his forehead had deepened and his skin was a sickly pallor. His rheumy eyes looked out from behind a painful threshold and his bottom right eyelid had drooped. His bottom lip also drooped upon occasion, and so he dabbed at his spittle with a linen napkin.

Father's entire body was merely skin stretched over a skeleton now, his skull only covered by skin, and sometimes he cried from the pain of this horrible disease. A'dair sat and held Father's shriveled, crow-like hand much of the time and clenched his jaw to force back tears when his father rocked back and forth from the pain.

He begged the Healers for something, anything, but they had given him everything they had, and his body had adjusted to the medicines.

The entire chamber reeked of sickness.

"Father. You wished to see me?"

"Ah." Father reached a skeletal hand up and beckoned A'dair closer.

A'dair sat down next to him.

"Tell them to go away," whispered his father hoarsely.

"If you would, leave us. Thank you." A'dair swept his arm about the room to dismiss all of them. Without a word, the Healers closed the chamber door.

"Ah. They do as you tell them now," his father noted in a whisper and a ghost of a smile slipped across his face. "Treat them like puppies, train them, and they will come to heal. Never –" and a wracking cough shook his body. "Never let them bark back at you. And if they growl at you, dismiss them at once, without mercy. Treat them gently, and you will have excellent dogs who protect you and always stay by your side. My – my grandfather taught my father that, and – it works."

This information had fascinated A'dair, though it had winded his father. A'dair would certainly put it to good use.

The first few times he'd visited his father in here, when A'dair dismissed them, they'd said, "But, Your Highness, the King...." Now that A'dair was accustomed to ruling, he expected to be obeyed without questions, King or not, and the Healers had noticed the change in him, for they immediately scurried for the door whenever he visited his father now, whether he dismissed them or not.

Father had regained his breath. "A'dair. I want you to know some things...."

"Father –"

"Listen to me, A'dair, while I still have breath in my body, for I am still King," wheezed his father.

That was what was left of the Royal tone, and A'dair immediately bowed his head.

"It has been too quiet of late. Quiet," panted his father, "is not good." He shifted a bit on his pillows.

"What do you mean, *quiet*?"

"I mean, that it's been nearly twenty years since the last war, son of mine. And that means that things are not actually quiet, they only – only *seem* quiet." His father coughed alarmingly then, and spat spittle up that was speckled with blood.

"Father, let me –" A'dair stood up and leaned over Father but he smacked at A'dair.

"Back, back, get off me! I have enough to deal with Healers hovering over me, stay off me," he wheezed.

"I – yes, Father." And A'dair sat down.

"A'dair. What I am trying to tell you is that someone, somewhere is planning something. This land never goes this long without a war. Send your – your cousins to – to Arzua and to Corstarordan. Tell them to listen and look around, report back. But not to tell anyone," Father panted.

"It's been too long. Build more ships. You need more ships. You don't have nearly enough for a war."

A'dair's eyes popped out. "A war? Father –"

"Listen to me while I can still tell you these things. Trust me. You need ships. War ships. In the Billoughby Bay, keep them all there, from prying eyes. That's what I did, and other kings." He coughed a little.

"But build ships."

"Father, the lumber alone…."

"Is worth the coin. There is more than one fund than the Cabinet knows about. That's just the Cabinet's money. My money – which will be your money – has a war fund. And I keep it where you played with your wooden horses as a child. Do you remember? If you do, don't say it aloud, you never know how many ears the walls have. But every king changes it up, so you change it up, too –" a wracking cough seized him, but he held up a hand to keep A'dair back. After he finished coughing, the King panted, "All your most important things, papers… war finances…."

A'dair knew exactly where his Father was referring to.

"And A'dair, ask your advisors. And Cabinet members. If they all say there's only peace in all the Land, fire them. Right away. Fire them."

A'dair stared at his father. "*What?* Fire them?"

Father's rheumy eyes were serious. "Dismiss them. Use any reason you like. But there is no peace. I don't have much of a gut left, but I still know," and he reached out for A'dair and grabbed A'dair's surcoat. "There is no peace brewing. War is bubbling."

Exhausted, he let go of A'dair and fell back upon the pillows. "Believe me. I may be sick but – but – I know."

Father laid against his pillows and panted for a while. A'dair sat in his leather chair in shock. War! His biggest concern was governing a bloody country – what did he know of – war!

A'dair glanced at Father. Could it be... that maybe he was... dramatizing, since he was ill.... But... it wouldn't hurt to send his cousins all the same. Dismissing his Cabinet members, now that was, that – that was excessive.

Perhaps Father needed his rest. A'dair leaned a bit forward, as if to get up.

"A'dair."

He froze. "Yes, Father."

"Another thing."

"Of course."

"You need a wife. You need to get married. Now. Right away."

A'dair coughed and cleared his throat. "Married. Right away," he questioned.

Father's eyes opened tiredly. "Now. Secure our bloodline. Marry, get her with child. Before the year is out, have your throne cemented. And don't look to Tortoreen. Thanks to your mother, now she's in peace, for you and your sisters and your brother, but we have had enough of Tortoreen for now. You notice, don't you, that –" and his father panted for a bit. "You notice that they never sent us a betrothal inquiry about their daughter, long of marriageable age, for you. Again. Bubbling. If all was peaceful, you and their daughter would have married years ago. If you don't believe me, believe that."

A'dair's mouth suddenly dropped. That couldn't be more true. And not a word from them. Why was that...?

"Ahh. Now you're understanding. Believe me now, do you?" His father laughed weakly, which turned into a cough. "Tortoreen always stirs the slops pot. King Almeric wants his princess wed to whomever gives him the best advantage in this upcoming war. He knows, like I do, what's ahead, and he wants ties to whomever will keep his stingy arse in the clear.

"And we don't have ships, so we can't help protect him once war comes around," A'dair's father finished.

A'dair felt as if a blanket had been yanked from his eyes. This actually was happening.

"My poor A'dair," and the King gave a ghostly smile. "There is more to ruling than just governing. No ruler is ever ready for war."

A'dair lifted his widened eyes to Father. "Is it... really...?"

Father nodded slowly. "I may be sick, and I may be closeted in here, but I still get occasional reports. The Ormon Queen – they're calling her the Ice Queen now. She killed the King herself, they're saying, and is ruling Ormon on her own. No sign of the Prince, they think he's dead as well. Stay away from the North. I've –" and he coughed for a minute, bloody spittle landing into his handkerchief. Father lay back against the pillows, panting for a little while.

Suddenly, he said, "Where – where was I? What was I saying?"

A'dair wasn't sure whether he should just take this time to leave and allow his father this time to rest, or actually tell him what the conversation had been about.

"Ah. The Ice Queen," his father recalled. "You – you just stay away from the North altogether, A'dair. I know we are adjoined to them through the Northern-Coastal Partnership, but only have anything to do with them if they insist, and at the last moment. I don't trust her. And I've heard strange things out of the Shield as well. Stay out of it all. Marry, quick as you can. This month even. A good bloodline out of S'hendalow, maybe Coral City…."

"I won't be with you much longer, A'dair, but heed what I'm telling you. War is brewing. Dismiss anyone who tells you otherwise. Appoint your own advisors. Build ships. Stay away from the North. And marry a S'hendish girl as soon as you can, right away. Give me the – grandchildren I'd – have loved to have seen," he coughed. "Do you understand all that, A'dair?"

"War. Dismiss people who claim only peace. Appoint my own staff. Build ships – I know where I played as a child, Father. Stay away from the Northern Countries. Marry a S'hendish girl and have children immediately to secure the bloodline." A'dair stared into his father's eyes to reassure him.

And he thought governing was going to be rough.

His father took in a deep, rattling sigh of relief. "Good." He patted A'dair's cheek. "It's time I sleep now. I am – exhausted. You, A'dair, will make a fine, fine King, of that, I am absolutely – certain." His father nodded to himself and fell back against his pillows.

A'dair was not so sure - he could only hope to rise to his father's example. He placed his footing carefully on the rich carpeting, trying not to wake his father as he left.

A'dair stopped at the door. He leaned an arm on the chamber door jamb, then turned placed his back on the door.

"Father."

Father woke and looked up at him from somewhere deep inside, and understood.

"Please, my son," he whispered. He reached out with both arms.

Tears streamed down A'dair's face as he hugged his Father, the Royal King Mend'alair Beaudalain of S'hendalow as tightly as he could, and his father hugged him with skeletal arms. He whispered in A'dair's ear, "My son, I would do the same for you."

A'dair pushed down on his father's face with a pillow until he could no longer breathe, then covered the King's eyes, for he was finally in peace.

Hettie

She shaded her face against the late afternoon sun. There – up on the far hill.

"Marthur... Marthur –" she called lowly. *"Marthur!"*

"What, woman!"

Her Marthur had just come up from the fields. Brushing the ground from his arms, he gave her an expectant stare.

"Lookit. Up there."

Marthur glanced just long enough, and then pushed her around the corner. "Git the kids inta the cella. Now. Hurry up." His low tone brooked no disagreement.

"Rindy, Tarry, into the cella." She forced the cella door open and strained to pull it up.

"Mum, let me." Her oldest son, Mickel, fifteen now, he towered above her, amazin' how he'd sprouted. Just a few weeks ago, seemed like he was ten and yankin' on her apron.

"Mickel, get them down there quick and keep them quiet," Hettie whispered.

"I will, Mum, I remember how," he whispered as he urged Rindy and Tarry down the ladder.

Hettie let out a breath. She hated this, oh how she hated this. She spread the rushes over the cella door and then rearranged the ancient, threadbare rug so it would cover the rug.

The first time them soldiers came, they ate up half of what Hettie and Marthur had. Of course, there were six of them, plus her and Marthur and the three kids.

Hettie had started to get a bit mouthy when she asked what country they worked for. They all at once told her, "None of your business!"

Well, maybe so and maybe not. What if she was harborin' criminals? Her face must have shown her suspicions, for whoever their leader was got up and grabbed her. Marthur immediately stood up but the other soldiers pushed him back into his chair.

"Let's just say you make sure no one knows we've been here, or your children won't be able to say anything at all," said the leader, and he grabbed Hettie's youngest, Rindy, by the arm.

They'd insisted on staying the night, and Hettie and the fam had had to sleep in the barn. She and Marthur huddle together in the hay for warmth, while Mickel had wrapped Rindy and Tarry together in a horse blanket and covered them with his own body.

Those bloody bastards. Claimin' to be they was soldiers. Well, so they was, Marthur said, 'cause lookit their hair, all chopped, and actin' like they owned the joint. But Hettie was friggin' hacked off, 'cause they wasn't wearin' uniforms. Soldiers wore uniforms 'til they got to their own homes. And they didn't travel around in common clothes, askin' people to step aside, like they was friggin' Royals or somethin'.

The second time they came through, they stayed at the top of the first hill, with the elder couple, and then was gone in the mornin'. Hettie didn't find out about that 'til the next day, when her neighbor run over and told her about it.

"They said it were the weirdest thing," said Chyda, "said their comrades had stayed there before, a house wit' kids. You know the Mister and the Missus over there – they ain't had their kids there for fifteen years some now, all moved on, kids of their own."

"Aye," agreed Hettie thoughtfully.

So the next few plainclothsed soldiers as came through, Hettie and Marthur had a plan. Right off, they threw the kids down in the cella and told them not to make the first peep, not one, and if they had to squat, do it in the corner. Mickel kept them quiet, and they had a skin of water down there for just such an occasion.

That group of plainclothsed soldiers came in, tracking mud everywhere. Their leader asked if they had children.

Marthur stood atop the cella door and lied. "Aye, we have. We got the fever here, so we sent 'em off to my sista', over in Roos to stay. Don't want 'em gettin' sick, you know." And he'd coughed a bit, as if still a bit sick.

The men looked nervously at each other. "Fever, Sir?" whispered one to the leader.

Hettie curled her arm about Marthur's, and said, "We got a son in the Navy, though. Just joined up. Down at Arzua." Hettie had acted like a proud mother, parroting any other of proud mothers she'd heard with sons who had joined the Navy. Odd thing, when she said that, though. They looked at each other and laughed. "Busy boy, he is."

Hettie had asked, "Why is that?"

They just glanced at each other knowingly and smirked.

Mickel truly did want to join the Navy, but was a year shy of sixteen, so now he counted every day 'til sixteen, for most of his friends were gone now. He was such a good lad, still helpin' his pop in the fields like he ought, and trainin' Tarry how to take his place one he was gone.

That group of soldiers took some vegetables just pulled out in the garden and a few eggs from the hens, and was gone, for fear of fever. Hettie expected they stayed with some other unlucky couple, but she didn't let her children up outta the cella 'til the next day, just to be safe. They stayed down there with their blankets and extra lanterns and Hettie stewed them some apples she'd been hoping on makin' a tart with, just to ease the night with.

Another group of soldiers came through caught them almost unawares. Good fortune had put together planning for another night such as the last two nights, and so Hettie and Marthur had dried some dried meat and packed vegetables, and even a bit of cheese, all just in case they came back.

And that sneaky group – Hettie and Marthur had barely enough time to grab the kids and shuffle them downstairs. Why, it was Mickel who pushed her to the window and put a finger over his lips, his eyes wide. He'd heaved the cella door up and she had ushered her younger two children down into the dark. Hettie had had barely enough time to edge the rushes back over the cella, but she hadn't had enough time to pull the rug over top o' them.

She had heard Marthur talkin' to 'em outdoors on the porch, shiftin' his weight purposely side to side so's the squeak o' the wood might warn them inside in case they didn't already know. Hettie smiled faintly. How she did love that man – he would do anything for his fam.

That group o' shits, they stayed for a meal and said they had t' be on their way. But while Hettie had been spoonin' out stew, their leader said, "I heard this house, you two had children."

His soldiers had stopped, spoons in the air, and had glanced from him to Hettie.

"We do, we do," she smiled proudly.

"We do." Marthur's voice was quiet.

"I heard from our last unit that you was the ones had the fever, so you sent 'em away to some sister in Melm." The commanding officer eyed Marthur with an evaluative gaze.

Marthur snorted. "Melm. Melm? Don't got no kin in Melm. No. Hettie, you ain't, either. Roos, yes. Got a sister in Roos, sent my kids to stay with her while she was sick and her place needed a bit of a repair, so they stayed on to help her a bit 'til they come home. Fam does that, you know."

The commanding soldier nodded slowly, though his eyes narrowed. "So it does."

Hettie had attempted to lighten the intensity of the mood. "We do got a boy who joined the Navy not too long ago. You boys hear anything about the Navy?"

All of the soldiers scoffed into their stew, smirking.

The commanding soldier arched an eyebrow. "What, he don't send a bird home now and again? Bein' your 'fam' and all?"

"Just two – that they kept him constantly busy. Building on ships, I think. Don't remember, the message was read to me," she had lied.

All four of them smirked.

"Soon enough, he'll be floatin' on one," scoffed one, and they all chortled.

Marthur caught Hettie's eyes in such a way as to tell her to keep her mouth shut. He himself had said nothing.

Hettie had cleared their stew bowls and dumped them in the water barrel. As she did that, the four soldiers stood up behind her.

"Well – you got a fine barn out there. A fine one."

Melm and Hettie had found this a curious statement, for it was only mid-afternoon. Hettie suddenly worried. Maybe they thought to search the barn for the children. Or did they plan to put the torch to the barn? Worse, the house?

The commander then started unlacing his tunic. "Boys – take her to the barn."

Marthur stood up and stepped in front of the commander. "Over my dead body!"

"That, peasant, can be arranged. Stay in here, and you'll keep your life. And your wife, once we're done with her. Fight us, and you'll both be dead." The commander pulled his tunic out of his breeches.

Marthur had stared wordlessly as two walked out, one by one, of the house, in the direction of the barn. Two had stayed behind, to guard Marthur.

What had happened next was a blur, for the commanding soldier had forced her arms behind her, and Hettie had started screaming. The second soldier clubbed her, and the last thing she saw was the dirt on the wooden porch beneath her dress as she was carried toward the barn.

When had Hettie awoken from her hazy black spell, what she had seen first was Marthur and Mickel staring down at the hay of the barn. Hettie herself was lying over two bales of hay.

She had sat up slowly, woozy, wondering why her son was out in the barn….

And then she had seen the bodies, and Marthur leaning on the pitchfork… and the tines of the pitchforks had been dripping with blood.

Hettie's movement caused them both to turn around.

"Mum!

"Hettie, my love!"

And they had both run to hug her and support as she sat down on the stack of hay beneath her.

Then Hettie had seen the stack of bodies.

She'd screamed wordlessly, clutching at Marthur.

"Shh, shh, shh, Hettie, sh

h, you're all right, everything is fine." And he'd held Hettie's shocked head against his chest and rocked her, just as he might a child.

Later, Hettie had learned that Mickel had pushed the cella door up and between him and Marthur, had overcome the two soldiers – though she had a good bit of rushes that needed to be switched out due to blood covered on them. A good thing the rug hadn't been over the cella door after all, for Mickel wouldn't have been able to get out so fast.

But then Mickel and Marthur had snuck into the barn before anything had happened to her, and killed the other two soldiers, Marthur with a pitchfork, and Mickel with a scythe. And oh, but they had been bloody!

"You hearin' what they said?" Marthur said. "That sounded like war to me. War."

Hettie had nodded mutely.

"You know what happens to people like us, out here on the borderlands, when soldiers like them march through. Like they already been doin'. Like they tried today. This ain't good. War ain't good." Marthur looked far away just then, out the barn door. "We might have to leave here, if it comes to that. An' it just might." His eyes focused suddenly. "Next time any o' bastards come through, I want you goin' down wit' the kids. Hear me, Hettie?"

Hettie had nodded.

"You send birds, send birds to all your kin, over in, where's that, Corstarorden, your cousin and your auntie, and I'll send word to my sister. Tell them to watch out and listen, and tell them to spread the same word, to all their kin, just as we are. It's the innocent people get hurt in war." And so Hettie had.

Today, Hettie stood, looking over their new planted radishes thoughtfully. Not a one o' this fam would be eatin' 'em, that was sure, though they'd had some specially good fertilizin'.

Cartie

The woman before marked her "X".

"Yes, then, this is from…" and the scribe scanned down the pigeon parchment down to the end… "Hellia." Then he read,

"Dear Great Auntie, I'm so sorry, but Great Grandma has passed just one and a quarter weeks ago. Her last thoughts were of you and of all of us. We gave her a lovely burial, lots of flowers such as she liked. We love you so. Hellia."

Then the scribe let the parchment roll up in his hand and handed it to the woman.

"Missus, you have my condolences."

Tears ran down the wrinkled older lady's face, her bottom lip quivering with grief as she turned away.

Cartie hoped with sudden desperation that whatever her parchment said, it wasn't anything to do with a death in the family.

The scribe looked up at her expectantly.

"Yes, sir, a courier called by my home? I have a bird, he said?"

The scribe nodded. "Name?"

"Cartie."

He pushed through the parchments and found hers. "Very well, Cartie, have it here. And do you read?

"I – have my letters. Don't use them much, but I can read when I need to."

"Well, then – I could read it to you, if you'd prefer…." The scribe trailed off expectantly.

"No, no. I'll just – my husband can read it if I can't. Here, I'll put my mark here, shall I?" And she put a "C" instead of an "X". Her cheeks stained with color. It had been a long time since she'd written anything. She decided just to leave it with a "C", and grabbed the pigeon parchment.

Outside, she unrolled it. After a time, Cartie finally worked the entire message out. It was from her cousin, whom she hadn't seen in a day and ten.

Cartie,

Soldiers been comin thru regular. They say theres lots of ships bein built and soon they'll be floatin – but they mean not in a good way. They been stayin at our house lots of times now and they talk like maybe theres war comin. Watch and listen, see if you hear the same where you are. Send this same message to all your kin too, just be quiet about it. Be safe – love to all – Hettie and the fam

Cartie looked up from the message, alarmed. War! Her boys were in the Navy. How was she ever goin' to sleep now?

Morlond

The old lady hobbled up, leaning on her cane and a younger woman.

"This is Ma'llelia. A courier stopped by and told us she had a bird," the younger woman told Morlond.

"Ma'llelia? What's a fine S'hendish lady such as yourself doing in ArkenHeights? Corstarorden's quite aways from home," Morlond addressed the old lady, trying to be kind. He could see she was wearing mourning black from head to toe.

Ma'llelia smiled sadly, and the younger woman patted her arm. "It's okay, Grandma."

"Followed my husband here, many a year ago," the old lady said, and she looked down at her dress. She brushed it off. Then she looked up. "Who is it from?"

"Uh," and Morlond leaned toward the granddaughter. "Has she her letters?"

The granddaughter shook her head. "Is it from Melm? We've got from kin there, my sister was hopin' to get with another child...."

"Ah. Well then, I'll just read it to her, shall I?" He cleared his throat as he unrolled it.

Morlond scanned the note. He always did in case he had to soften the blow – some of these peasants were just too blunt when it came to telling their kin that someone had died.

Great Auntie,

Soldiers been comin thru regular. They say theres lots of ships bein built and soon they'll be floatin – but they mean not in a good way. They been stayin at our house lots of times now and they talk like maybe theres war comin. Watch and listen, see if you hear the same where you are. Send this same message to all your kin too, just be quiet about it. Be safe – love to all – Hettie and the fam

Morlond arched an eyebrow and glanced up at the grandmother and doting granddaughter.

"Ah. Yes, from Melm." And he pretended to read, *"Dear Grandmother, I have... lovely news. I am with child now. Hoping for a son. Can't wait – will send news soon –* and uh, the ink's blotted a bit throughout, hard to read." He crumpled it and threw it in the tossbasket.

"Oh!" and the grandmother clapped her hands. "Another one!"

"See, Grandmama, what wonderful news?" the granddaughter said, then she leaned over and asked for the parchment. "The parchment, sir, please?"

"Oh, so sorry, I've just tossed it. It was covered in ink blots, so I crumpled it. I could fish about, if you like...?"

The customer behind them cleared his throat with impatience just then.

What splendid timing, thought Morlond.

The young girl shook her head. "No, thank you, sir." And she guided her grandmother from the clerk's office.

"This is from outside Heatherlocke. In S'hendalow." Captain Novland sat back in his chair and stroked his beard. "What is going on up in Heatherlocke?"

"I don't know, sir. That's why you pay me to check on these things for you, and bring it all directly to you, sir," Morlond told in respectful tones and a bowed head.

Captain Novland did not miss the hint. "Yes, Morlond, so I do." He passed a bronze coin to Morlond.

"Read everything else from this point henceforward, Morlond."

"As you wish, Captain." Morlond bowed and exited the Captain's office.

Morlond had found it just as puzzling as well. War? Soldiers? Building and manning ships? Not in S'hendalow, of all places. They'd just lost a King. The old one wasn't building ships before, and the new one wouldn't know better to build ships now, much less man them. So who was it these soldiers were talking about? He hoped he found out soon.

Of course, the Captain need not know that, per usual, Morlond had already passed this on to his two other sources, and they paid much, much better....

Helmm

"Right, then, here to pick up message, a parchment." Helmm rubbed his calloused hands together. This was taking up his break time, it was. Apprentices never did half so well work as a master.

The scribe eyed him. "Name, please?"

"Well, it's for my wife, Kay'lay, but she's bedbound with our next babe. Know how it is? So if I could pick it up, I'd be much obliged, sir, got to get back to work," Helm smiled at the scribe. Smiles would always get a customer, he told his apprentices, every time.

"As you say. I'm thinking then, that you can read, sir?" asked the scribe.

"Read? Oh, yes. Have to in my line o' work."

"Well enough then, sign here," and the scribe pushed forth the official receipt document.

Helmm wrote his name and when he collected the pigeon parchment, he handed the scribe back his business card: *Roos Town Cobbler – Fine Cobbling by Helmm.*

The scribe cleared his throat and nodded as he took Helmm's card.

Now who would be sendin' Kay'lay a bird? Helmm walked along back to the store, thinking of all the people Kay'lay knew. He unrolled the tiny parchment and, squinting, read:

Kay'lay,

Soldiers been comin thru regular. They say theres lots of ships bein built and soon they'll be floatin – but they mean not in a good way. They been stayin at our house lots of times now and they talk like maybe theres war comin. Watch and listen, see if you hear the same where you are. Send this same message to all your kin too, just be quiet about it. Be safe – love to all – Marthur and the fam

Helmm's eyes grew wide. War! Fine time for war! He did not doubt his brother-in-law, they'd tried times over to get him and his fam to move here to Roos, in a proper town, but that stubborn man, wanted to make his living off the land, like their pop had. Well, now look, they had soldiers marching through up there.

Well, Helmm had nothing against farming, nothing at all, but up there, on the border so close to the Free Lands, too far away if bandits came through. But Marthur said it was close to Pavilion City come harvest time, and they got better coin there than just regular Market Place. And what could Helmm say to that.

But this... soldiers, soldiers comin' through. And war. War. Soldiers would come through the city and demand he resole their boots, that's what would happen. And they'd burn the town, and, and.... Damn.

Well, for sure Helmm would look and listen, he didn't want anyone to be taken by surprise, and he'd send birds to all his kin... but as for Kay'lay. She didn't need to know about this. It'd upset her, and with her with child, no. This he'd keep to himself, at least for now.

Renfry

With a sigh, he closed his eyes. He tried so hard to shut out negative emotions. But irritation, frustration, anger – they just rose so quickly to the top, like fat in the kettle.

And that boy. For he was a boy, yet. Kept following him. What had Renfry done to deserve this? The boy was like a puppy, following after its mother. A little lost duckling. What was this fuckery? Renfry shook his head in annoyance. Was it idolatry of some sort?

Clearly, the boy was a runaway from the Silent Brothers, though few would recognize that now. So he was no moron – in fact, the boy was likely quite intelligent, for the Silent Brothers trained their Order in nearly every subject.

Yet the boy persisted on trailing him. Overtly, Renfry thought sourly as he thought of the boy's fire some hundred yards from his campsite last evening. And the night before that.

Finally, with no small amount of ire, Renfry stopped in his tracks at noon today. He stood there, waiting to see what the boy would do. Believing the boy would also stop, surprise overtook Renfry when he found the boy continuing forward.

In fact, when the boy passed Renfry several yards away, he gave Renfry a mild, two-fingered salute.

"Headed in the same direction." And then he kept traipsing ahead.

Renfry recognized that as a dig, for the boy had told him as much back in Landy's Hollow.

He'd seethed at the time. Cheeky little bastard. So Renfry had broken camp for a half hour, for damn if he was going to follow in the footsteps of an untried lad.

Yet he found footsteps here and about as he trudged along down the grass. Renfry wasn't walking the road to Roarden North, and, as was obvious, neither was the boy. Which meant neither of them wanted to be found along the way. The kid for life and death reasons, but Renfry always kept to himself now. Just how it was done.

When Renfry had set up camp for the night, he saw the boy's campfire glowing some hundred yards or more away. Renfry stewed over it, and then finally could not resist. He wandered across the grass to where the boy was warming his hands over his fire. He glanced up.

The boy looked up at him, shadows of the camp fire flickering over his face. "Can I offer you some roasted parsnips?" He held up a sturdy stick of parsnips, seared on the edges.

So that's what Renfry had been smelling the last two nights. He hated parsnips, boiled, roasted, or otherwise.

"No." Renfry placed his hands on his hips and stared down at the boy's camp fire. It was pathetic. But he gave the boy credit for trying – at least he'd even got a flame started, much less enough to cook food with. He really ought to help the boy – it was the right thing to do. Ah – his conscience – Renfry really hated the damn thing…. Got him in more trouble than just living regular life.

"You know, that fire there is pretty pathetic."

The boy looked vaguely surprised and then down at his campfire. "You think so?" he asked with curiosity.

Renfry rolled his eyes. "Boy. I'm giving you some advice here."

Then the boy said, "Well, it's just that your campfire," and he leaned far around Renfry's legs to peer down across the grass at the campfire in the distance, "is actually what I'd call pathetic."

Renfry's mouth fell open. Did he just hear correctly? What a cheeky little bastard!

"And how is that?"

The boy looked down at his campfire and gestured. "Well, this has everything I needed to ignite it, and I can still put more in there, but I built a sort of cabin over it, so I can cook on top, a platform. And it will still be burning in the morning, because it's protected. Yours, from the smell of the smoke, will just be ash and coal come morning. So, unless your definition of *'pathetic'* is entirely different than mine…" and the boy trailed off. He shrugged. "You sure about the parsnips? I have more."

There were few things that Renfry truly hated, but being wrong was one of them. Especially when a boy was right. It had been a sheer effort in will, and restraint, that had forced him to agree to sharing a campsite. Some part of him did point out that pooling resources was the smart thing to do. But Renfry didn't have to like it.

And now, Renfry scraped a hand across the stubble on his chin and studied the boy in the flickering campfire. Why was an escaped Silent Brother headed toward Roarden North? Had he kin there? Surely he knew that anywhere escapees had kin, Silent Brothers would be first to watch.

Finally, he ventured, "What's your name, boy?"

The youngster smiled toothily and replied, "You first."

Renfry scoffed. "That'll never happen."

The boy shrugged then, his arms out.

"Well, what do you want me to call you? Boy?"

"Arithist."

"Arithist," Renfry repeated.

"Yes, that's my name," said the boy, defiance creeping into his tone.

Renfry snorted and shook his head.

"Are you making fun of my name?" the boy demanded.

Shaking his head, Renfry eyed the boy. "You know, your Order isn't the only one who studies the ancient scripts. I know what that means in the old language. And if I do, there will be others who recognize it. Maybe shorten that. Just go by Ari."

The boy was glaring at him. "It's not my Order."

"Really. So you wouldn't mind if I bound and gagged you, shore your hair off, and took you to the nearest Order, asking for coin for an escaped Silent Brother?"

The boy said nothing.

Renfry nodded. "That's what I thought. Your hair's still growing out. I won't tell anyone, and no one will think to ask, but what you're thinking, going to Roarden North, I can't imagine. More Silent Brother collections there than I can imagine, and if you got kin there, I'd bloody well turn around and head in the opposite way now, right now, before they catch you there."

"I have no kin," returned the boy quietly.

"Ah." Renfry nodded a bit as he studied the boy over the campfire. Sparks flew up as one of the logs caught fire and fell.

Renfry had no kin as well, but he didn't guess Ari, or whatever his name was, had anything in common with why Renfry was orphaned. No one ever did. His own father had been a drunkard with a heavy hand, one that grew heavier as the years passed.

Most often, Renfry had stolen bread and vegetables off the streets just so they could eat, for his mother was rarely in shape enough to cook. Often, Renfry's aunt down the street slipped over a pottage for them while his father was out drinking, and made it look as though his mother had prepared it.

More and more, Renfry's little sister stayed with his aunt, just to keep out of sight of his father.

Renfry would never forget the day he arrived home to find his mother staring sightlessly up at the ceiling. Renfry was just short of sixteen then, but he'd always been a big-boned lad. And his father sat there on the floor, nearly passed out, his head lolling about.

"Ah. You! Where you been, boy! I said, *where you been!*" His words were hardly intelligible.

Renfry lifted his mother and sat her into one of the few chairs that still stood reliably. She was still warm. He placed his hand over her eyelids and pushed them down, so she wouldn't look so horrible. Thank all the gods, she finally was free.

"Boy!" Renfry's father attempted several times to stand up, his arms windmilling wildly. "I said, boy! Tell your mother to start dinner! Dinner should be ready by now!"

Renfry stared at the man who was his father. This man, who finally thumped back down on the wooden floor, this despicable man was his father.

No longer.

Renfry crossed the room in three short strides and hauled his father up to his feet. He stank of alcohol, vomit, and piss.

"You – are no man. You – are a monster." And then. Renfry sighed. He didn't like to recall what he'd done – he wasn't sure if it was an accomplishment or... but that was the day his conscience started nagging at him.

He winced inwardly. For he'd pummeled the man. Over and over and over, until the man's face was no longer recognizable. Blood covered Renfry and the man who had been his father. And then, Renfry took the candle burning in the center of the room, and lit the entire house to the ground, from rafters to rushes.

He left that place forever, but he made one stop. At his aunt's house. She already smelled the smoke and was frantic. Renfry picked up his eight-year-old sister and hugged her close, so tight.

"Ren – what have you done," whispered his aunt.

He just shook his head back and forth. "Shh, shh, shh," he'd told his sister.

"Auntie, she'll need to stay with you now. I'm going to join the Army. I'll send you money as I can."

"Rennie – don't said money. She's been ours for so long – she's family. Rennie, don't you forget – you are, too, love." And his aunt tried to hug him, but he was covered in blood, so he'd held her back.

She brought him one of his uncle's shirts. "Just – just tell me. Is she at peace now?"

He'd nodded. "Forevermore."

She'd patted his cheek. "Good. Good, baby. And – and," she struggled with emotion. "Is that bastard, tell me he's in hell now."

Renfry had nodded slowly. "Forevermore, Auntie."

His aunt sniffed and the tears started rolling down her cheeks. "Good. *Good!"*

Commotion in the street arose. "Baby, honey, you go. I'll tell them you joined the Army yesterday. You've made us so proud. We love you so, Rennie. Hurry, lad, go, before you're seen...."

Today, Renfry knew that out there, somewhere, he had nieces and nephews, but where, he knew not.

And for years, he had struggled with the idea of whether to do the right thing, should you do the wrong thing? Or was that backward – to do the wrong thing, you should do the right thing?

Renfry had wrestled over it for years and finally, one night he'd had an epiphany. It was a single moment, not an answer, not closure, but decided, *"fuck it."* After that night, he had felt much better.

The campfire popped and sparks rose up. "And the story for your short hair...?

"It's not *that* short," returned the boy defensively. "But – it is noticeably shorter. I'm going to join the Army, like my brother. I cut my hair short like him because I can't wait to join. And now that I'm sixteen, I'm going to Roarden North to sign up."

Renfry lifted his eyebrows and shook his head. He still thought Roarden North was damn stupid place to go for a boy with a past like his, but he was bent on it.

"Well, it might work," he commented neutrally.

"People always love a patriot," the boy declared with a winning smile.

"Until you're actually in the city and nowhere near the recruiter's office...."

"I'll think of something. I have more than one idea," said the boy.

Renfry shrugged. "It's your arse on the line, not mine. And just to be clear – once we get to Roarden North – you go your way and I go mine. We will not know each other. Understand?" He stared the boy down.

"Completely."

Nodding then, Renfry poked a bit at the fire.

Suddenly the boy asked, "Want me to take first shift?"

Renfry frowned. "Shifts? Why would be we be taking shifts? We're in the middle of nowhere." He gestured about them to the wide expanse of grass and trees.

"True. But you're not the only one who's perceptive. You act like you have eyes in the back of your head. You watch the trees and the open ground to the side of us. And I'm sure you know how you'd attack if someone snuck up behind us in the dark, and where you'd run if you needed to. Same as in the pub. All you did was watch."

Damn. He did not like people seeing through him like that.

"So I offer shifts so you can get a real bit of sleep without worry about someone sneaking up on you."

Renfry studied the boy. True sincerity there. Why not. "All right. Wake me at half-moon."

—⁓—

Suddenly, Renfry opened his eyes. Where was he? A campfire – almost morning... Renfry sat up. The boy!

"You were supposed to wake me at half-moon," he growled.

The boy shrugged. "You needed the rest. I can go without." He poked at the fire with a stick.

Renfry grudgingly admitted that he'd slept far better than he had in months. Not that the boy had to know that.

He sat up and brushed leaves and dirt free of his tunic and cloak. "Why would you do such a thing?"

The boy's eyebrows rose in inquiry.

"I'm a complete stranger," Renfry explained. "Why would you do something like that for a complete stranger?"

Shrugging, the boy said, "Human compassion. I'd want someone to do the same for me if I was falling asleep in my boots and didn't know it."

"You're a real smartarse, you know that."

The boy smiled and shrugged. "Sorry. Haven't had lots of practice."

Cheeky little shit. "Are all of you Silent Brothers smartarses, then?"

The boy leaned forward. "It was hard to tell. We were all silent."

Harvick

"Your Majesty," curtsied the servant. She was wearing light blue, which meant that she was one of his organization of spies. When she met his eyes, she blinked twice, which meant that she had information for him. Ah. Wonderful, wonderful.

Harvick liked to think of his spies as a second kingdom, a secret kingdom. Though it most often gave him news he didn't care to hear, he enjoyed the thrill of the unknown, the intrigue. There was finally some excitement, some adventure, for governing over pesky Cabinet

members bored him so…. His country ran itself.

But his underground organization… that required – harmonizing. Harvick exceled at that…. For example, Varley had no idea that the reason everywhere he went, his two young brothers seemed to also appear was because their nursemaids were Harvick's spies. And Harvick cradled his hands with that thought so he could hide a faint smile.

Until two years ago. A bird from Ormon sent here, its parchment from the Queen herself. Imagine, he'd thought, whyever would the Queen of Ormon be sending me correspondence….

And then he'd read it. It had actually been addressed to Varley, but the pigeon loft servant had mistakenly delivered it to him. A happy error indeed, for the Queen had outlined, in quite serious detail, plans she expected to set forth.

Those plans quite took Harvick's breath away. For a number of reasons, though the main few were that, above all, she was addressing this communication to his son, the heir to his throne, a neutral country. Also, that she planned to kill all of the heirs to the Ormon throne. That alone shocked Harvick, for she had a son and a daughter.

Sending such plans to his son, the heir to the throne of a centuries-old neutral country, had shaken Harvick to his core, for the letter was of a nature that implied familiarity. They knew each other by this point.

What did this mean for the future of Storden? Storden was a neutral country, had been a neutral country for hundreds of years now. Was his son conspiring to change that? With a Northern Country, of all the damnable countries in the Land?

Harvick loved his only son. Of course, for he was his father. But as the years passed, certain things, character flaws call them, or better yet, personality quirks, had emerged out of Varley. Doting and adoring one moment and then cold the next. Arrogant and prideful.

Last year, there was the matter of the courtesan, which was a kind word for her. Varley had – impregnated her. Harvick closed his eyes and shook his head. Perhaps it was not simply that which bothered him, for numerous lords and nobles did so, but it was the information gleaned about how Varley acted in the brothels.

Harvick was no stranger to the idea of men, royal or noble, in brothels, though it was smarter of them to have affairs with ladies-in-waiting instead, for they were less likely to acquire sexual diseases. Nor did men have to leave their homes. However, men of reputable status still visited brothels, and Harvick was ashamed, and disgusted, to learn how often the Heir to the Throne of Storden visited them.

So when this "courtesan" was brought to a secret audience, it was not due to the fact that she was carrying the Prince's child, but another matter altogether. The brothel madam was asking for a favor from him, the King.

Of course, he'd wanted proof that the child was Varley's. The woman told him of a number of identifying marks, but the main one was the cherry birthmark on his lower back, near his spine, in the shape of an elongated crescent moon.

At the time, Harvick wondered just how many bastards Varley must have fathered at that point that had not been brought to his, or even Varley's attention.

But the brothel madam, with the greatest of courtesy, curtsied and begged Harvick's pardon for what she was about to tell him, for it was on behalf of her girls, and certainly on the behalf of the other girls, that she asked.

Harvick had, by then, been impatient, and certainly ready to give the young girl whatever she needed to have the child, but he was not ready for what sounded like extortion.

Then the madam asked the girl to turn around and slide her dress down. Lash marks and healed scabs covered the girl's back.

"Beggin' Your Majesty's Most Royal Pardon, I'd show ya her front, too, but that'd be indecent." The Madam pulled the girl's dress back up and put an arm around her.

Horrified, Harvick had said, "And you know, you know, Madam, for a fact that my son did this?" And he gestured up and down at the girl.

Tears rolled down the girl's face. The Madam nodded. "It's not just her. But she's with child now."

"Well, we'll take care of her, give her all the expenses she needs –" Harvick began.

"No, if it please you, Your Majesty, we take care of our own, less you want the child yourself. We'll take care of her and her child, it's what we do. But we can't – you know – this just ain't...." And she gestured up and down at the girl's back.

Harvick nodded with understanding. And horror. The girl hung herself, he was told, three weeks later. Probably for the better, he'd mused at the time, a child of Varley's in the Land, and by a, a whore no less....

Drinking, whoring, wild parties, and now conspiring....

Of late, Varley's behavior had calmed some, though Harvick found that suspicious rather than impressive. Varley never did anything without recompense. Harvick believed, based on the information his spies were bringing him, as well as his personal knowledge of his son, that Varley was planning something, and needed to cleanse his reputation of its sordid past.

Ha. That could be anything. Conspiring with a woman who had killed her husband to take over the throne? Harvick believed daily that his life was now in danger... and from his own son, no less. Gone was that laughing little boy who ran after bluebirds in the courtyard. Gone was that smiling little boy who played in the puddles after the rains....

The very first thing Harvick had done once he'd read that parchment was marry again. One of his Cabinet Members from Kipper Cove was a Wescarl, and what ships there at the docks and at sea that Lord Wescarl didn't own, he had the coin to build. So Harvick married his daughter. Young for him, yes, but by the gods, Harvick would have more children by the time the year was out.

And so he had. Those Wescarls were fertile if nothing else. Twin boys, Harvick could hardly believe his luck.

And unknown to Varley, Harvick had cut him out of the line of succession. Harvick's Uncle Dordonas would serve as Regent to Harvick's older twin son, Tollard, and second in the line of succession was now Tollard's twin brother, Jonnard. The Throne would then pass to Harvick's brother Irving and his children, and, if necessary, Harvick's Uncle Dordonas, then Uncle Connald. In no way was Varley ever to sit the Storden Royal Throne.

Harvick had a very serious and private conversation regarding all of this with his uncle, and told him that, if he suffered an untimely death in the near future, immediately arrest Varley and place him in a traitor cell, with no trial, and allow no one to know where the boy was. Uncle Dordonas' eyes grew wide at this last, but he nodded his head very slowly in agreement. Harvick rewrote this new line of succession paperwork, stamped it, and Uncle Dordonas witnessed it. He would keep it himself, rather than Harvick.

Harvick feared for the lives of his young sons. And for his new wife's life as well. She must think him a crazed lunatic, he mused. All he wanted was more children. He hated to think of her as only an heir producer, but that was his main reason for marrying her, aside from any need of ships in the future.

Since the babes were born, Harvick would leave her alone for a bit, but as soon as it was fair to start trying for new babes, he'd be on her again, twice a day. He'd not have that traitor sitting in his home expecting to take over his country. The more heirs Storden had, the better. And the sooner he could get Varley out of his plans, the better....

Ellia

"Ah, my dear," said Nona as Ellia stepped into Nona's flowing pavilion. "I have news for you."

Ellia tried not to frown, but the last time Nona told her she had news for her, they had three people to guest and Ellia had been given a half hour warning. She had had to choose her gown, her hair ornaments, everything and meet them on the lawn early while not appearing flushed.

Nona stood and placed a hand on Ellia's shoulder. "My lovely girl. You are beautiful. You are truly beautiful."

Ellia curtsied a little and thanked her, but was immediately on the defensive. She sniffed a plot....

"Ellia, child, you were to stay here, at Emberly, for three months. But I have been instructed to send you in three weeks...." And Nona trailed off. Nona was rarely speechless.

A breeze teased Ellia's hair across her face and she brushed it aside. "Three weeks...?" She suddenly felt a cold dread spreading across her.

"You are wanted at the Palace, to join your family, my dear. In three weeks."

Ellia's mouth fell open, mindless of her manners. "Three weeks? But that's... that's... so soon...."

She could not imagine herself at any time at the Palace, but now? She still had not finished her instruction with Nona....

"I'm not ready..." Ellia implored.

Nona bestowed a gracious smile upon her. "Unless you were born into this position, you can't expect to be ready for it. And," she added gently, "no one is ever ready to meet the King and Queen for the first time, especially when they are one's parents....

"And that is why you now have your first lady-in-waiting. Her name," and Nona beckoned behind Ellia, "is Kimbur. She is extremely fluent in all the Courts of the Land, as she has learned at my own hand, and she will be at your side at all times. Never dismiss her, dear, for she is your greatest ally, and my greatest gift to you.

"Kimbur, my dear, this is Ellia, or, from today henceforward, we shall call her Mirelle, unless others are about, for she will need to adjust to the name as quickly as possible. Lady Mirelle, please meet Kimbur."

And Ellia found a girl of an age with herself, standing behind her in a rose gown trimmed with silver embroidery. Her chestnut hair was arranged simply down her back and her brown eyes looked very kind and though her they hid an intelligent spark behind them.

"Your Highness," Kimbur curtsied flawlessly.

"Mirelle, part of what Kimbur will do is assist you at Court. She is well-versed in all that a Royal Princess will require, be it a slight blunder, a walking social disaster, which invitations to accept, which gowns to choose, and... oh, so many other tiring things that Court life demands of a young girl, indeed, a Princess."

Ellia swallowed. Perhaps there was still time to run away and disappear somewhere, somewhere pretty in the country, where she could live as a maid with a nice couple....

"Now, from today forward, we will focus our time on Court expectations and those whom you will meet there. For while the history of the Lands is certainly required knowledge for a Princess, being suddenly emerged in Court life will be far more important. In fact, I would expect many of them have forgotten their history and much more...."

Ellia lounged on her bed, leaning her arms on her knees as she stared through the window. Moonlight spilled across her bed, the only thing that calmed her just now. Her mind was numb. Not another thing could enter it, for it was entirely full, as a sponge full of water. In fact, Ellia expected it was probably dripping, dripping with information she would need to recall at some near instant and there she would be left, gaping like a fool.

Why couldn't some other girl have been Princess....

"Your Highness," said a soft voice across the room, "would you like me to draw the curtains against the moonlight?"

Kimbur. Her new lady-in-waiting. She – Ellia, oh, if you please, she was now *Mirelle* - now had a lady-in-waiting. A lady's foremost lady-in-waiting always slept in her rooms with her, in a separate alcove of her own that she might always be available.

Kimbur stood suddenly. She crossed to Mirelle's windows and pulled the curtains closed. "Begging Your Highness's pardon, but it's proper to draw the curtains at night," she said softly.

Mirelle sighed. Of course it was. "I don't know how I'm going to learn all this in just three more weeks."

"You will. Of course you will. And Nona and I will make sure you do," Kimbur told her in an encouraging tone from her bed across the chamber.

Hmph. Mirelle doubted that. She certainly didn't doubt Nona's abilities, nor even this Kimbur – nor their combined efforts. But her own abilities? Sponge dripping. Mirelle could only take in so much at a time, and she was beginning to suspect just lately that her sponge was rather small....

"Perhaps. But three weeks just seems so very... soon."

"But you shall take to it immediately," Kimbur responded with confidence. "You've learned so much so soon."

Mirelle wrapped her arms about her knees even tighter. She was only a good actress. Flashing a pretty smile for strangers had taken up the better part of her life, so it seemed she would continue to do so, merely in a different setting.

"Aye, and so much more left..." Mirelle trailed off thoughtfully.

Kimbur cleared her throat delicately.

Mirelle directed her attention to Kimbur.

"With all due respect, Your Highness... your, your... accent is creeping in."

Mirelle frowned. "My accent?"

Kimbur cleared her throat again, daintily. "From South Fairview."

Mirelle took that in for a moment. Then she smiled. Then she giggled. That was the best news she'd heard in a long time. At least something of the old her remained.

But Nona had gone to enormous pains to teach her to speak correctly, to lose that exact accent to which Kimbur now referred.

She practiced aloud for Kimbur's sake more than her own. "My... *AC*cent, my *AC*cent, my *AC*cent," she spoke slowly, flourishing her hands.

Then Mirelle sniffed and rolled her eyes. "Oh, bloody hell with my accent. You know what my Pappy would say if he saw me all done up in gowns and jewels? He'd laugh and say something stinks in the fish kettle." Mirelle smiled for a moment as she pictured Pappy's face. Then her eyes filled up and her bottom lip quivered. But, of course, ladies weren't ever to cry, so Mirelle rolled her eyes up to the ceiling and took in several deep breaths. What a stupid rule.

Mirelle shook her head slowly. "That's why this is going to be so hard. You can put the castle in the barmaid, but you can't put the barmaid back in the castle."

Gently, Kimbur asked, "What was it like?"

Mirelle thought of everything that she could say to that. There was no easy answer. She took in a deep breath and a faint smile slipped over her face. "It was... freedom. Love. Playful. Laughter. Singing and dancing. Family. It was... just..." Mirelle couldn't think of anything that properly could possibly describe her home. "Flat out." And everything this life won't be, she added to herself.

"You know, don't you, that you can't go back there. It wouldn't be safe for you now," came Kimbur's quiet voice.

"I know," Mirelle rolled her eyes. How many times that had been explained to her before she finally had understood! "More importantly, it wouldn't be safe for them," she returned.

Kimbur stayed silent to that.

"But one day, a long time from now, when it's safe, and no one knows who I am or where I'm going, I will return," Mirelle vowed quietly.

Rhutgard

"Are you sure this really is a good time?" worried Principea at his side.

She was everything a man could want in a wife, and everything he wanted in a Queen. Gracious, compassionate, elegant, diplomatic, and tactful.

Tact – a quality he had been losing over the years. Rhutgard found he wanted everything explained to him immediately, directly, and forget long, drawn-out details. Is the man dead or alive? Is there plague or no plague? Bandits or imposters? Because of this, he depended upon Stanyard for much of this now.

And now Rhutgard pushed down the irritation he felt at Principea's question.

"Yes, my love, I am." He kissed her on the forehead to assuage her.

"But Rhutgard, perhaps after the ball, rather than before it…? It will be such a terrible time for her to adjust…."

"I realize the stress she will be under, and if I could ease her discomfort, I would. But from a practical point of view, it is best. The more who see her and interact with her, the better. This is the biggest event of the season, after all. And I want her here now. If only you knew what I knew…."

Principea frowned. "Does Stanyard agree to this?"

Rhutgard frowned. "Whether he does or does not matters not. If it eases your mind, both of us had the same idea."

Principea stood away from him, her lips drawn tight. She placed her hands behind her.

"Of course, Your Majesty. As it please you. I will remind you, however, that she is also my daughter." Principea's blue eyes narrowed as her chin lifted. "Do be sure to allow my daughter to retire early if she must. On that – I insist. Make note of it."

Principea's gown swished behind her as she stepped away from Rhutgard as if he were fresh street excrement and exited his solar promptly.

Bloody hell. There were few people in the Land that truly intimidated Rhutgard – the two at the top of his list were his mother, who was second, now passed on – and his wife, at the top of the list. He rolled his head back on his back and stared at the ceiling. How was he going to make up for this one?

Stanyard snickered, then outright laughed. "Well, Your Majesty, I'd say you could share my bed, but it's a bit snug."

"It's not bloody funny, Stanyard! I need to make up for this somehow," Rhutgard snapped.

Stanyard snorted. "When have I ever served as a Royal Marriage Ambassador? What makes you think such a quality is even an ability of mine?"
"Well, there was that one time –"

"That one time, Your Majesty, was when you forgot the day the two of you married. Anyone could have helped you out on that blunder, even a guard – a blunder, I might add, of idiotic proportions –"

"Stanyard. Did you just stand here and call your king an idiot?"

Stanyard snorted again and shook his head. "No, Sire, I called the blunder itself idiotic."

Rhutgard glared at him.

"This one on the other hand, perhaps… apologize? I know not…." Stanyard trailed off.

"Apologize?"

"Yes, with flowers or some such. Women like flowers. Just…." Stanyard shrugged. "And she has a point – allow the girl to retire half-way through the evening if she prefers. This is, after all, her very first Court appearance, Sire. She's not ever been around these people. Think of her not so much as if she were sixteen, but ten years of age. Would you not allow your ten-year-old daughter the chance to retire early?"

Rhutgard nodded slowly. He wanted to show off this new daughter of his, especially to the faces of the spies he knew would be among the Ball. But there would be several other events during the entire week that she would be seen.

Ah, but messages would be flying to and from that week, and his network would be watching every move. He knew he had a number of spies from other countries in his Palace. Only because Rhutgard allowed them – he made sure they were fed information that he wanted their countries to hear. Three Ormon spies at last count. That Queen of theirs really did think him brainless. To his knowledge, nothing had come of the bird he and Stanyard had sent to Ormon instead of Ambsellon, though they wondered often.

It was far harder to infiltrate Ormon. Especially now that she had changed up the guard as well as appointed new staff. All anyone knew now was that she was believed to have killed her husband and probably her son as well – for now she was Queen and no one doubted her Rule. She just went about here and there, taking over everything and all there seemed to live in fear.

Rhutgard held his hand up in annoyance. "Have we any recent news to report?"

Stanyard shrugged slowly. "Nothing of note. A ferryman gone missing."

"Missing? Is this the extent of it?"

"Yes, Your Majesty."

"Missing how? Did he fall overboard?"

"They investigated, found neither hide nor hair of him at his home. They thought it odd, for he'd reported for duty every night. Ran the Night Crawler. Former Naval man from Storden, I believe, retired here. Just up and left – odd, they thought. Not a word."

Rhutgard frowned. "They should have asked him about all the bodies washing up."

"They did, I believe, Sire. He thought an amateur was dumping them, but more he couldn't say. Just that the Rosh River has been awash with bodies."

"Awash with bodies…." Rhutgard repeated, rubbing slowly at his chin.

"Sire?" prompted Stanyard.

Rhutgard suddenly strode to the wall and pulled one of his swords free. He tucked it under his belt. "Sword?" he held another to Stanyard.

Stanyard, wide-eyed, shook his head. "I – no. I have a –" And he patted his surcoat, where a dirk was clearly outlined.

"Come, Stanyard, we are going to see sights," Rhutgard strode to his study door, oblivious as to whether Stanyard followed him or not, for at least two Crown Guards would follow him regardless.

Stanyard hurried after him. "Would you like to tell me where –"

Rhutgard held a hand up to cut him off. Who knew how many ears and eyes the walls had. As always, two Crown Guards stepped into place behind him. He loved to walk at a fast pace, just to annoy them. It was terribly rude of him, Rhutgard knew, but it was for a few reasons. One – he didn't know who he could trust, and if one fell behind, that might be an infiltrator.

Two – it was a small way of rebelling, however childish – he himself was once a member of the Guard and he would despise this post.

And three – just a small bit of exercise. Rhutgard so rarely got out anymore, the way his sons did, the way the nobles of the Court did. Utterly pathetic – walking fast just for exercise, and only to annoy the guards who would protect his arse should he need their assistance. His logic here was a bit faulty, Rhutgard had to admit....

Stanyard was accustomed to Rhutgard's fast pace but as they headed downward, he suddenly whispered behind a hand, "Sire, where are we going?"

Rhutgard replied, "I told you back in my study, Stanyard."

Still behind a hand, Stanyard whispered, "Yes, but if we're going sight-seeing, the stables are that way," and he nodded to the opposite side of the corridor that they had just passed.

"Oh, no, Stanyard, I told you something different. We are going to do something different – remember how I told you? Keep up."

Soon, they arrived at the very bottom level of the castle. As they stood before the dungeon gates, the Crown Guards saluted. While one turned the key to the door, Stanyard muttered, "Not my first choice for either sort of sights, Your Majesty...."

The Guards saluted Rhutgard and he stepped inside. An earthy, underground smell accosted him immediately and he hid his nostrils under a hand. With the other hand, he picked up a lantern from the wall to light their way down the main corridor.

He glanced at Stanyard and saw that he had done the same.

"Do, please, tell me what we're doing in a dungeon, Sire...." Stanyard's voice sounded muffled behind his sleeve.

They came across a man in an ill-fitting Guard uniform.

Stanyard stepped forward with the lantern and said immediately, "His Majesty the King wishes to see the Warden."

The Guard said, "Yah, and I'd like to blow my nose up His Majesty the King's arse'ole, but that ain't gonna happen, is it? Now git the fuck outta 'ere. Warden," and the Guard snorted.

Stanyard coughed and stepped aside, holding his lantern high so that it illuminated Rhutgard's face.

 The Guard's mouth dropped open. "O my gods. O my bloody gods." Then he fell to his feet before Rhutgard. "Your Most Royal Majesty, sir, I didn't mean that, sir, I, I, am so – so sorry, I –"

Rhutgard stepped backward before the man started licking his boots. In distaste, he rolled his eyes upward.

"The Warden, please?"

From his kneeling position, the Guard replied with a trembling lip, "The – the Warden. He – he takes time off. Now and again, Your Most Royal Majesty."

"Stanyard, please?" Rhutgard stepped back and motioned for Stanyard to get information from the man.

Soon, they were walking down damp, dungeon corridors, along with the piggish Guard and a parchment that supposedly listed the names of each prisoner in each cell.

"Where is this prisoner?" Rhutgard gestured at the empty cell.

"He – he ain't in there, Your Majesty, sir," replied the guard."

"So I see. What I want to know is – where is the man who is supposed to be in there? Is there no record of him leaving? Dying, requiring medical assistance perhaps? Why is this man not in his cell?

"Or..." and Rhutgard strode to three more cells. "This man? Are they dead? Did they die?"

 He strode down the entire cell block and found five empty cells, though according to the roster, all had inhabitants.

"Where are the guards who guard this cell block?" asked Rhutgard, angry now.

"Your Majesty, I – I don't know." The dungeon guard was terrified.

"Give it your best guess. Where are they?"

"Your Majesty, I don't know what they do in they's off-time...."

Rhutgard frowned. Then he noticed a common mark next to each prisoner's name. "What do these marks mean?"

"Oh, those. Those mean they had a visitor." The guard was relieved to have been of use finally.

Rhutgard showed the roster to Stanyard. "See how recent the ink is compared to the others."

Stanyard looked at Rhutgard and nodded. In a low voice, he said, "Inmates are being smuggled out."

"While the guards are paid to look the other way."

"And the inmates are killed once freed –"

"Because they know too much for someone's comfort."

"Yes, Your Majesty, but now we have another puzzle on our hands. What do they know and how many of them know it? And who is it endangering?"

Rhutgard sighed. How many people were in his dungeon? Fifty? Seventy-five? Who was running this operation right beneath his feet, and why? A network of counterspies. This was intolerable. He would clean this dungeon, and its counterspies out, starting today.

Nona

"And? What is your personal opinion?"

They were strolling through Nona's small grove of plum trees. Kimbur glanced at her beneath Nona's parasol.

She shrugged a shoulder. "For as far as she's come… she can't do much better."

"*'Can't do much better?'*" My darling Kimbur, that sounds dismal for a Princess about to emerge onto one of largest Court seasons of the year."

Nona had debated over whether to tell Mirelle that just a week after she arrived at the Palace, an enormous ball would be held. Nona told her, in the end, for finding out on her way there, or once she arrived – well, the girl was delicate enough, they didn't need her to balk and run. Nona thought of Mirelle as a newborn foal; her legs still wobbly.

Ah, Rhutgard, Rhutgard. While she questioned the boy's ideas all around – both his idea of raising Mirelle in an alehouse, and suddenly demanding her back with next to no warning, he was still the King, and they had no choice but obey him, Nona mused.

But she would be a beautiful Princess, that, Nona knew.

Once she got her legs under her.

"Truly?" she questioned Kimbur. "So bad as that?"

"No – no. It's just – her heart's not in this. I think that's what keeps her back. You know, most girls would love this opportunity, and she hates it. She wants to go home."

Nona nodded slowly. "Well, her whole life has been a lie. That will take some adjustment."

Kimbur cocked her head to the side in contemplation.

"Yes, my dear?"

"She said something once, that I found interesting. She said, *'You can put the castle in the barmaid, but you can't put the barmaid back in the castle.'*"

Nona smiled a little. "When was this?"

"Three weeks ago, when I first arrived."

"Well, unfortunately, the barmaid will be returning to the castle, and tomorrow, whether she's ready or not, I'm afraid. You have quite a job ahead of you, my dear Kimbur."

"So does she. But I think she's up to it," Kimbur mused.

Myrischka

Her Seneschal blinked rapidly at her. He had that anxious tendency, and it grated on her nerves. If she saw him too often, she might have to replace him.

"I've stamped all of these, if you – would just care to sign them… Your Majesty?"

Myrischka knew what they called her. The "Ice Queen." She rather liked it, though perhaps another would arise that she preferred better.

She was simply passing through, and he'd caught her like a rat smells cheese.

"You do know my signature by now, do you not?"

The Seneschal nodded.

"Then by all means, employ it, for if I have to sign this stack of papers, it will end up as the last." Myrischka had sent that stack fluttering into the fire. This was the Seneschal's purpose, one of many, and running the small, trivial things such as food shortages in parishes, bear attack increases, and tariff proposals on minimal things fell to him.

"Yes, of course, Your Majesty." He bowed and stepped aside.

Today, she left for Helm Port. She had to know what resources she had and she wanted to see for herself. And refused to take other people at their word. This required her personal sight.

After they got on their way, one of the Captains rode back and told her, albeit respectfully, she should be aware of possible threats to her person, exposed as she would be. But the Captain's biggest concern was that the ride ahead would be difficult and demanding, exposed to the elements, especially for one of her important stature.

Myrischka told him then to break the way ahead and make sure that all before them knew of her arrival, and that she expected to see him there when she arrived. She wondered personally if he would survive the ride.

She knew what he referred to about threats to her person. She was wearing ring mail designed specifically for her person, of course, over a fine woolen shirt. Myrischka did hate it by now, for it was so heavy, but she knew that it might very well save her life should some miscreant decide to exact vengeance.

The Captain was, of course, right as well in regards to demanding weather. The weather was most uncooperative for the first two days. All the troops covered themselves, from head to toe, and the horses were covered in wool blankets as they rode. And during camp, snow leaked through the canvas above the wood of Myrischka's tent. Before the night was over, the wood was sodden and dripped in places.

But Myrischka was no cream puff. Handling inclement weather was not an issue for her. As long as the drips didn't land in her fire, all was well.

The third day was much easier for travel. The sun was out in a clear blue sky, and, though the air was cooler, there wasn't as much snow on the ground. The men even unwound their scarves from their faces for short bit of time during the afternoon.

A Captain had arrived, she was told, once she arrived at Helms Port, though he was recovering from severe frostbite. She was impressed – the man had survived. That spoke of a true Ormish Captain – the ability to survive. Myrischka made a mental note to have his needs seen to and a medal bestowed upon him. A promotion was unlikely – the man would likely have difficulties walking again, much less be well enough to fight.

Rooms at the local tavern had been made ready ahead of time for her and her men, along with the very best food the town could offer.

But first, Myrischka wanted to see her ships.

"Your Majesty, if it please you, this is the Official Chronicle of all our current Ships-At-Sea," said the Commander as he offered Myrischka the leather-bound book of parchment. He bowed stiffly, as was the wont of his station.

Myrischka accepted the book but was not going to stand and read through names. "How many seaworthy warships are there, docked and at sea, Commander?"

"Four hundred and two, Your Majesty."

Hmm. She liked precision. But so few ships. She had hoped for more.

"Commander, how long does it take for a shipwright to build a warship?"

The uniformed man paused to consider all alternatives. "Six months, Your Majesty."

Six months! That was far too long!

"Therefore, three shipwrights would halve that time. Commander, I need one hundred more warships, even better than what I have out there now." She ignored the man's balk. He immediately returned to his soldier's demeanor, though his eyes were still round at the idea.

"Find me shipwrights. Import lumber. Take as many men off their current ships as you need to assist the shipwrights, but I want this done. I will give you… six months. No longer. One hundred ships, six months.

"Now. I want to step aboard one of my ships."

Her black mourning furs billowed out behind her as she strode down the gangway. Once she had climbed aboard, Myrischka took in the fresh sea air and walked around above deck with a pleased expression. Gulls called all around her as they flew pasts. Yes, she would have one hundred more of these ships, and another hundred by this time next year.

"Your Majesty." The Captain saluted her stiffly.

"Captain?"

"Would you like to go below decks now?"

"That's why I'm here, Captain," Myrischka told him.

The Captain stepped down the ladder with a practiced ease. Once he stood at the bottom, he bowed and held a hand toward Myrischka. She brushed it aside – she was perfectly able to ascend and descend ladders.

Then she turned around. Two hundred-fifty of her men stood at full salute.

In one voice, they all said, "YOUR MAJESTY!"

Myrischka smiled. Now that she liked.

Ishbel

She heard the clink of two silvers on her bureau. Sleepily, Ishbel opened her eyes.

Then her eyes grew wide. Rogue!

"You're early," she commented.

He arched an eyebrow. "Have you fit me into a routine, then?"

"Well. Six weeks in

between the last two." She stood up. Had it been two weeks or three this time? Ishbel placed her hands on his shoulders and turned him about. "Just want to see how my handiwork turned out."

Ishbel stood on her tiptoes and inspected the knife wounds she'd stitched up. He, or someone, had pulled the thread out, but they appeared to have healed well enough. Ointment or no, those would probably leave scars, like the others on his back....

"Not bad," she commented as she sat back down on her bed. "Now that, I've got nothin' for," and she pointed at the purple eye Rogue had.

He snorted. "I don't need anything for it. The other guy's got two."

Ishbel raised an eyebrow. "I'm surprised Gobin let you back here, lookin' like that. Normally, he wouldn't."

Rogue shrugged a bit. "I told him my horse did it while I was trying to shoe her. Told him I was also in the market for a new horse, and he said they had a whole pavilion of them here now. But I told him you were my favorite, and he took me straight back, said he knew he recognized me."

"Right then. You ever going to come in here completely healthy?" Ishbel asked as she slid his rucksack off his shoulder. She thought she saw him wince, but she could have been mistaken.

Rogue scoffed. "What did you call it? Occupational requirement?"

"What, getting beaten, getting knives in your back? What sort of occupation is that?"

"You were the one sleeping on the job," he countered.

"Ah," Ishbel said, "but I was up for two days with no sleep. I get a little sleep now."

"Fair enough. I could use some myself, as it happens."

She sighed. "I can't ever figure you out."

Rogue stared at her with gray eyes. "You wouldn't want to, trust me." He sat down on the edge of her bed then and winced, then set his face solidly. She watched his jaw clench.

"You did it again, didn't you? You realize that I'm not a Healer, don't you. Those tents are far along in the other direction."

"Yes, I'm quite aware. One of many reasons why I'm here and not there. Healers talk too much. How many of them would have talked the second I'd walked out of there with those wounds last time? Word would have spread in an hour that I was here. I'm trying to stay invisible, Ishbel, not obvious."

As he told her this, Rogue pulled his boots off and swung himself up on her bed. He winced as he did so, for he clearly had broken ribs.

Ishbel sat down next to him. "Well, you're obviously not doing a very good job of it, are you? Knife wounds last time. Broken ribs this time. What'll it be next time, hey?"

"Woman, you don't need to give me any grief. I'm paying you to not give me any grief. I get enough of that out there. The last time I was here, you forced me to take a bloody bath. This time, just let me relax, all right then?" But Rogue was shaking his head in a mild snicker.

"All right, all right then." Ishbel laid down beside him. "We'll just have a little sleep, then."

He yawned. "You know something. Everywhere I went, I heard the same thing you told me. Anything new here?" He laced his hands beneath his head.

Ishbel shook her head on the pillow. "No. Same as before. Crates comin' through, now, but I don't know what's in them. I saw one of them stamped, "Iron". They're all about so big," and she gestured four feet by four feet. That's the only new thing."

Rogue was silent for a moment. Then he quietly said, "Un-uniformed soldiers traveling through. Excess horses. Lumber. Iron. What does all that say to you?"

Ishbel looked over at him from her pillow. Together, they both said, "War."

"No," she whispered. Pavilion City was always the first hit in wars. Now she was nervous. She curled up next to him.

He sucked in a little air from the broken ribs, so she slid herself up higher, onto his shoulder. Together, they both fell asleep.

But Ishbel had nightmares of soldiers coming through and burning Pavilion City to the ground – and worse.

When she woke, Rogue was gone. Slipped right out without her even noticing. Damn! How did he do that! He had gently arranged her on the far pillow of her bed and – curled in her downward palm, were two more silvers.

Ronan

He gave a covert glance at Mirelle. She sat with her hands folded atop each other in her lap as she looked out the coach window. One would think she had always been a lady, as calmly as she sat.

Ronan suspected that her tranquility belied her. He believed that inside, she was bubbling with anxiety. Enough that she had been taken from Luvian and Ruthie, South Fairview, and The Brew House and Tavern she had called home her entire life. But to find that the King and Queen of Romeny were her true parents? Ronan couldn't imagine anything more severe.

But in two months, Mirelle had transformed completely. A new girl, a Princess now sat before him, dressed in full Court attire, a pale blue gown of lace and silk, trimmed with cream and cloth of gold. Her golden hair was piled atop her head, ornamented with hair combs. Two golden ringlets hung gently around her neck.

And those Romeny blue eyes that hid her true feelings stared out the window.

Ronan remembered her first week at Emberly. He was leaving his chambers for a late-night snack one evening when, down the hall at the Ladies Quarters, he spied several maids rushing away from what would only be Ellia's chambers.

He had stridden over to her chambers and knocked. The maid outside was horrified. Ronan had asked, "What's wrong with her?"

She had whispered, "The lady has been crying, most every night. We bring her warmed milk, sugared with honey, and mulled cider, to help her sleep at night."

"I'm a friend. I should be able to help." Again, the maid was horrified at a man's presence outside a lady's quarters.

He placed his hands in the hair. "I'm only going in to speak with her, relax. Please leave us."

The maid curtsied and left.

Ronan knocked at the door again. "Ellia, it's me. Open the door."

Ellia came to the door, her face red and wet with tears. "Ronan! What are you doing here! It's not fitting! Go away before someone sees you!" she hissed.

"Ellia, let me in," he told her and placed his boot in the door. "I'm not going away."

"Ronan, it's not right! Go away!" Ellia stuck her head out of the door and looked down both sides of the corridor.

"Ellia, let me in, it's all right." And Ronan pushed the door open gently. "It's easier than me standing in the hall begging."

She stood in her night dress and robe, her hair let down in waves, her face blotchy and wet.

"What's wrong? Why are you crying?" Ronan asked, though he suspected he knew.

Ellia's lips quivered and her eyes filled up. She sniffled. Ronan handed her his handkerchief.

"Come on, you can tell me."

"It's – it's this –" and Ellia swirled her arm all about her at the chamber. "It's you, it's me now, it's, it's everything."

Ronan's heart went out to the girl, for then she started crying again. "Oh, Ellia." He knew it was wrong to hug a lady.

"Come, come here." And he pulled her down against her bed, for he certainly wouldn't be found *atop* the bed should a maid walk in. He would never stain her reputation before she ever entered the highest of society, whether Lady Elenorina trusted these maids or not.

Ronan held his arm about her shoulder. "Just – just forget it, all right, now? Just think of yourself as Ellia, and me as Ronnie right now. And just cry, let it out, girl."

Ellia looked up at him with her blue eyes and then leaned on his shoulder and cried herself out. Occasionally, he said useless things such as, "There, there" and "You'll be all right," but she wasn't listening.

Finally, as a storm blows past, Ellia sniffled a few times and the last of her tears rolled down her cheeks. She looked up at Ronan, then down at his surcoat. "I'm sorry," she whispered as she tried to dab at it, for its green woolen shoulder was wet clear through.

At a weak attempt at humor, he smiled a little. "I have others." He stood up. "Now, let's see about putting you to bed, shall we?" And she took hold of his outstretched arm. Ronan lifted her up and placed her in her bed. She stared at him as he pulled her covers up. "You get some sleep, now, you know she'll have you busy tomorrow."

Ellia had nodded and Ronan left. A maid carrying a tray of milk saw him leave.

"Shh," Ronan said. "I've just put her to sleep." The maid's eyes grew wide but she saw Ronan's wet, tear-stained shoulder and nodded. She curtsied and told him "Yes, my lord," before she turned to leave.

The next morning, Ronan was summoned for a private meaning with the Lady of Emberly. He was not surprised.

"Ronan," she'd greeted him. "Tea? Fruit juice?" she'd offered him from her breakfast table.

"Thank you, no, I've already eaten."

She nodded. "I admire early-risers. They get their days started soon, with the sun, before anyone else is about to pester them. A nice, peaceful, quiet time."

The Duchess of Emberly poured fruit juice into her tea cup. She really knew how to draw out the suspense of a moment. Finally, she looked up at him. "I understand you went visiting last night, young Ronan." She sat back against her cushioned chair, holding her tea cup with both hands as she studied him with those implacable gray eyes.

Ronan had had the feeling she would find out. "I did. The Lady Ellia was in need of consolation, and I am a familiar face. She was crying, my lady. I only gave her a shoulder to cry on."

The Lady of Emberly took a tiny sip from her tea cup and lifted her eyes back up to Ronan again. "Ronan, child, I understand how true your intentions were. But you were seen by two maids of mine. As fortune would have it, they are faithful to me only, and so will not repeat such a story. But imagine if they were to.

"However honest and true your intentions, and however kind a friend you are, I must ask you never to do so again. You must remember that she is, whether she wants to be or not, a Royal Princess. And you are both a Crown officer of Romeny and a Crown Prince of Ghiverny. I expect you to act as such at all times. Her reputation must not be stained in the least, ever.

"I'm sure you understand me, Ronan."

And Lady Elenorina bowed her head and looked down her nose at Ronan, implying a suggestion that Ronan understood only too well.

He'd seethed at the implication but understood an elder's need to remind him of it.

And then spent the most boring two months of his life there. Shooting pheasants, practicing swordplay, a bit of hunting on occasion. Ronan was responsible for teaching Ellia her horsemanship, which had turned her into a fair horsewoman, so long as she never went on a hunt. That was probably the most interesting time he'd spent there.

But now. Kimbur and Lady Elenorina had worked out a plan with him. Should at any time Mirelle be in some sort of danger, Ronan was to take her immediately and covertly back to Emberly. He'd balked at that initially. For that was treason, stealing a King's daughter, that was kidnapping, and Ronan liked his neck attached to his body, and he also wanted to live the rest of his life freely, not in a dungeon. He suspected no amount of bargaining between King Rhutgard and his own father in Ghiverny would make up for kidnapping a royal daughter.

But the Lady of Emberly consoled him by telling him the King expected her to keep Mirelle safe at any cost, and she would intervene. After all, Mirelle would be safe at Emberly, as opposed to anywhere in the Palace. The entire reason for all of this was to protect the Royal bloodline, after all – daughters carried the bloodline truest, she reminded Ronan, and how could Mirelle do that from the Palace if some plot arose to harm her or worse?

So, unbeknownst to Mirelle, and indeed, her royal parents, a plan was ready to steal her off to Emberly if necessary.

Abruptly, Mirelle took in a deep breath and stared at a place inside the coach between Ronan and Kimbur. At the same time, the bumble of cobblestones they had been traveling on suddenly stopped and the horses started on a smooth pavement.

They had arrived at Fairview Palace.

Ronan stepped forward. He saw his uncle, somehow related, he knew, and his aunt, King Rhutgard and Queen Principea standing on the landing of gleaming landing of a back staircase.

Ronan knew this castle almost as well as he knew some of his own, for he'd spent so much of his time with his cousins, Keldrick and Kendrick here. He didn't recall this back staircase, but he enjoyed returning to what was a second home for him. Its highly glossed marble and gold trim, beautiful ornamented candelabras, all were welcome sights.

Ronan strode forward.

"Your Majesty Rhutgard, Your Majesty Principea." He bowed very low.

"Ah, Ronan," called Rhutgard. "You look more like your father each time I see you."

Ronan had only a glance at them but saw that age had treated them both kindly over the last few years.

Ronan bowed again for the courtesy. Then he called, "Your Majesties, I have the pleasure of introducing your royal daughter, Her Highness, Princess Mirelle Ginnessa Rochilda Firthing." Then he stepped back and held out an arm for Mirelle to move forward.

Ronan saw Rhutgard and Principea grin. Principea grabbed his arm and they laced hands.

Mirelle stepped forward daintily, her eyes staring up at her royal parents.

"Your Majesty. Your Majesty."

Then Mirelle dipped into a flawless curtsy before them.

Mirelle had met her parents.

Myrischka

They were a day out. She expected to be home by this evening. Myrischka wanted a hot bath, a warm fire, and her own bed. And decent food. She was content now that there was a time table for her new ships.

"Your Majesty, I – pardon, Your Majesty, I have a message for you." A courier was trotting alongside her.

Myrischka took in a deep breath and turned to stare at him. "Do you not see where I am?" She gestured to the wide expanse of snow, to the billowing banners at the front of her train, the men riding three by three before her to protect her, and the guard to either side of her.

"Begging all pardons, Your Majesty, I do. This was important enough that the man who gave it to me said it was urgent. He said you needed to see it immediately, so you could consider its contents on your way home."

Myrischka lifted an eyebrow. If nothing else, it sounded curious. She accepted the message and brushed the courier aside.

Her mouth dropped open at its contents. Well, well, well. "Go back," she told the courier, "and tell him he was right to send me word."

The courier set off immediately.

Oooooo. Rhutgard. The man was far slyer than she had credited him for.

This changed the gameboard dramatically....

Hewart

Ah. That was Sturgund.

"Father? You called for me?"

"I did, my son, I did. Here." Hewart waited until Sturgund slid into a seat before Hewart.

"Tell me what you make of this."

Sturgund looked mildly annoyed. "This isn't another tariff proposition, is it, Father? I've seen more of those than I ever care to."

Hewart told him, "Just *read* it." He waited in silence while his son read the words but enjoyed the different facial expression he suddenly took on.

Sturgund sat back in his chair, open-mouthed. "Is this for real? I mean, this is reliable?"

Hewart nodded. "By two different accounts, in fact."

Sturgund considered the long-term implications for a moment in silence, a serious look on his face.

Then he suddenly grinned and held the parchment up. "You haven't got another one of these stashed around anywhere that I should know about, have you Father?"

Kendrick

They hiked their way up the stairs.

"You have no idea what this is about?" asked Keldrick.

Kendrick shook his head. "No. Although if it's another meeting, I will scream. I'm *'just putting that out there for consideration,'*" and they laughed at the familiar phrase that lords used when they wanted their idea to be personally considered by the King, rather than turned around and around in an Assembly meeting.

Kendrick knew he, and Keldrick now as well, were being included in more and more of Father's duties as King so that they might learn more of their responsibilities as princes. But much as Kendrick appreciated Father finally trusting and respecting him enough, he missed his freedom.

The Crown Guards saluted and Keldrick pulled open the door to Father's solar.

"Ah. Boys. Well, my sons," said Father, who was standing behind his leather desk chair. "I suppose I will always consider you my boys, though you are grown now."

Kendrick shrugged noncommittally and was relieved to see no lords in the room. He did see Mother, however, that was odd. She stepped forward to join Father behind his chair.

Kendrick had started to sit down, but now he smelled a plot. He remained standing and stared at them. Keldrick stood before the desk as well.

"My sons, I would like you to meet… Princess Mirelle…"

A lovely girl who had been hiding in the far corner of the room strode gracefully forth. Lace trimmed with cloth of gold and embroidery covered a rose gown which brought out the blush of her cheeks, and her golden hair was arranged artfully atop her head. Dainty but yet she had a strength to her. She reminded Kendrick of his mother.

"…your younger sister," finished Father.

Kendrick's head jerked toward Father. "Our what?"
"Sister, did you say?" Keldrick asked at the same time.

"She was born at the same time you were," Mother said, with an enormous smile upon her face. In fact, Kendrick saw, her eyes were glistening…. "The two of you are her brothers. Twin brothers."

Keldrick looked lost. "How…?"

Even as shocked as he was, Kendrick never missed a chance to tease his brother. "It's a very simple process, really, Kel –"

Keldrick dug him in the ribs. "I know how, you prig, I just –"

Father took in deep breath and shook his head. To Mother, he said, "I had envisioned this going much better."

Kendrick finally asked, "Where – where? Where has she been all this time? I mean, why have we not known?"

Then he realized how rude he was being. "But I'm being so rude. Let me first welcome you… Sister." He bowed. The word seemed so odd on his tongue, *sister*. She, of course, had Father's eyes – *Romeny blue always breeds true*, Kendrick mused. And she looked just like Keldrick, but a female version. Or himself, that was to say.

She curtsied. "Thank you, Brother." Kendrick could hear the hesitation behind her speech and knew that the word *brother* was just as awkward for her as *sister* was for him.

Keldrick, of course, immediately welcomed her as well.

"If you knew then what was happening, you would know it was necessary. And much of it still is, current happenings of which I will speak to you about very soon. But a daughter's blood runs truest, and it was necessary."

"Of course, of course, Father." Kendrick recognized that tone as his Father getting irritated. As always, there was a disconnect between his brain and his tongue, however. "But where has she been all of this time?"

Keldrick prodded him in the ribs to stop talking.

Two things happened then – Father drew in breath to reply, with that look, that Royal *I will brook no disregard of my authority* look – and his new sister stepped forward. Clearing her throat just as Father started to say something, she said, *"She* is right here and need not have anyone speak over her."

Father blinked. He was not accustomed to being interrupted when he gave that *look.*

Kendrick would have successfully kept in his laughter. The look on Father's face –

was just – so comical. No one ever interrupted the Royal Fatherly "We" when he started on his supreme rampages and there he stood, interrupted and by his own daughter, no less. She'd taken the words right from his mouth, and he stood there, literally speechless. And if it were not for his damnable brother snorting, Kendrick would have kept a straight face, would never have burst into laughter....

Kendrick's new sister had yet to understand what she had just done.

"Boys," came a mild rebuke from Mother. Father had given up and looked to her, shaking his head.

"I think we may just have a new conspirator, Brother," Keldrick said to Kendrick as he outstretched his arm toward their new sister.

Mirelle smiled a little uncertainly.

They stopped laughing. Keldrick looked from her to Mother.

"She looks a lot like you, Ken, but she has Mother's face."

"You're an idiot, of course she looks like me, she's our twin. And Mother's daughter." Kendrick knocked his brother behind the head.

"Again, I have ears. I can hear you just fine."

"Oh, oh, right. So sorry about that," said Kendrick. Her lips were tightened and her blue eyes narrowed.

"Oooooo, she's got Mother's temper. Mother, you have a conspirator, now," laughed Keldrick.

"You idiot!" hissed Kendrick. He knocked Keldrick behind the head again.

Mother's eyes narrowed and her lips tightened, too.

And Father laced his hands atop his head and walked toward the window, saying *"Bloody hell."*

A'dair

"Your Majesty?"

Still, A'dair did not answer to that immediately. His first impulse was to turn and look for his father in the room.

"Yes. What is it?"

"Your Coronation details for next week. Also," and the man cleared his throat rather stiffly.

A'dair stood up and looked him in the eye. "Finish your statement."

"The list of marriageable women in the south you required, primarily Coral City." He handed A'dair a parchment of women's names and details.

"Thank you, if that's all, you may go." A'dair had been so busy with his father's burial and full assumption of royal duties that marriage had not taken place within the month that his father had asked. But he had immediately begun arrangements for ship construction in Billoughby Bay, and quietly.

He was frankly amazed at how many of Father's advisors believed there to be peace throughout all the Land. A'dair would be replacing a full half of the Cabinet, if not more, for he wanted his own staff in place. The problem was finding men of equal qualification and standing to take over the empty posts.

A'dair was also wrestling with the idea that a Cabinet run his Kingdom. That men run his Kingdom rather than him – well, was he King or no? He felt there was going to be a shake-up in how things were run, and very few people would appreciate it.

The first complaint at the top of the list would be, he knew, "But, Your Majesty, it's just not tradition." And the second would be the guilt stab, "But, Your Majesty, this isn't how your father ran things."

A'dair grew exhausted just thinking about his responses to those objections.

People were already horrified at the thought of him marrying so soon. And certainly, so was he. He, of course, had expected at some distant point in time, to wed, have children.... But within just months? And he was of the same mind of the people. So soon after his father's death, it was unfitting. But it had been one of his father's last wishes, and he would not go back on that.

And so he scanned the roster of marriageable women. A'dair groaned. Some of them were old enough to be his mother.... Who of them were at all seemly enough to sit the throne beside him, give S'hendalow a continued legacy of heirs? Who, he wondered, were at all comely in any way? Securing a continued legacy did require a little something specific to get out of the gate, much less win the race.

At least at his Coronation, he would be able to view them. Imagine, shopping for a wife during his Coronation just three months past his father's death. He couldn't be much more unbecoming than that. What the history chronicles would say of him, he mused.

Hopefully, they would say that he turned the entire kingdom upside down, shook out the spies like pepper from salt, and protected his people from all the war with his fantastic new warships, and that he had an amazing brood of children with his beautiful Queen.

"Your Majesty," came another servant at A'dair's side, shaking him from his wonderful reverie. What a nice daydream….

"Yes…."

"This may be of interest to you."

A'dair retrieved the parchment from the silver platter and dismissed the servant. Many of his father's informants, at a loss, A'dair supposed, as to what to do, continued to send him information as they had his father. Although A'dair wondered how many no longer served S'hendalow now that his father had passed on.

He smoothed the parchment open and took a tired breath, expecting some trivial tidbit.

"What?" he breathed aloud.

A'dair knew the Eastern Shield was canny, but he would never have guessed on this. Well, he mused, daughters did carry the bloodline truest.

Then he snorted. Maybe he should marry this new Romeny princess. Wouldn't that piss off the Northern Countries….

Theldry

"I don't know why he lets her in there."

"Nor do I. A woman, after all –"

"Not even, still a girl."

"What is he thinking, letting her in like that –"

"They think her cute, you know."

"Harrumph. Just wait until she counters them at the table. How does she know – she just always seems to know…."

"Like the iron shipments. Who have you told about that, I'd like to know?"

"Me? I was going to ask you the same – I've told no one at all but you, fool. So why would she propose raising customs duties on incoming iron and steel?"

"Did you see the look on Lord Darnish's face when she proposed creating a new Bill of Entry register, one that would catalogue each and every item aboard the ships specifically, so that nothing might get left out, *'for the good of our Tortoreen'*?

"How much has he been skimming all these years? I thought he'd be sick on the floor right there." Rolling laughter.

"I don't know, but his wife and daughters might – the very best of fashions – quite a lot of silk finds its way off those boats." Sniggering.

"She needs to removed. She shouldn't be in there –" came the last remark as boots disappeared down the corridor.

Theldry, who had been flattened against the wall, suppressed a triumphant grin as she glanced around the corner.

Theldry had become quite the sleuth. She had learned the art of invisibility. Following others about and listening to their conversations as she just had was more difficult that she imagined it was for other people, for she was a Princess, and dressed as one. Servants would stop to bow or curtsy and "Your Highness" her in the corridor, which, of course, ruined whatever she was listening to, for then they would run off. And the servants were beginning to think her a bit odd, for she was always standing up against walls.

Which was how she found out about the new daughter who'd been hidden away all these years in Romeny. What Theldry wouldn't give for a new sister suddenly....

But Theldry found out information on these horrible Council Members one way or another. When she could not follow them about in the Palace, she started throwing small garden parties, and invited their wives. Whom, of course, Theldry spent a good deal of time speaking with, drawing information from in all innocence.

And of course, Lord Darnish was sneaking a good deal of extra materials in off his ships in the harbor, including silk dresses, Lady Darnish confided after just a bit of wine as a secret between "us ladies."

Theldry's mother was thrilled at her daughter's lovely behavior, but, Theldry knew, if only she were aware of Theldry's true intentions. Theldry's actual motives were as impure as the men whom she sought to bring down. And she smiled just a little again.

Her new lady friends would invite her to their homes in response, and so Theldry had the chance to remark on all that she saw in the Councilors' personal estates, remarking on how much they had on a Councilor's income, which on two occasions left the wives curious. The third brushed it off airily, for they both came from money and her husband serving as a Council Member was merely a favor to the King, and a bit of a social hike.

Theldry had rolled her eyes privately, for this was the exact type of woman she hoped never to become. She really hadn't thought of herself as a girl anymore. She was attending Council Meetings regularly and even if not considered a complete equal, she was given the floor whenever she wanted to speak. And they never liked what she had to say, for Theldry always worked ahead of time to find out their secrets, then prepared full counteractions for Council.

Holding garden parties wasn't a favorite activity of hers, but if it gleaned the information she could use in Council, then it was a necessary sufferance. And men never actually recognized that their wives had attended parties with Theldry – for if they had, they would know the culprit, the actual root of their downfall. But men never thought of women beyond their little parties and their embroidery and their paper fans.

How Theldry would enjoy the next Council Meeting....

———⌒⚬⌒———

"Mother? Father? You wished to see me?"

Theldry stood before them in their favorite balcony. They took most of their private meals here. Breakfast they insisted on eating with her and Bronn.

Theldry could no longer stand to look at any of them. Bronn, for obvious reasons. But her father – he knew all of what was occurring, here in Tortoreen, his kingdom, and he, as King Almeric, did nothing at all. Nothing. That just horrified her. Disgusted her, in fact, Theldry thought, and now she could no longer bear to look at him, for she had no respect for him.

And her mother, who meant so very well as a gracious lady, and performed so very well at it.... Theldry thought of her mother as a... a mouse. A mouse – perhaps she had a brain, but she had never used it, for she had been told all her life that, because she was a woman, she was not supposed to use it, at least not for anything other than setting up invitations, choosing gowns, and noting which of the Court were seemly and unseemly company. Theldry loved her mother, of course, but never wanted to be like her.

"Theldry, we have wonderful news for you!" Her mother's green eyes sparkled and her hands were clasped together.

Then her father, reclined back in his chair, told her, "Yes, my dear, you have finally gotten what you have always dreamed of...."

Theldry experienced a second of confusion – she couldn't think of anything she had always dreamed of....

"...you are to be married. And soon, I might add," her father finished.

None of it registered. Theldry heard his words, but they didn't sink in.

Married? Was that what he had said?

"Oh, Theldry, isn't it marvelous?" Her mother clapped her hands with excitement.

Theldry's mouth was open. No! No! Not... not *now!*

Her father harrumphed. "Look at the girl. You'd think she'd be happier."

"Oh, she's just in shock," her mother patted her father's arm.

But things – were just falling into – place! She couldn't marry – *now!*

"Who – who is it?" Theldry finally asked. It was so surreal. She licked her lips.

"He's a Duke, over in Corstarordan."

"Yes," rolled her father's voice.

Did he sound smug, Theldry suddenly wondered....

"He's a fine man, a Duke. Older man, but he's a good man. He's just lost his wife, but he'll treat you kindly. He's over on the sea there, so you'll still have a breath of ocean air." Then he cocked his head at Theldry. "You know Corstarordan. You've been fighting for them in Council. Now will be your chance to really make a difference, Theldry."

Again, she detected a note of smugness in his voice. She had been sold – merely because of political pressure. She blinked. Swallowing, Theldry asked,

"And – when is the wedding?"

"Two months. You're to be married in two months," her father told her. His face was stone.

Theldry's breath was taken away. Months? Two? Months? It was always a year, at least.

"You've been waiting so long, dear, aren't you happy?" Her mother got up and embraced her.

"Oh. Ever so...."

———

Back in her chambers – for Mother could not resist accompanying her back to her chambers – Mother told her more of what the next two months would entail. Theldry believed wholeheartedly that Mother was more excited about this betrothal than she ever would be.

"But – Mother.... An older man – in Corstarordan? Could it not be someone more local? Someone in Tortoreen, perhaps, or even S'hendalow? We have a relationship with S'hendalow. And they have a new King, he's unmarried. Why would Father not send me to S'hendalow, where his Princess could be a Queen, rather than to some old Duke, where I'll be some out-of-the-way Duchess...."

Which was, of course, why he was sending her to Corstarordan... to be as far out of the way as he could get her. Theldry would shrivel up and grow old out there, with some pruned-up old man who'd lost his old, pruned-up wife.... Surely, Father knew how terrible he was being. Someone, someone on the Council had forced him to do this.... Her eyes narrowed.

"No, my dear," Mother patted her cheek. "We already have a relationship with S'hendalow. Undoubtedly, that is why he did not send a betrothal inquiry."

Well that, that – that just made no sense at all, Theldry fumed. A king who doesn't want his own daughter to be Queen of a neighboring country?

Ha. That was exactly it. Father knew that Theldry knew everything about Tortoreen and would level his Council once she was given the first spit of power as a Queen, even if in name only.

No wonder Father was sending her to the other side of the Coastals, she fumed. Well, once she got her legs under her over there, she would see that he and Tortoreen got exactly what he had coming to it.

She could have been Queen. What a perfect arrangement that would have been…. Maybe she'd work her way into the Court of Corstarorden…. And even make friends with the new S'hendalow king. *Oh, Father, what a mistake you've just made….*

———

Mother had declared that Theldry as no longer a Princess, but a woman betrothed, and so all her garden parties and other social engagements were, as of now, canceled. And certainly, all of her guests would understand and rejoice for Theldry, as this occasion only came along once in a young woman's life. Theldry had rolled her eyes behind her mother's back.

"And that includes those dreadful Council Meetings, too, my dear. They're not fitting for a woman," she held Theldry's hand and looked at her sternly. "We have much to plan now, and you'll have no time for such unseemly pursuits. You don't want your husband-to-be to hear of such activities so soon before your wedding, now, do you?"

Theldry put on a pleasing smile. "No, Mother."

Her mother hugged her. "That's my darling girl. Now, we have so many details to work out – of course, your gown…."

She nodded and shook her head, smiled and laughed when required as if in a daze.

Then her mother said something that broke through. "And, of course," and cleared her throat delicately, "we'll have those *ladies* stay with you so you can," Mother coughed, "practice, of course."

Theldry stared at Mother. "Ladies? What practice?"

Mother had turned a delicate shade of pink and her hands fluttered at her throat. "Well, you see, *those* ladies." She drew in a breath. "Theldry, dear," and Mother covered her mouth with a hand.

"These ladies will teach you – about – well, pleasing a man. Because, of course, you need to know that, before the actual wedding night, don't you dear. Oh my, it's hot in here, isn't it?" And Mother shook her fan out and fanned herself, looking across the room from Theldry.

Theldry suddenly realized what her mother was referring to and reddened herself. "No, *Mother* – I don't want any such – *ladies* – staying here with me. Gods! Ugh! Mother!"

"I'm sorry, dear, it's tradition."

"Tradition? Who turned *that* into a bloody tradition? A man, I'm sure! And no! Don't send anyone to my chambers!"

"Theldry, how dare you curse! Never, ever curse!" Mother was horrified.

"Mother, can we just continue with the wedding details, please!" Theldry begged.

"Yes, dear, of course."

Theldry had received permission to walk through the Market Place, to enjoy the flowers and the breezes and the salt of the ocean on the cliffs before she had to leave, as long as she went with Palace Guards.

The salty air blew her hair from her face as she turned her face to the sun. She took in long breaths of fresh air. Would it smell the same in Corstarorden?

In just three weeks, she would be a married woman. Married to some dried-up old prune. She didn't even know how old the Duke was, nor was she being told, she suspected, on purpose.

In fact, Theldry suspected a lot of this entire betrothal on purpose. Just a two-month betrothal before the wedding? That was unseemly if anything. That only happened when people thought you were with child. If it wasn't for the fact that Theldry and the Duke had never met, and that the Duke was on the other side of the Coastals, and, of course, that he was some blind, deaf, wretched old man, Theldry sulked, then people would, of course, think her with child.

Well, they would be disappointed to find out that she wasn't at all with child, nor would she lose her figure. In fact, she doubted her marriage would even be consummated.

She and her ladies-in-waiting had all whispered of tales of using chicken's blood upon the wedding sheets, to make it seem as if the groom really had – well – taken the bride's virginity. They did that if the woman wasn't a virgin, and of course, if the man never fulfilled the evening's requirements.

Spinning the handle of her parasol idly, Theldry wondered whether she would need to hide some chicken's blood away to do the same, for if drunken Lords came to in to stand outside the door, they might be bored, for her groom might pass out atop her. If she could only find out which bed would be the wedding bed, she could hide the sack of chicken blood there....

Such an awful outlook for the start of her marriage....

And then she was shoved aside – a man flung himself in front of her, and Theldry saw the silver of a blade slash down, once, twice. She nearly fell over into the cart behind her, breathless. Blood flew into the air.

Theldry stumbled on the hem of her gown, trying to stand straight. Her basket fell to the white-washed cobbles and fruit rolled everywhere.

A man in a neutral colored tunic and a black vest turned around. "Were you hurt?"

"No, I, no –" Theldry's breath was coming in short gasps. Those men had – tried to kill her? But why?

"Good."

But the man before her – blood spread across his arm quickly. He'd saved her, stepped before her while two men had tried to kill her. He bent down and picked up one of the knives. As he stood up, she saw another slash across his chest growing red from the blood flowing freely beneath it.

"You're hurt – you're terribly hurt!" she told him, appalled.

"Come –" and the man grasped her arm. He pulled her behind the vendor's cart. "Hold that up," he said, gesturing to Theldry's parasol.

"But – you're wounded –"

"I've had worse," he said dryly as he pulled out some strips of cloth from his rucksack. As he tied the wound on his arm, he glanced up at her. "What are you doing, walking around the Market Place without any protection?"

He yanked the strip of cloth off and then pulled his tunic up.

All Theldry saw was blood running down from an open wound, running into his trousers. He immediately began dabbing at it.

Then he looked straight at Theldry in the eyes. Theldry saw he had what was left of a black eye. "You're not afraid of blood, are you? Not going to pass out?"

Theldry took in a deep breath then, more out of defiance than anything. She'd just never been so close to a man before. An idle part of her thought – *oh, if Mother saw her now....*

"No, I've just never – seen it before. What can I do to help?" She reached out a hand, but he slapped it back.

"Just what you need – to go back up there –" and he jerked her head in the direction of the Palace "with blood on your hands. No, you just keep that parasol up." He found a long wrap of cloth and wrapped it around himself. "That'll have to do for now.

"So – these Palace Guards of yours. Did you, by chance, dismiss them? Because there wasn't a single Guard to be seen in the square. Not one." The man's gray eyes stared steadily at Theldry.

Her mouth dropped open. "What? But there were four! Where did they go?"

"Well, I suggest, Your Highness, that the first thing you do, is get back to that Palace. Immediately. And don't leave it." He stood and held his arm out to pull her up.

"You knew? Who I was? How did you know?"

He looked up to the sky, then back to her. "Let's just say I have a knack for these things and leave it at that.

"I'll follow you back to the Palace and make sure you arrive safe, but after that, I'm gone."

"But, but you're terribly hurt," Theldry protested. "We have Healers, and you've just saved my life, my parents will want to meet you –"

"No, no thank you, though the invitation is appreciated. The farther from a castle I am, the better I feel. Obviously, someone wants you out of the castle. Why would that be, as you are just a Princess?"

Theldry flared, "I am not *'just a Princess'*. I've made a lot of people very uncomfortable of late – oh...."

The man snorted. "You don't say."

"Well, I've been attending Council Meetings lately, and –"

"Really? Your father, allowing you, a Princess, to attend Council Meetings? That's a first, I'd have to say."

"Well, he never really got a say in it. They liked me being there at first. Then I found out everything they were actually involved in, and I moved to stop it all. And so, my father has me betrothed to some ancient old lord across the Coastals, just to get rid of me and make them happy." She sighed.

He sounded interested behind her. "What sorts of things do you find out?"

"Well, for instance, that the white fish in Emerald Lake and the ocean fish off the docks cost exactly the same, pound for pound, but I discovered that for myself - certain Council Members are vying for a higher market price on lake fish when there's no difference at all actually. I countered them in Council when I found out. I also found out there was no blight on the Corstarordan vegetables, even though they wanted to impose a higher tax on incoming vegetables. Three ships owned by a Council Member don't report all of what's actually brought in, so I proposed a new Bill of Entry register. Incoming iron is supposed to line their pockets as well. A few other things from their wives."

"Really...." Her new protector sounded fascinated. "And who has your father betrothed you to?"

"A sudden two-month betrothal to some old lord who lost his wife, on the Corstarordan Coast." Theldry gestured helplessly. "I'm fifteen. Who knows how old he is?"

"Really," said her protector. "I mistook you for fourteen. A brave fourteen, at that, but all the same. And extremely gifted. I'm sorry to hear of your upcoming nuptials. Hmm."

"What?"

"Curious, rather. A young, attractive, unmarried King in S'hendalow? Did that not work out? Perfect arrangement, I should think."

"Father didn't want me going there. He said that we already have arrangements with S'hendalow."

"Hmm. Well, it seems you have angered someone enough to take attempt on your life, Your Highness. Stay in your rooms. And watch the Guards."

"What about all the people coming for the wedding? How will I know who to trust?" Theldry worried.

The man chuckled. "Want to put a knife in their back? Have the wedding at the Duke's estate. Leave right away. A princess killed on her way to her wedding? All too odd – no one would believe it. The people who attempted your life today – they know everything about this place. Its people, the Market Place, you, the Guards.... If I were you, I'd change your plans immediately. It just might save your life.

"And you are nearly at your Palace as we speak."

"What is your name? You've saved my life, and I don't even know your name." Theldry turned and looked at the man with the fading black eye. She wondered if she had seen him in the Market Place before, for he seemed familiar. He reminded her of someone she knew, somehow, but whom?

"Well, I've had a number of names." He snorted a bit. "The most recent one, probably the most appropriate one, is *Rogue*."

"*Rogue!* That's awful! You've just saved my life! Are you sure you won't come in then? You are wounded, and from saving my life...." Theldry implored over her shoulder.

"Oh, quite. Quite sure."

"Whom should I tell about this? What if I tell no one?"

"Well, if you suddenly turn your wedding plans upside down, you should have a reason, shouldn't you? You should go immediately to your father. And, I'm sure, your mother. Any idea who might have ordered this attempt on your life, Your Highness?"

A terrible thought crossed Theldry's mind and she looked high up at the top of the Palace.

"What if it was my father?"

Selby

"And..." This was far, far worse than she had dreamed. This. This was a nightmare. No.

"Your Majesty?" Durain wasn't sure what to say.

"This is all – reliable?"

"Our source nearly died getting this information through." Durain's voice was quiet.

The Gods hated her. They must, Selby knew. Bad enough she was now an orphan, running a country alone.

Storden, centuries-old neutral country to her immediate South was building both an Army and a Navy.

It was thought, though not verified, that the new S'hendalow King was building a new Navy.

The Ormish Queen, widely believed to have killed her son and husband in order to take power, was planning to launch her four hundred warships within months and building one hundred more. She was amassing troops as Selby stood here.

And Ambsellon, as always, would add its might to Ormon, which would mean at least seven hundred warships were headed to Clemongard in just months. That was just Navy. And Selby had no timetable for a meager Navy of scanty means.

Selby had no knowledge of war. Her father had exceled at war strategy, tactics…. Her father had also been trained for this office. She leaned her arms on the balcony guard rail and hid her head inside them. Why? Why not some other ruler? Why not some other country?

"I need men," she said aloud. "I have no hope to retaliate in war against battle troops in that amount. I only now have Crown Guards up to capacity from the Twenty Years War." She shook her head.

"You have Ericorian, Your Majesty."

Selby stood up and looked up Durain. "How many Ericorian does Clemongard have?" She needed to distinguish between her and Clemongard, for Ericorian fought for Clemongard, not just for her. They were not her personal guards.

"Sixty thousand the last I knew."

Selby stared at Durain. "Did you say sixteen or sixty thousand?" Undoubtedly, she had heard him wrong.

"The latter, Your Majesty."

She leaned against the balcony, facing him. "Well, that helps quite a bit. Quite a lot, I should say. I thought it was far less, something like fifteen or twenty thousand."

Durain said, "We purposely mislead people for circumstances just such as these. We always have men in training."

She was silent for a few moments.

"Well, I am afraid that Clemongard may soon have need of her Ericorian."

Selby looked at every one of her Council Members as they sat at her wooden Council Table. Today would be an historic day, she knew. And not one she wanted. At least her Coronation was over, so she was truly and fully Queen.

She took in a deep breath. "My lords. Today will be a long Assembly, I fear. I have had refreshment brought in for you to avail yourselves of. Cold chicken, grapes, other assorted fruits, cheeses, and bread of course...."

They would wait until she ate before they chose something to eat, but now they were all curious, she saw.

"I know you all have propositions and other such parchments of interest that you would like for me to see, and ultimately, that you wanted this Council to consider, but I will go over those at my own leisure. Send them down to me now." Selby rose and gestured for her Council Members to slide their parchments to her down the table.

Immediately some of them became defensive and others irritable, but, as it was ultimately her vote that cast the approval, it really did not matter whether they turned it about endlessly in Assembly or not. A few of them sent their proposals down with a sullen glare and others sat back in their seats with curiosity.

Selby stacked her carefully inked proposals and set them on the side table.

Then she stood. "This Council Meeting is now in adjournment. I now call to order our first War Council."

Selby looked down and watched the expressions on each Councilor's face register shock. For a few instants, only silence hung in the air.

Once the clamoring began, Selby tuned them out and waited until there was silence again.

"A War Council?" huffed Lord Wharfstead to her right. Selby had often found him her adversary during Council Meetings. "We haven't had a War Council in nearly twenty years, Your Majesty."

"Nor have we needed to, Lord Wharfstead," Selby answered smoothly, "as we haven't had any wars." She locked eyes with him until he frowned and looked away.

"If I may, Your Majesty?"

Lord Barstann now took the place of the previous Council Member who had refused to put bridges up where she had asked him to.

Selby held a hand out to acknowledge him.

"While we're all aware we've not had a war in nearly twenty years, is there a war that is bringing us to this council together now?"

"Excellent question, Lord Barstann." This was the reason she had appointed him. "And the answer to your question is... yes."

And Selby took her seat amidst yet another chorus of clamoring.

Once it was silent again, Selby steepled her hands on the elaborate wooden table. "It may surprise you to learn a few things. For example, Lady Ormon – which I think we all know is a kind expression for her – has four hundred warships that she's planning on launching within just months. Another one hundred warships should be ready in about six more months. And her troops, I'm told, which are four to our one, have amassed.

"Naturally, Ambsellon usually joins its Navy to Ormon's and so, at the least, we can expect... 700 warships sailing toward Clemongard within the next six months. I don't have a current number on King Hewart's troops, but in the last war, they were three to our one.

"Of most interest, and possibly even more concern, is Storden. Hundreds of years neutral – they have been our neighbor, and upon occasion, an ally of sorts. Storden now has a full Navy and a full Army. Other than that which they keep to protect itself. I'm told a guess at their troops might be two to our one, though their troops are on the move, and we know not where.

"I even have a report, more of a candid sighting and not something too much of concern just yet, that the new King of S'hendalow has built more warships.

"Frankly, my lords, this reeks of havoc," Selby finished.

Again, the room was silent.

Lord Garrath finally asked, "And these reports of yours, Your Majesty, are they from credible sources?"

She nodded. "The most. In fact, one nearly died getting some of this information to me."

It was too quiet. Well, who knew what they were thinking. She herself had been repeatedly shocked with each report, but to get all of that bad news in one sitting....

She pulled the board of cold chicken closer to her and selected a few grapes. Still nothing. Selby popped a grape in her mouth.

"Come, my lords, I have never known you to not have an opinion."

She popped another grape in her mouth.

"How do we know that Ormon is even headed toward us?"

"How do we know Ambsellon is going to join them?"

"How do you know Ormon is leaving any time soon?"

Selby started to slice a piece of cold chicken but stopped.

Just as she took in a breath to answer some of her Councilors' questions, Lord Wharfstead at her side laughed heartily. He said, "So you've had reports of a wolf. You only know there's a wolf. You don't know anything about the wolf, only that there is a wolf. And now you want to call a War Council?"

Selby kept her temper in check. The pompous bastard. "I'd rather take care of the wolf before it attacks me. As long as I know there is a wolf, I'm going to do something about it, not sit around and hope it doesn't head my way. Wolves do hunt in packs, after all. Where there's one wolf, there's sure to be another."

Lord Wharfstead snorted and shook his head. "I don't know, Your Majesty. There may be no need for this War Council. Rhetoric in the Council Chamber is one thing –"

That was it.

Selby took hold of the cleaver she'd been cutting with, hurled it upward, and slammed it down into the Council Chamber table, just inches from Lord Wharfstead's fingers.

It had sunk into the wood, and his eyes popped out at just how close the blade had come to missing his fingertips.

"Lord Wharfstead, you have disrespected your country and its Queen for the last time. You will either stay in this War Council and offer advice worthy of a Council Member and Lord of standing, or you will go home to your estates, hereby thus removed of all titles and entitlements, including your lordship. All income will be revoked, you and your families' estates will be hereby denied you and taken back by the Crown, and you shall be banished from Clemongard. Permanently. If you cannot protect the country you sit here in Council for, you will be banished."

Selby's face was stern and her arms crossed.

"That is also offered to the rest of you who sit at my Council Table."

Every eye was on her.

Except Lord Wharfstead, who stared still at the cleaver. "By the gods," he breathed. "You have your father in you. You have your grandfather in you, Your Majesty." He swallowed and looked around the table. "Do any of you recall what her grandfather was called?"

Many of them smiled, albeit nervously.

"The Cleaver King."

"We have a Cleaver Queen," roared Lord Wharfstead. "By the gods, we have a War Council. Let's get down to it!"

———

Selby knew what they were calling her. "The Cleaver Queen." After her grandfather, King Rorbann. They started calling him that during the Ambsellon/Ormon Clemongard skirmishes, for his favorite weapon of choice became the cleaver, when soldiers set upon his camp unexpectedly while they'd taken time to eat. Reports listed Grandfather as having killed eight enemy soldiers with his cleaver alone in camp, and so he considered the cleaver as his good luck weapon from that point on, carrying one at his belt everywhere he went. Of course, he also swung a broadsword as well, but he became known by all of Clemongard as the Cleaver King.

And now, Selby knew that everywhere her Councilors went, they would be spreading the word, particularly Lord Wharfstead, that they now had a Cleaver Queen. She supposed it could be worse. Lord Wharfstead, formerly her long-term adversary, was now her fiercest advocate and loyal subject.

Selby was certainly glad of it, for he held Clemongard's southernmost ports and even a number of ships there.

Lord Barstann, she was pleased with. Articulate and intelligent, he was a fierce advocate of the Riverlands, both the Roarnebourke and the Trellis, where his predecessor had only known the Roarnebourke. Selby's bridges were already standing, in fact. Barstann, when approached, offered insight and ideas, but had not wanted to leave his post as Riverlands Administrator. Why had he not been approached before for his expertise, and indeed, this post altogether, Selby wondered.

In fact, he hadn't wanted to leave "his rivers." It was then that Selby appointed him as Council Member. Lord Barstann only agreed if he could still approve how "his rivers" were being overseen in his absence. Selby had been impressed at the man's insistence, for most men would have jumped at the chance to become a Clemongard Council Member. She had found herself negotiating and agreed to allow him a certain amount of time per month to travel to the Riverlands to see that they were being maintained properly by a deputy administrator of his choice in his absence.

So Lord Barstann also had balls as well, for he stood up to not only Her Majesty of Clemongard, but Lord Wharfstead, and Selby wasn't sure which a man should be more intimidated of. However, the two worked well together, which at this point in time would be crucial.

In fact, during Assembly, Lord Barstann offered an excellent point.

"If I may, Your Majesty –"

Selby acknowledged him with an outstretched arm.

"It may be that my predecessor did not want bridges to be erected because he knew that soldiers would be traveling east, or perhaps west, upon the rivers. May I suggest then, that Crown Guards be posted at each bridge, along with perhaps, an honorable Ericorian, to discourage – ahem – well, any unsavory activity?"

Selby recognized to what Lord Barstann referred – bribery of the Guards, or even the killing of them and taking over of their uniforms. Ericorian present would certainly discourage such behavior. "Absolutely. Have the bridges modified with gates so that no one can come or go without approval, and I want two Ericorian present, one on each side. Get started immediately."

"Also, Your Majesty, something I considered –" began Lord Barstann.

"By all means, please continue." Selby wanted to smirk at this point, for her new bridges were going to anger a lot of people... she only wished she knew who.

"This idea is only a notion, not necessarily something at all possible. I –" and he looked to Lord Wharfstead, who suddenly looked interested, "realized that our rivers have no bridges of consequence where the sea enters them, merely ports and ferries. Would it not behoove us, particularly with such Naval activity as we are like to see soon, to build some very impressive bridges at the mouths of both the Trellis and Roarnebourke? To discourage incoming soldiers from the sea, of course? This would be a project Lord Wharfstead and I would work on easily," and he turned to Lord Wharfstead briefly.

Selby smiled slyly, for she loved the idea. "How many men will you need to accomplish this within the month? I will supply you with whatever coin is required, and you will, of course, send me ongoing reports of your progress. Guards and Ericorian both will accompany you."

She had downplayed the amount of the Ericorian by half, just a precaution, for she had had a spy at her very own Council Table once before feeding information to the enemy, and she would not risk sending out such specifics again.

Her former Councilor now sat in a Treason Cell below the Palace in the Royal Dungeon. If he died of poor conditions down there, Selby wouldn't care a spit. Since her first impulse had been to draw and quarter him, then her second to crush him into a small enough ball and toss him from a trebuchet over to King Hewart, Selby believed the bastard was making out quite well, as he had a roof, four walls, and regular meals. And if there were rats down there, then he could rejoice in spending time with those of his own kind.

As for those to whom he reported, they all smiled a new smile, a red one, and laid deep down in the earth where no one would ever tell them secrets again.

The problem, she explained to her Assembly, was that they had to act on the belief that they would be attacked from both east and west, and possibly even the south now.

Which meant that they had to divide their forces to the east and west. What Navy Clemongard had could not hope to withstand such an attack as what might be leveled against them.

Her Council agreed that they had to operate with the worst scenario in place, but consider other scenarios as well. Selby instructed them to reach out to strategists whom they trusted, both Naval and Army, and war in general.

Selby told them outright, "My lords, you and I both know that I have no knowledge in the art of war, though I would not call it an art but the atrocity of war, for that is what it is. Name it as it is. While soldiers fight soldiers, the people of our towns, villages, and cities are killed, their livelihoods destroyed, sickness and plague run rampant as bodies pile up, and men, women and children all over the country starve. While soldiers consider war an art, I as Clemongard's Queen consider it an atrocity.

"And make no mistake, I, as Clemongard's Queen, will fight this war as an atrocity, not an art, for it is my duty to consider all of my people, not just my soldiers in battle. See that, in the coming months, when we strategize and plan tactics, you keep that in mind.

"I shall also fight this war to win, for it matters not that I am young, Queen, inexperienced, or naïve to war tactics. Clemongard will never fall while I have breath in my body.

"Because of this, and because we are desperately out-numbered, I have already sent word to Romeny, asking for an alliance request. Obviously, I could have simply sent my congratulations on their new daughter – however, our need is more dire.

"We have allied with the Eastern Alliance in wars past, though not recently. I hope they will consider that. I know, my lords, how proud we in Clemongard are, but there is a difference between being proud and being smart.

"The Eastern Alliance is accustomed to fighting Ormon and Ambsellon, as are we. We can share information, such as what we know of Storden, what we know of Ormon and Ambsellon, should they not already know it, that is. Such an alliance would only prove fruitful for both of us. I am waiting, as we speak, for a return answer."

Not a sound. Her Council Room was silent as they stared at her. It was a lot to take in, Selby admitted. She actually had not sent word to Romeny yet, for she wanted Durain's informants – her spies now, she supposed, to follow whoever panicked and immediately ran to some unknown source with this information, or any of it. She hoped none of them would, but if so, well, certainly there were more empty Treason Cells in the Royal Dungeon....

After the Assembly was over, Selby looked down at the cleaver stuck in her Council Table. She nodded to herself. Cleaver Queen. She sniffed and shrugged. Why not? Selby took hold of the cleaver handle and pulled.

Well, it had certainly gone in much easier than it was coming out. She rolled her eyes, wondering if the Ericorian behind her were holding back laughter. She drew in a breath, then heaved the damn thing out of the table, where a deep wedge was left behind. Selby turned the blade over. Bits of wood clung to it. Cleaver Queen. Very well. She'd have a thong made and have it hung at her side as Grandfather had worn his. That should make for interesting portraits....

Selby wanted to go up to her chambers, dismiss all her maids, ladies-in-waiting, Ericorian, and just cry. Just fall on her bed, and cry into her pillows. She wasn't even eighteen, and she had no family, she was running a country, and now she was going to be fighting a war.... Alone, with no guidance at all.

Other rulers, of course, took over thrones amidst or at the start of wars, Selby knew. But they had wives, or even Regents if necessary, and they had been trained their whole lives for such a thing, tactics, politics, strategy.... Selby didn't even own a suit of armor.

She dismissed all her servants and her Ericorian, who looked skeptical. Selby finally told them, "Then – go down to the ends of the corridor – I want total privacy!"

They immediately bowed and obeyed.

Selby stood and looked about her personal chamber, warmed by a quiet, crackling fire. Her father had been an excellent tactician – he should be doing this, not her.

She stared at her bed, where the plump pillows lay, inviting her.

Selby grabbed an ivory bust next to her and hurled it at the stone wall, where it exploded into chunks and pieces – screaming as loud as she could.

Harvick

Canny old man, Rhutgard. Hiding away a daughter. That hadn't been done in, what, decades. He couldn't remember the last time, not recently, that someone had done that, either a son or a daughter. Harvick understood why, of course, preserving the bloodline through the daughter.

Harvick wished he had a daughter, or another son even, of age to spring out of hiding suddenly. That would be sure to piss of Varley. Oh, the jealousy.... Of course, knowing Varley as he was coming to, Harvick would have to lock this other son or daughter in their chamber all day, every day, or they would find themselves dead at the bottom of stairwell, having suddenly "slipped"....

That was right after the Twenty Years War, mused Harvick. What made Rhutgard decide to do such a thing.... He pulled the most recent book of history from his shelf and blew the dust from its leather. He knew next to nothing about Eastern history besides its changing of the guards, who fought whom during what war....

Harvick cut a few slices of bread, loaded his plate with cheese and fruit, and poured a goblet of wine. He pulled his boots off and laid back upon the chaise lounge next to one of his chamber windows.

Well, well, well, Eastern Shield, Harvick thought as he thumbed through the History of the Era book. Finally, he arrived at Romeny.

Damn. Rhutgard's first wife and child died before she was fully to term. His next wife, while with child, was entirely bedridden and gave birth early, during which she died. His father, King Galvin, died while choking on a fish bone, of all the bloody things.

Rhutgard remarried once more and had two more – well, now the history would need to be updated, - three more children, two twin boys and a triplet girl. That was quite a line of succession.

Still, a bit dramatic – possibly simply coincidental – to be sending a daughter off so mysteriously. Was he reaching? Actually, in speaking of mystery, Harvick hadn't heard a thing of Rhutgard's first son – ah, there was his name, Merridon. Crown Prince. All it listed in the History was "Served 2 Years Posted in the Royal Romeny Army."

Harvick rose an eyebrow. That was all? For a Crown Prince? All first-born princes were expected to serve a tour of duty in the military, be it Army or Navy. Even Varley had served his two years of duty. In fact, now Harvick's eldest twin son, Tollard, would be expected to serve, since he would be the new heir to the throne. Though when it was written, "posted," it was a euphemism for "served somewhere that little or no action would be seen."

For Kendrick and Keldrick Firthing, numerous listings were inked in, such as "Assisted with Flooding Victims of Ivy Gate After Storms" and "Assisted in Building of MantleTown Hospice After Plague."

Harvick sighed. What would they write of Varley's accomplishments? Impregnating whores? Dismissing servants for bowing improperly? Importing massive amounts of silk? He swallowed several more sips of wine.

Since he had the book before him, Harvick decided to flip through the entries of other Shield countries.

His eyebrows drew down suddenly. During the same timeframe as the deaths of Rhutgard's family members, the Queen of Shaw died, the King of Ghiverny's brother, first in line to the Throne, died under the ice, while no one could reach him, and four of the Ghiverny King's closest advisors died, all within a six-month period.

The Hardewold King's youngest sister died of "Illness, Cause Unknown," meaning the Healer didn't know what the illness was. The Delsynth King's daughter nearly died of a fever, but according to the entry, was listed as a "Miraculous Recovery," which usually meant that the individual was on the brink of death before recovering.

Harvick glanced through the Northern Countries and found that only the great aunt of the Ambsellon King at the time passed away at eight-six in her sleep, listing of "Old Age," and one advisor in Ormon passed away of the wasting disease.

In fact, no other deaths of note were listed about the Land, other than those fighting in skirmishes, who, of course, were not noted in Histories of Eras.

King Reaghann of Hardewold – only atop his throne a few years now – his father died of, choking on his food while dining, was it? How humiliating a way to die. The book here was not yet updated, but Harvick had read that from both his source's pigeon and the official courier. Hmmm. Harvick looked into his wine goblet and swished it around a bit, arching an eyebrow. That suddenly smelled as fishy as the fishbone – food poisoning? Poison? Harvick looked down at his plate and swallowed uncomfortably. He was immediately going to hire a new chef and a personal taster. He was leaving nothing to chance. He would not have it said that he choked on his wine or some such nonsense.

At least King Munsolrysche had been slaughtered to death, stabbed multiple times by knife, even if it was by a woman, his own wife, no less. With a slight bit of humor, he knew an awful lot of men were suddenly eyeing their wives with a slightly different outlook – and hiding the knives.

Perhaps, Harvick thought, now that he knew of all the deaths happening around Rhutgard at the time, hiding his infant daughter seemed like the right thing to do at the time. Well, all the Land was fascinated with the thought of her, he knew. In fact, Varley was on his way to the Romish Court for their Spring Seasonal, in hopes of worming his way into her favor.

Ha! If the girl had even half her father's brains, she'd see through him and send him back home, whining and whimpering and licking his wounds.

But in the meantime, Varley's absence gave Harvick time to look over this new Navy Varley thought Harvick oblivious of....

Perhaps Harvick would send it to sea somewhere out of Varley's reach.

Varley

Ah. How nice to get away from his father. And those damned babes – crying every bloody place he went. Finally, he was going to relax and enjoy himself. And while the Ormon bitch was busy recovering from blow after blow, Varley was maneuvering an entirely new scheme, one that didn't require Ormon at all.

He'd had word sent ahead of time that apartments to suit a Crown Prince were to be made available for him in advance. Varley was traveling across half the Land for this Spring Seasonal, or whatever they called it. So whatever Duke was quartered in Varley's soon-to-be chambers would need to find new arrangements. When Varley arrived, he expected a fine, roaring fire, the best wine these Easterners could provide, a sideboard full of bread, cheeses, fruits, and sweets, and a bed with freshly laundered linens, for Varley was tired of carriage travel.

The Free Lands offered very little in the way of overnight accommodations, and twice they had camped beneath the stars. Which, Varley mused, a man should do from time to time to remind him of his true roots, his masculinity. Just not in the Free Lands, where at any time bandits or Free Riders might discover your camp. Steal the horses, your luggage and finery, even your food, so stories told. Leaving you with just your carriage or not even that, for it was mainly the wealthy they prayed upon.

But finally, here at Fairview Palace, he had arrived. If this new daughter of King Rhutgard's was at all comely, then Varley would steal her little heart and before she knew it, have her locked up in a betrothal.

And why not? The daughter of a King, matched to a Crown Prince – she would be a Queen herself. Why would Rhutgard say no?

Varley wasn't sure what he liked best about it all.

A new Court to emerge himself in.

Or having a new jewel to put in his crown once he got this new Princess married to him....

Or the fact that once he got this little girl on his arm as Queen at Storden, then he would, through her, hold the key to not just Romeny, but the Eastern Shield, and thus all of the East. And that would give him the West as well as the East and that Ormon bitch would be down on her knees begging for anything Varley felt like giving her, which was exactly what she was supposed to be doing... begging for it.

Scollard

That little bitch. If he ever found her, ever....

He had spent years customizing and building connections as Lord Drury. Now he would have to reemerge himself in another Court, after a significant, proper period of time had passed, of course. He would take the time to draw up the identities of false references. Perfection required time, and time such as he required fortunately he had the means to provide, for he had two modest estates, though neither under names he'd used in the last decade.

He kicked the inside of the carriage in an uncharacteristic display of temper.

One of the coachmen leaned toward the window. "Sir? Is everything satisfactory?"

"Just drive!" Scollard snarled.

If he ever found that little bitch – or perhaps it would be when. Yes, when. When he found that little bitch – he would look into her eyes and flay her. If he let her keep her eyes – scooping their eyes out while they stayed conscious was always a treat. But he would peel her skin, roll it back, quarter inch by quarter inch, and listen to her scream the entire time....

Shadow

She eyed the cow. Who knew that cows snored? Every time Shadow nearly fell asleep, something in this dreaded barn made a noise. She was just not a farm girl, that much was clear.

In all honesty, the barn was shelter from the rain, and, were it not for the animals, the steady pitty-pat of rain on the roof would have lulled Shadow to sleep. However, the roosting hens reshuffled themselves occasionally and that bloody rooster nearly found himself roasting on a spit, cocky little monster. She'd shooed him away several times, so now he glared at her from the other side of the barn.

Shadow would sneak out before dawn, with a few eggs, of course. As best as she could tell, she still had about a week of travel, if by foot, to Port Stanton. She'd lifted a few silvers, a few coppers, and a bronze for her trip before she left HarCourt, for she didn't know how much a trip aboard a ship would cost, but she hoped she had enough.

Since HarCourt, Shadow had gotten the occasional wagon ride, by permission and sometimes hidden among its goods, under the canvas covers. Those were the easiest – she just rolled off stealthily as the wagon turned into a village or town. Riding was the best alternative, for the soles of Shadow's shoes were starting to thin. They weren't meant for long-distance walking, after all.

Upon occasion, when asked for her name, Shadow had a few identities constructed, just so people wouldn't remember the same girl all the way down the same route, if inquiries arose. At first, she used the name Lynza, just for old times' sake, since she and The Shrew bore each other such deep love and devotion.

But then, Shadow felt a pang of conscience, for she didn't actually want The Shrew to get in trouble, should anyone question local villagers and make the connection. Lynza may be a bitch, but she didn't deserve Drury's wrath. No one did.

So Shadow changed her stories around. If she didn't like the looks of the people speaking to her, then she was Mitzie, on her way home from visiting her Auntie, who'd died of the fever. And Shadow would cough or sniffle a bit. That sent people scurrying off hastily enough. Other times, she was Salla, off to visit her cousins for the first time. Most times, no one asked, or else they talked more about themselves.

Shadow snagged a donkey once, which had turned out to be more trouble than he was worth, for he started hobbling not three hours after she'd taken him, and Shadow had wound up leading him. The irony was not lost on her – a shadow leading an arse instead of trailing behind it. She'd finally left the poor beast in a village where someone would know what to with him.

Of course, it wasn't the first time Shadow had been in the immediate vicinity of an arse, but she'd take the donkey rather than Drury any time.

Shadow wondered often what had become of Rilstrom, whether he made it back to Shaw safely. For in a number of villages, Wanted signs of him were posted on poles, with drawings of him and his name beneath. Obviously Drury's men.

So whenever Shadow saw these Wanted signs, she waited until she wasn't being observed, then cut the Prince's name off the papers with her knife. Next, with a piece of charcoal, she wrote, "Lord Drury" and added to the sketches a bit to liken the pictures more to Drury's appearance.

Probably by now, if King Reaghann was true to his word, Drury was no longer at HarCourt. It didn't matter, for Shadow was free of him. As soon as she set foot on a ship at Port Stanton, she would be gone from the East altogether. Shadow felt certain that wherever Drury went, he would still stay somewhere in the East, whatever country he reemerged in.

Shadow had no ties to any country, be it the Eastern Alliance or somewhere West, but she thought warming her toes in the sand of some sunny beach of a Coastal Country sounded wonderful after hiding behind the miserable, cold, stone walls all this time....

Theldry

And now she was Theldry Eochair, Duchess of Mendellion.

She closed the door behind her and leaned against it. Or she would be, as soon as… this… happened.

She swallowed. All the wall sconces were lit about the chamber, and a warming fire lent a calming atmosphere.

Theldry realized her chest was heaving with anxiety and struggled to breathe normally. It was a nice sort of chamber, she supposed, trying to steady her nerves.

Theldry's new *husband* – now there was a word that would take some adjustment to – was not half as old as she had anticipated. He was thirty-one – still old enough to be her father, but Theldry had thought of him as in his mid-fifties, or worse.

Theldry's new husband entered the chamber from the side. He must have some sort of access from another chamber, she thought vaguely. He – Cathall – was dressed in bed linens, rather than his wedding attire, as she was. This awful gown – gods, her mother had delighted in its design, and all for what, four, maybe five hours of wearing it? And Theldry could hardly breathe in it, her waist was cinched so tight.

She cleared her throat. Would he – want her to – disrobe, or would he want to do that himself? Oh gods, she hated this.

Cathall placed a hand against one of the bed posts and looked at Theldry, taking her in for a moment. Then he sat on the bed and held an arm out toward Theldry.

"Come here, my dear." He patted the bed next to him.

Theldry picked up handfuls of her gown and walked slowly over toward him. It was everything she could to sit down.

"My dear." He looked into her eyes. He had kind eyes, she thought vaguely….

With a hand under her chin, he raised her head. "Do not think that I am unaware of what you are going through. You are still – young yet. You will sleep alone tonight, unless you want me to be here with you. I won't touch you at all. Nor will I, until you feel you are ready, and when you are, you come to me."

Theldry was amazed. Cathall was not a handsome nor a striking man, but good-looking in his own way. He was personable, easy to be around, people enjoyed his company she had seen during the reception. While he was older, he was not old, though he had what people called "laugh lines." And that meant, Theldry decided, that he smiled a lot and maybe even laughed a lot.

"But – what if I –" and she looked down. "Never want to?"

Cathall took in a long breath. "Well. I hope that you will change your mind. For I do want children. I had a daughter once, she died when she was three. And I will want children, as it's right and proper to pass on my bloodline and birthright.

"I might add," and he paused delicately, "that because people know I've had a daughter, they know I am able to have children. Whereas, if you do not conceive, they may consider you barren...."

Theldry took in another deep breath and nodded.

"Now. In order for everyone to assume we have consummated our marriage –" and Cathall held up a small leather sack. "Chicken's blood." He gestured at the white linens on the bed behind them. "Would you like the honors or shall I?"

Theldry stared at him.

"Oh, come my dear, you don't think men hear of such tales as well?" Cathall smiled gently. "Let us pull the first sheet off the bed and we'll use that, shall we? That way, you'll have a fresh bed to sleep in for the night and I'll sleep in the other room. The servants can't get in if I've locked them out, and they are, of course, locked out."

And so it was that Theldry slept her wedding night alone in her own shift, untouched, unspoiled, and still a virgin, though the next day, all of the entirety of Tortoreen as well as half the court of Corstarordan believed her fully a woman wed.

No longer a Princess. A wife, and a Duchess.

Rogue

He swung past the carts. Gobin – what a foul little man. All whore peddlers were foul. One day, Gobin would get his. If Rogue didn't see to it himself, then someone else would, but Rogue despised the man just the same. Such a travesty required just to get your boot in the damned door.

Rogue knew the way down the packed pathway by now. He inserted his head between Ishbel's curtains. He wasn't sure what kept him returning. Perhaps it was that she was – genuine. In a Land of so many insincere folk – the girl was genuine. Direct, perhaps a bit too much so.

He had always enjoyed the environment of Pavilion City – the billowing silks and amazing smells and sights. One could easily get lost in here, which was both a boon and a peril. Invisibility was both a proclivity and a requirement for Rogue and he found it here more often than not.

Ishbel was brushing her dark hair absently, her green eyes staring out at the vast, far-reaching grasses of the other side of her pavilion. She was wasted here. Silently, he laid the requisite two silvers on her bureau. Sneaking up on people was part of the requirements of his occupation.

"Well, come on, then, if you're coming in," she said.

His eyebrows rose. "How did you know?"

Ishbel turned around. "Heard the boots outside stop in front of my entrance. Some men, they like to just – watch." She shrugged. "That it was you, though, that…." She smiled. "You're almost becoming a regular."

Rogue scoffed and let his rucksack slide to the ground. Ishbel stepped over and inspected his face.

"Well, the black eye's gone." She stood back and looked him up and down. "And you're still standing, and there's no blood." Ishbel cocked her head to the side and nodded. "You're making progress."

Sarcasm. He knew noblewomen would never mock a man, nor speak so in such a tone. Nor would most women, nobly born or no. But Ishbel, a slave, a whore, had no reason to speak otherwise, and had certainly earned the right to speak as she liked, especially as she had no other rights. Perhaps it was her repartee that he enjoyed, Rogue mused off-handedly.

Although, if it were not for this business arrangement, he thought as he sat down to pull his boots off… there would be much, much more of Ishbel that he would enjoy.

But business was business, and you never mixed business with pleasure. That was the first thing he had learned in life, Rogue mused as he rubbed at a small scar on his hand.

"So. You're back so soon," Ishbel commented as he sat down on her bed.

Rogue was back – three weeks, if that. He leaned back on the pillow, thinking. For some reason, the blowing of the breeze and the scented jasmine in here always helped him relax enough to think. Today, though, he just could not concentrate….

"Have you learned anything new?" Rogue asked. Perhaps Ishbel's information would prod his jumbled mind out of its confusion.

"Oh, and haven't I," she told him. She sat down behind him on the bed. "And I made special note of it – I knew you would want to know. More furs and silks and satins and gowns and frocks than you can imagine went through here last week, and I think the week before, but I wasn't paying too close attention at the time. If I guessed, I'd bet even some nice men's outfits slipped on past. Somewhere, some royal or noble gave quite a party. I haven't seen that much go through in a long time. Not since – I can't recall."

Rogue sat up and nodded. "A wedding party traveled through from Tortoreen to Corstararorden."

Ishbel leaned back on the pillows. "A long trip," she commented.

"Gods, it's hot in here." He stood up and rolled the reed blinds down part way to shut out some of the afternoon sun. Then he pulled off his vest and tunic and folded them on her bureau. Much better.

Just as he started to lay down again, Ishbel tut-tutted at him. "And I thought you were making progress. Look at that. And that...." She traced a finger across his half-healed knife wounds from the Market Place in Tortoreen.

Rogue slapped her hand away and told her, "If I wanted a woman to nag me, I'd get a wife."

Ishbel hmmphed at him and told him, "Maybe, if you had a wife, you wouldn't have all these —" and she waved her hand up and down with disdain at his torso.

Rogue looked down. A few scars stood out worth making note of. He glared at her.

"As it happens, that's part of the reason I'm here. I wanted to know if you'd heard of anyone in that wedding party. They would have traveled past not long ago, and I wanted to know if you'd heard any information."

Ishbel sat back on her knees on the bed and shook her head. "Sounds like they traveled through when they bought all those clothes, but I never heard anything about a destination. Why are you so concerned?"

Rogue shrugged. "What we spoke of before." He laid back on the pillow and crossed his hands behind his head.

All traces of levity left Ishbel's face. "Hard to forget."

"I think I've got more of that puzzle now." Rogue sighed, then looked at Ishbel. Odd, the way he trusted her. He couldn't imagine anyone who would agree with the idea to trust a whore with such secrets, but there was just something about her. He couldn't unravel her.

Rogue paused for a moment. Then, "I happened to be in the Market Place in Tortoreen. Call it a very opportune moment. The Royal Princess of Tortoreen was suddenly set upon by assassins – her guards missing, paid to leave. And – well," and he gestured at his wounds.

"You saved her life?" Ishbel asked.

Rogue rolled his eyes. When she put it like that, she made him out to look like some bloody hero. He glared at her and nodded.

Ishbel smiled slyly. "You see, what's it like to have a conscience, Rogue? I knew you'd find one soon enough." She patted his arm.

"A conscience. Really."

"Of course. You saved a Princess's life. If that doesn't count as a conscience, I can't imagine what does." And Ishbel leaned over top of him and placed a tiny kiss at the very top of his hairline.

Rogue rose an eyebrow. That was the most forward she'd ever been.

"What was that for?"

"An award for merit."

He shook his head. "Right." He coughed, uncomfortable suddenly. "Well. So – this Princess. Nearly assassinated, and because she'd found out a lot of information about the important nobles on the King's Royal Council. She told me a good deal of it – illegitimate trading, smuggling, a few others. Fifteen years old, and she'd found out all these things about the Council Members. Suddenly the King marries her off to an older, minor Duke clear across the Coastals who just lost his wife. I suggested she change the venue to the groom's home instead of the Royal Palace, so the wedding party traveling through is what you probably witnessed last week.

"What say you to that?" he looked at Ishbel, who had laid against some pillows next to him.

"Simple. I'm the King, my daughter steps out of line, my Councilors complain, I send her as far away as I can. You have to please the people," was Ishbel's nonchalant response. She'd propped one leg up on the other and was studying her hand.

Of course. From a – well, a slave's – point of view – he just couldn't bring himself to consider Ishbel as a *whore* – she put it not from the Princess's point of view but the King's. He did it to please his Councilors. As someone who had worked her entire life pleasing others, Ishbel offered a unique perspective.

Rogue, of course, had arrived at that conclusion himself. However….

"Well then, next to Tortoreen is S'hendalow. A young, attractive, unmarried King just took the throne. S'hendalow and Tortoreen have kinship already between them. Now, Ishbel, you're the King, with your daughter…."

Rogue watched her. He loved watching her consider ideas – she was so wasted here.

"And he didn't marry her off to the King next door?" She paused. "You know why, don't you? With all the information she has, she and the S'hendalow King would hold it all over Tortoreen. And S'hendalow could act on it at any time. Or not. With other countries, even. Tortoreen would always be worried. Give a girl a little power, you better step out of her way," remarked Ishbel casually.

Rogue had come to the same conclusion as well, although he hadn't thought too much about a woman having power being so intimidating suddenly.

"Why do you say that? About women in power?"

Ishbel rolled a green eye up at him and snickered for a second. "Even down here, we've heard of the Ice Queen. I heard a song about her just last week with the minstrel troupes playing. *"Now every man, Bows all that he can, They hide all the knives, From all of the wives, Oh, what's a crown to a King?"* Ishbel sang.

Well, that was one he'd not heard yet. Rogue traveled too much to hear many tunes sung.

"Not just that," she added, "but a woman with knowledge could be dangerous. She might not even decide to share her information with her husband the King, but act on it all by herself. That's what I'd do. Why give a man all the credit for everything I've done myself?

"All through history, men have been Kings, but it's women who are truly the power behind the throne. A woman can make her man unhappy no matter who he is, King or stable hand. And if he's a King, then his country's in for a rough time of it, until he makes up for himself."

Rogue had enjoyed this commentary, realizing, of course, that Ishbel was right. Once again, her unique perspective proved instructive.

"But –"

And Ishbel stopped. She laid a hand on Rogue's. "What I don't understand is – if the King announced this pathetic little betrothal all the way across the Coastals to get her out of the way, to some little Duke, then that made all of his Councilors happy, which would have made the King happy. So then why would someone assassinate her? She's already been neutralized."

Rogue sighed. "When I dropped her off at the Palace, she wondered if maybe her father the King had arranged it...."

Ishbel sat forward, indignant. "What! What a bloody animal! Assassinating your own daughter, and right before her wedding!"

Then she settled back, thinking. Suddenly she sat up and turned around on the bed to face him. "You know, it's actually brilliant." Her face was serious. "Disgusting, but brilliant."

"Why do you say that?" he asked, curious.

"Well, if he's engaged his daughter to some man all the way across the Coastals, that makes his bloody Councilors happy. But if she's killed in the square there right in plain view, or anywhere at home, it could be made to look as if the Duke ordered an assassin, because he's mad with grief at having just lost his wife, and he wants to get out of the betrothal without upsetting the King.

"So she's dead, with all her information, no one will know what really happened, to the relief of the Council, and Tortoreen can then kill the Duke and take his estate for bride price. Isn't that how bride price works? What's he got that the Tortoreen King wants? Anything? Or just an out-of-the-way location?" asked Ishbel.

Rogue stared at her. Why the bloody hell had he not puzzled that out? That was exactly what he had been trying to figure out – and missing.

He shook himself for a moment. After asking around enough, he'd learned of the Duke of Mendellion that Princess Theldry was to marry.

"The Duke's estate is the northernmost estate in Corstarorden, on the water...." And then Rogue leaned his head back against the bed with a sudden revelation. "...On the Storden border...."

Ishbel's mouth dropped open. "Storden. And there are still plenty of those little shits running through here. And everyone knows it's pirates that the Tortoreen really are. An ideal location, across the Coastals. Perfect arrangement, the location and the Stordish," Ishbel proclaimed.

"Tortoreen – and Storden...." Rogue mused. "I didn't see any Stordish while I was in Tortoreen, so unless they were hidden somewhere...."

"Nothing of S'hendalow?"

Rogue shook his head. "No, all I hear is that the new King is shaking things up in his government, and that war is not first on his mind. I did hear that he's building ships, but...." Rogue shrugged. If the new King was smart and had heard anything new going on around the Land, then he was preparing for it like an incoming storm, the same as every other country.

"Then Tortoreen is aiding Storden somehow, or else those boys are hiding in the Free Lands...." Ishbel shrugged.

Rogue shook his head. "Not many of them in Free Lands. They're headed East somewhere."

"So, with horses, lumber, iron, Stordish soldiers heading East, and a Tortoreen princess sitting off the Stordish-Corstarorden border...."

Ishbel's eyes grew wide.

This was truly taking shape. Rogue normally kept to the South, but this was information he had to pass along, and certainly more he had to confirm....

"Ishbel, I may be gone a while this time. Here –"

Rogue sat up and rummaged around in his rucksack. He pulled out a small book, something she could easily hide. "I've been meaning to give this to you."

Ishbel accepted it gingerly and made a face at him. "What's this?"

"Something to do during your off-hours. When you know you won't get caught. I know you can read, just – something else to pass your time."

Hmmm. She was still giving him that look.

"Let us say that it is part of our arrangement, shall we?"

Ishbel looked with distaste at the book and wrinkled her nose. "Very well," she sighed, and stuffed it deep under her mattress so that Gobin wouldn't find it.

Rogue knew that whores – slaves in general – were rarely allowed to better themselves, and so she would need to be cautious, but if anything, he knew Ishbel to be clever and she would see that Gobin never found the book. It was only a child's version of the History of the Lands, after all, but she had such a keen mind.

"Right, then. My time is nearly up as we speak," Rogue stood and pulled his tunic on. As he stuffed it in his trousers, he told her, "Listen for anything about ships, or water, Navy and maritime information. Most of this wood is being used to build warships. But it might also be used to build war machines. Neither is good." He pulled his vest on and shouldered his rucksack.

"Remember – go forth and commit more acts of meritous behavior," Ishbel held up a finger to direct him as he started to leave.

"Meritous behavior." Rogue smiled faintly and shook his head.

"Yes, it's called a conscience."

He rolled his eyes at her. "I know what it is. Even if it is a bit rusty."

Ishbel cocked her head and smiled primly then. "I could – help with that, you know."

Rogue understood exactly what she was referring to. He had women whenever he wanted them. This one. Damn all the gods. Business was business.

He smiled. "That – isn't rusty at all. But I don't mix business with pleasure."

Rogue took her hand and laid two silvers in it this time, so she wouldn't be offended, and rolled her fingers over them. Ishbel caught the implied meaning behind the gesture and smiled.

As he left her pavilion, he wondered whether the line between business and pleasure wasn't blurring a bit....

Gerard

"Ah," he said as he stepped up and slapped his cousin on the back, "two of my favorite people."

His niece turned and kissed him on the cheek. "Uncle, I'm so glad you made it!"

"As am I, my dear, as am I. Looking lovely as you ever have, child."

She beamed – she had always been a sweet girl.

"Gerard, it's been too long –" and with a smile, he and his cousin hugged each other tightly.

And it had – far too long. *"Business had a way of getting in the way with pleasure, whether the smaller or the larger of either,"* Gerard remembered his grandfather instructing him, *"but without pleasure, you will have no business."*

Unfortunately, business was taking up a lot of time of late.

The three of them leaned upon the grand balcony overlooking the Great Hall.

"Well, Rhudy, I've come to see this new niece of mine." Gerard dug Rhutgard in the ribs. "You sly old bastard, you could have sent her to me."

"Gerard, you're the first place they'd have looked." Rhutgard half-smiled at him.

Gerard conceded that point. Ghiverny and Romeny were so close as allies, they were nearly brother states.

"Fair enough. So, then, where is she?"

Principea leaned out and Rhutgard stared intently into the colorful kaleidoscope of dancers below.

"There – do you see her!"

"Rhutgard, don't point!" hissed Principea.

"Principea, just this once it warrants it –"

"Uncle, in the blue and purple gown, there, in the center," Principea told Gerard.

Ah, and there she was. Lovely girl, of course, and why wouldn't she be. Stunning in royal blue and amethyst, trimmed in cloth-of-gold. A dainty tiara peeked through the golden curls arranged atop her head.

"Why, Princie, she looks just like you, except with blonde hair. Are you sure she's yours, Rhudy? No offense to you, of course, my dear, anything can happen in the turn of the moon. But Rhudy, I don't see anything of you in her at all...."

Principea laughed. "Uncle!"

"Gerard, you are a bastard –" Rhutgard grinned and shook his head.

"Except for those bloody blue eyes. Romeny blue. Even got some of them up in Ghiverny."

Rhutgard snorted. "You should. Those are folks of quality."

Gerard laughed and then sobered as he watched the girl swirl about on the Great Hall floor with a new partner. Mirelle, that was her name. And the feminine image of her twins.

"She is beautiful, my friend."

Rhutgard nodded quietly and smiled the smile of pride that only a parent knows. "I know."

Well, it had gotten far too serious. "You know what they say about triplets, don't you, Princie, Rhudy?"

Princie rose a single finger. "No. Do not breathe a word of that aloud."

Rhutgard rolled his eyes. "Not that tripe."

Gerard shrugged. "Parents swear by it. *The youngest of three smiles prettiest but plans the evilest plots?*"

"Uncle –"

"We are hoping that since she didn't grow up as a triplet that might prove untrue."

Gerard snorted. "For your sake – and with that face," he glanced at Mirelle on the Great Hall dancing, "– I hope so." He grinned.

A servant stood behind them with drinks, and each of them accepted a goblet of wine.

"I remember being one of those men down there, many a year ago, don't you?" Gerard remembered aloud fondly. Romeny's Spring Seasonal was always the place each year for members of the Court to show themselves off.

Today, he thought it a bit frivolous, but he enjoyed the merry atmosphere. And such a thought he found depressing, for that was a sure sign of growing old.

Rhutgard laughed aloud. "Oh, I do, and so well." He laughed some more.

Principea sat to one side in her chair. "Oh, no. I get the distinct feeling that I don't want to hear any of this...."

"Ah! Our first Seasonal," laughed Gerard. "We were 'Lurking and Dangerous' –"

"Which by the end of the night became 'Looking and Desperate'!" Rhutgard slapped his lap with laughter.

"And the second Seasonal, we were 'Manly and Motivated' –" Gerard started laughing.

"– Because neither of us had laid with a woman yet –" Rhutgard was laughing with hilarity.

"Oh, my dear gods, why must I hear this?" Principea covered her face.

"And we fell asleep trying to figure out which we were less of, manly or motivated...." Gerard laughed at the memory. "But the third Seasonal – what did we call ourselves – oh, of course – 'Clever and Cunning'!"

He and Rhutgard had called it out in unison. "Because we said it so many special different ways – gods, how those girls must have hated us. No wonder we never got any women," and he laughed some more.

On his other side, Principea had rolled her eyes with the utmost of disgust. "I can't even imagine why...."

Rhutgard said, "Our fourth Seasonal – oh gods."

Gerard groaned. "Ohhhh."

"'Hard to Get' – that became 'Deserted and Drinking'." Rhutgard chuckled.

"And then 'Drinking and Heaving'...." Gerard finished. That had not been a good night at all.

"Where was it your father found us that one time?" Gerard asked as a memory sparked him.

Rhutgard laughed aloud. "Oh, gods, I still think of it every time I pass by there – on the third floor, passed out against that seven-hundred-year-old suit of armor. That *you* threw up in –"

"Can I help it if his cod piece came off – it was at the perfect level –"

"And he hauled us up to my rooms and wouldn't let us out," finished Rhutgard.

"Actually, I believe, that year, we called it 'Kneeling and Heaving.' That was the Delsynth wine. I still will not drink that shit," Gerard mused as he rubbed his chin in memory.

Of course, after that, the Twenty Years War had gotten out of hand and it had not been seemly to continue, as Crown Princes, dancing about at seasonal balls when their countries were in the thick of fighting for their nations and the Alliance itself.

But of all the people in the world, Rhutgard was one of the men he treasured most, for they'd grown up together as cousins. He's spent more time in these hallowed Fairview halls then his own at Martmain some years.

"Speaking of young men, I do want to see my son. That is, with your leave…?" Gerard smiled, for his son Ronan was serving as a Ghiverny Ambassador in the Romeny Royal Guard. He may not even be present tonight but was sure that Rhutgard would make sure Ronan was present. Gerard hadn't seen his oldest son in over three years now.

"Gerard, of course, of course!" Rhutgard gripped Gerard's shoulder. "And let me tell you, he looks just as you did at his age – almost exactly the same! Wait 'til you see him and tell me he doesn't," Rhutgard nodded to Gerard.

"Really. Well – as long as he doesn't act like I did at his age, then he'll be fine." He chortled.

"No, no – military life has done him wonders, you'll be very proud of young Ronan. You, at his age, on the other hand –" and Rhutgard chuckled.

Gerard grinned. "Well, I always did have an eye for the ladies and a tongue for the wine. Or – hmm. Was it the other way around… Rhudy, help me remember…."

Rhutgard collapsed with laughter, but Principea slapped his arm.

"Uncle! How dare you dishonor your dead wife that way! You are so offensive – shame on you!" She smacked him repeatedly with her little fan with each of her last words.

Silly little thing, Gerard did love the girl. She was so easy to harass.

Then she turned her attention on Rhutgard. "And you! Don't you encourage him so!" Principea smacked Rhutgard around Gerard's back.

Rhutgard held up his hands in placation. "Yes, My Lady."

But he and Gerard burst out into laughter again.

"My Lord…." And there was that wifely tone that all wives used to control their husbands. Gerard saw it still worked splendidly upon Rhutgard, for Principea was staring down her nose at him. Gerard missed his dear Ismanna always, but most often at such events as these.

"Oh, of course." And Rhutgard adopted a stern expression.

"Care for a dance, My Lady?" He bowed before Principea and picked her hand up high above their heads.

Ah, thought Gerard. The King and Queen of Romeny would be gracing the floor. What a sight for the Seasonal goers. Traditionally, they only sat in their seats to watch.

"Come, Gerard, let us two reacquaint ourselves with that Seasonal Silliness, shall we?" Rhutgard slapped Gerard on the back.

"And possibly even a back hall or two with bottle of wine one night, eh?" Gerard muttered under his breath.

"I heard that…" called Principea.

Gerard grinned.

As Their Royal Majesties of Romeny stepped up to the Great Hall floor, all hushed and the dancers immediately parted down the middle.

A new waltz began, and Rhutgard spun Principea into the center of the polished floor. Gerard saw nothing but admiration on faces all over the Hall, for this was quite a treat. Rhutgard had always been the better dancer than Gerard, and Principea swirled about in his arms.

Then he bowed to his wife and stood in front of another guest, leaving Principea bereft of a dance partner. What was the man thinking?

And then Gerard nodded. Rhutgard led out a strikingly beautiful young woman, dressed in royal blue and purple velvet, trimmed with cloth of gold. Rhutgard bowed before her and kissed her hand. The young girl curtsied before him, and they began to dance.

Gerard loved it – a Father-Daughter Dance – for all the Seasonal to see.

He immediately stepped out to dance with his niece, who was so happy to see her daughter, her eyes were glistening.

"She's beautiful, Principea." Gerard spun her around.

Principea looked up at him and smiled. "I know."

It was good to remind himself that pleasure made a business run, not the other way about.

Ronan

As the dance required, he drew Mirelle forward, then apart, then twirled her about. The intricacies of the dance steps did not allow much time for conversation, but, Ronan thought, dance was not meant for conversation.

"And how is Ellia faring tonight?" he asked, deliberately using her former name to jolt her out of what seemed a daze.

She looked at him suddenly and smiled. "Both Ellia and Mirelle's feet are so sore, she probably won't walk much tomorrow. But –" and then she returned to his arms, "I have danced with two Kings of State, one, of course, being my father, and the other yours, two Crown Princes, five princes, and so many Dukes that I've lost count.

"But –" and she returned to him in a swirled flourish of blue and purple velvet, "I haven't yet danced with any Guards. Are you supposed to be out here, Ronan, I mean, as a Guard?" asked Mirelle.

"Only because I serve as a Diplomatic Military Ambassador to another country," Ronan replied, and he patted the medal pinned to his chest that showed the Ghiverny colors on its ribbon.

"Oh, of course," Mirelle said, and she patted it. "It's – actual gold, isn't it…." Then she looked up at him. "Of course, in the shape of a crown."

Ronan shrugged a little. "So you can say you've danced with one Guard and –"

"Three Crown Princes tonight. Right."

He smiled a bit. Then the music ended. Ronan bowed lowly before her hand, and Mirelle curtsied daintily.

Ronan instinctively realized that they were being watched. "I'll say *Good Night* now, or they'll all talk, you know."

He stood up as stiffly and properly as he could.

"Talk? About what?" Mirelle asked with confusion.

Ronan couldn't help but smile. "Nothing. Nothing at all. Good evening, Your Highness."

— ⚜ —

Ronan stepped into his father's guest quarters. Truth be told, he hadn't seen his father in nearly four years if he figured right, and to have seen him dancing out there on the floor with Queen Principea had made him smile.

"Father? You wished to see me?" He was still, after all, on duty.

"Ronan! My son! Finally – I'm so glad to see you!"

"Yes, sir."

"What? Sir? Toss that. There will be no *sir*. You are only in that post because I put you there and I'll just as soon take you out. Now forget that bloody uniform – you are off duty until I say otherwise."

Ronan had just been issued an order from higher than any commander in Romeny, including King Rhutgard's, so his face split into a grin and he stepped forward to hug his father.

His father enveloped him in a bear hug, then stood back and held Ronan by the shoulders.

"They told me you were like looking into a looking glass of myself at your age. Damn near it. You're a bit taller, though, and you've got a look of your grandfather to you. Have you seen your brother? He's here, somewhere about."

"Yes, Father, I have. I can't believe how tall he is! He's taller than I am!"

"Oh, yes – and still growing – eating the kitchens out of the castle, they tell me. And an excellent hunter, fine horseman, fine horseman."

Father was so proud of Petran. Ronan remembered days when Father spoke of Ronan like that. Then Ronan entered the military on this assignment for Father.

"It's good to see you, son." Father leaned against the table and gazed at Ronan. "I would love to have you back at my side at home, planning with me." He sighed a great sigh. "Truth be told, my son," and he trailed off and studied the fur on the floor.

"Father?" Ronan was suddenly worried.

Father inhaled deeply and bestowed a tired look upon Ronan. "Truth be told, Ronan, you are doing better for us out here, in the land wide than you could ever do for me at home back in Ghiverny right now." And he nodded vaguely, suddenly pensive.

"What exactly does that mean?" Ronan asked slowly.

"I put you out there – here –" and Father twirled his hand about suggestively in the air – "to learn more about what's going on in the land. The military, the Army, yes, that has served you well, but that last assignment of yours, down in... where was it?" He cocked his head.

"South Fairview?" Ronan felt a slight pang, for he'd almost said, *South Fair....*

"Yes, yes. You may have hated it, but you learned quite a lot. And look who you turned out to be guarding, hey, my boy?" And Father chuckled.

Ronan scoffed. Who would have guessed that a Royal Princess was growing up in an ale house? Well, she was certainly well-guarded – between Tank and Luvian, no one would ever have harmed her, whether they had guessed her identity or not.

"But I need you to use those skills still. While you're here – you'll still be Lieutenant for the Romeny Royal Guard as a Diplomatic Military Ambassador. But now you will be serving a new assignment, one for me."

Ronan grew somber. An assignment for his father meant a personal assignment for the King and Country of Ghiverny. And while on Romeny land, as a Royal Guard.

"Yes, Father."

"Oh, Ronan, nothing so dramatic as that. But one day, Ronan, you shall be a King –"

Ronan's eyes rounded with horror. "Not any time soon!" he interrupted forcefully. He hated when his father used that sentence.

Father scoffed. "Don't worry, my son, don't worry. There is far too much wine left in the land to be drunk before you become King, never fear." He smiled and gripped Ronan's shoulder.

"However – you do need to know – as all Kings must – you need to listen, and watch, and think. Your grandfather and his father before him called it trusting their gut. I call it that myself, but others call it instinct. Either works as well. If you think you know something, act on it.

"And right now, my gut," here Father patted his belly, "is telling me that something is awry. I don't know what. And I don't like not knowing. But whenever my gut told me something was awry, it was always right. And I think it will not fail me now.

"I have my spies and I have my soldiers – some of them are one and the same. And I move them about, as I taught you to, before you left for Romeny. But now you are here in the Palace. Your Uncle is family, of course. Somewhat tangled, but he is dear to me. His daughter is now arisen, from a past he sought to hide her from, and now I look back, I think he might have been right to do so.

"People, Ronan, people of all sorts will emerge from all sorts of corners. Not just because of her, either, though her sudden arrival will have changed a great many plans, that I can guarantee you."

"Plans?" Serious concern had just settled on Ronan's shoulders with the enormity of this assignment, and it hadn't even been fully explained yet.

"Yes, Ronan, plans. A good number of threads have just been yanked from embroidery clear across the Land, I'd say – and a lot of snarls have been left in their places.

"Which means that a lot of moves are being planned and negotiated even as we speak, my son. I am going to have a few of my men report to you as well, since you are in a unique position to respond. And, of course, you are here, rather than in Ghiverny, which makes you far more accessible to them.

"What I want you to do is listen for troop movement of any sort, from any direction, any at all. New men at Court – ladies, too, I suppose, after all, we do have a new Queen next door."

Ronan nodded. "Did you hear the new song about her?"

Father chuckled. "Which one?" Then he grew serious again. "It's exactly significant movements like hers, for example, that I want you to listen and watch for.

"Also, I want reports regularly. I brought new birds here, so use them instead of the other Ghiverny birds, just to be absolutely certain my people receive them and no one else. They're in the back, and the first one has a white ring about its neck. The second has two large black spots on her wings. I also brought a third, though it's not remarkable in sight. However – it flies to LongStaff. Use that if you must."

Ronan stared at Father. "LongStaff? We never go there."

Father said, "And thus I said, *'if you must.'*"

Ronan leaned against the table next to his father and nodded. He was trying to take in the implications of what Father was hinting at.

"So… troop movements, of any kind. Odd individuals in the Court. Watch over Mirelle. And anything out of the ordinary. Just – go with my gut." Ronan was tempted to make a light joke here, but his father was more serious than he could recall seeing him. Ronan knew exactly what Father meant in regards to a gut feeling, for it had served him well on the streets of South Fairview. But he found the idea of using it in Romeny for Ghiverny and the Eastern Shield, in fact, enormously… intimidating.

Father took Ronan's pensiveness for uncertainty.

"Just remember, Ronan. If you think you know something, *act on it*. Unless, of course, it's a woman. If it's a woman – don't act, my son. Just drink." Ronan saw his father's eyes cloud over with pain at the loss of Mother. Ronan stepped forward and grabbed two goblets and filled them with wine. He handed one to Father.

"To Mother," he raised his goblet.

His father looked old to Ronan then. Father nodded slowly, his eyes sad. Then he sighed and raised his goblet to Ronan's. "To your mother."

And they both drank.

Reaghann

As he walked away from the Council Room, Reaghann thumbed through all of today's parchments. He immediately shuffled them according to which he really felt were worth looking at, which he'd heard them discuss repeatedly today, which were just reworded versions of another Council's proposal, and which he wasn't even going to bother looking at.

He had begun this habit ever since Lady Green Eyes had arranged his paperwork for him. He thought of her often and wondered where she was now.

Part of it was sheer intrigue. She had fascinated him, he had to admit.

But the rest of it was – that she had been correct about all of it. And all under his own nose. He, the King, in his own Palace, had known nothing of crimes taking place right before him, and in his own home, his own Council….

Reaghann had promised the Lady of the Green Eyes that he would give her until the next day at noon to check the treason cells, but he had not slept at all that night. Instead, he had taken every file he had on each of the lords she'd provided him with and pondered over them in his personal solar. What a dark night that had been… and yet so illuminating….

By the noon bells, Reaghann could hardly contain himself. He took two guards with him, two non-descript, random guards from along the corridor and took them down to the Royal Dungeon. And the turnkey led him down to the Traitor Cell Block, where a disgusting guard nearly pissed himself at the sight of Reaghann.

Reaghann shoved him aside and stalked down the cell block with his lantern held high. And once he stood before the last cell, he saw that an inhabitant had indeed spent recent time there.

Once the dungeon guard had disclosed that the man had simply disappeared and also that he had not alerted his superiors that a traitor was missing, he was arrested and put into a cell of his own. Reaghann also switched out the other dungeon guards to different castles, as he suspected them culpable as well.

A man had lived in that Traitor Cell for – according to his Lady of the Green Eyes' account – nearly six months. And no record of him arriving, being tried, convicted, nor even his crime, nor even his bloody name, Reaghann fumed. She claimed he was Prince Rilstrom, that he had been captured on his way here on a visit of State. Yet no such visit was arranged. But… King Rickstan had been wearing mourning for his brother for… six months, now that Reaghann thought of it. So perhaps Lady Green Eyes was right.

She had certainly been right about Lord Drury. As soon as he'd left the Royal Dungeon, Reaghann had immediately left for Lord Drury's quarters. He told the Guards that, upon entering, they were to kill upon command should he give the order. Their eyes rounded but they acknowledged his order.

And Lord Drury was gone. The entire chambers – rich, lavish – could have belonged to anyone. No personal identifying characteristics or paperwork were left to distinguish the chambers as Lord Drury's.

As a point, Reaghann sat down at Lord Drury's desk. He pulled the top drawer forward and felt about underneath. And damn if the girl wasn't right – just as she had described… a hidden compartment. That alone verified the girl's story. Reaghann had to force it open a bit, but found nothing inside.

And so the bastard had slipped through Reaghann's fingers.

Well, at least he was gone.

As for the Prince, he too, was gone, and Reaghann's men had combed the woods along the main road to Shaw looking for him, but to no avail. There were no tracks, wagon or horse, on the road, and their search came up empty in the woodlands. So Reaghann was left to wonder what became of the man. Did he escape? Was he hiding in plain sight, perhaps? Maybe he decided not to return to Shaw at all? Or perhaps he was with Lady Green Eyes somewhere….

He had always thought of HarCourt Castle as a temple, his temple, and to find out it was riddled with spies and secrets and – tunnels, even… sickened him. Reaghann with no notice at all, dismissed half his Council Members – those he knew or believed to be complicit with Lord

Drury. The other Council Members left were a-tremble at the thought that they at any moment might be dismissed as well.

And as for tunnels – Reaghann could not help but glance at the stone floors upon occasion whenever Lady Green Eyes sprang to mind. Twice, he actually saw chalk against a wall and he'd reveled in the knowledge of its true nature. But he couldn't very well go skulking about wherever he saw chalk.

But he did remember to use candles and brought chalk of his own when he finally snuck into the corridor in his Study. And he covered up the Spy Hole.

Rhutgard

Laughter erupted all over the courtyard. Mulford's *"Three Wise Wives"* now had a new take on it, for one of them was costumed to resemble the Queen of Ormon. Rhutgard had always enjoyed the Spring Seasonal, but the plays were the best of all the entertainment. Since he had taken the throne, he had added two more plays, for his father had always enjoyed the circus acts instead. One could only watch so many acrobat troupes perform without getting bored, Rhutgard believed.

"Your Majesty," came one of his servants behind him.

Automatically, Rhutgard handed up his goblet.

A voice cleared and his goblet was not refreshed nor taken.

Rhutgard turned his head over his shoulder. The servant had a dusty letter on a silver tray.

Annoyed, Rhutgard looked up at the servant. "Man, put that in my study at once." He brushed the servant away and turned back toward the play. This was the Seasonal. Rhutgard would not be attending to business during the Seasonal, particularly not during theater.

The servant coughed and whispered, "Lord Stanyard bade me give it to you at once, Your Majesty."

Stanyard had passed it along to him. Hm. "Now?" Rhutgard swiped the letter off the tray. "Very well." The servant bowed and hurried off.

He watched the play for a minute longer, then down at the letter. Clemongard. Rhutgard never received correspondence from Clemongard. Perhaps someone had passed on. For that country's sake, he hoped not, they'd lost their entire Royal Family in what, two months? Now their sister sat the throne, poor girl….

Inside the letter, he found another letter, this stamped with the Queen of Clemongard's Royal Seal. Rhutgard rose an eyebrow. Now he really was intrigued. He ignored the laughter about him and popped open the wax seal.

What he read made him sit up straight. Rhutgard no longer saw the courtyard before him, nor the theater, nor anything of the Seasonal.

He heard Gerard at his side burst out with laughter. Rhutgard laid a tight hand on his arm. "Come with me."

Gerard looked over at him with surprise.

"Don't say a word. Just come with me," Rhutgard insisted. He rose from his chair with an enormous smile and a wave, indicating that the play should, by all means, carry on.

Principea tugged at his sleeve, whispering, "Surely this can wait." She rose an eyebrow at the letter, though her lovely smile belied what he knew was surely annoyance.

"No, it actually cannot. Just tell them, that – that I – was ill or some such thing. I will be back as soon as I can, that I promise," and Rhutgard kissed the inside of her hand.

Principea relented and watched them leave.

Once they were alone in the corridor, Gerard turned a wide-eyed look at him. "Rhudy, what the –"

"Come. Walk with me."

Gerard snorted, trying to match Rhutgard's pace. "I would walk with you, if you were walking, but you're running…."

Finally, they arrived at his Study. Rhutgard closed the polished wooden doors and turned to look at Gerard.

Gerard, for his part, was strolling about the room with his hands behind his back. "I remember this room well. Though the last time I was in it, 'twas your Father's room, may peace be with him." He turned to Rhutgard. "Like what you've done with it. But I suspect showing off your Study isn't why you've run me up here." He looked down his nose at Rhutgard expectantly.

"Here. Read that and tell me what you make of it." Rhutgard shoved the letter at Gerard and then sat down behind his desk.

He watched Gerard's eyebrows shot up. Gerard turned his green eyes up to Rhutgard. "What the bloody hell!" He stared for a moment, then said, "Are we sure this is real?"

"I broke the seal myself. And that's her stamp."

"Why, I –" Rhutgard watched as all the energy seemed to drain from Gerard. He collapsed down in one of the chairs across from Rhutgard and flung the letter across the desk.

"That. That cannot be right."

"Well, if it wasn't Gerard, why would she write?"

A Silent Game of Spies

And he read it aloud:

Dear King Rhutgard,

First, let me express my heartfelt congratulations you on your daughter Mirelle. Undoubtedly, blah-blah-blah,

I apologize for writing during your Spring Seasonal, which I have myself attended before, blah-blah-blah but I am afraid that my need is most urgent.

I am asking for the assistance of Romeny as an Ally. It has been many years ago since our countries last allied with each other, but we as countries together found it a most beneficial mutual Alliance and I am hoping to renew that symbiotic relationship.

Today, I write for your assistance, for I find my country besieged on two, if not three sides, and by two, if not three nations.

As Romeny may itself have suffered, after the Twenty Years War, all of my troops, both Army and Naval, were decreased in numbers. Clemongard's Army is only now to the capacity it once was prior to the Twenty Years War.

I have received reliable intelligence that Ormon is launching its Navy of 400 warships within just months. Ambsellon, should they accompany Ormon, will increase that number to 700 warships. Clemongard has no such Naval ability to withstand such an attack.

Furthermore, Ormon's new 100 warships will be completed six months hence from the date of this letter, and my intelligence informs me that yet another 100 will begin construction after that.

Ormon's troops, I am told, are amassing for release soon as well, and they are three to Clemongard's one at best, as are Ambsellon's, who will also attack.

As for being attacked by a third possible nation, I add Storden to this   list. While I find this as incomprehensible as I am sure you do as well, given its many centuries of neutrality, I have excellent information that its Naval presence is three to one over mine and twice what it once was itself – new warships.

Storden also has a new Army, two to one of my own.

Obviously, Your Majesty, you see that Clemongard's need is most dire, and that if not so, I would not write asking for your assistance. I am happy to share all information, as the release of Ormish and Ambsell troops affects the Kingdom of Romeny. It is also quite possible that Stordish troops may affect the Kingdom of Romeny, or perhaps another Eastern Shield country.

I hope that you will seriously consider my Alliance Request, Your Majesty, as Clemongard will soon need all soldiers available to protect her.

A Silent Game of Spies

With Greatest Mutual Respect,

Her Royal Majesty of Clemongard

Selby Cylysse Stevanrhut, First of Her Name

Rhutgard looked up from the letter at Gerard. "That can't be more specific."

"Four hundred warships? That crazy bitch. Have you heard any such thing?"

"Not as such, no. That they are planning something, yes. What, I've not found out yet. Ormish intelligence is damnably difficult to ferret out," Rhutgard muttered.

"Well, that I'll agree with you on." Gerard rubbed at his beard absently. Then he said, "Well, Rhudy, what are you going to do?"

Rhutgard tossed the papers across the desk. "What do you mean, what am I going to do! Gerard! Bloody hell!"

He had hoped his reign would never see such a thing, never. He'd already fought once, and survived, thank every god, and Luvian, mainly, for that matter. *Bloody fucking hell.*

"You're going to help her," said Gerard quietly.

"What the fuck, Gerard. Of course I'm going to! Wouldn't you? What if you needed help and wrote Clemongard? Wouldn't you want them to help? Besides –" and Rhutgard pointed at Gerard across the desk – "those Green Fucking Gates are going to open, according to her, and who knows which way those soldiers are going to turn. They just might turn your way.

"So you'd be wise to jump in as well."

"What!" Gerard roared. "Ha! Fuck that, my friend. I've got problems of my own to worry about."

"Really? Such as?" Rhutgard demanded.

Gerard's expression became belligerent, but he knew not to push Rhutgard. He just shook his head.

"Gerard, I'm telling you, you should jump in on this. That Ice Queen may be sending her people your way and it'd be good to get intelligence from across the Land. It could help you."

Gerard's belligerent expression did not fade. Between clenched teeth, he demanded, "Is this Rhudy or King Rhutgard talking?"

Rhutgard raised his chin a bit. "Both," he said evenly.

"Then let me ask you this. We are all recovering from the Twenty Years War – I've recruited widely, but if those bastards come in my direction, and yours, what makes you think I should send help halfway across the bloody Land? Sending her help while she's outnumbered by the troops of their Navies will leave us outnumbered while we send troops to help – and that lets Ambsellon and Ormon take us by Army, just like the Twenty Years War. And I don't know about you, my friend, but I don't know half of what my father, or yours, did about fighting a war. While we send help there, they'll attack us here. That's the truth of it." And he pointed a finger at Rhutgard for emphasis.

"But Gerard, we have all the rest of the Shield to back us up. And she has no one," Rhutgard told him. Then he said, "And just what are these *troubles of your own* that you're referring to?"

Gerard looked away with a sulky expression. "She might be right about the Stordish," he finally commented.

Rhutgard sat forward. *"What?* And how would you know that?"

"My men – underground men, spies, that is – have been seeing a lot of movement. Stordish men, soldier types, complected the same, headed across the Coastals and the Free Lands through Delsynth, best as we can tell."

Rhutgard's signet ring clanged as his arm fell against his desk in amazement. "And you didn't think to share this information with me?"

Again, Gerard grew belligerent. "Who's asking this time, King Rhutgard, or the Eastern Shield?" he demanded with downdrawn brows.

"Both!" Rhutgard roared, standing up. "Stordish troops? Storden soldiers, in Delsynth, and you never thought that once of relevance? My friend, that is why we have an Eastern Shield! If nothing else, Delsynth should like to know of their presence, don't you think? Or have you told him already?"

Gerard looked a bit cowed. "No. I have not told him yet. I wanted to be sure, and I had not yet verified the information. Think of it, after all, Stordish troops, wouldn't you want to verify it?"

"I would tell the Eastern Shield that possibly Stordish troops have mobilized and are moving through its countries unknown and to an unknown destination!"

"What! Tell all of them? And if I was wrong?" Gerard spluttered.

"I am the Eastern Shield, Gerard! Never lose sight of that! It is for me to decide how to tell them, and whom, if necessary."

Romeny was the center of the Eastern Shield, and the King, or the Queen as may be, inherited the seat of the Eastern Shield. Romeny made all of the decisions for the entire Eastern Shield, as a ruler might. It was odd that the country of Romeny was shaped as a shield, but it shielded the other Eastern countries on almost every front from their enemies, and so whoever was King or Queen of Romeny was also known as the Eastern Shield. The first Romeny King called the capital of Romeny Fairview City "Fairview" because the city was situated so that he had a "fair view" of all of his enemies, and so it did, being bordered by the Mantle Mountains to the west, and Ormon and Ambsellon to the North. Over the years, the other Eastern countries had formed and in return for a mutual respect and arrangement, the Eastern Alliance had formed between the countries against the North. But Romeny was its first line of defense and the office of Eastern Shield had formed, to oversee the Alliance.

It was an enormous amount of strain, some days, Rhutgard's father had told him, but such it was. On days as today, Rhutgard felt that strain.

Rhutgard glared at Gerard. "Better to have been wrong than taken unawares."

He stood and paced. "I will be sending my reply forthwith. I immediately accept her Request for Alliance and will provide her with troops."

Rhutgard half-glanced at Gerard over his shoulder, then continued. "You, of course, may or may not send the Queen assistance, however you see fit."

Gerard took that in for a moment, then said. "Mm-hm. That's a pit-trap. That's a do-whatever-you-want-and-keep-your-troops-Gerard when actually you mean if-you-don't-send-troops-as-part-of-the-Eastern-Shield-Alliance-you-will-regret-it-for-years-to-come. Fine. Fine, Rhudy. But if Genwith City or Martmain falls, on your head be it."

"That's why we have an Eastern Shield Alliance, Gerard," Rhutgard told him as he studied the maps on his wall. He would have to send a bird to Reaghann. That would not be a fun letter to write. *Need troops – but possibly troops are moving through your land.* Hmmm. No. This required Reaghann's presence. And Rickstan, and Driscoll. Bloody hell. A fucking War Council. Why? Why his reign? Why could he not just pass this off to some other King, a hundred years from now?

And that meant – his sons. Kendrick and Keldrick would be involved, and Ronan, for that matter, just as he had been once. Those fool boys – how would he keep them from running off and doing something ridiculously foolhardy?

"You know what this means." Gerard's voice was tired.

Rhutgard turned around and eyed his old friend.

"A War Council. You have to invite them all."

Gerard always could read his mind. Rhutgard nodded. "I was just thinking the same."

"I remember our first one." Gerard looked pained.

Rhutgard remembered as well, for they had finally been allowed to attend, considered old enough, mature enough to attend. He nodded slowly.

"Now we'll be the old folks." Gerard cleared his throat then. "Rhudy, if you haven't already, you need to change your line of succession, stamp it, finalize it."

Rhutgard sighed. "You're right. I will. But before we act on anything of note," and he turned his head back to the maps, "let us talk to our mutual men of the Shield, and pool all of our information… and I'd like to hear yours as well."

Gerard nodded. "You'll have to call in Ronan."

Keldrick

"Oh, I –" and Mirelle had turned pink.

That lady-in-waiting of hers, Kimbur, she was a smart one. She had been dismissed by this gentleman – though that was euphemistic – but had then immediately insisted upon his and Kendrick's attention.

Keldrick swung around one side of the pillar while Kendrick swung around the other.

"Dear Sister, it's been just a few hours since we saw you last and yet it seems like days," Keldrick ventured.

Mirelle yanked her hand back.

"Varley, have you met my brothers?"

The young man stood straight and, it seemed to Keldrick, almost did not smile.

"No, no I have not. Perhaps another time," and he backed away.

"Not at all, Lord Varley," Kendrick stepped forward smoothly and rounded Varley's shoulders with an arm.

Varley coughed and looked distinctly uncomfortable with the familiarity. "It's actually 'Prince' – Crown Prince."

Kendrick walked him away from Mirelle. "Really? Then we have that in common, being princes, that is. Although I can't say I know which country you're a Crown Prince of. Are you visiting from a Coastal Country, then?"

Whatever Varley's answer, they were too far away to hear it. Keldrick snorted laughter.

"What's so funny?" Mirelle asked.

"Him – that – Prince Varley. Of Storden." Keldrick shook his head.

"What of him? I thought he was very – nice...." Mirelle turned pink again.

Keldrick looked down at her. Adorable but so very naïve. They had a lot to teach her. "He was practically licking your hand. Perhaps they do it differently in Storden," he trailed off and shook his head. "But here in Romeny, we don't corner young girls and make people question their virtue, especially when those young girls are Princesses."

Mirelle's mouth dropped open and her hand fluttered at her throat. She stared after Kendrick and Varley.

"He said he just wanted to talk...."

Keldrick grinned. "I've done a lot of *talking* in the back corners of the Palace. Lots and lots of it."

Mirelle smacked his wrist smartly. "Shame on you!"

Keldrick laughed and shrugged. "What? It were just talking…."

Mirelle arched her eyebrow. "Oh, sure it was –" and then she looked frustrated. "I can't remember your name."

Keldrick laughed. "Don't think that's the first time that'll happen. It still happens to Mother and Father. That's why, when twins are born," and he held up his left hand and pulled his signet ring up to reveal a tiny scar in between his ring finger and his index finger. "To keep track of first and second. Kendrick's is between his pinky and ring finger. And yours, dear Sister, because you are youngest, is between your two first fingers, though you originally thought it a scar.

"But something about him –" Keldrick nodded in the direction that Kendrick and Varley had just taken.

He put his arm through his sister's and escorted her back toward the main Great Hall. "There's something about him I don't like. I'm not sure what it is, but – just stay away from him. And if he wants to 'talk,' or any other man for that matter, don't leave the dance floor, stay where everyone can see you. A real gentleman won't ask. Never go anywhere alone with a man – not unless it's family. All right, then?"

What a sweet thing she was. They were going to have to keep a closer watch on Mirelle from now on, for just reasons like that Prince Varley….

Renfry

The boy talked endlessly. About everything. Renfry supposed if he had spent six years not speaking, then possibly he would talk for hours just to hear the sound of his own voice as well, but Renfry could not keep up. After a while, he just tuned out. Birds. Clouds. Grass. Do you think this? Do you think that? Why bears hibernated. The stars. The best way to press parchment.

The gods had sent this boy as a true test of Renfry's patience. He could not wait to get to Roarden North, if only to rid himself of the incessant yammering….

What was that?

Renfry heard something, and for once, it was not his young companion.

Up ahead.

"You. Shut your mouth and do not utter another word."

Ari looked at Renfry, his mouth frozen in mid-stream of whatever he had been discussing.

"What?"

Renfry rolled his eyes. "I said, do not speak another word. Listen, but do not speak."

He saw the boy swallow as he nodded. Renfry kept forgetting that technically, if found, Ari, or whatever his known name was, could be executed where he stood.

Yes, the boy had been a Silent Brother, but to Renfry's way of thinking, he was no longer a Silent Brother. Nor certainly silent. He'd really forgotten about the boy being a member of the Order. Well, Renfry wasn't going to turn him in. Everyone deserved a second chance, after all.

Renfry adopted a casual expression and continued walking down the dirt road. The terrain had changed, and only grasses and meadowland swept the side of the road to Roarden North, so they walked the road now.

Soon, three men showed around the bend in the road. Renfry cracked his knuckles.

Instead of passing and just tipping a head in civility on their way past, they stopped, causing the dust in the road to cloud up around their boots. They were walking in a triangular formation.

"Where you headed?" asked the first.

"Wherever the road takes us. Where are you headed?" Renfry asked in a tone just short of defiance.

"What's your name?" asked the first with narrowed brown eyes.

"Ren," Renfry told him. Soldiers. More and more of them. Where were they going?

"Yeah? Who's he?"

"My kid brother."

"He don't look like your brother."

Renfry spit on the dirt road. "He hears that a lot."

One of the others opined, "What, he don't speak for himself?"

Renfry scoffed. "Most days, I can't shut him up. But he's got a real good recipe for brewing beer. Want to hear it?"

The three soldiers suddenly grinned, jostling each other.

"Go ahead, tell them." Renfry nodded at Ari, who looked confused, for this was going against the directions he'd just been given.

He drew in a breath. "Well, you see, what you need first is – oh my – what – what – did you! Holy God above!"

"Relax, boy. It's all over." Renfry planted his swords into the dirt road.

The three soldiers' heads were lying askance, staring sightlessly, bleeding into the dust. Renfry walked over and nudged them away from the bodies. Then he looked up at the boy.

His arms were clasped behind his head and he was pacing back and forth across the road.

"What did you – what did you *do* that for!"

"Simple. They would have killed us."

"You don't know that. How do you know that!"

Renfry looked at the boy. "It's been my experience that they would have." He nudged the heads away over a little further so that their blood wouldn't spill onto their uniforms. The second soldier's head spun around in a full circle and bumped into the third soldier's head, causing it to wobble a bit more. Beheading was almost more trouble than it was worth.

"Well, come over here and be of some use," called Renfry. So far, the boy had not wretched. Renfry was impressed. He kneeled down next to one of the bodies.

Slowly, the boy approached, an accusatory expression all over his face.

"You don't know that they would have killed us. You could have let them go."

Renfry shaded his eyes against the sun as he squinted up at Ari from his kneeling position. "I could have. And they could have mentioned us – you, especially – to someone. Who might pass it on to another someone. Who might pass it on to someone else. I don't care to be in that position, do you?"

The boy stared at him stubbornly. "We need to bury them."

Renfry scoffed. "Bury them! I'm not burying men who wouldn't have the decency to bury me. You bury men you love, serve with, and respect. I don't give a kick of shit for these arseholes, nor did they for me. Or you, and you think about that before that guilt sets in.

"Now I'm going to be bone-picking and you can turn around and pretend it's not happening, or you can get to it with me, and we'll be on our way quicker, and eliminate the amount of time that anyone can connect them to us.

"Or you can go retch in the field there. As you like."

"I have a strong stomach," Ari retorted. "I've helped butcher animals before."

"Well, these men were animals dressed in clothing, so you think on that. Now here –" and Renfry tossed the soldier's coin purse to him. "Count it."

By the time they had taken all they needed off the soldiers' bodies, including two shirts for the boy – which he had immediately recoiled at the idea of – they had amassed a fair number of items.

Renfry generously gave the boy half of the money, which for a boy who had never had money before, was a great deal indeed. Now he had money and two shirts as well, for they were in a city style rather than those rough-spun country shirts that would mark him surely as a country boy in the big city of Roarden North. Eventually, the boy accepted the shirts, however gingerly, mainly because he recognized the logic behind the idea, not because he wanted the shirts themselves.

A few more items Renfry kept himself – a fine compass that he was certain the officer had stolen, a knife, and another cloak, for his own was ragged now. And they both had new rations, though Roarden North was only a two-day walk now at most.

Once they set out again, the boy asked him, "Why do you carry two swords?"

Renfry looked out over the vast grasslands, searching, though for what, he wasn't sure yet. "Because I'm good at using them both," he said. It was his usual reply for that question.

He watched as the boy took off his rough-spun shirt and bagged it into his rucksack. Renfry was surprised to see a fair muscle tone. The boy held out of one of the shirts with clear distaste but pulled it over his frame. After he rolled up its sleeves, he threw his rucksack over his shoulder and strode forward.

"You can stop calling me *"boy"* and *"Ari."* My real name is *'Topher.'*"

Driscoll

As he cut his meat, a servant stepped up to him. Driscoll noticed that he was not liveried in the same serving attendant apparel, but thought nothing of it, until the man said in a low voice,

"Your Majesty, a pigeon parchment arrived for you."

Driscoll chewed his meat and then swallowed. "You – are in the wrong place. That goes to my advisors, starting with Pastorn and, if necessary, Hensfeld." Driscoll eyed the servant's livery. It was not crisp and fresh as a new servant's, but worn upon the man easily.

Driscoll sawed off another piece of roast. "You know that, you're not new here."

"No, Your Majesty, all pardons, Your Majesty. The parchment is arrived from the Eastern Shield, however, Your Majesty."

Driscoll's bite of roast arrested in mid-air. "Let's have it." He dismissed the servant and wiped his hands clean of food and grease. A servant stood by for him to cleanse his hands in a bowl of water. Driscoll shook them clean and dried them before he popped the seal and unrolled the parchment.

What he read rounded his eyes. Driscoll sat back in his chair, disbelieving.

Once finally he had digested the contents of the letter, he scraped his chair backward. "You," he said to the nearest servant. "Find Hensfeld. Tell him to ready a retinue and horses for a week's stay. And I will be traveling alone." Driscoll watch the servant scurry off.

Then he threw the letter into the fire, watching as it burned into ash.

Mevrin

"I must insist, Lord Yelvin," said Mevrin in his most imposing voice, "but this is for *His Majesty's eyes only.*"

"Captain Mevrin, you are but a member of this Royal Guard, and I am the King's Chief Advisor. I will have that parchment. For that matter, from where did you get it? What has a Captain been doing in the Royal Pigeon Loft, may I ask?" Lord Yelvin was infuriated.

Mevrin told the man, "If the King cannot view this parchment, then I am under strict instruction not to give it to anyone else." And Mevrin slipped the parchment into his uniform.

Lord Yelvin's face turned a shade redder. Mevrin then decided at that moment on Lord Yelvin as his personal choice as conspirator number one for keeping back information of magnitude from His Majesty.

Which was why, some months ago, King Rickstan set up Mevrin's personal pigeon loft. Mevrin, of course, was in no way a Captain, nor any way a member of the military. Just a loyal subject and highly knowledgeable in the means and ways of pigeons. He'd trained them for years, in fact.

When King Rickstan approached him not long ago while on a ride about the countryside, he asked Mevrin to set up a personal pigeon loft so that all correspondence go through him instead of to the castle now, to *train the birds*, he'd said. But the King gave him a sharp look, a *read between the lines* look that meant he didn't trust the pigeons in the Royal Pigeon Loft.

King Rickstan also gave Mevrin strict instructions that if any pigeon should ever fly from the Eastern Shield, then Mevrin was to immediately find him and give it to him, for Rickstan's eyes only. Not Lord Yelvin's, not anyone's. Should anyone interfere, take the message back and refuse to give it, burn if need be. Mevrin had blinked at that but solemnly agreed. He left Mevrin with the Captain's uniform so that he might be admitted immediately. And, of course, when he brought these pigeons to His Majesty, he was never to reveal their sender under any circumstance.

Mevrin lived only an hour from the Capital, and so this arrangement was simple enough. He was afforded with more than enough to provide for the birds and his own personal living needs.

But today was the first time anything from the Eastern Shield had arrived and he was suddenly unnerved at just why the King had made this personal arrangement with him, for this

Lord Yelvin seemed a man to be reckoned with. Now Mevrin understood exactly why this arrangement existed.

He would not, of course, disclose that there was also a letter from the Eastern Shield inside his uniform as well, which the King had set up, too. Mevrin wondered why, if the King believed there to be such conspiracy surrounding him here in the Palace, did he not just dismiss all the servants, or advisors, Councilors all? But what did Mevrin know of politics….

"I shall have you arrested, sir!"

Mevrin was worried now….

"Your Majesty! It is Captain Mevrin, with a message for you!" Mevrin yelled. The King had best be in that Study….

Lord Yelvin nearly throttled him. "How dare you!"

Suddenly, the King himself appeared and paced down the few darkwood steps to his Study, an alarmed look on his face.

"What is this? Lord Yelvin, this is a Captain of our Royal Guard, what do you think you are doing to him!"

"I – he said that he had a message for you, Your Majesty!" Lord Yelvin insisted as he tugged his surcoat back down.

"Well, by all means, allow him in! Whyever should we disallow Captains of the Royal Guard to give messages to their King? Captain, I must apologize," King Rickstan told Mevrin.

"Your Majesty, he would not give me the message, and I ordered him to," Lord Yelvin was not to be dissuaded.

Mevrin bowed low and then saluted. "With all due respect, I told him, as I must now tell you, that I was instructed to tell you that it is for your eyes only, or none at all."
That was exactly how the King had instructed him to tell him that it was an Eastern Shield letter, after all.

"Very well. I'll take a look at it," the King said dismissively.

Was it Mevrin or had the King put on a bit of weight? Hm. He looked much better than he had the last time he'd seen him, anyway.

"Also, Your Majesty, I was instructed to give this to you, for your eyes only as well."

"I see, Captain. Thank you for carrying out your duty so well," mused the King as he read the parchment.

Suddenly, he crumpled up the parchment and tossed it into the fire, rubbing a hand over his eyes in what looked like tension.

Then he sighed and popped open the seal of the letter. Whatever he read there, Mevrin thought, was no more gratifying than the pigeon parchment, for he crumpled it up and tossed it into the fire as well, watching it burn into ash.

The King stood away from the hearth then and said, "Captain, you've ridden a long way and under great peril. Take some rest a few days before returning to your regiment. Possibly, I may even reassign you."

"Lord Yelvin, ready a retinue for me and horses. I'll be gone for at least a week, perhaps more. Alone, no servants."

"Excellent, Sire. I'll see to it at once. I should like to get out of the Palace for a bit. Where will we be going, then?" responded Lord Yelvin.

King Rickstan looked at him. "Lord Yelvin, perhaps you did not hear me when I said, *'no servants.'* That means you as well.'"

Mevrin held back a smirk.

Reaghann

No. No. And leave the rats of his Palace to scurry about unattended while he was gone? No.

Bloody hell. A Royal Fucking Summons from the Eastern Shield meant he had to pack tonight, leave tomorrow, sit in a bloody carriage for at least a bloody week, change out horses....

Why now? When he was sniffing out spies and searching for replacements for his Council that weren't going to assassinate people in the dead of night? When he was making sure that no one was watching him through spy holes in every room he went?

Fucking War Council.

War. Not in Hardewold, there wasn't.

He balled up the parchment and tossed it in the fire, watching it burn into ashes.

Ronan

Sprawled on the floor outside King Rhutgard's Study, they were trying to stay quiet. Getting caught would only mean that they'd never be involved. A real War Council!

Keldrick and Kendrick sat across from him, and Dougall next to them. They had their own small council out here on the floor, their ears pressed up against the wall and the door of King Rhutgard's Study, where all five Kings of the Eastern Shield had just met for the first day of the War Council.

"They're just laughing," Ronan shrugged.

"Give them a moment to reacquaint with each other. When was the last time they were all in the same room with each other?" Kendrick whispered.

Ronan thought on that.

"King Reaghann's Coronation?"

They glanced at each other and shrugged. "Could be," Kendrick whispered back.

"Wasn't my father's Coronation. He's old enough to be everyone's grandfather," Dougall grinned.

"I'm just sharing this with you because we're cousins – somehow – but," whispered Keldrick as he put a hand on Dougall's shoulder, "your father scares me." Then he grinned.

Dougall grinned. "My father scares everyone."

Ronan waved at them to stop talking. "They're talking."

They all pressed their ears against the wooden paneling.

"Laughing. Discussing wines. Do you believe that?" Kendrick rolled his eyes.

"Oh, here we go – women," whispered Keldrick. Then, "Ew, she's ancient. Old enough to be our mother."

"Oh, gods – may I forget I heard that…" Kendrick whispered.

Ronan buried his head in his knees. Only his father would share a story like that. But they were all laughing hysterically, even King Driscoll.

"And you – Reaghann – Hound of the Eastern Shield –" King Gerard's voice was clearly heard outside of the Study from drink. "You Hardewold men are ever the dogs. What's your number up to this time?"

Kendrick and Ronan's mouths both dropped. "Thirties! Impossible!"

Kendrick looked at Keldrick. "Have we ever had thirty ladies-in-waiting even in residence here altogether?" he whispered.

"Is that really what the "Hound" of Hardewold has actually meant all these years?" whispered Dougall.

Ronan grinned. "I think they try to out-do each other – it's a family tradition of some sort, how many by the end of their lives. I can't imagine what their wives must think."

Keldrick and Kendrick looked at each other and grinned. "Oy – I sense a competition arising – get it?" And Kendrick dug Keldrick in the ribs.

Ronan snorted. "The only thing my father and I could compete in is wine-drinking," he whispered.

"What are they saying now?" Dougall whispered.

Ronan pressed his ear up to the door. Then he shrugged in disgust. "They're all just laughing. Oh – wait, no, Reaghann just made a toast to –" and then he laughed.

"To what?" asked Dougall.

"To all the working units of a King."

"Cheers to that," Keldrick raised a fake toast.

"True, and then some," snickered Kendrick.

"All the working units of a King?" Dougall asked.

"A King's working units –" and Ronan gave a meaningful glance at Dougall's groin and upward again.

"Oh, bloody hell."

Ronan grinned and then whispered, "Oy – if we ever have to have a War Council, then it sounds like to me that we just to need to bring wine, women, and get totally racked."

They buried their heads in their knees and laughed.

"Oh – right – your father's calling them to order," Ronan whispered.

Kendrick pressed his ear up against the wall.

Ronan's mouth dropped suddenly, as did Kendrick and Keldrick's.

"He didn't just say that!"

"Shh – keep your voice down!

"What'd he say?"

"Ormon has 400 fucking warships! And they're getting ready to launch!"

"400! Where is she sending them?" whispered Dougall.

Ronan waved at them. "Shh!"

"Clemongard…" whispered Kendrick.

"Clemongard?" whispered Keldrick.

"Alliance treaty –" Ronan whispered.

"An alliance with Clemongard –" whispered Kendrick as he pushed his head to the wall even closer.

"That's Queen Selby. Did you see her a few years ago at the Seasonal?" whispered Keldrick.

All of them nodded.

"She's what, our age, or just older. All that blonde hair. Wow."

"Yes, Kel, and now she's the Queen of Clemongard, fighting a war alone against Ormon and Ambsellon, and our Ally. And look at all of us, sitting on the floor with our ears pressed up against a wall. Pathetic, aren't we," remarked Kendrick in a whisper as he glanced around at the four of them.

"A Stordish Army attacking in Delsynth?" And Ronan sat and looked at Dougall.

Kendrick and Keldrick looked at Dougall as well.

Dougall's mouth fell open. "How is that even possible? Storden is neutral. They don't have an army."

"That's what they're saying," Ronan pointed a finger at the door and stared at Dougall.

"But – we'd know." Dougall's face was suddenly very serious.

"How did they get there? By sea? They'd still have to travel up river. Or up land. They'd still have to travel across Romeny," Kendrick mused. "Or up north of Romeny and into North Delsynth. Surely the Queen would have made note of that somehow. Or they would have attacked her...."

Ronan suddenly made sense of all the soldiers coming upriver while he was in South Fairview. "They came upriver, disguised as commoners. I was on assignment and saw a number of them for myself, but no one knew what direction they were traveling, or who they were fighting for. My assignment was just to watch and report, so I did. I don't know what was done with the intelligence I sent, but if those men are in Delsynth somewhere, then you can bet they're well-hidden and that there a lot of them. Several units of them, in fact."

"Then who are they attacking? Not Delsynth? Surely they know how irrational that is. We have Crown troops alone that would be five to their one, at least. And that's before our Stafford Spears. Are they going elsewhere, then?" whispered Dougall.

Ronan felt suddenly very cold, for Ghiverny was a small country. Not as small as Shaw by any means, but it had always depended upon the Wolf Wall to the West to keep Ormon out, the Ice Isles to the North, and the EverWinter Mountains to the East to keep attackers from invading. Ghiverny was only vulnerable from the South, where it faced both Romeny and Delsynth. If Ormon wanted to attack from the South....

King Rhutgard's Study Door opened just then. As King Rhutgard, the Eastern Shield, stood looking down at the four of them sprawled upon the floor, he lifted a slightly amused eyebrow and said, "Perhaps you lads would like to join us now."

Reaghann

He breathed in the fresh night air. Finally, they had come to an adjournment for the evening. War Council or no, Reaghann admitted that it was nice to be out of his own Palace, even out of Hardewold after all.

King Rickstan stepped out onto his balcony as well, which adjoined his own, evidently with the same idea as Reaghann's. Fresh air and relaxation.

"Ah. King Reaghann. In the flesh, as it were."

Odd choice of words. "That I am. How was your trip?"

Rickstan smiled suddenly and looked down as if at a personal joke. Then he leaned on the marble guard rail, enjoying the night sky. "A bit long, but I'm sure your trip all the way from HarCourt was far longer."

"A bit, yes, but a smooth one just the same."

Reaghann realized then that Rickstan was not wearing his mourning clothing anymore. He never had replied to Reaghann's birds asking of his brother's safe return. Reaghann was unsure how to approach the subject.

"I think that, unless summoned by War Councils or wars themselves, I shall stay at home more often. Not that Fairview Palace isn't a beautiful castle."

Rickstan gestured to the grandness that surrounded them. Reaghann would have to agree. HarCourt was built more to sustain than to impress, but at some point, it, too, had been beautified by some Queen and her ladies.

"Well, I can't boast nearly the beauty of Fairview, but HarCourt does have a bit of beauty to it, at least in some areas of her. Perhaps one day you'll visit." He smiled.

Rickstan smiled vaguely. "I remember my last visit quite vividly, as a matter of fact."

"My Coronation, yes," Reaghann had hated that day. What a blur that day had been.

"Yes, I remember that day very well, and what a feast," Rickstan recalled. "But –"

And he offered Reaghann his hand, as if they were strangers, to meet for the first time.

Reaghann accepted it, and Rickstan gripped it tightly.

"I visited HarCourt very recently, for quite a lengthy stay, in fact. Unbeknownst to you, of course."

Unbeknownst to me…. Then Reaghann's eyes grew wide and he looked down at Rickstan's hand.

Rickstan held up his hand, where no scar sat between his pinky and ring finger, but his ring and middle finger, to indicate that he was the second twin.

Rickstan was in fact… *Rilstrom…!*

Rilstrom shook his head ever so slightly and said aloud, "Say nothing."

His Coronation ring covered his Second Twin Scar and his signet ring, designed with Rickstan's initials, covered the space where the First Twin Scar would be.

Reaghann's breath was taken away. He was speechless – he had no idea what to say. This was a plot, a conspiracy, regicide even, possibly....

Rilstrom stood and watched as Reaghann took in the implications of this.

"But – where...?"

"It turns out my dear brother, my own twin, wanted me out of the way. Just in case I wanted the throne. Which I don't, I actually despise it. But he had me seized, my wife and child killed. He told everyone that I went to stay at one of our other castles, and was set upon by bandits, kidnapped, killed, my body never found. He wouldn't have me stay in our own Dungeon, for I might have been recognized, so he sent me to yours. He kept me alive in case he should need me, or so he explained to me when I returned."

"He is, at this very moment, occupying a traitor cell at a location known to me and three others, which is three better than I'd like and where he is far better taken care of than I ever was. And he is also quite mad now."

Rilstrom sighed and looked down at his coronation and signet rings.

Reaghann stared at him. "I am afraid I don't know how to respond...."

"Oh, don't. I still don't. Except that each day, I am glad to be out here, with fresh air and good food and...." Rilstrom trailed off and shrugged.

"You have my deepest regrets and apologies." Reaghann suddenly asked, "How did you escape? Was it with the help of a young girl?"

Rilstrom nodded, a smile spreading across his face. "Yes, and I – and my country, in fact, shall be forever grateful to her."

"I spoke to her just once. She was behind the wall in a tunnel, looking through a spy hole at me. Whatever was her name?" asked Reaghann, as he fought to keep eagerness from coloring his voice.

Rilstrom laughed a little. "Oh, those tunnels. Thank the gods for them." Then he shook his head. "Saucy little minx. She never did tell me her real name. She went her way and I went mine. But I thank every god for her every day."

Reaghann nodded. So Lady Green Eyes she would forever remain.

"And what of his wife? His children? Surely some people recognize the difference," Reaghann commented.

Rilstrom nodded. "Apparently, they noticed immediately, for I like dogs, and he did not. Also, it seems, he liked tea, while I do not. He was not an early riser while I am. A few other subtle differences. The Queen finally cornered me. She said she and the children really hadn't cared for him in years, yet still, he was her husband, their father. So she would go along with the charade, for she was far happier now with me."

Reaghann was taken aback by the entire story. Someone had been complicit in the entire arrangement, he knew, but he would have time to ponder that later.

"You will need to establish your own bloodline for a succession to the throne," Reaghann commented.

Rilstrom shook his head. "No, the real successors belong to the first twin, that's only right. As for my own bloodline, well – I wouldn't expect any wifely duties from the Queen, we agreed upon that. Unless she were willing, of course. That would be untoward of me. And besides, you're the Hound of the East, not me." Rilstrom smiled.

Rilstrom smiled, but Reaghann could see lines on his face and gray in his hair that shouldn't be there – and the man was of an age with him.

Reaghann scoffed. He shook his head.

"If anyone needs to establish his bloodline, it's you." Rilstrom – or Rickstan as he would still need to be called, said, "Reaghann, Hound or not, you need to marry, my friend."

Reaghann exhaled. "Not you, too. I already got this lecture the night I arrived, from Rhutgard."

"From Rhutgard, or from the Eastern Shield?" asked Rilstrom.

Reaghann frowned. "Both, I think."

Rilstrom slapped him on the back. "Well, then, start looking around. Shaw is already recently tied to you. And I can't imagine that there's a lady in all of Hardewold that you've not slept with by now...."

Reaghann sighed and stared up at the stars again.

Shadow

Here she was, hiding in the shadows, yet again.

She didn't have tunnels this time to protect her, nor did she have spy holes to listen and watch with. And so, Shadow was crouched in the bushes after twilight, watching the soldiers teeming above board the ships, as well as those cascading down onto the gangplank. And all of them common-clothed.

Larcy was right. Shadow couldn't take passage to the Coastals from Port Stanton.

Shadow had finally arrived in Port Stanton late last night and slept in a wagon. She had never smelled the ocean before – salty a little, but fresh, with the waves crashing every few seconds upon the shore.... She could grow very accustomed to that. A small cabin on the ocean somewhere in the Coastals....

Shadow woke to the sound of birds crying overhead. Gulls, and wind in her face. She heard the roaring of the ocean in the distance and could not suppress a spark of excitement.

Shadow wasn't really sure how to procure passage on a ship, so she'd walked about the streets a bit, letting the wind blow her hair around her face. Her dress finally stopped flapping about her when she stepped into the tavern closest to the docks. The Laughing Pelican. Bells tingled above the door as it closed.

"We're not open for business yet," called a woman. A tan-faced woman with her hair pinned up hauled a basket of linens before her. She eyed Shadow from head to toe.

"What you need, lass?"

Shadow thought of a lot of answers to that question but asked, "I was just wanting to know – how to book passage on one of the ships in the harbor. I want to go to – S'hendalow." Shadow didn't want to be too specific in case someone asked.

The innkeeper studied Shadow's face and nodded a little. "Well, I hate to tell you this, lass, but there's no passage on ships headed out of Port Stanton. Not no more, anyways. 'Less you want out for the day on a fishing berth."

Shadow's face fell. "But – why not?"

"Lass, why are you so keen on takin' a ship to the Coastals when you could walk? Easier – cheaper, to walk."

Shadow glanced away.

"All right, all right. You got your own business, I don't pry. But I'll tell you this, my young friend, Port Stanton is closed for pleasure travels. They don't say it like that, but we towners know it."

"What about the next port? How far away is it?" asked Shadow. Maybe she would just follow the water line to the next port, then.

"Hey, Larcy – who's that you're talkin' to?"

Larcy glanced over her shoulder quickly, then pulled Shadow over to the bar. She motioned Shadow to kneel down.

"No one, just someone headed out the door. You know I talk to myself," Larcy called. "I'm headed back upstairs with these fresh linens, right? You'll have the pub."

"Yes, yes, go on, then, woman."

Larcy waited for a minute, then beckoned Shadow to follow her silently. "Come on, then," she whispered as she directed her up the tavern stairs.

"Inside here, this is my own room –" and she opened the door of a well-kept, cozy room. Shadow snuck in. "What's your name, lass?"

"Mitzie," Shadow said. She was amazed at how quickly the lies came now.

Larcy's gray eyes narrowed just slightly, but she said, "Well, *Mitzie*, my name is Larcy. I been the innkeeper here with my cousin here nearly my whole life and before that, our parents. And we've seen a lotta strange stuff, but what's goin' on now beats all. And Mitzie, you need to hear me when I tell you, you don't want to be here tonight."

Shadow's eyes grew round. "What? Why not?"

Larcy sighed. "Where you comin' from, that you don't know this?"

Shadow glanced away again.

"Mm-hm. That's what I thought. Well, whatever you're runnin' from, you're runnin' the wrong way, lass. This here is what we've been calling Port Soldier lately. Just amongst our own personal selves, those we trust, that is. We got soldiers from somewhere West comin' here to Port Stanton and goin' –" Larcy shrugged and shook her head. "We don't know where. But they're not dressed in uniform, and every week, a new ship drops off more of them. And they stay here, and you know, we appreciate the coin, sure, but – something about them stinks worse than bad fish on a beach.

"And my young friend, they should be docking about two hours from now. Which means that you – you cannot be down there, nor anywhere on these streets. Not 'specially near those docks.

"There's two things soldiers want when they get onto land from a long voyage. Regular food is number two." Larcy looked Shadow up and down and gave her a sour expression. "Hate to tell it to you so."

Shadow rolled her eyes, disgusted. This was horrible – all of it, horrible. She'd spent nearly three weeks traveling, her shoes had holes in them, she was exhausted, only to finally get to Port Stanton and find it overrun with soldiers who, if they saw her, would –

She glared at Larcy.

"I'm so sorry, lass. They'll be here for two days before they move on. You cannot be seen, you understand that?"

Shadow heaved an enormous sigh. She had hoped to be aboard a ship this afternoon. "How far is the next port from here?" she asked tiredly.

Larcy told her, "Ferrisport? I'd avoid it like the plague if I was you."

Then she stood back and looked Shadow up and down, really studied her. "How long you been walkin'?"

Shadow eyed her. She really wanted to tell this woman, for she seemed kind and concerned, but even the nicest of people would believe the worst of rumors and turn you in for a coin or two.

"Well, I don't know for sure, and I can see you'll not tell me. But those shoes aren't goin' anywhere much longer. I know where I can get you a pair from someone who owes me a favor. And that dress needs serious washin'. As, little lass, do you, and I don't mean that roughly.

"My Karly, she lived here with me once, she left this frock behind," – she gestured to a calico dress left in a small closet – "but she's had her babies now, and she'll never fit into this frock again. You wear this and I'll launder your dress that you're wearin'.

"Now. That's a tub of clean water that I was planning on usin' myself, but – seein' as how you need it far more than me – you help yourself and I'll get more water later. Here now, here's a clean shift.

"And you – you stay up here. You stay up here for today, and definitely do not come down tonight, whatever you do – these men, they ain't nice men, Mitzie. Now. That bed – you get some sleep. And there's water there on the bedside table, you drink all of it you need. I'll bring up somethin' to eat later. Just pretend like you're not up here. I'll be back around," said Larcy.

Shadow's mind was spinning – it'd been so long since someone had been randomly kind to her that she was speechless. But soldiers moving north – she wished she could send a bird somehow to King Reaghann. If the people here didn't like these men, and thought there was something wrong about it all, and the port was completely closed down, King Reaghann should know. He would do something about it.

And then Shadow stepped into the tub of water. She pulled her knees up to her chin and watched the dirt float away from her skin. She was by no means as dirty as Prince Rilstrom had been, but she certainly felt it. Ah… to be clean again….

And to sleep on a bed…again…

Durshkin

These uniforms. Durshkin riffled through the neatly folded tunics that had just arrived. They were Kingsmen, not Queensmen. If scouts told them the Ice Bitch was coming, then his men would change into these uniforms, but otherwise, they'd still wear their Kingsmen uniforms.

Durshkin snorted. Women. All women were supposed to do was suck cock. And shove out babies. Not strut around running countries and planning out wars.

And these Stordish. Durshkin could not get past how pathetic they were. All he kept remembering was that they were, after all, the first spit of military a country hundreds of years neutral could cough up. That made the total amount of men twenty-five hundred men, agreed upon in some treaty between Ormon and Storden. As for the other Stordish back West – they'd fall faster than snowflakes in steam.

But his men were training these shits. They were pathetic, all of these Stordish. Difficult to watch, even harder not to laugh at. Ormon bought and paid for them and Durshkin owned them now, not Storden, and he made that clear immediately. And until each one of them convinced him that they were worthy of being in his ranks, then they were only women dressed as soldiers.

Durshkin saw the Stordish glaring at him when they thought he wasn't looking. And still they stood in formation, sloppy, loose. This morning, where the Stordish troops stood next to his Ormons, Durshkin heard as he walked past, one Stordish whisper,

"Why do they call him Colonel LD?"

"Because," whispered his Ormon soldier, "they say he has such a long dick."

"You!" Durshkin pointed at the Ormish soldier.

"Colonel, yes sir!"

"Run in place until I tell you to stop."

"Colonel, yes sir!"

The Ormon soldier began running in place, staring sightlessly at nothing.

Green, yes, but not untrained.

"You." Durshkin pointed to the Stordish man.

"Colonel, yes, sir!"

Durshkin just despised these Stordish men. They did not even salute, nor snap to as Ormish soldiers. Well, perhaps that would change….

"Advance, soldier," Durshkin called to him in a bored tone.

The Stordish soldier finally about faced before him.

"Kneel."

The soldier's eyes grew round, and he threw a half a look over his shoulder at his comrades, but slowly, he knelt, swallowing, for he knew what was about to happen.

Durshkin unlaced his trousers and thrust his dick down the man's throat.

"Now suck my cock until I tell you to stop."

Durshkin let his thoughts drift as he rammed his dick down the man's throat.

He heard their songs around their campfires along with their laughter and forbade them to sing them, though the songs had also caught on to some of his own men. And if he was honest with himself, he found them humorous, but he was commanding this entire ragtag Army division, and so it fell to him to keep them in line.

And trained. His own men weren't bad – he'd fought with worse. Green, but through no fault of their own, for there had been no wars, no battles in years. Nearly two decades, in fact. Durshkin remembered The Twenty Years War. He'd only fought during the last ten years of it, but just the same – battle changed a man.

These Stordish… they had no idea that they'd be divided up and used as his vanguards. Suicide soldiers, one and all, and not a one of them knew it. Durshkin permitted himself a small smile as he surveyed the Stordish camp. One thousand of them, ugly red-haired and blond freckled bastards, undisciplined, untrained – sent as a measure of good faith for this maneuver. Half of these Stordish Durshkin would send as the vanguard into Ghiverny, and the other half he'd split evenly when they attacked the Delsynth….

Durshkin looked down at the soldier before him. Vomit streamed down the man's chin and puddled in the snow. Couldn't suck worth a damn but he'd gotten the job done. Women were made for sucking cock, not men.

"Now stop. Next time you're in formation, soldier, keep your mouth closed."

"Colonel, yes, sir," the soldier choked.

Shadow

Larcy had strictly instructed her to stay out-of-sight and hidden. And now Shadow knew why.

Last night, she had slid her knife inside her dress. Then she'd leaned out Larcy's window, searching for soldiers. Finally, she climbed down the rope net underneath Larcy's window that served as décor.

The inside of the bar reverberated with the laughter and banter of drunken soldiers. Shadow sniffed. Soldiers-who-were-not-soldiers. What a mystery. Why pretend to be common folk? From what she heard of them, they acted as if they were soldiers, and made demands upon the waitstaff and innkeepers.

Shadow lingered in the darkness up against the wall of The Laughing Pelican until she was sure it safe to step away. No soldiers.

She threw the cowl of her gray cloak over herself and stole through the shadows of the town, keeping to the darkness.

As she passed one couple on the street, she heard them say,

"Back again, obnoxious shits. They should stay in their own country."

"Huh. Wherever that is."

Shadow listened to another couple while she hid outside their window in the bushes.

"Why Port Stanton? This used to be a decent town. Now we all just stay indoors when they come 'round," grumped the husband.

"Too bad they don't stop at Ferrisport, or Chesterport instead. They've got docks size enough for that boat."

"Allie, I keep tellin' you, it's not a boat, it's a ship. An' a wicked big one, too. Besides, Ferrisport and Chesterport are the same, same as we are, locked up tight. That's what I heard on the docks, anyways."

"It ain't right. It ain't right. I mean, what if Della wants to visit?" Allie fumed.

"Then she'll be walkin', same as everyone else now."

Shadow stepped silently away from the home, watching up and down the narrow street for just the soldiers Allie and her husband were complaining about. Obviously, if everyone knew they were soldiers, they shouldn't bother covering up anymore, Shadow snickered to herself.

But shipful after shipful after shipful, each week? And in the ports just south of Port Stanton as well?

How did King Reaghann not know of this? Or did he know and was turning a blind eye?

No. She could not believe that King Reaghann would allow his ports and his country to be overrun by strange soldiers from an unknown country.

Shadow spent the next hour looking for a clerk's quarters. Perhaps the scribe there had not sent word to King Reaghann at all, and only said he would. How simple would it be to install a clerk, or pay him, to send no word at all to the King about the incoming soldiers?

It took Shadow half the evening, and a long time spent hiding in the bushes from passersby, but she finally found a small clerk's office, where she saw pigeons asleep under a roof.

Well, it meant breaking in, and for that, Shadow could be jailed, hung even, if she was caught. Perhaps she could get in through the pigeon keep.

Success met her and a number of pigeons fluttered their wings at her or cooed as Shadow held her lantern up inside their pigeon keep. Well, waking up pigeons was the last thing Shadow was worried about....

Did this pigeon keep even send pigeons to Romeny?

Selby

She accepted both pigeon parchments and the servant left her alone in her Study. One was only from... she eyed the seal closer. Just a Romeny Seal. Selby heaved an enormous breath.

That did not bode well. That did not bode well at all. For if she got no militaristic assistance in this upcoming battle, she feared for her people altogether….

Selby slid her finger beneath the wax seal and popped it open.

Inside it the parchment was another sealed parchment, though this one was stamped with the Royal King of Romeny's Seal. Hmm. If nothing else, Selby's curiosity was piqued.

To: Her Royal Majesty Selby Cylysse Stevanrhut, First of Her Name

Queen of Clemongard:

Your Official Alliance Request with the Kingdom of Romeny has been accepted.

More Official Correspondence will soon follow.

Send detailed Correspondence as necessary.

Your Ally,

His Royal Majesty of Romeny

King Rhutgard Anghus Firthing, First of His Name

Eastern Shield of the Eastern Shield Alliance

Selby's heart soared and her legs nearly gave way beneath her.

Now, for the other.

To: Her Royal Majesty Selby Cylysse Stevanrhut, First of Her Name

Queen of Clemongard:

As per your recent Alliance with the Kingdom of Romeny, the Eastern Alliance has agreed to offer to Clemongard an Official Alliance.

Send appropriate Correspondence promptly.

Best Regards,

King Rhutgard Anghus Firthing, First of His Name

Eastern Shield of the Eastern Shield Alliance

Selby's mouth fell open in shock and she dropped the parchment. Tears of relief formed and trickled down her cheeks.

Perhaps there were gods after all....

Rhutgard

Nearly a week. All five of them were exhausted. He'd never seen Driscoll this... relaxed. Usually he was stiff and stern. Now, his surcoat was loosened and he should have shaved this morning.

Gerard, of course, was never stiff and stern, the exact opposite of Driscoll. Gerard was always merry and lively, but after these last few days, he was grumpy and had drunk more than normal, Rhutgard suspected. Understandable, of course, for sending any of his troops to Clemongard depleted him should Ormon cast its attention his way. Driscoll would be watching over South East Ghiverny, and Rhutgard knew, if the others did not, how much that rankled Gerard.

Shaw had far too few troops to send, and so his task was merely to guard the Riverlands – as it always had.

Hardewold was the biggest country in the East per mile, bordered by the EverWinters, Delsynth, Shaw, and even a portion of Romeny, with the Singing and Rosh Rivers to the West, the WetLands, and a massive amount of coastal waters. Reaghann's Southern Shield Castle had never been breached, the very entry to Hardewold that wasn't a part of another country, but the Free Lands instead.

Reaghann could supply troops to Clemongard and probably not even miss them, Rhutgard mused. Reaghann was mainly vulnerable from the coast, and rarely did anyone have a Navy of note large enough to mount an attack on Reaghann's Naval fleets.

He'd sent the Clemongard Queen an Alliance Acceptance from Romeny and also sent an offer of Alliance from the Eastern Shield – they were only waiting to receive her reply now.

It was an historical event for Fairview, hosting all of the Eastern Alliance at the same time, and for this long. Principea wished a portrait could be painted – ah, she did love portraits. Once Rhutgard thought of it, he thought it an outstanding idea, but certainly not under the circumstances. Furthermore, not a one of them would ever be able to remain still for so long. And Gerard would make them laugh constantly... Rhutgard could imagine it now, the artist would be driven mad.

No one knew of the real purpose of the Alliance's assembly, save their sons. And how enamored they'd been with the idea at first. Rhutgard snorted. Not so enamored now. He had set the four of them to studying books of war tactics and strategy in the library. Which was more he had ever had, he mused. At noon and at the close of the day, they reported what they learned to the Alliance and offered their thoughts.

Much of what they were studying was quite old and but had been tried and used successfully in battle in war after war, from the Battle of the Banners straight up to The Twenty Years War.

Rhutgard had them studying Naval Stratagems as well. They were now officially allied with Clemongard and at minimum, Queen Selby had four hundred war ships sailing her way. Furthermore, if Queen Selby elected to accept the Eastern Alliance's offer, then Reaghann might well be sending some of his own warships west, and that meant the boys needed to familiarize themselves with the seas and the oceans as well as naval attack strategies.

It was not humorous at all, but Rhutgard found some small humor in how tired the boys looked at the end of each day. No more did war hold such appeal. Even less appealing would war be the day the first sword swung.

Rhutgard's Study was now a makeshift headquarters, where military maps, maps of each country, both wide and detailed, and lists of information from resources were pinned to his walls. They were referring to his Study as the War Room now.

Lord Stanyard walked in with two pigeon parchments. Stanyard had been ensuring that no one overheard what was spoken of in the Study, the way the lads had. Guards were stationed farther down the hall, and they made use of the old bell system – just a simple ringing of a regular bell, to let food in and out, messages for the King, and people approved to be let in, such as Principea and the lads.

Rhutgard unrolled one of the pigeon parchments – it was on fine parchment and he knew it was from Clemongard before he even saw the wax seal.

To: King Rhutgard Anghus Firthing, First of His Name

Eastern Shield of the Eastern Shield Alliance

Clemongard accepts your gracious offer of an Alliance with the Eastern Alliance.

I await any Correspondence, as requested.

Your Ally,

Her Royal Majesty, Selby Cylysse Stevanrhut, First of Her Name

Queen of Clemongard

"Ah," Rhutgard nodded as he held the parchment up for all to see. "She accepts."

Around the War Room, sounds of acknowledgement resulted from his announcement.

And then the bell rang out in the foyer. Stanyard stepped outside briefly but walked in with several steaming trays of dinner. Was it evening already? Just as well, for Rhutgard was famished.

Now that Clemongard had officially allied with the Eastern Alliance, even if for what might turn out to be nothing at all, an exchange of information would prove very fruitful....

"Your Majesty, the other message…?" Stanyard pointed to the parchment Rhutgard was still holding in his palm.

"Where is it from, do you know?" He looked the parchment over, for it was dusty. "What does… 'PSt' mean?" he questioned Stanyard.

Stanyard shrugged. "Never heard of it, Sire," he replied.

Rhutgard shrugged. "Might be it got lost and came here by mistake." He popped the mysterious seal open.

To: King Firthing of Rhutgard

I write to inform you that Port Stanton, Ferrisport, and Chesterport, all on the North Hardewold coastline, have been shut down by incoming soldiers. They are dressed in common clothing but all know they are soldiers. They arrive in large ships each week and then travel north by land, and no one knows where. No one is allowed to leave from ports, only soldiers are allowed in. No one knows what country these soldiers come from and their ships are unmarked. King Reaghann may not know of this so I write to you as birds to HarCourt may not fly. – Anonymous

Rhutgard stared at the page. "…What? No." He read it again and then took in an enormous breath. PSt. Of course. Port Stanton. *Bloody hell.* Troops, through Hardewold, each week, from three different ports. *Bloody hell….*

"Reaghann." He said it quietly. Reaghann was the youngest of them all, had the least of time as a King, but times were, Rhutgard thought him the cleverest of all of them.

But this.

Reaghann was just laughing at a joke with Gerard and Rickstan.

"Reaghann." He tried not to sound angry, but did add a tone of insistence to his voice.

Reaghann heard him this time and approached. "Rhutgard?"

Rhutgard reminded himself that Reaghann was both young and had been on the throne what, five, six years? Nevertheless…

Rhutgard placed a hand on Reaghann's back and steered him toward the Information board, where they had put up all their resources, discovered from informants, learned on their own, and pooled together.

"Reaghann, what is the state of your Navy at present?"

"Near capacity. Two ships were lost in a storm, but shipwrights are rebuilding." Reaghann did not inquire as to the nature of the inquiry but lifted his eyebrows, clearly curious.

"When was the last time you visited a Naval Port?"

Reaghann rubbed at his chin as he thought. "Five months ago, I'd say. All was well, nothing out of the ordinary. I run Naval Port visits quarterly, to see for myself the state of my fleets, my Naval Yards, my men." Reaghann crossed his arms and looked directly at Rhutgard. He was clearly annoyed at what seemed like a questioning of his capabilities but refused to show it, out of respect for Rhutgard's office as the Eastern Shield.

And quarterly visits were an excellent practice, Rhutgard believed.

"How often do you receive reports?"

"Twice monthly from each port. Forgive me, Rhutgard, and accept my pardons, but is there a point to this interrogation?"

Rhutgard frowned. Bi-weekly, and nothing mentioning incoming soldiers. Perhaps this was a ruse.

"Rickstan," he called.

Rickstan hastened to join Rhutgard at the Information Board.

"Did the two of you not share an informant who went by the name of Anonymous?" asked Rhutgard quietly.

He watched the two of them flick a glance at each other. Now his temper was starting to fray. This was like trying to drag information out of Kendrick and Keldrick. Neither wanted to admit anything for which both were complicit.

"Obviously, both of you know more than you have shared with me, and that we will address shortly. First, there is the matter of this informant with whom you have both worked. Do you both trust this... *Anonymous?*" And Rhutgard pointed to the Rickstan's pigeon parchment and Reaghann's list of lords, both from Anonymous, both written in the same hand.

Immediately, both Kings nodded emphatically.

"And neither of you have any reason to doubt this informant?"

"None whatsoever," said Reaghann.

"That informant has my complete trust," added Rickstan.

Rhutgard's eyes narrowed. He'd heard more convincing lies from Keldrick and Kendrick. Something was not right. If one of them said, "Honest, Father, I promise," next, Rhutgard would not find it at all amiss.

"And we have established that both parchments are of the same handwriting." Rhutgard did not wait for them to comment.

"Since that is, indeed, the case, then I think we will establish that this – informant – of yours, whom, by your own words, you trust completely, you have no reason whatever to distrust – has also written this. I'm sure you will agree that the handwriting is the same.

"But first," and Rhutgard pinned it the wall next to the others, *"I want you to read it."* His dangerously low tone was warranted, Rhutgard thought.

He watched Reaghann's jaw drop open. He watched Rickstan close his eyes and sigh.

"I think that you two and I have a few things to discuss. Starting with whatever you haven't told me. Outside. Now."

—⸺—

"I would crack your skulls together if I thought that might make a difference," growled Rhutgard.

"I beg your –"

"No, my lords, you will, both of you, remain silent." Rhutgard held up a single finger and stuck it in both their faces.

"If either of you had bothered to open your stubborn mouths back when this had occurred, we might be a little better off than we are now. A little. You – masquerading as a mad man after he had you thrown into a prison under your dungeon. It reads like a tale. What both of you failed to do was report this to me. It is my responsibility to find out why these things happened. Why an assassin on your Council assisted your brother to imprison you. And now that your lives have returned to a semblance of normality, have either of you attempted to find the men responsible? Surely your brother was not working alone.

"Now, explain how I am to go in there and explain that my lord of Hardewold has had hundreds of soldiers sneaking into his country under his very nose for months now? More to the point, where are they going? Are they stationed in Hardewold? Have they gone to Delsynth? Do they plan to attack Ghiverny? Romeny? Join the Ormon forces? Hundreds and hundreds of soldiers, Reaghann. Fifty men per ship, each week, at three ports for four months – Nearly five thousand men have made it through the Eastern Alliance, and we don't know where they are now, who they are, why they're here, or what they're going to do. And those are just the ports we know of.

"Now, you tell me how I'm to go in there and tell them that."

Neither King said a word, though Rhutgard believed they were too shocked to say anything rather than out of his instruction to remain silent. In fact, all the blood had drained from Reaghann's face.

"Worse, I just offered troops to a seventeen-year-old Queen so that she doesn't lose her country. How am I to go back on that vow now I discover we need our own troops at home.

"What do I tell them in there?" He pointed emphatically toward the direction of his study.

No one said anything for a few seconds.

A light twilight breeze blew across the side garden.

Rhutgard saw Reaghann's auburn hair riffle a bit before he said quietly, "What would you like me to do, Rhutgard? Fall on my sword? Would that make it easier? Or I could kneel and you could execute me, behead me."

Rhutgard stared at him. The audacity!

"Why, you little –!" He punched him in the jaw.

Keldrick

He was so tired. If he never saw another printed word, it wouldn't be soon enough. His brain was mush. They were all dining in his chambers tonight, mainly so that they could eat all they wanted and consume large quantities of wine and, quite possibly, pass out. The kitchens were accustomed to such behavior from him and Kendrick, though not four princes all in the same room, so they had brought up an enormous selection of food and were probably hoping not to be rung for.

"Hey!" Ronan stood at the window. "Hey, come look at this!" He pulled the curtain back farther across Keldrick's window. He started laughing. "Two drunks down there, socking it out. Ooo – ouch!"

The four of them stood at the window watching the men near the end of the side courtyard, whaling on each other. They were really pounding on each other. Perfect entertainment for the evening! Keldrick mouthed down into another bite of his turkey leg.

A third lord in the courtyard stood about wincing and covering his hands at every blow. A stand-in, obviously.

The four of them laughed as the two men beat each other blow by blow. One of them picked the other up and dumped him on the ground. By this time, Dougall was taking bets.

Neither man had given up.

"They're doing pretty good, maybe they're not drunk," commented Kendrick.

"Maybe it's over a woman," Ronan suggested.

"Hey – hey!" Dougall pushed the curtain farther back even more. "Hey – oh – you know who that is? That's your father! That's *King Rhutgard* down there! Wow, what a punch that one was!"

"What!" Kendrick immediately ran to the end of the curtains.

"Who? It is not!" Keldrick pressed himself against the glass.

Ronan and Dougall burst into uncontrolled laughter.

"Ow, that was a good one!" laughed Ronan.

"Oh, that one's going to hurt, who's that he's with?" Dougall asked.

"Oy – that's King Reaghann! And that's King Rickstan with them," Ronan noted. "Wow – your father's still got it." He laughed again.

"Not for long once Mother finds him," Kendrick snickered. "Wow – that one is going to hurt - I don't who's winning."

"And he tells us not to fight. What's he call that, down there? The Eastern Shield, King of Romeny, out there, with the Hound, pounding on each other?" Keldrick snorted.

"Just wait 'til Mother sees him, all bloody and bruised up. She'll throw him in the dungeon," Kendrick scoffed. "Damn, good cross, Father! Way to give it back!"

"No, Mother won't throw him in a cell," mused Keldrick as he continued to watch the fight, "she'll just have a portrait commissioned. *'King Rhutgard Angus Firthing, After Getting His Royal Arse Handed to Him'* and she'll hang it in the Great Hall."

"It's a pretty even match, actually," Ronan said, and Dougall agreed.

"Well, it can't go on forever. I mean, where is Stanyard?" Keldrick wondered.

"Oh, look, look, look – what is he saying!" Kendrick pointed.

"Rickstan's breaking up the fight. Damn. Best entertainment I've seen in years. Look at him," Ronan laughed.

Dougall sat back and laughed as well. "The Eastern Shield just got dunked in a fountain!"

"And the Hound! Wonder who started it," Ronan wondered. "Look – Rickstan's dragging them inside like children."

"I will never forget that – the Eastern Shield and the Hound pounding on each other in the garden," Dougall proclaimed.

"Nor will I," Kendrick laughed.

"Nor I – who knew the old man had such a good right hook?" wondered Keldrick.

"That was a fierce fight – I wonder what brought it along?" Dougall asked.

"I want to see what the others do when they walk in like that…. Too bad we can't be the wall's eyes for that!" Ronan chortled.

Principea

She arrived with the servers and found Lord Stanyard with the Guards and the bell.

"Your – Majesty." Stanyard cleared his throat. Principea and Stanyard had, on occasions, found themselves at odds. But surely not over a morning meal.

"Come along, Stanyard, grab the other sideboard, here's a tray." Principea gestured to the other tray of food. If the boys were in there, more food would need to be sent up, but likely they were still asleep, for one of her ladies-in-waiting told her there had been quite a ruckus down in the Lords' Quarters. Principea had sighed and known it to be her sons. Hosting two other princes, she expected when they rose around midmorning, red-eyed and achy, last night's merriment would be a woeful memory.

At present, however, Stanyard's expression looked a combination between hilarity and apprehension.

"Relax, Stanyard, it's only breakfast." Principea pushed the double doors to her husband's study open. Stanyard held them open for her as she wheeled both sideboards in.

"Your Majesties, I've brought you breakfast. You have all been closeted in this room for a week now, and in able for you to think clearly, you need to have a good meal to start off the day.

"You, my lord of Delsynth, need a shave. This is a Council of Kings, after all, not a hunting trip with your best mates.

"Uncle, the same for you as well, and tighten up that surcoat, Sir. My lord of Romeny," she called to Rhutgard. "Were you all here so late then? I don't recall you coming in last night."

He was facing the wall, fascinated by a map, it seemed. She circled her arm about his shoulder.

Rhutgard's entire face was a mass of purple and black bruises. Two black eyes. His lip split in two places. Marks on his face where a ring looked to have hit it. Scratches upon his neck.

He wouldn't meet her eyes but had the grace to look guilty.

She sniffed and shook her head. "Ah, I can see where you did spend the night. If it was in a bed, it was in the Healer's Wing...." Principea wouldn't have thought he still had it in him. Truly, the stress in here must have been insurmountable.

"Really? That's all the sympathy you have for me?" Rhutgard wanted to know.

Principea smiled and walked away. "That depends upon your opponent." She stood in the front of the Study the men had styled the War Room. They and the lads were the only people in and out of here, and Lord Stanyard, of course. So who else might there have been....

Ah. "My lord of Hardewold. How fare you this morning?" She glided across the Study to King Reaghann, who was staring out the window, his back to her.

Principea stepped next to him and looked up at his face. Reaghann heaved a guilty sigh and looked down. His face looked quite like her Rhutgard's. Black and swollen eyes, bruises all over his face, split lip, small cuts most likely, she thought, from the rings of office Rhutgard wore. It would be a while before either of their faces healed.

Well, good. Fighting like boys.

To the rest of the room, she rose an eyebrow and asked, "Dare I ask what this was about?"

"Principea, 'twas nothing but a boxing match," came Rhutgard's voice.

Her gown rustled behind her as she stepped to the side of the room where Rhutgard cowered.

"A boxing match?" She chortled.

Rhutgard turned and glared at her from between red, swollen eyelids.

"Don't you turn those lying Romeny blues at me, my lord of Romeny," she scolded. Principea turned to Uncle. "What do we say in Ghiverny, Uncle? *Romeny eyes hide the best lies?*"

Rhutgard turned around and glared at Uncle. "Are you taking up with her now?"

Uncle coughed and took a step back. "I'm on nobody's side in this – keep me out." He held his hands up.

"So what really was this about, boys? What started it?" Men – all of them the same. It didn't matter if they were eight, fifteen, thirty, or fifty, they never got past that need to prove themselves. And she had two twin boys, both exactly like their father, so it had been much like raising male triplets, just one of them older in years.

First came Uncle – "Wine."

Next came Rickstan – "A woman."

Then Driscoll – "The length of their –"

Principea immediately interrupted him. "Lord Driscoll!"

"...swords. I was going to say, swords, Madam. What? I was," Driscoll insisted. Rarely had Principea ever seen this group in such a state. And Driscoll had always been the most stately of them all, the Silver Statesman, Rhutgard called him a few times in private with her, for the elder king was always so dignified and so skilled at diplomacy.

Uncle snorted laughter suddenly, as he was wont to do. "Possibly all three."

Principea glanced in the direction of her husband. "My lord of Romeny, I despair of you. I ought to send you to your bed to rest and then I might take over as Eastern Shield for a day. And I guarantee you," Principea pointed at all the Kings around the room, "half this Land's problems would be solved in a day. All it takes is a woman's perspective on things."

"A woman's perspective – ha. Just what we need," grumped Rhutgard.

Suddenly, Rickstan and Reaghann coughed in unison. Rhutgard shot them both a nasty look.

Uncle cleared his throat then. "Rhudy, it's actually not a bad idea," he said in a steady tone.

Her husband surprised her by nodding, though she could see his head was probably pounding. As was Reaghann's. Ridiculous. She wondered what had truly brought them to blows.

"Very well, then. Lord Stanyard, if you would ring for a servant to have the boys sent to us, please."

She wandered over to King Reaghann. "You, my lord Hound."

He looked down at her warily. He probably thought she was going to scold him. And, of course, most people were wary of her, for she was the wife of the most powerful man in the Land, after all.

"You need a wife."

King Reaghann started to laugh but saw her insistent glare and immediately changed his laugh to a cough. "So I've been told, Madam."

"You shall need to do so soon, before your... dog... can no longer... hunt." She glanced downward briefly, then met his gaze again. Principea enjoyed watching his green eyes grow round at her meaning, for she was being quite direct without being outright specific.

He swallowed and finally replied, "I enjoy a – great deal of – hunting, and I don't anticipate any issues arising, so to speak. I thank you for your kind regard."

Principea chuckled. Privately, Rhutgard had wondered about which country the Hound would eventually cast his eye upon. She smacked the Hound in the ribs with her fan. He winced.

"Rhutgard always has had a wicked upper cut," Principea smiled sweetly.

Merridon

He heard her long before she tiptoed into view. At first, he was unable to establish who the visitor was, merely that it was female. But soon, he eliminated all possibilities.

And there she was before him.

First, a guilty look slipped across her face. As she emboldened herself, she took in the sight of him. Most newcomers did. Merridon was neither twisted nor disfigured, but, he knew, he was not pleasing to behold. Perhaps when he was a child, but today, no more.

Now, she realized her rudeness and smiled a little.

Merridon beckoned her closer. "I don't bite." He smiled tiredly.

Even in the dimness of the room, he saw her cheeks flush with embarrassment as she approached.

"You would be my new sister. I knew you be up here soon enough. Please, have a seat." Merridon gestured at the chair across from the table. Mostly, only Father visited him, and they played a game of Ice or two, talked of the happenings in the Land.... Occasionally, Stanyard visited, but not of late.

Merridon's new sister. That had been quite a shock. He wasn't sure if Father had been paranoid at the time, or if the move had been warranted. Merridon had looked into the History of the Era and found how many deaths had occurred around the Eastern Alliance, and decided that possibly Father might have been both, with the end of the Twenty Years War still resonating in his mind. Merridon had read much about the lingering after-effects of wars and tragedies on soldiers and citizens. This library of his dwarfed the Royal Fairview Library by three times, he believed, and he knew he would never have enough time to read it all.

Mirelle. There was no doubt her resemblance to the twins. What there would be was doubt upon the people's reaction once they found out where she'd lived her entire life. An ale-house? Just hiding her away was an odd choice, for Father might have sired more children at his age, should she have passed away. But an ale-house.... Merridon saw an interesting twist to that. If anyone knew of her birth at all, they would never think to look for her among the poorest and underprivileged of all the city, where villains and offenders flourished. Father entrusted his only daughter to that innkeeper, a mate from the war, so if Father trusted that man, then the rest of them were right to as well.

Merridon saw she was studying him.

"I'm sorry I've not come earlier," she said. Her voice was light and lilting. "I didn't see you at the Seasonal."

He smiled wryly in reply. "Do I look like I should attend a Seasonal? I'd scare them away."

"But – you're the Crown Prince," Mirelle responded. She wasn't scolding him, but she sounded suspiciously like her mother, the Queen. Did she inherit that, Merridon wondered off-handedly, or did she learn it where she grew up....

He gestured idly with a hand.

Mirelle's brows drew together. "And there's an Assembly of the Eastern Council going on. You should be attending that. Even Kendrick and Keldrick are there." Now, Merridon believed she was scolding him.

Aloud, he said, "An *'Assembly of the Eastern Council'?* Is that what they're calling it?" He shook his head and scoffed.

Mirelle frowned. "Yes. We were told it was a tradition."

Merridon shook his head. "Well, they are assembled, and it is a tradition, I'll give them that much."

Mirelle's eyes studied him. "Well, what else would it be?"

"It's a War Council."

Her mouth dropped. "A what?"

"It's a War Council. They are discussing war tactics and strategies. For we are not at war yet, Sister, but we will be soon."

Finally, she recovered. "Then – then… you are Crown Prince. All the other princes are in there. Why are you not in there, Brother? Are you not…" and Mirelle gestured all about the stacks of leather-bound books that he loved so, "… learned? Have you not learned something of war in here and in your education as a prince?"

"Oh, quite a lot. I have actually contributed a number of works –" and he waved his hand to the books that surrounded him, "to the cause, as it were. For my brothers, and the other princes to read, assist with…" he trailed off.

Mirelle continued to stare at him. Once, long ago, Merridon had that same stare, full of vigor, interest in the Land about him. Now, he was just so …tired.

"In all fairness, in all honesty, Sister of mine – but I have forgotten my manners. Welcome to the family, Sister. It is nice to have a Sister – you will be a pleasant addition to our family."

Mirelle smiled faintly. She did take after Principea, merely a blonde version.

"Now, as I was saying, Sister… in all fairness, in all honesty… do I look capable of sitting the throne of Romeny? I, King of Romeny, Eastern Shield of the Eastern Alliance?"

Merridon watched as she dropped her eyes. When she finally looked back over the table at him, he told her, "I can't even remember the last time I left this room. My bed is in the far corner back there," and he nodded behind him.

And there was the look. It always came. Pity. Merridon didn't want it. He had his blankets, his books, his bed – he was perfectly comfortable here. Except that he felt sick more and more often now, and the sickness itself had grown worse. He would never tell Father that, though.

He continued. "Soon enough, I will abdicate the throne. Kendrick is far more capable than I. If I were to hazard a guess, I would believe most common people, even perhaps the nobles, have forgotten I even exist."

"Abdicate…." Mirelle was absorbing this news.

"I can't rule Romeny from in here, nor certainly act as Eastern Shield." He smiled a little. He wouldn't admit to Father now that even playing a game of Ice exhausted him, but he stayed awake for Father's sake. "Mirelle, I'm sick. Certainly, you see that."

She nodded.

Merridon had no looking glass here, but he occasionally caught his reflection in a window when he passed. He knew his skin had a pale, sickly pallor to it, and that much of his hair had receded from his temple. He'd not needed to shave for almost two years now.

Bravely, she asked, "Is it – the wasting disease, then?"

Thank the gods it wasn't that.... "No. I don't believe I was ever fated for a long life to start with, given the circumstances I was born under. But now. Now fate is being helped along, since we are coming to the start of a war."

"I – I don't understand." Mirelle looked puzzled.

"Arsenic. A little each week, at first. I recognized it once I saw the powder now and again along the sides of a plate or bowl when it hadn't been mixed in completely. Now I see it about four times a week."

"Poison! Why do you continue to take it?" She was horrified.

Merridon shrugged. "Clearly, someone wants me out of the way. I've not been dying fast enough, it would seem."

"You've not told him! What if – whoever it is – is poisoning someone else! How dare you not tell him!"

"And what if he ordered it?" Merridon asked.

Mirelle's mouth dropped open. "No," she finally said. "I don't believe he would do that. He loves all of his children. He would never do that," she said firmly.

"As it happens, I agree with you," Merridon responded. A yawn overtook him before he could stop it. "I'm so sorry – it's not the company, I assure you."

Mirelle sat and glared at him.

"My sweet Sister. War is upon us, thus the reason for this War Council. And I will soon abdicate the Throne, in favor, I assume, of Kendrick, whom I believe to be next in the line of succession. Please believe me when I say that I welcome this opportunity, this – hastening of my demise, whether that be known to my poisoner or no. Some did not expect me to live as long as I have, minus the poison, of course. So, my dear, you must not tell Father, and on that I will have your word, please."

"My word. To not tell the King that someone is poisoning one of his sons. You're mad. That – poison – has made you mad. You cannot expect me to turn a blind eye and watch you just – fade away because someone, some traitor is killing you slowly each week. How can you ask that of me?"

Merridon sighed deeply. It was so hard to stay awake anymore during the day. Could she not just do as he wished....

"Have you seen any other people who are ill? Who look as I do?"

"No," she responded with reluctance.

"Then watch with persistence. I beg of you this favor. A dying man asking his Sister a boon. For I am, you know, dying."

She swallowed.

"Just let it alone. I'm quite sure it will pass once – I do. Please – as a favor. Do not tell Father," Merridon insisted.

Mirelle looked down at his table stubbornly. Ah, he remembered that stubborn expression from the twins, that set of the jaw stubbornness. He would miss not watching her flourish as a member of the Court, marry, become a mother. Merridon took in another deep sigh. Inhaling was getting harder and harder to do....

When she looked up at him, she nodded slowly. "But only because you insisted as a favor."

"Your word?"

"My word," she said, though she was unhappy about it.

Good. "Next time you visit, Mirelle, I shall have to teach you to play Ice. I have a feeling you would be a worthy opponent. But for now, Sister, I must rest...."

Rhutgard

He had survived Principea's scolding, at least her public one. She always knew what to say, and yet what not to. His head was pounding. His whole head was, to be sure, but he'd never admit that. The Healers had given them both enough dullwort last night to cut the pain a bit, and for today as well, though Rhutgard had not yet taken it, for it was to be taken with a liquid. Of course, they had absolutely laughed. In their King's face. And a visiting King's. What was it with Healers that made them believe themselves infallible to the law of the Land? Rhutgard, the most powerful man in the Land, had fallen asleep to the sound of Healers laughing over him. He really did hate Healers.

Finally, the boys trooped in. Well, mused Rhutgard with some satisfaction, at least he wouldn't be the only one with a pounding head this morning. Each of the lads looked tired and as hung over as he had ever been, wincing from the sunlight, bloodshot eyes. Principea had ordered them out of bed and down here to join them in all haste, along with a breakfast for each of them as well.

Finally, tea. He surreptitiously slipped some dullwort into his tea and swirled it around before he downed it.

Across the room, he heard Reaghann wince aloud at the hot tea he'd downed. If Reaghann's face was anything to judge by, then Rhutgard knew he looked just as awful – swollen and black-eyed, split-lipped....

Principea glided over to Reaghann. He grimaced as he held his jaw.

"Loose tooth, my lord of Hardewold?" she asked with sympathy.

He prodded about with a finger on his face and nodded slowly. "Possibly."

Rhutgard suddenly couldn't resist saying, "You know there's a cure for that. Works every time...."

Reaghann's eyes narrowed, but he waited for Rhutgard to continue.

"Pulling the fucker out."

Reaghann glared at him across the room, while Principea, horrified, called out, "Rhutgard! Your language! What has happened to you!"

Rhutgard just could not help but grin and heard snorts of laughter from the boys in the corner, though they turned around to hide their expressions.

The other Kings in the room had far more practice schooling their demeanors but even Driscoll looked amused.

The last time someone had actually punched Rhutgard was, in fact, Luvian. At least Rhutgard had not lost a tooth this time. Rhutgard worried a bit about Luvian over the last few weeks, though there was nothing for it. But whenever Rhutgard saw his daughter, he saw her confidence, her good-natured personality, her quiet dignity, and knew he'd placed her with the right man....

He cleared his throat and called the Council to order.

"First order." Then he paused.

Three Kings were staring at him with expectant looks on their faces, while all four lads, hung over or not, were drinking in the sight of the King of Romeny, Eastern Shield, purpled, blackened, bruised, cut, scratched up, and split-lipped.

No. That was not an item up for discussion.

"Details surrounding last night's – boxing match – will not be disclosed." He looked meaningfully at each person in the room, including Principea and Reaghann, to indicate that incident was sealed and thus over, closed.

Reaghann's face was unreadable.

"Now. An item we will address is of a nature far more disturbing, to say the least. We have just received excellent information from an extremely credible source that – as many as possibly five thousand troops have entered Hardewold via its northernmost coastal ports, and have headed north on foot. According to our source, they are unmarked troops, from unmarked ships. Those three ports have been locked down for approximately three to four months.

"We do not have any information yet as to where these troops are. They may be in Hardewold. The first half may have made it into Delsynth.

"We also do not know their intentions. Are they planning a strike against the Eastern Alliance in more than one country? Just one country? Or are they traveling through to Ormon? Even Ambsellon?

"And that is a new development that we must immediately face and conquer."

Every face was disbelieving, from his sons to Principea. Even Reaghann looked a bit sickened at the presentation.

The room remained silent for just a few seconds more. Rhutgard waited....

And then the pandemonium erupted. Many of them demanded answers from Reaghann and others babbled at each other in astonishment.

Reaghann flinched a bit but stood his ground, for he had already suffered through condemnation earlier for having unsavory characters on his Council and an assassin in his midst.

Rhutgard held his hands up high and yelled, "ENOUGH!"

All in the room stared at him.

Rhutgard walked over to Reaghann and stood beside him. He held an arm around the Hardewold King and announced, "There will be no denouncement in this room by anyone of anyone at any time.

"Reaghann has a very sound plan for checking his Naval yards and fleets, and immediately after he inspected these ports, they were shut down and troops came in. He gets bi-weekly reports from all military operations in his country. His Naval ports have all been telling him that nothing new has occurred and that all has been as usual. He has been given no reason to expect otherwise and would have left for another inspection in just three weeks.

"That is a very sound way to run a country and all of us might do well to imitate it if we haven't already such a singular operation ourselves.

"May I remind you that Reaghann's country is larger than any country in all this Alliance, and if people are paid to infiltrate it, it would be very difficult to discern.

"What has happened to Reaghann could easily have happened to any of us. It may actually have happened to any of us at this moment. We are appalled now because of the ramifications, and what appears to be proof. But this could have happened to any of us – getting false reports from anywhere, anyone, not so hard to imagine, is it? Therefore, be not so quick to judge.

"Reaghann has my full support, as would any of you, had this occurred to you in your countries. Hardewold is in need right now, and as an ally, and a friend, we will immediately move to strike back.

"But –" Rhutgard let his last word linger.

"We must also consider what these people might be doing. Where they are likely to be, how they are likely to get there.

"War is no longer on the horizon. We are at war.

"Until we know where these soldiers are, we don't know how to fight them, and so we need scouts. Fast ones. Dispatch them immediately, each of you. No one leaves until we know who we're fighting and where. No one leaves until we all have a solid battle plan."

Rhutgard pointed at the lads against the far wall. "You four. You are now each a full part of this War Council. Mind your manners and don't act like men, be men. The time for acting is over.

"What I want to know first – is who are these soldiers? Who are they? And why are they taking ship around the WetLands to as far as Port Stanton... rather than sailing in the opposite direction, or walking in any direction?"

Ronan interrupted him then. "If I may, Your Majesty –"

"Ronan!" Gerard cuffed him. "Manners, boy!"

"I beg your pardon, Your Majesty."

"It's all right, Ronan. Had you something relevant to offer on this subject?"

"You know of my previous assignment, Your Majesty. I was only to observe and report. Over the last six months, unmarked soldiers with fair complexions traveled up the Rosh River from what I believed was the west, always in groups of three and four. I occasionally heard a Western accent, but other than fair complexions, nothing gave them away."

"Fair complexions," mused Rhutgard. He walked over to the maps of the West.

"That could be any of the Coastals," Driscoll observed in his dry tone.

"Why would any of the Coastals be sending troops here?" Principea chimed in.

"Not King A'dair?" wondered Rhutgard. He was just about to expound further upon S'hendalow when Ronan spoke up again.

"Your Majesty –" and Gerard cuffed him again.

"Manners, boy! This is the Eastern Shield you're talking to!" Gerard hissed. "I apologize, Your Majesty, we did teach him manners, he's just lost them somewhere, I'm so sorry."

"Begging your pardon, Your Majesty." Ronan looked down immediately.

Rhutgard sighed. He couldn't remember what he was going to say anyway. He rubbed his forehead and gestured at Ronan. "Young Martel? If you mind your manners from henceforth, I would like to hear what you have to say."

Ronan looked up, troubled. "I apologize, Your Majesty. Living as I did for so long, I grew accustomed to speaking out whenever I pleased. I most humbly apologize.

"I do, however, have a number of my own sources whom I made and I learned through one that the new S'hendalow king has completely changed everything there. He got rid of his Council and only has Inner Secretaries now, who report to him with information that he requires each week, and they have people who supply them with information with what they need to do their job. He refuses to have a group of old men tell him how to run his country, was what my source said when he disbanded his Council Members.

"A'dair is also betrothed and will wed soon, and is building warships of his own, but it would seem only for protection, as he is not building in large quantities. My source says A'dair also recruited new armed forces recently, but again, only to booster S'hendalow's defensive abilities.

"So, with my humblest respects, Your Majesty, I would offer that S'hendalow is neither sending troops nor aiding in any design of conflict, present or future, though that is not for me to say."

And with that, Ronan finished.

Rhutgard took all of this in. He nodded. Again, he was impressed with Gerard's son. That boy would be an excellent king someday… many, many years from now be it.

The others were silent as they made sense of Ronan's information. Rhutgard smiled inwardly as he saw Gerard place both hands on Ronan's shoulders with pride.

"Well, then. I think it safe to rule out S'hendalow," Rhutgard announced to the members of the War Council and gave a quick nod to Ronan. Gerard should be very proud of that young man, very proud.

"Then where does that leave us?" asked Principea. "Corstarorden? He's a canny old man. But does he have so many ships that he could send troops to such account here?"

"I could see the old vulture resupplying them, perhaps, but where are they coming from, Ambsellon? Why would they sail this far? Why not just attack?" Driscoll ventured.

"Ronan told us they were of fair complexions, which cancels out both the Northern Countries. That leaves us only with Tortoreen. And, of course, Storden, but –" Rhutgard rolled his eyes about Storden. Everyone knew Storden was neutral.

"And Tortoreen only does anything that benefits it the most," Gerard observed dryly.

Suddenly, Rickstan – or *Rilstrom*, Rhutgard thought to himself - stood up and stared at the maps. Rhutgard made nothing of it. Tortoreen was, of course, on the opposite side of Shaw, divided only by the Silver and Singing Rivers. Rickstan then glanced at Reaghann.

Reaghann raised his eyebrows. Rhutgard heard Reaghann say lowly, "That's a bit of a leap, don't you think?"

Rickstan shrugged. "Possibly," he returned lowly.

Aloud, Rickstan called out, "King Harvick in Storden now has twin boys. To his Crown Prince Varley."

Principea laughed. "Those will some very long nights for his wife."

Ronan, Keldrick and Kendrick all stood up. "Varley is here," they all said.

"I don't like him."

"Nor do I."

"He's a tool."

"All right, all right, I did say to mind your manners."

"Father, it's a fact, the man's an arse and he's been all over Mirelle. He hasn't left her alone," Kendrick insisted.

"I'm surprised you haven't received a betrothal request yet," Keldrick said.

Rhutgard snorted. "Mirelle will not be marrying, nor betrothed to anyone, for some time to come. Particularly to someone you've described so thoroughly."

Rickstan coughed. "He is... fair complected. As are his people. Could it be that his father doesn't want him to sit the throne, in favor of the twins? That is what we call a – motive? Brothers in favor of other brothers. Perhaps Varley found out his father's plans to disinherit him and is now dismantling Storden in return... and the Clemongard Queen was right after all. She is going to be assaulted on three fronts, and it is Storden soldiers who have sailed in to your ports, Reaghann..."

"Moving north to Ormon as an ally?" continued Reaghann with widened eyes.

And Gerard finished by saying, "And here he is in your Court, Rhutgard, courting your only daughter."

Principea looked over at him with fright on her face and ice ran through his veins....

Merridon

Father walked in and sat down before him. Merridon had heard him long before he had appeared. He'd grown used to Father's footsteps long ago, a brisk, purposeful stride, not a heavy one but focused.

Merridon stared at him for a moment.

"For once, Father, I can easily say that you look worse than I do."

Father snorted and shook his head. "On that score, you're right."

"Tell me you won." Merridon leaned forward. Father's face a mess of bruises – not one but two black eyes, so someone must have had a good one-two swing. A split lip with a slight scab. Purpled bruising... Merridon wished he'd seen that fight. There's a man awaiting trial down in the Dungeon somewhere, if he hasn't already been hung, he thought with amusement.

Father sighed. "Between you, me, and these dusty books of yours – I think it was a bit of a fair fight. But I knocked a tooth loose, so, there's that." Father gave a bit of smile but stopped when it stretched the scab on his lip.

"And has he been hung yet? Or is he at least sitting in a cell?" Merridon could not take his eyes off his father. Father had trained his sons in a bit of boxing when they were boys, but apparently, he'd forgotten to keep up his guard.

"Well – can't do that, not either of them. Or at least, it hasn't been done in, probably two or three centuries...." Father licked his lower lip.

"Hanging? You may be as sick as I am, too, Father. A good blow to the head may have rattled your brains."

"No – not that. It was Hardewold. Cheeky little runt. Can't hang a king of the Eastern Alliance."

Merridon's eyebrows shot upward. "No! You and the Hound, going at it! Over... what, policy? Please, Father. At least tell me a fight like that –" he threw his hands up toward Father's face, "was over a really good reason, a woman, or because you were completely racked." Merridon laughed. Best visit in years.

Father rolled his eyes to one side and considered. "I suppose you could say it was over a woman, but not in the conventional sense...."

"Oh, Father, please. Stop being so boring and tell me. Were you at least racked?"

"No! I was sober and I was pissed off, are you happy, then?"

"Well, what about the Hound? Him, it could be definitely be a woman. And racked."

"No more so than I, I'm afraid."

Merridon sighed with disappointment. Then he brightened. "Speaking of women, how did my step-mother take it?" He had never met another person so proper and mannerly. "I'll bet you got your arse handed to you again once she saw you." He laughed.

"Did you call me here for a reason, Merridon, or was it simply to jest at your father?"

"I actually did have a reason, but jesting at the most powerful man in the Land looking like shit takes a bit of precedence." Merridon could not help but laugh again. He had rarely seen his father appear at all unseemly, perhaps a few times unshaven... a few times. This – was quite memorable.

Father smiled a little with affection. They had come to a point in their relationship where Merridon was an adult and they could speak with each other as adults now. He accorded Merridon the respect he spoke to other adults with. Merridon suddenly recognized it for such two or three years ago, for Father was not just being a father, or a king, but speaking of random adult matters as friends did.

But at the moment, he saw that whatever was happening in the War Council was taking its toll on Father and he looked exhausted, and even beneath the bruises, Merridon could see lines of worry. Well, this wasn't going to help.

"But, Father, I did have a reason for asking you here." And Merridon handed him the sealed parchment.

Father stared at it and then looked up at Merridon. He took it but didn't open it.

Gesturing with it, he asked, "What, Merridon, is this?"

"Read it, Father."

Father didn't glare at him. But he did heave in a long sigh.

He popped open the seal.

To: His Royal Majesty of Romeny,

King Rhutgard Anghus Farradan Firthing, First of His Name

Eastern Seal of the Eastern Seal Alliance:

I, Merridon Angus Tallard Firthing,

First Son and Crown Prince

of King Rhutgard Anghus Farradan Firthing, First of His Name,

Eastern Seal of the Eastern Seal Alliance

Do Hereby Abdicate and Renounce all claims to the

Royal Throne of Romeny, all of its Titles, and Responsibilities Therein,

to include the Title of Eastern Shield of the Eastern Shield Alliance.

On This Day, I Do So Swear:

"Merridon. What is this?"

"Father. I am abdicating the throne. I believe that makes Kendrick the Crown Prince now," Merridon replied quietly.

"But you needn't do this, Merridon. You may yet –"

"Father!" Merridon slapped the table with both hands. He loved his father dearly, but he clung to his ideals, he never saw the truth of things unless it was shoved up in his face, and even then, he would refuse to confront it.

That had gotten Father's attention. Merridon reached out and placed his own, weak, pale hands atop Father's hands. "Father," he said gently. "I am dying. You know this, whether you want it to be true or not. Soon, I won't be able to leave my bed." He stared intently into his father's eyes. "I cannot ever be king. We both knew that many years ago. With war starting, it is best that I abdicate now, so that you teach Kendrick, and Keldrick as well, all they need to know about running a kingdom. I am doing this now, so that you needn't deal with – unnecessary paperwork – later."

Merridon smiled gently. He was suddenly seized by emotion – he hadn't realized how hard this would be.

Father stared up at the ceiling and swallowed. Merridon saw his jaw clenching.

Finally, he looked back down at Merridon and nodded shortly. His eyes were bright with emotion he was struggling to hold back.

Merridon took a deep breath and twisted off his Crown Prince signet ring. It was too big for his finger now, anyway. He offered it forward to Father.

Father pushed his hand back. As he spoke, his voice trembled. "Crown Princes – who abdicate – wear their signet rings on their other hand." Tears spilled down his face. "*Damnit, Merridon –*" and he pushed his chair back with such force that it fell over as he left the library.

Merridon heard something in the corridor crash into pieces.

Ronan

While they were awaiting news from Eastern Alliance Scouts, Ronan had returned to his Guard Duty. And while he had been in the War Council, word had finally been released that Mirelle had grown up under the constant watch of a retired Lieutenant of the Twenty Years War... who just happened to run a very reputable tavern. Though where she had grown up would never be released, the Palace wanted to release this information now rather than it be discovered elsewhere by other individuals. It was hinted that she grew up far, far away from the Palace, and thus searching for her origin home would prove a futile endeavor.

This information was accepted with mixed reactions. Obviously, members of the Court were both fascinated and scandalized by this tidbit. They loved anything to gossip over and seized upon this as a juicy treat. Although they had found Mirelle easily a member of their own formerly, now they eyed her with curiosity, for her manners and graces were impeccable. Salacious questions had arisen as to whether she was legitimately born, though all could see the resemblance to the twins, Ronan fumed.

Even the common people were taken with her, though now more so, Ronan believed, for they thought of her as someone who knew how they lived, what their lives were like, a Royal who truly understood the commoners for once. Rumors were floating about that they were calling her the Princess of the People.

Ronan's gaze found Mirelle on the terrace below, surrounded by the noblewomen of the court. She glided easily among them with a poise that belied the artless, laughing young girl from South Fairview. None would guess that the refined young Princess below had lived her life behind the bar of a brew house, taking orders from bawdy customers, cleaning tables, and serving ale.

He watched the young women of the court dance about her, hoping to divert her attention long enough to engage her in sycophantous conversation. An association with the new Princess of Romeny would prove advantageous amidst their social circles. Ronan flicked his eyes away, all that outwardly revealed his disgust.

The particular detachment of the Royal House Guard next to him whispering and snorting laughter amongst themselves was liveried more than armored. The House Guard was reserved more for men of high birth who were no longer Squires and continued to stay on at the Palace until their contracts with the King were severed by their lord fathers. No House Guards would ever be stationed at battle posts nor be assigned life-threatening missions, and most of them would stay on here during the war, Ronan was sure, or protect their own homes. Sugar, most of them.

While they were well trained in weaponry by the best of ArmsMasters, Ronan scoffed inwardly at the idea that any of these men would brandish a sword about for more than entertainment in the immediate future. Though not all the House Guard was so lacking in combat acumen, the poorly disciplined detachment of men next to him was hardly more than courtiers in uniform to Ronan's mind.

"Oy, so, Sergeant Martel," called Corporal Tarleton as he leaned lazily on the dusty sill of the bailey with a slow, cocky half smile. "Is it true that you knew the Princess before she was, well, the Princess?" Tarleton jerked his chin toward Mirelle in the courtyard below.

Ronan's eyes narrowed as he faced Tarleton. "She was an acquaintance," he returned shortly.

Tarleton's smile widened. "A guard for an ale girl. I'll bet you knew her, Sergeant. I should have applied for that station. That's a girl I'd get to know real well," he snickered as he threw a lewd smirk over his shoulder to the rest of the men.

Ronan nodded slowly, then stepped forward, the gravel of the bailey stones beneath his boots crunching. Private Hampton stood before him, alarm growing in his eyes.

"Private."

Private Hampton immediately stepped behind Corporal Tarleton, fumbling in his haste.

"Corporal Tarleton."

Ronan advanced slowly until he was staring into Corporal Tarleton's brown eyes. A light breeze riffled the fringe of blond hair across his temple. Silence fell over the unit, each man stiff with anticipation. Corporal Tarleton's normally condescending expression finally faded. "Sergeant?"

"Corporal Tarleton." Tarleton finally blinked hesitantly. "You are speaking of a member of the Royal House of Romeny." Ronan kept his tone low and harsh.

Tarleton's demeanor relaxed. "Yes, Sir, Sergeant."

"Do you find this amusing, Corporal?" Ronan's gaze bore into Tarleton.

"I, no, it's just –" And then that cocky smirk crossed his features again.

Ronan grabbed him by the lacings of his uniform and slammed him into the cold stone bailey wall. Tarleton's head bumped forward off of the rock and the man winced with pain. Then fury crossed his features.

"What the –! What was that for!" Corporal Tarleton immediately rubbed the back of his head, his eyes wide with outrage. "It's just what everyone else is talking about!"

Ronan punched him in the face. He took immense pleasure in watching the Corporal slide to the gravel, bright red blood spurting from his nose, dripping down his usually smug countenance.

"Corporal Tarleton, you have grievously insulted Her Royal Highness of Romeny. Offending any member of the Royal House of Romeny constitutes a treasonous crime, punishable by execution or imprisonment. I trust that, as a member of the Romeny Royal House Guard, you know this.

"You will immediately report to Colonel Daxton. You will, at his convenience, recount all that has transpired here in full, and await my arrival. You are dismissed." Ronan turned his back on the belligerent corporal.

"Private Hampton, advance."

"Sergeant Martel, sir!" The young private awaited Ronan's command. The entire company now stood a formal attention, their faces expressionless.

"You will direct this company of House Guardsmen in Corporal Tarleton's place until directed otherwise." The young private saluted smartly and stepped to the front of the House Guard.

Ronan would wager none of them would speak ill of the Royal Family again. Grimly, he looked out over the courtyard again.

—⊱※⊰—

"Your Royal Majesty." Ronan bowed. King Rhutgard nodded in acknowledgment.

"Sergeant Martel." Ronan inwardly was glad the King had not called him Ronan as he was wont to do.

"Colonel Daxton, sir!" He saluted Colonel Daxton firmly.

"Sergeant," replied Daxton mildly.

"Sergeant, I understand why you did it, but did you have to break his nose?" King Rhutgard asked. He and the Colonel chuckled. "I need Lord Tarleton's good will."

"As you say, Your Majesty," Ronan replied.

"Ah, cut the shit. Colonel?" Rhutgard gestured impatiently to Colonel Daxton.

"Sergeant Martel, please relate the events that occurred between you and Corporal Tarleton this afternoon."

"Yes, sir. The Corporal's speech was offensive to Her Royal Highness of Romeny. I disciplined him and sent him to you, sir."

"He'll make a politician yet. His father would be proud," mused the King.

"With all due respect, Your Majesty, his only parent is Romeny now," Colonel Daxton replied.

"Yes, that's so. But both parents are proud of him today, I'll say," returned King Rhutgard gruffly.

"Sergeant, please relate with *specifics* all that occurred this afternoon," Colonel Daxton told him.

So Ronan carefully recounted the events that led to Corporal Tarleton's dismissal from the House Guard. "Allowing others to speak maliciously of the Royal Princess is hurtful to her and to the Royal Family, Your Majesty. I felt it should be immediately addressed." He turned this last comment to King Rhutgard.

"You were right to do so. We expected some – opposition, of course, but within the ranks…." King Rhutgard trailed off, his face stern. "Well, then. We shall work quickly to dispel this – rumormongering."

Ronan expected to be dismissed, but instead, Colonel Daxton asked, "And how would you punish the young man, Sergeant?"

Taken aback, Ronan replied, "It is not for me to decide his punishment, sir."

"I did not ask who should decide the punishment of the young man. I asked how you would punish him," returned Colonel Daxton solemnly.

Ronan thought for a moment. "Muck the stables for the rest of the afternoon. Sleep with the pigs this evening. All officer rank and rights revoked. Bunk with the men-at-arms. Promotions possible only six months' minimum at a time each. Any further infractions of any kind will incur the severest of sentences."

Colonel Daxton and King Rhutgard exchanged an amused glance.

"I was just going to send him home with a dishonorable discharge," chuckled King Rhutgard. "Why not just send the boy home?"

"Your Majesty, in these uncertain times, we need every soldier we can spare." Ronan answered gravely.

Rhutgard harrumphed, a slow smile crossing his face. "Sergeant, I like your way of thinking, it shows foresight. I've decided your punishment is much better," he announced. "Colonel Daxton? Anything to add?"

Colonel Daxton shook his head. "Nothing, Your Majesty."

"Good. But forgo the stable mucking. Let the boy have his face tended to instead. I don't need Lord Tarleton's complaining of his son not getting proper medical attention. If the boy lasts a month in men-at-arms' quarters, I'll be surprised. That will be all. Sergeant, Colonel, you are dismissed."

———— ·ᴥ· ————

Ronan stepped into the quiet alcove. He had been summoned by the Colonel, but found instead another uniformed soldier. The soldier's decorated uniform identified him as a field Colonel, but Ronan did not know him.

"Colonel, sir."

"You would be Sergeant Martel, I'm assuming," the Colonel said drily as he returned the salute with firm precision. Sharp gray eyes studied Ronan, and Ronan found himself admiring the Colonel, plainly an experienced career soldier. Bald with a slight but precisely trimmed fringe around the side of his head, his weathered face bore a strength that came only from combat.

"Yes, sir."

"Colonel Daxton was –" here he looked down his nose and stared frankly at Ronan "unexpectedly reassigned – to one of our posts in North Romeny. I arrived here this morning to replace his command. I am Colonel Gregorick."

Ronan took this news in with interest and noted Colonel Gregorick's unmistakable emphasis when informing him of Colonel Daxton's reassignment. So soon after Corporal Tarleton's demotion, too. The Corporal had just left for home two days ago, Ronan had heard. He was sure the two were linked. King Rhutgard was crafty that way. Ronan decided the King was taking no chances with loyalties when it came to his daughter. Colonel Daxton's reassignment was not punitive in nature as far as Ronan could discern, for little if any fighting would be seen there. But the post was far from political gain.

"Colonel, sir."

"Let us hope you and your unit have no further incidents such as what I was recently informed of. There is rank, and there is leadership. Be sure not to confuse the two.

"Dismissed."

Ronan saluted smartly and turned on his heel. The Colonel was right. If Ronan had led that unit better from the start, those soldiers never would have considered insulting Mirelle, but been her fiercest advocate.

They were going to be very busy today....

Rhutgard

After Ronan's information of rumormongering in the ranks, Rhutgard wanted immediately to speak with Mirelle. He had seen her in passing, of course, and during the Seasonal.

And she was beautiful. So much like Principea. And the boys as well – her mannerisms somehow, so odd how she would somehow mirror them upon occasion, even though she'd never seen them until two months ago. And she had Principea's laugh.

Rhutgard had wanted to let Mirelle settle in before he and Principea pressured her. But since the Seasonal, with the War Council... he sighed. Time had flown past.

He wanted to check on her and see how Mirelle was handling the stress of the Court's reaction to where she had been raised. Rhutgard made sure, in the statement, to say that she had grown up far away from Fairview Palace.

So far as everyone at The Brew House and Tavern knew, "Ellia" went to stay with a sick aunt down south in the small town of Himbledon and then married a man just recently. A woman matching Ellia's description was, indeed, now living in Himbledon with a gentleman there. All, of course, financed by the Crown.

A number of nosy people had stopped in Himbledon recently, according to Rhutgard's undercover guards. Many of the townspeople there, not knowing better, confirmed that a young woman named Ellia was, indeed, living among them now, and recently married.

Ellia's actual stand-in stayed home quite a lot and rarely went to town now, preferring her quiet, married life after such a busy life in the city of Fairview, and no one thought anything of that.

Meanwhile, the real Ellia, Mirelle, had adjusted beautifully to Court life and was working unbeknownst to all, with a tutor on many subjects she had not learned with Nona. Her tutor gave Principea reports and Principea adjusted her education as needed.

But now that the gossip had begun, Rhutgard feared her carefully structured face of self-assurance might crack. It was one thing to adjust to a new life, he thought, but another when those in it were whispering terrible things about you.

Rhutgard had hated to announce such information, but he and Principea had agreed that it was necessary, for if they did not and she was recognized by someone in Fairview, then it would look as if he had simply been unfaithful and Mirelle adopted as a between-the-sheets illegitimate child that he had just discovered. And also best to announce it immediately, while the people were still adjusting to the thought of her, rather than after they had formed a solid opinion of her.

And before the war, he thought with a grimace, for now she was last in his immediate line of succession. He knew half of the country wondered why he had hidden her away, but he needn't explain his actions to anyone. Daughters carried the bloodline truest. They hadn't been present at the time she and the twins had been born. But he knew a number of people had read the most recent copies of the History of the Era's. Perhaps that would serve to convince them.

"Father? Mother?" Mirelle asked as she stopped before them. They looked over the empty Great Hall.

Rhutgard could see Mirelle studying the last of the bruises on his face, though she said nothing.

"Mirelle," said Principea, "we wanted to speak with you and see how you've been faring recently. We know things haven't been... easy for you... and for that, we're so sorry, dear."

Rhutgard took in the sight of Mirelle's lady-in-waiting, posed respectfully several paces back in honor of Mirelle's current company. More of an attack dog, he thought, than a lady-in-waiting. Rhutgard recalled that Mirelle arrived here at Fairview with the girl in place, so quite possibly Nona had installed her with Mirelle, in which case, he whole-heartedly approved.

Mirelle bowed her head with respect. "I am doing well enough. It was nothing I did not anticipate. I have dealt with worse." She smiled slightly, and Rhutgard suddenly recalled that the girl had, after all, worked in a tavern with loud and bawdy drunks on a regular basis. Between Mirelle's growing up under Luvian's watchful eye and her attack lady-in-waiting, Rhutgard wondered with a tiny bit of amusement if it wasn't the Court he should be inquiring of their health instead.

"And your brothers? Are they minding their manners, I hope?" Rhutgard inquired. "Because if not, tell me, and –"

"Rhutgard, don't scare her," Principea tugged at his arm.

Mirelle smiled. "They are wonderful. They have been very kind."

"Excellent," Rhutgard relaxed. They were good boys, his twins, but they did have a penchant for pranks. And teasing. They had run this Palace ragged when they were young lads – he couldn't count the amounts of glares he'd get from the servants because of those boys. It wasn't his fault they were wild.

"We just want to make sure you feel as much at home as we can here, dear," Principea told her.

Mirelle nodded and smiled. "I know."

Though she had smiled, Rhutgard thought she looked a little sad.

"What is it, child? Is it the Court? You needn't make regular appearances right now."
Mirelle shook her head. "No, no, I can handle the Court." She looked up as she told him that.

Pleased, he had just enough time to wonder what upset her before the girl said, "It's just that – I miss my cat...." The sides of her mouth turned down sorrowfully.

"Oh, Mirelle. I'm so sorry." Principea's voice was full of sympathy. "We have a number of cats about the Palace...."

"I know. But this one was mine. He was a stray cat that we took in. Pappy named him Captain, and everyone there would salute him whenever he came around...."

Rhutgard coughed then and cleared his throat, trying not to glare. Luvian. What a –

Principea's voice was decidedly merrier when she said, "I can't think of a better name for a stray cat. He sounds like a wonderful pet. Why don't we find you a kitten, darling, and you can have a new cat."

Mirelle nodded and smiled, sentiment still clouding her eyes.

"You be sure to tell us, or your brothers, if you need anything at all," Rhutgard told her as she was retreating down the steps.

After she was gone, Principea let out with her burst of tinkling laughter.

"Captain. Luvian, that man –" Rhutgard shook his head.

Principea told him, "Rhutgard, it was out of affection, you know that. Just his way of having you around a little. And for her." She laughed again. "What a great name. And they all salute him."
He snorted. "I'm glad you find this so amusing." Then he looked down at her. "You know what? I'm going to get a huge, giant, hairy dog – a Wolfhound, that's it. And I'm going to name it Lieutenant. And he'll have to follow me everywhere I go. What do you think of that, Sweet Pea?" Ha. Rhutgard thought that was funny. Take that, Luvian.

She laced her hand in his as they started walking away. "Why would you do that? He'd just bark at you and bite you in the behind."

Harvick

Harvick strode about the castle. Paranoia was starting to grip him, but he knew that it was not altogether unwarranted. There were new faces in this castle, after all, faces he did not recognize.

Now, he knew it was the Castellan's responsibility to replace servants, but... surely, not so many as Harvick had seen recently.

New Stordish Guards among the Royal Kings Guard ranks. New menservants in the Great Hall during meals. Even a few among the grounds....

And he'd caught a few glances, glances from these new men that had snapped back forward.

If the intention was to make him paranoid, why, then, they had succeeded, though Harvick was standing his ground and refusing to change his routine or act differently.

But – Varley had been gone over a month now in Romeny. And Harvick didn't like it. Courtship did not take so long as that. Either the girl liked him or she didn't, and either he had applied for a betrothal request or no. Harvick wouldn't say no to a Rommish daughter on Storden soil, though he couldn't remember the last time that had happened. And certainly not a Rommish Royal.... Hmm – Romeny blues, clear over in Storden, who would have thought. That would shake up the bloodline a bit.

Or else Varley had his head stuffed up the Eastern Shield's arse. Somehow, Harvick didn't think Rhutgard would rub elbows with Varley. Rhutgard's boys, though.... Perhaps Varley was just making his rounds about the Eastern Court....

But Harvick just did not think it likely. Varley never did anything without a goal to pursue, one that met his needs.

And now that Harvick saw all these new faces about the Palace, he knew that Varley had moved his piece on the gameboard. Varley's perfect alibi.... Visiting in Romeny for over a month.

Well, a shame he didn't know that he'd been disinherited, Harvick thought smugly. But now that all these new men were in place, he wondered what the play was.

Moving against Clemongard was the obvious choice, but how much had he aligned himself with the Ormon Queen? Harvick didn't think him able to organize an entire militaristic movement on his own without help. Yes. Harvick believed Queen Ormon had Varley on her little leash, and, if she knew what she was doing, she'd better keep him on a very tight collar....

These new troops of Varley's, all in common clothes... as if no one would recognize them unmarked. Harvick sighed. Most of them were congregated in South Storden. Once he'd discovered them, new faces began showing in the Palace. Harvick knew too much now.

Harvick knew as long as Varley stayed in Romeny, his own days were numbered. His sons had left with their mother for her maternal residence soon after Varley had left for Romeny, but Harvick had met with Uncle Dordonas last week to tell him to move the Queen and the twins to an old estate not on the map. They'd have to stay there alone for some time, until Uncle Dordonas deemed it safe, but better than their deaths. And Uncle Dordonas would act as Regent until Tollard was old enough to take the throne.

Yesterday, Uncle Dordonas told him as they walked upon the green, pretending to be jolly over goblets of wine, that they had been moved successfully. Harvick gave Uncle Dordonas strict instructions to carry out, rolled up in a thick parchment, which his uncle then snuck up his sleeve.

"You recall what you do if I die suddenly?"

His uncle regarded him steadily. Then he sighed. "Aye." He took a long gulp from his goblet. "Harvey, my boy, how sure are you of that?"

"Of disinheritance? Or arresting him?" Harvick took a sip of wine himself.

"No, Harv. The other."

Harvick took another swallow of his wine as he studied Uncle Dordonas. Then he raised his goblet. "To family."

Uncle Dordonas returned his toast. "To family."

———

Harvick stood upon his bedchamber balcony, enjoying the crisp night air. Behind him, he heard the popping and crackling of his fire, enticing him to come to bed. He missed his babes – he wished he could hold them.

Harvick looked at the stars in the sky one last time and then turned around on the balcony, ready to go to bed for the night.

And there was a Kings Guard, standing there. In his bedchamber.

The man never said a word.

All Harvick saw were the whites of the man's eyes as he picked Harvick up over the balcony and threw him over it.

Harvick envisioned the smiles of his baby boys....

Selby

"Your Majesty, these arrived for you." The servant bowed and left after she dismissed him.

"Your Majesty," Lord Brinlett insisted on being allowed into the Council Chamber.

Her Ericorian men, now doubled, stepped forward to surround her. Selby held up a hand. "Lord Brinlett?" He was a part of the War Council, with a number of ties to the Central Coast towns.

The Ericorian at the entrance of the Council Chamber allowed him through, and he glared up at them as he stepped inward, righting his surcoat.

"Your Majesty, at least one hundred ships were spotted in the Bandle Bay off the coast of Little Wharton!"

Selby's mouth fell open. She grabbed at her throat. "No... no." She shook her head. This was not happening. They had barely begun mobilization of troops....

Distantly, she heard a voice ask, "Your Majesty?" with concern. But it just did not process. How?

With incredible effort, Selby heaved in a sigh, forcing herself to breath slowly. Now was the time to appear strong. And thank all the gods ever in creation that it was only Lord Brinlett standing in here with her and not a full Council. And her Ericorian, of course, but she thought of them more as formidable statues who came to life when called upon or if the smallest threat was perceived.

Aloud, Selby said, "Little Wharton.... That will be a direct hit once they make land. And from there, they would march directly here... in just – two days, no less." Selby felt sick.

The nearest Ericorian grabbed for the tossbasket in the corner just in time for Selby to empty the entire contents of her stomach into it. She heaved one last time, then stood straight again, holding her pounding head.

"Water," she croaked.

Lord Brinlett supplied her with a cup of water.

Once she stopped panting, Selby sat down. Was it too late to abdicate the Throne? Run away? Crawl into a hole and hide?

She took another deep breath. "How did our Cliff Watches miss this? Are they compromised, all of them? I should think I would have heard if they had been demolished...."

One hundred war ships.... That was five thousand men, just two days away.

"No report of enemy ships passing through, Your Majesty, and Naval Guards report that the Cliff Watch Towers are all functional," Lord Brinlett replied. She heard the fear in his voice.

"Lord Brinlett, call the other Councilors here at once."

"Yes, Your Majesty."

Once he left, Selby leaned her temple down into her hands. This could not be happening. They would have to retreat....

And then she saw the letters that had been given to her by the servant.

She picked the first one up and flipped it over, sinking back into her chair to read it.

A Storden seal. This should be interesting.

To: *Her Royal Majesty Selby Cylysse Stevanrhut, First of Her Name,*

Queen of Clemongard:

As your long term neutral Southern Neighbor, I, His Royal Majesty of Storden, Harvick Whittemore Goddard send to you a gift of good will of three hundred newly built warships. One hundred have a destination of Clemongard's Bandle Bay, for your personal protection should your Northern enemies suddenly strike.

Two hundred other warships await your use northwest of Clemongard's Ainsley-by-the-Sea. The troops aboard these ships are yours in whole now as my gift to you, in hopes that you might make use of them in these troublesome times ahead.

Please know that I in no way ordered the construction of these ships nor the enlistment of their troops, nor any of the Army which has mobilized in my centuries-neutral nation. My eldest son, Varley, once my Crown Prince and heir, ordered this unbeknownst to me. I had no design in this whatever.

He has been disowned and removed from my line of succession in favor of my infant twin sons, Tollard and Jonnard Goddard, who will, gods be good, rise to my throne through their Regent, Dordonas Willam Goddard. Should anything happen to me, and you are able, I hope you might watch out for them, as they now are in hiding.

I believe my eldest son to be allied with Ormon and possibly Ambsellon as well. As to his immediate plans, I know not, though he is no longer welcome in Storden. Know that he will react poorly once he knows that his Naval fleet no longer exists, so you should consider possible militaristic action on his behalf.

With this gift, I hope you will remember me as a neutral neighbor who has always meant you and your country well over the centuries, as you and your country has always meant Storden well in return. I wish you a long and fruitful Reign.

With the best of will always,

His Royal Majesty of Storden,

King Harvick Whittemore Goddard

Selby took a deep breath. Her mouth had fallen open while she had read this letter. Harvick's own son! The Crown Prince of Storden, not welcome in Storden, disowned, in favor of Harvick's twin infant children… who were now in hiding.

And even more so – Harvick had stolen all his Naval fleet and given it to her. If each ship had a minimum of fifty men, and they were all hers… then… Selby smiled. She now had fifteen thousand more troops. And three hundred war ships.

Was it her, or did Harvick write in such a way as if he was fearful for his life….

Selby could not believe her luck. She would need to thank Harvick in some way. And absolutely watch somehow for his sons, if she ever heard whisper or word of them.

But the idea of Varley attacking, that was frightening. That was cause for alarm, and once her Councilors were assembled, they would immediately plan possible defensive maneuvers all along the borders. Her bridges at the mouths of the Trellis and Rournebourke Rivers were nearly complete now, so they would post full watches all along the coast as well, and mobilize troops at the Cliff Watch towers....

Then Selby recalled the second message. She popped the seal open.

Also another message from Storden, though it was not King Harvick's Royal seal personally.

She read it, then dropped the message on the table.

King Harvick was dead.

———

"Well, at least he died peacefully in his sleep," remarked Lord Wharfstead.

Selby had very different ideas about that.

"He was quite young to die in his sleep. Perhaps it was a brainstorm," remarked Lord Garrath.

Or a pillow pressed upon his face, thought Selby.

"I remember when he took the throne," Lord Dansherd declared as he sat back in his chair.

"Well, whatever it may have been, Varley Goddard, formerly Crown Prince of Storden, is not to take the throne, nor is he even welcome in Storden itself. Dordonas Goddard is the Regent for Harvick's son when he is old enough to take the throne, so we shall be dealing with Dordonas henceforth, and he will see that Storden continues to be a neutral country as its tradition holds.

"Varley, however, is a problem. Now that we have all of his Navy, along with fifteen thousand of his men, it's likely that he will strike at us, if only as a show of strength. And so, we need a solid battle plan."

Selby now had four tacticians, three war experts, a retired Navy Admiral, and a retired Army colonel from the Twenty Years War, all serving on her War Council, and she let them throw ideas about.

Finally, she spoke up and told them, "I want troops all along the Stordish border, the rivers, and spread evenly around the Cliff Watches as well."

"Your Majesty, that will leave us spread thinly...."

"With fifteen thousand new troops out on the water? Whom we can call to land at any time? Possibly not. We have thirty thousand Ericorian as well. If anything, we will be open at the mountain passes, and that's where we can send our Ericorian troops if must be – let them meet our incoming Northern host until we can move our men around accordingly and our Alliance troops arrive."

"We could also attack Harbour Town, it's his northernmost port as well as a fort. He has soldiers there, I guarantee you that. We could take out –"

"No, my lord Garrath. We are defending Clemongard, not attacking Storden. We do not actually know if Varley will even cast his eye toward us for sure yet. He may simply consider Clemongard as a lost cause and ride to attack the Eastern Alliance.

"We are defending ourselves from Varley's offensive actions, not the peoples of our centuries-neutral neighbor."

Colonel Gormmick coughed and cleared his throat. "With all due respect, Your Majesty, you have to consider that this young runt may now rule Storden, whether it was his father's wish or not. The commonfolk all over Storden don't know that his father disowned him. I'd be willing to rejoin the Army as a Private again if half of the commoners knew the King was father to twins now. Had been, as the case is now. So long as they have food in their bellies, they're just going to keep farming their fields, fishing, and minding their children, and if the big guy on the throne decides neutral's not the way to go anymore, then half of them won't like it and half of them won't care, but they'll all have to go along with it anyway.

"So they're likely to believe that Varley is their rightful King now, unless the Regent does something immediate. If those boys are in hiding, they're already one step behind. They ought to be in the Castle, where everyone knows about them.

"We need to stay one step ahead. Deploy scouts to the mountain passes and northern Cliff Watches, for with warning enough from scouts, our men, Ericorian or otherwise, can meet the Northern Countries in the same time it will take for them to get through the passes or to one of our towns on the Coast. We need more men in the RiverLands, and thick units all down the border, from Port Collier, Brewer's Field, clear over to Elm Haven. And Ainsley-by-the-Sea.

"Once that little runt sees our borders are impenetrable, then he'll just ride his sugar arse – oh, pardons, Your Majesty – he'll just ride on out and south of here somewhere, and then we can set to planning for the Northern attacks."

Selby nodded slowly. It sounded sensible, though she had no frame of reference by which to judge it, so how could she refute it? "Very well."

The Colonel's eyes narrowed and observed her shrewdly. "Your Majesty, this boy is what we in the Army refer to as a 'wiggler.'"

Selby rose her eyebrows. "A 'wiggler.'"

"Yes. A "wiggler" is like a worm on a hook. This runt, he wiggles back and forth, he doesn't know what he's going to do next, he doesn't know how he's going to do it, he wiggles back and forth, round and round, 'til a big fish swallows him up. The whole time, he don't know he's bein' used as bait. You follow me?"

Pleased suddenly, Selby smiled. "I do, Colonel."

"And the big fish, I'd be willing to bet, is that Ice Cu – uh, Queen, up in Ormon."

A number of the other Councilors and members of her War Council were nodding their heads.

"Unfortunately, Your Majesty," Colonel Gormmick's deep rolling voice paused, "and this is the bad news. This little wiggler's on a big damn hook, and that hook is Storden. Meaning, he's got a lot of power behind him. He can do a lot of damage before he gets swallowed up."

Selby's smile turned immediately to a frown. Her lip curled upward with distaste. Varley. She sniffed. She had met the little... wiggler... years ago, during a state visit, when her father and King Harvick met. He was just a few years older than Selby, but he had such a sense of self-entitlement even then that Selby distinctly recalled disliking him immediately and avoiding him as much as possible. Hmm. She had only been perhaps ten at the time. Who would have guessed she'd be going to war with him in just a few more years....

Lord Wharfstead spoke up then. "Well, that little wiggler is no match for the Cleaver Queen, now, is he?" and he grinned, causing the rest of the War Council to chuckle and roar with cheers. Selby sighed and smiled for Lord Wharfstead's sake. He was now her fiercest supporter. He had recruited widely down in the Coastal areas and even brought forth one of the men sitting here at her table. However, he had spread talk of the new Cleaver Queen of Clemongard everywhere that people had ears....

Interestingly, an impressive cleaver had been gifted to her by her War Council at the last meeting, with her full name and title inscribed in gold upon the hilt, along with "Cleaver Queen of Clemongard" below it. It even had a beautifully preserved leather scabbard, that she might wear it without the blade causing damage to limbs or anything else. So now she wore it at her side wherever she went, more to appease her Councilors then out of a sense of pride.

Ah. Perhaps she could test out her new cleaver on the Wiggler....

Theldry

She was so bored. Theldry felt as if she were just a marble, rolling around in this whole estate, alone, by herself.

How odd, for not so long ago, all she'd wanted was to be married... the romantic notion of some wonderful man who would take her away from StoneScape, from Kelving City and her family was all Theldry could think about. Just months ago, in fact.

Now, here she was, and it was nothing like what she'd dreamt of. Of course, Theldry sighed, she was clear across the Coastals, nowhere near any of her friends. Visiting with her friends would be quite an undertaking, and two of them were even with child now, according to their letters.

Theldry grimaced. It was possible, now, at least, that she could be with child, for three weeks into their marriage, she had finally recognized her wifely duty, as her mother put it, and approached her husband one evening in his bed chamber.

Cathall was slightly more than twice her age, though she would be sixteen in two more months. But he been very gentle. It hadn't been anything at all like what ladies all whispered and giggled about, so Theldry wondered if she was doing it wrong and Cathall was simply being kind by not telling her. Just thinking of it made her blush.

But he wanted children, she knew, so she visited him each week. That had been last month. This month, he'd been home only once.

Theldry only had one lady-in-waiting and several maids. Her maids were more talkative than her lady-in-waiting, Mila. They laughed and sang songs. She didn't realize how much she'd miss Cathall until he was gone for weeks at a time. There was no one at the table to talk to, so she took her meals in her chamber, or outside under a pavilion.

At least there was a breeze. The estate literally sat on the ocean, and Theldry loved to go down and walk barefoot in the waves. Her lady-in-waiting was horrified at this unladylike behavior and Theldry was on the verge of dismissing her, but for having no one to speak to if she did.

She couldn't help it – she loved the water flowing over her feet and the grainy sand between her toes. Theldry would never have been able to do this in Tortoreen, but now she was a woman, a lady married, and a Duchess as well, so if she wanted to go barefoot in the tide, then she would. She could hear her mother – *Theldry! A newly married Duchess and going barefoot in the ocean! I despair of you!*

Theldry finally wandered about the estate last week, looking for rooms she'd not yet entered. She found a conservatory on the far end of the estate with furniture that was covered in dust sheets, so she knew no one used the room. Theldry wandered about, letting her fingers trail along the richly paneled walls as she studied the portraits. Then she came to one that caught her breath. It was her husband – Cathall. With his hands on the shoulders of a beautiful woman and a young child. All of them were smiling, a happy family…. Ayrissa, that had been her name, though Theldry could not recall the child's name.

And then one of the maids, Jeanie, came in behind her. "Oh! My lady, you gave me such a fright! No one's ever in this room."

Theldry gestured up at the portrait. "He's never home because of me."

Jeanie walked up beside Theldry. With a hand on her hip, Jeanie studied the portrait. Then she shrugged a shoulder. "That was right before the little one passed, you know. It changed them both. They had ten long years together, and they were happy, even though she was sickly a lot of the time. But that ain't why he's gone so much, my lady."

Jeanie put a gentle hand on Theldry's back and steered her out of the sitting room. "He goes to visit all his properties."

To Theldry's confused expression, Jeanie responded, "That's right, my lady, the Duke has a number of properties, from here almost to Roarden North and clear down to Meadow Stretch." She patted Theldry's shoulder. "I know you don't know where lots of those are yet, now you're in Corstarorden, but the Duke, he's very wealthy man, my lady. You married real well. He goes to visit lots of his holdings to make sure they're functioning how they're supposed to, provides them with what they need, represents them even in Court.... He's a real good man, the Duke. I been workin' here since I was just older than you and I ain't ever known him to be different. He just stays busy is all, my lady. Don't you think on it more." Jeanie rubbed Theldry's back kindly.

Theldry knew it was because she was so young that Jeanie felt comfortable being familiar with her. And to be honest, Theldry felt a certain solace in the maid's presence, one that Mila had not provided. Mila was content discussing her stitchery patterns and the news she'd heard from her family in various parts of Corstarorden. Theldry had fallen asleep twice while listening to Mila. She couldn't help it. Theldry had been a shark, and now she was locked up inside a bowery with a goldfish. Or worse, a minnow. Mila the Minnow. Theldry wondered if she could get her lady-in-waiting a lady-in-waiting just so that she could be left on her own.

Of late, she had been sneaking past the bowery altogether and sitting with the maids in the kitchen, for they were funnier and far more companionable. Theldry suspected Mila preferred it that way herself.

Finally, they received a message that Cathall was returning, so of course a full five-course meal was ready for his dinner that evening. Theldry had been glad of intelligent conversation, of hearing news in the world outside the estate....

"Perhaps I could accompany you on your travels," Theldry offered. She hoped she didn't sound too desperate....

Cathall smiled at her. "Perhaps I will take you to Roarden North for a holiday someday soon. You are accustomed to a city life, and you must feel like a stowaway here." He placed his hand on hers with affection briefly.

Theldry tried not to look disappointed and smiled for him.

Later, when she lay next to him, under his arm, he saw that she was pensive.

"My dear, something is troubling you. I saw that when I came home earlier. What has you worried?"

Theldry stared off. Thinking of the portrait, she wondered if she should say anything at all.

"Theldry...?" Cathall prompted her. He moved so he could see her face.

"You still love her, don't you," she blurted.

Cathall drew in a deep breath and was silent.

"There is," he finally said, "a part of me that will always love her. But she belongs to my past, and I don't live in my past. You are my present, and my future."

Theldry looked up at him. Then she smiled.

That was the first night they made love.

Mirelle

"Perhaps you will come to visit us in Storden next. We, of course, would love to host you."

From behind Mirelle, Kimbur sniffed just slightly. That was an indication that Varley was overplaying himself and being, as Pappy would put it, a jackarse. Oy, she thought, this bastard just will not give up....

Aloud, Mirelle smiled with tolerance and told Varley, "What a kind invitation. You're so thoughtful, Your Highness."

"Varley! I heard you were returning to Storden. We here in the East will miss seeing you at Court." One of her brothers – Mirelle hated that she could not tell the difference yet – stepped up and encircled her under a casual arm.

Varley's face started to sour, for he rarely got a moment alone with Mirelle now. She had never left the company of others, nor had Kimbur left her side during this War Council while the boys were unavailable to chaperone her. The man unnerved her. If Tank had been present, she would have asked him to throw Varley out on his arse.... However, Varley was a Crown Prince and so had to be babied and treated with all the etiquette that any visiting Crown Prince was accorded.

Mirelle was disgusted. Crown Prince this, Crown Prince that. Ronan never spoke that way. Nor Dougall, Crown Princes both. Hm. She'd like to stuff that crown up his princely arse.

"Well, Your Highness –" Varley started.

"Please, it's Keldrick, Varley."

Mirelle knew the twins did this merely to aggravate Varley, for he was so stiff on titles and condescension. Plus, it put him at a disadvantage, for he was unable to determine which twin he was talking to, and so he was made to look foolish.

"Right," Varley replied from gritted teeth.

Mirelle linked her arm into Keldrick's. "Varley just invited us to visit Storden. I was telling him kind it was to invite us. When was the last time you two visited Storden, Keldrick?"

"I've never been." He turned to Varley. "Perhaps we will take you up on that invite. When do you leave, mate?"

Mirelle saw Varley's eyes had turned cold. "Not for another two or three days."

"Well, then, I'm sure we'll see you about before you go. A good evening to you," Keldrick called as he escorted Mirelle away.

"Thank you, Brother, again," she whispered as soon as she knew Varley was out of earshot.

"You're quite welcome, again. Why would you possibly want to visit Storden?" He scoffed.

Rhutgard

The bell in the hallway rang. They stopped talking so that Stanyard could leave the room. When he returned, he looked puzzled as he stared down at a pigeon parchment.

He handed it to Rhutgard. "It's from Clemongard, but not sealed with Her Majesty's Royal seal."

Rhutgard glanced around at the men in the room with whom he'd been closeted for nearly two and a half weeks now. He raised an eyebrow and slid a finger beneath the seal.

It was from Queen Selby – she was just being cautious, he decided. He had done the same more times than he could count.

What he read took his breath away.

"Kendrick! Find Mirelle and bring her here immediately. And Keldrick."

To: King Rhutgard Anghus Firthing, First of His Name

Eastern Shield of the Eastern Shield Alliance

His Royal Majesty of Storden, Harvick Whittemore Goddard recently died under what I consider suspicious circumstances. As you know, Clemongard's neighbor to the south, Storden, has been a neutral country for centuries.

King Harvick wrote to me not three days ago, telling me that he had disinherited and disowned his oldest son Varley, formerly Crown Prince. King Harvick and Queen Talia recently had two twin boys, and the oldest of these two will take the Stordish throne when he comes of age. His Regent is Dordonas Goddard. The two twins and the Queen are in hiding with the Regent now.

King Harvick just sent me a good will gesture of three hundred warships, all built privately by Varley. King Harvick informed me that he suspected Varley to be allied with Ormon, if not Ambsellon as well. He was unaware of Varley's militaristic recruitment and was never involved in any part of it.

Immediately after I received this notice from King Harvick regarding the three hundred Naval forces sent to me, I also received notice that King Harvick died in his sleep. The King warned me in his letter that, after Varley finds out his Naval fleet is gone, he may well strike at Clemongard.

I know that Varley has been visiting you in Romeny and I know not what designs he may have, especially so close to the Northern Countries. You should know, however, that by his father's own hand, Varley is not welcome in his home country of Storden.

May this information be of use to you.

A Silent Game of Spies

From Your Ally,

Her Royal Majesty Selby Cylysse Stevanrhut, First of Her Name

Queen of Clemongard

Reaghann was the first to respond after Rhutgard finished reading the letter aloud. "So... it's true then. It's the Stordish who have been heading East."

Gerard said, "I have a question. Does the little bastard know that his father is dead?"

Rhutgard rose his eyebrows. Damn good question. The whole of the War Room was silent.

"Because if he does, then he thinks right now that he's King. And if he doesn't, then he thinks he will be soon. And either way, he has no idea that he's been removed from the line of succession, unless some source sent him a bird here, which is unlikely. Harvick took that secret to the grave with him, so only the Regent and the Queen know about that, I'd bet.

"So right now, he thinks he's got an extra fifteen thousand men ready to command and that he'll be King... and you know, him being here as long as he has, perfect alibi. She said, suspicious circumstances, didn't she?

"So the real question is, what will he do now, whether he becomes King of Storden or not?"

Driscoll sighed, staring off. "You know, I remember Harvick's father. Good man. Only met him twice, he let us resupply during the Twenty Years War. That was right before he died and Harvick was about twenty or so. I'll rule for suspicious circumstances on this. Too young to die in his sleep.

"As to this Varley – what he does comes down to whether he gets into Storden at all. If he's not welcome, then he'll have to take it by force. Somehow, I don't see that happening. The commoners won't know he's been disinherited. My guess is, he'll find out his Navy and his troops are gone. He'll head right into Kingston and take Pikes Keep as a show of force, to strike back. Then he'll either head north to Clemongard and find the Stordish-Clemon border heavily fortified with the Queen's troops, or he'll head south to the Coastals. He is an ally of Ormon, now, so essentially the Coastals have to accept him by extension.

"I expect he's done being told what to do by the Ice Queen, now that he's sent her some five, maybe six thousand troops by water and land. His father moved a few pieces on the gameboard he didn't see coming and now he has no Navy, so he'll just strike out at random. My guess is – he'll head around the Coastals toward our RiverLands."

Kendrick, who had walked in with Mirelle and Keldrick during Driscoll's proposed theories, spoke up then. "To what end? He has maybe twenty thousand troops left."

Rhutgard had informed Kendrick and Keldrick at the same time that Merridon had abdicated the throne, which made Kendrick the Crown Prince and Eastern Shield-to-Be. He'd also informed them that the time for laughing and playing around was now over, they were to be at his side to learn all things Kingdom-related and Eastern Shield-related henceforth, Kendrick to one day replace Rhutgard, Keldrick to serve as Kendrick's Chief Advisor if Kendrick so wished and, of course, if needed, as a possible King of Romeny and Eastern Shield himself.

Rhutgard had never seen either of them so solemn, nor so grave. Kendrick had then placed both his hands on Rhutgard's shoulders and said quietly, "Father. Please. Live *forever*."

Keldrick had also been intensely earnest when he agreed with Kendrick.

Rhutgard had waited to inform Kendrick that he was now the Crown Prince until a new signet ring had been crafted – which had been done in extreme haste, but which was nevertheless, exquisite – and he took Kendrick's hand and put the ring into his palm.

Kendrick had moved his other signet ring to his right hand and slid the new one on. He'd stared at it for a few seconds and then breathed out. He'd glanced at Keldrick and then at Rhutgard. Then he'd taken in a deep breath. "Thank you, Your Majesty."

Rhutgard had been quite pleased. Kendrick and Keldrick grew up overnight. Gone were his laughing boys suddenly, now replaced by sobered, serious young men. Rhutgard, with some sentiment, would miss those laughing young twins though....

Reaghann spoke up. "He'll want to join the troops he sent East. I'll need to send more men down to the Southern Shield. As will the rest of you – send men South."

Rhutgard held his hands up. "Do not send men South just yet. First, we need to wait and see what he does once he returns to Storden. If he attacks Clemongard, then men you sent to the South was for nothing. If anything, fortify the Southern Shield, but do not brace the entire border."

Reaghann conceded with a nod. Then he looked at Driscoll. "My lord of Delsynth. You've fought in more skirmishes and in the entire Twenty Years War. You have more battle experience than all of us. What do you suggest we do while we wait?"

Driscoll smiled a bit. "Son, you're looking to the wrong man. I was a scout during the Twenty Years War. I rose up the ranks sneaking around in the grass and the woods and the hills."

Reaghann cocked his head. "But does that not then make you the perfect man to direct our movements? You know what is like to see from all sides, both hostile and friendly territory, rather than soldiers, who – forgive me –" and he nodded toward Rhutgard and Gerard – "only fight against men while upon one field of battle."

Rhutgard nodded. Reaghann was a young King yet, but he was clever. For all this nonsense that had just taken him by surprise, he was a clever man and would rule Hardewold well, he mused.

Driscoll was rubbing at his chin, considering.

Gerard spoke up. "He's right, that's sound thinking. Without scouts, soldiers are blind."

Rhutgard couldn't help but remember his own experience in the war. Why, it was a scout that brought Luvian to him all those years ago.

"Driscoll? What say you?"

Driscoll shrugged. "I don't think my old uniform fits like it used to, might be a little tight about the middle," here he looked down and patted his stomach. Rhutgard wanted to scoff, for the man was still as slender as he'd ever known him to be.

"But I'm up for it."

"Well, then. While we wait for Varley, let's take down these soldiers who snuck their way in. And open up those ports of yours as well, Reaghann."

Varley

Ahh. That was much better.

He hauled her up and shoved her away, letting go of her blonde hair at last. "Go on now," and he tossed his head in the direction of the door.

Ugh. Varley extracted a strand of the maid's hair from his hand and shook it to the floor. Maids. He was reduced to maids, he scoffed as he tucked himself back into his breeches.

But ladies-in-waiting would talk, complain even, and in a foreign Court, who was to say whether he would be believed over them or not.

Stupid girl, she'd slobbered all over his breeches. He'd have to discard them. But he would wear them for the rest of the day, just in case, for his surcoat would cover it, he thought.

As he stood lacing the silken buckles of his blue surcoat, one of his servants called to him from outside the door. Varley had taught them never to enter his chamber, given that he was often occupied.

"Your Highness?"

"Enter," Varley called in a bored tone. This had better be worth his time.

The servant bowed and presented a pigeon parchment. Varley already recognized the paper as Storden's.

"For you, just arrived, Your Highness." The steward immediately exited.

Varley pulled the seal off the parchment and unrolled it.

To: Your Royal Majesty, Varley Whittemore Goddard, First of His Name

King of Storden

Your Royal Father, King Harvick Whittemore Goddard of Storden, died peacefully in his sleep less than one week ago. We of Storden eagerly await your arrival so that you as the new King can acknowledge his death and that we may Change the Guard.

With All Due Respect,

Varley stopped reading and smiled. At last. The old coot was dead.

Rhutgard

Rhutgard leaned on the marble guard rail of the balcony that overlooked his Great Hall.

He knew Varley had received a bird, for he'd specifically instructed the Palace Pigeon Loft keeper to inform him when any correspondence arrived from Storden. And the Guards informed him that the Stordish horses had been made ready immediately, along with the Stordish coach. Luggage was being loaded onto it, Rhutgard was told.

Rhutgard left instructions for the kitchen to give Varley as much as he wanted to take with him on his journey home. Anything to make him feel as if nothing were out of order.

He stood above the Great Hall, for Varley would have to pass through on his way out.

Finally, Varley strode into the Great Hall.

"Leaving us so soon, Your Highness?" Rhutgard called down.

Varley almost jumped at the sound of Rhutgard's voice. If you centered yourself just right, and used the right tone of voice, Rhutgard had learned years ago, your voice would echo down there....

Varley stood up straight then and faced Rhutgard, his chin up. "I am, actually. I just received word that my father died a few days past. You understand, of course, why I must leave with all haste."

Rhutgard held back his distaste for the young man. "I'm so sorry to hear. How did he die?"

Varley looked Rhutgard straight in the eyes and said, "In his sleep. He went peacefully, I'm told."

Rhutgard concealed his disgust as he nodded. "Well, then, Your Highness...." Rhutgard drawled, careful to use only the honorific *Your Highness*. You must get back to Storden in all haste. For the Changing of the Guard ceremony. Do have a safe trip." Rhutgard smiled then and stood up straight.

Varley barely smiled in return as he bowed and left the Great Hall.

Rhutgard felt sure they would be meeting soon, under far less amicable circumstances.

He signaled Stanyard. "You see him leaving finally?"

Stanyard nodded.

"See that he is followed, very discretely, to the Romeny border. I want to know who he sees and what he does before he gets there. And then I want a guard posted all along my border.

"Varley Goddard is no longer welcome here, nor is he to be admitted into the Kingdom of Romeny, or the Eastern Alliance."

Dordonas

Peacefully, in his sleep-like. He blew a belch threw his lips. Or... was that, in his sleep, peaceful-like. Dordonas thought that sounded better. Somehow. He was stumbling, almost fall-down drunk on shitty rum. He tripped over his own foot and laughed. There was no such thing as shitty rum. Ha ha!

Really, Dordonas knew he shouldn't be here on the grounds of Pikes Keep. But he'd snuck in the way Harv had snuck him in these last few weeks, where guards rarely patrolled.

He should be back with his niece, watching over them babes. Now they was out of the enemy's eye, they actually slept better, he thought. Odd, or no....

But a day later, just a day after seeing him and Harv was gone. Dordonas remembered Harv as a little lad, running about screaming, with a huge grin on his face, as if he knew one day he would rule a nation, go to war....

It was that memory of Harv that he kept in mind, that little seven-year-old lad running all around the terrace, full of laughter, that tortured Dordonas now.

Finally, he stumbled his way through the shadows of the looming, moonlit hedges to the back of the castle, where Harvick's rooms were located. Dordonas stared out at the green where just days ago, he and Harvey and had toasted, "To Family."

And that was why he'd come all the way here.

"One last toast, mah boy, ya good lad, you. One last toast, to family," he whispered. Dordonas leaned against the spruce hedge behind him and raised his bottle of rum for a few moments, envisioning all the memories of Harvick Goddard, from his birth to his Coronation, straight through to just nights ago. A few tears trickled down his face. Then he gulped down several more swallows of rum.

"Ahh," he winced as it burned on its way down. He wiped his mouth on his sleeve.

Something caught his eye. To be sure, his mind was so sodden and blurred right now, if his hand caught his eye right now, it'd be a good thing, for suddenly that walk all the way back down out of the hedge rows was a long one with his legs all jelly-like.

But what was that on the terrace, there, in the moonlight?

That was men. Royal Storden Guards. With buckets. They was splashin' water there on the terrace. Well, wasn't that a gardener's duty? One of them scratched at the cement with a boot and shrugged.

Finally, they left.

Dordonas looked up above the terrace. Those had been Harvick's chambers. All the windows was dark now. He snuffled and looked around. No guards. Of course not. No King.

Dordonas stole onto the terrace to have a look. The puddles of water were... he looked up. Right below a balcony in Harvick's chambers.

Dordonas leaned upon his knees to look about in the water. He knew if he knelt or sat, there'd be no getting up.

What...

What the bloody fuck was that....

In the crack of the terrace there....

Dordonas threw caution to the wind and knelt down on one knee. He looked real close.

He pried it up out of the crack and, with a lurid fascination, studied it.

Bloody fuckers. Those bloody fuckers. It was Harv's hair. His hair and his scalp.

Dordonas was suddenly as sober as he could be. He looked at the water. The white circle of the moon reflected in the puddle, but the water itself sat upon... dried blood. King's blood.

He knew it. Harv hadn't died in his sleep peacefully. He'd died right on this spot, and here, in Dordonas's hand, was proof.

He needed to get back to the estate and move those boys immediately.

Hewart

"So. The Rockdale pass is fortified." Hewart drummed his fingers on his chin. That seemed quite a bold move to him. That was, after all, the best way through the Mourning Mountains into Clemongard.

"We should strike as soon as possible, Father." Sturgund wanted blood. At this point, mused Hewart, Sturgund didn't care whose blood it was as long as it was red. Patience was now by the wayside, what little of it Sturgund had possessed previously. Levonroth had expended enormous effort on discovering the plot that had nearly killed Hewart's son, but it and its players were long in the wind, gone.

Sturgund insisted it was the Ormon bitch. Hewart was not ready to dismiss the idea, but nor was he willing to jump aboard with it, either, for to do so meant accusing the ruler of their ally of hundreds of centuries. And so he was faced with the uncomfortable task of finding excuses to put off his son's sharp accusations, while neither rejecting the idea when only in the company of Levonroth.

What would the bitch have to gain? Hewart had quietly added more troops to the home guard here in the Castle just in case an attempt on his own life was made. Surely an attempt upon Sturgund's life, which was supposed to have beheaded him, was meant to symbolize the end of his bloodline, from Crown Prince down, as beheading a snake, or so Levonroth suggested.

Well, whoever sent the order out didn't send someone capable enough, for Sturgund survived the attack. Although his arm was still healing even now, and what a scar that would be....

Hewart wondered why Sturgund was so convinced it was Ormon. To be sure, women should never sit the throne, anyone with half a brain knew that. They were too flighty. Best for running a household, be it hut or castle. But a country, Hewart scoffed. Women knew their place, and it wasn't on a throne, unless there was a man underneath them.

He gave Myrischka her due – she'd done fairly well on her own, but they were waiting until they found someone to take over. After all, they hadn't found the son. And there had to be blood kin somewhere. If that fool Munsolryshe had kept better records, they'd have a king on the throne by now, not his Queen directing his men.

What's worse, all he'd heard was how she'd killed the poor bastard. Stabbed him, slaughtered him in his sleep with a knife. Songs written about her, he'd even seen a puppet show last week about her. Why, she had the whole Land laughing at her.

Except, perhaps Sturgund. He wanted her head.

He also wanted to march west, with or without Ormon's involvement.

Hewart was inclined to agree. Myrischka, she had her four hundred warships and at least as many troops as Hewart did by land. But why wait for a woman to authorize Hewart to march on Clemongard, or even south on Romeny? He scoffed. He thought not. On that much, he was in agreeance with his son, though not for the same reasons.

He had almost one hundred thousand infantry, a combination of cavalry, archers, and infantry, though mainly infantry. Cavalry he sent along the coast as mountains were no places for horses.

The main bulk of this battle was going to be Naval, Hewart thought, for the Western Queen had no Navy and he had three hundred ships who could fire on her coast and drop off men. Yes. He smiled. Yes.

Then he realized that he had just decided to declare war on Clemongard, and without consulting Ormon. The latter of which he couldn't recall having happened. And the former... well. It had been far too quiet of late. Perhaps he would send a few troops back east and harry Romeny just for the fuck of it....

Rhutgard

Bloody hell.

"I won't ask about the credibility of this source, Driscoll, but…." Rhutgard trailed off.

"Yes. Absolutely certain. Chose him myself, he's a scout." Driscoll's voice behind him was devoid of expression, tired.

Tired, yes. They had been locked up in this study, this War Room, for three weeks now, and Rhutgard couldn't bear the sight of it anymore. Nor could they, of course. They took frequent breaks out on the green as often as they could but still. And people were beginning to talk. An Assembly of the Eastern Alliance – the five of them had never been closeted up with each other like this, nor had they visited so long. And no feasting, no entertainment….

Stanyard shrugged and told Rhutgard that he could only circulate so many plausible rumors. People were not stupid. They started gossiping, though he had not heard the words "War Council" yet. A small boon, Rhutgard supposed.

Rhutgard, still leaning on his fists on the table, did not see what happened next.

Gerard yelled, "That is my country, you flea-bitten bastard! If you had half a brain, and had paid attention to those fucking ports, there wouldn't be five thousand fucking men sitting on my border!"

Rhutgard turned around to see Gerard point a finger at Driscoll. "And you – could you post a few fucking men in your damn mountains so they'd send you a bird or two, let you know, *'Your Majesty, thousands of fucking soldiers are marching north to Ghiverny, you want us just to wave while they pass by?'*"

Oh, *bloody hell* – once Gerard gets started, there's no calming him down – Rhutgard stepped away from the map table in alarm.

"But you, you fucking Hound, you were too busy up womens' skirts not to notice –"

"Oh, all right, that's it –" and Reaghann flew at Gerard.

A mess of parchments went flying up, scattering all about the two Kings as they wrestled each other. Gerard slammed Reaghann into the wall and a small, framed painting fell to the floor. Reaghann shoved Gerard off of him and swung at Gerard, but his fist was caught by… Kendrick?

"OY! *That's enough, from both of you!"* Kendrick shouted. His voice bounced off the walls and the room was silent for a second.

Rhutgard's mouth dropped open. Kendrick had separated both Kings and held them away from each other at the end of each arm, and his face showed pure disgust.

"If you can't act like men, and the Kings you are, then leave until you can. Gerard, drink less wine, we need your best game in here. Reaghann, this is not a brawling ring, this is a War Council – stop being such a hothead. War is not going to be easy on any of us, so stuff your tempers and pick these parchments up off the floor."

Kendrick gave them each a small shove backward and stepped away from them.

Rhutgard's jaw was open. He immediately turned around and acted engrossed in the map on the wall before him.

That signet ring had changed his boy. Rhutgard smiled a bit. What a king he would be....

———

"And now all we know is that Hewart's men have mobilized. They are not ready to march, but both the soldiers we have in place gave the same account. *'Marching on Clemongard, Romeny possible as a side attack. Singular move,'*" Levonroth announced.

The room was silent, but the faces of the men in it spoke volumes. They were grave, solemn. Worried now. 'Twas one thing for five thousand Stordish men to be huddling north of Delsynth in the northern EverWinters. But quite another for this coinciding correspondence from two sources in the Ambsellon ranks.

"Singular move?" asked Dougall.

Ah. Rhutgard forgot about the lads. They were new to the some of the terms of war. Well, war was without doubt upon them.

"Advancing, or making a move without notifying the commanding officer, or the units you fight alongside with. In this case, Ormon."

Driscoll whistled. "I have never known that to happen."

"Well, there has never been a Queen on the Ormon throne, either. I expect that has a good deal to do with Ambsellon's choice," Rickstan said.

Rhutgard nodded. Then he approached another issue, directly related to their troop movements. "We need to send Clemongard troops. She is our ally."

Immediately, all four Kings shook their heads and scoffed.

In a firm voice, Rhutgard insisted, "Whether we like it or not – she is our ally and we promised her aid." He let a stern stare rest upon each of them for a few seconds.

Finally, Driscoll said with reluctance, "I can send some Stafford Spears."

Reaghann let out an impatient sigh but announced, "I can spare some troops as well."

"Excellent. Now, with my lord of Delsynth's valued contributions, let us plan some fortifications for all of the Eastern border, and focus on the Ghiverny-Delsynth conflict.

Raegan's ports will soon be open again, so his coastline will need to be fortified as well.

"Let us begin there. Ronan, Keldrick," Rhutgard finished by waving the two lads forward.

Both young men approached Rhutgard with curiosity.

"The time has come for us to speak with the Queen of Clemongard."

Rhutgard watched their faces. No change. They continued to listen to him, waiting. Ah. Well, once they heard what he had to say next, they would certainly have a response, each of them.

"My son and Ronan, we need to speak with Queen Selby. However, given the state of things, between

Varley's unpredicted actions and Ambsellon now making its move, we cannot arrange a simple visit of state, as we have here our assembled Kings of the Alliance. Aside from sheer distance, both Clemongard and we have militaristic issues that we cannot leave our countries for on extended visits of state. Travel time alone would be far lengthier than either she or we could afford to be away from our nations during wartime.

"Which brings me to why I have called you here before me. The two of you, Ronan, and you, my son, Keldrick, will be serving as Eastern Alliance War Time Ambassadors for me. Keldrick, you will be speaking as my voice on this mission.

"The two of you will traveling alone, just the two of you, and undercover. You will not be using your actual names until you arrive at FalconRise."

Rhutgard paused and took in their faces. Stunned, as if they'd been told they'd be living underwater from now on. Part of him wanted to laugh. But this assignment would make men of them, that he knew.

Ronan cleared his throat. "And, if you please, Your Majesty, what identities will we be using?"

Ronan

"This is something only the two of you can do." King Rhutgard paused and looked between the two of them thoughtfully.

Ronan's curiosity was piqued but he was also wary now.

Then the King said, "I will be sending you to Clemongard."

Ronan, from the corner of his eye, saw Keldrick's eyes grow round with interest.

"Clemongard!" repeated Keldrick.

Clemongard, indeed! Misgivings immediately arose. Whatever for? Under normal circumstances, a trip west to visit a new ally would be quite the experience. But when war was sprouting in every direction….

"Yes. We have a new ally, and it is time to make her acquaintance. Since I myself am unable to meet with her, I am sending the two of you in my stead, as Ambassadors of the Eastern Shield.

"You, Keldrick, will be serving in two capacities, as my son and as an Ambassador to the Eastern Shield. You, Ronan, will be serving in two capacities as well, though one will be far more… complicated, I expect."

"Yes, Your Majesty," Ronan uttered with respect. Why could he not simply stay here with the War Council? Complicated how?

King Rhutgard said then, "The two of you will be traveling alone together, no retinue, for speed and safety's sake. Because of the nature of your prior mission and experience, the second task I am charging you with – is to keep my son safe."

Neither Ronan nor Keldrick said a word for a moment. But Ronan knew what the King meant. But then Keldrick let out an outburst. "Father! I am perfectly able to protect myself!"

King Rhutgard looked at Keldrick steadily. "Of your weaponry skills, I've no question, Keldrick. It is your ability to –" And he turned his attention to Ronan.

"Blend in with the commoners," Ronan supplied.

"Ah. Exactly. And thus why Ronan is accompanying you, for he thinks quickly on his feet."

Keldrick threw a bewildered glance to Ronan before he trailed off, "Blend in with the…."

Ronan could not help but draw in an enormous sigh. Why? Why him? King Rhutgard read his expression at the time and told him, "Ronan, I know you feel like I'm punishing you –"

"Punishing him? By being with me? You can't be bloody serious," interjected Keldrick.

And King Rhutgard knocked Keldrick behind the head.

"Father! What the hell was that for!"

He did it again. "Keldrick, stop cursing."

Bemused, it was all Ronan could do to keep his jaw from falling open. The Eastern Shield was full of surprises these last weeks.

"Now. Across the land, you will be traveling as a Rommish lord, Ronan. While you, Keldrick," and King Rhutgard took in a deep breath. "Will be traveling as his steward."

For one second, Ronan was able to control himself. And Keldrick, for one second, said nothing at all. But after that, Ronan could not keep a grin from overtaking his features. Try as he might, he could not stop grinning. He wanted so badly to laugh….

"You can't be bloody serious!"

"Ronan," and the King gestured to Keldrick.

But Keldrick stepped out of the way. "If you try hitting me anywhere, I will break your bloody hand."

"Tell me, Keldrick, if your steward spoke to you in such a fashion, how would you respond?" asked King Rhutgard.

"You can't – you cannot be serious." Keldrick amended his speech at the last moment, but then demanded, "Why can we both not simply go as Ambassadors? Or he as my steward?"

Ronan watched that famous icy glare that King Rhutgard was known for slide into place across his face and instantly, Keldrick was cowed. "I need answer none of your questions, son of mine. However, should you think to no longer act as the role I have given you, you should know that, even in the West, in the Coastals, and in the Free Lands, there will be people who will recognize a son of the Eastern Shield. But no one will recognize a servant, whether they have blue eyes or no.

"And so you will act as a servant, for servants tend to be overlooked, invisible. Until the two of you reach Queen Selby's court, you, Keldrick, will be steward to *'Lord Galland,'* the name that I have chosen for Ronan. You will follow the directions on the map I provide you, unless Ronan believes it necessary to change the course.

"This is a mission that requires your utmost in abilities, my son, for you will be serving as a War Time Ambassador to the Eastern Alliance. You may not like the journey, but you must learn it and perfect it nonetheless. My father told me that when I was not much younger than you, though he was speaking of life itself.

"Now. Keldrick. Ronan. Can you perform the duties of War Time Ambassador to the Eastern Alliance that I have given you?"

"Yes, Father." The words *War Time Ambassador* seemed to have sobered Keldrick.

"Yes, Your Majesty," replied Ronan quietly.

King Rhutgard then placed a firm hand on Ronan's shoulder and told him, "If anyone can do this, I know it's you, Ronan."

And Ronan had looked at Keldrick, and back to King Rhutgard. "All due respect, Your Majesty, but how am I supposed to…. I mean, in enough time to, pass muster…." Ronan would have to teach Keldrick how to act like a commoner the entire way there. Until they arrived at Queen Selby's court, when Keldrick would take over as the Ambassador to the Eastern Shield.

"You're a very gifted young man, Ronan, you've lived in both worlds, and you'll see the both of you there and back safely."

Then King Rhutgard smiled faintly. "I knew a very stubborn prince, a very long time ago, who learned a lot in just a few days. Believe me, Ronan, when I say that if that prince could, this son of mine can." And he had clapped a sullen Keldrick on the back.

They would be riding out this morning, Ronan as Rommish Lord Galland, and Keldrick as his steward.

They would be riding on just two horses, no carriage, no servants, so they might speed their trip and more easily report what they saw on their way there.

Ronan recalled with interest, however, the reference to another stubborn prince that King Rhutgard made and wondered who it was.

"Boys," came King Rhutgard's voice. He was standing there in the stable.

He looked at them both and smiled a little. Ronan had just a little time to think how perfectly dressed Rhutgard always was, nothing too lavish, nor never underdressed – never bejeweled nor perfumed like many of the lords at Court….

And then the King hugged them both. "Good will go with you both. Come back to me, safely."

Myrischka

"On their way, Your Majesty." He bowed deeply.

Ah.

She forgot most of their names – they weren't relevant, after all, they simply bore news. But this was the best news she'd heard in some time. Her ships had been launched. Ahead of all schedule.

Or at least ahead of what the rest of the Land believed.

Myrischka was no fool. She knew she had a few spies within her ranks. A few, but not many. And she preferred that. Let the Land live in fear of her and let them wonder what she was doing next.

She had let them believe that in two more months, she would launch those ships, when today was her actual send-off. A smile curled her lips.

Two hundred should take care of the little Queen nicely for now, with her next one hundred sailing in to finish her. Combined with the twenty thousand troops she'd send by land, that should assuage Ambsellon and give the Clemongard Queen something to juggle, for she knew most of her troops were sitting on the Stordish border ready to strike against Varley.

She scoffed. Varley had served his purpose. Sent five thousand near useless troops to the northeast EverWinters. Utterly useless, or so her Colonel there reported. In return for those troops, Myrischka had the little runt's father killed for him. Any man who didn't have the balls to kill a man himself, particularly his own father, was not only useless, but a coward. And he expected to rule. Myrischka shook her head minutely. She would take his country as well, for his country had no experience in war, no more than he. Her other two warships would be sailing far away from the fighting and would stop at Storden to, among other things, resupply.

Myrischka had heard disturbing reports of the runt. Any man who felt he needed to demonstrate his sexual prowess by harming women during the act to prove his masculinity was no man at all. Why, any man who did such to her – but there was no man who would do such to her. Quite the coward, Varley.

Well, let the Royal Runt think he had the upper hand for now. Until she arrived at the Green Gates, no warmongering had yet to be accomplished, and she had but a four day's ride hence.

Ambsellon was already moving into Clemongard. He had even sent his three hundred ships off. For Hewart refused to take orders from a woman. He and his clan were even more intolerant of women ruling anything but the head of a man's dick than Munsolrysche was.

So Myrischka had some small number of troops to send to the EverWinters, and some small amount to harass the Eastern Alliance, some twenty thousand to send off behind Ambsellon, so Hewart would think it was all his idea, that she was just the eager, wagging tail of his dog....

And then, once Hewart was fully occupied warring with Clemongard, Myrischka would set up a blockade with her last one hundred ships in Hewart's harbor, to block him from returning home, and the rest of her troops into Ambsellon. It was time to expand, starting with the land immediately west of her.

Dordonas

Irving caught his arm in the darkness. Dordonas nearly jumped out of his skin.

"Dordonas, what the hell is this about?"

"Well, Irv, my boy, glad to see you, too." Dordonas scoffed. It was, actually. He looked his nephew head to toe. Still had that slender figure he'd had back – well, he was ashamed to say, seven some years ago it'd been since Dordonas had checked in on the boy last. Well, he was no boy, father of three midling boys. Thirty-five, Irv might be now.

Irving shrugged with a bit of guilt. "Sorry, Uncle. It's good to see you." They hugged. "But what, you drag me out here," and he gestured about the old ruins of a burned down church, "in the middle of the night, in all privacy. What's gotten into you, Uncle? Are you mad!"

Dordonas snorted. "You heard about your brother, I know."

A troubled look crossed Irving's face. "'Course I did." His voice was quiet. After he took in a deep breath, he said, "Died in his sleep, they told me."

Dordonas frowned. "And who was that who told you?"

Irving's eyebrow rose. "Two Guards from Pikeston. Why do you ask?"

Dordonas shook his head noncommittally. "Just – woulda' been nice if it had been that way."

Irving stared at him. "And what's that supposed to mean?"

Dordonas pulled out the piece of scalp he'd kept wrapped up in his breast pocket.

Irving leapt back. "Bloody fucking hell, what is that!" He stared at it, then at Dordonas, then back at the piece of dried scalp dangling from Dordonas's fingers. The blood was dried now.

Irving's mouth was open in horror. Dordonas held it higher up in the moonlight. Irving stared at it a few seconds, his eyes round.

"What the bloody fuck! Uncle! You sick bastard!"

"You know it's his!"

"Did you kill him, then?"

"Did I kill –? You really are thick, boy! Of course I didn't kill him! What the!" Dordonas wrapped the piece of Harv's scalp again.

"Well, who did! That – that is… that's regicide! Murder of a king!" Irving spluttered.

"You know, funny how I knew that? What you think we're here for and not in a pub? Not in your fancy estate?"

Irving was still wide-eyed and open-mouthed. Well, and why not. Not only had his brother been murdered, but the King….

"Now, here. Drink up." Dordonas handed him his bottle of rum.

Irving looked at it and shook his head. "I don't usually –"

"I don't care if you *'don't usually.'* Finding out your brother, our King's been murdered is a good fucking time to. Don't you think?"

Irving looked at the bottle, then held out his hand. He drank several swallows.

"Who?"

"Oh, my boy, have I got a lot to tell you…. But first, drink a little more."

Irving drank a few more swallows. He sat down on an old bench.

"All right, then. Let me start by givin' you these to read." Dordonas gave Irving the documents Harvick had given him to hold.

Irving unrolled them and started to read by the light of Dordonas's lantern. It didn't matter if he tore them up, for Dordonas had his separate copies of each. Canny, Harv had been, there in the last few weeks. Thinking of that piece of scalp, now Dordonas knew why.

He watched as Irving's face changed. "Varley, not welcome here in Storden? Disowned? To be arrested, imprisoned, or banished should he not return? But, he's my nephew...."

"Dordonas, I hate to ask, but... was Harv in his right mind? Is that even his... well... you know what I mean?" Irving asked.

Dordonas nodded slowly. "Got it from below his balcony. They were trying to get rid of a blood stain on the terrace there. Couldn't help myself, I snuck in, looked at his body –"

Irving interrupted him, horrified. "Uncle, you did what? You could have been arrested! Thrown in the Dungeon! Hung! I know that Palace, I grew up there. Guards posted everywhere...."

Dordonas grimaced. "Not around a dead King's quarters, there aren't...."

Irving's mouth was still open with shock. "Still, guards would have been posted."

"Relax, boy. I climbed in, climbed back out. What you need to know is, the back of his head is bashed."

Irving's mouth worked, but no sound came out. Dordonas realized he could have said that with more tact, they were – had been – brothers, after all. But aloud, he said, "Irv, I talked to him a number of times over the last several weeks, and he was quite sane. Worried, but sane."

Irving took a breath. "Well, then, this says I've moved up in the order of things. And my boys."

"Irving. You see, don't you, Varley's turned Storden into a military state. We've always been neutral. That last act of Harvick's, sending that boy's warships to Clemongard.... What you think he'll do when he comes home?"

Irving's eyes grew wide again.

"In fact, Irv, who you think it was ordered Harv's death?" Dordonas said as gently as he could.

Irving rolled his eyes and stood up. "Come on. Come on, now. I see what my brother wrote, I hear what you're saying. But Varley's his son. Crown Prince. My nephew. And King now."

Dordonas had expected this. "Aye, with at least twenty thousand troops. You think on that, Irv. Twenty thousand. Harv saw them himself. Three hundred... not three, three hundred warships. That's thirty-five thousand men. Storden recruited thirty-five thousand men. What's Storden need thirty-five thousand men for? It keeps a Navy to protect it, what, fifty ships at most, and five thousand men at most to protect the King...."

"Irving, aren't you hearin' me, boy? Allied with Ormon, fifty thousand men, three hundred warships… your brother murdered. That boy was disowned by your brother. Not a Crown Prince anymore and not King now."

Irving turned around, rubbing at his beard, thinking. "I should move my family as Talia and the boys have been moved…. Where to go…."

"Not a bad idea," Dordonas said quietly.

"This, this place that's not on the map – that's our old grandma's estate – you should move them at once. Varley may know of it. There may be a document that mentions it…."

Dordonas raised an eyebrow. "I'll do that immediately. I know a place, I think."

Then he took a breath. "Irving." Irving turned and faced him in the moonlight.

Shaking his head, Dordonas said, "Irving, I'm no Regent. I can't be Regent to those babes for another some sixteen years…." He trailed off.

Irving's eyes narrowed. Then he said, "Is that what you brought me out here for, so you could ask me to be Regent? Oh, no, Uncle. I've my own life to live. I'm quite happy living my life at my estate in the country with Gerry."

"You mean, Gerranne."

Irving gave Dordonas a strange look. "Well, of course I do. I call her Gerry. And I will not play Regent. Harv left that to you, he couldn't have written it clearer right here in this document then he did," and Irv gestured with it at Dordonas.

The most stubborn man alive sat right before him, Dordonas swore. "Irving. Those babes aren't six months old yet and this country is going to war, starting with Ormon. And our country, Storden, is a part of that, allied with Ormon. When Varley gets back, you think he'll care about that?" And he pointed at Harvick's last line of succession parchment. "He'll try to take the crown by force. He'll take this country to war, against Harvick's wishes and against Stordish tradition. And Storden needs to keep him out.

"We can't do that with a six-month-old on the throne and me as Regent."

Dordonas watched sudden realization dawn upon Irving.

"You need to make a claim for the throne, Irving."

"What!"

"You. You need to make a claim for the Stordish throne. You were the next in line for it after Harvick; most in the Land will know that. And if the Crown Prince has been disowned, then the Crown falls to you.

"Irving, you know it's the truth. You know it is. You grew up there, you got the same education Harv did, you're the son of the King-before-the-King. You're Royal Blood. And

Varley is no longer a member of the Royal Family. He is disowned. Banished. Right now, he is outside Stordish borders, so he is no longer allowed back in. Banished for life.

"Make your claim for the throne, Irving. You're the proper King," Dordonas insisted.

Irving was nothing if not proper. He stood with Harvick's line of succession in his hand. "And what of *this*!" he spat. He smacked the succession parchment as he said so.

"And what of war!" Dordonas roared. "I'll eat my left nut if Harvick knew Ormon was on its way already. I'm here now because I heard two guards say that she was circling around Clemongard to come here! We need a king on the throne now, Irving, you selfish prick! Now step up and make your claim. No one will know of Harv's line of succession to the twins first. I've already rewritten it, you just need to read it. I'll convince the Queen, who is already petrified, and you find her a nice estate somewhere where she and the twins can live their lives freely, but anonymously.

"The time to move is now, Irving. Get in there. With your wife and your sons. Claim the throne, read the document for all to hear. Banish Varley. And fight this war that's coming at us. You know Harv would see the sense of it." Dordonas pulled out Harvick's royal wax, seal, stamp that he'd stolen, along with parchment. He held it out for Irving to read.

Irving took in a deep breath. He met Dordonas's eyes, then he took the document and read it.

He nodded once.

Dordonas made as if to stamp it, but Irving held up his hand.

"Let me."

Dordonas bowed and held out the wax, seal, and stamp. Then he bowed.

"Your Majesty."

Varley

"Your Majesty – I have most important news for you." The soldier wheeled his horse alongside Varley's so that he might speak with him.

"Parchment please," Varley held his hand out to the soldier.

"Begging your pardons, Your Majesty, but I was to relate these to you verbally."

Varley raised an eyebrow. That was different. At least it promised a slight bit of change. His trip from Romeny had been a long one thus far and he was tired. Still two days from the Storden border, too. A slight smile tugged at his face. *His* Storden border now.

"Very well, then. What is it?"

The soldier eyed Varley briefly before he began. "Your Majesty, by King Harvick's hand, Irving Whittemore Goddard took the throne in the line of succession. He has now installed himself in Pikeston Keep as King of Storden, along with his wife and sons.

"He has a document given to him from your father, King Harvick, written, stamped, and sealed by His Majesty, King Harvick, that says you, Varley, were disowned and are banished from the Country of Storden for the Crime of Warmongering. The entire country is talking of it, Your Majesty. Irving read the document before all in the City of Kingston and says your crimes against the Country of Storden, as they are Treasonous, are punishable by Execution only. The folk are already calling him – forgive me, Your Majesty – they are already calling him King Irving. He even rang the bells and they Changed the Guard...."

With that, the soldier urged his horse away from Varley. Well, Varley wouldn't have driven his sword through *that* soldier, he thought, for he had informed him of such news that without it, Varley would have walked into a trap, or worse.

Disowned. His head spun. That couldn't be. Where were those ridiculous, howling little brats? Or had the Queen taken them and run? Undoubtedly a forgery. Father would never have known ahead of time. He scoffed a bit. Warmongering.

"If you please... Your Majesty, I've more news." The soldier eyed Varley warily.

Varley's eyes narrowed. More news than such as what he had just heard? It had best be good....

"Carry on."

"Three hundred warships, seen last in the harbors of Port Dembledon and Port Senswick, are missing, and sources from both Naval ports report that King Harvick sent them and the troops aboard them to join Clemongard's Navy, as a neighborly gesture to Queen Selby."

Varley did not hear this last. It washed over him, like a tide, and it did not sink in. His entire Naval fleet, the man said. Three hundred warships – all fifteen thousand troops. Now in... Clemongard.

By his father's hand. As a neighborly gesture.

And Varley now himself a man to be executed if seen upon Stordish soil.

He let this sink in, slowly. Slowly.

The Ormon woman's ships were on their way, so those former ships of his would get blown from the water in just two weeks hence, while her other ships would be stopping at... Storden. His... former home. Very well. King Irving, fight those twenty thousand men of hers, for Varley would be taking his own twenty thousand men and riding south.

As another... neighborly gesture.

Romand

Romand tilted his head to the side and swiped the razor down his face again, keeping his hand steady. Terrence had been his steward since the days before time, and as such, Romand could tell when Terrence had that look in his eye. Terrence never spoke a word of his own life to Romand, and the steward kept his private concerns to himself. He kept himself healthy and never asked for time off unless he believed poor health might endanger Romand.

Romand stopped the razor just short of nicking himself and grimaced. This morning, when Terrence had woken him, there had been an odd expression on his face. Terrence was always expressionless. Always – much to Romand's displeasure over the years. Romand had taken a look at the man he'd called steward for the better part of his life and dismissed him from the day's duties. Terrence had regarded him for a few moments, considering perhaps whether to object, but in the end, he had excused him.

Romand swirled the razor around in the bowl of water to free it of lather and began again on the other side of his face. Odd, the things one grew accustomed to. Perhaps he would shave himself from now on, rather than Terrence. He splashed water across his face and toweled dry.

He inspected himself in the mirror. Not a bad shave. Not a bad shave at all. He smoothed his bed-tangled white hair into a semblance of normalcy.

Romand padded into his bed chamber and found that Terrence had spread the day's clothing out on the bed for him. As he slipped his airy robe over his silken vest, he mused over what might have caught the steward's attention to such a degree. He ducked to pull the clanking chains of his office over his head. Then his KingsGuard met him outside his chambers. Today was going to be a long day.

His staff wanted to relocate him to ArkenHeights, for it afforded more protection. He spent much of his time here at his Roarden North residence. He preferred the hustle and bustle of the great city to the prosaic seaside. At least he would see his lady-wife at ArkenHeights. Years ago, it had been much the opposite. When he was a younger king, he craved the peace and quiet that the secluded ArkenHeights offered, where his queen, basking in her social standing, enjoying all that a city the size of Roarden North offered, preferred their city dwelling.

Looking back now, the Twenty Years War had taken much out of her. Running a household that had to deal at times with the Northern Countries, other Coastals, or even Eastern armies, as well as protecting their children, had proven a difficult task. She had only wanted to live quietly after that. Women were not meant for war.

Now that he was older, a king confident in his own right, twenty years of war for experience, two grown sons and a daughter a S'hendalow Duchess now, Romand enjoyed the hustle and bustle of one of the biggest gems in all the West – Roarden North. But Romand knew his entire household would be packed and relocated within the week.

And Romand knew why. All the city, all of Corstarorden was talking of it. A sour grimace overtook his expression. The Northern Countries.

He'd heard all about Munsolryshe. Hell of a way to die. Pierced like a suckling pig and left to stew in his own juices. Romand knew of the songs and even the plays, but he had denied entry to entertainers who boasted them, and refused for them to be performed in his Court. Corstarorden was the first Coastal Country that the North called upon, either by land or by sea. If they were to find out that Corstarorden was mocking them – Ormon, specifically – in the slightest....

Romand had heard, as had everyone, that Munsolryshe had died at Myrischka's hand, and that not a member of the entire royal family, extended or immediate, was found to step up to the throne. Perhaps Romand was just a traditional old man, but he wanted his wife, his sons and daughter, their children, all to live healthy, long lives – and he wanted the succession to his throne to remain in place as well.

And Romand was quite certain it wasn't just the Northern Countries he needed to watch out for now. Munsolryshe's death had been a shock, yes, and that his wife was commanding all of Ormon, more so.

But what really stunned him was the death of his neutral neighbor on his northern border. The Storden king, Harvick – had disowned and exiled his son... for the crime of warmongering, of all things, in a country hundreds of years neutral. Harley, Romand thought the boy's name was. And then Harvick's brother took the throne. Under different circumstances, Romand would not have thought much of that except that not two years ago, Harvick had married a woman from a village on the Corstarorden border, Kipper Cove, and unless Romand was mistaken, twins were born.

No matter. Romand would need to meet this new King Irving, for Corstarorden and Storden did an enormous amount of business together. Still, mused Romand, warmongering.... With whom was the boy conspiring? Certainly not the East, nor Clemongard either, for that little Queen had her hands full. Two interesting and far more plausible possibilities rose to mind....

Warmongering. If it had been his Kreston and he in Harvick's shoes.... He shook his head a bit with disgust. To disown a family member, bad enough. To disown your own heir, banish him.... If Kreston had committed treason against the Crown – gods, what Harvick must have faced in making such a decision. Had it been Romand, well, how hard to separate King from father, for Kreston was the jewel of his eye. But to turn against his country and commit treason to the point of committing war crimes with the enemy. The Exile Isles wouldn't even be good enough. It would have killed Romand, but he would have had Kreston executed. Publicly. Very publicly, to serve as an example. Treason was treason, and no one was exempt, particularly those born to royals and nobles. King Harvick had shown weakness by simply banishing that boy, for now the lad was free to run about the land creating havoc.

Romand considered the children of the rest of the rulers. Why, A'dair was now King A'dair and just a few years ago, he was a squire. That Queen Selby. He scoffed inwardly. Romand had no idea why no male kin had stepped forward for the throne. She was just a girl, staring war in the face. Ambsellon would carve Clemongard up soon enough, whether someone stepped up in her place or not. The Cleaver Queen, they called her, in the spirit of her forbear. They must be desperate for encouragement up there.

But the Eastern Shield now had a new daughter, hidden at birth. The Pop-Up Princess. He'd caught the second part of a mime show in the Great Hall depicting it. Of course, everyone thought the girl was just a springtime between-the-sheets Rhutgard was embracing, but t'was said she looked exactly like her twin brothers, blue eyes and all. He'd finally given in to curiosity and blown the dust off of an old History of the Era volume. Mayhaps if a man was just paranoid enough, after fighting in the Twenty Years War, losing two wives, a father, a child, and enough peers, he might spirit his only daughter away. Rhutgard had been a young man, that wife a young queen. Plenty of time to make more babies. Odd. Well, what's done is done, the tide already rolled in, and that Pop-Up Princess had captured the imagination of people even in the West. Romand thought at first that they would roast her and the girl would need to retire from public life before she'd even begun it, but the common people loved the idea of a royal girl who knew what their lives were truly like, and so what little dramas he'd seen depicting her were more fanciful than harsh.

Romand now had the Tortoreen princess married to Cathall Eochair, Duke of Mendellion. Romand had not liked the prospect one bit, not at all. There was enough Tort blood flowing through Corstarorden veins. The fewer ties he had to King Almeric, the better, for that man was as slippery as a greased eel, whether by land or by sea. What had possessed Duke Eochair to marry out of the realm, indeed, a Tortoreen princess, Romand could not fathom.

Eochair enjoyed boundless amounts of wealth for a Duke, rivaling the Crown itself in fact, and so Romand held his tongue. The Duke pulled in a fair share of that wealth from his holdings – in large part productive agricultural lands. He owned prolific properties all over the west and he worked hard to see that they remained fruitful.

Romand could not help but respect a wealthy man with a work ethic. Too many men of affluence enjoyed their fortunes by living in coastal and Roarden North estates, spending time at Court among other lords, and traveling. Duke Eochair had a rather remote familial estate out on the northern border, and now his fifteen-year-old Tortoreen wife was the Duchess. Barely more than a child. It couldn't have been wealth he'd been seeking, and if so, Tortoreen would be the last father-in-law to wed. Pirates under the guise of bankers. Romand scoffed, wondering if Eochair would have to pay a marriage tax on his wife each year.

Romand knew little of the children of the rest of the Land. King Hewett had three young lads. Harvick's boy must indeed have been conspiring with Ormon. That took a sturdy set of balls. He frowned. If Storden was closed to the boy, and Clemongard risen up against Storden now, as it rightfully should, then the little shit was likely to turn to his new allies. The Coastals. Romand grimaced.

Well, he had his own problems to worry about now. He turned the corner, his robes rippling behind him, and stepped into the foyer.

"His Royal Majesty, King Romand of Corstarorden!"

Romand strode into the Cabinet Room before the announcement was complete, a bad habit he'd developed over the last several years.

They all bowed before him. He waved them all down with a precursory flourish of his arm.

Ah. The first War Council he'd assembled in nearly twenty years.

"I now call this new War Council to order."

Rojimar

Rojimar studied the leaf a little a longer, then twirled it between his fingers and wondered what was delaying his source. Tardiness as a rule was not an acceptable working quality of a spy. It caused wrinkles of unknown proportions in others' missions, such as his own, and he was beginning to get restless. He would stay another fifteen minutes and then, though he hated to leave without word of any sort, he would leave.

Rojimar flung the leaf away. At least he wouldn't be discovered in his position here in this simple little sunlit farmer's field. He leaned his elbows on his knees with impatience. He took pride in the network of spies that he had created. Like ivy, it had trailers in directions even Rojimar was now unsure of, but the information was pure. But if one root died, an entire branch could die.

Rojimar cared for his network and if any of them needed anything at all, he provided it if he could. After all, he reported to the highest authority in the realm. It would not do to have no information, or worse, deliver false information. Lives depended on what his sources reported.

If Rojimar was proud of anything, he was proud of his BridgeMaster. Rojimar had never been so surprised than when he'd seen Durain's tall frame in his doorway, but when Durain explained why, Rojimar was immediately taken with the idea. He'd not seen Durain for near a decade, but it had been good to see him as a freestanding entity and not part of the Ericorian unit.

It had been clear, Rojimar mused, even as children that Durain's chance to serve Clemongard lay through his strength. Rojimar grew up two doors away and was a year older but Durain towered over all the children more and more the older they grew. As an Ericorian, he more than met the height requirement. A shame, Rojimar thought, for the smiles he remembered on Durain's face as a boy were now replaced by a stern and solemn countenance, typical of the Ericorian. Rojimar, as a businessman, knew everyone in Woodhill, and so was able to serve Clemongard in a different capacity. Where his old friend had the brawn, Rojimar liked to think he had a bit of brain.

He wished Durain would tell him the story of Queen Selby when she'd nearly cut off old Lord Wharfstead's fingers, since it was all anyone talked of, but he knew Durain would never speak a word of it. Ha. The Cleaver Queen. So much better than the Ice Queen. Rojimar chuckled a bit where he sprawled in the grass. Queens were getting feisty these days.

Rojimar shifted his weight. He'd give it another minute or two. He just couldn't wait, whether he wanted to or not.

Millick whistled behind him. Rojimar nearly startled from his skin. Sneaky bastard had snuck up on him.

Millick sat down on the other side of the tree. "Sorry for the delay."

Rojimar rose an eyebrow. "What kept you?"

"Well... it was worth it. But I was recognized." He frowned. "Think I need to lay low for a bit. Or maybe relocate." He gave a shrug of indifference. Then Millick withdrew a rolled-up parchment from his tunic and handed it to Rojimar.

Rojimar accepted it but paused.

Millick rolled his eyes. "Yes, I know. Perfume oil. Belongs to the madam who recognized me. May my wife forgive me," and he looked skyward for forgiveness.

Rojimar did not laugh, for Millick's wife had passed on some years ago. "So what is this?" He unrolled the parchment.

"Well, you were right about Rockdale in terms of numbers. But that's a list of the men who have family on the other side. Might be best to weed them out. Don't need men passing along our numbers and sensitive information and such through the pass to the Ambsellon border. I wrote that list myself. I wouldn't have gotten caught otherwise."

"What's done is done, and this makes up for it," Rojimar told him. "You go home and rest up. I'll decide on a new destination to relocate you in the meanwhile. Watch out for yourself... things are going to heat up quick."

Beard

He glanced around at everyone on the street. After all these years, he'd never thought he'd see this old Tower Town full of folks again. And it had blossomed overnight. Just a few months. After the Twenty Years War, everyone thought there would be no need for war, and thus no need for lookouts. People had deserted the town in just about a year, leaving a skeleton crew to run the tower. Which was as it should be.

But now, the town was full of youngsters, much as Beard himself had been back before the Twenty Years War. All of them excited for war, all wanting to see galleons, enemy soldiers, all wanting to send up the fire signal, send out the alarm. Truth be told, it was boring work, sitting there day after day. They were in for a rude awakening, Beard mused.

He'd raised an entire family here, and now they were starting to raise theirs. His wife was a tough lady and Beard was proud of her. That was Tower Town families for you, he mused. But even she shook her head the other night in wonderment. If the town was full to capacity, it must be serious. Tower Town folks were among the hardiest there were – military wives and fams grew accustomed to their fathers sleeping in the Towers every other month. It was what they signed up for. But his wife was the toughest woman he knew, and she was not looking forward to what lay ahead. For when all the Tower Towns were full to capacity before the war even started – and it was a war – well. That was fearsome.

And the Queen's worst kept secret down in Ainsley-by-the-Sea… quite the laughing stock there for a bit. Still good for a chuckle now and again. No one but the Towers were speaking of it, for it was a military town, thus a military matter, naturally. But the Queen wanting to gut the old Ainsley estate? And a call for all the best shipwrights silently sent out? Worst kept secret in the Navy. But a brilliant idea nonetheless. All of the channel now housed warships, those being built, and those completed.

As well as a number of those that had suddenly sailed up from Storden. Now that was a treat. He had no idea why Storden should want to send some three hundred manned ships to Clemongard – they still puzzled over it in their cups – but they were grateful for it nonetheless. Those Stordish men were trained and paid for, a gift to Her Royal Majesty from King Harvick, chosen specially. The Tower Towns wondered privately what new King Irving thought of that but what was done was done.

Beard was now a Captain. He just got the promotion last month. Captain Masterson. The younger men, those new to Cliff Watch North, were calling him Captain Masterson, and Beard felt like looking over his shoulder for his father, though his father was dead these fifteen and some years now. Older men and men he knew were still going to call him Beard, for the beard he grew. Julie had huffed and said it was about time he came down from that tower.

But Beard was not happy about it. Cliff Watch North was the first seaside Tower Town to sound the alarm for Northern enemy ships. What if a rookie missed the attack and didn't ring the alarm bell, didn't light the fires? All the rest of the Cliff Watches would miss the alarm….

Driscoll

"Parchment for King Driscoll," called the servant at the entry of Rhutgard's War Room.

Thank the gods. Driscoll hoped it contained news of interest, for he was tired of this room. They had given him certain concessions, given his age, as he was the eldest king not only in the Eastern Alliance but possibly in the Land, though he took no comfort in this latter.

Driscoll believed he was of an age with King Romand over in Corstarorden. There had been King Mend'alair Beaudalain of S'hendalow, who had been about ten years their senior, but he had recently passed from the wasting disease, or so the reports sent out claimed. Driscoll grimaced. No one should die in such agony.

"Lord Berringer," Rhutgard said dryly as he handed the rolled-up parchment to Driscoll.

The five of them had come to an impasse as to whether to announce a War Council or not, but the truth was, they could not continue to cloister themselves inside this War Room of Rhutgard's. Sequestering themselves thus, having meals brought to them, it was as if the War Room was a hospice. He and Gerard believed a formal War Council should be called, whereas Rickstan and Reaghann believed it too soon and the more privacy they had to plan, the better. Rhutgard had abstained for the moment and would call for a vote again after more information had been obtained, for he believed both arguments had merit. Perhaps if Rhutgard's country was not being immediately threatened, he would feel differently.

And fighting – bosh! Rhutgard of all people in the land should have known better. Reaghann was young enough yet that he didn't have a firm enough grip on his temper. Though it had made for good sport, Driscoll had to admit. And no one had said a word of rebuke to Rhutgard, for they were quite sure his wife had words enough on that subject.

Driscoll accepted the parchment from Rhutgard and unrolled it. Finally. Word from Ormon. He had two men placed inside Ormon but of late, reports had been skimpy.

He felt the eyes of the rest of the Alliance Kings watching him.

Driscoll looked up and met their gaze. Then he sighed. He did not like to be the bearer of such news. He addressed Rhutgard next. "I think it may be time to call a formal War Council."

Quietly, Rhutgard nodded at him to continue.

"I have two men living within the Ormon borders. One finally reaches me," Driscoll held up the unrolled parchment. "He writes that the Ice Queen is marching toward the Green Gates, but that her force is divided. Most of it will be headed West, but a small division of it will be sent East to the EverWinters." He paused and glanced at King Gerard, for another detachment of Ormon and Stordish men was already stationed at the northeast border of the EverWinters. That surely meant that Ormon wanted access to Ghiverny, or to his own country, or both. Either was about as bold a move by the Ice Queen as Driscoll could imagine. Second to regicide, that was. Murdering her husband in cold blood the way she had, well, would that her spouse had boasted half the balls she did or they wouldn't be sitting in this position, Driscoll thought with disgust.

Rhutgard frowned and glanced all about the room at the Kings of the Eastern Alliance. He nodded shortly.

"Then it is not simply time to call a War Council. It is time to call our Armies to their fighting stations, as we have planned." He gestured at the strategies they had designed. "And… it is time to announce to our people that we now at war." Rhutgard's blue eyes were cold. "I will declare a formal Proclamation of War against Ormon this afternoon."

The words echoed in the study.

Ronan

A cloud of dust was growing larger on the horizon.

"We have company." Keldrick nodded in the direction of the oncoming group of people on the road. They were still too far away to detect whether they were military or merchant in nature, Ronan mused, and with luck, they were not bandits.

Yet again, Ronan wished King Rhutgard had sent them through one of the southern Mantle Mountain passes instead of the Free Lands. Bandits and Free Riders ran the Free Lands regularly. But while the Mantle Mountains were clear of Ambsellon and Ormon, it was the Mourning Mountain passes on the Clemongard border that were growing more and more thick with enemy soldiers.

Ronan glanced at Keldrick. This would be a true test of Keldrick's abilities. Ronan had quizzed him much in the manner of how he personally had been trained. How to fit in with commoners, how to serve noblemen.... Ronan had trained for weeks, however, where Keldrick had trained just the week since they'd left Fairview. He had learned quickly enough, thought Ronan, but he wasn't happy about it. And now that they were past the Brace Fort in the Free Lands, who knew whom they might encounter....

"Behind me, then," Ronan told Keldrick warily.

Keldrick's blue eyes narrowed in understanding, though he slowed his horse.

From behind him, Ronan heard Keldrick say dryly, "If you ever tell anyone about this journey, you will rue the day you opened your mouth, I promise you, Ronan."

Ronan hid a small smile. "Just remember you're supposed to say when you open your mouth."

Keldrick scoffed behind him. "Yes, *my lord,*" he intoned with disgust.

Finally, the party ahead of them rolled into view. A merchant and his train of wares. Ronan relaxed. A very well-to-do merchant, now that he studied the merchant a bit more. Three sturdy wagons, two full of wares and one full of travel gear for the merchant and his retinue. Two men rode a-horse next to the wagon, rented mercenaries by the look of them, thought Ronan. The merchant pulled the horses in and a small puff of dust arose around the wagon wheels as they rolled to a stop.

Ronan reined in his horse.

"My young friend! How goes your travels?" called the merchant.

"Well enough," returned Ronan. "And you?"

"Much better now that we are closer to home. Tell me, youngster, where are you headed through the Free Lands without protection?"

"Corstarorden," called Ronan. He and Keldrick had previously agreed upon any other destination but Clemongard, to keep their mission secret but also to find out as much information about the West as possible, should they meet people along the way.

The merchant's face changed. He climbed down from the wagon. Ronan had no choice but to slide off his horse. He sensed that Keldrick was conflicted so he patted his horse and whispered, "Stay here."

"Kayson Talvert, at your service."

"Lord Galland, at yours," replied Ronan.

Talvert grasped his outstretched arm. "My lord, I'm not sure what sends you to Corstarorden, but the entire West is talking war. I've a practiced eye and it looks to me as if you hail from the East, begging your pardon. If you're traveling alone without protection, you'd be wise to turn around and return to wherever you came. I don't know a lot about the East or politics and certainly not a thing about war, but I haven't heard that the East was involved in any war. Best, my lord, if you and your man turn around while you can. There's been trouble on the road of late." Talvert turned his head back toward his mercenaries, who nodded shortly.

"What trouble do you mean?" asked Ronan.

"Why, just this morning, we came across an east-bound carriage who'd met a group of mercenaries. They managed to hide in time, they said, off in the grass, but they were lucky to have a mercenary traveling with them. Most folks do nowadays. He scouted ahead and found a band of mercenaries headed north to Corstarorden, wearing Corstarorden colors. Patrolling, they thought. We've had a right bit of trouble out here, out West just these last few months. You Easterners probably don't know it yet. My lord, dressed as you are, they'll spot an Easterner sure as I did, and they won't be nice."

Talvert's expression was solemn.

"I thank you kindly for your warning. I have kin in Corstarorden. My mother sent me to stay with my aunt as she's all alone now. We'll be sure to look for trouble on the road," Ronan told the merchant.

"Well, my lord, I can't fault family values, but I'll tell you this, if you really love your mum and your auntie, pack your auntie up and move her back East. Corstarorden is no place to be right now. All people talk of is war. Me, I stay, I make money no matter if it's peace or war."

Then he said, "In fact, have you boys ever been to the City?"

Ronan had to grasp for a moment to follow Talvert's meaning. Then he realized that the merchant was referring to Pavilion City, where merchants and buyers from the entire land traveled year around to buy, trade, and sell goods of every type, from fine wines to exotic spices to livestock to art to cheese. It was said one could buy and sell anything in Pavilion City.

"No, we have not," Ronan answered.

"Well," Talvert said, "it's a sight everyone should see once. But the two of you really must go. I insist." And he pulled out a credit piece from a pocket and held it out.

What was the man playing at? They weren't children to be spoiled, Ronan thought bemusedly.

"Thank you, my friend, for your kindness, but –"

"No. I insist. You remind me a bit of my son. And I wouldn't let my son go about dressed in such clothes. Stop at Pavilion City, get clothes made for a man of the West. I have so many of these credits I can't count them all. So this credit will dress you and your man over there appropriately and get you a good meal and anything else you need.

"Now, you boys take the next road south to the City, you can't miss it. It will take you a little out of your way, but it's better than the mercs or the military thinking you as Easterners." And he pressed the gold credit into Ronan's palm.

"My friend, you have been most generous. How can I repay you?" asked Ronan.

"Bosh," and Talvert chortled. "I've got money enough. Take care of your auntie and take her out East. Methinks I need to visit the East one day, get past the Silver River. But I just don't like those damn taxes of King Almeric's...." He chuckled as he climbed up into the wagon.

Ronan smiled as he swung up into his saddle. "The East is a beautiful place. May good will follow you."

"And good fortune follow you."

Ronan waited until Talvert's wagon train was out of earshot.

"Keldrick," he said as he fingered the gold credit, "change of plans. We're stopping at Pavilion City first."

—⚡—

Yet again, Ronan struggled to keep from gawking. Easily the most inclusive market he had ever seen, Pavilion City disgraced even the very best of markets Ronan had visited. Overwhelming in size alone, silken pavilions in every color served to divide each vendor from the next. Miles of merchants stretched out in a magnificent tangle all about them. Scents and sights of every imaginable variety accosted them as they walked through.

He saw other first-time visitors staring about the market much as he and Keldrick were attempting not to. They were trying not to call attention to themselves, for if Talvert had recognized them as Easterners, anyone might recognize them, and anyone might recognize Keldrick for the son of the Eastern Shield. Though dusty as they both were from their ride through the meadows of the Free Lands, Ronan mused, it was unlikely. Keldrick's golden curls were weighed down by dirt and bits of grass sprinkled in it from sleeping under the stars. How Kendrick would laugh at the sight of his twin.

But yet another marvel for Pavilion City – it was built on two natural hot springs. Ronan planned on taking advantage of those before they left tonight. Right now, they passed a stand of a number of natural oils, useful for bathing and health, called out the vendor. Grape seed oil, pomegranate seed oil, sandalwood and hickory oils....

Mounted tapestries of varying sizes were guarded carefully by a merchant. Another merchant tried to coax them to purchase fine linens, silks and damasks. They passed stalls selling books and parchments, spices, herbs, and teas, lotions, perfumes and incenses, jams and jellies, potions, powders, and medicines, even lumber of all sorts. Ronan smelled the unmistakable odor of livestock growing in the distance. But still they had not found a clothier.

Finally, a glassware merchant directed them to the north and also recommended that they try the cheese in that quarter.

"Gladly," muttered Keldrick under his breath as soon as they were out of earshot. To his credit, he had directed his gaze downward for the most part out of respect to the role he was playing as Ronan's supposed manservant, though at stalls with more odd and sundry items, such as pickled bear claws at one stand and torture devices at another, he couldn't help but pause to scrutinize as they passed. "Bloody hell," he'd whispered, trying not evince his disgust.

Finally, they arrived in what could only be described as the clothier's district, for silks, satins, laces, velvets, calicos, cotton, and completed clothing of every sort stretched out before Ronan and Keldrick, all busily attended by customers and merchants. Ronan glanced back at Keldrick and sighed. Who knew this would take half the afternoon?

After being shouldered and pushed about for an hour, Ronan's temper began to fray, but they found a woman selling an enormous assortment of finery, both Eastern and Western clothing. Some of it was far too foppish for Ronan's taste, but he saw a few outfits that he liked.

A sharp slap to his wrist startled him. "No touching! That's crushed velvet!"

Ronan blinked. The merchant had just slapped his wrist. He really was not in the mood. "Begging your pardon, Madam, but that," and he gestured at the material he'd just fingered, "was not velvet."

A combined snort and cough came from behind him. Keldrick was holding in a laugh. Now Ronan really was not in the mood.

A small woman with salt and pepper strands of hair falling out of her done-up bun glared at him. "Of course it wasn't. That was satin. Keep your oily hands off the satin. That over there," and she gestured impudently at the last outfit he had looked at, "is crushed velvet. You think I make a living with people fingering this clothing? Who buys satin with dirty fingerprints on it? Who buys ruined velvet? Now go on. Go to the cotton stand. You can't afford any of this. Go!" And the little merchant waved her arms at Ronan to shoo him and Keldrick away.

Keldrick was seized with a sudden sneezing fit, which he turned around to hide.

Incensed, Ronan pulled out Talvert's gold credit. "As it so happens, Madam, I can afford it." He held it up before her so that it flashed in the light. With great satisfaction, he watched her face change. The little woman's mouth dropped into an "O" and for a moment, she was speechless. Keldrick turned back around to observe this interaction.

"Oh, oh my. I'm so sorry, sir." She reached for the credit.

Ronan stuffed the credit back in his vest and shook his head. "I don't think so. Under normal circumstances, I would take my business elsewhere, but fortunately for you, I am in a rush and need clothing immediately, for both myself and my steward here. So. I need Western wear fit for my station of the very best quality and fashion. Have you that here, Madam, or shall I find another vendor of a more pleasant temperament? Did I mention I will be purchasing more than one outfit for myself and for him?"

The little merchant tried to conceal her irritation at his rudeness, since the promise of making money was more attractive to her than a retort. She settled for a glare and invited Ronan and Keldrick back behind the stall front.

Once she quizzed Ronan on what he wanted, she pulled out several outfits for him to choose from. Perhaps it was the Western style, but they were a bit too garish for Ronan.

The little merchant chewed on her lip thoughtfully. "Ah." She dug around and pulled out two more ensembles and laid them out for Ronan. He liked them only marginally better, but her eyes narrowed and annoyed, she blew a sweaty strand of hair away her face.

Keldrick, behind him, cleared his throat. Ronan decided that was a signal to purchase the attire. Once the clothier found two Western outfits to Keldrick's size, Ronan gave her Kayson Talvert's name so that she could extract payment from him when he visited again. She had just made a month's profit this afternoon.

"You didn't have to be so harsh on her," noted Keldrick.

"She didn't have to slap my wrist," returned Ronan.

Keldrick snickered. "When was the last time anyone did that?"

Ronan scoffed. "Never."

They had purchased new boots in the style of the West and were now headed in the direction of the baths, but a familiar scent caught his awareness. And if he recognized it, Ronan knew Keldrick had.

Ronan cleared his throat to remind Keldrick of his role, for the distinct smell of horseflesh was in the air, and Keldrick loved nothing more than he loved horses. Ronan shot a look over his shoulder at Keldrick.

Keldrick glanced from side to side. Once he determined that they were not being overheard, he said lowly, "It would be a travesty, would it not, to go to Pavilion City, to the West, and not see the horses? Whatever types there are, we might infuse with our own stables, purchase for our own cavalry...."

Ronan admitted Keldrick had a point and so they found their way toward the whinnies and scent of horses.

Stables of horses squeezed together surprised Ronan and Keldrick. Ronan did not like what he saw. He stepped up to first row of stalls, where at least a dozen horses stood in straw that needed to be changed out.

A fly buzzed past and a greasy vendor observed their approach lazily.

Behind a hand, Keldrick told Ronan, "Ask him what sort of horses he has."

"What sort of horses are these?"

The vendor turned and spit into the straw before he answered. "Gold chestnuts."

Keldrick cleared his throat to indicate to Ronan that the vendor was full of shit, but Ronan did not need Keldrick to tell him that. These horses were coursers. Ronan was no equestrian as was Keldrick, but even he knew the difference between a gold chestnut and a courser.

"Mind if I have a look?" Ronan asked.

The vendor shrugged and with great effort, stood up to walk Ronan over to the first horse. Ronan reached out to check the stallion's teeth, but the vendor immediately showed a sign of life by blocking Ronan's arm. "What you doin'?"

"Just wondered how old he was," Ronan commented.

"They's all between six and eight years old," the vendor snapped. "Is you lookin' to buy?"

"I have an employer is extremely interested," Ronan responded. King Rhutgard would want to know about the number of coursers for sale on the open market in the West, after all. As soon as they got to Clemongard, he would apprise him of what they had seen here.

The vendor's attitude changed, just as the clothier's had. "Well, I'm gettin' more horses in next week, tell your employer that. I got the best selection of anyone here. Name's Vincick."

Ronan nodded and backed away. "I'll be sure to tell him that."

Once they left, Keldrick could barely contain himself. "Gold chestnuts! Did you see them! Those were coursers and destriers!"

"Yes, Kel, I know, now keep it together," Ronan hissed. "We're here at the baths and this is the last place we can talk about personal business."

"The baths," Keldrick repeated.

For the first time today, Ronan smiled. "Afraid of a bit of water, Kel? Plan to bathe with your clothes on, do you?"

Keldrick said nothing for a moment. Then he said, "Fine. Just so long as I get food and ale afterward."

They walked into the only actual building they'd seen so far. Curls of steam rose from an enormous natural bath. Several people were already sitting inside, beads of sweat rolling down their faces. Ronan could not wait to immerse himself inside the water and soak all the dirt from the journey off himself.

Then Keldrick ruined it by whispering, "You do realize, don't you, that all those horses we saw have already been bought? That's why their heads all faced toward the backs of their stalls. Someone is just waiting to pick them up. That's at least a four-dozen horse cavalry unit."

Theldry

The Duchess of Mendellion was still not with child. Theldry wondered if that was what they whispered of her. It had been nearly six months, after all. It mattered not that Cathall wasn't home that often; people only knew that Theldry, young as she was, was not yet a mother.

Her friends were all expecting or mothers already. And when she was quite honest with herself, Cathall married her so that he might have a family. Theldry placed her hands upon her belly and attempted to imagine herself with child. Or a mother. She just couldn't see it. But she did want to please him, and so, when he was home, they tried as often as possible. She wondered if perhaps he was too old, or she too young. But Mother had borne her already at fifteen. And so Theldry brooded.

She kept herself busy, however. At first, she had been bored, given her only company had been Mila the Minnow. But three months ago, Theldry found Mila sprucing herself up one day and could not imagine why. Then the scribe visited and Theldry had had to hold back amusement at Mila's awkward attempts at flirtation. The scribe seemed to stay overlong and Theldry excused herself briefly to give them the privacy she would have wanted had she been Mila.

They spoke mainly about rare books and interesting parchments written by great masters of art and music. Theldry decided the young scribe was completely innocent in his attentions toward Mila and, before he left, she asked if he might return the following week at the same time with any works from Tortoreen, for she missed her homeland so.

She saw the young man glance quickly at Mila and then immediately agree. Theldry thanked him and sent him on his way, but didn't miss how Mila's eyes were shining.

First, however, Theldry inquired of her kitchen maids what sort of character the young scribe's family was of. She hadn't married for love, but she recognized it when she saw it, and if she could facilitate it, then why not?

It took a few days, but Jeanie reported that the scribe's family was well-to-do, owning a prosperous printing business which the young scribe was due to inherit one day, aside from his own scripting abilities. In these days and times, in Corstarorden, especially the way people were talking war, it was best to marry a young girl off as soon as possible so that she'd have the protection of her husband and new family. And in Northwest Corstarorden, big fish didn't swim around all that often, said Jeanie, so you had to grab what you could. He would support Mila just fine, thought Jeanie.

So after numerous picnics, during which Theldry stifled yawns and pretended amazement and interest, young Engard worked up the courage to ask to court Mila formally, and Theldry, of course, obliged. Within a month, he asked for Mila's hand in marriage. Theldry told him she accepted the betrothal request as long as he could provide suitable living arrangements for Mila that suited her current station, and so he was now scrambling to find the best for Mila that he could.

Jeanie and the other maids were thrilled, as was Theldry, for it was one of Theldry's duties as the lady of the household to see to the needs of the people living at the Mendellion Estate. And Mila was so in love she could hardly sleep at night.

Cathall, however, was not pleased at all. Tonight over dinner, he explained that she was new to Corstarorden still and should not make decisions of such great consequence without his consent. He would have planned Mina's marriage himself in due time. Theldry returned this with an impassive nod and remained aloof.

Cathall's fork settled onto his plate with a clang. "You disagree."

Theldry looked across the dinner table at him. What was she to say? She was reminded of her father again. Her father would say Theldry had no say in such matters. "I have no opinion in such matters," she answered in a quiet way she thought would please her mother, then turned her attention to the roast duck on the sterling plate before her.

A sigh erupted from Cathall. "You are angry. I know you well enough to see that."

When Theldry said nothing, he said, "Speak, wife. I must deal with my people's troubles all the while I am traveling. I would not return home to see you glare at me across mine own dinner table. Speak, or I shall retire early."

Theldry lay down her utensils. "Very well." She met his eyes and raised her chin. "I did not betroth that girl to some neighborhood apprentice. Engard stands to inherit a prosperous printing business and is already a learned scribe and businessman in his own right. He cannot marry her until he can provide for her a home that is worthy of her. Before I allowed them to court, I first approved his family. I chaperoned all of their outings myself.

"Husband, in Tortoreen, I was raised to run a household such as yours. Running a household such as this included seeing to the needs of my ladies-in-waiting. A husband would have had little to do with the needs of ladies-in-waiting, except to see to their finances, which, as Mina has no family but us, I hope you will continue to act as. Having been educated thus, I saw no reason to consult you, and as you are rarely available to consult due to business concerns, I have never thought it necessary to bother you with the smaller happenings in my life, such as the courtship of my lady-in-waiting."

Theldry had kept her tone even, but Cathall was right. She was angry. She disliked having to justify her actions. He remained quiet for a moment, sipping from his goblet. Finally, he nodded.

"Very well. I will honor the betrothal. I had planned to do so anyway – they are good for each other."

Theldry relaxed.

"But." And Cathall took another sip. "Do not betroth, or dismiss, anymore of our servants without my consent. Not until you have been in Corstarorden, and Mendellion, for some time more to come. Then I will turn that power over to you completely. You hail from Tortoreen. Allow yourself time to adjust to Corstarorden's cultures. They are not so very different, but they are different.

"Are we agreed?" Cathall asked her.

Theldry nodded, glad that he was honoring the betrothal. She did not want to have to tell Mina why Cathall had broken it.

"Which leaves us with another problem," Cathall told her then. "You will need a new lady-in-waiting."

Theldry was unable to stifle a grimace.

Cathall read her expression. "So bad as that? I chose your current lady-in-waiting based on what Ayrissa would have enjoyed...." And he stopped, for he realized that Theldry had cast her glance aside. Not only had he referenced his first wife in her preferences, but he realized that perhaps Theldry was quite different than he thought her to be.

In a quiet tone, he apologized. "I was quite unsure of whom I would be marrying, and so I was blind in that respect. I chose a young lady I was familiar with in regard to Mila. What would you like in a lady-in-waiting?"

Theldry gave him a hopeful smile. "None at all?"

Cathall chuckled as he sliced his asparagus. Then he eyed her. "Why would you say that?"

"I enjoy riding, and singing, and theatre. I appreciate humor, and conversation about other topics than stitchery and fashion and gossip. I have more in common with our maids than most ladies-in-waiting," Theldry told her husband.

Cathall's fork of gingered carrot was arrested in midair. "The kitchen maids? Why is that?"

Theldry paused. She did not want to get Jeanie and Kallia in any sort of trouble. She shrugged a little. "They are easy to talk to. I have actually taught them their letters better when they have some extra time. And they have taught me about Corstarorden." Theldry did not add that they had sung songs together, including one that made Theldry blush once she recognized what it really meant, "Ribbons Around the Maypole". They had also taught Theldry a little about cooking and preserving, enough that Theldry hoped she would never need to fend for herself in the kitchen.

But Cathall was looking at her with a look of interest on his face. Finally, he nodded and said, "You say they teach you about Corstarorden?"

"Mina hates to leave the estate. I've taken them into the village with me and they've proven invaluable. I've met a number of the village people," Theldry pressed on when she saw Cathall's face darken. "Sitting here, day after day, why shouldn't I go into the village? I am the Duchess, am I not? And two guards accompanied me each time. I know half the merchants in the market now. I go perhaps each week or two.

"You should know, the Burdan family, who sells sea shell art, just welcomed two twin girls last month. I congratulated them, of course, but I think if you paid them a visit, it would mean so much more. And the fruiter's oldest son broke his arm two weeks ago. One of our kitchen maids told me that he broke it repairing the wagon wheel on the fruit cart. They haven't the money for a Healer, and it was quite an awful wrapping. His name is Darvel, and he was in terrible pain. I paid for the town's Healer to wrap and tend to it correctly," Theldry continued in a firm tone. "Neither you nor I would know such things if I did not go out to see the village."

Thoughtfully, Cathall nodded. "Well, that would explain the congratulatory remarks on my marriage. I thought them rather enthusiastic for people who had never met you." He waited as a platter of hot, fragrant bread and a small bowl of honey butter was placed before him. "Nevertheless, maids are not ladies-in-waiting. Mina may prefer to stay at home, but I shall find you another lady-in-waiting who has more of a taste for short outings."

Theldry gave her husband a pained look.

"I shall not change my mind. When we have guests, or visit others socially, and we will, you must have a lady-in-waiting of the proper social standing. Which brings me to a problem, for in Northwest Corstarorden, there are few ladies-in-waiting worthy of a princess of Tortoreen and Duchess of Mendellion to be had."

Cathall read her expression. "But I shall search for one who is an equestrian, who prefers wit and conversation to stitchery and gossip. Perhaps even one who might like to stay in the village, yes?"

A smile overtook Theldry's features. If she had to have a lady-in-waiting, one who wasn't underfoot at all times would be perfect.

Cathall returned her smile. "Now, something else I think you will be pleased to hear. I checked into what your father's Cabinet members were talking about. The blight – was no blight at all, just as my farmers insisted. I have advised them to raise their prices on all their outgoing produce so that they might recover the money they have lost in recent years. And we will no longer be dealing with Tortoreen until they bring their new tariffs down. I spoke with King Romand personally. I am uncomfortable delivering such a financial ultimatum when it comes to a Coastal Country, but nor will I deal with crooked partners."

Theldry nodded. So much for making money off of Corstarorden, Father, she thought snidely, though she refrained from expressing her personal triumph. What had Father kept telling her? *Duty before love, Theldry, duty before love.* Ha.

Blakeson

What a man the Duke was. Fine man. Fine man.

Last night the Duke had told him and Richland Fields and Sweet Trees all about that bloody blight those years ago. Blight. That was no blight. Everyone in all of Corstarorden knew it. Anyone who'd ever put their hands in an ounce o'earth. Blakeson packed another burlap bag of seed in against the cellar wall.

"Then what did he say?" pressed his wife as she held up the lantern. Neasa was just as surprised as he was by their good fortune.

The root cellar hadn't been in use since the Twenty Years War, back when his father and the fam had hidden inside it. You could barely tell it existed, so well was it crafted. His father said they never knew which country's soldiers had camped out in the house above, but the fam had hidden inside for three days, eating everything they could find, and sneaking out only once for water. Then the soldiers were gone. They counted themselves lucky the house and Blakesly Farm hadn't been put to the torch, like so many other farms.

"The Duke told us there was war comin' and to go to his estate for shelter."

Neasa shook her head at that. "We'll not be goin'. Not and leave the farm. No. We'll just take the boys and hide in here, like your fam did," she said resolutely. "What did the other two say?"

 Sweet Trees and Richland Fields, the only two farms of the Duke's that bordered Blakesly Farms for miles and miles, weren't about to leave either. In fact, Richland told the Duke that a farmer was like a captain – you don't leave your ship. The Duke nodded and told them, "I respect that, and I thought you'd say that. That's why I've brought you this." And he'd uncovered the wagon with enough seed to help them plant for next year, "– in case soldiers ruin or burn what you have now. And if not, then you have enough to expand what you have now or keep it for a future date. Do with it as you will. I suggest you hide it in your root cellars or barns, where it cannot be found by soldiers, so that you have enough to replant. Store it safely for next season. I give you this in place of coin, as soldiers might find coin and assume you stole it. If that were to happen, not only would you lose your farm, but a hand or even your life, and that I cannot protect you from."

Neasa listened to this as she watched Blakeson pack one of the last burlap bags of seed against the root cellar wall. "What a man he is. Do you suppose he realizes he's given us more than we need to replant?" she asked thoughtfully.

"Of course he does. He's no fool." Blakeson topped the stack of seeds with the last burlap bag and brushed his hands free of dirt. He studied his wife in the shadows of the dusty root cellar. "He seems sure war is coming here. We need to stock up some dried meat and preserves, some tallow and lanterns, blankets, have a plan so we can stay in here. Get some food from the pantry and bring it down here."

"Like your fam did." Neasa gathered her shawl about her and climbed up the ladder, but not before Blakeson saw the nervous look on her face.

He felt bad for Sweet Trees – all those fruit trees. If soldiers took to burning, why, it would take years to regrow a fruit tree. But the Duke had a half a wagon full of seed of some sort for him, too, and the two had held a private conference of some sort. Something to plant in the interim. A good man, the Duke of Mendellion. What luck it was that the Duke was their landholder and not some bloody tax collector type.

War, Blakeson thought as he threw hay over the entrance to the root cellar. May it not last twenty years like the last one.

A'dair

A'dair stared into her brown eyes but saw nothing. She was neither buxom nor curvy, nor beauteous, nor did she hail from Coral City as Father would have preferred. He had tried that option already and her head sat atop the castle upon a spike as a warning, though few in the realm realized it.

It had been a very small wedding, for A'dair had planned to announce the marriage after the fact. Very few people had been invited, and even fewer attended, for he had given virtually no notice. The wedding itself had transpired without incident, and the new Queen of S'hendalow gave A'dair no cause to believe that conspiracy might be afoot.

But come the reception, after A'dair presented his new bride with lands for her family, she presented him with a rare wine, a vintage from his great-grandfather's lands.

A'dair, as a new husband and groom, did as a gentleman ought and presented his new Queen with the first goblet.

Numerous times since, he recalled a panicked glance from her to her father across the room. And her father had nodded gravely. A'dair had thought that odd, but she looked him straight in the eye then, raised her goblet, toasted A'dair's good health, and drank every drop.

A'dair had found the glance to Lord D'alwar distinctly unsettling, for they had been regular adversaries before A'dair had dissolved the Cabinet, and so had set his goblet down. And rightly so, for the new Queen fell to the floor, convulsing and frothing.

Half the Kings Guard lined up before A'dair, and half behind him, to hide the event transpiring. A'dair insisted someone take Lord D'alwar into custody.

And so, his marriage not even two hours old, his Queen tried to kill him, assassinate him, just as the Ormish Queen had her own husband. Regicide. Perhaps he should feel fortunate that he had not been in their wedding bed, stabbed to death, as King Munsolrysche had been found, but only an attempted poisoning.

He ensured that no one knew what had occurred – it looked as if she merely choked to death. Ninety percent of S'hendalow didn't even know he had been betrothed, and of those present that day, most thought the girl simply choked. A'dair took away her lands all the way back to her great-grandparents, as well as any supporters' lands, and shipped them all to the Exile Isle. When they cried and begged before him for mercy, he turned a deaf ear, and showed them instead the severed head of the annulled Queen he had married, before it was mounted upon a spike and raised above the highest Palace tower, their wedding rings nailed into her mouth. He insisted each of them look at it, particularly her father and mother. Lord D'alwar stubbornly said, "You didn't deserve her." A'dair returned with grit, "Interesting. I thought the same of you."

And he had them all chained together for the voyage. The voyage to Exile Isle was a long one and the captain and crew had not yet returned. It was said that exiles who lived there, brought there from all the realms, stood a low chance of survival and often turned to cannibalism.

The priest cleared his throat with an expectant tone. A'dair blinked and glanced at the priest. He knew the correct words to say this time. He lifted this girl's gauzy veil from atop her face and bowed before her. Cannibalism. A'dair scoffed inwardly. Hardly the right subject to reflect upon while marrying. He wished – for a second time – that his father might be here to witness his wedding. A'dair and his father shared the same quirky sense of humor.

Je'hanna curtsied before him. He placed a ring upon her finger and covered her shoulders with a velvet cloak that depicted the royal crest of S'hendalow. Together, they stood before the priest. The priest pronounced them man and wife, King and Queen, King A'dair and Queen Je'hanna of S'hendalow.

Scores of wedding guests applauded when they turned around, for A'dair had made this a very public wedding. *Well, Father, be pleased*, thought A'dair. His new bride was not from Coral City this time, but Billoughby-by-the-Bay, and her father owned a great deal of ships and coastal property.

Now A'dair would secure the bloodline and would also surround both his Queen and himself with guards. Separately, of course. He would do his regal duty as often as it took to impregnate his new bride, then retire to his own quarters. Trust would take a long time to build after the last matrimonial disaster.

Though first he must live through his second wedding reception.

Selby

She had dismissed most of her War Council and stood looking now at its wary remainder. Who remained were more important – their lands were border lands, towns, parishes, rivers, and trade supply routes that stood to be encroached upon first. Coastal and mountainous lands mainly, though she retained the services of Lord Sandewyre, whose lands were meadowlands. Having an entire room of Council members talking all at once at such a late date only served to add to the fray.

Selby did not need an entire Council to vote. Her Councilors served as advisors only, steering the nature of Clemongardian politics by vote, though Selby knew they would not appreciate being described thus. As for war, some of them wanted to be heard more and others less, but ultimately, they were largely uninformed on war strategy.

Of course, this was why Selby had employed experts to advise her. Such as the Admiral and Colonel who were looking wary as she stood against the maps of Clemongard on the finely paneled wall.

She swallowed down her annoyance at what seemed sure to be a disruption, for they stood side by side together. Selby shouldered her hair back and leaned against the map on the wall. "Admiral Droyce. Colonel Berold. It seems you have a point to make. Have out with it so we may continue."

Selby noted then that her manners had slipped away. Not three months ago, she might have asked these men to *please do so* and *thank you*. Now, she simply issued commands and expected them to be carried out. Hmm. Perhaps it was the stress of this war, or perhaps it was the weight of the Crown. Selby decided it was both.

Neither the Admiral nor the Colonel appreciated being addressed so, she decided, for they glanced at each other. Selby raised her eyebrows expectantly.

The Admiral gave a brief shake of his head and looked down, thereby assigning the responsibility to the Colonel, who took a deep breath.

"At risk to life and limb, Your Majesty," said Colonel Berolt, eyeing Selby's cleaver, which she wore at her side each day, "I would say to you that this is a war we are going to fight, and that people throughout Clemongard will be hurt regardless of how we fight it. You cannot romanticize war."

Ah. They felt she was basing her war strategies based on the placement of her populations, so that people would not get hurt. Selby felt her anger rise.

"I would say the same to you, Colonel, Admiral. It is one thing to win a war. It is another to send enemy soldiers home and have so few remaining survivors in your own land that it wasn't worth the victory. You will not center this war around highly populated areas unless absolutely necessary. Soldiers fight the war, but the people suffer for it. They endure poisoned wells, burned towns and cities, loss of lives. They starve for years afterward. Livestock and crops are ruined when soldiers march through, sickness and disease spreads. I realize that our men must feed themselves, and supplies must be amassed as you march through. I have studied war, these many weeks since I called our first War Council. But I will not have our own citizens suffer at the hands of Clemongard soldiers more than must be, with Stordish and Northern soldiers attacking as well.

"And, Admiral Droyce, Colonel Berolt, if either of you find this a principle you unable to strategize by, then you will take a demotion and retire from the military. I suggest that, if you choose that option, you then leave Clemongard, as she will be besieged in merely a matter of days. Do make your choice in a timely manner, so that I may appoint another in your place.

"And do understand – while you are each in charge of Clemongard's Navy and Army…" Selby paused and stared at each man before she continued, "I am in charge of you and your decisions regarding Clemongard's Navy and Army, just as I am in charge of Clemongard and her people, whether in peace time or in war. Strategize away from highly populated areas. Am I understood, Admiral, Colonel?"

They returned her query with stiff salutes. Neither of them was happy at all, Selby saw, but she did not think either of them would furnish her with their retirement papers. They were men of honor and had each fought in the Twenty Years War with distinguished service records, else neither would be before her now. Neither would leave a country they had fought for and spent their entire lives serving as officers in over a difference in principle.

Lord Wharfstead had, during this speech, stepped up to join her. He cleared his throat at her side as if to lend support. She marveled inwardly, not for the first time, how nearly chopping off the man's fingers had earned her the man's undying loyalty.

"Had you anything other points you wished to make?" Selby asked pointedly. Had she been a King, no one who had earned a seat in this room would question her directives.

Another glance between the two officers occurred before Colonel Berolt told Selby frankly, "Just this, Your Majesty. Within the week, we expect enemy troops to be within Clemongard's naval borders and make landfall elsewhere. Your Majesty, it is time to mobilize our troops."

Prickles chilled her flesh. His words hung in the air.

The time had finally come.

They had wanted to dress her in gold plated, highly ornamented armor, adorned with ridiculous accoutrements.

Her answer was to ask them if gold dented more easily than steel. Her armorers' jaws dropped in horror, telling her a woman was in no way expected to be on the field of battle. Selby had then replied that she was not going to war to win a fashion show, but to kill her combatants, should they make it past her guards, and to start again. Then her armorers protested that she would not be fighting at all, for women did not fight.

But Selby had begun lessons in private, against strident objections of Durain, who insisted that Ericorian would protect her.

And so Selby now owned a steel suit of armor and a chain mail suit, both of which were quite heavy. She also owned a sword that was made to her measurements.

Selby found the idea of wearing the chain mail and armor unimaginable, for their sheer weight alone. But she insisted upon their making, for her only heirs were two cousins who were not trained in statescraft. Her survival was crucial to Clemongard, particularly so soon after the loss of her brothers and father.

Her master armorer was insistent upon her breastplate being quite ornate, however, if she would not garbed in gold. She must appear to be the Queen of Clemongard in some aspect, he insisted. She told him that was why she did not want ornate armor – she did not want to be taken as the Queen of Clemongard. Selby would stay back with her Generals and her Colonels and would be well protected by her Ericorian, but would not call attention to herself. The officers would fight this war, not she. All she would do was approve final movements.

Durain had indeed, voiced objections at the idea of Selby learning to fight. But, at her insistence, he found a discreet Armsmaster with whom she had trained several afternoons a week in a quiet, deserted alcove of the Palace, under Durain's watchful eye.

And at the start of each session, Armsmaster Andeval told Selby directly that, Queen or no, he strongly disapproved of women fighting. And Selby shrugged it off, for war was approaching and she would not be defenseless if an enemy soldier broke through. The opinion of a single Armsmaster mattered not to her when it came to the lives of her people. Her people must have a ruler.

One of the first things Armsmaster Andeval taught her to do was use her cleaver. "Before you chop off some unsuspecting Councilman's fingers," he'd told her dryly. Selby narrowed her eyes at the salt-and-pepper haired Armsmaster, for she had purposely missed.

"Narrow your eyes all you will, missy, but the next time you go to use that knife, it may not obey you," Andeval returned her glare with a disapproving look that made her feel the seventeen-year-old she was suddenly.

He'd brought her to the barn. No one knew they were there and he supplied her with a horrid leather apron, stiffened with what Selby suspected was dried blood. Once they were inside, Andeval walked her down to the end of the stable, and she'd wrinkled her nose at the smell of manure. He'd scoffed at a private joke.

Then she saw three suckling pigs, hanging from a hook, dead, their red eyes staring sightlessly. Andeval tied a leather apron around himself and told Selby, "Get your cleaver out, Your Majesty."

Selby had been horrified, but she had wordlessly obeyed him.

"You want to know what it's like to hit a man with a blade?" Andeval pointed at the first pig. "Go on, then."

Blood had spilled on the hay and her first few hits had been clumsy, weak. Then he told her to hack at the pig. She felt her cleaver hit bone several times and was partially dismayed, but partially intrigued. When she drove her cleaver into the pig's soft belly, its guts spilled out onto the ground and blood splashed up onto her apron. Selby looked up at Andeval, her breath whooshing out of her in disgust. She tossed down her cleaver.

"That, little missy, is what it is to kill a man. Pigs are very similar to men. Are you sure you want to carry on?"

Selby had swallowed down her disgust and taken a deep breath before she nodded.

Andeval shrugged and nodded. "Here." He handed her a short sword and gestured her over to the second pig.

After stabbing the second pig several times with the short sword, she moved on to the third pig and slashed and hacked at it.

Armsmaster Andeval reached out slowly with a calloused thumb and wiped away a small bit of pig's blood from Selby's face.

"Still sure you want to learn to kill men, Your Majesty?" he asked.

Selby was staring down at all the carnage she'd wrought, seeping into the hay. If she just imagined it as Ambsellon and Ormon… then perhaps….

She had swallowed and nodded. Though she had waited until she had gotten back to her chambers to vomit, several times.

Andeval had taught her nearly every afternoon since, how to avoid incoming attacks, how to use her shield, how to use her cleaver, her sword.

Today, after leaving Admiral Droyce, Colonel Berolt, and the few others remaining on her War Council to hammer out a few more plans for the North, Andeval had told Selby that, starting tomorrow, she would practice in her ringmail, so that she might get accustomed to its weight. Until today, she had only been using leather armor and wooden weapons.

Selby whirled out of Andeval's sword attack. She was getting better on her left defense but she hoped she would never have to test her abilities on the actual battlefield.

Durain suddenly cleared his throat and Andeval stopped his assault.

Seneschal Mandewel stepped into the stone alcove. "Your Majesty, I apologize for the interruption, but I've brought this."

Selby drew a forearm across her temple and held out her hand. The Seneschal brought her a pigeon parchment, which she could see immediately came from the Eastern Alliance.

A Silent Game of Spies

"I thought you would want to see it right away." The Seneschal bowed.

To: Her Royal Majesty, Selby Cylysse Stevanrhut, First of Her Name,

Queen of Clemongard:

I write in hopes this find you in good health. I have sent you two representatives from the Eastern Alliance who should arrive within a day to two days of the reception of this communication. Prince Ronan Martel and Prince Keldrick Firthing travel to Clemongard to meet with you as War Time Ambassadors in my stead. They will share information such as the Eastern Alliance has for you as its Ally. Please confirm their arrival.

From: King Rhutgard Anghus Firthing, First of His Name

King of Romeny; Eastern Shield of the Eastern Shield Alliance

Visitors from Romeny. At last. She nodded slowly and looked up at Seneschal Mandewel. "We will be receiving two – high profile – lords visiting tomorrow. Have guest quarters according to their rank in the Lords Quarters freshened tonight.

"And send Jennelle to my chambers. I'm through for this afternoon."

─────

Selby drew her knees up to her chin and slid further into the steaming bath.

"I don't understand why we would suddenly receive guests from the East," Jennelle mused aloud as she pulled at Selby's wet hair with a comb. "Even in the East, they must have heard we're going to war."

Selby smiled a little and said drowsily, "I expect they won't stay long once they find out how soon we will be facing enemy soldiers." Which was true. They would only be here to gather information too sensitive to send by carrier pigeon and find out where she wanted any troops they could supply sent.

Jennelle was her chief lady-in-waiting, and the only one Selby had time for. Selby no longer had time for an entire gaggle of ladies-in-waiting, and so it fell to Jennelle to entertain the whole flock, until Selby sent for her. And while she didn't tell Jennelle everything, she did gloss over certain things, such as the details of the Eastern lords visiting tomorrow.

Jennelle interrupted Selby's reverie by saying, "You know, Your Majesty, with all due respect... it's been almost eight months." She trailed off.

Selby sighed. She knew what Jennelle referred to. The deaths of Selby's father and brothers in RainsCourt.

Selby cleared her throat. "And...."

"Well, Majesty, perhaps, while the people can still see you, perhaps it's time for a bit of... something extra."

"Jennelle, say what you would, please, it's been a long day."

"Only this, Majesty. You have five black velvet gowns –"

"For mourning."

"Of course, for mourning, five black velvet gowns, but, what if, just one, had maybe a little bit of gold to it? Some cloth-of-gold embroidery trim, that the people might see you wear before you leave for the war?"

Selby was quiet. Thoughts of her brothers and father flashed before her.

"You'd still be in mourning, only a little trim after eight months," commented Jennelle. "And you've company from the East visiting soon."

Perhaps on special occasions.... "Very well, see to it. Nothing too ornate," Selby rolled an eye over her shoulder toward Jennelle.

Jennelle started squeezing Selby's hair dry with a thick towel. "Good. It's been seen to already. You should wear it tonight, for we've entertainers guesting with us." Jennelle was pleased.

"You've already done it?"

"You never noticed. What were four black gowns to five?" Jennelle began winding Selby's hair carefully about. "And we'll put your hair up as well. You've been wearing it down ever so long. Don't fuss, nothing special, nothing ornate, just something that says 'pretty,' not 'plain'".

In the end, Jennelle had her way with a simple gold clip and two braids wound round Selby's head. Selby admitted, she missed dressing up, but a mourning period was a mourning period.

But she didn't realize just how her people had grown accustomed to her in mourning and 'plain,' as Jennelle called her, until she descended into the Great Hall with Jennelle for dinner. The entire Great Hall hushed when they saw her.

Perhaps it was time to leave her mourning behind.

The Seneschal leaned in briefly and whispered, "Your Majesty, your – high profile guests – arrived earlier this afternoon. Their rooms are being readied as we speak, but I made sure they had rooms to rest and refresh themselves in prior to dinner."

Selby started. "They're here? Now?" She was exhausted and hadn't prepared for an Eastern Alliance accord.

Seneschal Mandewel nodded just slightly and answered behind his hand, "I believe they are here only to relax for the evening. The gentleman in blue and gold near the end of the table introduced himself to me as Lord Galland of Romeny." The Seneschal flicked his brown eyes behind him briefly. "Perhaps a name he traveled by, then?"

"Understandable," mused Selby. Who would want to go by the name of a Prince through the Free Lands when bandits, mercenaries, and military men from any side were traveling through?

"Shall I schedule him for tomorrow?" asked Seneschal Mandewel.

"Yes, first thing in the morning." Selby nodded and the Seneschal retreated. Her mind ran over the entire evening's entertainment. Had it been pleasant? Had the feast been worthy of Eastern Alliance guests? She had never had such high-profile guests before. A few Dukes, most of the several generations removed, two Duchesses. King Harvick had meant to attend her Coronation but sent his deepest regrets, for his wife gave birth to two twin babies that same weekend, and so he instead sent her enormous gifts in place of his absence.

So now, in her Great Hall, sat the son of the most powerful man in the Land, as well as the Crown Prince of Ghiverny. And what had been served... ugh. Nothing of note, spiced pheasant with oranges, cucumber soup, and roasted tomatoes stuffed with cream cheese and dressed with sage and bacon. Cherry and cheese tarts along with fresh melon had been served for sweets.... Selby sighed with annoyance. If she had only known.

At her side, Jennelle slid into her chair next to Selby, where she sat most often. Dancing had been going on all evening, and thanks to the gods for that, thought Selby. Jennelle had enjoyed herself thoroughly, given how breathless she was.

"I do wish you could dance out there as you used to, Majesty," Jennelle said.

"As do I," Selby replied absently. Then, on a whim, she told Jennelle, "Stay here."

Selby could not have two members of the Eastern Alliance sitting in her Great Hall, under a clandestine identity or not, without introducing herself. She kept to the wall so that no one would bother her with deep bows and curtsies, nor she they with the stoppage of the music and entertainment.

Once she stood next to her recently arrived guests, Selby cleared her throat. They both turned around.

"My Lord Galland, I believe? Welcome to Clemongard," she said.

Both of them bowed lowly. Selby only experienced a moment of curiosity in wondering which prince was which, for she recalled the old saying about Romeny blues always breed true, and the second prince looked back at her with quite startling blue eyes. Prince Keldrick, she recalled from King Rhutgard's communication. She would need to send an immediate communication telling him that they had arrived safely.

"Your Royal Majesty," both men intoned, and they kissed her ring when she held it out, though Prince Keldrick met her eyes as he did so. Was he told to do that? Her stomach fluttered.

"Let us speak elsewhere, Lord Galland," Selby tore her eyes from Prince Keldrick's blue gaze to Prince Ronan's.

"As you wish, Your Majesty."

She led them from the clamor of the Great Hall to a deserted dining hall.

"Durain, please see that no one disturbs us," Selby directed Durain and her other Ericorian, then turned to her allies. "We may speak privately in here."

Prince Ronan stood back then and nodded to Prince Keldrick. Interesting.

"Your Royal Majesty, we come from Romeny on behalf of the Eastern Alliance and King Rhutgard, the Eastern Shield. I am Prince Keldrick and this is Prince Ronan. We are sent to speak with you in his place, as War Time Ambassadors and your allies."

The two of them bowed to her again.

"I am most grateful for your presence, as well as your affiliation," Selby told them with as much dignity as she could muster. She had no idea this would be so hard, asking for the help of other countries....

Prince Ronan cleared his throat. "How bad is it?"

Just like that? Selby considered him. Shrewd green eyes contemplated her, and he had just sliced through all the diplomacy that all her advisors and Cabinet members usually took such delight dancing around.

She swallowed. What to say? She felt a child again, and any answer might be the wrong one.

"I'm not really sure where to begin." Her voice was hoarse. "Ambsellon killed my father and brothers last year. That's why I'm Queen." She watched as they exchanged a glance. "So you see, I must win this war. I've no heirs. I can't let them take my country.

"I won't."

She took in a deep breath and after she steadied her nerves, Selby continued. "They'll be here in about a week, by land and by sea. I've had bridges built all along my rivers and put my Ericorian along them to keep back enemy soldiers –"

Prince Keldrick held up a hand. "Ericorian?"

Selby nearly smiled. Ericorian were the crown jewel of Clemongard. She turned and gestured at Durain and the other Ericorian standing at the door. "Ericorian are Clemongard's personal, highly skilled, highly trained militia. Only those who survive the training become Ericorian."

Both princes eyed the Ericorian with curiosity and then Prince Keldrick gestured for Selby to continue.

"Ericorian guard my bridges. I have four hundred galleons with fifty more being built yet. I have eighty-five thousand Crown Guard and a total of sixty thousand Ericorian.

"But whether King Harvick's first son, Varley, disowned, wants to invade my country, I know not. I have information that he has upward of fifteen thousand men. I stationed ten thousand men all along my southern border. No one knows where Varley is just now, but I don't want to continue holding ten thousand men along my southern border waiting for an enemy who may not show when I have much more disturbing problems to the northeast and northwest."

Prince Ronan nodded and Prince Keldrick crossed his arms and leaned back against the table.

"As for the north –" And she sighed.

"Ormon and Ambsellon will sail into my harbors within the week. Whether they will put to there, or sail further south, I've no idea. My men have made plans, of course, but nevertheless, Ambsellon will show first, then Ormon will follow, and where any of those ships pull in, I've no idea.

"On the other side of the Mourning Mountains sits Ambsellon and his bastard army."

Oh! Was this the way of it then? First her manners, and then her language? Would she be cursing like a common drunk next? And in front of allies, too!

But they hardly reacted at all. Only Prince Keldrick – a slight curve of his lips lifted, hardly noticeable, but she caught it. Selby! Take hold of yourself!

Primly, she continued as if she hadn't cursed at all. "Rockdale Pass exists on both sides of the Mourning Mountains, and my men have blocked it up. But again," and she paused deliberately, "King Hewett comes with his army through the Mourning Mountains, and then I've very good information that the Ice Queen will be following or joining his forces.

"Clemongard does not have the size Army she once did, before the Twenty Years War. She has finally recovered economically but does not have the two hundred thousand men that are bearing down on her by next week.

"My War Council has made plans, and it may be that we might sustain a war with the North, but with Varley, and Coastal Country military as well?"

Selby stopped. That was all of it. The stuff of her nightmares at night, what kept her awake at night, the source of the circles under her eyes....

And, Andeval said, the reason she kept hitting so hard when she was only supposed to be practicing. Selby had cracked three wooden swords in two weeks.

Prince Ronan looked down and shook his head in sympathy. Prince Keldrick stood up and said, "We have good news for you, Your Majesty. We will be sending you troops –"

"Please, any ally that can assist me in any way during this time period I insist call me Selby. I cannot imagine dancing upon formalities when I am accepting the aid of other countries who need troops themselves."

Prince Keldrick cocked his head and then said, "Your Majesty, if you please –"

"Prince Ronan, Prince Keldrick, I beg of you one thing, do please, call me Selby. In informal settings, at least. We have been children together, after all, and we will rule this land together and all grow old with one another. As allies, shall we not be on social terms?"

Prince Ronan nodded and smiled, while Prince Keldrick gave a small bow. "As you will, my lady." He smiled, then continued what he had been telling her before he'd interrupted. "The East will be sending you a total of forty thousand troops. At this time, it is unknown whether we can send any Naval assistance, so we will only be sending Army assistance. Some of that is made up of Stafford Shields, some cavalry, some archery, mostly infantry.

"I regret that it will not be here in the timeframe you hope for, within a week, that is. But it has already mobilized and is on its way from different countries. We have specific numbers and locations that we can share with you, though –" and he cleared his throat. "Not on our actual persons. We had planned to share those specific details with you in a War Council or such, if you will."

Selby stood motionless, hardly hearing the last few remarks. Had he said forty thousand? Or four? No matter… any aid, any at all….

"Your Majesty?"

"My Lady? My Lady, are you well? I'm sorry forty thousand is all we could manage, we've a bit of a new crisis that's developed ourselves, but the troops are on their way. Tomorrow, we'll go about working out the finer details with you if that's agreeable…."

"Forty thousand men…. I've no idea how to thank you…" said Selby faintly.

Keldrick

They followed the chamberlain provided for them down the polished marble steps. Finally, they would be able to ascertain the needs of this country so they might report back to Father. Both they and the Queen – or Selby, as she had bid them call her – sent birds back to Fairview last evening, but carrier pigeons didn't fly far in the evening after they'd been fed, so it was hard to tell how far the birds had gotten.

"Beautiful palace," remarked Ronan with an eye to the artwork as they passed.

Keldrick snickered at his lifelong friend. Ronan always had displayed an eye for the arts and music.

Ronan shouldered him, knocking him a bit off balance on the steps. "Just because you're a cretin doesn't mean the rest of us are. This is an oceanside country, and that was a portrait of her whole family by the sea when she was a girl, which you'd have seen, if you noticed details more often. A shame we can't see the sea while we're here."

And that was why Ronan was in the position he was in – he noticed the little things. He would make a good king someday, mused Keldrick, a very, very long time from now. No one ever wanted to think of the passing of their parents, but when it came to having to look at your friend and know that he would be the man to step up and change the guard after his father… well, you couldn't help but assess him a bit. Until then, Uncle Gerard was as hale and hearty a man as he would ever be.

The chamberlain led them to what Keldrick assumed was the Queen's War Room, for it was heavily guarded by Ericorian. Now, they were a sight to see! He and Ronan had only seen men that tall in carnivals during celebrations, but these Ericorian men were formidable warriors in the white and sky blue of Clemongard, with specially cropped hair. Ronan had told him later last night that Ericorian were trained in most all weaponry but was surprised to see them guarding the Queen.

Keldrick thought not so much, considering the circumstances of how he had just gained a sister. When the Queen told them how she'd lost every heir to the throne, just like that, he thought it wise of her to surround herself with the most lethal fighting men Clemongard had to offer, as she had no heirs. Ronan conceded to that.

Two Crown Guards stood before the War Room. They bowed low and then asked for Keldrick and Ronan's weapons.

Keldrick raised an eyebrow and placed a hand on his sword hilt. "We're allies."

"So is everyone in that room, Your Highness. Weapons, please, or I shall have to ask you to leave." The guard stared at him with insistence.

Of all the –

"Kel," Ronan said lowly as he detached his sword from his swordbelt.

"Very well." And Keldrick removed his sword and scabbard and handed them to the waiting guard, who placed them in a bin.

Still, they blocked the way.

"Ah. Bootknife," Ronan realized, and bent to pull his bootknife from his boot.

"You can't be serious," muttered Keldrick as he pulled his bootknife from his boot and surrendered it to the Crown Guard.

"We are very serious about Her Royal Majesty of Clemongard, Your Highness. You may enter."

Keldrick glared at the guard as he passed.

Inside Queen Selby's War Room sat several men, some in decorated uniforms, others her Cabinet members and advisors. And all about the walls were inked parchments and maps of various types, most of Clemongard, some of the ocean, some of Storden and Ambsellon.

A hush fell over the room as he and Ronan entered.

Queen Selby, her hands on her hips in a confrontational stance, suddenly relaxed.

"My Lords of the War Council. We have visitors." And she gestured Keldrick and Ronan further inside the room.

"Let me introduce to you our allies from the Eastern Alliance: Prince Keldrick, son of the Eastern Shield, and Prince Ronan, son of King Gerard of Ghiverny. They will be sitting in our War Council with us."

And for the first time, Keldrick saw her smile. It was a lovely smile, but out of place in her tired face, framed by long waves of platinum hair. Well, perhaps he could change that drained expression.

Ronan, behind him, had cleared his throat. Damn. What had he planned to say?

"My lords of the War Council, we are glad to be here with you, to help you in this fight. And, to help you win this fight. We all have a common enemy, and we cannot let that enemy win, nor even survive. Let us not be afraid of what we can overcome."

That was nothing at all like what he had planned to say, and Keldrick wondered if his father would approve. The uniformed men looked skeptical but several of the Lords nodded their heads with approval.

Then Ronan muttered under his breath, "How'd you pull that off?"

Keldrick smiled then.

An older lord stood up and said, "It's glad we are of having you both here, Your Highness, glad of this Alliance with the East." He had long, white whiskers that rode down the sides of his face. "You know our beloved Queen is a tough woman. You know what we call her?"

Keldrick and Ronan exchanged a brief glance. This might not be a good question to answer... and Keldrick saw Queen Selby look down and shake her head slightly.

All in the room broke into grins.

The older lord said, "She's the Cleaver Queen, after her grandfather. I nearly lost my fingers to her, right here at this very table." He waggled the fingers of his left hand and then pointed to – was that a gash – in the wooden Council Table? Even Ronan was staring.

"That's why she wears that cleaver at her side now. She can take care of herself, she can," said the lord proudly.

Keldrick shook himself and could not resist a smile, for Queen Selby – or should he refer to her as the Cleaver Queen – was looking quite rueful. And there was indeed, a cleaver sheathed in a fine leather scabbard hanging from her slender waist.

A beautiful woman who was determined to win a war, a Queen who was his own age, who cursed, who used a cleaver to make a point? Keldrick liked this woman very much....

Renfry

Renfry didn't think he'd find anyone in here, but it had been worth the look. More dogs looking for bones to pick over than mercenaries, and certainly not soldiers. The few soldiers he'd found in the last three months had been on furlough or assignment in plain sight. Mercenaries, on the other hand, were more common than fleas in a haystack in high summer.

And that Renfry didn't need.

Enough was enough. What he did need was a meal before he left.

He scanned the noisy pub as he waited for a bar keep to take his order. The sooner Renfry was out of Roarden North, the better. Out of Rorden North, out of Corstarorden –

"What the bloody hell are you doing here?"

Renfry peered through the smoky haze of The Red Fox to find a familiar face staring down at him. A bar keep held a wooden tray that balanced two pitchers of ale stood before him.

Topher?

His brown hair had grown out a bit more, tied back with a leather thong behind his neck. Topher wore a stained apron that spoke of many a night serving ale and whatever greasy pottage the pub offered as fare. How had Renfry missed the boy?

"Me? What are you doing in here?"

"I should think that's obvious. You want a meal or an ale or both?" And Topher smiled, for the phrase was something he'd repeated often.

Renfry, disturbed that he hadn't seen the boy in this dingy pub after he'd traveled with him for weeks, glared at him and said, "Both. What are you doing, in here, of all places –"

Topher said, "People who don't want to be found hide in places like these. Know what I mean?" And his brown eyes flicked about briefly as he set down an ale before Renfry.

Renfry scoffed. "This seems eerily familiar." But he swallowed down a bit of ale nevertheless.

"I'll be back with your stew."

Renfry was amazed at the change in Topher. He had acquired something that he had before lacked – confidence. Perhaps serving dirty, sweaty drunks in the worst part of Roarden North did that.

"And what brings you to The Red Fox, my friend?" asked Topher when he returned with a hot bowl of pottage.

Renfry shook his head. "I was searching for someone but I won't be staying. I'll have to leave as soon as possible."

"Ah, this is eerily familiar," Topher smirked. "Avoiding chaos and bloodshed?"

Renfry grimaced and glanced about. Seeing no one of note, he told Topher, "Keep your voice down." He handed Topher payment for the meal.

Topher shook his head and said, "Keep it. As it happens, I am leaving myself, so consider it on the house."

"Leaving? What for? Off for the evening?"
Topher rolled his eyes. "For good. Out of the city." His voice was hushed.

"And why is that?" prompted Renfry. The lad was stubborn – why could he not just out with it!

"Bar keeps stay quiet, keep their eyes and ears open and their mouths shut if they want to keep their jobs. And me, I don't want to keep my job anymore. There's – well, people like you – coming through town, a lot more of them, let's say. In organized units. Very soon. I'd just as soon not be here when they do. I'm leaving tonight. You might want to join up with one of those units," commented Topher. "I hear it's very lucrative." He tossed his towel over his shoulder.

Cheeky little bastard. "What makes you think they're people like me?"

Topher shook his head and scoffed a bit. "I know a merc when I travel with one, Renfry." He glanced at where Renfry had belted both his swords beneath his cloak for emphasis.

Renfry took several more swallows and then vowed to lay off, as he had a long night of travel before him. "For your information, bar keep, I am no merc. I am looking for someone of my status, however, which I was doing before I even ran across you.

"As it stands, I am leaving Corstarorden tonight, and I suggest you do the same."

Topher's brow furrowed. "Corstarorden. Altogether?"

"Aye." Renfry threw a glance about the room. Topher ran his towel over Renfry's table to appear busy, but his face had taken on a concerned expression.

"I leave in twenty minutes. Will that be enough time for you to finish your meal?"

Not again.

Well, the boy had matured. "What, this greasy shit?" He smiled a bit. Then Renfry said, "I don't want to be seen out there with you, understand me?" He nodded slightly in the direction of the street.

Topher looked scandalized. "Who would leave town that way? You must be bloody mad. Finish that slop and meet me two back alleyways down. I've money saved and a travel bag. I'll meet you there. I can get us out of Roarden North safely – but you, you get me out of Corstarorden. Do we have a deal?"

In shock, Renfry finally nodded. The new Topher was going take some getting used to.

Rhutgard

"Come in, son."

Kendrick glanced about, curiosity registering on his face when he saw that none of the other members of the War Council were present.

"I thought you might like to read this first before I read it to the rest of the Council." And Rhutgard handed the correspondence from Clemongard to Kendrick.

Kendrick recognized it immediately but accepted it stoically rather than eagerly, when just a few weeks ago, he might have grabbed for it. He and his twin had never been separated for so long before, or at least, not for such a reason. They had squired at Mountain Shield and Martmain Palaces for a few months each, but never had either been in peril of any sort, nor planning a war.

Where Kendrick's new title of Crown Prince might have been merely a title in peace time, and he might have retained his boyhood laughter and charm, he now was a man grown, circles of worry beneath his blue eyes already, with no trace of the boy, and little laughter or smiles. Rhutgard would miss that boy, but the times of today needed his son the man....

Rhutgard watched him read Kendrick read his twin's letter.

To: His Royal Majesty, Rhutgard Anghus Firthing, First of His Name,

King of Romeny, Eastern Shield of the Eastern Shield Alliance:

I and Prince Ronan Martel of Ghiverny, having arrived safely in the land of Clemongard, have been welcomed by our Ally, Her Royal Majesty, Selby Cylysse Stevanrhut, First of Her Name at FalconRise Palace. We have been working steadily in her War Council with her advisors to determine the best choice of action for her military, so that we may advise you which of our troops to send where.

I am sending a map of all of Queen Selby's military strong holds as well as where the Clemongard War Council knows the North to hold passage, with particular respect to the Rockdale Mountain Pass. Clemongard has had reports of growing numbers of Ambsellon soldiers manning the Blood Fort in Southern Ambsellon, that they might use that Mountain Pass as in times past, since across the border is Stormsguard Castle in Clemongard.

Clemongard is armed with sixty-thousand Ericorian, 500 cavalry, 500 archery, 150,000 infantry, and thanks to the late King Harvick of Storden's gift of Varley's Navy, 500 warships.

Ten-thousand men are stationed along the southern Clemongard border, though the Queen hopes to use these men elsewhere as no one is aware of Varley's movements at this time.

We expect to see Ambsell ships in the Northernmost of Clemongard's naval borders within a day to three days of the writing of this letter. The Queen's Royal Navy is already in position to engage in combat and attack as necessary.

We expect to see Ambsell troop movement through the pass within a day to three days of the writing of this letter also, as marked on the map I send you. Queen Selby plans to leave FalconRise with her troops and will be protected by Ericorian.

The War Council believes the two best ways for Eastern Alliance troops to enter Clemongard are through the FreeLands along Stone Crossing south of the Mourning Mountains and then north to StormsGuard, to bring in any cavalry, or divided further into Clemongard toward the coast. The Roarnebourke and Trellis Rivers have bridges that are heavily guarded, but any infantry headed toward both East Rockdale and Jernigan City would be welcomed, as seen on the map I've provided.

I believe the best way to serve as Eastern Alliance War Ambassador would be to remain here and coordinate our war efforts with Clemongard's. Please send a prompt reply if you prefer me to take on a different role. May this information be of use to you.

May this find you in the best of health; good will and good fortune to all of the Eastern Alliance.

From: Prince Keldrick Anghus Firthing,

Eastern Alliance War Ambassador to Clemongard

A troubled look crossed Kendrick's face and was gone. He looked up at Rhutgard and said gravely, "He means to stay over there."

It wasn't a bad idea, thought Rhutgard, but he didn't want his son out of his reach. So very, very far from his reach, during war. Not just one, but two, possibly three countries were trying to bring Clemongard down, and his son Keldrick in the center of it.

Rhutgard the father said, *absolutely not, come home immediately!*

But Rhutgard the Eastern Shield was intrigued and swallowed down the parental fear, for he knew that it was a good idea. He'd only sent the boys over for a few days' discussion with the Queen, that they might get a feel for the country and its needs, introduce themselves to the Queen on behalf of the Eastern Alliance to lend her support and then return home.

Not lose them to a lengthy stay in a permanent position.

"What think you?" Rhutgard asked.

A long sigh sounded from his son. Kendrick studied the map his twin had sent. "It's very detailed. He put a good deal of effort into this. This will be of great help to us." Then he placed both the letter and the map upon Rhutgard's desk.

Deflecting the question. "True. But what think you of his staying on there?"

Kendrick scowled. "It has merit. A good deal of merit. But I don't like it." He paced away. The back of his neck was red, a tell-tale sign of anger, thought Rhutgard.

"Go on."

"Well, in peacetime, why not," and Kendrick rubbed the back of his neck as he walked about the study, as if he knew the back of his neck was defying him. "But, Father, he's our line of succession. If something happens to both of us, and he's over – there, all the way across the damned Land, because he feels sorry for an orphaned Queen with a pretty smile, well, then what have we got? Mirelle?" Kendrick turned around and raised his eyebrows at Rhutgard. "Another orphaned princess with a pretty smile."

"You think he's being selfish?" questioned Rhutgard.

The world *selfish* seemed to change Kendrick's outlook. "I don't know if he's playing at fairytales or if he really does believe this is the best way to serve." Then he shrugged. "Maybe both. That's for you to determine, Father, not me."

Rhutgard nodded. "True. But if you had to make this decision now, instead of me, what would you do?"

Kendrick's scowl returned and he sat down before Rhutgard. His blue eyes stared off for a few seconds and then he told Rhutgard, "You know, I can't decide right now. He's the only one who can piss me off totally and completely, and until I can calm down about it, I ask to withhold my vote until later."

Rhutgard chuckled. "A wise decision, son. Use that choice as often as you need to when it's your time to sit where I have to, and it will serve you well."

Kendrick smiled a little and relaxed. Then a trace of his old self returned when he said, "Unless it's the Hound?"

Wryly, Rhutgard held a finger up and told him, "That subject is not up for discussion."

They both chuckled a little.

Mirelle

Mirelle held the book she'd been reading aloud and watched as his eyes drooped. He tried so hard to stay awake for her, she knew. She held her breath and didn't move, waiting until sleep claimed him. And like that – he was gone again.

She met Kimbur in the columns of books that stood outside Merridon's makeshift bedroom. Kimbur read her face and reached out for her hand.

"There's nothing you can do for him, you know," she said softly, her brown eyes sympathetic. "He wants this."

Mirelle sighed. "I know. If only… if only… I don't know. He can hardly breathe, now, Kimbur. It makes me want to drink air as if it were water."

Another time, Mirelle had arrived for her morning visit and found Father sitting at Merridon's bedside. Just as Mirelle was pondering the possibilities of the two of them visiting Merridon at the same time, a cheery sort of visit, she saw between the rows of books her brother's head loll upon the pillow, asleep. Her father began to sob, great, quiet, racking sobs. Mirelle stole in silence from her vantage point immediately, horrified, for she'd intruded upon her father's privacy. She'd witnessed the Eastern Shield crying by the bedside of his dying son, and the guilt she felt for that could not compare to anything she could think of.

The Healers came each morning with to plump Merridon's pillows, bathe and clothe him in fresh, clean clothing, and bring food that he ate little of, as well as a new medicine that he took a great deal of. One morning, Mirelle waited until the Healers had left to explode.

"This is ridiculous!"

Merridon looked at her pityingly. "What is, dear sister?"

"All of it! You, refusing to eat. This, this stupid medicine is all you'll take in. This stupid War now. Sending two princes half-way across the land into a – a war zone completely unprotected when they're going to be hit by the Northern Countries any day." Mirelle had gestured futilely.

"And what about the last do you hate most – that it's a dangerous mission, or that you didn't get to say good-bye…?" Merridon asked, his blue eyes studying her.

Ugh. She hated it when he did that. "Well, I'm going to miss them, of course," she had fumbled. Merridon was far too shrewd.

"You mean Ronan," he said and smiled like a small boy. "You've only known Keldrick a few months. You've known Ronan what, three years…?" he had suggested. "Pass me a glass, will you, dear sister," he had asked in a very pleased voice.

Mirelle had glared at him and told him, "You have no idea what you're talking about. And you take far too much of this." She'd shoved the glass into his hand so that he could pour the medicine himself, when normally, she would pour it herself.

"As you say, love, as you say," Merridon had replied, still inordinately pleased with himself. "Lovely shade of pink you're wearing."

And Mirelle had actually been wearing blue. To know that she had blushed did not help matters, and she had looked up to see Kimbur disappear behind a stack of books. Of course he was wrong! Merridon Firthing was not right about everything in the land.

Just a few days ago, Mirelle found Kendrick in the corridor near Merridon's library. He looked surprised to see her emerge from within.

"Kendrick?"

"You – you've been visiting him, haven't you?"

Mirelle had nodded. Kimbur, behind her, stepped aside to allow for a personal family conversation. The gesture was not lost on Kendrick. "How," and he cleared his throat gruffly, "how is he, then?"

Mirelle had wondered how to answer. Her years at The Brew House had taught her that some people wanted the brutal truth while others wanted the kindness of a lie. Even others wanted a combination. She wondered what Kendrick was looking for.

She had decided upon a tactful combination and told him gently, "He's dying, Kendrick."

His blue eyes, so like her own, bore into her. Then he nodded. "I haven't actually visited of late, not since, well –" and he held up his hand, which had its Crown Prince signet ring on it.

"I want to see him, but do you think he'll be… angry? That I've taken over after him?"

Mirelle had reached out and taken his hand. "I think he is relieved to know that you are carrying out the duties he never wanted. He never wanted to be Crown Prince, you know. He has been sick a very long time, Kendrick, and you taking over for him is a great relief. Especially now, with the Alliance on the brink of war."

Kendrick had nodded, visibly relieved, and then looked over at the door to Merridon's library.

"But, Kendrick, don't visit now. I've just left him asleep. He sleeps most all day. The best time to visit him is early in the morning, after he's woken and eaten breakfast."

"You see him twice a day, then?"

"I had him take over as my tutor, until just recently, anyway, when he's become bedridden. Now, I read to him twice a day and he corrects me while he's awake. Or sometimes we just talk. He taught me to play Ice at first. Perhaps someday, I will find as good a competitor as he is," and she had smiled gently.

"Merridon is the most gifted of all of us, an extraordinary mind he has. I wish I had seen him more often, as you have…."

"He is not dead yet, Kendrick," Mirelle had reminded him softly, trying to keep the reproach from her voice.

His jaw had clenched with emotion. "I will see him tomorrow morning," Kendrick said hoarsely.

Mirelle nodded and thought how glad Merridon would be to see his little brother.

———

Today, as she was reading to Merridon, he suddenly gasped and sat bolt upright. He heaved in a breath.

His arms fluttered about him. "Mirelle," he gasped, trying to suck in air. "Mirelle!"

"Merridon? Merridon, what is it!"

His chest continued to heave as his lungs gasped for breath. She had never seen him so. Petrified, she leaned over him and asked, "Merridon, I'm here, what can I do?"

He pointed at the pitcher of liquid on the table next to the bed. It was water that medicine had been added to, and he drank from it regularly. But she had never seen him have a fit before. Immediately, Kimbur had filled a glass and handed it to Mirelle.

"Merridon, here, drink. Carefully," and she held the liquid to Merridon's lips.

He slurped at the glass at first and liquid ran down his chin, but as more and more of the medicine got into his system, he calmed and his gasping stopped.

She was still alarmed, for Merridon had drunk most of the glass. He usually only drank half.

"Mirelle. Get Stanyard," he panted, and fell back against his pillows.

"Lord Stanyard?" Mirelle quizzed him.

"Please, Mirelle. Get... Stanyard." Though he lay against the pillows, Merridon continued to pant.

"As you say, Brother. I will be back."

She stood and gestured for Kimbur to follow her. Once out of earshot, Mirelle told Kimbur, "Stay here, watch him. Give him anything he needs."
Kimbur nodded, her eyes wide, and then turned toward Merridon again.

Lord Stanyard. Whatever would Merridon want with him.... He would be in the War Council right now, which was down one floor and halfway across the Palace.

After taking the back stairways and corridors, Mirelle was able to arrive at Father's study, only to find the foyer to the study doors heavily guarded.

All the Crown Guards immediately saluted her, but none moved to allow her passage. Mirelle blinked with indignation. "If you please, I need to speak with Lord Stanyard."

Two of them exchanged a dubious glance. "With all due respect, Your Royal Highness, you are not on the list."

"The list?" Mirelle repeated. She had not run half the way here on behalf of her dying eldest brother for a guard to stand in her way because she was not on some silly list. And all these men in front of the door so no one might listen in at the door? The fairytales all said people heard plans through the walls, thus the phrase, *the walls had eyes and ears.* Silly.

"Yes, Your Highness, the list of approved people allowed to come in."

"I assure you, this is of utmost importance, or I would not be standing here." Then she spied a gold bell in the hand of the guard nearest her. May the gods, and her father, forgive her....

Mirelle reached out for the man's hand and, before he knew what she was doing, vigorously clanged the bell, calling out as loud as she could, "Lord Stanyard! I need to speak with you! Come out here immediately! Lord Stanyard!"

The guard yanked his arm back, but the damage had been done, for the door to Father's study opened and Lord Stanyard, his face livid, stepped out into the foyer and closed the door.

He marched up to Mirelle. "Just what do you think you're doing, young woman? Do you have any idea what is happening in there!"

Mirelle grabbed his arm and thundered, "Walk with me. Immediately! I insist upon it, Lord Stanyard!"

Lord Stanyard took stock of the rage in her eyes, considered that he had just been issued a command from a princess, and then said, "Very well, Your Highness."

As soon as they were out of earshot of the guards, he started to ask why Mirelle had summoned him but Mirelle was suddenly struck by an idea. She stopped his query with a finger in the air.

"It's you. You. You give him the medicine, don't you?"

Mirelle watched the man's entire face change.

"Lord Stanyard, if you don't tell me true, I shall go in there now and tell Father everything. Think what it would do to Father if he knew. Merridon told me all but who. So do not lie to me. He is asking for you. He had some kind of dreadful – fit just now and begged me to bring you to him.

"Shame on you, Lord Stanyard. Shame on you. If only you saw what your supposed medicine has done to him. Now come with me, quickly. Or do you need to get more medicine?" Mirelle spat.

Cowed, Stanford replied, "I'm not going because you've threatened to extort me. I'm going because he is asking for me. And I need make no other stops."

"Good," she replied, her voice snippy.

After Mirelle led him around several corridors, Stanford, his voice breathless, told her, "You know, he asked for this. I never wanted to do this."

Mirelle stopped. "What do you mean?"

"He would have died some time ago, but for the War Council. You said he's told you all?"

She nodded, suddenly very unsure she wanted to be party to whatever he was about to impart to her.

"He knew he was dying. First, he only wanted to die and the process wasn't happening fast enough, thus the so-called medicine he asked for me to have given him each week. Then, the War Council happened and he wanted to slow the process. He wants to live until your father and brothers are away from the Palace and can't come home for a state funeral. He wants a small affair – he doesn't want your father to go off to war with his death on his mind, or worse, if he dies, he doesn't want your father to stay here and not go off to war where he's needed most. And so, I have been keeping him alive until your father has left for war. There will be no state funeral, only the barest of necessities. You, as his half-sister, are his nearest relative once all his brothers and father are away from the Palace. He only wants a burial, no formal announcement. The paperwork is formally drawn up. You may read it over now or later, as you wish. But do not discuss it with him, I beg you. His was a life never meant to be lived. I can't tell you how many times I have heard the boy say that. All I have done these last two months or some is keep him comfortable. I see I must strengthen the dosage, for he is slipping away.

"We leave in three days. If he can hold out for five, then...."

And to Mirelle's surprise, tears formed in the lord's brown eyes. "Whoever would want to assist in the life and death of a young man? I never thought I would have to do such a thing." He shook his head and fingered the tears from his eyes. Stanyard took a deep breath. "I shall, of course, once he passes, ride back on behalf of your father to assist." He cleared his throat hoarsely, then gestured ahead of Mirelle. "Shall we continue?"

Myrischka

Finally, they had passed Salmon Ridge, the last small town to Gatesfield. Gatesfield controlled the Western Green Gates. Never had Myrischka experienced such a high before. She was splitting a quarter of her army off to send to the northern EverWinters, to join Colonel Durshkin's ragtag army of Stordish and Ormon soldiers.

And possibly sack Genwith City and Abelruth from there.... Anything so long as she could get into Ghiverny. She was tired of that bloody Wolf Wall on her eastern border. It couldn't be burned down, for it was far too vast. And the Ghivern Army always met them half way through. Trying to burn the Wolf Wall, or the Wolf Wood, as it ought to be called, would be an immense waste, thought Myrischka, and she didn't understand why rulers before her had even bothered.

Myrischka was sure that Romeny and Delsynth would offer resistance, assist their ally Ghiverny, but now that she was free of Ambsellon, she would keep the bulk of the Eastern Alliance busy by circling around and attacking at its north and west.

Clemongard. Ah, Clemongard. Ambsellon would do most of her work for her, ramming through the mountains. Just as the little Queen finally fell and Ambsellon moved in, Myrischka would move in to Ambsellon. She smiled slowly. And she would own the North.

Not only was Hewart doing her work for her by land, but she was letting him take credit for the naval war he was about to rain down upon Queen Selby. Myrischka's war ships, far out to sea unseen by the Clemongard Navy's formation, had already passed Cliff Watch North by now, but that runt of King Harvick's had lost his navy and so her Navy would be stopping at Central Cliff Watch....

In the center of both the Clemongard rivers, Central Cliff Watch commanded all the Coastal Cliff Towers of Clemongard. The young queen had built new bridges, all fortified, along those two rivers, in just the last five months, a very cunning move, thought Myrischka, especially having only been upon the throne for eight months.

The Cleaver Queen, they were calling the girl now, and she carried a cleaver, no less, at her waist. Myrischka could not help but admire that, but she doubted a seventeen-year-old girl had the strength to command such respect as her forbear. It mattered not, she unlike to live the next few weeks. Hewart and his army would not stop until they had her in their hands, and then – well. Myrischka almost felt sympathy for the little Queen – that cleaver of hers would be Hewart's war trophy for sure.

But while they were otherwise engaged, Myrischka's Navy, after fighting its way past whatever was left of the Clemongard ships at Central Cliff Watch, would dock at Gull Port, cross the Trellis, and sack Jernigan City. Such a simple thing, really. It would serve two lovely purposes – take the Clemongard capital for herself, and infuriate Hewart. Ah. After she took Clemongard, well – Storden did have a brand new ruler and that brat Varley was at large –

"Your Majesty, we have arrived at Gatesfield."

The Lieutenant who informed her of their arrival seemed wary.

"I'm aware of our location, Lieutenant. Why have we stopped?" The Green Gates were the official border between Ormon and a free travel land, neutral territory, which beyond it lay Romeny. Why should they have stopped?

"There's a problem with the gate, Your Majesty," the Lieutenant told her stiffly.

Must she do everything herself?

Myrischka stepped out of her coach and approached the gatehouse. A small group of men stood clustered near the wheel that would otherwise serve to crank the three-hundred-foot high green gate open.

Behind her, almost all of the entire Ormon Royal Army stood. Before her stood a three-hundred-foot high green gate that stretched for all the length of her southern border... and a small handful of men by the gate control. She refrained from rolling her eyes. Men were such childish creatures. Why, she wondered for yet another time, was it that merely having a penis allowed a man to rule a country when they were such imbeciles? No mind. She was ruling Ormon herself, and soon more than just Ormon. A problem with the gate control, indeed.

Myrischka boots crunched as she advanced forward in the snow. The man who stood before the gate wheel, protecting it almost, she thought, stared at her.

"And your name is...?"

"Belvart Mindal, Your Majesty. My family has controlled the Green Gate here for generations."

Dressed warmly in a fur coat of some sort, Belvart stared frankly at Myrischka with a steady brown gaze as he relayed this information.

"And Belvart, these men, these children, they are your sons?"

"They are, Your Majesty."

"Well, Belvart, it would seem that you should know your art, as it were, by now. Or are you suddenly unable to turn a wheel?"

Belvart looked at his assembled family and then said, "Your Majesty, there are some as don't believe women should be ruling, much less going to war. Lots believe that, in fact. And dissolving our pact with Ambsellon, lots believe that ain't right, Your Majesty."

Myrischka was impressed. Her dead husband didn't have a tenth of this man's balls. But it mattered not.

"Belvart, do you know what I believe?"

The man shook his head slowly.

She walked down the line of his family and then looked back at him. Then she drew her sword and sliced the youngest child's head clean off his body. Somewhere, she heard a woman cry out.

"I believe that a man who cannot open a gate when asked is ignorant."

She stepped away from the child's head, which lay bleeding in the snow, his innocent little eyes now sightless.

Her men moved to keep Belvart's family in place. Belvart's eyes had popped out of their sockets.

She continued. "I believe that a man who cannot perform his job when asked is ignorant." Myrischka stepped up to the next child, about thirteen. She cradled his chin, looked into his small brown eyes, and saw fear there. The boy was trembling. Then she nodded to the soldier holding him. He stepped away and Myrischka sliced the boy's head off with her sword, mindful of where the head fell.

"No!" screamed a woman, presumably the family's mother. Crying soon ensued.

Her soldiers had chained the next two men.

Tiredly, she said, "Belvart, I believe that a man should perform his duty at all times." This time, Myrischka did not even look at the teenager, though it was harder to slice his head off his neck due to his age, so the soldier had to hold him solidly. Blood spurted from arteries and Myrischka stepped immediately to the side to avoid it. She made the child to be approximately seventeen. Not actually a child at all, was he, she mused as she stepped to the last son.

The last son spat at her. She caught the spittle before it landed on her face and smeared it on the man's face. He was young, reckless still, approximately twenty, not old enough for a full beard yet.

She heard Belvart whisper, "No, no, please, no...."

Myrischka looked at Belvart. Tears streamed down his face. "Belvart, I believe men who do not do their duty to be ignorant." She gestured for the eldest son to be forced downward.

"Noooo!" Belvart cried as she swung her sword downward. Her sword sunk into the eldest son's neck, through the bone, and out below so that finally the head rolled off. It bumbled into the snow and hit a soldier's boot. With distaste, the soldier nudged it away. Myrischka wanted to laugh, but she was not done yet.

Her sword was dripping with bits of bone and scarlet blood. She would give it to someone to clean once she was done. Myrischka stepped up to Belvart, who was trembling, his face wet with tears. Yet still, he stood his ground. Fool. Men who stood for the wrong ideals were wasted.

"Belvart Mindal, what else I believe? That you are ignorant. You were responsible for your family. You were responsible for the carrying out of your duty and you failed. You were responsible for obeying your Queen and you failed. Therefore, all generations of the Mindal family will be executed so that none will inherit this post. This post from here on out will be run by the Ormon Royal Army. The heads of your children will be placed upon spikes above the Green Gates so that all will recall such ignorance, learn from it, and know it to be intolerable." She gestured at the soldier, who bent Belvart forward.

Myrischka had the feeling she would be sore after these beheadings – beheadings were best done with an axe, but, she thought, in the absence of such a weapon....

She took in all of her breath, raised her sword high, sent a prayer to whatever gods might exist that she would sever the man's head with one cut... and sent her sword arcing down in the sunlight into the man's neck.

Blood spurted onto her knees but she cared not, for, after forcing her sword through, she finally got the idiot's head to roll. Another guard had to step out of the way that the bloody head not hit his boots.

Ah. 'Twas done. "Clean this –" and she handed her sword to a sergeant, who accepted her sword and immediately saluted.

A soldier approached her holding all four sons' bloody heads by their hair. "Would you like these mounted on spikes, then, Your Majesty?"

Myrischka nodded. "Yes... but not so high up that they can't be seen." She directed him further and sent him scurrying off.

The Lieutenant asked her, "And as for him, Your Majesty?" He nodded downward at Belvart's bloody, mustached head.

She smiled. "Nail his head to the center of the gatewheel."

Then she climbed back into her coach.

Myrischka watched the Green Gates crank open, watched as her EverWinters detachment turned east behind her. She could not help but smile again as her army headed west toward Ambsellon.

Today was the day the Green Gates turned red. She might just rename them the Red Gates.

Hewart

Hewart listened to all the jingles of the ringmail, the leather creaking of the saddles, the thud of the horse hooves as they hit the grass, and the occasional low conversation of the men surrounding him. He loved it. He lived for it. It had been far too long.

It had been quite the battle to urge Sturgund westward when he wanted to wait at Newcastle for the Ice Queen. Ultimately, just as Hewart was on the verge of ordering his son a Royal Command, Sturgund resolved to change his course for Rockdale Motte all on his own, in such an innocuous manner that left Hewart suspicious.

Sturgund's shield arm was entirely healed but the scar nevertheless served as a daily reminder that someone wanted him dead and had nearly succeeded. The encounter had left Sturgund a changed man. Whether the architect of that plan was the Ormon Queen or not was immaterial, for she had made combat plans – and mobilized her troops – without consulting, nay, even advising Hewart. In fact, Myrischka had reached out to Storden, of all the countries in the land, a neutral country, and bought the little runt Varley's loyalty. Hewart was not happy with Myrischka.

Part of Hewart saw the brilliance in that, for that would secure her Storden easily. But what was left of the Ambsell-Ormon Alliance, an over two-thousand-year-old treaty? Hewart never once dreamt that he would wonder if Ormon would be casting its eye at his country....

And so Hewart went to war for Ambsellon, without Ormon. The Ormon Ambassador advised against it, but had no new information, nor no ideas of merit, given the circumstance.

Odd to see only his own banners, his own country's colors among the ranks. He'd been fighting since he was a squire, and always there had been both Bear and Moose banners on the field. Well, the Ormon bitch had chosen her path, she could march down it.

Spies and scouts alike told him that her own large force was headed west behind him, but that she had divided some of it to add to a detachment of men in the EverWinters. The better part of her ground force would be following his some two days behind him.

Hewart had also dispatched his Navy, which he knew that right now, should be arriving within Clemongard waters. However, he had needed to rethink his attack, for the Western Queen was suddenly in possession of as many warships as he was, so for now, his best attack plan was the element of surprise. Hewart's Army was stronger by far than Clemongard's, so he would use that first, and his Navy second.

But – he would give much to know what his eldest son was thinking. Perhaps Sturgund was keeping his mind off the Ice Queen by educating his younger brothers of war. For truth, Treskin was too young to be out here. At fifteen... but he would not be in a command post of his own, he would be stationed with sixteen-year-old Stegreth.

What a blow to a boy's pride, to be left at home at the start of a war just three months shy of his manhood birthday. Hewart would not do that to his youngest son, but nor would he allow him to serve in a camp without a brother to watch for him. Stegreth would take care of him. Stegreth had served nearly a year in the Army now.

However, war was war, and the line of succession must be secured. While his boys thought they would be in the thickest of the fighting, Hewart's generals and colonels would be ensuring the most serious of protection. And Sturgund... Hewart was unsure of Sturgund yet. He'd watched the boy return to fighting condition in the castle practice ring. The boy – nineteen, but still a boy to Hewart – had practiced with an intensity twice a day until he'd overcome his injury and perhaps even bested his prior ability.

But Hewart knew his son. Something was driving him. Hewart would have to have a word with his back Commanders about making sure Sturgund stayed with the Army and didn't leave in the middle of the night, or worse, attack on his own once the Ormon Army arrived. Once Sturgund got an idea in his mind, he was loathe to leave it alone, and Hewart could envision Sturgund looking for Myrischka....

The foolishness of youth. His son in particular. He just wouldn't be able to leave it alone, would he....

Aleck

They were all on high alert, of course, and had been since Cliff Watch North had been under attack. So chilling to hear. He'd heard of war from his grandfather, his father. Even read about it a bit when he was learning his letters. He never thought he'd ever come to a time in his life when it actually occurred. Eighteen of their ships lost at Cliff Watch North, last report. It seemed impossible.

But not a thing to see from the Bourken Rock Isles, and Aleck's shift was drawing to a close. He heard his relief shift draw the boat up on the shore below the tower. He sighed with relief. It seemed Cliff Watch North was keeping the North well-contained.

Aleck heard Danwick's boots on the bottom of the Bourken Rock Tower stairwell, and stared through his scope into the twilight all about the horizon again, expecting to put it away and greet Danwick when he climbed into the room.

And so he did, he slid the scope together and started to place it in his vest pocket.

But something – instinct, perhaps – urged him to pull out the scope again and peer into the twilight one last time.

What… was… that….

Aleck focused carefully on a speck due north.

A speck that moved further in toward the Isle….

He stared as hard as he could.

It was a bloody fucking warship. Enormous!

"Fuck!" he yelled and procedures he'd only trained for raced through his mind. Where was the bloody torch!

"Aleck?" asked Danwick, who had just emerged.

Aleck yelled, "Ring the bloody bell! They're coming for us! Cliff Watch Central is under attack!" He lit the torch so that the Cliff Watch Central's Tower would see.

The oil in the torch finally flared up and Aleck heard the enormous bell jarring behind him. He peered through the scope at Cliff Watch Central's Tower. "Come on, come on, come on wake up over there…."

Finally! Cliff Watch Central's Tower flared up with flame to alert the Navy, the Army, and the residents. Distantly, other Cliff Watch Towers would soon flare up with the message, and reports would be sent to and from by land. He let out an enormous breath. Aleck's job was complete.

Riggs

Ah. Another afternoon…. He blew out a puff of wonderweed, humming to himself. Another white cloud drifting by…. Riggs formed his hands into a make-believe scope and peered through them at the sky. And another cloud. That one looked like a turkey leg. He giggled a little. Another perfect day.

He moved his make-believe scope down about the horizon of the cerulean ocean, casting it east and west. Nothing to see, nothing to see, Riggs yawned, as usual – wait.

What was that? Riggs scrambled to sit upward in the crow's nest. A gull landed on the rim of the crow's nest and cocked its white head at him. Normally, Riggs would enjoy the company, but he shooed the bird away as he patted at his faded vest for his real scope. The gull fluffed its feathers, gave Riggs a baleful look from a golden eye, then launched itself into the air and flapped away.

Ah. Riggs pulled out his scope and zoomed in on the northern horizon.

What the bloody hell was that….

He stared a bit longer and then whistled to himself. Riggs shoved his scope into his vest and leaned over the side of the crow's nest. "Mutt! Mutt!"

As usual, the crew was surprised to see him. His actual name was Rigsby but he'd started off doing the rigging and been so good at climbing the ratlines, that he'd just taken the look-out station. Most men hated it, as there was no one to talk to, but Riggs, what they'd started calling him, was happy enough in the middle of the sun and the sky, looking out at the water above everyone else. They sent someone climbing up with a meal and some water, and kept him well supplied with wonderweed, so he had no complaints.

"Riggs? Whatsa matter, man?" Mutt yelled up from his station below Riggs.

Riggs yelled, "Get the Captain!"

When the crew heard Riggs call for the Captain, they always ceased activity for a moment.

"Call for the Captain!" Mutt screamed Riggs's message back down.

After a time, Captain James D. Hartley himself appeared. The Captain shaded his weather-tanned face as he stared up with an intense blue-eyed gaze. The breeze riffled his gray beard. "Riggs! It's important, is it?"

"Enemy ship, thirty clicks to port! War ship, Captain Hartley!"

Riggs had seen plenty of warships – pirate ships, especially – in his time aboard Captain Hartley's ship. And the Royal Sea had seen more battles than Riggs thought it would survive, both in Banker's Bay, and against his fellow pirates. But he had never seen a warship the size that gargantuan warship was.

Riggs waited for a few minutes as the Captain looked through his own scope, knowing Captain Hartley was shitting his pants at the sight of that beast.

Then the colors for Tortoreen were hoisted and the ship took a hard turn to starboard. No one could fight that bastard and expect to live.

"Good man, Riggs! Cove us!" And the Captain stalked off down the deck.

"Riggs, we headed for a cove – first sight of land you see, send us to cove. Think they saw us?" Mutt called up then.

Riggs shrugged. "Fuck if I know. I just hope there ain't any more of them." He peered again at the warship through his scope. Brand new warship, biggest ship he'd ever seen. Even Captain Hartley had said *"Fuck it!"* when he'd got a look at that ship and he'd seen plenty of warships in his time.

Riggs had never known the Captain to back down from a fight, but then, the Captain wasn't stupid, neither, especially if there was more than one of that ship. They'd just sit a'cove and fish for a while, and let that massive beast, or fleet of beasts begone.

Keldrick

He was still taking it all in. For two days, they'd been riding due east in a sea of glittering armor and waving banners. He was outfitted in perfectly fitted Western-style ringmail and armor, and were it not for the constant breeze from the ocean, Keldrick would be sweating like a pig. The more he saw of this land, the more he loved it. A constant breeze, but not humid and sticky, like the RiverLands, nor muggy and mosquito-ridden as the swampy WetLands, nor hot and sweltering as the Coastals. Romeny was landbound, and only warm in the spring and summer. Queen Selby's Ambassador told Keldrick and Ronan that often the autumn here was seasonally warm as well.

Suddenly, they came to a stop. They had arrived at the tiny town of Thistlegood, where they would rest the horses. Infantry all around Keldrick took small sips of water. Ronan flashed him a look. Ronan was furious, there was no other way to describe it. But Keldrick's mind was made up.

Ronan swung off his horse, his cloak flapping behind him. Tiredly, Keldrick dismounted, awaiting what he knew would be another of Ronan's tirades.

Once he stood immediately before Keldrick, Ronan stared at him with furious green eyes. "Are you mad!" he hissed.

"No, and keep your bloody voice down," Keldrick shot back in a whisper, for directly before them, the Queen rode, and she had just swung out of her saddle and onto the grass.

"Keldrick –"

"He's right, you know," said the Queen quietly as she tossed her long, blonde braid over her shoulder. "You needn't stay. It's going to be a bloodbath."

Ronan turned about and had the grace to look ashamed.

"Oh, you needn't apologize. You need to know, I cannot protect you if you do stay. I am grateful for every last man who will fight on this field. But I cannot protect you, who are the son of the Eastern Shield. I need every man on this field to fight for Clemongard, not to protect the son of the Eastern Shield. Know that, should you choose to stay." A small, wry smile crossed the Queen's face briefly and was gone.

"I serve as the Eastern Alliance War Time Ambassador to Clemongard. In what way would I be performing my duty if I turned tail and ran home once the war began?" Keldrick asked quietly.

Ronan turned and walked away, his hands laced behind his head.

Queen Selby let out a long breath she must have been holding. She nodded shortly. "Thank you. A direct communication with the Eastern Alliance will be most welcome." Her blue eyes looked afar to where Ronan had stridden. "Your friend does not approve."

"No, he will not understand. We are cousins, and he will worry. No more so than I about him when the war starts in the East," Keldrick returned.

The Queen nodded. "To worry about one country will be hard enough; to worry about five, and now my own – a lot of pressure to add to your plate, Ambassador Keldrick."

Prickles raised upon Keldrick's arm. That was the first time she had ever called him that.

The Queen turned and ventured forth to speak to a Colonel. It was time to move out.

Ronan stepped up to him. "Please, Kel – tell me you'll change your mind."

Keldrick shook his head slowly. "No, Ronan. We talked about this last night."

They had near come to blows over it last night. But Keldrick was positive. Ronan had jabbed him by saying, "And what if she was a man? Or an arsehole? Or a total bitch? Or an ugly shrew? Would you want to do this then?" Which was when Keldrick nearly punched him. Ronan caught his punch and they struggled to keep from hitting each other, and the truth became quite evident, but Keldrick had growled, *"Yes!"*

If Keldrick was entirely honest with himself, chances were, not so much. But there was still a country that was part of the Eastern Alliance, and he was his father's son. Kendrick was the Crown Prince, and he had a lot of responsibility so far as becoming the next Eastern Shield. However, Keldrick had a responsibility as well, as the son of the Eastern Shield during a war... and he took it seriously. And Ronan simply did not understand it. Keldrick had not recognized it until they'd arrived here and the woman had nearly fallen apart before them. That was when he recognized that he had a duty to fulfill. After the war, then he could return home. Unless his father called him home before then.

"Still – you can still come back with me." Ronan sounded hopeful.

Keldrick shook his head.

The Queen approached. "Your Highness," and she bowed her head with deference to Ronan. "It is time for you to leave if you still plan to leave. I've supplied a retinue protection unit of twenty guards to take you to the Romeny border back through the Free Lands." Her voice was gentle but firm.

Ronan was nothing if not proper. "Your Majesty, it was an honor to serve you. I thank you for the protection unit." He bowed deeply before her.

"The honor was entirely mine," Queen Selby returned.

Ronan turned to Keldrick. They embraced each other tightly and clapped each other on the back, their ringmail rattling with each pat.

Keldrick grasped Ronan by the shoulders. "Good will go with you."

"And good fortune with you," Ronan responded seriously.

Ronan swung up into his saddle. Then he looked down at Keldrick. "Stay alive, cousin." He stared at him for a moment longer, then kneed his horse south. His Clemongard protection unit followed him and they raced away from the Clemongard Royal Army. Keldrick prayed they would see each other again soon.

⁓

Finally, they arrived at Rockdale Pass. The rest of the Clemongard Royal Army stationed there had tents and command posts already set up.

A mobile War Council had been held en route just an hour ago, when one of the scouts met them. A Command Station had been set up for the Queen and was awaiting her. Half the ten thousand men who had been stationed upon the southern border were now stationed at Cliff Watch Central, spread out between the Trellis and the Roarnebourke Rivers, as ordered. The Queen and the War Councilors who were present were pleased. Keldrick was still getting a feel for the geography of Clemongard but he thought moving the men to Cliff Watch Central was a sound idea.

Many of the men posted at Rockdale looked at Keldrick curiously, until he was introduced as the War Time Eastern Alliance Ambassador. Many of the men did not even know they had allied with the East, and so he was welcomed openly by the new additions to the War Council. A hastened Council was called, if only to familiarize the Queen with the new members of the Rockdale Pass War Council and her own from FalconRise.

Keldrick recalled all of Ronan's lessons in how to blend in with commoners and infantry, and instantly saw the soldiers there had relaxed once they noted that he curried his own horse, for they had expected that they would have to protect a spoiled lordling, as Ronan had referred to it. He also fetched his own meal, though he might have asked the guard detail outside his tent to bring him one. He needed no steward, though the services of one were offered.

Keldrick recalled, too, the Queen's words: *"I need every man on this field to fight for Clemongard, not to protect the son of the Eastern Shield."* He would not have expected preferential treatment out on a battlefield, in the midst of a sea of armored men, himself included. And so, he acted as any other man-at-arms would. He almost felt guilty for the placement of his tent, which, due to his position as Ambassador, was next to the Queen's.

But during the War Council, when Queen Selby introduced him, he knew he had made the right decision. Information such as "thousands of men on the other side of the pass" and "marching toward the Blood Fort even as we speak" and "sailing toward Cliff Watch North" had all but washed over Keldrick until he had addressed them. He'd looked at each of the men in there, mostly field Captains, Lieutenants, scouts. And then he'd told them, "I've come to coordinate your efforts with the forty thousand troops who are on their way as we speak from the Eastern Alliance. Communicate through me to the East."

The entire War Tent had been silent, for jaws had dropped. And he had seen hope wash over their faces. To have brought hope to an entire country.... Keldrick knew he had made the right decision.

Such strength she had! His mother was strong in a different way, Keldrick thought as he stared at the hypnotizing flames of the dying campfire. Mother would sweep into a room, her gown aswirl around her, and everyone took notice. Mother was a very powerful woman in her own right, married to the most powerful man in all the Land, and women flocked to be near her, men bowed deeply before her, and she was gracious, kind, tactful, and generous. Yet she had a steady gaze that could become dangerous should she become angry, which was rare, and men turned from it, even Father himself shrank before it. Keldrick and Kendrick had provoked it many times. Mother ran that entire Palace. She set the fashion standard for the entire East, coordinated entertainment, supported literature, arts, and music, donated to charities and hospices all over the East, and assisted the poor and poverty-stricken. Mother was a force of nature.

But the woman – *Selby* – she had insisted on Keldrick calling her, though it felt far too unseemly, even for him – was a force of nature all in her own right. And of an age with him, as well, which he could not help but like.

In the twilight, Keldrick stole a glance at her as she sat across from him in the grass and immediately froze, for she took that moment to bite into an apple she'd brought out of her tent. Her clear blue eyes met his over the fire and held his gaze for a moment. Selby said nothing but sighed instead and returned her gaze to the fire.

Selby had lost her mother some years ago to fever, he knew. But Keldrick wondered what it was like to lose all her remaining family all at once, leaving her a ruler and worse, having to take her country to war, with so little knowledge and training. He could not fathom losing Father and Merridon and Kendrick and Mother in just six weeks' time. And Mirelle. To leave him King of Romeny, and Eastern Shield, and in charge of the war....

Keldrick remembered meeting Selby years ago… they had been perhaps thirteen. Keldrick hardly remembered her, and only recalled her because the Clemongard Royal Family had made the trip for a Spring Seasonal. Keldrick and all the boys were more interested in tourneys and jousting, and the entertainment that year than they had been the young girls, but he did remember Selby as a lighthearted and laughing young girl, the center of attention as a Western visitor.

This woman sitting across from him, crunching into an apple, staring into the fire, there was neither lightheartedness nor laughter to her. She was tough and hammered, strong as the steel that encompassed her, as the cleaver she wore by her side. There was only wariness and distrust, and what Keldrick deemed exhaustion. Stray wisps of hair had escaped her braid and the plait that bound it. He wondered if she would sleep at all tonight.

Just then, a horse cantered up into the Queen's camp. Two QueensGuard moved to hold the horse's reins while the rider threw himself over the saddle.

Both Keldrick and Queen Selby stood up.

The rider eyed Keldrick suspiciously. "Your Majesty," he said, and bowed.

"Have you a message?" asked Selby.

"It is – for Your Majesty, with all pardons," and the rider bowed with respect to Keldrick.

Selby replied, "He is my Ambassador from the Eastern Alliance. Whatever you have to tell me, he may hear as well."

"As you please it, Your Majesty," and the rider bowed again. He took a breath and then the words spilled out. "Cliff Watch North is under attack from Ambsellon! We've lost three ships, but taken two of theirs and boarded two. They've boarded two of ours as well. I was told to tell you, Your Majesty, by the Cliff Watch Tower, that we are holding our own and keeping to the plans we put in place. No ships have made it to land. That was the message as of my leaving three hours ago to give you this message."

Queen Selby nodded throughout this. "Thank you for getting here so quickly, Sergeant." She waved at a soldier. "See that his horse is seen to immediately and that the Sergeant is brought to the War Tent. Bring him some nourishment as well." She waved at another soldier. "Call the War Council to the War Tent."

Queen Selby looked across the fire at Keldrick. She drew in a deep sigh.

"And so it has begun."

Selby

She emerged from her tent to see the blue sky before her. A fine day for war. She scoffed. Was there such a thing a good day for war?

Selby wondered how many of her ships were left since last night. How many men were alive, wounded.... How many Ambsellon bastards had stepped foot upon her beaches. And if they were headed here, or further east.... No further riders had come in the night, which concerned her. She'd barely slept after the War Council had concluded last night.

At that moment, the Ambassador stepped out of his tent. He yawned and stretched. Selby immediately looked away lest she be caught staring. Keldrick. He was – interesting. She had been sure he would leave when the other Prince had. That he had not had taken her by surprise. But she was... comforted by his presence. Selby hated to admit it, for it felt like weakness, but there it was.

She believed it was that he was of an age with her, and that he supported her actions and directives, as an Ambassador, rather than many of her advisors and councilors, who offered second opinions and often condescended her. The Ambassador's primary responsibility was to support her as an Ally, and he had done exactly that so far. He had even cleared his throat once last night in the War Council when they diverged from Selby's actual plans. The Ambassador had said steadily, in a firm tone that brooked no argument, "I believe Her Majesty has already set out our plan of action. Any further discourse on the subject is a waste of our time, gentlemen." Selby could not help but find him... comforting.

At the same time she found him distinctly unsettling. Perhaps it was his eyes. Cobalt eyes that, with a glance, figured you out completely. Selby wondered if that was why he had been chosen as an Ambassador.

But she found him curious, as well, for he fetched his own meals, saw to his own horse and bath water, insisted he get no preferential treatment. The men liked him. He had an easy smile and, if Selby hadn't known he was a third son of the most powerful man in all the Land, she would have taken him for another soldier.

A Lieutenant approached her. "Your Majesty." He bowed low.

"Lieutenant." Instantly, every nerve was a-jangle. Selby glanced at the Ambassador, who had heard the Lieutenant's approach. He immediately stepped to her side.

The Lieutenant eyed Ambassador Keldrick but said, "There was a second rider late in the night. We chose not to wake you, for the Ambsells retreated. We are holding them off, according to the rider. He said they retreated but look to be regrouping. Nine more ships lost, five boarded. They lost twelve ships and we have boarded eight of their ships, and had them surrounded until they retreated. That was at about three hours past midnight." Then the Lieutenant bowed low.

Retreated. Selby closed her eyes for a moment, but only a moment. Then she nodded. "Thank you, Lieutenant."

The officer turned and left and Selby turned to Ambassador Keldrick. "What make you of that?"

He looked surprised. "I – think you should take your wins when you get them, Your Majesty."

Selby huffed. "Spoken like a diplomat." She turned around to go into her tent. They were riding out as soon as possible today.

"Very well," she heard the Ambassador say. Selby turned around. He was a bit pink in the cheeks. Had she made him angry? Intriguing. She stopped to listen.

"That was the first thing that came to mind, and something I've heard at Court more times than I can count. But true, nonetheless. If you want the truth, then... what I also think is – that they have probably regrouped and will continue fighting today now that they have a feel for our fighting maneuvers. Last night was a practice. Today, they'll come at us hard, wins or losses."

"Us?" queried Selby.

He faltered for a moment, then recovered with, "Are you not an Ally?"

She nodded.

The Ambassador continued, an eyebrow raised. "Was that too direct, Your Majesty?"

"I prefer the truth. Layering the truth with lies does me no good, especially now. I need direct answers from my advisors, and I rarely get them. Direct is refreshing, and, let me say, a requirement of your office. Are we agreed?"

He regarded her with something like respect. "Agreed, Your Majesty." He nodded his head gravely.

She shook her head at him. "Please. Have I not told you to call me Selby?"

A half-smile brightened his face and he looked away. He seemed a very carefree person, she thought.

"You have, Your Majesty," he returned.

She tossed her braid over her shoulder. "Then I request that you do so." A smile almost came to her lips and she began to advance into her tent again.

But the Ambassador said, "I'm sorry, Your Majesty, but I can't do that. It's just – unseemly."

Now Selby looked up at him square on. She placed her hands on her hips. "Unseemly. Are you calling me unseemly?"

He refused to look at her. "No, Your Majesty, it's just that – as you are my Commanding Officer – it's unseemly of me to call you by your first name, particularly when you are the Queen."

Selby narrowed her eyes at him. She realized suddenly then that Mother did that to Father when she wanted him to do something for her. Immediately, Selby's brow furrowed in consternation. She let her eyes relax, but asked the Ambassador then, "Very well, Ambassador Keldrick. But tell me something."

He looked down at her.

"Are all of you Easterners such prudes?"

The question caught him entirely by surprise and his jaw dropped in a grin. Then he remembered himself and cleared his throat. "No, Your Majesty." He struggled to hide the grin.

Selby recalled her brothers, all full of laughter and life, not unlike what she'd just witnessed in Ambassador Keldrick here. "Good. Perhaps there's hope for you yet, Ambassador." And she ducked into her tent.

After several last-minute briefings from various field officers, Selby was now stone silent as she rode her horse toward the front of the line. All she heard was the plodding of her horse's hooves beneath her, the jingling of his trappings, and the victory marching songs her men were singing behind her. "To the Victors" was a drum song she personally despised, but military men loved it, and on the first day of war, who was she to deny them a song that enthused and encouraged them?

And there it started again. Selby sighed aloud.

"To the Victors"

In the end, the victors take the daughters

In the end, the victors take the sisters

In the end, the victors take the wives

To the victors go the swords (Da-DOOM!)

To the victors go the blood (Da-da-DOOM!)

In the end, the victors take the sons

In the end, the victors take the brothers

In the end, the victors take the husbands

To the victors go the armor (Da-DOOM!)

To the victors go the weapons (Da-da-DOOM!)

In the end, the victors take the wells

In the end, the victors take the livestock

In the end, the victors take the farms

A Silent Game of Spies

To the victors go the crops (Da-DOOM!)

To the victors go the lands (Da-da-DOOM!)

In the end. the victors take the villages

In the end. the victors take the towns

In the end, the victors take the cities

To the victors go the plunders (Da-DOOM!)

To the victors go the possessions (Da-da-DOOM!)

In the end, the victors take the churches

In the end, the victors take the clergies

In the end, the victors take the priests

To the victors go the relics (Da-DOOM!)

To the victors go the riches (Da-da-DOOM!)

In the end, the victors take the forts

In the end, the victors take the towers

In the end, the victors take the keeps

To the victors go the banners (Da-DOOM!)

To the victors go the standards (Da-da-DOOM!)

In the end, the victors take the ale

In the end, the victors take the mead

In the end, the victors take the spirits

To the victors go the flasks (Da-DOOM!)

To the victors go the tankards (Da-da-DOOM!)

In the end, the victors take the duchesses

In the end, the victors take the princesses

In the end, the victors take the queens

To the victors goes the gold (Da-DOOM!)

To the victors goes the treasure (Da-da-DOOM!)

In the end, the victors take the palaces

In the end, the victors take the fortresses

In the end, the victors take the castles

To the victors go the kingdoms (Da-DOOM!)

To the victors go the countries (Da-da-DOOM!)

In the end, the victors take the dukes

In the end, the victors take the princes

In the end, the victors take the kings

To the victors go the SPOILS OF WAR! (Da-DOOM!)

To the victors go the SPOILS OF WAR! (Da-da-DOOM!)

To the victors go the SPOILS OF WAR! (Da-DOOM!)

To the victors go the SPOILS OF WAR! (Da-da-DOOM!)

To the victors go the SPOILS OF WAR! (Da-da-Da-da-Da-da-Da-da-DOOM DOOM!)

Ambassador Keldrick rode up next to her and just caught her expression of distaste.

"Do you have such songs in the East?" Selby asked.

"Of course," he returned. "This very one, in fact." The leather of his saddle creaked as he sat forward a bit. "Though I cannot say I ever expected to hear it during an actual war."

Nor had she. Selby studied him. He made a handsome figure in his blackened steel ringmail, with the breastplate burnished with the rose sword of Romeny, his cloak flowing behind him. "Are you afraid?" Selby asked. She gestured at the thousands of men about them.

A breeze riffled a blond lock of hair as he regarded her. "I would be a fool to say 'no' after all the war stories I've heard from my father and my uncle and countless others about the Twenty Years War. But I think perhaps a bit of fear is natural."

Selby looked down at her horse and smoothed his neck. She had never grown up hearing such stories, for she had sat in the bower or out on the terrace with her ladies-in-waiting, speaking of new fashions and visitors to Court, holding garden parties, and working at her stitchery. If she could go back to those days and tell her younger self that one day she would lead all of Clemongard to war as Queen, why, her younger self would collapse with laughter....

"And you? Are you afraid?" asked Ambassador Keldrick.

Odd question.

She looked up high at the perfect blue sky above them, then out at the waving banners to either side of them, the scores of horses and infantry....

"No. Not afraid." Selby looked at the Ambassador, searching for a word. He waited patiently. "Angry."

His eyebrows rose, taken aback.

Selby stared back over the men advancing toward the mountain. "There was a time, especially at first, when I was afraid. Now, there is just... anger." Selby shrugged. There was nothing left but anger.

The Ambassador told her, "You know, my twin and I, we learned a great deal of responsibilities over the last few months, just before we learned of the war. And my father told us this. A best mate of his in the Twenty Years War told him that anger can be either a tool or a toxin, we have to be sure to make it the former."

A tool or a toxin. Hm. Well, she would try to keep that in mind when she ordered her men to slaughter the people who had come to kill them with no provocation, mused Selby.

Aloud, she wondered, "The Twenty Years War. I wonder what they will name this war, and what we will tell our children about it."

Ambassador Keldrick's head jerked around to look at her. She glanced at him. He seemed surprised for some reason. So she said, "Perhaps this will only last a year at most, and be equivalent to a skirmish, hardly be worth a paragraph in a History of the Era text."

"Let us hope so, let us hope so," he returned. "Let us hope, more importantly, that there is an enormous victory for Clemongard today."

Two Generals rode up. "Your Majesty, the men are in their places." They would be protecting her, along with ArmsMaster Andeval, a small detachment of Royal Guard and Ericorian both.

But first – she had to address the Army.

Selby rode forth between the two Generals until her horse brought her to the center front of the entire line of the Clemongard Royal Army. She waited until all the Army – her Army – was staring at her, focused on her, before she yelled out at the top of her lungs,

"See this mountain? See this mountain that stands before us? It is in no way as strong as you are! We fight an enemy who hides behind this mountain! That enemy is the Northern Countries! Time after time they come for us, by land and by sea, and time after time, we push them back. The Northern Countries want Clemongard! Last year, they killed our King! Now, I, your Queen, stand before you, and I urge you to fight them! Just last night, Ambsellon opened fire on our Navy at Cliff Watch North! Our last communication was that our Naval formations are holding them back!" Selby heard cheers sound all over the ranks. She continued.

"Brave men, and women too, for I know you to be out there –" and random whoops went up from women all over the Army assembled before her – "Let us fight this Northern enemy, you who stand before me, Clemongard's fighting forces, you protect Clemongard from the North, and the Coastal Countries! But you are more than just fighting forces! You are its brothers and sisters, sons and daughters, fathers and mothers, farmers, businessfolk, you are Clemongard's lifeblood. All the land has need of a good queen, but what Clemongard needs is a great queen, and today, I will be that queen, for I will lead you against our Northern enemy!

"You are Clemongard!" A cheer went up from all the ranks. *"You are Clemongard!"* She rode up and down the entire row of the Army before her as another cheer rang up. *"You are Clemongard!"* The men roared their approval.

"ATTACK!" Selby screamed.

Rhutgard

The sturdy knock at his chamber door he knew was Gerard's. "Enter!" he called, and then he dismissed his steward. Damn, he'd forgotten how heavy ringmail was.

He heard the heavy oaken door open, then swing shut.

"The last time I was in this area of Fairview Palace, 'twas your father's chambers, and I never did get an invitation," called out Gerard.

Rhutgard smiled a little. Only Gerard would remember such a thing. Ah, how he missed Father, especially at a time like this....

"Are you going to come out, Rhudy, or – oh." Gerard took in the sight of Rhutgard in his full ringmail once he emerged. He grinned a bit. "I'll bet the last time you wore armor, you were a bit thinner around the torso, hey?"

Rhutgard snorted and glanced down at his midriff. "I looked an awful more like Kendrick, I'll tell you that."

Gerard said, "Oh, please, Rhudy, you don't look that far off. Me, on the other hand," and he guffawed, patting his belly. "I've a wine belly that Ronan couldn't hope to put on in twenty years."

"Well, you'll lose that wine belly in two weeks, I guarantee you. Wearing a suit like this every day, swinging a sword, constant exercise – you'll look like Ronan again in no time," Rhutgard gibed. He moved his arms about. The jingling of the steel rings was a little exciting, he had to admit....

Gerard grimaced. "Yes, and only water to drink. I don't want to think about it. You'll be back to being a skinny runt again in a week. I won't be able to tell the difference between you and Kendrick."

"Of course you will. Kendrick hasn't got a beard yet. I couldn't keep a full beard until I was – hmm, twenty-one," chortled Rhutgard as he ran his hand across his beard. He needed this lightheartedness before they rode out tomorrow, perhaps that was why he'd called for Gerard up here.

Unfortunately, however, there was still business to attend to….

"My friend, on that side table," and Rhutgard pointed. "is a communication you need to read."

He watched Gerard's face immediately change to one of concern, both for his son and his country. In two quick strides, Gerard had approached the side table and swept the communication up. As he read it, Rhutgard watched his brow furrow. Finally, he looked up.

"You're letting him stay? Are you mad?"

"Gerard. What would you have me do?"

"Do? Rhutgard, he's your son. Issue him a Royal Decree or some such whatever you would do. Send for him to come home. That country is about to get sliced to pieces, and your son in the middle of it."

"He is my son. He will not return, I am sure of it. It is an honorable thing he does –"

"Honorable! Shit on that! You know I love him like my own, he's my nephew, Rhudy. I don't want to see him get killed or worse, become a prisoner to the Northern Country soldiers. Once they find out who he is – Rhutgard, send for his stubborn little Rommish arse to come home. He's done his Ambassador duty. We got the map, we got the information. What's he doing there, playing at fairy tales with the Western Queen?" Gerard slammed the communication down on the side table. "That's it, Rhudy, you know. He wants to swoop in and save the Queen. His fool head is in the clouds –"

"That will be enough," Rhutgard said lowly. It was one thing to express concern for Keldrick, much of what he was already experiencing. But he – and Principea – were the only two people who could insult any of his children. Not even Gerard had that right, uncle or no.

Gerard said nothing for a moment, aware that he had pushed Rhutgard too far.

Then he said quietly, "I am only concerned for the boy, Rhudy. He doesn't know any more of war than you and I did when we stepped foot onto the battleground the first day. And out there, whether she's an ally or not, he hasn't got anyone at his back. Here, he has you, Kendrick, all the Alliance."

"All of what you say is nothing I haven't thought of constantly since I received that communication. But his reasoning is sound. We need an Ambassador –"

"Then send one, and send your son home –"

"–That we can trust, who won't be swayed by the enemy."

"Send a loyal man who won't be swayed by the enemy, who isn't your son. Rhutgard. See sense in this, I beg you. I'd send for Ronan were it me. Ronan may be seasoned by the street assignments he's had, but he's never been in war before."

"Answer me these two questions: What would you have done at his age, and is the position he's chosen an honorable one?"

Gerard glared at Rhutgard.

"The position he's chosen has merit. If I send for him now, it will seem that I don't trust him or believe in his abilities to serve the Alliance. He would lose face. He will have to learn. You and I did. Do you think I want him half way across the Land in a war-torn realm, Gerard? But I trust him. I trust his instincts, and I believe in the boy. Keldrick wouldn't stay in a war-torn realm just to play at fairytales. This will make a man of him. He's smart, he knows our ways, and he can advise her. He may just know what he's doing, Gerard."

— ⚬ —

Two Kings flanked him to either side, and two Crown Princes behind him rode. Rhutgard appreciated the uniformity, if nothing else. He found himself thinking how Principea would find yet another opportunity for a portrait, though the artist would have a hard time portraying the grimness of the Romeny Royal Guard that surrounded them on all sides, like a tide bearing them forth to war.

To his left, Rhutgard felt sure Gerard was sulking. And unless he missed his guess, the ever-dignified Silver Statesman, Driscoll rode silently, keeping his concerns to himself after conferencing with several of his personal advisors. Both men would turn off to the north and the east, respectively, to meet their own Armies in due time.

Rhutgard had dismissed both Rickstan and Reaghann a week ago, shortly after he had announced to the people formally that the East was now at war with the Northern Countries. Neither Rickstan nor Reaghann had any experience with war and he sent them home to get their affairs – and their castles – in order. They had been away a month now, and Reaghann had expressed concern over that especially. His ports were now clear and ingoing and outgoing ships of all sizes were docking from each port throughout his entire coastline. His own army occupied the coast now, so any further Stordish who had attempted to come in to Port Stanton, Ferrisport, Chesterport, or any others were immediately dissuaded, though the damage was already done, for a sizeable faction of both Ormon and Stordish troops awaited them at the northeasternmost corner of Delsynth, in a pocket of the EverWinters. And undoubtedly more arriving from Ormon, if Rhutgard were to judge.

And that was where they rode.

Principea had not understood at all, and these last few days had been difficult for them both. He'd spent as much time with her as he could, and a long, tender night last night that unfortunately had a morning today. This morning, as his steward dressed him in armor, Rhutgard reminded his SweetPea that while he was away, she would be taking over as many new duties as necessary. Principea already ruled the much of the Fairview household, and what she did not, the Seneschal did. But Rhutgard also reminded her that she would have Mirelle to lean on, and Mirelle would need to lean on her as well.

Rhutgard hated to leave his Principea behind as upset as she was, but there was nothing for it. He was the Eastern Shield before he was a husband, a father, or a King. And today the Eastern Shield led the five countries of the Eastern Alliance to war.

Varley

The east Corstarorden border and the Free Lands had been the perfect lay-low location for Varley. He had recruited men as they impressed him – men, he scoffed. Neither bandits but not quite mercenaries either. However, they took his coin and populated his ranks. He now had thirty-five thousand men, which made up for the ten thousand he'd sent the Ice Bitch in the North.

Ah – rumors swirled about her. Varley heard them all, mainly from the ignorant in his ranks, who hailed from any of the Coastals, to as far away as Clemongard. Their diversity gave him a wide range of information. Most of it agreed with each other in the end. Ambsellon was marching upon Clemongard, which any fool with the capacity for thought knew by know, and that the Ice Bitch had killed her husband that she might start the war.

What they didn't know was that she was docking in Clemongard, and so Varley chose to keep his men out of Clemongard. He knew now that Clemongard was the sixth Ally of the Eastern Alliance, and it was just bad business to fight in Clemongard with Eastern and Northern soldiers there. Who knew what arrangements might have been made in regard to him and Storden? Kill on sight? Dead or alive? Capture and deliver? No, he believed it best to stay out of Clemongard. Especially if the Ice Bitch were there, for she was not known for her patience. She covered up her back trail and Varley was quite certainly a back trail, knowing all that he did of their arrangements.

So he would be staying south of the fray. Which meant… Storden. And the Coastals. King Irving had no idea how to rule. And the people would accept Varley's claim to the throne, should he choose to make one. With over thirty-thousand men, Varley believed he stood a chance at taking back the throne from his uncle.

If he wanted it. He was more interested in Corstarorden of late….

But he had to bide his time. Riders were watching for Myrischka to land in Clemongard. Once Clemongard was fully occupied, by both Ormon, Ambsellon, and the Eastern Alliance, then Varley would make his move, for no one would be able to stop him. He would take what he wanted from Storden, and move into the Coastals, one by one….

Topher

He was curious to know why Renfry wanted out of Corstarorden. Was he running from someone? Wanted for a crime? The man seemed desperate to leave.

Topher knew that unless Renfry was willing to speak on the subject, asking him for answers was a futile endeavor, so he did not pursue the subject. Until they arrived at Middleborough, just a day from the Storden border, and an equal distance east to the ocean and west to the FreeLands.

So nice to sleep beneath a roof again and eat warm food. Just a tiny town, with a small, three-room inn, The Mid-Point Inn. They nearly had to sleep in the stable until the proprietor threw a man out for his rowdy behavior, bags and all.

"You two," and the irate innkeeper pointed at Topher and Renfry leaning against the stable wall, "a room just opened up. You want it, you got it." And Topher and Renfry brushed themselves free of hay and scrambled up the stairs for the tiny room.

After a three-day trek from Roarden North, the thin, greasy broth, mainly devoid of vegetables, was welcome, and they said little to each other while they slurped it down. Topher watched Renfry study the innkeeper and the other customers, but none of them raised an alert, so Renfry relaxed – minutely. The innkeeper was largely disinterested in his clientele – as long as everyone paid and behaved in an orderly fashion, Topher decided the balding, aproned man was lost in his own thoughts as he kept to his tasks.

The next morning, as Renfry and Topher stood outside of Middleborough's town limits, Renfry confronted Topher. "I've gotten you most of the way to the Corstarorden border. Have you an idea which direction you're headed?"

Topher hoisted his rucksack over his shoulder. "Anywhere but Storden. East, to the FreeLands, then perhaps…."

Renfry studied him.

"The FreeLands. Whatever for? Did you not say not four days ago that you were trying to stay away from "mercs" like myself? The FreeLands are full of mercs."

"Aye, but they're all headed west," Topher returned. Every whispered conversation he'd heard as he'd served ale was the same – mercenaries in Roarden North.

Renfry looked actually concerned for him. "Why, then head north. Storden is neutral again, it's got a new king –"

Topher blanched. "Ren, where have you been for the last three months? Storden may have a new king, but its last crown prince still wants that throne, I guarantee you that. And he'll still want to make war. That Varley, he's still got that Army ready at his command, new king or no. I would rather shave my head than go north to Storden." And Topher gave Renfry a meaningful look, for his traveling companion knew what dire consequences shaving his head would bring about. If Topher was going to be executed, he'd rather be executed by a member of the Silent Order than soldiers who might torture him. And everything he had heard in The Red Fox from those mercenaries looking for hire told him over twenty thousand soldiers sat in Storden awaiting Prince Varley's command.

Renfry stared at him. "The FreeLands are not safe."

"Far safer than Corstarorden or Storden. And just where are you headed?" returned Topher, a bit incensed.

Renfry's brown eyes narrowed. "North."

"North," repeated Topher. "That's so specific."

Renfry rolled his eyes and turned forward on the road, shaking his head at the sarcasm in Topher's voice.

"Actually, I am headed toward the Eastern border, by 4 Kings' Fortress, and then North, so you can continue with me, if you choose, to the Free Lands. I will be heading North from there."

Amazed at this scrap of news that Renfry had shared, Topher hastened after him. "North from 4 Kings Fortress? That brings you into Clemongard. And you warn me of safety. Whatever would convince you to walk blindly into the one country that's being attacked by what is probably not one but two, and possibly even three other countries? You've clearly lost your bloody mind, mate."

Renfry threw a glare at him. "Did all of you talk this much or is it just you? The whole Silent thing, just a ruse, yeah?"

Topher, now angry, for that was an enormous secret, glanced about. Seeing no one on the road anywhere, he retorted, "We communicated other ways, by signing the old, unspoken language, and by writing. Thus the callouses." Topher held up the two first fingers of his right hand, which were roughened from six years of constant writing in order to communicate.

Renfry stopped suddenly and grabbed Topher's fingers, inspecting the callouses. Then he looked up at Topher with a pensive expression. "What subjects did they train you in?"

Taken aback, Topher blinked and tried to recall all the way back to his first year with the Silent Order. Renfry began walking again, that same pensive expression on his face.

Topher listed on his fingers, "… calligraphy, scribery, animal husbandry, agriculture, law and legal studies, health and anatomy, basic medicinal studies, history of each country in the Land, heraldry, political studies, art and literature, language, accounting, upper arithmetic, basic architecture…. And, of course, continuing studies of the One God," he added.

"And no study of weaponry? No… archery? Pole axe, perhaps?" asked Renfry ahead of Topher.

"It's a peaceful, religious order. Why would they teach acolytes to maim and kill?" asked Topher.

"Oh, I don't know. In case their members fear for their lives, perhaps," replied Renfry dryly.

"Then they offer their souls to the One God freely," answered Topher.

"And you? Do you offer your soul to the One God freely, should it become imperiled?"

"Imperiled? I made my peace with the One God before I left. I told Him that I believed in him and his teachings, but that I was not willing to offer myself to a life of silence. He, in return, was silent. I thought that was a sign as loud as any other, so, I decided to keep my tongue. Should my life be in danger, I'll fight for it. Will I fall to the ground in prayer to the One God? No."

Up ahead, Renfry nodded a little.

"Just why are you asking?"

"I'll be turning north to deliver an extremely – important – message to someone in Clemongard. You're welcome to join me, though it will be dangerous, very."

Topher rose an eyebrow at this sudden revelation of Renfry's, and his offer. But the man was – crazed. "Clemongard. A message. Renfry, you have lost your brains, man. Can you not send a pigeon?"

He watched Renfry give a firm shake of the head. "This must be delivered in person. As soon as possible. It is of dire importance that I get this message delivered."

Topher was impressed at Renfry's conviction but thought him crazy nevertheless. "Did you not hear me when I said that Clemongard was being attacked by two, if not possibly three countries?"

Renfry said nothing.

Topher jogged up until he was even with Renfry. "Just why is this so important? Who is this going to?"

Renfry sized him up for a moment and then replied, "I have a message for the Queen."

Topher stared. Perhaps Renfry was kidding. He was waiting for Renfry's face to break into a sarcastic grin. But it did not, and his pace continued.

"The Queen. Of Clemongard. Queen Selby." Topher was disbelieving. This man walking next to him wanted an audience with the actual Queen of Clemongard.

"You're mad." Topher shook his head. "Mad."

Renfry stopped in the dirt road, a small puff of dust arising around his boots. Topher stopped and stared at him.

"Let me put it to you like this. I have to deliver this message. It's my duty, Topher."

He stared at Topher a few seconds longer, then drew the crisscrossed swords from behind his back out. Topher stared at them, glinting in the sun. Then Renfry whirled each sword around and caught them by the hilt, once, twice, three times.

Topher tried not to look impressed.

"Let's just say you're not the only one who's a member of an order, mate."

And Renfry stashed his two swords into their scabbards on his back, staring at him the entire time.

An order? What? There were no other orders, no orders with swords like that. And Topher would know.

Renfry had started down the road again, at a brisk pace this time.

"Wait! You're a member of an order? A real order? Or just a –" Topher thought it best to stop talking before he got himself into trouble.

"Yes, a real Order," replied Renfry tiredly.

"Well, I've never read of any Orders like – like that."

"That's because we keep it private. The Silent Order is not a private Order. Ours is and has been around for centuries." And Renfry stopped in the road. "We are the Brotherhood of the Two Blades. We serve with partners and we travel the Land. And we serve a number of important purposes, including protecting the Royals as necessary. Right now, I have a message I must get to Queen Selby. In fact, I will need a horse soon, so if you choose to come with me, you will be riding, not walking. If you choose not to accompany me north to Clemongard, then you keep your mouth shut about me, and I shall keep my mouth shut about you."

Topher nodded slowly. If either of them exposed the other, then they had simply to turn the other in. Topher would never do such a thing, but it was a safety clause. And as learned as he was, he had never heard of the Brotherhood of the Two Blades....

"What is this message you bear?" he asked quietly, respectful of this mission that Renfry was on.

"I overheard a plot by a group of Stordish soldiers to see that she was murdered, leaving the entire country without a ruler. She is the last of her family. If she is on the battlefield, it will be easy for her to be killed – a stray arrow, for example...." Renfry sighed. He looked at Topher. "You have no weaponry experience save what little I taught you myself. Where I go, to Clemongard, there will be war on all sides. I suggest you stay your course – stay to the FreeLands. You lived off the land easily enough before. Stay out of the way of soldiers and you should be fine."

"The Coastals will be called in once the Eastern Alliance starts fighting. The whole of this Land will be at war. Where will be a safe place to hide? A rabbit's den? I can help you, you know. I know all the heraldry banners, geography, who you're like to meet on the battlefield. Take me with you." Topher suddenly could not believe what he heard himself saying.

"Did you not hear me say it was dangerous? You know nothing of weaponry. As you yourself said, twice, Clemongard is besieged by as many as three countries."

"Yes, and all three countries the wrong side. That Queen needs all the assistance she can get. She lost her whole family in less than a year. They're trying to kill her, you say. That is plain bloody wrong. Teach me how to use those swords on the way there. I learn fast. I'd not have it said that I turned away when I could have helped a Queen who needed assistance when three countries were attacking her and a plot to murder her was afoot.

"Consider it a matter of honor," Topher finished.

Renfry nodded slowly, considering. "Very well, then."

———

Topher's mind was spinning. They had come across more traffic than he'd thought possible on the road West. Renfry hadn't been kidding when he'd said the way would be dangerous. Two small bands of mercenaries who, once they took Renfry's measure, decided to leave them alone. Topher knew it. The two sword hilts poking over Renfry's cloak and the quality of his ringmail shirt told common mercs that he was not a man to be trifled with. They each acknowledged Renfry with a short nod as they passed, like dogs in the yard. Topher they didn't even notice. Renfry said he would train him a bit each night.

A family headed for ArkenHeights nodded pleasantly enough, though they seemed apprehensive. They asked if any trouble in ArkenHeights had been heard of, but Topher and Renfry had no news for them.

And near the end of the day, a five-man group of Stordish soldiers nearly overtook them on the road.

Topher fully believed they only wanted a bit of sport. But, unlike the last time, Renfry gave neither Topher nor the soldiers any notice. He beheaded all five of them within less than two minutes.

"Field's over there if you plan to retch," Renfry had shot Topher a meaningful look.

Topher had taken in a deep breath and nudged the heads aside while he bent to rag-pick. Much of the coin he had now came from the two men Renfry had killed on the road to Roarden North all those months ago, so who was Topher to judge how bounty was delivered?

After a moment, Renfry had bent to do the same. Both of them now had ten more silver pieces and over thirty or more coppers. But the most distasteful part followed, for Renfry insisted Topher wear one of the men's ringmail shirt. As it had a splash a blood upon it, he had swallowed down his disgust and pulled the ringmail over his head.

It was impossibly heavy and smelled foul, for undoubtedly, the group had been traveling for some time together. Who knew the last time the man had bathed? The next opportunity to bathe presented itself, Topher would be first in line, for he could not abide uncleanliness. Renfry scoffed at him and threw a belt at him to cinch the shirt around the waist, for the ringmail shirt hung on him loosely.

And lastly, Renfry handed him a sword and dagger, with the oddest expression upon his face.

After they had lumped the bodies off to the side of the road – and the heads – the two of them had continued. Topher could not believe he was wearing armor, even ill-fitting as it was, much less a sword belt and sword.

Suddenly, out of curiosity he asked, "Did you not say that those in the Brotherhood traveled with partners?"

He saw Renfry grimace. "Aye."

"Then, where is yours?"

Renfry did not break his stride, but he looked up at the sky. "I left him in Tortoreen. Six feet in the ground."

Topher's eyes bulged at that. After a few minutes, he said, "I'm sorry."

"Don't be. He died a grand death. We were ambushed at the last moment but we still completed our mission."

Topher took this in. He recalled what Renfry had told him at The Red Fox in Roarden North. *"...I am no merc. I am looking for someone of my status, however, which I was doing before I even ran across you."*

"Who have you been looking for all this time? In the bars and pubs, that is?" asked Topher. He wondered if Renfry was looking for the man who had killed his partner.

Renfry said nothing at first. Then he shook his head. "I must be mad." He turned toward Topher. "I've been looking for another partner. Interested?"

Mirelle

She sat speaking with another lady-in-waiting when Kimbur cleared her throat in such a way that made Mirelle look up. "Your Highness," whispered Kimbur, "the Healer across the terrace seems most urgent to gain your attention."

The Healer.... Mirelle shot a meaningful look over her shoulder at Kimbur, who looked quite somber. Undoubtedly, this was related to Merridon.

"Do excuse me," Mirelle told the lady-in-waiting and, without waiting for a reply, carefully made her way across the terrace. The closer she got to the Healer, the more upset the Healer became.

"Quiet yourself, dear Healer," Mirelle said in a calm voice, pulling the Healer around a pillar that they might not be seen by anyone else on the terrace. She recognized the woman as one of Merridon's regular attending Healers.

The Healer curtsied and said, "Your Highness, if it please you –" Tears formed in her brown eyes and she began to wring her hands.

"Come, come, let us go where we cannot be overheard before we speak," Mirelle interrupted her.

Kimbur placed an arm on the woman's back and Mirelle led them to an indoor sitting room. She closed the windows and the door and then sat down next to the Healer, who was trembling. Odd, that the Healer was so disconcerted. As a Healer, Mirelle thought she might be accustomed to the idea of a patient's death.

Death... this meant that Merridon was... dead, then. She let out a breath she hadn't realized she'd been holding. She swallowed down tears, for she had to be strong for this woman. She'd read the paperwork Merridon had drawn up with Stanyard.

Mirelle's mind was suddenly a-whirl. She would need to send for Stanyard, and plan this small burial down in the Royal Romeny Tombs... and how would Mother respond to all of this, would she cry or –

Kimbur coughed slightly. Mirelle took the Healer's hand. "How can I help you, Madam Healer?"

"As y-y-ou know, Y-Your Highness, I have been attending your eldest brother, M-M-"

And the Healer began to cry. Kimbur offered the Healer her handkerchief. The lady took it, trembling. Whatever had happened that had this woman so terribly disconcerted?

"Go on, Madam Healer," Mirelle prompted in a quiet voice.

"If you please, Your Highness, I'm so sorry to fall to pieces like this. Your brother – we knew he hadn't long left – begging your pardon, Your Highness."

"Go on." Oy! Would she ever just spit it out!

"I'm so sorry, Your Highness, your brother Merridon, he has – has passed on."

There, thought Mirelle, was that so terribly hard to say. She controlled her facial expression. "Thank you for informing me, Madam Healer. He has been struggling for some time. I know he is at peace now. I will see to his arrangements."

The Healer's eyes grew large again, however. What now, wondered Mirelle.

"He – His Highness, he – he didn't pass – like he ought to have, Your Highness...."

"In his sleep, then, perhaps? Elaborate, Madam Healer."

The Healer glanced all about the room nervously, then at Kimbur, before whispering, "His Highness was murdered!"

Immediately, Mirelle thought of the white powder she knew Merridon had asked to have given him – and wondered whether this woman recognized arsenic when she saw it. What a tangle this would be. Stanyard would have to talk to the Healers about this. This was all Stanyard's doing, damn the man.

Aloud, Mirelle responded, "Murdered! What makes you say such a thing? How do you know?"

"We came in this morning and –" the Healer looked horrified suddenly – "he had a –" She ran a line across her throat. "Someone cut him from behind across the throat! In the night! It's horrible! We've covered him up and not let anyone in. You're the first to hear of it, Your Highness, as you're his only blood relative here."

Merridon! Murdered! On the brink of death and – murdered! And – and neither Father, nor Kendrick, nor Keldrick, in the Palace…. What was *she* to do?

⸺ ⌘ ⸺

They had been very good about – about covering Merridon. The Healers had simply placed a collar over his – wound, and dressed him in one of his best outfits. Merridon looked to be asleep now. Even at peace.

Here, in Merridon's library, things seemed much calmer somehow. Kimbur encircled her shoulders and led her away from Merridon's bedside, and a Healer moved to cover his face up.

Mirelle began listing what had to be done in her mind. There was a murderer still in Fairview, either in the Palace itself, or the city. How was she to deal with that?

All the Healers were accounted for, and both she and Kimbur agreed that, judging by the tearful, pathetic state of the Healers, none of them had killed Merridon. At least not in the way that had actually taken his life in the end. Mirelle wondered if any of them knew they had been administering poison to him all these months.

That left only the Guards, for they had intimate knowledge of where Merridon slept, his daily routines. Perhaps one had been bribed. She told each Healer to act as if Merridon had died of his disease, not murder. They were to tell no one what had occurred in this room, including the Her Majesty, the Queen.

Some of them looked doubtful, so Mirelle said, "Her Majesty is distraught already with the King having just left for war. Would you add this horror to her grief, needlessly? I will tell her myself what occurred here when it is time. Until then, you will only speak with me and Lord Stanyard about what has actually happened to His Highness." And all of the Healers nodded immediately, for Mother was well-loved and regarded among the Healers.

"Your Highness, we are concerned for you. What if the – monster – who committed this act is still in the Palace? He may attempt to kill you, or your Royal Mother, Her Majesty," said one of the Healers.

Kimbur caught Mirelle's eye. Even Kimbur seemed emphatic on this point. "Very well, I shall see that more guards are assigned. And what of you? Are any of you afeared for your lives?" she asked.

A few Healers raised their hands, shaking.

Mirelle nodded. "Very well. I will see that guards are assigned to you as well – discreetly. I will be sending for Lord Stanyard and he will interview each of you. Once he speaks with you, you are free to leave the Palace. See that you remain in the Healers' Quarters. Guards will be stationed outside there."

Mirelle took a deep breath, for she had no idea how she would accomplish all of this. But she looked at the small group of Healers then and told them, "I'd like to thank you for your dedicated service to my brother. I know how much he appreciated your assistance in his time of need, and how much my Father, the Eastern Shield, will appreciate your continued services at this time. Take time to rest until Lord Stanyard arrives, and he will advise you further."

Mirelle saw them relax a bit. She gestured for them to leave ahead of her. Once they had all filed out of Merridon's library, she and Kimbur turned to the two guards at the door. "Where is the key that locks this door?"

The Guard on the right produced a small gold key, holding it in the air before her.

"I will take that now." Mirelle held her hand out for it.

Wordlessly, the Guard surrendered it, then saluted. Mirelle locked the doors to Merridon's library. Then she told them, "Should anyone want entrance, they will require my permission."

Both Guards replied, "Yes, Your Highness."

And she and Kimbur returned to her chambers.

"Mother," Mirelle called. She had only been in her mother's chambers once, and had been so new to the Palace that she hadn't taken stock of her surroundings at the time.

This time, Mirelle had a chance to take in some of the interior while her mother crossed the room. A plush, plum carpet covered the chill stone floor, and a number of detailed art pieces hung upon the walls, including a wedding portrait of her and Father.

A crystal vase held freshly cut red and white roses from the garden below, and Mirelle suspected that they were replaced daily. A dark, mahogany mantel surrounded the hearth, where a lively fire snapped and warmed the entire chamber.

"Mirelle, dear. How are you this afternoon, child? Have you taken lunch yet? I just rang for lunch. Come, come into the solar with me." And Mother guided Mirelle by the elbow into her solar.

Mirelle had a chance to glance at Kimbur, who gave the tiniest shrug. Lunch was not the ideal way to tell Mother the news of her stepson's death, especially now that Mirelle saw the red rims about her eyes. She'd been crying – concern over Father – and Kendrick and Keldrick – at war. And now she was going to tell her that Merridon had passed away. Such rotten timing, not just over lunch but so soon after Father had left.

One of Mother's servants appeared. "Lunch for three, please, thank you," and the servant hastened off immediately. "Wine?" Mother offered Mirelle and Kimbur goblets of white wine, but they both declined.

Mother glided to her balcony with her goblet of wine. "I do love the view here. You see the Royal Forests and even some of the Mantle Mountains beyond them. Don't you like it?"

"Of course, Mother," answered Mirelle automatically, standing at her side.

"Now," Mother said around a sip of wine, "did you want to see me for something, or was this a social call? I do hope it was the latter." And she smiled.

Mirelle's heart sank. She drew in a deep breath. "I'm afraid I come with bad news, actually, Mother."

Mother huffed and raised her eyebrows. "Bad news? You mean worse than your father and brother off in the EverWinters at war, and Keldrick in the West who knows where in Clemongard at war? Worse than that?" She shook her head and sipped again at her wine, staring out over the balcony of her solar.

Mirelle rolled her eyes to one side. Would a murderer on the Palace grounds count? But she wouldn't tell Mother that.

"Actually, Mother, it's Merridon." And she paused.

Mother turned and stared at her. "Merridon! Is he well? Is he asking for me?"
Mirelle wondered just how close Merridon and Mother had ever been. "No, Mother," she replied gently. "He – passed on – in the night." Such a kind way to phrase it, given what had occurred.

Mother's mouth dropped into an "o". She was silent for a moment, but then asked, "How is it that you know of this before I do?"

"The Healers informed me first because I am his only blood relative remaining on the grounds. I told them that I would tell you myself."

"Of course, of course. I should have thought of that," mused the Queen. "And Rhutgard so far away…" She sighed. Tears formed in her eyes and she immediately produced a handkerchief to dab them away with. "I – should have seen him more." She sniffed. "You were – using him as a tutor. Such a brilliant mind he – had." She stumbled over the need to speak of him in the past, then she looked down. "Your Father and he played Ice together each week, and most often, your Father would come back amazed at just how exceptional Merridon… was. His was a life wasted, he would tell me. Your Father will be so crushed…."

"Merridon made me nervous at first, when I came here, a blushing young bride. For he was the son of your Father's first wife, and a daily symbol at first that I needed to bear fruit." She smiled through the tears that rolled down her reddened cheeks, though she was still beautiful, thought Mirelle. Aware that Mirelle was watching her, the Queen shook her head at the thought of her younger self's folly. "I was hardly older than you, my dear, just nineteen. Eighteen when

I was betrothed, nineteen when I wed your father, and just past twenty when I bore you three. I was never so relieved. And Merridon was a very sweet child, he loved me immediately, even though I was only his stepmother."

Mirelle thought then how Merridon's personality had not changed, for he had immediately welcomed her, tutoring her daily, when he normally preferred to speak to no one at all. He really had been very kind. But she could not allow emotion to overtake her now, for she was here to walk through the coming few days with Mother.

"I've sent for Lord Stanyard," she told Mother. "Merridon drew up paperwork that insisted on very little ceremony, only the bare minimum, which Lord Stanyard knows how to assist with," Mirelle ventured.

"Ah, Lord Stanyard." And Mother swallowed at her wine. Mirelle took that to mean that they had navigated through their differences in their past.

"Well," Mirelle pointed out delicately, "Merridon's paperwork specifically calls for him, and he is Father's chief advisor. He will need to serve in Father's place, for Father cannot return now."

Mother pursed her lips with distaste. "I understand." Then she stared out at the view from the balcony again. "It's almost as if Merridon planned this - waited to pass on until Rhutgard was away at war and could not be present," she mused aloud, her face thoughtful.

Lunch arrived and Kimbur busied herself assisting the servant, though her face was alarmed. Mirelle found her mouth dry and had nothing to say. Mother was not stupid, but neither would she imagine Merridon capable of what he had planned over the last two years, much less three months.

"Come, Mother, lunch has arrived, you'll feel better with food in your stomach," Mirelle coaxed. Chopped chicken and strawberries, toasted wheat bread and garlic butter with chives, creamy cucumber soup, and a board of several cheeses with sliced pears and plums, along with several cherry-cheese pastries were laid upon Mother's solar table.

Mother sighed and said, "I suppose you're right." Then she took Mirelle by the shoulders, looked her up and down, and lifted her chin. She smoothed Mirelle's blue and ivory dress out. Then she sighed. "My poor daughter. Not even here a year yet and you'll be wearing mourning."

Ishbel

She heard boots stop inside her pavilion, silver clinking on her bureau. Again? Gobin was outdoing himself this week. And Ishbel was not in the mood. This one was going to get a handjob and that was it. And if the bastard complained, then it was his word against Ishbel's. Most of the time, Gobin believed Ishbel.

A voice cleared behind her.

Rogue? Ishbel turned around in amazement. "Well, you took your time returning, didn't you?" she drawled. She wandered over to him and looked him up and down.

He raised a sardonic eyebrow. "I did tell you I would be a while returning, did I not?"

"Aye, so you did. I didn't expect you to take two months, though."

"Perhaps you'd like me to rent a carriage, next time," Rogue returned. "And just what are you doing, jabbing me about like that." He grabbed her hand. "Looking for contraband?"

Ishbel sniffed. "If I cared about every man who snuck in here with some form of contraband, I'd be a nun. Checking for broken ribs, open wounds, gashes, and the like."

Rogue grinned. "Of those, you won't find any."

"Expect me to believe you went near two months on the road without a drop of blood spilt? Not falling for that one."

"I didn't say that. None of my own blood was spilled. I can't speak for any others I came across, though."

She sighed and patted his face with her free hand. "What happened to 'go forth and commit more acts of meritous behavior?'"

"That might have fallen by the way side. And whatever are you doing to my hand?" He pulled his hand up where she had laced her fingers between his.

"You've a bump, between your middle two fingers, is it a callous?" Ishbel asked. She'd never noticed it before, that was odd.

He unlaced his fingers and said, "Callous, yes, a bit," his voice odd. Rogue turned away and said, "So, am I forgiven? For I have a gift for you." He sat down on her bed, looking at her expectantly.

The breeze blew the tiny bells in her pavilion so that they tinkled ever so slightly. "Rogue, you know I can't accept gifts." Nevertheless, she crawled onto the bed out of sheer curiosity.

He produced from his rucksack another book. A book? Again? She despised reading. Due to the terms of their arrangement, she had read the first book, and she knew it perfectly now, but only because it was business, not pleasure. And so, Ishbel was now acquainted with all the history, however basic, of the whole of the Land. After she'd read the little book from front to back and no longer had to follow along with a finger to pronounce words, she recognized that the book was likely a child's book. She didn't care. It was stuffed in the exact center of the bottom of the mattress, in a small rip, so that if Gobin for some reason pulled the mattress up, he would see nothing.

Over the last three weeks, with all these horrid mercenaries, Ishbel found herself thinking of the words on the page rather than pleasing the bastards, and that was dangerous. An educated whore was a liability to her master, and she did not want the lash on her back. A bored whore, however, was even worse when it came to mercenaries such as were buying armor in the City, and then taking their pleasure with the whores. They were barbarian. Gobin was even afraid of them. Ishbel had twice been to the baths this week.

"Ishbel?" Rogue inquired. "You are distant today."

She sighed. "I read the other book – I know it perfectly," she added in a low voice.

"And?"

"A History of the Lands – a child's version, I expect."

"Nevertheless. This book is not a child's version, it is a History of the Era of this Era. If Gobin finds it, tell him you can't possibly read it and that I forgot it when last I visited, so you are holding it until I return."

"This book will be harder for you to read, but I know you can read it."

"Why do you want me to read anything? Find you a wife, teach her to read. Rogue, my job isn't to read, it's to...." And boldly, she laid a hand on his upper thigh.

He didn't startle at her hand, which surprised her, but he did ask, "And do you like your job, Ishbel?"

Shrewd, damn the man. "I'm good at it."

"That's not what I asked. Do you like your job?"

"...Sometimes, yes. I've no choice, it matters not. I perform my job either way, for I belong to Gobin."

"And you also belong to me –" Rogue laid his hand atop hers where it rested on the inside of his thigh. He picked her hand up and sat it in her lap. "But I pay you as an employer pays an employee, not as a slave. And so I ask that you read this book, so that you might learn more of the world around you. For war is happening, and you need to know why and who and where. Just as I need to hear what is happening inside this City, you need to know what is happening outside of it."

Ishbel stared at him. He was using her as an actual employee. That was why he paid her all the time. Finally, she nodded. "Give me the book."

Rogue smiled. The leather-bound book – ha! Was enormous. She would never read the entire thing. She stuffed it under the mattress and he took the child's book back. Ishbel would have to cut a larger hole in the mattress for this book.

"Now, tell me why you look so exhausted," Rogue said.

"Mercenaries and Free Riders. Brutes, the lot of them. No more Stordish, no soldiers. Just mercs and Free Riders."

"Then why does Gobin allow them in?"

"They scare Gobin, too. Pavilion City is overrun with them, here to buy armor, ringmail, weapons and such, then they take a whore before they leave. Even the horses are mostly gone now. But they're all here in droves, and hardly a decent one of them in the bunch." Ishbel grimaced.

"I've heard," Rogue commented experimentally, "that the one way to tell the difference between Free Riders and mercs is that Free Riders don't get involved in the wars."

"Well, whoever told you that was a bloody idiot," returned Ishbel. She yawned and immediately said, "So sorry – it's not the company."

Rogue's eyes narrowed. "Are these mercs, are they abusive?"

Ishbel smiled – he was being protective of her, even if it was just because she was his employee. "Rarely. Gobin would throw them out, bare-arsed and all. Can't bruise the fruit, least not on the outside. But what men don't understand – snatches are like horses, you can only whip them so many times before they fall down. They have to get a bit of rest, a bit of water, before they can go back to haulin' men again."

"I learned that my first year, from a woman who'd been a whore near twenty years." Ishbel paused, remembering that woman, now long sold away. She never thought to tell that to a man before. But perhaps it was as Rogue insisted on this platonic relationship that made her blurt out such a thing.

She glanced sideward at him. His expression was comical, a mixture of interest and distaste. She grinned and stood up to light the candles in her room. He was her last customer of the night and already the sounds of Pavilion City were quiet, customers had left for the evening, and merchants were packing up their wares. The time between twilight and evenfall was her favorite – no more customers, just the quiet of her own thoughts, the tinkling of the bells in her pavilion, a cool breeze to lull her to sleep....

Ishbel woke in the middle of the night. A quick glance saw that her linens had been changed out.... Rogue had set up wet linens so that they might be changed out for her. He was an amazing man, she mused sleepily....

Then she heard even breathing from – beside her. She looked to the side on the floor. Rogue. He had snuck back in and was asleep on the grass matt where he'd slept the last time he'd stayed overnight. He was using his rucksack for a pillow. Ishbel studied the outline of his face in the darkness. He seemed at peace, probably the only time he ever was at peace.

Somehow, she felt much better knowing he was in the room. She fell asleep staring at his face.

Selby

The hell of every god had opened up once Rockdale Pass let out the Ambsells. The clanging of swords had rung all about her and her Ericorian stood before her to protect the flight of arrows. Several had actually hit within her range, even struck her Ericorian right before her eyes. Such was why she wore a helmet, she thought, even though it felt unwieldy. But she was moved whenever the fighting line pushed forward, even though she would have preferred to be on the battlefield itself, fighting with her men. Now her tent was on the top of a small copse, which offered a bit of protection and gave her a better view.

For the most part, it seemed interminable, watching her men slash their swords in the air, duck behind shields, and fall to the Ambsells. At times, they pushed the Ambsells back, and others the Ambsells drove them back. And all the while, she heard a drummer drum war songs out. Had he nothing better to do?

Her colonels occasionally consulted her, and Selby numbly directed them to drive eastward or westward.

Finally, a lull came at midday. The Ambsells withdrew toward Rockdale Mountain. Men drank greedily from waterskins and attended to wounds. Selby called for a War Council.

When only half of her Council met her, her brow furrowed. "Gorgovish? Tellanar?" She looked around. "Millick?"

The Council members coughed and looked down or away. Selby sighed. "I see."

Ambassador Keldrick joined them just then, ducking under the tent flap. "My apologies for my tardiness, Your Majesty. I was on the other side of the camp." He bowed.

Selby removed her helmet. "Casualty count? Reports?"

"Six thousand dead, some two thousand wounded, Your Majesty," replied Colonel Berolt, whose armor was encrusted with blood, though Selby suspected it was not his own.

"Reports?"

"I've three scouts who tell me that more troops are coming through the pass, Your Majesty...." The Lieutenant who told her this looked sick as he reported this.

"No matter, we have siege weapons on their way – they will be here by end of afternoon," reported Captain Tomerond.

"Captain, all due respect, what good will that do if our camp has been overrun?"

"Do you really think we will be overrun by late afternoon, sir? So soon?"

Selby spoke up and told them, "Both of you, enough. We cannot count on what we do not yet have. Plan for it, yes, count on it, no. Assume we will not see those siege weapons. But also plan to keep the whole of our fight on the pass. We cannot let more of them through or any siege weapons we may have will, if we are overrun and have to retreat, fall into their hands, and that we cannot afford."

"Your Majesty, a rider has arrived," called a guard from outside her tent.

"Send him in," she returned.

In came a harried-looking scout, exhaustion plain upon his face.

He bowed before her. "Your Majesty."

"Have you an update?"

"Yes, Your Majesty. Central Cliff Watch has been breached. Men on the beaches at Gull Port. We were ambushed there. By Ormon ships. We lost fifteen ships. They lost twelve, but four ships made it to the beaches of Gull Port."

No one said a word for a moment at first. Selby's heart plummeted.

"They're caught between both rivers... they won't be able to get far, not right away," she said faintly, glad she had pushed for moving her men on the southern border to Central Cliff Watch.

"They'll be able to get through the fortifications soon enough," General Stonefield told her.

"But our own ships will land at Gull Port in response as well, General. We agreed upon that." Selby sighed. Her head was throbbing suddenly.

"Are you well, Your Majesty?" asked a Lieutenant whom she did not recognize.

"No, Lieutenant, no I am not. There are Ormons on my land from the East, having burned my ships to get there. There are Ambsells who have killed my men all over the battlefield just out there, and they wait to kill more men. They all want Clemongard. So no, Lieutenant, I am not well." Selby turned and looked about the tent. "How do we drive them back?"

The men in her tent glanced at each other uneasily.

"Very well. If we have no answers, then I shall supply one, at least. Send two riders, one to Holland Fort, one to Moss Grove, have them split their strength and send it Gull Port. The second half, send here. Are you in agreeance?" Selby barely waited for ayes and nays before she stepped outside to dispatch a Guard with the message.

"Your Majesty – this is just a lull. We need to see you safely back to your quarters," pointed out General Stonefield.

"A lull."

"A break in the fighting."

"I'm aware of what a lull is, General. But we must see to our men on the field, those wounded, those dead. And reform in a such a way that gives them pause to think we have more men – until we are spelled by those from Holland Fort and Moss Grove. That won't be at least two hours yet."

"Yes, Your Majesty. But you must return to your quarters. The fighting may resume at any moment."

Ambassador Keldrick stepped forward. "If you please, Your Majesty. I'm not commanding a unit, I can escort you to your quarters."

"Very well," Selby returned, feeling like a child out of bed after curfew. Ambassador Keldrick gestured before him, but she waited for her Ericorian to follow her.

As soon as they stood before their horses, the Ambassador grabbed her reins. "If Your Majesty would be so kind as to replace her helmet...?"

Selby glared at him but saw that the Prince from Romeny was not going to relent. He had gone from Ambassador to body guard. If they made it out of this alive, she would be sure to speak highly of him to his father for this.

As she wound her braid about her head so that she could replace her helmet, Selby studied the Ambassador. Blood was encrusted in several places on his armor, and she didn't think it was his. Sweat had trailed down through the grime on his face – he had fought dearly for his life out on the field of battle – for her country – and won. Selby could not help but respect him.

He handed her the helmet and Selby fit it onto her head. She swung up onto her horse and waited until he was ahead of her on his horse.

The battlefield was littered with soldiers. While many of them were her Clemongardian, and even a few Ericorian, a fair number were Ambsell. Her nostrils flared with distaste when she saw the gore, the opened wounds still seeping, the indelicate nature of some of the death wounds.... And everywhere upon the grass was blood; her horse's hooves were slick with it.

And then there was a distant *"Take cover!"* screamed from the tent halfway down the hill they had just vacated. Selby didn't recognize the sound of arrows whizzing through the sky at first but they landed in the grass about her with tiny thuds.

Then her horse reared, screaming in pain. An arrow protruded from its neck.

"Selby, jump!" yelled Ambassador Keldrick.

Her horse was falling to the ground beneath her and she had just enough time to launch herself from her saddle lest she be crushed beneath him. Ambassador Keldrick wheeled his horse around and held out an arm. It was so surreal....

But an Ambsell was running toward her. How had an Ambsellon soldier gotten this far? A scout? Running directly for her, running like a mad man – and she had no time to draw her sword!

Her cleaver – she pulled it from her waist. She recalled ArmsMaster Andeval's lessons – what it was like to kill a man.

Selby saw the Ambsell's sword arc up and saw her opportunity – she reached inward and sliced the man's neck open. Blood sprayed all over her. She jumped to the side to avoid his sword, narrowly missing it.

Somewhere, in the back of her conscious, she heard the Ambassador yell, *"Selby!"* again. Looking at her dripping cleaver, and then at the man whose life she had just taken, she chastised herself for not using her shield instead.

"Selby!" It was the Ambassador, in front of her, on his horse, ducking arrows.

She held up her arm and he hauled her up into the saddle before him. He kicked the horse into a full gallop and immediately, they dashed up the hill toward her quarters. Ericorian were surrounding her from the back and guards had packed up her tent, moving it back out of range.

Finally, they were out of arrow range. "Thank you," she told the Ambassador breathlessly. "You've saved my life."

Over her shoulder, he cleared his throat awkwardly. "Of course, Your Majesty."

Selby was struck then. She glanced at him over her shoulder. "You called me Selby back there."

He coughed. "It was shorter than Your Majesty. Necessary. Your Majesty." But he smiled a small bit. "We shall have to find you a new horse once we break for camp. A good, strong courser, I think, trained well."

Then he paused. "How – how are you?"

"I'm not injured, if that's what you mean."

"Well, many people, after they've – taken a life for the first time, they are – a bit upset by it."

Ah. Understandable, mused Selby. "I don't have the time to be upset about it. He would have killed me. It was him or me. Although I am covered in his blood, aren't I…. Bother."

"Truly the Cleaver Queen now," remarked the Ambassador. "Your first weapon of choice when killing a man was your cleaver."

Mirelle

"I will be seen – tell her I am out here before I make more of a racket!"

Mirelle blinked sleepily and sat up. In the shadows of her bedchamber, she saw Kimbur advancing toward the door as she pulled her robe about her.

Who would be banging on her door at this time of night?

She heard Kimbur in the corridor, oblivious to the apologies of the Guards, say, "Lord Stanyard, you will lower your voice! Her Highness is asleep! Whatever business you have with her can wait until the morning hours!"

Ah. Lord Stanyard had arrived, and in excellent time. He would not stand for Kimbur's excuses much longer. Mirelle slid from her bed and pulled a mantle about her.

"Lord Stanyard, 'tis an odd time to be visiting, don't you think?" She yawned as she stood in the open door of her chambers. All her guards saluted.

"Don't you play coy with me, Your Highness. You –"

"Perhaps we can speak down the corridor, yes? That is, if you can contain yourself?" Mirelle raised her eyebrow suggestively.

Lord Stanyard, incensed, nevertheless followed her down the corridor a bit, along with Kimbur. Kimbur stopped the guards at a respectful pace.

"You, young woman, had best have an incredible reason for insisting I return in all urgency. I rode three horses to get here, one near foundered. If I find that you read that paperwork and are simply confounded as to what to do, you shall bear my wrath," he hissed.

"My lord, need I remind you to whom you speak?" snapped Kimbur.

Lord Stanyard continued on relentlessly. "Explain yourself, Your Highness. For once I returned, I found the Capital City still standing and Her Majesty, the Queen very much alive and in good health and now we stand whispering in corridors like thieves. What required such urgency on your part?"

Mirelle was irate now herself. She bowed her head that she might whisper to the stubborn man. "The walls hear all, do they not?" She cleared her throat. "Merridon was found murdered. His throat was cut in the night. Is that urgent enough for you, my lord?"

Incredulity replaced the wrath in Lord Stanyard's face. He stared from Kimbur to Mirelle, his mouth agape. "But how – why?"

"Only one of those questions I have an answer for. When he was so close to death, it seemed a waste of effort, a terrible risk to take."

"Is that why I was denied entrance, then," he wondered aloud. "You have locked the library purposely."

"Of course. Regardless of how, Lord Stanyard, a member of the Royal Family lies dead in that room. No one should be allowed in to see him without permission of his next of kin, and that is me. Until we move him for burial purposes, there is where he will remain."

Lord Stanyard did not look happy but agreed. "I need to see him," he said, "for official purposes."

Mirelle nodded and pulled her mantle tighter about her. "Let us away to the library, then."

Kimbur handed Lord Stanyard a wall torch and the three of them walked somberly to Merridon's library.

She produced the golden key that Mother had given her a chain to keep about her neck on. Lord Stanyard held his hand out for it, but she refused him. His eyes narrowed in the torchlight, but he stepped aside.

Mirelle clicked the door lock open, and torches held high, the three of them entered the darkened library together.

The Healers had provided blocks of ice near Merridon's bedside to keep his body cool. He was wrapped in silk and linen, awaiting burial in the tombs beneath the castle.

Kimbur stepped back, for she did not want to see the body again. Nor did Mirelle, but she had a duty to perform. She hoped this was the last time she would need to. She watched as Lord Stanyard delicately unwound the silk wrappings, but looked away as he studied Merridon's face and throat.

Must he take so long, she wondered irritably. Then she realized that perhaps he was saying good-bye, for he remembered Merridon as a child.

Finally, Lord Stanyard sighed. "Merridon, my boy, you didn't deserve this, not any of it. May you be at peace now." And at the corner of Mirelle's eye, she saw him rewrapping Merridon with great care.

She stood aside, waiting for Lord Stanyard to ready himself.

"Your mother, does she know?"

"I thought it best not to tell her. She is very – fragile, just now," answered Mirelle. "Besides, the fewer people who know, the better."

"Just as well, just as well. She would not take lightly to this."

"The Healers are waiting for you to speak with them. Some of them are concerned that the killer may come after them for knowing too much. I have told them that they are free to leave the Palace as soon as you have interviewed them. That is why they have extra guards outside the Healer's Quarters."

"Why would an assassin kill a Healer? Nonsense," said Lord Stanyard in a dismissive tone.

Irritated, Mirelle responded, "Why would an assassin kill Merridon?"

"Hmm, yes. It is my guess that whoever killed him did not know that he had abdicated the throne in favor of Kendrick. Perhaps whoever it was thought to strike out at your Royal Father. In fact," and then he paused and wandered around, stroking his chin.

"Lord Stanyard?" Mirelle prompted.

"With Merridon gone, Kendrick at war in the East, Keldrick at war in the West...." Lord Stanyard glanced up sternly at Mirelle. "We shall need to keep a very close guard on you, for all know just how much effort Rhutgard went into protecting you. Daughters bear the bloodline truest. And now, with your father and all three sons out of the way, where something as simple as a chance arrow might kill them, that leaves you out in the open, unprotected. I think that assassin may only have been delivering a message. And I think that he may still be in Fairview, either on the grounds or in the city.

"Your Highness, we shall need to keep a very close guard on you."

Mirelle stared at him in the torchlight. An assassin! To kill her!

— ⸎ —

Merridon, now entombed with his forbears beneath the Palace, his bedroom now no longer a bedroom but a second library of sorts. And he had been right; few people recalled he had still been alive, so certainly there had been no need for a ceremony and funeral. Mirelle missed him already. Though these black gowns did not help. When others asked why she and the Queen dressed in mourning, they simply replied that a beloved family member had passed away.

Lord Stanyard directed her specifically, and later the Queen as a matter of caution rather than what it truly was, to watch for ice and water on stairwells, strange people and guards, odd people about the Palace, and anyone with weapons. The Queen had been dismissive but promised to be more careful now with no male family members in residence, while Mirelle promised to exceptionally more careful, to the point of not eating new dishes or even anything that smelled odd. If Lord Stanyard was concerned, than Mirelle believed she, too, should be concerned. No more long rides, no visiting destinations outside the Palace. A long list had been given her privately that he had insisted she promise to obey, as the King's daughter and the truest of the bloodline. Kimbur promised to watch for her as well, so Mirelle felt something of a prisoner and a little paranoid as well.

Lord Stanyard had been dispatched back to Father's side, where what he told Father, Mirelle could only imagine. As to a would-be assassin, she was sure such a person was gone, but Lord Stanyard thought he might be waiting for time to pass before striking again....

Shadow

She had worked the floor for a week at The Laughing Pelican to make up how much she owed Larcy for the shoes, though she'd had to wait until the Stordish soldiers had left town.

And what a celebratory mood the Port Stanton was in. When the skippers of two different fishing berths came in, reporting that they had seen Royal Navy ships sitting in the bay, the whole town whooped and hollered, supposing that maybe the Navy had chased off the Western soldiers' ships, and that maybe they wouldn't be visited by the Westerners anymore.

Shadow wondered privately if the message she'd sent to King Rhutgard had gotten through, and if so, if these ships were the result. She certainly hoped so, for then these people could leave and return again by ship. But not Shadow. She had had enough of soldiers, no matter whose they were. She would walk as far as she could along the coastline, then take a boat across the RiverLands to the Coastals. Shadow wanted out of the East and all its deceptions.

Larcy remarked one day, "Mitzie, it's as if you were born to work tables, you're so good at it." Shadow had kept a smile to herself, for she wasn't born to wait on anyone.

But finally, when Larcy told her that her debt was paid in full, Shadow said she'd leave in the morning. Both Larcy and her cousin said they could use the help around the bar during the off-season, if she was willing to trade for room and board, but Shadow wanted to be off.

"Well, all right then, have it your way. Lots of girls would want a roof over their head and free room and board, Mitzie. I don't know where you're going that's got a fire lit under your tail so, but you need to be careful. A girl traveling alone – she's not safe, you know. It's not just soldiers you have to watch for, it's dishonest types in general."

In the end, the next morning, Larcy's cousin arranged for Shadow to ride with a pickled fishmonger and she could catch a ride with him the next morning, for he was going to Ferrisport and then stopping at Chesterport, where he would restock with his supplier. It would be a three-day trip, if she didn't mind traveling with him, but at least she wouldn't be walking. Of course, Shadow had accepted gladly, and took a place in the back of the wagon.

Eventually, she got used to the rumbling of the empty barrels, the faint leftover smell of pickled fish, the stony road, and the occasional spitting to the side of the road that her traveling companion, Wilhelm, made.

Mostly, Shadow dozed under the wagon cover, though once Wilhelm was stopped by a pair of Royal Crown soldiers who asked where he was headed. Once he told them he had a wagon full of empty pickled fish barrels he was taking back to Chesterport to restock, they seemed inclined to believe him and told him to be on his way. Shadow wondered what about Wilhelm made him more believable. Did he have an honest face, or just appear to be a merchant more than others on the road? What would Wilhelm have said if they had looked under the canvas wagon cover?

They arrived slept under the stars the first night, and Wilhelm allowed her to sleep in the wagon, while he slept on the grass in a horse blanket. The second night, they reached Ferrisport, and he slept in The Barn Owl Inn, while Shadow slept in the stable, glad of a roof above her head that did not smell like pickled fish and moldy canvas. She had enough copper chips to buy herself a bowl of fish soup and a cup of mead. One last day would get her free of her silent traveling companion, though she had no idea what Chesterport had to offer, nor if soldiers were camped there.

But Ferrisport was much in the same celebratory mood as Port Stanton – Shadow heard talk of the Royal Navy ships sitting offshore, and townspeople wondered if that meant the Western soldiers would not be returning.

Chesterport was a half day's ride away. Shadow attempted to pay the fishmonger, but he shook his head. She suspected that money had already exchanged hands on her behalf back in Port Stanton. She also suspected that he was quite glad to be rid of her. Well, she was glad to be in Chesterport on her own, though she kept Larcy's words to heed – watching for soldiers.

It was after she had determined that the town was safe from the Western soldiers that Shadow felt free enough to explore Chesterport for an inn. She paid for a room at the Cast-A-Net Inn, though the innkeeper looked at her with a stern eye. Shadow glared back at him and made as if to leave. He finally said, "Third floor, back room. No trouble." Ha. She couldn't agree more.

But as she was exploring the town on how to find a way to the next port, Shadow fell in behind a group of Crown soldiers. She had learned to walk silently and so they never knew she was there.

"Hey, Bandster, I know of a way to make a little extra coin on the side. Sound like somethin' you'd be willin' to take part in?"

The other soldier studied him for a moment. "Nah. This don't sound legal-like. My wife, she just had our first child and I can't get in no trouble for nothin', leave her on the high and dry. But I tell you who, who might would be interested, you know that Ragom? We always call him Rag. He's just the kind who'd help out on this, ah, venture you're talkin' about. Big guy. Bald. Scar by his left ear. Tell him I sent you so he knows you're legit."

Shadow sighed to herself. Soldiers were soldiers. This didn't sound good at all. And if she saw a bald man with a scar behind his left ear, she would avoid him like the plague.

She hated dishonesty. But she couldn't turn in all the dishonest men she ran across, could she. She wondered what the proposal was. Probably smuggling or some such idiocy. An arrangement with the local fishermen, or the Navy for a cut.

Maybe she'd follow the first soldier and see what sort of scheme he was involved in. But Shadow was more interested in moving south. She hoped that not all the soldiers she ran across were involved in schemes and rackets. She just wanted to get to the Coastals.

Reaghann

Reaghann paced about his study. He had sent out so many directives, he was unsure of what was left next. He was exhausted, as well. Much of his work he had accomplished on his way home from Romeny, but a fair pile he found awaiting him when he returned. Damn this war.

Finally, he flung himself into his chair and drummed his fingers upon the mahogany.

Almost guiltily, his eyes strayed toward his upper right-hand drawer. He knew no one would have opened it or gone through it... but....

On a whim, he pulled it open and riffled through the paperwork inside it. Still in the same order he left it. Lady Green Eyes had left. But he had held out some hope when he'd seen her handwriting, signed *Anonymous*, back at Fairview Palace.

Idiot, he scolded himself.

Well, at least he knew he wasn't being observed. He'd covered up the spyhole from the outside. Listened to, well, that Reaghann would never be able to guarantee. But he had dismissed half his Cabinet as well as the members Lady Green Eyes had warned him about. He'd replaced them with new Lords and Councilors, some of whom, it seemed, had truly taken their new posts seriously in his absence.

He wondered if Lord Drury had been seen, or if he was colluding with anyone. Reaghann hoped neither, especially the latter. Hardewold was immensely difficult to police due to its size. Worse, no one would believe that a man of Lord Drury's integrity would be capable of such crimes, and so no Wanted posters were distributed. Only word of mouth among select individuals.

His Crown Captains reported that Prince Rilstrom had not been found. Reaghann started a bit at the news, then nearly smiled. He now had a loyal Guard. He dismissed the search on the part of King Rickstan.

No Western galleons had been spotted in his waters, neither along the coastline nor in the Treasure Sea. Reaghann was not sure if only the number of soldiers who had been sent through to the EverWinters had been previously agreed upon, or if they knew they had been discovered and stopped sending men. In either instance, Reaghann's Navy now owned the sea again. He distinctly believed that something under the table had taken place, allowing those galleons through, keeping his own men far out at sea, unaware of what was transpiring. However, it was too late to unravel the mystery now, with him going to war. At least ten ships would be docked at each port, and another ten stationed in that port's waters, watching for incoming ships from the West. Two hundred more would be stationed around the Sea Straights, and two hundred more at sea in random formation at the south of the Wet Lands. If – if he had to send the Clemongard Queen ships, he could spare one hundred and that would make it tight... but sending ships around that far would likely be seen by the Coastals, especially if they were going to be called in to war by the Northern Countries. Undoubtedly, they had assumed attack formations to prevent assistance from the East as his Navy had from the West. And by attack formations, he meant for his Admirals to fire at will. There would be no Twenty Years War if he could help it....

But his Captains had given him strange reports from the South. People going missing, ships and merchants, both by land and sea.... From Southend and west. He didn't like it, he didn't like it at all. Not pirates, too bold for pirates. There was no reporting it to Rhutgard now, of course, that the Eastern Shield was already in the EverWinters somewhere. Reaghann would have to take care of it himself. Damn.

And what was he to do, when he had a war to plan?

He sighed and slammed the right-hand drawer of his desk shut.

Driscoll

An entire army marched at his back. He couldn't say that made him feel any better. Driscoll had felt young and invigorated nearly forty some years ago, the last time this had happened. He'd fought the entirety of the Twenty Years War, fought it and had the scars to show for it. And his daughters.

Now, the Heir to Delsynth, the Crown Prince rode by his side, Dougall, and Driscoll couldn't be prouder of him. His son had acquitted himself as a young man staring at the start of a war should during the War Council in Romeny.

Driscoll had five daughters, one of whom had married Rhutgard all those years ago when he was still a prince, Aolynn, but died in the child bed. If he tried, he could just remember her voice....

He still had four daughters older than Dougall, all married, and three sons, two of them squires at fourteen and twelve, and one ten. Of two wives, both now deceased, Driscoll would one day depart the land having left it with nine children. He thought that a fine legacy.

His first son would ride only another day with him, then split off with the Stafford Spears and archers, that they might follow the mountain line and come about to flank Driscoll's formation two days' hence. He himself would stay with the cavalry and infantry. They were riding slower than preferable, but they also had siege machines from Blade Fort. He'd sent two catapults and a trebuchet to the Clemongard Queen, and so he felt himself quite justified in keeping the rest for himself. They'd had no word back from Keldrick before Driscoll had left, so he had no idea if the Queen needed such weapons or not, but the more, the better, in his opinion.

And, in his opinion, he was quite glad it was not Driscoll being attacked on all sides by Ambsellons and Ormons and possibly even Stordish. Driscoll stole a glance at his son, who looked both pensive and stern in his armor as he rode next to him. Driscoll couldn't imagine what Rhutgard was thinking, or Kendrick, without Keldrick. And Gerard, for that matter, for Ronan had not yet returned, and Ronan was his heir.

War. This had not even begun and he hated it already.

Gerard

The last time he rode to war, he'd been a prince, and cocky, full of life at that. He'd ridden with his father, The Wolf of Ghiverny.

Now Gerard was The Wolf of Ghiverny, and the Wolf Claw sword rode at his hip. Was he a coward for wishing his father here with him? And where was his own son? Ronan should be here, along with Petran. The gods only knew where Ronan was, and if something had befallen him, then Eastern Shield be damned, Rhudy would pay for that fool's errand that left Keldrick over in the other side of the Land.

Instantly, Gerard felt terrible for that thought. Rhudy was in mourning, after all. Merridon had just died last week. Gerard would never forget Rhutgard's face when he read the news of his son dying.... Gerard had immediately sent everyone from the tent. Poor Rhudy – his face had just – fallen in on itself. And he'd tried so hard to maintain strength, out here, at war. Gerard had only seen Rhutgard's face like that once before, and that was when his father had passed.

Gerard had read the communication and immediately crossed the tent to envelope Rhudy in a bearhug. Some things you just put off when it came to the death of a child, and war was one of them. He wondered how his lifelong friend was faring. He was wearing a black cloak emblazoned with the Rose Sword of Romeny and few thought to ask why – they probably assumed it was his battle cloak, mused Gerard.

"Your Majesty, we have sighted scouts up ahead!" a serjeant broke into his thoughts.

"Whose scouts? Ours?"

"They wear Ormon colors, Your Majesty," claimed the sergeant.

"They weren't scouts. I'm a better scout than they are. They wanted to be seen." He sighed. "Which means, then, that they know we are here and want us to know that they know.

"Ormons aren't stupid soldiers. Their scouts would never be caught. Follow and pursue," Gerard told the sergeant. "Sergeant, send word to King Rhutgard."

The sergeant saluted and departed immediately.

Scouts were scouts only if they were not detected. Something was wrong here. Did the enemy think them so stupid as that? Was this an attempt to lure them into a trap?

And then an arrow whizzed past. Gerard hadn't heard the sound of an arrow for over twenty years but he certainly couldn't mistake it – it wasn't a sound he'd ever forget.

"Your Majesty! Take cover!"

Rhutgard

Rhutgard held his sword ready, its cross-guard already wet with blood. Where was Kendrick? Kendrick's directives were to stay behind him, not ride forward! Rhutgard did not need to lose another son, in particular, the Crown Prince and Eastern Shield to Be. He would deal with Kendrick later.

Another bloody bastard rode forward, whom he neatly dispatched – the man slumped forward as his horse carried him away. These were not Ormons, thought Rhutgard wildly – they fought with green and red checked shields. Stordish, he thought. They couldn't fight for a damn.

That was it, thought Rhutgard, they were sending the Stordish out first, to exhaust the Eastern Alliance Army. Then the Ormons would attack.

He wheeled his mount around and called for a withdrawal of troops. As he did so, an arrow took his horse in the leg.

Rhutgard had enough time presence of mind to jump from the horse before he was trapped beneath it.

An infantryman crept up to him, sword ready. Rhutgard swung and their swords clanged. Rhutgard threw his shield up to avoid the man's parry, then drove a forward stroke that slid between the soldier's ribs. He pulled his sword out of the man's body, watching the soldier slide onto the ground, dead, and turned for another opponent.

Rhutgard never thought to use the Rose Thorn sword in war – yet here he was in the middle of battle. Oddly, he wished for Luvian just now, for the last time he'd swung a sword, Luvian was behind him.

Another Stordish soldier raised his sword against him. Ha! Hardly more than a boy, thought Rhutgard with disgust as he swung his own sword about to dispatch the soldier. He moved to disengorge the soldier.

"Father!"

"Kendrick!"

Kendrick galloped into view. "Get on!"

"What the bloody hell are you doing out here! I told you –"

Two arrows whizzed past.

"Never mind that, Father, get the fuck up here!" Kendrick leaned down with an arm.

Rhutgard climbed upon his son's horse and they galloped out of the battle.

———

"Never mind I saved your bloody life –"

"By not following orders, you put your own life at risk. Did I not tell you to follow behind –"

"Do you want to hear what I found out, or do you want to keep giving me the Royal Chastisement?"

"Nothing I haven't figured out with my men already, Kendrick."

"These Stordish –"

"Are meant to serve as a vanguard only, to tire our troops out, yes I know, Kendrick."

"Were part of an arrangement between Varley and the Ice Queen – she is sending more troops as we speak down the Northern Countries Crossland. A dying soldier admitted that to me. That's why I came to find you."

Rhutgard was silent. Gerard! They had to get word to Gerard!

Kendrick voiced his thoughts. "We must get word to Uncle Gerard, Father. Runners, immediately."

"Sergeant! Find me scouts, now, and two cavalry men."

The soldiers who had witnessed the spat between Kendrick and him had been previously invisible but now sprang into action.

He directed each of the men what to say once they found Gerard's troops and then looked at his son.

"Walk with me."

Once they were out of earshot, he told Kendrick, "You did well to act as you did; such were the actions of a field captain. And I think you know how grateful I am for rescuing me – also the actions of a field captain. And a son." He permitted himself a small smile. "But son, Kendrick. This is a war – and you are under the command of the Eastern Shield. You cannot argue with the Eastern Shield, particularly not before the men. Do you understand that?"

"Even when he's wrong?" asked Kendrick in a low voice.

Cheeky little shit. So like himself. Father would have cuffed him for saying that, as would have Grandfather. But those were different times.

"Your next outburst of disrespect will cost you your Captaincy, Captain Firthing. Consider whom you're addressing." Rhutgard watched Kendrick's eyes grow round and the boy stood straighter, with the air of a soldier who had just been dressed down.

"Yes, sir!" There was no disrespect in Kendrick's tone and he stared straight ahead properly as a soldier should.

Ah. Much better. He would not have his soldiers complain of nepotism in the ranks.

But one thing remained.

"Thank you, Captain Firthing, for saving my life today."

Varley

He had remained camped west of Durcomb's Last Stand. People tended to overlook it due to its nature – Durcomb, who had changed sides in the Ten Legions Battle, was forever after known as a turncoat and his last stand, at the 4 Kings Fortress, was what brought the castle down to near rubble. Varley thought camping near Durcomb's Last Stand was quite apropos, given who was going to war against whom, and how his father had turned upon him, and how he would enjoy watching Queen Myrischka turn Storden to rubble. Yes, Varley quite preferred his location.

However, he had become impatient with it. He knew from reports that Myrischka's Navy had landed in Clemongard and also that she herself had likely landed in Northern Clemongard and set up camp, possibly even at Hewett's side, though Varley thought that unlikely.

Varley's men were also impatient. They had waited long enough. They wanted action, and they wanted blood. Soon enough, thought Varley. Soon enough. They would skirt the Stordish/Clemon border and take what was theirs. And then, he would turn south.

And take the Northern Countries' reserves. He knew the Ice Bitch was underestimating him and that made his plan all the more easier to carry out.

This time next week, the ground would be wet with blood.

A'dair

Je'hanna had settled into her role as Queen more easily than A'dair had anticipated. Of course, she had a veritable host of ladies-in-waiting at her side wherever she ventured, which assisted her. To his knowledge, she had made no faux pas of any serious degree.

He didn't pay close attention to her daily schedule, though, either. A'dair visited her mostly each night so that he might beget her with an heir. Now that war was upon them, the need for an heir was ever more vital.

And war was indeed, upon them, for A'dair had received a notice from the Queen of Ormon, demanding of him his Naval services as their partnership of old required. As to when and where he should send his Naval forces, he would receive word soon, but he was expected to be ready.

A'dair nearly threw the letter into the fire, but it had been Je'hanna who had stayed his hand. She warned him against such an action, and so, with great distaste, he looked at the letter daily upon the desk in his study. Nearly every ship he had would be going to this fool's errand.

He admitted that had been a clever move on the part of his new wife. A'dair liked that about her; she was smart. He hadn't courted either wife, this one he'd hardly searched for longer than two weeks before he'd begun betrothal proceedings. His advisors, those left, of course, were scandalized, but A'dair had not been concerned at all. War had been on the horizon, and he had had an oath to fulfill.

This wife was shrewd; she understood politics. Yet she had a sweet face, and kind brown eyes. Je'hanna was modest, and though she wore fashionable clothing, she didn't wear the plunging necklines that were stylish. She did not gossip amongst her ladies from what he had seen and she was well-liked by the servants. She had so far been a good Queen and A'dair was impressed. She would need to be a strong Queen, once the war started, however, for undoubtedly, he would be called away from the Palace and she would need to run Coral Palace on her own....

Romand

Romand walked the halls of ArkenHeights restlessly. He had known the day would arrive, it had only been a matter of when. The Ice Queen had finally sent her communication. His infantry and naval forces were to be made ready for her use at her command. Interestingly, he had not yet heard from Hewett, and it had been Hewett with whom he had most often communicated. Bother.

The Ormon Queen's communication was short and demanding, and told him that details would be sent forthwith, only to have his forces mobilized and alert.

Well, Romand had been fighting in wars since both monarchs' parents had been children and he knew a thing or two. All of Corstarorden's major cities were fortified and had been for years. After the Twenty Years War, Romand had seen to that, for troops from every nation had marched through Corstarorden to resupply. War was hardest on the little people, the commoner people, and while he could not protect his farmers, his parishes, and his villages because of this centuries-old Northern-Coastal Partnership, he could at least see that the towns and cities were stronger so that the farmers, parish folk and villagers might seek refuge there.

Romand expected he would be following his army into battle in Clemongard. Ah, he was too old for war. At sixty-five, he had no interest in it. His sons, Niall and Mandard, would be following him into war, for they were well-versed in war themselves, both being veterans of the Twenty Years War. Except this time, Romand would allow them far more latitude than when they were merely princes with rounded eyes, staring with amazement at the world about them. They had grown up in the era of the Twenty Years War – a painful way to mature, to be sure, watching men die at your hands. War changed every man, and twenty years of war made its mark upon his sons.

Romand had yet to inform his lady wife. Though a strong soul, Normandra, too, had lived through the Twenty Years War, and it had made its mark upon her. Such a kindly woman, he mused as he observed her across the morning table where they had begun taking their morning meals since he had arrived back at ArkenHeights. At sixty-five, she had aged admirably. Her hair, once platinum and shining, now was a beautiful white, and her cheeks were hardly lined at all.

Suddenly, Normandra smiled at him across the breakfast table. "Romand, you've been so quiet of late. What troubles you?"

Romand shook his head to shrug off his concerns.

"Romand, I know you better than that. I have been your Queen for almost fifty years now and I can tell when you're hiding something.

"It's the war, isn't it? Has the North asked for troops finally?"

Dumbly, Romand stared at her.

She tittered and set her napkin down on the table. "Romand, Romand. In all this time, you have learned so much about the land but never a thing about women." She stood up and placed a kiss on the top of his head. "I've been through twenty years of war already, I think I can handle a few more years."

Theldry

Cathall was good to his word – he had married Mina off to Edgard, and with a handsome wedding gift, as well. But the search for a lady-in-waiting went on. Jeanie supposed it had to do with the war. Cathall had fortified the estate, reinstating the old guardhouse and barracks with guards well beyond those who already lived upon the grounds.

As often as he traveled, Theldry felt better with guards posted at all the gates, as the estate had originally intended for. There was still room for more guards to be brought in, should the war come close, Cathall assured her, but he thought they were safe with the double guard he'd hired for now.

He'd taken to lavishing her with gifts of late. The finest of silk, satin, and cloth of gold gowns, trimmed with delicate lace and embroidery, in tasteful hues of green and blue that would bring her eyes out. Scents for her bath made of petal oils, special teas and honeys.

And gems – diamond earbobs that caught the sunlight as they danced below her ears, a new sapphire ring, and a gold and amethyst necklace.

Theldry felt guilty, for the one thing she knew Cathall wanted was a baby. And they tried every day that he was home, yet she still was not with child. Jeanie thought that it was due to Theldry being too young yet to conceive, and that she shouldn't fret so.

Theldry also suspected that many of these gifts were the result of Roarden North merchants selling their wares cheaply so that they might leave Corstarorden altogether for the East, or even Pavilion City, and that these merchants were in some way beholden unto Cathall.

"Relax, little duckling, enjoy it," clucked Jeanie as she brushed off a new blue velvet dress trimmed with lace. Theldry did not comment, for all of these gowns were without doubt, the highest of fashion and beautiful, but who was to see them? She held no court here at Mendellion. Only the villagers would see her in the Market and they wouldn't know if she was dressed gaudily or in the best of fashion and class.

But Cathall surprised her when he commissioned – and sat for – a portrait of the two of them. She wore an amethyst gown with her new amethyst necklace and diamond earbobs, which pleased him.

Theldry finally confronted Cathall about the lavishness of these sudden gifts. He told her that he would normally have taken her on at least one trip by sea by now, and taken her shopping in Roarden North. But political tensions were high and for safety's sake, he could not take her anywhere. He knew she was tired of sitting about the estate, so he was trying to bring a little liveliness to the estate. What a dear man he was for that, she thought.

But by political tensions, Theldry knew what was actually meant was "war". War was going on all around them – the Ormons and the Ambsellons had attacked Clemongard by land and by sea just north of Storden, and who knew if King Irving would be attacked. Even the Eastern Alliance was at war now. It was all the villagers spoke of, though Theldry chose not to tell Cathall that she knew of this.

The Coastal Countries were always called to help defend Ambsellon and Ormon, and Corstarorden was the first country to be called, Theldry knew. Cathall was trying to shield her from what he thought would frighten her, but the truth was, she wanted to know more.

The villagers spoke of nothing else, for they were easily frightened and knew nothing of the outside land beyond the small village of Mendellion. Theldry tired of calming them, for they all had the option of staying at the estate should they wish if soldiers ever came to the tiny village of Mendellion, which was unlikely. Jeanie told her to be patient with them, but if Theldry had told them once, she had told them a dozen times.

She was more concerned for her husband, who rode the roads, which were unsafe now that mercenaries were looming about, and Free Riders....

Renfry

If someone had told him that his future partner would be a runaway Silent Order brother, he would have belly laughed for hours. Certainly, he would have laughed if so told when he'd seen Topher for the first time. But the more he thought of it, the more it made sense. Unfortunately.

'Twas unfortunate for a number of reasons – the number one being that the boy was from a peaceful order and was needing to learn his weaponry skills on the fly. Dual order partnerships were strictly frowned upon, though there were no more orders that Renfry was aware of.

Another reason – he had searched everywhere for both a partner and his chapter's mentor. Usually, once a Brother had lost a partner, a mentor assisted in providing a new one, and gave the final consent. But – there was a clause that stated that during times of war, a Brother might choose his own partner, as mentors might be killed in the war.

So Renfry had searched for six months for both a partner and his mentor and found neither, with the exception of Topher. He kept coming back to Topher, and Topher was well-learned in all and more of what the Brothers themselves were trained in, which meant that all he needed to learn was weaponry itself, and he was proving a quick study.

However – one of the first lessons to learn - be still, observe, report – which Renfry thought Topher would have adapted to immediately, he just could not be still. It must have been all the years of not talking, combined with his time as a barkeep, for now he was a gregarious fool. Observation and report, Topher was quite skilled at, but Renfry had the feeling that until Topher was placed in a dangerous situation which required silence, Topher would continue reporting before it was necessary to do so.

And they were on the verge of dangerous situations each day. Renfry believed Topher had the makings of an excellent scout, having lived off the land as long as he had. With Renfry teaching him weaponry, they would be an incomparable adversary, for Topher's education was boundless.

But first, Renfry had to get to Queen Selby, whether Topher was ready or not.

$$---\;{\rightsquigarrow}\;---$$

Renfry had never seen so many Ormons in one place. Topher, for once, was silent. Finally. From what Renfry could divulge, they had landed upriver at Gull Port and a bloody battle had ensued between them and the Royal Crown Guard of Clemongard. Judging by the amount of Ormon to Clemongard soldiers, it would seem as if the Ormons took the upper hand.

He had scouted the territory, after a very difficult time leaving Topher behind in the shadows. All he'd done was listen to conversations, and he'd finally insisted that Topher had no experience or training in shadow stalking and could easily get them captured, thereby ruining the mission before it was barely underway. Topher was also under strict instructions to carry on the mission should Renfry be unable to do so, however ludicrous he might personally believe it. Topher swore an oath to fulfill the mission and Renfry relaxed.

But it was Topher who found the horses unattended. Ormon soldiers who had left their horses unattended while going to the mess tent – Topher kept his head down and his cloak cowl up, praying to his One God the entire time, or so he'd informed Renfry.

Now, however, they had information and a mission. Fellow travelers told them the Riverlands were infested with Ormons, and Renfry wondered just how much the Queen knew of the Ormon presence here between the Roarnebourke and the Trellis Rivers, for all he had heard as he was scouting was that she was at war in the north of Clemongard.

Whenever they were asked for identification, Renfry introduced themselves as travelers, just him and his kid brother, which was not too far off the mark, though they acted as travelers rather than members of an order on a mission to save a Queen, and possibly a realm's, life.

It was Topher's idea to steal the horses.

Renfry had bought new horses in Storden in Kettlebrick but Topher was tired of dodging enemy lines and sleeping in the woods.

At Elm Haven, they finally met a number of Ormon cavalry troops. And that was when Topher got the idea. If they stole Ormon horses, they could fall in with the Ormon troops, and travel in plain sight, or even ride by night with no fear of being stopped.

At first, Renfry was violently opposed to it and said he'd rather feed his left nut to an Ormon before he rode with their troops.

But Topher insisted they needed to pick up speed, and the cavalry was traveling at a good pace, whereas he and Renfry on their own horses were skirting the Ormon forces continually. They only needed to fall in with them, not change sides. They already looked like mercenaries, so no one would know the better. The advantages were too plentiful to resist.

And so finally, Topher talked Renfry into stealing the Ormon cavalry horses. Now, they rode at a good clip, in a sea of Ormon enemy soldiers who were none the wiser. It made Renfry's skin itch. As soon as they were within range of Clemongardian or Eastern soldiers, Renfry and Topher were going to ditch these horses. Never did he think he would be masquerading as a Northerner!

Yet here he sat across from a campfire from Topher, surrounded by Ormons, just north of Moss Grove. He had to admit it was a stroke of genius, hiding in plain view. They would be turning east tomorrow, toward the mountains, and Molengrove, a town where they hoped to resupply. The sooner he and Topher could outfit these horses as normal horses and then make a run for the tree line, the better, for then they could travel at their own pace, without the watchful eyes of Ormon soldiers and mercenaries. They needed to get to Queen Selby as soon as possible and that required breaking away from the Ormon Army.

Assuming they could break away tonight, they had three days' hard ride before they met the Queen in Rockdale Pass. And every day counted.

Selby

She slipped the blade of her cleaver under the apple skin and peeled it delicately back. This cleaver had seen so much blood....

With precision, Selby unraveled the apple from its peel in just one red roll. She held up the curled apple peeling with great satisfaction and bounced it a bit in the twilight as she sat before her campfire. Then she tossed it into the fire, taking a small bit of delight in the sudden spark of crisped apple, a foreign scent to this gray and gloomy battlefield.

"Bloody hell!" came a whispered curse from the camp next to her. Selby bit into her apple and observed Ambassador Keldrick attempting to even his beard out in the twilight by the light of his fire. She shook her head.

She rose to her feet and, her Ericorian following her, stood at the bounds of the Ambassador's camp, her cloak rippling about her legs. Clearing her throat, Selby asked, "May I?" She gestured at the boundary of his campsite.

Ambassador Keldrick scrambled for a moment. "Your Majesty, of course –"

Selby rose a palm. "At ease." She stepped up to Ambassador Keldrick's campfire and knelt down, squinting at him in the twilight.

"Here, you've bloodied yourself," she said, and reached out to where he had nicked himself with the small razor blade. A trickle of blood ran down his neck and she covered it with her index finger.

Then their eyes met.

She had often avoided his gaze, for she found his eyes stunning to behold, such a bold blue. But just now, she saw herself reflected within them, and even the flames of the campfire....

He coughed and held her hand for a moment as he removed it from his neck. Selby took a deep breath and, in an effort at recovery, said, "I don't know why you want to shave your beard. You resemble your royal father more this way."

Ambassador Keldrick blinked. She had taken him aback. He rubbed his hand over his beard and mused aloud, "Yes, yes I do, don't I?" Then he said, "Regardless, I must keep it trimmed up. An Ambassador can't look like a heathen, can he?"

"No, I suppose not." Selby almost smiled, for she had heard her brothers and father say that they couldn't look like heathens themselves. She sometimes forgot just how gently born Ambassador Keldrick truly was. More royal than she herself was, for he was the third son to the most powerful man in the Land.

She found him staring at her again. She swallowed, suddenly nervous. "You're still bleeding. I haven't any scar ointment or I'd bring it over to you...." Selby trailed off.

He shook his head. "No need." His voice sounded odd, she thought.

She felt as if she couldn't catch her breath.... The Ambassador's eyes caught hers and shook his head. Try as she might, Selby could not look away. "Apple?" she breathed and held up the apple between them.

He suddenly leaned in, holding her gaze, and kissed her on the lips. All of Selby's authoritative persona dropped in an instant, no longer a Queen but a girlish princess again. His lips were rough and salty, but careful....

Then she reached out for his shoulder and kissed him back, the apple rolling onto the grass.... *This is Keldrick*, she thought, and pulled him close. He responded, leaning in and placing the back of a calloused hand on her cheek. His beard was rough against her chin....

A breeze blew then, sending snaps and sparks from the campfire into the cooling night air. Selby jumped.

Immediately, Keldrick pulled away. "I'm sorry, Your Majesty, that was – untoward of me," he apologized in a low voice. He glanced about.

She immediately said, "I apologize, that was unfitting of me."

Keldrick returned, "You've nothing to apologize for, it was I who started it –"

"No, no, not at all –" Selby began, but then she looked into Keldrick's eyes, and all she wanted was to be in his arms.

She read his face – he wanted the same.

"Durain, both of you, leave me," she called out in a low but serious command.

Durain turned to look at her. His distaste was evident at leaving his Queen unprotected, but in truth, she was in the midst of an entire Army and scores of Ericorian protected her.

The other Ericorian looked at Durain for confirmation, for this was a questionable command.

Durain eyed the apple on the grass, raised an eyebrow ever so slightly, and then looked at his partner. In silence, he jerked his head to leave. Satisfied with the action being taken so long as it was Durain's choice, the other Ericorian fell in line. Selby knew they would not go far, only out of earshot and visual awareness.

As soon as her Ericorian guards were gone, Selby, breathless, looked at Keldrick's tent. He held its flaps open for her to duck through, making sure they weren't observed, and then tied them shut on the inside.

Immediately, they fell into each other's arms with a rattling of chainmail.

Kissing and groping each other, they fell onto his blankets. His tongue was suddenly in her mouth, exploring it. He stopped and smiled gently at her. Selby froze.

"You taste like apple," he whispered.

She chuckled and smiled. She could not recall the last time she had laughed. He made her feel so... free.

He kissed her again, now slowly, and her entire body was crying out with the wanting of him. Damn this chainmail shirt. And there was no way taking it off, nor he his.

But in the end, he was very tender with her. She could not help but think that of all the times she imagined her first time, it was not this way – in a tent, on a blanket in the grass on the battlefield as Queen of Clemongard. She always thought it would be in a beautiful wedding bed, after a glorious wedding to a handsome Duke or Earl who was earnestly in love with her. As she looked into the strong face of Keldrick, she wondered with awe at the difference. He stared into her eyes the entire time and was so careful to keep from hurting her more than was necessary. And then.... Selby could not believe such sensations existed, but she wanted more, and more....

He was careful to spill himself on the grass, and once he had collapsed, he picked up her hand and kissed the inside of it.

Selby rose up on an elbow and studied him. He was panting from the effort of their labors, and perspiration dotted his temple. She could not control a silly smile from overtaking her features.

She slept very little, for they came together twice more, he always on the grass at the end. And then they spoke in hushed tones of small things, of each other, of their families, of how they'd grown up, but very little of the war. And sometimes, curled together as they were, they actually slept.

Selby knew the morning would come all too soon, but the night was glorious and she never wanted it to end, so she reveled in it as long as she could.

—⟶⟵—

The next morning dawned all too soon. Selby sat up from her warm cocoon amidst Keldrick's blankets and cloak. She looked down at him. He looked so peaceful....

She began to plait her hair back. He had unraveled it last night, loving its softness, stroking it.... But she couldn't think of that now. As she tied the bottom of her braid with the leather thong, she sighed softly.

Keldrick propped an eye open. "Watching me?" he asked, his voice husky with sleep.

A bit embarrassed, Selby shrugged. "You look so peaceful asleep."

He snorted. "Peaceful. You've no idea what I was dreaming of."

Selby flushed a bit, self-conscious.

He eyed her braided hair and sat up.

"We can't...." Selby struggled with words to say that weren't offensive. "We can't – do this – again." He only regarded her calmly. "I could... get with –" She trailed off, at a loss. *Child,* she wanted to say.

"I know," he said.

Selby breathed out with relief, glad he understood her plight. "And your royal father would...." Gods be good, her ally, the Eastern Shield, whatever would he do?

"Bust a gut," Keldrick finished for her, rolling a discomfited blue eye at the prospect.

"And my father, gods be good," and Selby looked skyward for forgiveness. *I'm sorry, Father, if you're watching, but he's a wonderful man....*

"You have to get back to your tent before you're seen," Keldrick warned her.

She nodded. "We can't – we can't speak of this, you know."

He smiled a bit. "Of course not, Your Majesty." His smile was courteous and professional, very much the Ambassador of the Eastern Shield.

Then he waved at her. "Go, go, before you're seen," he whispered.

She peered through the flaps of his tent. Few signs of life were about yet – smoky campfires and gray dawn hung in the air. Not even her Ericorian were to be seen. She wrapped her cloak around her against the chill of early morning. Selby gave Keldrick a last, longing glance, and a quick smile before she slipped out of his tent.

It seemed a hundred steps to her own tent when in fact, there were only fifteen, but when she, the Queen, might be caught sneaking from a man's tent, every step seemed a canyon to cross.

Her campfire had not burned down. The Queen's fire must always be kept burning. Did Durain think of everything, Selby wondered with awe, not for the first time. He was nowhere to be seen, but she knew he had stoked her fire before he had retired for the evening, to make it seem as if she was inside her tent. Amazed at his resourcefulness, she marveled privately at her luck in such a loyal servant.

Inside her tent, alone at last, an enormous smile spread across her face. She would be fighting on the battlefield yet again today, but for now, she reveled in this private moment. She had something to smile about again.

Gerard

All he knew was riding, riding, riding. And he was tired of it, and his horse was tired. Why, then, were they riding? Under damned attack – in his own country, in his own land.

Then it struck Gerard. That was the plan. That was what the damned Ormons wanted. Send out these measly Stordish bastards after him and tire them out, then let the Ormons finish them off.

He slowed his horse and the riders behind him were forced to stumble to a halt.

Gerard yelled, "ABOUT FACE!" and sent up the attack command with his arm.

"Your Majesty?" asked two generals, rearing in their mounts around him.

"You heard me! About bloody face! We're fleeing these bastards and that's exactly what they want us to do! We will not run from Ormon arseholes in Ghiverny! Now turn around and charge them! Fight! Fight them! *Fight!*" Gerard hollered. He would not back down from a fight in Ghiverny, no, nor anywhere else.

His men roared all around him and the words, "Fight!" rolled through the ranks like a wave.

And then Gerard knew little more but slashing and hacking, and blood. He led the fray into the midst of those damnable Stordish shits and he sheared through them like pigeon parchment with Long Claw.

Three grandfathers ago, King Nordon had preferred a pike, and of more notoriety had been several kings before that, King Crandal, the Axe-Fisted, named so for fighting Ormons during the Ormon-Ghiverny skirmishes with a hand axe rather than Long Claw. Gerard wasn't sure what action spurred him to using the hand axe, as the little Queen out in the West, now the Cleaver Queen as her grandfather was known to be the Cleaver King. But, Gerard thought as he sliced through another opponent, he had known infamy for it.

Gerard preferred to skewer his opponents at the end of his sword to gutting them with an axe, but if it killed it an Ormon, then he had no argument with it.

Gerard was more traditional in that he preferred Long Claw, his original forebear's sword. Polished each day that they had not been at war, this sword served him well, though it now dripped with blood all the way to the quillions. Gerard was a sizeable man and fought well with the sword, his best move being the Up and Cross, though the Martmain ArmsMaster who had taught him as a boy told him to watch out, for it left him open on his shield arm.

And so it did, for his shield was beaten and dented. If this went on much longer, he would need a replacement shield.

He swung at the man astride from him and watched as he fell off of Long Claw. Another Ormon down. Instinctively, he raised his shield and took another incoming blow. Enraged, Gerard wheeled his destrier about and sunk Long Claw into the neck of the man who had just hacked at his shield. Blood spewed forth upon the horse of the enemy and the life faded from the angry eyes of his attacker.

With haste, Gerard turned again to his side to meet another attacker. He cared not if he was fighting as a gentleman ought – if it had elk antlers or boar's tusks, Gerard was swinging, slashing, and hacking, and his reward was blood. The Wolf of Ghiverny was not playing nicely when it came to his country, his men, and his family.

Suddenly, galloping thundered upon the earth, and then there was a lull. The jingling of his destrier's armor rang out as he wheeled him about.

Fleeing! They fled! They retreated!

His men let up a roar of victory. All over the battlefield, vacancies of Ormons and Stordish were left, and Ghiverns stood shaking their fists and swords in the air, jubilant.

Gerard let out a long breath of exhaustion and slid down from his horse.

"Father!"

"Petran! You're okay!" He embraced his son as tightly as he dared. Petran winced, for his armor was bloody.

"You're wounded. Healer! I need a Healer for my son!" Gerard roared out.

"'Tis nothing, Father! A minor scratch. They've run! They've retreated!" Petran was caught up in his first after-battle triumph.

"Yes, my son, so they have. As long as you are well, 'tis all that concerns me now."

"Yes, yes. Are you? Look at you, you're bloodier than am I! The Wolf!" called out Petran suddenly, still elated. "The Wolf!"

"I am well, hush with that now."

"Your Majesty, your armor is torn on the side, it must be mended –" an armorer said, buzzing about him.

"Yes, yes, now is not the time. Later."

"I must insist that you see the armorer for that shield and that tear, Your Majesty," said a General at his side.

Your skin is only so thick as your armor, was what the ArmsMasters said. And his was exposed.

"Yes, later," Gerard growled. It was time to address the men.

"And you must see a Healer, before you take an infection, Your Majesty."

This General had balls of steel!

"And before night's end, I shall. See that I have a new shield," Gerard snapped to the armorer at his other side.

Then he roared, "Men of Ghiverny!" He let his voice echo and waited until every man within hearing was listening. "We were attacked today. Given odds we were not expected to live through! And we survived! We triumphed!" He let the word *triumphed* echo throughout the battlefield. Then Gerard yelled, "They came into the Wolf Lands and expected to defeat us by ambushing us! Do not underestimate them, for they may do so again! Take rest now! Care for our wounded! Be humble, be vigilant in your victory, for make no mistake but that the Ormons will come at us again tomorrow! And we must be smart, we must be strong, and we must push them back to where they are hiding and we must crush them! For we are Ghiverny, we are wolves, and we will not be defeated!"

His men cheered and roared then, with howls and cries of "The Wolf!" going up all among them.

And then it was time to walk the battlefield. Gerard joined his troops.

A gloom settled over the ranks as they killed those who were dying, and moved the wounded to the Healer's Tents.

A young boy, no older than fourteen, Gerard judged, watched him. Gerard was accustomed to being watched with awe, as men were impressed by royalty and rank. But then, at his feet, an Ormon soldier lifted up an arm toward him.

"Mercy, please," he called. The man was wounded terribly by a gut wound that had laid him open, judging by the location of the blood seeping through his armor. He would take hours to die.

Gerard said nothing, only stabbed the man through the heart. He waited until the light left the man's eyes and then stood to move on.

The young boy was staring at him, horrified. With no celebration, the boy whispered, "He begged for Mercy!"

Ah. Youth.

"And I gave it to him." He studied the boy. A squire if he wasn't mistaken. The boy's master was a fool for taking him out here so young. "Squire, how old are you?"

"Sixteen," replied the boy in a brave tone. Lying, of course, so he could fight. If that boy was sixteen, Gerard would fry and eat his left nut.

"Son, that man was a soldier of Ormon. He served his duty to his country. Didn't matter that he was of Ormon, he could have been of Ghiverny. All soldiers who serve their country fight for their king. That man was dying, son. All men bleed red, be they stable boy or king. And they all deserve mercy, which is what I just gave that Ormon soldier. Never forget that, son. All men deserve mercy, no matter who they are."

The squire nodded solemnly.

Gerard stepped over the dead Ormon soldier and moved on.

———

That night, the men played their drum songs and a number of them got drunk. Gerard sighed. He was quite sober, having only had a goblet and a half of wine. He did not entirely disapprove of their celebration, though one day's win was nothing. He was one of a minority on this battlefield who had fought in the Twenty Years War, and so he was a seasoned warrior. He knew that while today was a win, tomorrow they might easily lose, and they had lost a fair share of men today, and many men were wounded. But he could not bring himself to retire for the evening. Perhaps part of it was that he was lost in the memories of himself as a soldier in the Twenty Years War....

Finally, when he heard the beginning drum line of "To the Victors" begin, he wandered up to the celebration.

At first, the men around him did not recognize him. Then the men across the bonfire started to stare and the drummers faltered.

Gerard gestured for them to continue and when the first line started, his voice was the loudest.

"To the Victors"

In the end, the victors take the daughters

In the end, the victors take the sisters

In the end, the victors take the wives

A Silent Game of Spies

To the victors go the swords (Da-DOOM!)

To the victors go the blood (Da-da-DOOM!)

In the end, the victors take the sons

In the end, the victors take the brothers

In the end, the victors take the husbands

To the victors go the armor (Da-DOOM!)

To the victors go the weapons (Da-da-DOOM!)

In the end, the victors take the wells

In the end, the victors take the livestock

In the end, the victors take the farms

To the victors go the crops (Da-DOOM!)

To the victors go the lands (Da-da-DOOM!)

In the end. the victors take the villages

In the end. the victors take the towns

In the end, the victors take the cities

To the victors go the plunders (Da-DOOM!)

To the victors go the possessions (Da-da-DOOM!)

In the end, the victors take the churches

In the end, the victors take the clergies

In the end, the victors take the priests

To the victors go the relics (Da-DOOM!)

To the victors go the riches (Da-da-DOOM!)

In the end, the victors take the forts

In the end, the victors take the towers

In the end, the victors take the keeps

To the victors go the banners (Da-DOOM!)

To the victors go the standards (Da-da-DOOM!)

In the end, the victors take the ale

In the end, the victors take the mead

In the end, the victors take the spirits

To the victors go the flasks (Da-DOOM!)

To the victors go the tankards (Da-da-DOOM!)

In the end, the victors take the duchesses

In the end, the victors take the princesses

In the end, the victors take the queens

To the victors goes the gold (Da-DOOM!)

To the victors goes the treasure (Da-da-DOOM!)

In the end, the victors take the palaces

In the end, the victors take the fortresses

In the end, the victors take the castles

To the victors go the kingdoms (Da-DOOM!)

To the victors go the countries (Da-da-DOOM!)

In the end, the victors take the dukes

In the end, the victors take the princes

In the end, the victors take the kings

To the victors go the SPOILS OF WAR! (Da-DOOM!)

To the victors go the SPOILS OF WAR! (Da-da-DOOM!)

To the victors go the SPOILS OF WAR! (Da-DOOM!)

To the victors go the SPOILS OF WAR! (Da-da-DOOM!)

To the victors go the SPOILS OF WAR! (Da-da-Da-da-Da-da-Da-da-DOOM DOOM!)

At the end of the song, men screamed, "To Ghiverny!" and "To The Wolf!" and wolf howls erupted all around the bonfire.

"Speech, speech, speech, speech!" came the insistences of his men.

"Very well. But first – fill my cup!" called out Gerard. He held up his empty goblet.

The men cheered and someone dumped wine into his goblet.

Then the entire crowd was silent, awaiting his speech. Speech – bah! What was there left to say?

He downed his entire goblet in one drink, then howled at the moon for as loud as there was breath in his body.

Men erupted into cheers and roars and howls all about him. Another round of "To the Victors" started up.

Gerard slipped away as soon as he was able for his tent. Let them have this. They would need the momentum come the morrow.

Rhutgard

"Ah, Rhudy, Driscoll," came Gerard's voice.

"Gerard," said Rhutgard, nodding, falling in line with Gerard's horse. He nodded in dismissal to the Colonel who had led him to Gerard. "I understand there was a wolf in the vicinity last night."

"Yes, bloody loud one at that. Dirty, unshaven beast. Howled half the night." Gerard grinned as he rubbed a hand across his beard.

Driscoll snorted and Rhutgard laughed. Tales of King Gerard singing "To the Victors" with the men at the bonfire and howling like a wolf had spread throughout the ranks. Rhutgard wholeheartedly approved and could just envision Gerard baying at the moon though Driscoll considered it childish antics and foolery. Driscoll was ever the statesman and would never sink so low as to howl, thus continuing to earn the designation Silver Statesman that Rhutgard had coined. As King, Gerard was The Wolf of Ghiverny and what he had done last night breathed life into his ranks after the Ormons had ambushed them.

"We are bloody glad of the troops, let me tell you," Gerard commented as he waved an arm at the fresh infusion of troops that Rhutgard and Driscoll brought with them from Delsynth and Romeny.

"Something else you'll be glad of – we come with news," commented Driscoll. "Those Ormons you drove off with their tails between their legs, scouts tell us they are sitting off to the west stirring up a little storm, getting ready to attack again."

"You found them? Excellent!" Gerard's grin was almost bloodthirsty.

"Understand that this is not the full host, Gerard," cautioned Rhutgard. "We've reports that the full host is under command of a Colonel in the upper northwest of the EverWinters. Sizable, but not problematic."

"I don't care. I want these men out of Ghiverny."

Driscoll and Rhutgard exchanged a glance.

"Have you had no riders this morning?"

"No, none. Of course, if we had one yesterday, he was probably killed."

"More Ormon troops are on their way down the Northern Countries Crosslands, headed toward the EverWinters." Rhutgard took no joy in informing his old friend that Ormon troops would be marching through his country.

At first, Gerard was silent. Finally, he responded grimly, "Well, we just won the Battle of Rossdon, or that's what the men are calling it, since Rossdon is just miles from here. Should the men stay behind to meet them? What think you, will the Ormons be invading Ghiverny? Or are they headed only for the EverWinters?"

Martmain, Ghiverny's capital city, and Genwith City, were easily within marching distance of the Ormons' path, and Rhutgard knew how the Ghiverns valued their cities. Ghiverny was a country of art, music, and literature, and he knew how both cities would fair should the Ormons take it upon themselves to invade, though both cities were well fortified in times of war.

"I am told they are headed to join the EverWinter troops," Rhutgard told him.

"And just who is your source? How credible is your source?" asked Gerard.

It was hard not to be irked at that, but he squashed his irritation, for he would fear the same if Ormon troops would be passing through Romeny close to Fairview and Sherrigan.

Driscoll responded for him. "Captain Firthing is his source, actually. You might be interested in knowing that he got the information from a dying Ormon soldier."

Gerard seemed to take heart and realized that he was also in the company of the Eastern Shield. There were times when, like his sons, Gerard forgot that.

To dispel the awkwardness developing, Rhutgard said, "Well, the Battle of Rossdon may be won, but we have another battle to be fought. Let us use time to our advantage. Get your men mobilized, so that we can win another battle today. Then we can march for the EverWinters. If we hit the EverWinters before the Ormons reach them, they will know they cannot simply camp out in the East and expect to win."

Rilstrom

"So, you've finally come to visit, haven't you, Brother." This last was added in a nasty tone by his twin. Rilstrom marveled yet again at just who and what his brother had become, his twin, and right before him, when he hadn't even noticed.

"We are hardly brothers," Rilstrom responded, though he kept his voice calm. His twin was trying to bait him and he would not fall for it.

"Something I've been thinking for years," yawned Rickstan as he sat against the back of the cell. "So different, except you have my face...."

"That much, I agree with you on," remarked Rilstrom and turned around so he wouldn't have to look at the bastard who was his twin brother, who had taken part in imprisoning him in the HarCourt Dungeon for six months and passing him off for dead. Indeed, if the girl in the tunnels had not set him free, he still would be in the dungeons, subject to Joshik's every dim-witted whim. Hard to forgive a man for that.

"So what is the purpose of this visit? Have they missed me?"

Rilstrom scoffed. "No, Brother, actually, we are at war."

His twin raised an eyebrow. "We who? Us, as in, you and I? Or the family? Or... oh, so many possibilities, do be specific."

Rilstrom narrowed his eyes but refused to engage his brother. "You know of the war I speak. You had you hands filthy with the planning of it, did you not?" And he turned about to stare at the twin brother with whom he'd grown up, oblivious to such psychotic behavior.

Rickstan gave up. "At war at last, are we? I didn't think it would happen. Too many gutless lords holding back on their promises." He seemed pensive. "That doesn't tell me why you're here. You must need something from me. Ah. The keys to the Riverlands Stations."

"Don't kid yourself. I found those long ago," Rilstrom responded with disgust.

"Did you? I'm impressed."

Rilstrom turned and leaned against a wall. Just a tiny dark room, with a window outside the cell, and three deaf and mute guards, one who brought food and water daily, a guard for the nightshift, and a guard for the dayshift. Rickstan's cries literally fell on deaf ears and he was unable to get information here. None of the three guards even knew who Rickstan was, for they'd been hired from the West, and Rilstrom kept this prison separate from the castle. He visited once each month, only to see that his brother was alive and well, no more. 'Twas regicide if he killed the man, and he would not kill the father of his niece and nephews, though they cared not if he lived. Furthermore, Shaw might yet have need of him, should something happen to the royal bloodline. And so he made this trip each month, only to ensure that the man he once cared for still survived and was healthy.

"And the other safe?"

Rilstrom turned. He did not know of another safe.

"Ah. I knew I'd placed it well. You'll need the keys to the safe if you want the upper hand in this war."

Rilstrom raised an eyebrow. This would not come cheap. "And in return?"

"Well, probably a conjugal visit is out of the question –"

Rilstrom scoffed. "Try again."

"Early release perhaps –"

"You are getting everything I did whilst I was imprisoned, my dear brother, and frankly, you are being treated far better."

"Better! You must be joking. Do you see the slop I'm fed?" Rickstan spat onto the floor of his cell.

Rilstrom, seething, kept his rage from overtaking his features. Instead he turned about and unlaced his surcoat. His brother remarked, "I've no idea, Rilstrom, why you're stripping, but if it's for a boxing match, you might recall that I always was the victor."

Rilstrom said nothing but pulled his tunic off, revealing an entire back of scars from beatings.

For once, Rickstan remained silent.

"These scars are from the guard, who lashed me whenever he felt the need. Take a good long look, *Brother*, and tell me again that you are being treated unfairly in here. And now know that asking for anything such as I did not get is a pretty big ask."

Finally, Rickstan told him that the keys to the safe were under the tile beneath the throne.

"Though I would change that hiding place now if I were you." He paused. "How are my children?"

"Glad that I am you," returned Rilstrom evenly as he dressed. "I cannot fathom how you could do such a thing. To Shaw, to the Eastern Alliance. To Father."

"Father." Rickstan scoffed and shook his head from within his cell.

"Why do you say it like that?"

"Oh, don't worry, he died of natural causes. The last thing I wanted was the throne, though you may not believe it. That was it, you know. You, you paraded about doing anything you wished all the time, this social, that social. Whilst I, I was under Father's strict thumb. I finally snapped, and no one ever knew it.

"Because I was shrewd enough, smart enough to see that no one saw through me. Father, he had no political sense. I have political cunning and he had none. Like you, you have no political cunning, although you have lasted longer out there than I gave you credit for. My guess is that you are merely a good actor with a strong sense of survival. Perhaps you have a new group of advisors. That's what I would have done were I you, starting fresh in the same situation. But with my sense of political cunning, I brought Shaw to where she is now, and she will be safe in this war, or as safe as she can be. War was eminent, Brother, know that. I did not bring it upon us single-handedly. But I have set circumstances in motion that may save Shaw from being trampled upon in this war."

His brother's words chilled Rilstrom, and he looked pleased as a cat after a meal of fresh tuna.

"Your biggest fault, your whole life, Rickstan, has been that you are an ideal, greedy fool."

"And yours is your naivety," snapped Rickstan.

Rilstrom sighed and turned to leave.

Suddenly, Rickstan became placating. "I thought I would earn something for my cooperation."

Rilstrom snorted. "What would you like? A few lashings?"

His twin ignored that and said, "I think you'll find what I've given you to be of enormous value...."

"All right, I'm listening."

"These meals...."

"Careful, Brother, what you're getting is beyond compare for a prisoner who has committed treason."

"Could they be... a little better?"

His palate was exceptional, Rilstrom knew. He snorted his disgust.

"I'll consider sending you some cheese if I like what I read."

"You will, I know you will."

Rilstrom turned to leave.

His brother scrambled to his feet in the cell behind him. "Brother," he called out.

"Not another ask?"

Misery was clear on his twin's face as he gestured toward the tiny window across the room. "It's just – might I see the sunshine? I've missed it all these months...."

Rilstrom's lip curled with scorn. He recognized that yearning, but he hadn't seen even a window, much less been treated so gently.

He looked down at the stone floor and saw a rock. He kicked it into his brother's cell.

"Draw a picture of the sun on the wall. That way you'll see the sun shine every day, you bloody bastard."

And he let the door slam behind him.

———

So many lords – some who find themselves soon banished. He thought they were quiet in Council. He wondered if they knew he was not Rickstan. Probably not, if these papers were to judge. Rickstan had colluded with Lord Drury to see him dead and the paperwork was here before him on the desk, though a Lord Scollard had signed off on the matter. People were to be told that Rilstrom was dead in the bandit raid on the supposed state visit to Hardewold that never occurred. The fewer people who knew of the murder of a royal brother, the better, thought

Rilstrom darkly. Though he would love to know who Lord Scollard was. Any man who helped plan his murder, and the death of his wife and unborn child, was a man he wanted to meet. And categorically execute.

But most importantly, of the oddest names he found in this cacophony of his brother's was Almeric, King of Tortoreen. And what he read chilled him.

He would need to send a bird to Reaghann with all haste, in hopes that Reaghann had not yet left with his troops for the EverWinters. And then a bird to Fairview, for he was under the strictest of orders to share anything of the remotest importance with the Eastern Shield. Rhutgard was already at or on his way to the EverWinters, but a rider would need to send this message on. Rilstrom would not have it said that he had not performed his duty. And this could well change the outcome of the war....

Varley

King Irving. Who would have supposed he'd had it in him! The entire Corsta-Storden border, lined with troops. Troops whose orders were shoot to kill on sight if they saw Varley. He fumed as they rode. Irving had recruited mercenaries and given them raises in pay to work for him instead of Varley. And all of Storden was closed.

No matter. He still had twenty thousand troops and he led them through Corstarorden south of the Storden border. Corstarorden troops would not bother them, he knew, for they were too busy mobilizing for Her Royal Majesty, the Ice Cunt. If Varley saw her now, he would gladly slit her throat. She would get a nasty surprise in the end, though, for they had seen with their own eyes at least twice their number of Eastern Alliance troops marching for Clemongard, and with siege weapons. Let her and King Hewett fight their way out of that, for she had almost certainly set foot in the Land of the Falcons by now. While they were occupied with their cloaks flapped up over their heads like fools, boxed in by Clemongardians to the North and Easterners to the South, Varley's troops would take the Coastals. First, he would reacquire for himself a Navy, then take over Corstarorden with his own troops. Varley decided he would set up his own camp at Roarden North. So much city to be had....

They had finally blooded themselves at Middleborough nigh on a week ago, then drunk every drop of mead and ale the town had. Middleborough women left much to be desired, but were far better than the farmers' daughters they'd just left behind at Millsberg. If any of those women walked normally again, he would be surprised. Varley grinned. He was born for this.

According to the map, an estate lay on the coast, where he could finally sup and repose in the luxury a prince of his station warranted before he and his troops turned southward to gather the ships they needed. Just south of the estate was a fort, Hull Port, where, according to his information, twenty-five ships were stationed. That was a start. Those ships would be summarily seized and then become Varley's. Any issue taken with it could be taken up with the Ice Bitch.

And from Hull Port, he would move south, taking every port and ship....

Theldry

The guards had been killed first. Never had Theldry thought to see such blood, such violence. She had known there was war in the Land, and even known that Corstarorden was likely to be called upon as Tortoreen and S'hendalow would be due to the Northern-Coastal Partnership Agreement. But this... this... senseless brutality....

Troops! Mercenaries, more like, were camped inside the estate, and all about the surrounding lands! Many of them were wearing, if Theldry was not mistaken, Storden colors, and she knew her heraldry. The man who had sat at the Great Hall table was bedecked in Stordish colors and finery. The boar's head over a castle, that was the Storden family, yet Storden was neutral. How, then, Theldry's benumbed mind fumbled for answers, did this man command a ruthless, bloodthirsty army? Who was he?

As soon as the thundering of hooves had sounded upon the earth, Cathall and the guards immediately knew the estate was under attack and withdrew to the gatehouse to draw the gate down, shouting for men to man the baileys.

Jeanie and Kallia had pulled Theldry upstairs into her chambers for her safety.

"Quickly, now, change clothing with me," Jeanie had whispered.

"Whatever for!" Theldry had hissed. Kallia was already changing into a dress left behind of Mina's.

"So they'll think that I'm the lady of the house. If they think you're the servant, they're more like to leave you alone, and you can hide in the storeroom!"

Numbly, Theldry had stepped out of her dress and pulled Jeanie's maid dress over her head.

"There now, let your hair down a bit, and take those jewels off. Quickly, quickly!"

"Why don't we all hide in the storeroom –"

"My lady, if they find us, they'll think I'm the lady of the house. Now here, put those ruddy gems on me and we'll be out of here! The first place they'll look for the lady of the house is in her chambers, don't you know!" And then the three of them ran to the storeroom.

Soon enough came the sounds of men fighting and then of a battering ram. Tears had spilled down Kallia's frightened face. Jeanie swallowed. Sitting in the darkness on the storeroom floor in Jeanie's maid dress, Theldry reached out for their hands and squeezed them. These were the women who had taken her in here at Mendellion, even though she was the Duchess, and been kind to her in all her boredom and lightened the everyday tedium with their laughter and tales, shown her how a household was truly run... by the servants.

She heard running in the halls, the sound of boots. Soldiers. And then all was quiet.

Seconds passed like hours.

Then the purposeful stride of boots sounded in the hall outside the storeroom. A torchlight flickered beneath the storeroom door. And the door creaked open slowly.

A tall man stood, holding a wall sconce above him. Firelight spilled into the small storeroom. "Ah. What have we here?" Then he turned to the soldiers behind him. "You see, Colonel, General, I knew if we looked long enough, we'd find them." Then he returned his attention to Theldry and the women who cowered with her.

He gestured. "Up, stand up."

Theldry rose to her feet slowly. The other two women scrambled to help each other up, for they were frightened. And why not? They had never seen the insolent stare of soldiers, nor of a man such as this cowardly ilk as stood before her. But she had. Theldry had walked the Palace at Tortoreen and seen men such as them each day of her life, starting with her own father.

"A lovely estate, to be sure, but a dinner laid for two? I knew there to be at least a few of you about. And I would extend my compliments to the chef, but I'm afraid he ran." He sniggered. "Not very fast, I'm afraid."

Theldry seethed. Chef Nivell was one of the very best chefs in all of Corstarorden. But she would mourn his loss later.

"Come along, ladies, finally, true ladies. Except for you. But look at you, aren't you... exceptional. For a servant." The tall man led Theldry out of the storeroom and traced the back of his hand down her cheek. She jerked her face away. He smiled. "And spirited. Excellent." He led Jeanie and Kallia out. "Ah, the Lady of the house. Hm, exquisite gown, quite – tasteful. Silk. I do like silk." He fingered Theldry's gown upon Jeanie, who was too petrified to move.

He turned over his shoulder. "I believe I'll have this lovely servant for my appetizer, the Lady of the House for my main course, and this – come out of the shadows."

The man saw Kallia and immediately smiled. He reached out and lifted a breast. Kallia squirmed and cried out. "Yes. Yes, you. The lady-in-waiting, no? You shall be my dessert. Lovely little thing, aren't you. Don't cry, muffin, we'll have lots of fun." He turned and addressed his soldiers.

"Once I'm through with them, they're yours. But not – not the servant, keep her intact, we need someone to serve us meals while we're still here. Besides, I like her."

"Now see that they don't run, and don't so much as touch them until I call for them, understand?"

"Yes, Your Highness," said one.

"Yes, Prince Varley," said the other.

Prince? This man – was a prince? From – where? Theldry recognized the name only vaguely.

Varley reached out and grabbed her wrist. "Come along, darling, you have the privilege of being fucked properly tonight, and by a crown prince. You'll never get this chance again, so enjoy it while you can."

A Crown Prince? However did a Crown Prince come to conduct himself in such a manner? Perhaps he was lying, or a by-blow who had not been acknowledged. Still, his name sounded familiar....

He dragged her along behind him through the estate. She wondered what would happen if she resisted – tried to run, but the estate was overrun by his troops. Damn!

Finally, Varley pulled her into the Great Hall.

Then all rational thought left her as took in the sight before her. Soldiers stood randomly throughout the hall and there was blood upon the floor – obviously a great fight had taken place in here.

But her Cathall – her husband, the Duke of Mendellion... hung from the rafters above the head of the table. The one time he shouldn't have come home....

Theldry took in the sight of her husband's dead corpse above the Great Hall table and immediately she began to fight. "No! No!"

"Relax, little darling, it will go easier. Someone can cut the man down when we leave," Varley commented as he dragged her along.

"No!" She pulled against Varley's fist encircling her wrist but he clubbed her in the head with his free fist.

Everything went blurry. Theldry heard him instruct his guards to drag her up upon the table. Dimly, through a ringing in her ear, she heard the sound of the food and silver being pushed aside.

Then she was hoisted upon the table like a sack of vegetables. Immediately, Theldry began to kick and fight. She fought with every ounce of energy in her body, though her vision was blurry, though her ears were ringing. She threw punches at Varley, but he backed away. Was that him, laughing? All she could see in her mind was Cathall, swinging from the rafters above them....

For her trouble, she was slammed back against the table by soldiers who grasped her shoulders. Her head bounced off of the thick oak on which she'd eaten her meals so many times. And up, up, up above her, swimming blurrily, was Cathall.

Theldry began to fight again, but Varley laughed. "Hold her, I said! Two of you, each."

And two soldiers bore down on Theldry's arms. Then her bodice was ripped open, exposing her flesh. Theldry recoiled and squirmed beneath him.

Varley loomed above her, an ugly, unshaven face blotting out her field of vision. He inspected her flesh and she itched inside when he ran his hands all over her breasts. He squeezed them and said, "Not bad for an appetizer. Too small for my preference, though. Maybe you weren't fed well as a child. No matter." He unlaced his surcoat slowly, drinking in her exposed body the entire time. Theldry glared back at him the entire time, but he never met her gaze. Finally, he hung his surcoat on the main chair – Cathall's chair, Theldry thought, and she glanced up to where his corpse hung above them.

But Varley – Crown Prince Varley, she thought darkly – had unlaced his breeches and was looming above her. With every bit of strength, she fought against the men holding her down but they were too strong for her.

And then Varley pulled her legs apart and forced himself into her. Rammed himself. Theldry sucked in her breath with pain and her eyes were forced out of their sockets. Above her, Varley groaned with gratification. Over and over and over he rammed himself into her – Theldry felt her insides tearing with each thrust. She focused on the swinging corpse of her husband above her and tried to feel nothing. On and on it went – would he never stop!

She did her best not to cry out, for she refused to give him the satisfaction, but at times a whimper escaped her when the pain was too great. She knew blood was gushing from between her legs. He clawed at her and she cried out. Theldry distinctly saw him grin.

That was it, she suddenly recognized. He enjoyed her pain. It was her pain that he liked. She immediately went limp, pretending not to care.

After a few minutes, Varley slapped her. The side of Theldry's head bounced off the table and irritated the ringing in her ears that had begun to withdraw. But she remained uncaring. Finally, Varley withdrew and flipped Theldry over on her hands and knees.

"Hold her!" he growled to the soldiers to either side of her.

And then he thrust himself inside her again from behind. Theldry squeezed her eyes shut as he forced himself into her, over and over. She tried not to cry but tears formed anyway and dripped onto the oaken table as plentifully as the blood that flowed down her legs. Her arms trembled with the effort of holding herself upright while he rammed into her. But she did not cry out. There was nothing left in her. All she saw was the overturned vegetables on the table she'd been laying in while he'd violated her – spiced beets and honeyed carrots....

Finally, Theldry felt Varley release himself inside her. He felt like acid....

Varley pulled himself free of her and shoved her away. Thank all the gods, it was over....

"Go," he panted, as he climbed off the Great Hall table. "Get out of my sight." He gestured with disgust as he tucked his flaccid penis back into his trousers.

Theldry scrambled off of the oaken table, nearly falling. She felt for the bodice that Prince Varley had ripped open, pulled it up to cover herself, and limped out of the Great Hall.

— ⚜ —

She had hidden in the unused conservatory under a sheet in a corner until Varley and his troops left. Varley and his troops had stayed only the night, and for that, Theldry had been grateful. As soon as the estate was quiet, she came out from under the sheet, but sat against the wall with her knees pulled up to her chin, numb.

It was then that she saw that far against the room, either Kallia or Jeanie had thought to run in here and exchange the cover over Ayrissa and Cathall's portrait for that of his and hers, so that the troops would not believe her to be the Duchess. What amazing women they were, she mused absently.

She knew they had gotten the worst of it. She had heard their screams, particularly Kallia's. Of the three of them, Kallia was a lovely woman, with an hourglass figure, plump, blonde and blue-eyed…. The screams – Theldry had heard the screams sound throughout the estate half the night.

Finally, at dawn, the men rode out and silence pervaded the estate.

At least two hours slipped by in blessed silence before the whispered voice of Jeanie echoed in the conservatory. "My lady? Are you in here? My lady?"

Tears slipped down Theldry's face and she sniffled. She stood up on uncertain feet, holding her ripped bodice.

"Oh, my lady," breathed Jeanie. She immediately crossed the room and enveloped Theldry in a tight embrace. Theldry broke down and sobbed until she had no breath left in her.

How dare that – that man! How dare that man reduce her to tears! Jeanie was patting her back. "My lady, I'm so sorry, I'm so sorry…."

Theldry pulled away, her face wet. She took a good long look at Jeanie. The amethyst necklace was gone and scratches were left on her neck where someone had ripped it free. Her face showed the start of a black eye and her hair was frayed. The silken dress she'd worn now hung loosely off of one shoulder and was ripped down the front. A dark stain, undoubtedly blood, blotched what had once been a mint green silk.

Kallia stood behind Jeanie. She hugged herself and stared absently. Her lip was split and her face was bruised already. Her tangled hair was matted with blood from a cut on her cheek and her dress was stained in a number of places with dirt and blood. She had been used terribly. Even as Theldry took in the sight of Kallia, she trembled.

"Kallia –" and she outstretched an arm to her.

Kallia shrunk away. "No!" Her blue eyes had grown wide with horror.

Jeanie pushed Theldry's arm down gently. "She's in shock, my lady. She's going to need a lot of time, I think."

"Yes, I can see that."

Theldry shook herself. "We need new clothes. Have you other dresses?"
Jeanie nodded, her face solemn. "We need something else."

Theldry raised an eyebrow. It was too hard to think. Then she said, "Baths." What she wanted more than anything was a bath.

Jeanie conceded but held out her hand. "Wormwort." In her hand lay the root. It had to be crushed and immediately taken in a tea. But there wasn't enough of it for all three of them.

Theldry raised her eyes to Jeanie. She had just had her moon days. She was unlikely to have… gotten with child… by that monster. Especially after what he had done to her.

"There's not enough for all three of us. Begging your pardon, my lady, but given how she is –" and Jeanie nodded toward Kallia, "I forced her to take a cup of tea already. So this here is for you. You've got to take it right now, before we do anything."

Wormwort. It was powerful and it worked every time, it was said, but sometimes, it took a woman's ability to breed with it. Theldry wasn't likely to have gotten with child. She felt him – tear her – inside. That and coupled with just after her moon days….

"You take it. He only used me once. I just had my moon days, Jeanie. Take it. Besides," she added gently, "you need it more than I." Theldry reached out and closed Jeanie's hand around the wormwort. "Take it."

"But, my lady –"

"Take it. I'll not have you be gotten with child after such as what happened. He – hurt me inside. It's wasted on me."

Jeanie's eyes filled with tears. Theldry had never seen Jeanie become so emotional.

"Come," Theldry encircled Jeanie's shoulders. "Let us brew some strong tea, and then bathe. Then we shall put on fresh frocks and be rid of those bastards forever, Jeanie, shall we?"

—⁓⁓—

Cormber had cut down her husband's lifeless body from the rafters. Theldry promised Cormber that he could stay on as long as he liked, though he had no master to steward for anymore. She was personally glad of any male assistance.

She and Cormber wrapped Cathall's body in soft linen and a few of the guards who were left carried Cathall to the tomb beneath the estate, where they left him in a hastily constructed wooden coffin until they could commission a proper marble coffin such as his forebears lay in.

Then Cormber sat down at Cathall's desk. With shaking hands, the steward opened Cathall's files and finally found his personal will.

"With your leave, my lady?"

Silently, Theldry nodded. Just a day ago, Cathall had arrived home, and now they were about to read his last will and testament, his instructions for his properties upon his... death. Theldry swallowed.

"Oh. Oh my." Cormber looked up at Theldry. "He's changed this recently."

Theldry stared at him but the man remained mute. "Well?" she prompted, trying to keep her voice from being too sharp. He, too, had been close to Cathall.

"You see, my lady, Cathall died childless, and the last time that I knew him to speak of this subject, he had not yet remarried." He paused. "He had intended to pass the estate and the properties to a nephew." Cormber took a breath.

"He still does, but.... You, as Duchess of Mendellion, are to run the estate and all of its properties and extensions, including the village, until your death, unless you choose to relinquish your title and move away. After your death or relinquishment of title, then the estate and its properties and extensions, including the village, moves on to his nephew, cousin, etc., and he has a list of family members here who will inherit.

"My lady, you are now the sole proprietress of the estate. You, Lady Theldry Eochair, are the Duchess of Mendellion and all its properties."

Cormber's words washed over Theldry slowly. Her father's words rang in her mind.... *Duty before love, Theldry, duty before love....* Now she had a duty to perform. She only hoped she was half as competent as her late husband.

Hewart

Yes, he had been here before. The little upstart queen had withdrawn to RainsCourt. An excellent castle, built into the mountains. The first thing he would do once it was his would be to rename the damned thing. Perhaps BearsCourt.

He wondered offhandedly who was advising her to hide in the castle, for that was a mistake. He would just lock them in there and starve them to death. Hewart could wait that long. There was game aplenty to be had at the foot of the mountains, but not once up in them.

And speaking of upstart queens, Queen Myrischka had followed at his heels just like a bitch in heat, looking for a good fuck. He had refused to meet with her and sent his Ambassador to her. To be sure, she had not requested a meeting, which Hewart found odd. But she was trampling all over the thousands-year-old Ambsellon-Ormon Alliance and Hewart found he would be unable to look her in the eye should she request a meet.

And all the Ormons sitting in the Clemongard Riverlands. Hewart gave credit to whoever planned the move itself, sending ships around his navy to land upon the most fertile ground in all the country. But was she stupid? Allowing such a move? Trampling on the Alliance, that's what she was doing. Spitting on it. Spitting on thousands of years of friendly, international relations between their two countries. What was she thinking? She made it look as if she was making a play for Clemongard on her own. He shook his head. Women. Damn fools.

Sturgund was of the mind that they should punish her, but Hewart had to remind Sturgund that they were already at war with one Queen and one was enough. For now. Myrischka was a fool. Eventually she would fall in line. There was no sense kicking her when she was down.

Particularly when – and he had only shared this with Sturgund – no one was able to take the reins of her country over. Once they took over Clemongard, then who was to say they couldn't acquire Ormon? Sturgund had brightened considerably at that. Why not make it a revenge payment? He was so sure that it had been Myrischka holding the reins of the operation. Sturgund could take over Ormon while the Queen was away, thus dissolving the Alliance pact.

But for now, Sturgund had to fall in line himself, and Hewart insisted upon that. That meant keeping his two younger brothers out of harm's way in this war, and for that matter, out of harm's way himself, inasmuch as he could. Sturgund was unhappy about that, but with the prospect of taking over Ormon, determination took over in his eye and he agreed.

Whether or not they might actually take over Ormon, Hewart was unsure. He rubbed at his beard. The idea was fascinating. No monarch at home. No heir. A kick in the gut from the Queen. The more he thought of the idea, the more he liked it. But it would be exceptionally difficult, for Ormon had easily as many troops as Ambsellon did, and invading Ormon in the middle of a war with Clemongard – well.

He needed more answers first. Sturgund would be disappointed if they did not take Ormon, but he would get over it. Still… expanding to the west and – the east. Hewart found he liked the idea.

Keldrick

He could not believe the sight of the castle built into the mountain. He shaded his eyes and stared. So this was RainsCourt. Spires and flags towered from mountain peaks in its pride from a treacherous height. Keldrick wasn't sure he wanted to ascend to that height, lift or not.

He had tried not to glance at Selby ever since – those damnable nights. She had ruined his concentration. His focus had gone to shit now. Whenever she was near, he seemed to know, he could turn his head and see her there. But they rode side by side still, and Keldrick had caught her smiling from time to time.

After every night – three now, three extraordinary, incredible nights of glory, Selby told him, "We can't do this again!" Well, Keldrick knew the dangers of being caught, yet he was powerless to keep from seeing her. And in she snuck, into his tent both of the next two nights.

Finally, Selby grew solemn on the third night and told Keldrick that they were nearing RainsCourt, and that they would be staying in the palace once they arrived. They would be caught once they were at RainsCourt. Keldrick agreed, for what else could he do? She was right.

"Stop it!" Selby whispered.

Keldrick frowned. "What am I doing?" he whispered under his breath.

"You're riding too close!" she whispered back. But she smiled.

Damnable woman. But he immediately reined his horse apart from hers.

And then came the thundering of hooves. No! Under attack! Keldrick whirled his mount around while he drew his sword. "Get behind me!" he commanded, not looking to see if she had or not. This was going to be a difficult fight, for they'd lost a good deal of men over the last week to the Ambsells. And yet, they kept pouring through the pass.

But the banners... the banners were – Eastern. Red, blue, and gold... blue, green and silver....

Thank the gods! The troops from home had finally arrived!

Selby

"Your Highness –"

"Prince Keldrick, I must insist –"

"If you please, Your Highness," asked a general, "how are we to refer to you?"

"Captain Firthing will do," answered Keldrick mildly.

Captain Firthing, thought Selby. Interesting – she had not thought of Keldrick as having achieved a military rank.

But of course he would. As a third son, Keldrick would have been expected to serve in the military, just as her brothers had. Captain Firthing. She forced the smile tugging at her lips to keep from overtaking her face. Her stomach fluttered.

She could not help it – he captivated her. And as Queen, that was not good. Should anyone suspect – anyone but Durain, of course – her reputation, her integrity would be forever, irrevocably stained. Finally, Selby put her foot down, for they were to stay in RainsCourt now, and she could not be seen in any other than her chambers.

She watched Keldrick answer questions. He answered to Captain Firthing, Your Highness, and Prince Keldrick. Selby was not accustomed to his being the Royal in the room. He was so calm and firm, so strong... and they nearly forgot she existed. For once, she was practically invisible.

She tried not to sigh aloud. Another War Council. This one would take up at least an hour, while she wanted to press ahead and move on to RainsCourt. Selby was tired of feeling naked and exposed out here, camping where Ormish or Ambsell could attack her. She longed for the safety of four walls again. Though she did not relish viewing the walls where her three brothers and her father had died less than a year ago, and by Ambsell hands. Selby blinked, trying not to narrow her eyes with fury at the thought of that.

Keldrick – *Ambassador Keldrick* – introduced her to the Eastern Alliance men then. She smiled graciously and told them how grateful she was for their presence.

And she was. Near forty thousand men from the East had just joined her ranks. Forty... thousand. That took her breath away. Her ranks on the field were sorely depleted over the last week, fighting the Ambsells. At least five thousand men dead, some two thousand wounded. But Selby knew they had killed that many or more. 'Twas an equal fight, she was told by her War Council, or what was left of it.

And then the Ormons came through the pass. Once the Ormons came through the pass, the Ambsells paused in their fighting. That gave Selby all the time she needed to send her troops south toward RainsCourt. There, they could regroup themselves. They couldn't fight both the Ormons and the Ambsells at the same time. She needed more men.

And now she had them, thanks to the gods.

—⟡—

Finally. She had been able to slip out of camp.

Durain was not happy about this mission but he accompanied her nonetheless, as Selby had known he would.

Keldrick was oblivious, being surrounded by men from the Eastern Alliance. It had afforded her the perfect opportunity to leave camp without his watchful eye. And tomorrow night would be too late, for they would be in RainsCourt....

Selby loved the night wind in her face, the wildness she felt as they galloped across the foot of the Mourning Mountains, but they had finally come to a stop, for scouts would be posted here.

Durain signaled to her to wait until he checked ahead. Selby nodded and slid off her horse. She stared up at the full moon, watching as wisps of clouds drifted across it. Minutes began to stretch out interminably. Had Durain been captured? She couldn't turn around now that she had come so far.

And then a night bird sounded once, twice.

Selby glanced around. Ah. Durain stepped into view. He placed a finger upon his lips slowly, indicating the need for silence, then beckoned.

She sucked in a deep breath. Durain gave her a stern stare. He raised an eyebrow. Selby nodded and stepped after him.

Then… she lost track of all time.

When finally she found Hewett, she was sitting atop him, covered in blood, her knife to his throat.

"You!" he grated.

"Ah. Me." And she held her free finger up but drove her cleaver into his throat deeper. She placed her hand over his disgusting mouth again. "Just so you know, Hewett, I've nicked the vein in your neck so that if I move my knife even a little, blood will spray everywhere and you will die so, so fast.

"But first, I want you to know that, just as you took all three lives of Clemongard's sons, I have taken all three lives of Ambsellon's sons." Hewett's brown eyes widened in shock, then fury. He purpled with rage but didn't dare move. "Oh, you needn't worry, Hewart, they died hero's deaths.

"Now, however. Now it is your time. Just as Ambsellon took a King from Clemongard, now Clemongard will take a King from Ambsellon. A father and three sons for a father and three sons. I quite like it, don't you? No?" Selby asked. "Hm, that's too bad, Hewart, perhaps you should have thought of that when you decided to have my father and brothers killed, for now I am killing you and I've killed your sons as well.

"Did you know, Hewart, what they call me now, in Clemongard? The Cleaver Queen. I think that, after tonight, I will have earned that title."

Hewart's eyes in the lantern light of his tent were both furious and frightened.

"And no one, Hewart, to take over your throne, not a single son left. Pity, isn't it, knowing that you haven't anyone left to inherit Ambsellon. At least my father left the throne to me after my three brothers passed."

His eyes narrowed with disgust.

"But I know one Queen who might be interested in your Throne… they say ice runs through her veins, Hewart. I wonder if the Ice Queen will keep the name Ambsellon or if she'll change it to Ormon.…"

Hewart's eyes bulged in fury and Selby sliced his neck just then.…

Myrischka

She stalked the field and threw herself onto her horse. Behind her, Hewart's forces were chaotic and disorganized. She actually thought better of the man, given his penchant for control and thorough domination.

Myrischka had allowed the man time to meet in honor of the ridiculous Ambsellon-Ormon Alliance, but he had sent her an Ambassador. She had diplomats aplenty. That act on his part only told her that he was scared to treat with her. Well, Hewart's time had come and gone and now Myrischka was leaving.

She would stay longer but the little Western Queen now had an infusion of Eastern Alliance troops. Smart girl, thought Myrischka, allying with the East.

Standing and surveilling from her rocky point, all she had seen over Hewart's men was a sea of Eastern troops. Banners from all across the East – as far south as Hardewold, even Ghiverny had sent men. Which delighted Myrischka, for she had troops invading Ghiverny as she stood here in Clemongard. The fewer Ghivern troops on Eastern soil, the better. Romeny, of course, had sent men, as had Delsynth, and even the Stafford Spears were well represented. At least thirty-five thousand men had joined the fight, and Myrischka had no reason to believe that more Eastern Alliance men were not stationed elsewhere in Clemongard, or that they had not yet arrived.

Therefore, let Hewart and his men stay and fight this foe that had doubled in number. It had never been her intention to stay and fight, only to show her face behind him that she might convince him to attack Clemongard.

Now that his troops were distracted and exhausted, Myrischka was now plugging up the Rockdale pass and, with her own men, turning north toward Cliff Watch North. They would circle around the Mourning Mountains and attack Ambsellon now.

There had been an interesting moment, however, when she had laid eyes on who could only have been the Queen of Clemongard. Yesterday, in her scope, just as Myrischka determined that the new soldiers arriving were indeed Eastern Alliance, she had seen the young Queen. And indeed, a cleaver hung from her waist, just as Myrischka had heard. She looked strong and proud, wearing armor and ringmail. Cheeky little queen. Myrischka could not help but admire the girl, for she was only a girl. But soon enough, Clemongard would be hers. As soon as Myrischka left to take over Ambsellon, the rest of her men in the Riverlands would close in on Hewart's men and the Mourning Mountains....

Clemongard. Ambsellon. Ghiverny.

Myrischka breathed in a deep breath of satisfaction.

Selby

"I said, allow them to pass." She gestured to Durain, and he immediately stepped forward to wrestle a path clear.

Her generals were loathe to allow these two – travelers – near her, for they would not relinquish their weapons. Furthermore, they demanded a personal audience, an audience without her War Council.

She admitted being intrigued as they stepped forward. One of them, a bearded man, wore two swords crossed behind his back. He was not nearly as tall as Durain, but had a strong, sturdy build and muscled arms that undoubtedly knew how to swing those two swords.

His slender companion trod the floor of RainsCourt's polished Great Hall with an ease that suggested that he was comfortable in his own skin and not in the least intimidated by the senior military men demanding he relinquish the sword she saw hanging at his hip.

"And who are you?" Selby asked as they stopped before the throne.

"Two men with messages of extreme import for Your Majesty. We have traveled a great distance, at danger to our lives to be here," added the bearded man with the two swords.

That sounded foreboding. "And have you names?"

The man was silent, though his eyes flicked about the Great Hall to suggest he would say no more in the presence of the crowd.

She took a breath. If she dismissed all of the War Council, Durain and his partner Ericorian could dispatch these two should they try anything against her. Though the travelers looked highly capable of wielding those swords....

"Very well. All of you are dismissed." Suddenly, Selby called out, "Ambassador, please remain." Keldrick would be an added protection and an extra voice.

Grumbling, her War Councilors began to leave.

"Your Majesty, I really must object –"

"But, Your Majesty –"

Selby brushed her hands at them. "We shall meet later." Not for the first time, she knew that, if she were a King, many of these men would never think to doubt her commands.

Keldrick joined her at her side.

Selby saw the slender traveler studying Keldrick and wondered what the news they bore that was of such import it must be delivered in privacy.

"Now then, you have my attention, and I have even dismissed my War Councilors," she said.

The bearded man remained skeptical and glanced at Keldrick. "Him? And your Ericorian?"

"Surely you do not expect me to dismiss my own guard for two travelers whom I do not know? This is a time of war, and I have no reason to trust you, sir. My Ericorian I have every reason to trust, and this man, the Ambassador to the Eastern Alliance has already saved my life at least twice. I have no reason to distrust him politically or otherwise. Either they stay or you go."

The two considered and then the bearded men told her, "I am Renfry, and this is my – partner, Topher, Your Majesty. We are at your service." And they bowed low before her.

Selby bit back her impatience. "Thank you. Now, what have you come to tell me?"

Renfry frowned. "We have traveled through the enemy lines to reach Your Majesty, from Corstarorden. Ormon forces have massed in the Riverlands and plan on striking, though when, or where, we know not. But that is not what we came so far to tell you, Your Majesty." Here, Renfry exchanged a look with Topher.

He sighed. "I know of a plot to kill you, Your Majesty. Ormons plot to kill you so that no one sits the Clemongard throne."

His raspy voice hung in the Great Hall.

Selby stared at the man.

But before she could answer, Keldrick said, "She is a royal entity, man. Her entire family has been the object of Ormon death threats her entire life and yet she sits the throne. Tell me you have more than that."

She laid a light hand on Keldrick's to silence him. Her entire family was dead by the hand of a man whom she'd just killed. If there was a plot afoot to kill her, she wanted to hear more, and she owed it to her people to hear more....

"He has the right of it. I and my family have been the target of death threats my entire life. I think you need something more solid than just your word, sir."

A sour look crossed Renfry's face. "Very well. Overlooking the fact that we have crossed enemy lines at great risk to our personal safety to impart this information, I would ask a boon of you –"

"You dare! In mine own Hall, you dare to ask a boon of me after insulting me so," flared Selby.

"We are here for your benefit," said Topher.

Selby glared at him. "Before I grant you this boon, what is it, that I may consider it?

Renfry returned, "A simple one. That our identities be kept secret, and that what we discuss here before you be kept secret as well."

Selby stared at him flatly, tempted to say no. "And why is that? Are you hunted men? Are you wishing me to grant you asylum, when I hardly know you or your motives?"

"To my knowledge, we are not hunted men, nor are our motives impure," said Renfry in a quiet tone.

Selby considered and then said, "Very well. I grant you the secrecy of your identities and what may be discussed here. Ambassador Keldrick, your word on this."

Keldrick looked distinctly displeased, but gave his word nonetheless.

Renfry said, "We are part of a private order, a centuries-old order called the Brotherhood of the Two Blades. We are Land-wide and we assist and help people like yourself in their time of need."

"People like myself," Selby cut in.

"Royalty, nobles, individuals of importance and significance to the land, though very few Brothers assist the Northern Countries," Renfry answered. "We are instructed in weaponry and all levels of education –" here he looked at his partner, "some more than others, that we may be of service."

"I have never heard of the Brotherhood of the Two Blades, and I've had an extensive education," commented Keldrick with suspicion.

"It is a private Order. Secret, one that is unknown to those whom we do not serve."

With curiosity, Selby nodded at Topher. "He does not wear two blades."

"He is still in training. But I believe him to be more intelligent and more learned than most Brothers I have ever known."

Selby raised an eyebrow.

"Very well. How did you come to learn of this plot against my person?"

"We have traveled from Corstarorden. I overheard the plot being discussed by Stordish mercenaries. If Stordish mercenaries knew of the plot, you may be sure, Your Majesty, that the Ormish and the Ambsells are aware of it. We came to tell you that a price is on your head, and to offer our services. Stay as close to your Ericorian as you can, Your Majesty, for they are as impermeable a force as one might hope for."

"I shall, and I do. As for your services, what services do you offer?" Selby inquired, chilled. She had removed one threat, only to find out of another….

Topher said, "We will search for any threat against you. Quietly. Within your ranks, from your troops to your War Councilors."

"Many of my War Councilors just arrived from the East; they are Allies."

"Even Allies like the taste of gold, Your Majesty," Topher replied soberly.

How awful! "I agree, then, and accept your – assistance… provided you are quiet about it."

"We shall be," replied Renfry.

The Great Hall doors burst open. Both of her top Generals stood at attention.

"Your Majesty! Please forgive the intrusion, but this news is of an immediate nature!"

With impatience, Selby gestured for them to approach.

They hurried forward. Her top General nodded stiffly to Keldrick and then announced, "King Hewart and his sons are dead! All three of them!"

Selby pretended shock.

"What!" She turned to Renfry and Topher. "Did you know of this?"

But their jaws had dropped open in astonishment. "No, Your Majesty!"

"Dead!" echoed Keldrick, shocked himself.

"How credible is this news?" Selby asked.

"The entire Ambsell army has withdrawn, it's all their ranks are talking of. All our scouts have reported the same thing. Murdered in the night," the General reported.

"And they are retreating?" asked Selby.

"Retreating toward Rockdale Pass," replied the General.

Selby turned to Renfry and Topher. Her Brotherhood of the Two Blade spies, sorely needed, it seemed. "You will excuse me, this is of enormous import," she told them.

"Of course," Renfry said, shock still registered on his face over the death of the Ambsell family.

Retreating, Selby thought.

Good.

Varley

Now that he had taken the combined one hundred ships from Hull Port and Berring Point, he had something to work with. The Berring Point Harbor Master had been loathe to surrender the harbor, even with the might of Varley's men, until Varley told him, at sword point, to take his grievance up Queen Myrischka of Ormon. The Harbor Master had told him that he had not received word from King Romand to release the ships yet. It was like a game of Ice for Varley. He had improvised and said he was on his way next to see King Romand. Only after saying that did the Harbor Master release the ships. Fool.

Varley would be paying King Romand a visit in due time. After all of Corstarorden's ships were his. He still had three more stops to make, according to the map: South Port, MastView, and SaltySide, where at least fifty ships sat at each port waiting for him to take over, in the name of the Ormon bitch, who he was pretending to collect for. She would have quite a surprise when she found out he'd stolen her ships out from under her. He would eventually set up his own seat in Roarden North, for he'd visited the great city on more than one occasion and found it to his liking. But first, he would take over S'hendalow after Corstarorden.

That, mused Varley, proved to be possibly problematic. The new King A'dair had built new ships, yes, but would he capitulate to Varley's demands? Varley thought probably not. Those new ships would need to be taken rather than insisted upon.

Well, by then, he would have enough of a Naval presence that he could do so, he decided with a raised eyebrow.

Half of A'dair's troops would be focused by that time on Pavilion City anyway, as well as the cries of the farmers and merchants who would have no way to sell their wares as they usually did. No one was traveling the long distance to Pavilion City anymore because of the troops on the road, his among them. The rest of his troops would meet him at South Port. He wondered what King Romand thought of that.

Varley found that the sea life suited him; the cry of the gulls, the wind in his face, the waves crashing, and certainly the so-called cabin-boys. Who knew they were actually girls disguised as boys, and only for the enjoyment of the Captain? Ha. This Captain would be glad to see him go, Varley warranted, but he cared not.

What he did care about was finally owning the Coastals. But he must be patient. A trait he must cultivate, for he had precious little of it. He must spend his time warmongering, as his late father called it, wisely....

Shadow

Wagon rides were easiest. Shadow was more than three quarters of the way to her destination now and the more she was able to ride in the back of a wagon, the easier it was on her shoes. HarCourt seemed like a distant dream – a nightmare – to her now, and Port Stanton a hazy one.

She felt as if she'd been walking forever. But she had no money to take a ship around to the Coastal Countries, and so – walking was the only way. She replenished her stores when she could – in Padron, she had lifted a new dress that she hadn't worn until she was out of the town limits. She stole a whole loaf of bread, several eggs, an assortment of vegetables, and a wheel of cheese for her rucksack, which she rationed carefully, for there wasn't hadn't been another port until Southend and she was tired of fish. But she either fished or lived off of wild fruit and vegetables.

Now she had left Southend and Thrushport behind and arrived in Port Merrinor, thanks to a farmer on his way between the two towns. She jumped off but before she left, the farmer cleared his throat and called out,

"Iffn' I was you, I'd ah, go to The Beachcomber. And avoid the other places." He cleared his throat again and then snapped the reins of the mules he was driving. "Yah, mules, yah!"

Shadow thanked him as he drove by.

The Beachcomber Inn turned out to be two more coppers than she could pay. Five coppers for one night and a meal! Shadow scoffed. She'd rather steal a loaf of a bread and sleep in a barn!

The people she passed in the street would not meet her eyes – they almost seemed nervous, thought Shadow. Shifty-eyed. Nervous and suspicious were not a good combination for a town population. What would an entire group of people, from the merchants to the passersby, have to be concerned about? Even the Crown soldiers, the Navy, acted odd....

Just as she tired of walking the town, she found another inn. The Drift Inn. Shadow scoffed again at the title and saw the décor on the outside of the building consisted mainly of net with elaborately arranged driftwood. It seemed a bit of a ramshackle building, but she decided to enter anyway.

"Three coppers gives ya a room an' a meal, take it or leave it," called a mustached innkeeper from behind the counter.

Shadow hadn't slept in an inn since Padron, at the Silver Sea Gull. A blanket that didn't have sand in it, a pillow, a bed, bathwater, and a steaming serving of food all sounded wonderful to her. Shadow laid down her coppers and the innkeeper swiped them off the countertop.

"Room 4," said the barkeep in a disinterested tone, but Shadow felt his eyes on her back as she left with the key. She would be glad to leave Port Merrinor. The next sea port was Kallicove and from there, Shadow would finally turn north and away from the coast. She would follow the Singing River north and cross it where it became the Rosh River, once the land was no longer the WetLands but the RiverLands, and habitable by people. She wondered what it would be like to finally be out of Hardewold and in Tortoreen, the next leg of her journey.

But first, she had to get to out of Port Merrinor.

Almeric

This. This just received from Corstarorden. If he had to guess, it was another damnable tariff on incoming goods from Tortoreen. Almeric didn't even want to read the parchment. It smelled of something – something afoul. Ever since he married off Theldry, tariffs and excises had been leveled, higher prices had been charged... and all out of Corstarorden. The S'hendalow economy had remained stable. Corsta money was slipping between his fingers and he wanted to know why. And how. Almeric was tired of it.

His eyes narrowed. Ever since he'd married off Theldry. That was it then, wasn't it? Almeric sighed. If only the assassin had succeeded. She knew too much. Why those fools had allowed her to sit in on Cabinet meetings.... Politically speaking, a first-born child was allowed to do so, and so he had not sent her from the room, but the girl was too canny for her own good, unraveling plots and all but making bold accusations there at the table on three separate occasions. They'd finally told Almeric to stop the nonsense.

Tort law allowed women in Cabinet meetings... and even to take the throne if no other familial male descendant was left, but Almeric would die rather than let a daughter assume the throne of Tortoreen.

In S'hendalow, A'dair had taken the throne, and Nureen had been near rabid about marrying Theldry off to him, so that she might be a Queen, as she was a princess already, but with all the girl knew, Almeric just did not trust a new king with the possible knowledge that Theldry could hand him. If only she had stayed out of the way....

He hadn't relished the idea of killing off his only daughter, for daughters carried the bloodline truest, and Nureen was likely past childbearing age, should something happen to Bronn at nine. Almeric had only visited her ladies-in-waiting these last few years, which was quite fine with him, for after Bronn, Nureen had thickened about the middle and Almeric preferred his women slender. He wondered upon the odd occasion how often a lady-in-waiting got with a child of his and took wormwort. A bastard of his would be better to have than just the two children. Why, the Delsynth king, it was said, had nine children. Nine, and all legitimate, even if the first five were daughters. Almeric shook himself then. Imagine how horrible that would be. Five Theldries. Awful.

Even more awful if his Theldry knew of Lord Scollard and Prince Rilstrom. He'd offered for Prince Rilstrom to stay in Tortoreen, but the ride had been too long. Imagine... an Eastern prince, in Tortoreen. Almeric smiled. And eventually all of his ships were helping not this little cast-aside Prince Varley, but the Ormon Queen, to attack Hardewold over in the Eastern Alliance, as they had been resupplying ships with Stordish troops in months past. For his troubles, Almeric would be getting the lower RiverLands, south of Romeny, so Tortoreen could expand east to the Singing River. The Ormon Queen – Queen she may be, and brazen, but she was smart. Almeric just had to pass the time and allow that wiggler Prince Varley to think he was getting what he wanted. Fool.

Yes. This whole raise in tariffs in Corstarorden he would warrant had to do with Theldry. Almeric had betrothed her to the wealthy Duke of Mendellion, who lived as far away as possible. Unfortunately, to certain Cabinet members' chagrin, she had survived the betrothal. What good was knowing an assassin if the assassin was unsuccessful? Lord Scollard had returned the fee and written him that the *security surrounding the girl was too thick for another attempt, perhaps in the future.*

Well, mused Almeric as he considered the seven new tariffs and four new price hikes imposed upon Tortoreen by Corstarorden, that future was beginning to loom before him. Perhaps he would send a communication to Shaw and see if Lord Scollard was available again, for his daughter had become intolerable. Again.

Reaghann

According to this communication from Rickstan – the country of Tortoreen was responsible for putting him in the traitor cell of the dungeon, that was, him as Rilstrom. King Almeric, Lord

Drury, and this Lord Scollard, whomever that was. An assassin associating with Lord Drury, but Reaghann would bet the two were one and the same. Certainly, Lord Drury knew how to slip through society by means of more than one identity, thought Reaghann.

But what disturbed him far more was this collusion with the Queen of Ormon to attack Reaghann's coastline. Bad enough to have assisted the displaced Stordish prince via resupplying his navy and troops before sending them to attack the Eastern Alliance. But now, expecting not only to expand to the Singing River but attack Hardewold with Ormon's aid?

No, Hardewold would not be sending Clemongard naval assistance, Reaghann thought darkly, not when Tortoreen would be attacking him in the near future as Ormon's proxy.

He needed to double the Southern Shield's fortification as well as the naval stratagems. In fact, may the Eastern Shield forgive him, but this was proof that Reaghann needed to stay right where he was, rather than fight up in the north of Delsynth. Oh, he would send the troops he'd been planning on marching with, but he simply wouldn't be present. Like all Hardewold kings before him, he would see that the Southern Shield was impenetrable by the entire Western half of the Land, and he would risk the Eastern Shield's wrath to do it, for it meant obstructing invasion of Hardewold both by land and by sea....

Rhutgard

Rhutgard shivered and wrapped his cloak around him as he squatted by the fire. They were too close to the mountains for his comfort.

Of course, none of this was to his comfort. Merridon was dead and all he had been able to do to show he was in mourning was wear this black cloak, sent from Fairview. Not even a state ceremony had been held for his son, his first born. Rhutgard took a deep breath, remembering yet again the day Merridon came into the world, small, sickly, crying.

Even so, had Rhutgard been home, he would have insisted upon a small, tasteful ceremony to see his son to his grave. So odd, he thought, not for the first time. So odd, it was almost as if Merridon had held on until Rhutgard had departed. Stanyard assured him that all was done according to Merridon's wishes and Principea had everything firmly in hand. He even noted that Mirelle was assisting Principea, and for that, Rhutgard was grateful. He just wished he'd been there by his son's side at the last.

This miserable, biting cold.... They had not yet reached the EverWinters, but they would by morning. And then, with the might and main of all three countries represented, Delsynth, Ghiverny, and Romeny, representing the Eastern Alliance, they would attack the Ormons who were waiting for them.

The better part of the Stordish infantry had died in the Battle of Rossdon, as Gerard's troops referred to it. Kendrick, Driscoll, and the rest of the War Council believed more Ormons would soon follow down the Northern Country Crosslands and into Ghiverny, if they were not already in Ghiverny now. But here at the foot of the EverWinters, they had nearly two hundred thousand men, a fair portion of whom were Stafford Spears.

"Father," Kendrick greeted him quietly as he sat down on a log before the fire. He, too, wore a black cloak to symbolize his mourning Merridon.

"Kendrick, you stay away from the main line of fighting tomorrow, do you understand me?" Rhutgard told him. "I know how well you fight, and that you can take care of yourself, but I am telling you: stay away from the main line of fighting tomorrow. Stay with the generals instead."

His tone would brook no argument, nor was he in the mood for one.

Kendrick grimaced but nodded, giving him none. Perhaps he understood why. Rhutgard had just lost one son. He didn't want to lose another out here on the battlefield.

The mood on the night before a battle was always a morose one. Men stayed to their fires and talked lowly, rested while they could, prayed if they prayed, and stared into the flames for peace. Well he remembered these nights, thinking of the Twenty Years War.

Kendrick. So like him – he looked just like Rhutgard had at that age. Rhutgard wondered what Kendrick was thinking as he stared into the fire, and what Keldrick was thinking, where and how he was, and that hopefully he had found success in his post as Ambassador to the Eastern Alliance....

———

The most frigid part of the day – dawn. Rhutgard poked his head out of the tent and found Kendrick preparing porridge. Imagine that, he thought with wonder. A month ago, Kendrick would never have accepted porridge for breakfast, far less made it. Pride for his son filled him.

In silence, Kendrick handed him a bowl of porridge and scooped another bowlful for himself. They said nothing as they ate and Rhutgard relished the heat of the bowl in his hands, for the morning air was crisp and biting. Today, they would see snow, he had no doubt. He just hoped his troops were ready for it.

As he was shaving, he caught Kendrick watching.

"We are at war, Father. Why are you even bothering?"

So Rhutgard said, "Your grandfather and your great-grandfather always kept their beards neat, as do I. One day, you, too, will be the Eastern Shield, Kendrick, and your face will be the first thing people see. If you hide it behind a barbarian bush, people will notice. If you take the time to take care of yourself, people will notice that as well. Those are the words of your grandfather's father.

"I may meet the man who commands this Ormon Army today. If I, as the Eastern Shield, were to appear unkempt, why, that would cast a poor impression of my leadership abilities upon me."

"I haven't much of a beard to shave," Kendrick admitted ruefully. It cost him some pride to say that aloud, Rhutgard thought with amusement.

"No, not at first. What you have, you shape, and then, when it comes time, you trim it." He wiped his razor clean.

"I hope Keldrick learns that, wherever he is," said Kendrick, rubbing a hand over his thin beard.

"Something tells me that your brother has a lot on his shoulders as Eastern Alliance Ambassador, especially now that our troops have likely arrived. I'm sure that he is projecting a seemly appearance."

"A word, a scrap of information! Why has he not sent a report?" demanded Kendrick.

"Son, you forget that your brother is serving at the Queen of Clemongard's pleasure. Should she want to send a report, then she shall. Most notably, they are being attacked by both the Ormish and the Ambsells, by land and by sea, on more than one front. I believe he is likely too busy to send a bird or a runner just now. In war, updates can be few and far between," he chided gently.

He knew Kendrick only wanted news that his twin was well, and probably more so than anyone else did, for they had not been parted for so long, nor been placed in such dangerous positions. Rhutgard worried for Keldrick as well, but believed in his other twin son's cleverness and wit; his idea of staying on as Ambassador had grown on him and the troops were told to report directly to him when they arrived. But Rhutgard, too, hoped for news soon.

As the men were packing up Rhutgard's tent, he heard murmurs among the men of The Wolf and The Berringer and guessed that Gerard and Driscoll were nearby.

"Rhudy, a good morning to you." Gerard's voice sounded tired.

"Rhutgard," Driscoll nodded.

Rhutgard greeted them, welcoming them to what was left of the small camp that was being packed up as they stood there. Kendrick clasped arms with Dougall. A close friendship had formed between the two, for they had the commonality of both being Crown Princes and of an age together.

Driscoll eyed Rhutgard's black fur and leather cloak, flapping in the chill wind.

"Rhutgard, I never said this prior to now, but I'm sorry for your loss. You've lost a child and I know how that feels. And you know who that child was, because you will always be a son-by-law to me through her." Driscoll paused for a few moments.

Rhutgard was taken aback at this and unsure what to say. Suddenly, he felt a Prince again, cowering before his father-by-law, the King of Delsynth, who was only marrying off his daughter Hennolyn because she would be married to the Eastern Shield-to be and because it was the current Eastern Shield's desire. Driscoll had petrified him back in those days.

Then Driscoll said, "In fact, all of us are family here, this entire circle, united by blood, law, and Alliance. And we ride off today to fight a foe who has over and over attempted to divide us. So I have this – a little something for us –" And Driscoll withdrew an engraved steel flask from his cloak.

Gerard immediately grinned. "Where did you get that, Berringer?"

"A Colonel whose life I saved gave it to me, if it's the flask you're talking about. The bourbon, on the other hand…." And Driscoll permitted himself a smile of his own. "A little bourbon, to warm us up and start the journey off. And a toast. To family." He held the flask up as he said this, then sipped from the flask before he passed it around.

They each sipped from the flask. Ah, that Delsynth bourbon – it would burn a hole through your throat but it was damn good stuff. To family… all of his, thought Rhutgard, thinking of home and his wife and children.

"Are we ready to do this?" asked Driscoll as he accepted the flask from Kendrick, whose eyes were blinking from the strength of the bourbon. Rhutgard wanted to laugh. If Kendrick was going to be Eastern Shield one day, he would need to hold his liquor.

"Yes," said both Rhutgard and Gerard together.

"Very good. Then let us away."

—⟨⟩—

And there they were, at the foot of the EverWinter Mountains. Ormons. Bloody bastards.

"How many of them do you make?" asked Gerard, his face stone.

"Fifty thousand, more or less," replied Rhutgard.

"That's if no more are hiding elsewhere. Fifty thousand is just what's visible," commented Driscoll.

Gerard said, "Look at them, just milling about down there. No defensive tactics."

"You can bet an Ormish force that size knows we're here," observed Driscoll.

"Ideas?" asked Rhutgard.

Gerard scoffed. "We've lost enough men. That's a ploy. The Battle of Rossdon took too many good men. Let us sit here and wait for them to make a move."

Driscoll said, "They want us down there. Don't forget the men they have following up on the Northern Countries Crosslands. We have no idea the size of that army. We may be two hundred thousand, but that host may be two hundred and fifty or more."

"If I may, Your Majesty…?" asked Kendrick.

He had learned to only speak when given permission, something else Rhutgard was proud of him for.

"Captain Firthing, you have an idea?"

"Sending our entire force down there would be a mistake, I think. We don't know where the rest of their troops are, should they have any, nor do we know the size of the army they are sending here. If we send all of our troops down there, then we are playing right into their hand. They want us to think they are only 'milling around' and unprepared. They want us to think there are only fifty thousand, and perhaps there are only fifty thousand. My advice would be to send an assortment of our very best troops, say, sixty thousand down there, to meet them, some of that assortment to include Stafford Spears. And therefore, it will be an equal fight, rather than us ride down there, overtake them, and camp there, where we will be overtaken by an army from all sides and forced to fight with a mountain behind us and no way to retreat."

Was that his Kendrick who made such sense?

Driscoll and Gerard nodded their assent.

He called for the nearest Sergeant and instructed him to bring the War Council with all haste. Kendrick had just planned the first attack of the EverWinters Battle.

Ishbel

So restless. And tired of pacing. All she heard was war. War in Corstarorden, and certainly war in Clemongard, and she knew where they were now, damn Rogue and his books. She'd read that book over again in the daylight hours if she thought she wouldn't get caught but it would be her luck she'd finally get a customer.

Soldiers in the country closest to Pavilion City meant that Pavilion City was on their list of destinations, thought Ishbel, and whores were first on a soldier's list of priorities, before even food. All the soldiers who'd been through here over the last month had been righteous arseholes, and Ishbel wasn't afraid to say it. Not just to the whores, but the merchants as well, demanding lower prices, or even free. Violent, they were, too. One had dislocated Rosie's shoulder. She herself had a black eye that was nearly gone. And Gobin, useless shit of a man that he was, he wasn't about to fight back against these soldiers or he'd lose his life. Ishbel really did not want to be sold to some other whoremonger, especially the one who kept his whores chained in cages. Nor did she want to get sold as a slave again. As long as Gobin stayed alive, Ishbel stayed relatively happy.

But over the last month, business had dropped dramatically, and more so during the last week. Merchants had packed up, buyers refused to travel the roads. Ishbel couldn't blame them. And all due to the war. The Eastern Alliance was fighting the Northern Countries now, according to the gossip she heard in the stalls, and Clemongard was being attacked by both Ambsellon and

Ormon. But gossip was gossip, for she'd heard the Ambsell King and his sons were all murdered in the night and Ishbel knew that couldn't be true.

She gave up and flopped down on the bed. She felt like a caged animal.

Just as she did, someone hissed, "Ishbel!" from the entrance to her pavilion.

Rogue strode in. Ishbel was never so glad to see anyone as she was to see him at that moment.

"You are late!" she chided.

"And it's time for you to leave," he returned.

Leave? Leave and go where? Her face must have registered her confusion, for Rogue explained, "There are soldiers here. In Pavilion City. Putting the torch to the place. It's my guess they won't treat you kindly. I'm here to take you away from here. Now here –" He threw a violet calico dress on the bed. "Put this on. You can't be seen in public wearing – well, what you normally wear."

"They're burning the City?" asked Ishbel with alarm.

Rogue turned as she started to change clothes. "Just hurry up, Ishbel, before we've no time." How cute, she thought as she watched him turn while she changed her clothes. She couldn't count the amount of men who had seen her naked and this one turned his back to observe the niceties.

"And what does Gobin think of this?" she inquired as she pulled the dress over her head.

Rogue scoffed. "Let us just say that that sonofabitch whoremonger will no longer be a concern of yours, nor of anyone's."

Her eyes widened slightly at that, but she said nothing. She could not recall the last time she had worn a proper dress. "Very well, you can turn about now," Ishbel said lightly as she smoothed her dress.

Rogue studied her briefly. "Violet becomes you." Then he gestured. "Is there… anything here you want to take with you?" His voice sounded doubtful.

Ishbel thought for a moment, then lifted the mattress and pulled out the History of the Era book. In a regretful tone, she said, "I haven't yet finished reading it."

Rogue opened his rucksack and she placed it inside. Then she held up a finger. "Just one other thing." She stood on her tiptoes and felt along the far ledge for the linen pouch she'd created to hold the silvers Rogue had paid her over the last six months. As she pulled them off the ledge, they clinked.

"You won't need that where we're going," Rogue told her.

"Says you, who's always had such money to dole out," Ishbel returned, holding the linen to her as a cherished prize.

Rogue considered and allowed it.

"Does this mean, then, that I belong to you now?" asked Ishbel with curiosity. Ah. Another mark for her shoulder. But Rogue had been kind to her so far.

Rogue looked confounded. "Ishbel," and he cupped her chin with a calloused hand. "You are a free woman. I have set you free. Now, come, come, we must leave," and he beckoned. "Follow my lead."

Ishbel left without even looking back at her pavilion.

Rogue led her through the City that she had called home for years. A sense of panic was beginning to fill the air amongst the merchants, and green and red-check uniformed soldiers were seen throughout the stalls. Ishbel sucked in a breath.

"Follow my lead and stay calm," whispered Rogue.

He led her to a stable where an enormous black horse was saddled and waiting. He had paid the stable hand two silvers and a bronze for keeping the horse ready in the midst of the confusion in the City. The stable hand's eyes widened, then he bowed with respect just before he opened the far stall door.

"Can you ride?" asked Rogue.

Ishbel had learned to ride as a girl at the farm where she was first a slave, but it had been years since she had sat a horse. She nodded mutely.

Rogue climbed up and then pulled her up behind him.

And then they rode out, leaving the burning Pavilion City behind them.

———

She stared behind her for part of the way, watching as Pavilion City went up in smoke. Rogue had rescued her just in time. Ishbel felt sorry for the other women she had worked with. A huge cloud could be seen for miles over the wide expanse of meadowland. The burning of Pavilion City.

Finally, Rogue stopped the horse for water. He held out a hand for her to climb down the horse.

After the horse had drunk some water and she, too had drunk from a waterskin, Ishbel finally gathered the courage to ask,

"So am I no longer to spy for you?"

"No. I told you, you are a free woman, bound by no man."

Ishbel considered this. Not a slave? But such things always came with a price…. She moved closer.

"And… what do I owe you for this? How am I indebted to you now?"

Rogue looked angry.

"Ishbel, I set you free because slavery is wrong. Not because I wanted a servant bound to me for life. You are a free woman, free to go where you choose. In fact, if you like, you may turn and start walking away in any direction, although I don't recommend it. These are the Free Lands, and I know where we're going. If you stay with me, I'll see you to safety, and people who can see that you live a life of safety and freedom, as you were meant to. In fact, I even know someone who can remove those marks of indenture from your shoulder, should you so choose. I ask for nothing in return. You are a free woman, Ishbel."

Ishbel's stomach was giddy at this last. She flew into Rogue's arms and kissed him.

As a free woman – not a slave!

Mirelle

Mirelle envied her mother, for she had the gift of discourse on absolutely everything, and Mirelle remained spellbound just to listen, whereas she herself could only keep her audience listening to her so long as it required the necessity of purpose.

Suddenly, Kimbur grabbed them both firmly by the arms and held them back.

Both Mirelle and Mother turned to stare at her.

Wordlessly, Kimbur pointed at the water spilled on the stone stairwell just before them. A bucket sat to the side by the wall, yet no servant was to be seen.

Kimbur and Mirelle exchanged a meaningful look. Each morning, the three of them descended from the Ladies' Quarters near this time. A slip on those stairs would be painful at the least, for there was water on the stairwell itself as well. Who would clean this corridor and stairwell, wondered Mirelle with ire.

"Oh, Kimbur, thank you, we can't possibly trail our frocks down that staircase. We'll have to take this corridor down to the Center Corridor and go down the stairwell there." Mother lifted her black lace gown and smoothed it.

"Come along, ladies," she said, leading the way as she turned down the opposite corridor.

"Let us hope that we meet no other such spills on our way about the Palace," offered Mirelle. She shot a glance over her shoulder at Kimbur. Water on the stairwell. How many people had slipped and fallen to their deaths in exactly such a manner in castles? Or worse, said to have been?

Was it simply an error or was their assassin back within the walls of the Palace?

Ronan

Queen Selby was as good as her word. A group of twenty men had escorted him to the Romeny border, to the Brace Fort, and then turned back. He had attempted to get them to come with him into the East, as Ambassadors of sorts, but they had refused, citing their orders.

They were welcome, as was he, at the Brace Fort, for as long as they liked, being that they had escorted a Crown Prince of Ghiverny and a War Time Ambassador. The men took rest and stayed but a day, then turned and left for Clemongard, for, their Captain said, their country needed every able-bodied man to fight.

They had made good time – a one week's crossing was excellent given the amount of men and time it took to care for the horses. The Lord of the Brace Fort gave them food for their journey and then saw them off.

Ronan stayed an extra day so that he could write reports of what he had seen on the road, though he did not believe that any of them would reach the Eastern Shield soon now that he was in the field fighting. It seemed surreal, that the Eastern countries were at war fighting, especially Ghiverny.

So he rode for the EverWinters, to fight beside Father. And the closer he rode, the more restless he became. The border town of Rozier was larger than he expected and Romeny went on forever. His training took over and that was all that kept him sane right now.

He was nearly on the Romeny-Delsynth border, but as he rode for the EverWinters, he was to watch for an entire separate army of Ormons, according to the instructions left for him at the Brace Fort sent by none other than Rhutgard himself. If he saw a large army, then scout them and ride around them that he might send word of their number and actions....

Keldrick

He was frustrated. An entire army sat out there, wasting its resources, and still no word.

It had been over a week now. Over a week since the Ambsell troops had one morning simply withdrawn, retreated to the Rockdale Pass, with no warning.

It was said that King Hewart and his three sons had died in the night and so the troops were awaiting word on what to do. Surely they should know to continue attacking in their lord's absence, even whilst they searched for the next king to take the throne.

'Twas also whispered that the four were murdered in the night, but how could that be, said more logical minds, when they were surrounded by their own troops? Killed, murdered, indeed, regicide by someone in the midst of what was an undoubtedly heavy guard?

More like it had been poison, and poison was a woman's weapon. Or else they were too ashamed of the fact that a bloody assassin had been in their midst.

Well, Keldrick wished they would hurry on with it, find a new king. Half the War Council had voted for Selby to treat with them while they were crippled thus, and half of them voted against it. Selby herself cast the deciding vote, and an ambassador was sent to the Ambsell camp to treat but immediately was sent back in denial.

So over a week later, the Clemongard and Eastern Armies sat, wasting their resources and Keldrick his patience.

Meanwhile, the Ormish presence grew in the RiverLands and the South of Clemongard....

Theldry

She had learned so much these last few weeks. Only to realize she had so much more to learn. And if it hadn't been for the help of Cormber, Theldry would have been lost. She had promoted him to her personal business assistant, for he had been Cathall's steward and thus he had been present for much of Cathall's business transactions.

She had given Cathall a beautiful funeral, one representative of his station as Duke of Mendellion. The village people were greatly saddened at his loss, so she allowed them, fitting or not, to attend a small wake. Cormber said nothing, only raised an eyebrow. He did, however, surprise her, by joining them and placing a wreathe of flowers at the foot of Cathall's coffin.

The men and women who attended Cathall's funeral praised Theldry for the beauty of the funeral and offered her condolences for the terrible circumstances, for Varley's soldiers had rampaged all along the western coast. Women noticed the still-healing bruises of Jeanie and Kallia, whom Theldry insisted attend, and nodded to themselves knowingly. Not even powder could cover up the crimes dealt to them by Varley and his men.

Theldry and Jeanie both took care of Kallia, for Kallia had been treated terribly. She floated in and out of awareness now and startled easily. She did repetitive chores, such as chopping or skinning vegetables, but Theldry had already hired a new replacement for her so that Jeanie need not shoulder Kallia's work and her own as well.

Now that there was no one to chide her, Theldry often took trips to the ocean. She bathed there, as if the salty water could wash away what had been done to her. Somehow, it was healing in some small way – as if it washed *him* out of her, washed his thrusting and tearing out of her mind. The coolness of the salty water as it ran up against her, the grit of the sand between her toes, the wind tossing her hair about her face, made her feel so clean....

And when she stepped out, there was Jeanie with a towel to hug her dry.

They thought perhaps Kallia might enjoy the water as Theldry did. The day they tried, they walked Kallia to the shoreline, but the closer they got, the more agitated Kallia became, and so they stopped.

Varley and his men had devoured much of the estate's stores. Theldry finally gathered herself for a trip into the village, donning her mourning finery. Her first trip into the village since before Cathall had died. She and Jeanie readied themselves for a trip into town, leaving Kallia in the new servant's capable hands.

Theldry had not conversed with any of the villagers, nor seen them, since Cathall's funeral. As she wandered about the market, filling her basket with vegetables and fruits, she became aware of just how hungry she was. Perhaps they would –

And then Theldry dropped her basket and ran to the street corner, where she vomited every morsel in her stomach. Just as she thought she was done vomiting, her stomach rebelled again.

Finally, Theldry stood, panting, and looked into the concerned eyes of Jeanie. Jeanie held the basket of… vegetables and… fruits….

Theldry vomited once more. Ugh. She panted, bent over, staring at the puddle of vomit. All she could smell was overripe fruit and vomit and ….

Theldry's eyes grew wide and she laid a hand upon her stomach.

Standing straight, she looked at Jeanie, who stared at her in return, her mouth falling open.

Theldry was with child.

⸻

Jeanie begged her to get rid of the child, for she knew the babe was Varley's. And so would Kallia, once she knew. But how was Theldry to do that? It was dangerous, and no one in this little village was reliable enough for Theldry's preference. She wanted one day to bear children, and the terrible methods she knew of would harm her chances. She was a month along, and she didn't want to hurt her womb.

She was frankly astonished that she had conceived at all, given what Varley had put her through. She was sure he had damaged her beyond repair. While she did not want his child, nor did she want to lose this one possible chance at ever having a child.

Jeanie then begged her to claim it was Cathall's. But Theldry was horrified at the idea of claiming that that monster's child was actually Cathall's. And what if the rest of the staff figured it out, or the villagers? What if the child looked nothing like Cathall?

And Theldry – as a mother – the thought of herself as a parent to a babe was still giving her gooseprickles – lying from the start to her child… she just could not do it. Yet, what parent would want to tell their child that they were a product of…. And whenever she thought of that, that night, all Theldry could envision was Cathall swinging from hemp rope above her while Varley rammed himself into her.

But something good, indeed, she thought as she placed her hands upon her still flat belly, something wonderful had come of that horrible night, that horrible act. This child.

Jeanie said once, and only once, that Theldry should pray for a miscarriage.

Theldry's hand had itched, almost to slap Jeanie. She'd clenched it closed. Instead, she'd grated, "Never say that again."

Nor did she. But Theldry knew that's what Jeanie thought. It had occurred to Theldry as well, after all… having to explain one day to her child that it was the child of rape…. But also a child of summer. She sighed. If only it were Cathall's child.

"This child," she'd continued, "is a child of royalty. Through me, this child can inherit the throne of Storden, and the throne of Tortoreen." Jeanie's eyes grew round. "This child is the child of the Coastal Countries Alliance, of Corstarorden, and of the Northern – Coastal Agreement. Through me, this child will have ties to Clemongard by way of Storden's alliance, and, therefore, through me, this child will have ties to the East. This child, Jeanie, will be the most powerful child alive. The Eastern Shield is only King over five countries. My child, Jeanie, will have claim to all of the West."

Duty before love, Father. Duty before love….

Rhutgard

He wheeled his horse around, his pulse racing. If he survived this battle, then the gods were kind indeed….

All he knew was exhaustion. All those Ormish troops, spread out behind them, equally engaging them. Rhutgard saw a man bearing down upon him. With the exhaustion he felt, he reached out with his sword and slashed with all his strength. The enemy's arm fell off, his sword still in hand. The man howled in pain and gripped his arm with his one good hand, falling to the earth. Again, Rhutgard wheeled his horse around, this time hiding behind a mace that crashed down atop his shield.

"Retreat! Retreat!" came a familiar call. But was it his own side or theirs? He whirled his mount about, looking for direction.

"Your Majesty!"

"Your Majesty, it's gotten too dangerous for you to be out here!"

And two Generals escorted him toward a makeshift tent.

Well, that sounded familiar, he thought, thinking of Luvian.

"They've retreated," said one General. "But that won't last long, this is just for a break."

And thank the gods – he needed a rest. "Water," he said. One General gestured for a waterskin and Rhutgard nearly drained it.

"Have you any wounds, Your Majesty?"

Rhutgard let the remainder of the waterskin trickle down his face. "My son. Kendrick. Where is he?" he croaked.

"We'll find him. Have you any wounds, Your Majesty?" they repeated.

Rhutgard didn't think so. It was hard to tell with this armor. "Find Kendrick, find him now."

One of the Generals immediately left.

"There are more than we –" Rhutgard became dizzy, lightheaded suddenly. He bent over and leaned on his knees. He couldn't remember when last he ate.

"Your Majesty?"

Panting, Rhutgard continued. "There are – more of them than we can fight. We need a new – plan. Get me – my War Council. We can't fight them all."

Another waterskin was given to him but he pushed it away. They won the first battle, the first EverWinters Battle, but then the rest of the Ormon Army arrived, and it had been solid fighting since. They could not continue fighting this way. Something had to be done before they died out here....

Rogue

After twenty or thirty miles, he could no longer smell the smoke of what was undeniably Pavilion City burning behind them. He had gotten Ishbel out just in time.

She had turned to observe the cloud in the sky that had been her home from time to time at first. Then she had fallen asleep against him, her arms around his waist.

Rogue did not want to ponder the significance of his actions too deeply. What he had done was most unlike him. But, there it was, over and done with.

And now they were arrived here at the Capital City of the Free Lands, a place few knew existed, and few had permission to live.

Children ran freely, the smell of barbeque over afternoon cook fires accosted him, and somewhere, he knew, the Marigold River ran freely. Tents were pitched everywhere and the people of Capital City nodded or smiled at him in greeting as they rode through.

Ishbel stirred behind him now that their pace had slowed. He felt her immediately tense at the sight of all the people about her. "Rogue? Rogue, where are we?" she whispered as she stared from side to side.

"Welcome to Capital City, Ishbel, main homeland of the Free Lands," he announced.

"The Free Lands!" She wriggled about in the saddle, then whispered, "Are they not – dangerous?"

"No more so than you or me," he chuckled.

"But – but – the Free Riders…."

"Rob people of wealth, but do not kill anyone. Bandits and soldiers kill people."

Then a slap came on the horse's back haunch. "That's a fine bit of horse flesh you've got there, Armand, fine horse flesh. Kester will be wanting to see that."

Hammet. Of course he had seen his entry.

"That's where I was headed," Rogue said.

When finally they arrived at Kester's home, one of the few homes that was a mounded hut, built up against a hill and not a tent, he was awaiting them outside.

"Armand, Armand. It's been too long."

Rogue swung out of the saddle and the two embraced briefly.

"You have brought us a lovely horse, and a lovely young woman as well, I see," said Kester. He looked down his nose at Rogue. "You know our rules."

Rogue looked up at Ishbel. "She is homeless now. I think she will fit right in here."

Kester frowned and said, "Nevertheless, Armand, you know our rules."

Damn the rules. He leaned forward and said quietly, "I rescued her from slavery, the worst sort. Can she not find a home here?"

Kester stroked his beard for a few seconds and then said, "Perhaps we will find a home for her here after all." He walked up to the horse and extended a hand in greeting. "My dear, my name is Kester, and I, for better or worse, am in charge of this City. Please," and with that, he bowed with a flourish.

Ishbel climbed down awkwardly from the horse. "I am Ishbel." For the first time in all the months that he'd known her, Rogue witnessed a shyness in Ishbel. The first time that she was not in control of the situation, perhaps.

"Well, Ishbel, I am pleased to make your acquaintance," said Kester with a sweeping bow. It was this natural charm that put him in charge of an entire city and not Rogue. Rogue hadn't the patience.

"Thank you," came Ishbel's timid response.

Kester turned his attention to Rogue. "You, my friend, we must talk."

"I know, I know," replied Rogue. "But first, they've set Pavilion City afire. That's where Ishbel is from."

Kester looked with interest at Ishbel. "Is it? Afire, you say? That hasn't happened in years and years...." His face gained a faraway look. Then he said, "But you'll be interested to know that the King of Ambsellon is dead."

That took Rogue by surprise. "Dead? How?"

"No one seems to be talking on that subject, for it happened in the night beneath their own noses, so their pride is quite wounded as you can imagine. Come in, come in, tether that horse and come in. What's worse, for the Ambsells, that is, the three sons are dead as well. Murder, it's said."

"Murder! Of the entire royal house of Ambsellon! In the midst of a battlefield. No wonder they're not talking," snorted Rogue.

"I've known plenty of Ambsells. They only keep their eye on the ball and not on the field, so the saying goes," said Ishbel unexpectedly.

Rogue and Kester exchanged glances. Her unique outlook was why he liked her.

Kester snickered. "I think I'd agree with the lady on that." Then he grew somber. "Tea?" He offered cups of tea to both Ishbel and Rogue without waiting for their assent and sat down before a small cook fire. Rogue accepted his tea wordlessly and sat down, signaling Ishbel to do the same.

"What is worse, Armand... you are here. When Varley is out there, rampaging about –"

Rogue sighed. Kester was much the father he had never had. But he was tired and sore from a long, cross-FreeLands journey. "Kester, I don't need a lecture today, it's growing late and I just arrived."

"Don't you Kester me, Robard. That little wiggler is out there – his men have laid waste to half of Corstarorden and now to Pavilion City, you tell me. And he's asail, you know. On his way to S'hendalow, you know, Robard. Do you think to sit there and tell me he won't lay waste to King A'dair's country as well, and him with that new young queen? I wonder if she's with child yet?"

"Enough!" Rogue growled. "I'll not have the whole of the Coastals' damnable luck on my hands. You cannot guilt me into making a move!"

Kester glared at him and grunted.

"Who is Robard?" asked Ishbel.

Damn. "No one."

"Him," Kester pointed at Rogue.

"I am not Robard. Damn."

"Watch your tongue, boy. You may be a man grown, but you wouldn't have a place here if it weren't for me," Kester warned.

Rogue said nothing, only nodded with respect. Kester had taken him in and raised him himself when Rogue was found left to die as a babe thirty-two years ago. People of Capital City were amazed that their ruler had elected to raise a babe found to die.

Kester relented and studied Ishbel, who squirmed uncomfortably. "I see there's more than one reason you've been traveling afar."

Immediately, Ishbel sat up straight with indignation and started to respond, but Rogue held up a hand to silence her.

Kester watched this exchange with curiosity.

"Our relationship has only ever been platonic," Rogue informed him curtly.

"I have been his spy all these months," Ishbel said in a snippy tone.

"If it weren't for Ishbel, you wouldn't have known who and what was passing through the Coastals, for it was she who informed me of it in Pavilion City. She has been my spy all these months," Rogue told Kester.

"I see. We here in the Free Lands have thanks to give to you, young woman. Your actions have been more appreciated than you know."

Ishbel sat with her tea, taken aback.

Kester turned back to Rogue, as he had known he would. "But more than just one young woman has garnered your attention of late. Your niece has been gaining notoriety in certain circles...."

Rogue sighed long and loud. "Must you refer to her thus?"

Kester replied, "Is she not so?"

Ishbel asked, "You have a niece? Is that who got married not long ago?"

"Ah, I see why you like her, she is sharp."

"She is, very," said Rogue.

"Would you please stop referring to me as though I were a child," Ishbel snapped. "What is your name? Armand? Robard? And where have you lived your whole life?"
"Ah.... You did not tell her." Kester made a noise of disapproval.

"Of course I did not tell her. You are the only one who knows that," snapped Rogue.

"What do I not know?" asked Ishbel warily.

"Pardon, but if you did not know his name was not Armand, then what have you been calling him?" asked Kester to Ishbel.

Rogue looked at the ceiling.

"I have been calling him Rogue, for he refused to give me a name, and Rogue matched his personality best," Ishbel returned.

Kester laughed and laughed. "Oh, but doesn't it. And he answers to it, does he?"

She nodded.

"Oh, my. Oh, my. I do like that. Rogue, my boy. That is a perfect name for you."

Rogue glared at Kester and held his tongue.

"He refused to tell me his true name. He said we were together for business, not pleasure purposes, so perhaps that was why, that he never mixed business with pleasure. What is his real name?" asked Ishbel.

"He said that, did he?" said Kester thoughtfully.

Rogue continued to glare up at the ceiling.

"Well, good. I'm glad to know he learned something here at home." Kester chuckled. "Ah, I've made him angry."

Ishbel considered and said, "No, not angry, just irritated. See? If he's angry, he'll clench his fists."

Rogue had had enough. "Now who's speaking of someone as if they're a child?"

"You're an observant young woman. I hope he's never shown anger toward you." Kester said in a serious tone.

"Oh no, sir, not ever. But I've nursed him back to health a fair few times, and he's been frustrated about that." She smiled.

Kester said nothing at first, just shook his head. Then he said, "You may have noticed – he has a small bump between two of his fingers."

"Kester, don't."

"Between his middle two fingers, I know. I asked him about it, but he said it was just a callous."

"Robard."

"I am not Robard."

"At least tell her."

"Why?"

"Tell me what?"

"I believe the time is upon us. And if you truly search within yourself, Robard… you do as well. This entire Land is war-torn. It is our time. It is your time. There is no more denying it…."

Rogue curled his lips with distaste and glared at Kester for a moment. It was nothing he hadn't thought about over the last two months, with war churning across the Land. But he wanted nothing to do with it. Nothing.

He rubbed at the identification mark burned between his middle two fingers thirty-two years ago, then looked at Ishbel. Why tell Ishbel? Kester. He had good instincts.

Rogue – Robard – they sounded near enough – heaved an enormous sigh. Then he turned his attention to Ishbel.

He took in a deep breath. "Ishbel, when twins and triplets are born into royal – and noble – families, in order to keep the birth order separate for the succession to the throne straight, a small number is burned into the child's hand. The first to ascend the throne gets the brand between the pinky and ring finger. The second to ascend the throne gets the brand between the ring and index finger." Rogue cleared his throat. Then he held up his hand and spread apart his ring and index finger.

Ishbel's eyes widened and her mouth dropped open. "You –" she whispered.

He nodded. "However, shortly after my birth, and my branding, my father decided he didn't want there to be a fight for the throne, as twins often fight for the throne. And so – he gave the command that I be killed.

"The wet nurse was from a Free Lands family and couldn't bear the thought of having me killed. She arranged for me to be brought out to the prairie and raised by a Free Lands family, one who would not know my true identity.

"Kester recognized the meaning of the branding and knew from where I had come, found out my actual identity. And so, he personally raised me himself, so that should anyone ask questions, he would be able to pass me off as just a prairie child. Until the right time. He thinks I should take back my identity."

"But what country, what King –" Ishbel was spluttering.

"To whom am I a royal twin?" asked Rogue. "My birth name is Robard Turald, brother to King Almeric of Tortoreen."

Shadow

Why did she have the chills everywhere she went? In a summer month, no less? Shadow wanted to get her knife out of her rucksack and tuck it in her cloak pocket, but she didn't feel safe stopping. This was worse than Port Merrinor. The sooner Shadow could get away from the coastline and Kallicove, the better.

She met a few people's eyes directly while she ate at the Singing Dolphin Inn. They quickly looked away. Most people avoided her gaze altogether. Just as Shadow had decided to ask for her money for her overnight stay back, a man came in, calling out,

"Anyone who wants passage up the river, follow me. River passage, right here!"

Shadow's first instinct was to jump at the chance to leave this place, but the man looked unshaven. Three men in the bar got up to leave, however, and Shadow reconsidered.

Passage up the river. She only wanted to go to get to the Southern Shield, where the Singing and Silver Rivers converged into the Rosh River, in the rapids. If she couldn't get off, then she would be taken upriver and back into the East again. And she hadn't walked all this time and all this way only to be taken back where Drury might find her.

Shadow didn't like the looks of the man. Or her chances. She was heading west, not north. No. She would keep walking. Passage on a boat would be nice on the feet, but she just couldn't take the chance that the boat wasn't stopping at the Southern Shield.

So Shadow said nothing, kept her seat and looked out the window. The man made one last call, then left.

She watched the men leave in the street and felt relief. Somehow, she believed that boat would have taken her north without a chance of getting off at her stop. She had a bad feeling about this port, and the sooner she could set out, the better.

In fact, now that she had finished her stew, there was no time like the present. There was just something... not right about Kallicove. Shadow could not put her finger on it, but she wasn't staying another hour longer than she had to.

Shadow downed the rest of her mead, set her tankard down, and slipped upstairs to her room to get her rucksack. She could always wash up in the river, once she was on her way. She didn't need a bath here. She would just get her overnight coppers back and –

"Leaving us so soon, are you then?" asked a male voice. A heavy arm grabbed her from behind. Then something forceful hit her in the head and all went black.

— ⚘ —

Seawater. Shadow smelled seawater. And everything was black. Her head hurt....

Someone had clubbed her! Her head throbbed and her ear was swollen....

She struggled and found that she was bound by rope, bound to a pole. She was on a boat! And blindfolded.

"That one's comin' to. The girl."

Abruptly, Shadow's blindfold was lifted and an unkempt man squatted before her.

"Lookit what we have before us, hey? A girl. We don't get too many girls. Should be interestin', should be interestin'. If nothin' else, we can use you for –"

"Merold, shut up, you talk too much. So." And another man squatted down before Shadow. "I'm your Captain. I'll have the pleasure of your name, please?" This man had an oiled, black and gray beard, and his black eyes were shrewd.

Shadow said nothing, in shock. Certainly this was a dream. She was… she was… back in the tunnels and this a nightmare, that had to be right.

"No? Not speaking? Very well, I'll name you myself. We'll call you Skinny, for you are skinnier than a rail. Looks to me like you been walkin' a while, judgin' by them shoes. Not wantin' to take river passage, I hear? Well, that's a mighty good thing for you, as you are on my ship, the Destructor. Unless, of course, one of the Hound's ships comes around and then we are the H.M.S. Horizon. Same number of letters.

"You, Skinny, are currently on the Treasure Sea, and you have got a hard little head, for you took the longest time wakin' up."

Pirates! Filthy scum! Shadow lashed out with her feet, kicked and fought against her bonds.

The Captain chuckled. "Well, I see you have a little spirit in you. You're going to need it where you're going. I'll see you're fed once a day but if you cause trouble, I'll see you go in my brig, and I'll starve you once a day every day you cause me trouble. Is that understood, Skinny?"

Shadow glared at him.

"I'll take it for a yes. You people behave yourselves back here or it's the brig for you!"

And the Captain of the Destructor stalked off, his boots echoing on the wooden deck.

Shadow could tell they were still near land, for she could hear sea gulls crying somewhere in the distance. They must have set sail just recently.

She strained at her bonds, roped tight to the mast behind her.

"My advice, don't waste your energy. They know how to tie a knot – they won't have tied it loose enough for you to get away," came a voice behind her.

"Who are you?"

"Someone who's been on this ship longer than you. Since Port Stanton."

Port Stanton!

"Where are they taking us?" Shadow asked.

"I don't know. Some sort of deal they have. But we've been bought."

"Bought?" Her worst nightmare was coming true. She'd rather be back at HarCourt.

"Shh!" he whispered. "Don't let on that you know, for all the gods!"

Bought!

"What's your name?" he asked.

She wasn't going to give anyone her name now. What was the point? "Just call me Skinny," she said, trying not to cry.

"My name is Yuri. I've been aboard this ship for three weeks now. Don't fight them, whatever you do. I have learned that the hard way, and you can't imagine a more unpleasant place than the brig. You would not last down there. I barely kept my sanity. Do not fight them, just… just do as they say."

To have been captured by pirates, just her luck. She'd walked half of Hardewold to escape Drury, only to be captured by pirates. And now sold as a slave….

Selby

It was hard, hard to find time to slip away here in RainsCourt. There were so many visiting foreign dignitaries – Generals, Colonels, and just her War Council, all wanting her attention. But finally – she'd found a little bit of time to herself.

Taking Durain along was not just a given on this errand, it was a must. She held the wall sconce up so that she could see better.

Never did she expect to visit this area of RainsCourt Palace, but it was necessary.

The prisoner had been isolated from all other prisoners. There were so few prisoners in the dungeon here anyway, but 'twas necessary to isolate him. His head had been shaven, and the guards had been warned that he was utterly mad. All, or nearly all, of the prisoners here in RainsCourt Dungeon were Ormish or Ambsell, so were they not by definition, then, mad, thought Selby snidely to herself.

Finally, they arrived at his cell. Durain held up his wall sconce and Selby held up hers. The combined light shining in to the stone cell revealed her prisoner – Sturgund Merigund, Crown Prince of Ambsellon.

—⁓—

END OF BOOK ONE

<u>Connect with Me</u>

On Twitter: https://www.twitter.com/BrittannyDavis1

On FaceBook: https://www.facebook.com/officialBrittannyDavis

Favorite my book at Smashwords: https://www.smashwords.com/profile/view/BrittannyDavis

Please remember to leave a review for my book at your favorite retailer.

A Silent Game of Spies

Book One of

The War of the Royals

Map of the East

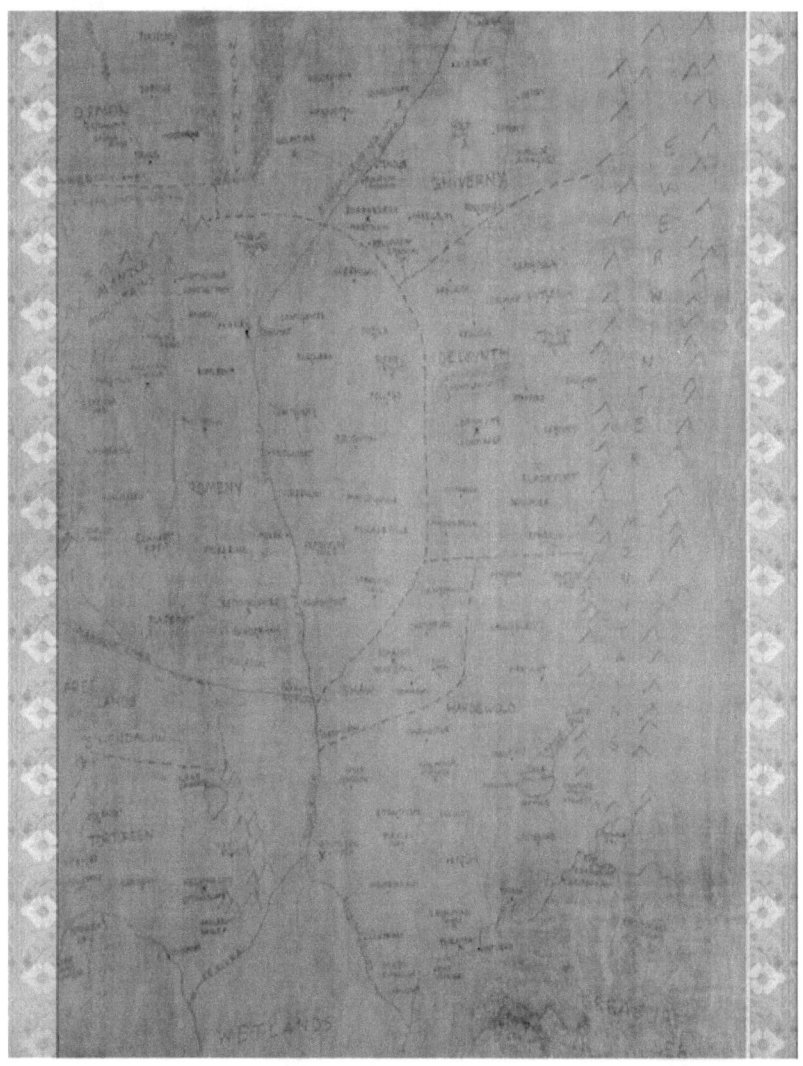

A Silent Game of Spies

Map of the West

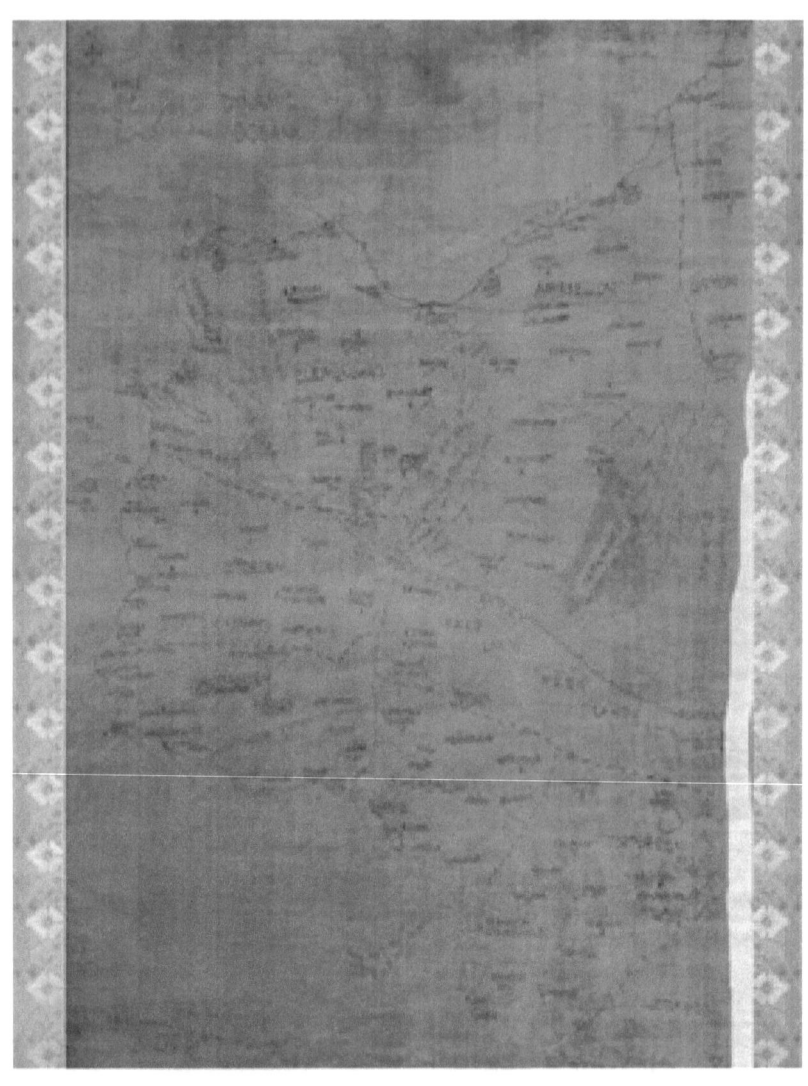

Map of the Northern Countries

Map of the Land

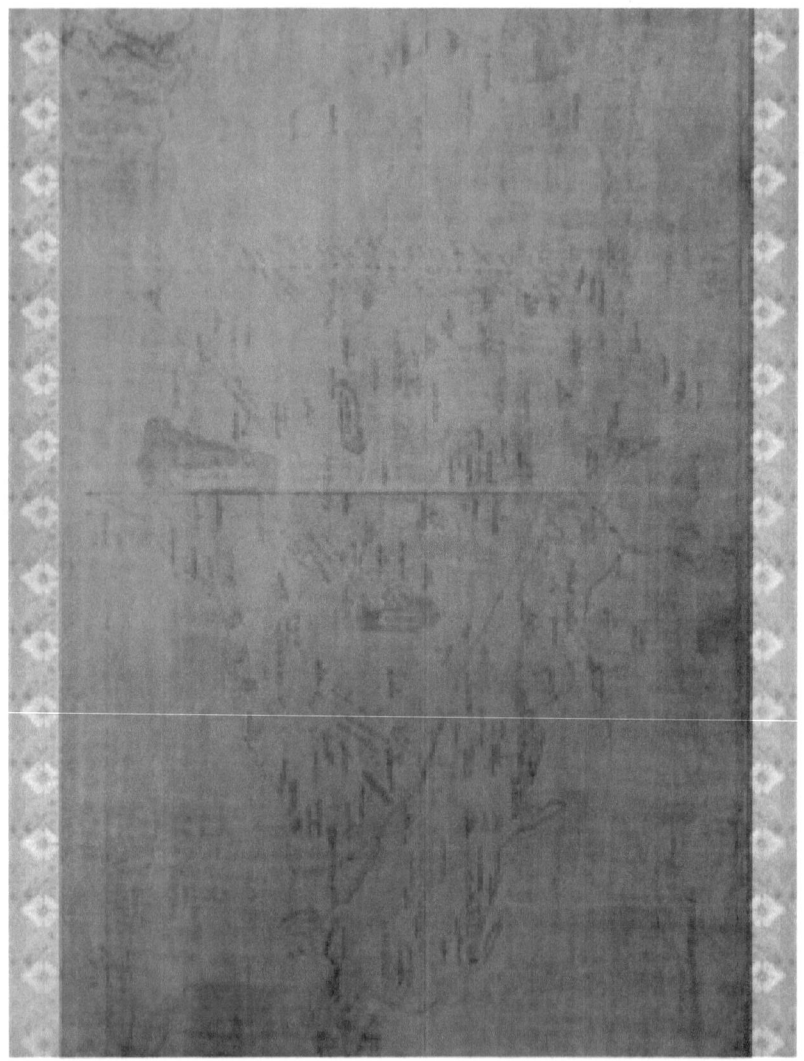

www.ingramcontent.com/pod-product-compliance
Lightning Source LLC
Chambersburg PA
CBHW020453020726
47493CB00001B/13